Also in the *Dynasty* series:

DYNASTY

13

The Regency

Cynthia Harrod-Eagles

sphere

SPHERE

First published in Great Britain in 1990 by
Macdonald and Co (Publishers) Ltd
Published by Futura in 1990
Reprinted 1991
Reprinted by Warner Books in 1993 (twice)
This edition published by Warner Books in 1995
Reprinted 2000
Reprinted by Sphere in 2006, 2009, 2010, 2011, 2013, 2014

ISBN 978-0-7515-0650-1

Printed and bound in Great Britain by
Clays Ltd, St Ives plc

Papers used by Sphere are from well-managed forests
and other responsible sources.

MIX
Paper from
responsible sources
FSC® C104740

Sphere
An imprint of
Little, Brown Book Group
100 Victoria Embankment
London EC4Y 0DY

An Hachette UK Company
www.hachette.co.uk

www.littlebrown.co.uk

FT
Pbk

*For Tony, with thanks for the support,
encouragement, home comforts, and many
questions answered.*

THE MORLAN

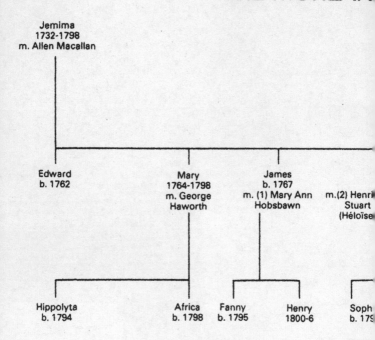

Jemima
1732-1798
m. Allen Macallan

Edward
b. 1762

Mary
1764-1798
m. George
Haworth

James
b. 1767
m. (1) Mary Ann
Hobsbawn

m.(2) Henri
Stuart
(Héloïse)

Hippolyta
b. 1794

Africa
b. 1798

Fanny
b. 1795

Henry
1800-6

Soph
b. 179

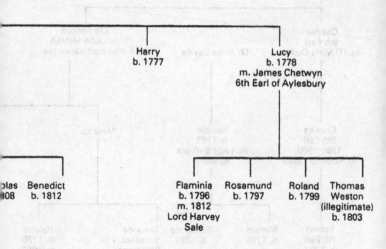

Harry
b. 1777

Lucy
b. 1778
m. James Chetwyn
6th Earl of Aylesbury

plas   Benedict
808   b. 1812

Flaminia   Rosamund   Roland   Thomas
b. 1796   b. 1797   b. 1799   Weston
m. 1812   (illegitimate)
Lord Harvey   b. 1803
Sale

THE CHELM

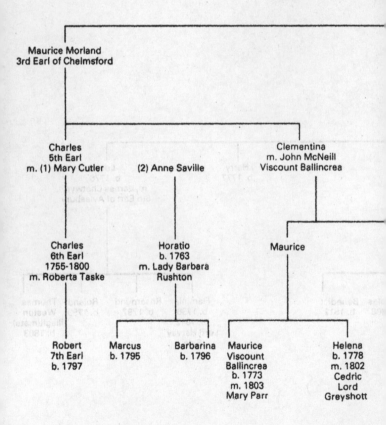

Maurice Morland
3rd Earl of Chelmsford

Charles
5th Earl
m. (1) Mary Cutler

(2) Anne Saville

Clementina
m. John McNeill
Viscount Ballincrea

Charles
6th Earl
1755-1800
m. Roberta Taske

Horatio
b. 1763
m. Lady Barbara
Rushton

Maurice

Robert
7th Earl
b. 1797

Marcus
b. 1795

Barbarina
b. 1796

Maurice
Viscount
Ballincrea
b. 1773
m. 1803
Mary Parr

Helena
b. 1778
m. 1802
Cedric
Lord
Greyshott

ORD FAMILY

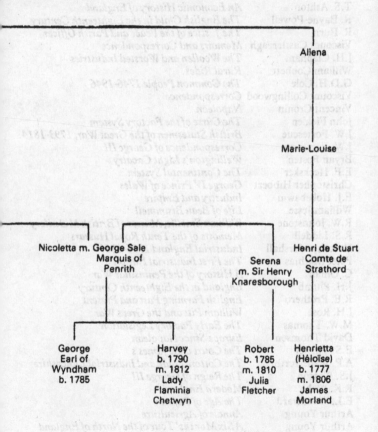

Allena

Marie-Louise

Nicoletta m. George Sale
Marquis of
Penrith

Serena
m. Sir Henry
Knaresborough

Henri de Stuart
Comte de
Strathord

George
Earl of
Wyndham
b. 1785

Harvey
b. 1790
m. 1812
Lady
Flaminia
Chetwyn

Robert
b. 1785
m. 1810
Julia
Fletcher

Henrietta
(Héloïse)
b. 1777
m. 1806
James
Morland

SELECT BIBLIOGRAPHY

T.S. Ashton	*An Economic History of England*
R. Bayne-Powell	*The English Child in the Eighteenth Century*
R. Burn	*The Justice of the Peace and Parish Officer*
Viscount Castlereagh	*Memoirs and Correspondence*
J.H. Clapham	*The Woollen and Worsted Industries*
William Cobbett	*Rural Rides*
G.D.H. Cole	*The Common People 1746-1946*
Viscount Collingwood	*Correspondence*
Vincent Cronin	*Napoleon*
John Fielden	*The Curse of the Factory System*
J.W. Fortescue	*British Statesmen of the Great War, 1793-1814*
J.W. Fortescue	*Correspondence of George III*
Bryan Fosten	*Wellington's Light Cavalry*
E.F. Hecksker	*The Continental System*
Christopher Hibbert	*George IV Prince of Wales*
E.J. Hobsbawm	*Industry and Empire*
William Jesse	*Life of Beau Brummell*
R.W. Johnstone	*William Smellie, Master of British Midwifery*
R.S. Liddell	*Memoirs of the Tenth Royal Hussars*
Dorothy Marshall	*Industrial England 1776-1851*
Peter Mathias	*The First Industrial Nation*
C. Oman	*A History of the Peninsular War*
J.H. Plumb	*England in the Eighteenth Century*
R.E. Prothero	*English Farming Past and Present*
J.H. Rose	*William Pitt and the Great War*
M.W. Thomas	*The Early Factory Legislation*
David Thomson	*Europe Since Napoleon*
E.S. Turner	*The Court of St James's*
A.P. Wadsworth	*The Cotton Trade and Industrial Lancashire*
J.S. Watson	*The Reign of George III*
R.K. Webb	*Modern England*
E.L. Woodward	*The Age of Reform*
Arthur Young	*Annals of Agriculture*
Arthur Young	*A Six Months' Tour of the North of England*

BOOK ONE

The Usurper

A springy motion in her gait,
A rising step, did indicate
Of pride and joy no common rate,
    That flush'd her spirit:

I know not by what name beside
I shall it call: if t'was not pride,
It was a joy to that allied,
      She did inherit.

Charles Lamb: *Hester*

CHAPTER ONE

March 1807

Héloïse woke, as she always did, when the housemaid came in to light the fire. The great ancestral bed of the Morlands in which she lay was a warm, dark cave. The red damask bed-curtains were too heavy to allow even a glow to penetrate them, but there was one vertical thread of white fire, like a fissure in a volcanic mountain, where they were not quite drawn together. Héloïse fixed her drowsy eyes on it, and listened contentedly to the muted, domestic sounds that came to her from beyond: the rattling rush of the bedroom curtains, the swish of hearth-brush, the crackle of kindling, the rustle of the housemaid's skirt as she rose from her knees, the soft click as she closed the door behind her.

This feeling of waking content was still new to her: she had been married only four months ago, in November 1806. It was bliss to wake to the awareness of James beside her, his warm body still wrapped in sleep. The dark cave was filled with the smell of him — not the *eau-de-Cologne* that Durban patted on after shaving him, or the sweet oil he sometimes used to discipline his fine, red-brown hair — but simply his own smell, the scent of his skin which she loved more than any perfume, and which was so intimately of him that to catch it filled her instantly with a warm flush of love, half tender, half erotic.

James woke now, feeling the altered rhythm of her body as lovers do, and turned to draw her into his arms, murmuring a sleepy greeting. Her body folded into the contours of his with accustomed ease, her head on his shoulder, her face against his neck. Their breathing ebbed and flowed to the same rhythm. Loving each other coloured every moment of their days, but of them all, she thought, these waking moments were the most exquisite.

13

At length he sighed and stirred, nuzzling for her mouth, and turned his hip towards her so that she felt the familiar nudging of his waking desire. She moved to accommodate him, turning her mouth up to his, and her body quivered in response as he pushed his hands in under her nightdress and closed them over her small, childlike breasts.

'*Je te veux*,' she whispered, and he made a sound in reply which was almost a groan, making her smile. Knowing each other, loving each other, their bodies eased together with the minimum of effort; he slid gratefully into her, and they moved together quietly like swimmers in a warm, calm sea. Passion and tenderness grew in an even surge, like the swell of the tide, and they held on hard to each other, clinging together as their movements grew stronger and faster. When the moment came, she cried out with the intensity of wanting him, and the sound pierced him as it always did, so that it seemed as if his very soul were being dragged out of him and emptied into her.

'James,' she breathed. She laid her hand on the nape of his neck, and he shuddered.

'I love you. Oh, I love you,' he whispered.

A long time later, it seemed, he raised his head to look at her. Her skin was lightly flushed, her eyelids moist, her dark eyes glowing, her lips curved in a smile of luminous sweetness.

'You're beautiful,' he said.

Héloïse cupped his cheek. It was a gauge of his love that he, who was truly beautiful, should think her so. 'So are you, my James,' she said.

'I love the way you say my name. It's absurd! Why should it affect me so much?' He kissed the end of her nose. 'What were you thinking just then, when you smiled like that?'

'I was wondering if we have just begun a child.'

'You said that last month, and the month before,' he said, and was instantly sorry. 'My own love, don't worry. We've only been married four months,' he said reasonably. 'There's plenty of time.'

'I know,' she said contritely. 'I am foolish; it's just that I love you so much, I want every time to get with child.'

'It will happen, in its own time,' he said, thinking that he was in no great hurry to have to suspend for a year the delight of making love to her. Of course he wanted them to have

14

children, but he was content to wait. Tactfully, he changed the subject. 'What do you do today?'

'I have some calls to make: first to return Lady Fussell's, who called yesterday, and then I must go to see Mrs Shawe, because she is very low after her miscarriage, poor lady — her second in two years, James, just imagine! And then to the village: I shall call on Widrith the weaver — oh, how hard it is to say that name! — and Abley the baker. I shall order one of his hams, I think.'

'My love, surely we killed a pig only two days ago? I may not have much of a memory for domestic detail, but I do remember Father Aislaby laughing about a fracas in the kitchen over the trotters.'

'Trotters!' Héloïse repeated, rolling the 'r's voluptuously. 'What a word this is, so touching, for pig's feet! But yes, it was because Monsieur Barnard wanted to make the feet into a special dish for me, and Ottershaw said they are not fit to be served to gentlefolk, which upset him. Barnard does not like to be told his business. And so there was a trouble.'

'That's putting it mildly, when the cook threatens the butler with a cleaver,' James observed.

'I don't think he would actually have *struck* him,' Héloïse said judiciously. 'Only it seems there is a tradition in your kitchens that when a pig is killed the *t-r-rotters* are always kept for the upper servants, and Ottershaw did not want to lose them. I like pig's feet very much, as Barnard prepares them,' she added musingly, 'but I think one could not serve them when there is company for dinner. They have not a very proper look.'

'Well then, why do you want a ham from Abley the baker?' James asked, remembering where they had begun.

'Oh, not because we need one, but because he has been ill. For several days he could not open his shop, so he has lost much money. I shall let him overcharge me for the ham, and that will make things easier for him. And I shall ask him what is the secret of his feeding, which makes his pigs taste so much better than ours.'

'Do they?'

'No, but it will make him feel more cheerful, because everyone likes to be asked about something they know well, and he must be in need of cheering. It is very wearing to have

15

the cold in the lungs, and cough all the time. And he truly loves his pigs, I think.'

James laughed affectionately. 'Madame Machiavelli! Do you know everything about every one of our villagers? You remind me of Mother.'

'Do I?' Héloïse looked pleased. 'I should like to be worthy of her, though I am mistress of Morland Place only until Fanny grows up. But I often think of your mother, and try to think how she would do things, and keep her kingdom for her properly. A sort of regency, you know.'

James looked down tenderly into her face. 'You are everything she could have hoped for, Marmoset. And everything I want, too.'

Héloïse sighed with pleasure and lifted her lips for kissing. 'But James,' she said, breaking off a moment later, 'speaking of Fanny, it really will not do, you know. She must have a governess.' James rolled off her, without making any reply, and Héloïse, regarding him thoughtfully, added, 'And Sophie, too, of course. A good governess for both the girls will make all the difference to them.'

'You haven't worried about a governess for Sophie until now,' James said expressionlessly.

'I was used to teach Sophie myself before I married you, but now at Morland Place I have so much more to do that I have not the time. And besides,' she added ruefully, 'my education was only such as girls were given in France before the revolution — needlework and devotions!'

James only grunted unhelpfully at the pleasantry.

'And besides again,' Héloïse went on frankly, 'you know very well that Fanny would not mind me. Yes, James, do not make faces and turn away your head! You know it is true. Fanny does not like me.'

'Nonsense! If you mean that business last week, there's no proof at all that it was Fanny who did it. I think it's very hard the way you all automatically blame her, just as if she were responsible for everything that happens in this house. And even if it were Fanny,' he added with the irritability of guilt, 'it was only a harmless prank.'

Héloïse leaned up on one elbow. 'James, she all but admitted it. And it may have been a harmless prank, as you say, to steal a knife and cut up two of my dresses, but me, I did not

16

find it amusing. Fanny does not like me; and Father Aislaby does not like *her*, and won't take any trouble with her, and *someone* must take trouble with her, *mon âme*, or she will grow up very strange, and be unhappy. I am sure she is not happy now, no, even doing what she likes all the time. 'Do what you will' is not a good thing for a child. You must engage a governess — *voilà tout*.'

'A gaoler, you mean,' James muttered. He stared stonily at the canopy for a moment longer, and then sighed and yielded, turning onto his side to look at his wife. 'Oh Marmoset, I worry so much about her! When she was born, and Mother first put her into my arms, I thought I should die from so much love! She was so perfect, so untouched and innocent. I thought I would devote my life to her. I thought she would make everything right for me. I was lonely when I was a child, and I determined she should never feel that way. And her mother never cared for her, so I had to care twice as much. But somehow, it didn't answer. She seems to get more wild and difficult all the time. When I saw your dresses all cut to shreds —'

He broke off, and his expression was painful. Héloïse understood the agony of divided loyalty he must have felt, and still be feeling: loving her, and loving his daughter, he must want so much to convince himself that Fanny had not meant ill by her 'prank'.

'Well, *mon âme*, I have told you what,' she said comfortably, making her voice matter-of-fact for his sake. 'Find a good governess — a woman of learning, whose character is firm, and whose heart is warm — and let her devote herself to Fanny, and you will see all will be well. I wish we might find someone like Lucy's good Miss Trotton! She is exactly the sort of woman who would suit.'

'Do you think so?' James said, already more cheerful. 'I am not averse from bribing Trot to change establishments, if you think it will serve! Offer her twice the salary Lucy gives her, perhaps? Or would a sum of money, cash to invest in the Funds, be more to the purpose?'

'Now it is you who are Machiavelli,' Héloïse smiled, and allowed herself to be engulfed again. How easily James was swayed into optimism, she reflected, when it came to his way-ward daughter; for herself, she had been much perturbed over the knife incident, though she had made light of her fear, not to put ideas in Fanny's head. She did not believe that the hiring of a governess, even one like Miss Trotton, would put everything right in an instant, but it seemed to her essential that someone should have continuous charge of the child. She must not be allowed to run all over the country unattended as she did now. It was not only the question of the harm to Fanny's manners and morals, but of the harm she might do to others. Where had she got the knife, for instance? It had not come from Morland Place. Héloïse had a mother's vulnerability towards her own little Sophie and Thomas. She could not really believe that an eleven-year-old child would actually do them violence, but she would not have them bullied or oppressed if she could help it, and Fanny was more than equal to that.

But she seemed to have carried the first point, at all events; James would no longer resist the idea of a governess; and as he was now giving serious consideration to the question of how much of his tongue would fit into her left ear, she felt obliged to leave further discussion for another time. The dressing-bell had not yet been rung: there was at least another quarter of an hour, she estimated happily, before they need get up.

The subject of her stepmother's musings was at that moment only a few yards away, in the chapel gallery. Crouching down, Fanny could look through the pierced-work of the balustrade without being seen, and watch Beamish, the altar-boy of the day, lighting the candles and setting things out for the early celebration. Yesterday Beamish had been held up to Fanny as a model of youthful piety and good behaviour by Father Aislaby, who had discovered her playing cat's cradle during vespers. Now Fanny meant to get even with him.

In one hand she held a short length of narrow pipe, which she had taken from the back of the blacksmith's forge, and in the other a few dried peas. When the moment came, and Beamish was in the right place, she would let fly at him. A dried pea, striking the right, tender place with sufficient force, could hurt a surprising amount. If he were to drop and break a candle he would find himself in trouble. At the very least, he would probably let out a yell, which would earn him a reprimand; and in the dimly-lit chapel he would never know what hit him.

The moment came; Beamish yelled, and though he did not drop the candle, he tilted it so wildly that wax splashed down onto the floor. Smiling with satisfaction, Fanny eased herself backwards and out into the little passageway which led to the spiral stairs, intent on putting as much distance between herself and the crime as possible. Then, finding herself opposite the door to the dressing-room of the great bedchamber, she stopped, and her smile faded.

Beyond the dressing-room, in the great bedchamber itself, in the massive, carved bed in which she herself had been born and would one day die, the ancestral Butts bed which belonged to her, as did everything in the house, her father lay at this very moment with *that woman*. Fanny's brows drew down into a scowl. She hated the Frenchwoman, not for taking her mother's place — for Fanny had never cared a jot for her mother, and did not believe her father had, either — but for stealing her father's love. Before the Frenchwoman came, all Papa's love had been for Fanny. She had come first with him, and she could not endure to lose her place to another.

Her hand went automatically to the doorknob, and for a moment she considered marching in, disturbing them, demanding Papa's attention, his love, his caresses. But common sense intervened; she paused, imagining the scene, seeing how angry he would be. He would side with *that woman*, against her. Grief came to reinforce anger; she clenched her hands with frustration. Her left hand still gripped the length of pipe; she frowned down at it a moment; and then suddenly jerked it up and used its rough end to score a short and violent runnel down the polished wood of the door.

I'll shew her! she thought. *I'll get even with her somehow!* She dragged the sharp metal down the door-panel again and again in an ecstasy of hatred. Somehow, someday, she would make the Frenchwoman pay for stealing her father away from her; she would make her suffer!

The dressing-bell began to ring, startling her out of her black passion. Fifteen minutes until first mass! Fanny stared at the door with faint shock. Had she really done that? The gouges shewed pale in the old, dark wood. It was seasoned mahogany, and though she had not managed to score it very

19

deeply, someone was bound to notice sooner or later. Well, let them, she thought defiantly. They couldn't prove it was she, any more than they could over those silly old dresses.

But there were footsteps on the spiral stair, the light running feet of Héloïse's maid, Marie, coming up to dress her mistress for chapel. Fanny looked around her for a hiding place. The stairs went on further up for another half-turn, ending in a blank stone wall, and Fanny ran quickly up and crouched there, pressing herself against the central pillar and peering down onto the landing below.

Marie appeared, her hair neatly hidden under a linen cap with long ribbons which Fanny's fingers longed to tweak, a silk chemise folded over her arm. She walked straight forward, opened the dressing-room door, and went in, without, apparently, noticing the scratches. As the door closed behind her, Fanny sighed with relief. The landing was ill-lit: perhaps the damage might go unnoticed for weeks, or for ever.

When nursery breakfast was over, Jenny always brought the children downstairs to the dining-room. Fanny, entering cautiously, could tell at once by the atmosphere that the damage to the dressing-room door had not yet been discovered. Breakfast was finished, but no-one seemed in a hurry to get up. Papa and Father Aislaby had newspapers open in front of them, and Madame and Mathilde were looking through a ladies' journal together. Even Uncle Ned, who always went straight about his business as soon as he had swallowed the last mouthful, was lingering. His face was normally dour and grim — Papa said he hadn't smiled since the death of Uncle Chetwyn, who had been his best friend — but today he looked almost cheerful, leaning back in his chair in the first patch of sunshine they had seen for ten days.

His new hound, Tiger, had its great foolish head jammed into his lap, its eyes closed blissfully as he pulled its ears over and over through his hands. Uncle Ned's old bitch, Brach, had had to be put down just before Christmas, and her long-time mate, Leaky, had simply pined away within a week. Tiger was one of their great-great-grandchildren, grey and wolf-eyed like them, but with handsome black-and-russet brindling over the quarters.

Fanny pouted a little at the thought of her own wolfhound,

Puppy, whom Uncle Ned had banned from the house because, he said, it was so bad-mannered. But he always brought his dogs in. And Madame had her hound Kithra at her feet under the table, too. Unfair!

Fanny would have gone straight in, but Uncle Ned and Papa were talking, and Jenny caught her wrist and frowned, and made her wait at the door.

'You can quite see why Grenville is so keen on the Catholic emancipation,' James was saying. 'He and his friends only ever had three policies; and now slavery's been abolished, and no-one in their right minds would advocate Parliamentary reform, when the country's seething with anti-Jacobin feeling, and all the new industrial nabobs are clamouring for representation —'

'Well, who in his right mind would have brought forward this Catholic Militia Bill, either?' Ned challenged. 'It hadn't a chance of getting through.'

'What else could they do?' James asked lazily. 'They hadn't another idea between them, and they have to talk about something in the Chamber, after all. And they nearly got it past the King.'

'By trickery,' Ned snorted. 'The King must have had a fit when he was told what he almost signed. Catholics allowed to be staff officers? Nonsense! The Duke of York would have died of rage! Saving your presence, Father,' he added hastily, seeing Father Aislaby's raised eyebrows. '*I've* nothing against the idea, but you know what these fanatical anti-papists are!'

'What's an anti-papist, Uncle Ned?' Fanny asked with interest. James, whose back had been to her, turned and smiled a welcome.

'Fanny, love! Come here and kiss me, you pretty thing!'

Fanny ran to him, glad of the excuse to omit the customary formal curtsey to Héloïse. Jenny bid the little children, Sophie and Thomas, to go to Madame, and glared at Fanny, who merely glared back, kissed her father, climbed onto his lap and repeated her question. 'What are anti-papists?'

'Silly people, Fanny,' Ned said shortly. 'Nothing you need know about.'

'Don't interrupt and ask questions, Miss Fanny,' Jenny reproved sternly. 'Speak only when you're spoken to.'

Ned pushed back his chair and got up. 'I must be off. But

21

it'll mean the end of this Government, Jamie, you mark my words. The King'll never forgive 'em. They'll be out before the month, and good riddance! Ministry of All-the-Talents, indeed! The only talent they shewed was in doing nothing.'

'Are you going out to Twelvetrees?' James asked.

'Yes — we've ten colts to cut. Want to come and give a hand?' Ned asked.

James laughed. 'No, no, I'll forgo my share of the treat, thank you. I've got that pair of bays to school for Mrs Micklethwaite, if they're going to be ready by the end of the month. I just wanted you to have someone bring the training-phaeton down for me, so that I can take them out this morning.'

'Very well, I'll see to it.'

Father Aislaby got up too, and he and Ned went to the door together, going out as Ottershaw, the butler, came in.

'Excuse me, my lady,' he said, looking at Héloïse, 'but Mr and Miss Keating have called, asking for Miss Nortiboys.' No inducement could persuade the English servants to pronounce Mathilde's name any other way. 'I did mention you were still at breakfast, my lady —'

Mathilde looked up, and her guilty blush clashed with her hair. 'Oh, Madame, I forgot to mention! Patience asked me on Sunday if I would spend the day with her today. She said she might persuade her brother to drive over and take me in to York, but I didn't know they would come so early.'

'It doesn't matter, *chérie*,' Héloïse and good-naturedly. 'We had finished anyway. Please ask them to step in, Ottershaw. And you may clear.'

'I beg your pardon, my lady, but Mr and Miss Keating are waiting at the door, in a sporting vehicle, my lady.'

'Good heavens, they must be in a hurry! Run and fetch your bonnet, then, Mathilde. Be so good as to tell them, Ottershaw, that Miss Nordubois is coming.'

'I imagine, knowing Tom Keating, that he's having difficulty holding his horses,' James said as Ottershaw went out. 'He has a propensity to buy horses he can't handle, which his father must deplore! I wish you may not be overturned, Mathilde. Do you entirely trust this beau of yours?'

Mathilde blushed even harder. 'Oh, yes, sir! I mean, he isn't my beau, but I'm sure he drives very well!'

'James, don't tease!' Héloïse intervened. 'Run along, Mathilde. And don't spend all your allowance in one shop! Remember you will want all sorts of things for the ball next week.'

'Yes, Madame. No, Madame.'

James halted her at the door. 'Who brings you home?'

'Oh, I expect Tom — that is, Mr Keating —' Mathilde stammered.

'Not alone,' James said firmly. 'If his sister does not accompany you, then a servant must. Do you understand?'

'Yes, sir. Of course,' Mathilde said, and dropped a hasty curtsey and hurried out.

Fanny, sitting on her father's lap, was an interested witness to all this, and thought with contempt that Mathilde was particularly ugly when she blushed, for it made her freckles stand out and drew attention to her horrible red hair.

Héloïse glanced reproachfully at her husband. 'I wish you would not tease poor Mathilde,' she said. 'She minds it, you know.'

'Nonsense!' James said. 'Every girl of eighteen likes to be asked about her beaux — unless she hasn't got any, of course. How long has Tom Keating been dangling after her?'

'He does not dangle,' Héloïse said. 'She is intimate with Patience Keating, that's all, and Patience and her brother are very close.'

'Mathilde will never catch Tom Keating,' Fanny could not resist commenting, 'not whatever she does.'

Héloïse frowned disapprovingly, but James looked amused. 'Why, what do you know about it, Fan?' he asked.

'Tom Keating would never marry a girl with *freckles*,' Fanny said contemptuously. 'He's a trump card! He has a capital grey hunter, and he said I have the best hands in the county.'

'Ah, now we come to the nub of it,' James grinned. 'Let me guess: you met him out exercising his grey when you were flying about the countryside on Tempest, and he paid you some outrageous compliment.'

'It wasn't 'rageous!' Fanny said indignantly. 'We jumped a stream to give him a lead, because he couldn't get his grey over. Tempest *flew* over, and then the grey followed, and he was grateful, and he said I was a splendid rider.'

23

'Well, so you are, chicken,' James said, 'but you'll do your reputation no good if you go about admiring young Keating's horsemanship. He ruined that chestnut his father bought from me two years ago, and he'll ruin the grey before the summer if he goes on the way he is. He's managed to get the brute so peppered up that either he'll break its neck, or it'll break his.'

'My love, I don't think this is suitable talk for children,' Héloïse said gently, and to Fanny, 'You must not speak so freely, Fanny, about people older than yourself. It isn't seemly, and you are old enough now to begin to behave like a lady. I think, James, that when I am out today I had better place an advertisement in the *York Mercury* on that matter we agreed this morning.'

Fanny looked at her with narrowed eyes. Something was being plotted against her, she thought.

'Yes, if you like,' James said, and feeling Fanny's rigidity, tried to placate her. 'It's time we were thinking of a new mount for Fanny: Tempest is a grand sort, but he isn't a lady's mount — what do you think, Fan?' Fanny drew breath to concur rapturously, but before she could speak he spoiled everything by adding, 'And while I'm at it, I must see about a pony for Sophie, too, as I promised. I think I know where I can lay my hands on just the right animal for her.'

Sophie flashed her father a dazzling smile of gratitude and pleasure; and Fanny was still reeling as James put her off his lap and stood up, saying, 'I must be going. I want to take those bays out to the Knavesmire and give them a good opener, to get the fidgets out of their feet. All this rain has played the deuce with their training.'

Jenny was holding out her hand to Fanny, but she ignored it, fixing pleading eyes on her father. 'Oh Papa, can I come too?' she asked urgently.

'No, Puss,' James said firmly. 'They're an untrained team — it would be too dangerous. Run along now with Jenny. It's time you were all in the schoolroom, anyway.'

Fanny's face contracted sharply with disappointment, and she watched her father kiss his wife and depart with such hungry eyes that for once Héloïse felt oddly sorry for her.

'I shall be going out later in my phaeton,' she said, as Fanny trailed after the little children, across the room to where Jenny was waiting. 'Would you all like to come with me for a drive?' Sophie and Thomas accepted eagerly, but Fanny said nothing. 'Fanny?' Héloïse prompted kindly. 'You can take the reins for a little, if you like.'

Fanny turned and regarded her thoughtfully. 'No thank you, Madame,' she said with a frosty dignity which looked odd on her usually animated face. 'I think I had better stay here and study my school books.' And she turned and stalked out, evidently feeling she had dealt an unbeatable card. Héloïse smiled — *school books indeed!* — and then caught Jenny's eye, and gave her a cautionary look which said, *make sure she doesn't get up to mischief.*

It was the first time the bays had been out alone together, without trained horses harnessed up to quiet them, and they gave James a lively time. His man, Durban, had the greatest difficulty in backing them between the shafts of the training-phaeton, even with the help of four other grooms; and when they were in position, and stood quivering like coiled springs, their eyes white and their quarters bunched for action, he was extremely reluctant to let go their heads and climb into the cart.

'I think we ought to weight the rig with some sacks, sir,' he suggested tentatively. The wild brown eye of the offside bay was staring down at him from a few inches away, and its ears were flicking back and forth like metronomes.

'No, no, I can hold 'em,' James said blithely. 'Jump in, man, and let's be off. It's only fretting 'em, making 'em stand like this. Once they've warmed the leather on their backs, they'll settle down all right.'

With an inward prayer, Durban let go and stepped aside all in one movement, and even though he was expecting it, their forward rush was so precipitate that he almost missed his jump as the rig shot past him, and the bays plunged off up the track, backs up and nostrils wide.

'Hoa, hoa, my boys!' James called to them, unperturbed, as the phaeton bucked like a mad thing over the ruts, and Durban fought to keep himself on the seat and his hat on his head.

'When were you going to deliver them to Mrs Micklethwaite, sir?' Durban asked obliquely as the bays lurched

25

forward and the rig hit a large stone and shot two feet into the air. The nearside horse tried to run out sideways, and managed to get his head under his partner's rein.

'End of the month,' James said cheerfully. 'We'll do it, you'll see. There's not an ounce of vice in 'em, you know. They're just green. Ah, here's the road coming up. Once we've made the turn, I'll spring 'em, and let 'em find their own rhythm.'

James eased the bays round the turn, held them for a moment, and then let them out into a fast trot. The road was in good repair — Edward in his capacity of Justice of the Peace, which included the office of Surveyor of Roads, saw to that — and the phaeton now bowled along smoothly, and ceased to alarm and fret the horses with its rattling and bouncing. The offside bay had a tendency at first to break into a canter every few steps, but James soon mastered him, and the pair settled down to find each other's rhythm.

A gleam of sunlight broke through the mild grey sky, and James suddenly felt a surge of pleasure and optimism. It was good that life had at last become something to look forward to with pleasure, rather than something to be endured. He whistled a few bars of *Lilibullero*.

'You know what, Durban,' he cried enthusiastically, 'I think they're going to make a good pair! Look how they're pacing each other now! Exactly in step!'

It was good to be driving these handsome horses along a smooth road on a mild spring day; to feel the speed and power running like lightning through the reins, to see the delicate ears pricked before him, and the harness jouncing on the glossy backs as they lifted their slender forelegs high. It was good to know that Héloïse would be presiding over the dinner table later, that he would hold her in his arms tonight and wake beside her in the morning. He was even looking forward to the small ball they were giving next week for Mathilde's eighteenth birthday. It would be pleasant to meet the new generation of young people — the grown-up children of his old friends and contemporaries — and watch their innocent enjoyment.

One day they would give a grand coming-out ball for Fanny, he thought. That would be an occasion! Miss Morland of Morland Place would be a considerable heiress and the catch of the Season. He thought with relish of the fortune-hunters who would inevitably dangle after her, and of the short shrift he would give them. With her beauty and her fortune, she might marry anyone — they might look as high as they pleased for a match for her!

Héloïse was right, of course — she must have a governess. He had always wanted her to be free to romp and play as a child, but it was time now that she began to acquire some polish, and learnt how to behave in company. At the back of the thought there was a hint of relief, too. He could never consciously admit to himself that his darling was anything but perfect, if a little high-spirited; but his capacity for self-delusion had been severly strained by the incident over Héloïse's gowns. The thought of someone's taking her in hand and preventing anything like that from happening again was deeply, if secretly, attractive.

Durban interrupted his thoughts. We're being followed, sir,' he said quietly. 'Miss Fanny on Tempest, coming along the other side of the beck. She's keeping to the trees, hoping not to be seen.'

James groaned and glanced round. Yes, there she was, coming out of the trees now, hopping Tempest over the beck and cantering towards them, grinning triumphantly. Even then he couldn't help a surge of pride at how well she rode. She had obviously taken Tempest from the paddock without asking anyone, and without bothering to saddle or bridle him, but even bareback and with nothing but a hemp halter round his nose, she had complete control.

'Papa! It's me! she called, and then several things happened at once. They had just passed Tyburn, the site of the old gallows, and a place where horses often became jittery. The bays' heads were up, and they were fidgeting a little, peeking about them. Then there was a rustling in the bushes to the right, and Fanny's dog, Puppy, came bursting out onto the road right beside them, and cavorted excitedly around the horses.

'God damn that bloody dog!' James cursed as the bays startled, bunching their quarters and trying to leap away. 'Get away, Puppy! Get off, you fool!' Durban's hands had joined his on the reins, and he freed one to lash out at Puppy with the whip. Puppy yelped, jumped aside, and then somehow became entangled in the horses' legs.

There was a moment of confusion. James felt the phaeton jolt, and the dog shrieked in pain. Fanny was upon them, shouting something and further exciting the horses. The bays struggled, trying to bolt, flinging their heads up and snorting in distress, and Durban was contemplating throwing himself out and trying to get to their heads.

And then a new figure entered the drama. A few yards further on, the road was joined by a track from High Moor which had recently been glorified by the name of Nelson's Lane, and out of it came a young man on a workmanlike road-horse, well splashed with mud as if they had come a long way. He summed up the situation in an instant. He turned his horse across the road and jumped from the saddle, flung the reins over the hedge, and stepped up to catch the bays' heads.

'Hoa there, hoa there, my beauties,' he cried soothingly. The bays surged against his restraining hands; the offside horse kicked out at Tempest, and he flinched away. 'Better take your pony out of the way, Miss Morland, before he gets hurt.'

Durban took the opportunity to jump out, and in a moment he and the young man had the bays at a stand. Fanny turned Tempest away to the side of the road and jumped off; left loose he trotted a few paces and then stopped to graze.

'Puppy's hurt!' she cried.

'I can hold 'em all right now,' the young man was saying to Durban, 'if you want to look at the dog.'

Durban left the horses and went past James, who glanced behind to see where Fanny was crouching in the road over the rough grey shape of Puppy. Damn and blast, he thought: if the dog's badly hurt, she'll be heartbroken. The bays were standing quietly now, aided by the example of the young man's road-horse, which stood peacefully eating the hedge and cocking one stout foot at its ease. James wound the reins, preparing the jump down, and only then looked properly at the young man who had come so efficiently to their aid.

The sun broke through the clouds again, and where a bar of sunlight touched the young man's brown hair, it lit a gleam of dark fox-red.

'I'm very much in your debt,' James said. 'John Skelwith,

isn't it? I haven't seen you for quite some time. It must be — oh, five or six years.'

John lifted his mother's dark eyes and looked at James steadily. The rest of the face, James thought, was not Mary's: dear God, how many people must notice the likeness? John was a little taller than he, more slightly built, but so like, so like! Did he know? Had any suspicion ever crossed his mind? James thought not; hoped not.

'I've been away a good deal, sir,' John said pleasantly, neutrally. 'School, of course, and then university; and I've been spending a lot of time in Leeds and Huddersfield lately, about my father's business.'

'Your business now, isn't it?' James said. 'Didn't you come of age in January?'

John Skelwith did not seem to wonder why James knew his age and birthday. 'My business,' he corrected himself with a faint smile. 'I've just come back from Leeds now, as a matter of fact. I was on my way home.'

'Lucky for me you were — another moment and I'd have lost these two. Durban!' He wrenched his gaze away from that frighteningly familiar face and looked over his shoulder. 'How's that damned dog?'

Durban, crouched with Fanny in the road, looked up. 'Not so good, sir. I think we'd better try and get him back to the house. Stand aside, Miss Fanny, and let me pick him up.'

Fanny's face was tracked with tears. 'Papa, he's hurt! I saw it — the wheel went over him!'

The horses surged forward as Durban came towards the rig with the dog in his arms, but John Skelwith's strong wrists held them.

'You'd better stay with Miss Fanny, Durban, and escort her back to the house,' James said. 'I can manage the pair myself now.'

'No, no! I want to go with Puppy!' Fanny cried at once. Durban rolled an expressive eye at his master.

'I don't think I ought to leave the dog, sir,' he said pointedly.

John Skelwith spoke up. 'Would it help if I led the pony home for you? It isn't far out of my way.'

'That's very good of you,' James said. 'I'm enormously grateful to you.'

'That's all right, sir. How would it be if I rode just ahead of you? It might calm your horses to see my old Trooper in front of them. Nothing ever startles him.'

He helped James turn the phaeton before catching Tempest and mounting his own horse, and taking up his position in front of them. The bays, sure enough, walked quietly with Trooper's broad rump directly ahead of them, while in the back of the phaeton Fanny kept up a crooning lament, and Durban parried her questions and evidently prevented her from examining the hound too closely.

James had plenty to keep his mind occupied on the short journey home; and only as they turned in under the barbican did he reflect that there was no-one but Ned left to be surprised at the sight of Mary Loveday's boy, Fanny's half-brother, leading the cavalcade home to what might so easily have been his house, his inheritance.

CHAPTER TWO

Héloïse called first at Fussell Manor on the Fulford Road, and did not find Lady Fussell at home; but making the second call at Foss End House in Walmgate, found her there, visiting her sister-in-law Mrs Crosby Shawe.

Lady Fussell, formerly Miss Lizzie Anstey, shared with Mrs Shawe, the former Miss Valentina Fussell, the distinction of having been very much in love with James Morland when they were all young, and he was in hopeless pursuit of Mary Loveday. It was not an exclusive distinction — James Morland had broken many hearts while occupied in breaking his own — but Lizzie and Valentina were perhaps the most willing of his lifelong captives, and were unusual in being sincerely glad that he had at last managed to marry the woman he loved. They liked Héloïse as they had not liked his first wife, and hoped, if wistfully, that he would now be happy.

'Lady Morland, how kind of you to come and see me,' Valentina said, holding out a welcoming hand from the sopha on which she was lying. 'Forgive me if I don't get up — I still suffer from giddiness if I move too quickly.'

Héloïse thought she was looking very pale and worn, and crossed the room quickly to take her hand. 'Oh, but you should not be up so soon! I made sure you would be in bed, and I meant only to send up my name and not disturb you. You poor thing! I am so very sorry! But the other children are well, I hope?'

'Yes, they keep very stout,' Valentina replied. 'I see you've brought your dear little ones! I'll send for my boys, and they can play together.'

'Thank you. Sophie, Thomas, come forward. Say good-day to Mrs Shawe and Lady Fussell. I have just come from Fussell Manor, ma'am,' she added to the latter. 'I left my card.'

'Did they not tell you I was here? I come every day. Poor 'Tina has been very low,' said Lady Fussell. She turned her

31

eyes hungrily on the children. 'And here is little Miss Sophie! I must tell you, Lady Morland, how I dote on her! And how quiet and good they both are — so different from my sister Celia's children, who are always squabbling and shrieking, and pull one about so, there's no bearing it. Come and give me a kiss, angels!'

Sophie obeyed good-naturedly, though Thomas, who was always rather shy, remained at Héloïse's side after making his bow to each of the ladies. Héloïse watched, amused, as Lady Fussell, fascinated by Sophie's bilingual abilities, attempted to converse with her in French, and was soon left floundering. Eventually Héloïse felt constrained to rescue her, and made Sophie recite from her repertoire of poems until Mrs Shawe's three boys were brought in by a nursery-maid. They were pale, undersized little things, Héloïse thought, with a pinched look about the eyes, and a shrinking air, as if they had been too often beaten. Beside them, Sophie looked strong and bright and vigorous, as though she had grown up in sunlight, and they in semi-darkness.

The children were introduced to each other, and taken away to another room to play, and the women were then free to converse more openly.

Valentina's miscarriage was naturally the first subject. She had been unlucky with her pregnancies, for this was the second consecutive miscarriage, and she had lost two of her children in infancy as well.

'But at least you have the dear boys,' Lizzie said mournfully. 'As for me, I have never shewn even the slightest sign of —' She sighed. 'I sometimes wonder if that's why Arthur is so — difficult.'

'No, love,' Valentina said, pressing her hand. 'I'm sure not. Arthur was always the same, even when he was a boy. Father was forever whipping him, but it never seemed to make the slightest difference.'

Arthur Fussell and Crosby Shawe had been schoolfriends. Lizzie and Valentina had made good marriages in the eyes of the world: for Lizzie, youngest of a large family and with only a modest dowry, to marry a baronet with an estate was considered brilliant; while Valentina, the baronet's quietest and least pretty sister, might have done much worse than Crosby Shawe, who had his merchant father's fortune to squander.

But Arthur, spoilt as a child, had grown up a thoroughly selfish, dissolute man, while Crosby Shawe, who was merely weak and impressionable, copied him in everything. Both men succeeded in making their wives very unhappy, and it was proof of how much the women had come to like Héloïse in the short time they had known her, that they could regard her evident happiness kindly.

Héloïse knew all about them and their husbands: Marie was a very good informant about everything that went on in the neighbourhood, and James in the course of their long conversations in bed had told her the rest.

'Arthur Fussell was always an arrogant little brute, foul-tempered and a fouler horseman. Worst hands in the Ridings! And a gamester! I was very sorry for Lizzie having to marry him. But their fathers arranged it all — they'd known each other for ever, and poor Lizzie at twenty-five was almost on the shelf. But I'm surprised at the way Crosby Shawe turned out. I always thought him a good enough sort of man: quiet, you know, and not much to him, but a dull and decent sort. But he and Arthur were bosom-bows at school, and I suppose the rest just followed. Valentina's a great deal too good for him. You might not think it to look at her,' he added, making Héloïse smile into the darkness at his naïveté, 'but she's a remarkably intelligent woman. The rest of her family were positively sheep-witted, but Valentina was always clever.'

Héloïse also knew, through Marie, that both women had been in love with James, and probably still were, but she gave no sign of that as she smiled and chatted easily to them.

'God moves in mysterious ways, Lady Fussell,' she said, embarrassing the ladies a little with the familiar way she introduced the Almighty into conversation. 'He has denied you children, which is very sad; but you are blessed with a great many nephews and nieces; and an aunt, you know, may sometimes have the best of it — all the fun and none of the sorrow.'

'Well, yes,' Lizzie said reluctantly, 'John's children bring me great pleasure, I grant you, and I'm fond of 'Tina's little boys.'

'My ward Mathilde is at this very moment visiting Miss Keating, who is also your niece, is she not?'

'Yes, Patience is my eldest sister Augusta's girl.'

33

'You must be very pleased with the way Miss Nordubois has turned out, Lady Morland,' Valentina put in. 'I have not had the pleasure of meeting her yet, but I hear good reports of her — a very modest, pretty-behaved girl, they say.'

'And her eighteenth birthday is next week, is it not?' Lizzie asked. 'I believe you are having a ball for her?'

'A very small thing,' Héloïse said. 'As she is my ward and not James's, it would not be proper at Morland Place to have anything very grand. But Mathilde looks forward to it very much.'

'Despite having her come-out in London?' Valentina said. 'She must be a modest girl indeed! And a trip to Brighton with Lady Chelmsford into the bargain, and all the glories of the military camp!'

'Ah yes, Brighton!' Héloïse laughed. 'She fell in love with a different officer every day!'

'Red coats have a dreadful effect on a girl's heart,' Lizzie said. 'I remember when the regiment was here in '79 — well, I was too young to care about officers, of course — but Augusta and your sisters, 'Tina, could talk about nothing else. They nearly broke their hearts when the regiment went abroad.'

'I remember!' Valentina laughed. 'Amelia and Caroline cried in each other's arms for a week over a certain Captain Matlock. If he'd favoured either of them over the other, they'd have hated each other, of course, but as he regarded them both with perfect indifference —'

'There is no better cure for a young girl's heartbreak than indifference,' Héloïse agreed. 'With Mathilde it was a certain Major Ashton of the Ninth.'

'We have a very decent sort of officer here at Fulford, you know,' Valentina said. 'A very gentlemanly set. Miss Nordubois might do worse than a handsome ensign.'

'There will be one or two officers at the ball,' Héloïse confessed. 'James knows the colonel.'

'Oh yes, of course. They all meet at the Maccabbees,' Lizzie said in a flat voice. The Maccabbees club was the source of a great deal of Lizzie's and Valentina's misery.

'James does not go there very often now,' Héloïse said, a little apologetically. 'He called on the colonel at the barracks, and the colonel invited him to dine.'

Just then the door was flung open, and Crosby Shawe walked in. He stopped short and goggled at them.

'Good God, what've I interrupted?' he exclaimed. It was evident from the first words that he was not entirely sober. 'It looks like that scene from that play — what's it called — with the three witches. You know — "Double, double —" or is it "Bubble, bubble —"? Never could remember. Shakespeare! Pa made me recite it for ever when I was in short coats. *Macbeth*, that's the dandy! The three wise women.'

'Mr Shawe, Lady Fussell and Lady Morland are visiting me,' Valentina said hastily.

'Can see that!' Crosby said indignantly. 'Wouldn't have come in if I'd known. Thought the room was empty. Damned if I want to listen to a lot of women's clacking!'

'Mr Shawe!'

'Anyway, Lizzie Fussell's always here. Nothing to make a fuss about. Is that your phaeton in the yard, Lady M? Wants its offside driving-wheel looking at, you know.'

'No, I didn't know,' Héloïse said with a calm good humour, 'but I shall tell my groom about it.'

'Told him myself, when I drove into it,' Crosby said, and laughed loudly at his own wit. 'Should think he knows now, all right.'

'Mr Shawe, do you mean you damaged Lady Morland's phaeton?'

'Not my fault,' he said sulkily. 'Damn stupid place for Brunty to put it, just inside the archway like that. Came round the corner at a hell of a lick and smashed — I mean,' he corrected himself fumblingly, 'I turned my tilbury in just as I always do, expecting the yard to be empty, and there was — this —' He paused again, looking owlishly round at them, aware that he was not shewing himself to advantage. 'S'only the one wheel. Got locked in mine, you see, and m'horse got in a panic, and wouldn't stand still.'

'I'm so sorry, Lady Morland,' Valentina said. 'You must send us the bill for the repair. I'm afraid our stableman is very stupid, and must have left your carriage in a very awkward place.'

In the irrational way of the drunkard, Crosby now grew angry with his wife for defending him. 'Yes, all right, I am a trifle foxed!' he said loudly, glaring at Valentina. 'Why not? I

35

went to the club for breakfast, and it's a cold morning. A man has to have something to keep the cold out, doesn't he?'

'Mr Shawe, I'm sure our guests don't want to know —'

'Don't want to know? I'll bet they do know, though. Arthur was there, anyway, Lizzie, so you see — and it isn't so long since Mr James Bloody Perfect Morland had his armchair by the fire every night. Founder member of the Maccabbees, Mr James Newly-Wed Morland!'

Héloïse, more in pity for the women than in shock at his behaviour, stood up, and said, 'I think, Mrs Shawe, that I ought to be going. I like Thomas to sleep in the afternoon —'

Crosby saw that he had gone too far, and became contrite. 'No, wait, don't go yet. I've got something to tell you.' He shook his head stupidly, trying to clear it. 'Wonder why I'm a little bit under the weather? Not foundered, you know — just a little windy! It's good news! Good news — heard it at the club — had to drink a toast, didn't we? It's just come up from London — Boney's been beaten!'

He stared at them hopefully, his dull and doggy eyes wandering a little. Héloïse heard the words with shock, and looked from Mrs Shawe's white face to Lady Fussell's. It was Valentina who took charge. She stood up and faced her husband, and her voice took on a ring of command which no-one but he had ever heard before.

'Beaten? What do you mean? Crosby, look at me, and tell me immediately exactly what you heard.'

'S'true!' he pleaded. 'Beaten to flinders, and some place called —' He screwed up his eyes with the effort, and then shook his head. 'Some jawbreaker of a name, in Prussia, anyway. Boney was in winter quarters, and the Russians attacked, and beat him completely. So we had some champagne — well, who wouldn't? And then Arthur said, he said, this is damn dull work without a drop of brandy to warm it up. Arthur said that!' His eyes swivelled round to Lizzie. 'It was the brandy that did the damage. All Arthur's fault!'

'Is it true? Crosby, look at me! Is it true? Is Bonaparte beaten?'

'Swear to God! Wiped out! The Cossacks hunted the Frenchies through the snow like rabbits! Thousands killed! Boney rubbed off to save his skin!'

'Thank God!' Lizzie said. 'Now perhaps the war will be over.'

Héloïse shook her head. 'Forgive me, but I cannot be so hopeful. Even if it is true, one defeat is not the end for a man like Bonaparte. If he is not dead, it is not all over.'

'Well, you may be right,' Valentina said briskly, 'but at all events, it shews he *can* be beaten, and that's something worth knowing. You did very right to come and tell us about it, Mr Shawe. And now perhaps you ought to go and change your necktie — it is a little crumpled, no doubt after your driving accident.'

She coaxed him to the door and her tact would have got him safely off, if a servant had not appeared at that moment in a state of great excitement.

'Oh ma'am,' she cried to Valentina, apparently noticing nothing of her master's condition or her mistress's pallor, 'there's a servant come for Lady Morland, ma'am, to fetch her home at once, on account there's been a terrible accident, and she's wanted, urgent as urgent!'

'Good God, what now?' Valentina muttered, putting a hand to her head.

'Accident?' Héloïse said, her lips paling. 'What accident?' Her mind offered her an instant image of the over-fresh, untrained bays, a splintered wreck, James carried home on a litter. 'Is someone hurt? *Nom de Dieu*, tell me at once!'

'Oh ma'am, m'lady, I should say,' the servant turned to her, eyes gleaming with relish, 'they're in a proper state at Morland Place, so the man said! It was Mr James, m'lady, took out a pair of young horses —'

'*Ciel!*' Héloïse cried. Her legs trembled, and Lizzie's hand caught her arm. 'Is he hurt?'

'Oh no, ma'am — m'lady — not him' the girl said, seeming unaware of the effect she was having, 'only that Miss Fanny followed him on her pony, ma'am, with her dog, and the dog got run over, and they're all in a proper to-do, and wanting you home this minute.'

Héloïse moistened her dry lips and took a firm grip of herself. 'Yes, I imagine poor Fanny must be very upset,' she managed to say. 'Mrs Shawe, if you would be so kind as to send for my children, I will go at once.'

'Of course,' Valentina said. 'Dora, go down at once and ask Mr Overton to have Brunty bring her ladyship's carriage to the door.'

'Yes, ma'am,' said the girl, but lingered, reluctant to let so promising a drama come to so little. 'The man says there was nearly a much worse accident, ma'am, for the dog was like to make the horses bolt, and there'd have been no holding 'em, and likely a terrible smash, but for Mr Skelwith coming up just at that moment and stopping them, and leading them home, too, safe and sound —'

'Dora, stop chattering and go at once!' Valentina said quickly, and even went so far as to propel the girl through the door with a hand in the small of her back.

The last words had meant nothing to Héloïse, but Crosby Shawe, who had been leaning against the door-frame listening all this while, grinned maliciously and said, 'Oho! Now we come to it! John Skelwith, hey? Is that what your husband gets up to when you're not there, Lady M?'

'Crosby!' said Valentina sharply.

'Ladybird, ladybird fly away home! Not quite so perfect now, is he, eh? Soon as you're out of sight, he starts bringing his by-blows home!'

'Crosby, you don't know what you're saying. Be silent!'

''Course I know,' he said, pushing himself upright, and curling his lip at his wife. 'I know you were in love with him — and Lizzie, too! S'pose you're still hankering after him — yes, I've seen the look in your eye when his name crops up! Well, if you're stuck with me, I'm stuck with you, too. And at least I never forced my bastards on you.'

The last words seemed to shock even him into silence, as he realised the lengths to which his drunken jealousy had led him. The silence seemed horribly long, and bristled with the unspoken and unspeakable. Héloïse felt her cheeks burning. It was impossible to meet anyone's eye. She thought for an instant that none of them would ever be able to move or speak again.

Then Crosby Shawe turned with an abrupt movement and went away. Lizzie's supporting hand was still under Héloïse's arm. She removed it cautiously, as if not wishing to draw attention to herself, and Héloïse, to her amazement, heard her own voice saying almost steadily, 'Perhaps if you would send for my children, Mrs Shawe —'

Valentina turned, her face white and shocked, but she followed Héloïse's lead. 'Of course,' she said steadily. 'You must be anxious to be off. Your carriage should be at the door by now. But I hope you will find things at Morland Place better than you fear. Servants always exaggerate.'

Lizzie was only just recovering her voice. 'Oh God!' she burst out, staring at them wild-eyed. 'How could Crosby say such things! Oh 'Tina —!'

'Lizzie, be quiet,' Valentina commanded.

'But he —'

'No,' Héloïse said kindly, touching Lizzie's hand. 'Nothing happened here. It's all right. Please, don't say any more.'

Somehow, she got away; took the children's hands and met Sophie's too-penetrating glance of enquiry; endured the butler's rambling explanation that her phaeton was not safe for a lady to drive, and that he would have it sent back, with her ponies, that afternoon; climbed into the carriage that had been brought round instead, and was driven home.

Sophie sat close, and slipped her hand into her mother's to comfort her, and Héloïse felt herself comforted. She was shocked, yes, but it was not as the other women probably thought. She knew James had had a wild youth, but nothing in his past impinged on her, or touched the deep core of love and trust that was between them. The shock had been at the words themselves, the spite and anger of them, and the dark, violent forces which had brought those words to be uttered. Crosby Shawe's crime was that he had rent the social fabric that bound them all and kept them in delicate equilibrium, an exact and tolerable distance apart.

Edward took less pleasure in despatching Puppy than he would have expected. The dog evidently had internal injuries, and was suffering, though only the occasional whimper escaped it, as it looked in pitiful entreaty from one face to another and occasionally licked its lips placatingly. Edward had often threatened to shoot the dog, and perhaps in a sort of irrational atonement for that he now insisted on taking the unhappy duty on himself.

Fanny, who could see no external damage to her dog, and who could not therefore believe that it was all up with him, screamed and fought when she understood what Edward meant to do, and had to be carried bodily away. Ned waited until she was out of earshot before doing the deed. He made the mistake of stroking Puppy's head before raising the gun, and the brute licked his hand and wagged its tail apologetically, as if it supposed the pain were punishment for a misdeed. Ned had had to despatch many animals in the course of his life, and he was damned if he could understand why this one was so hard. Puppy kept on looking up at him trustfully, so that his eyes actually misted over, and he had to wait a moment until his hands stopped shaking, before he could pull the trigger.

When he went outside again, the Skelwith boy was still there, looking troubled and at a loss.

'I'm sorry it had to come to that, sir,' he said. 'The little girl will be very upset.'

'It always was a useless dog,' Edward said shortly. 'Impossible to train it. I've threatened to shoot it many a time, but —' His voice disappeared.

'It doesn't make it any easier, though, does it?' Skelwith said with quiet sympathy. 'I remember when my mother's spaniel got too old, and I had to do the job for her. It's always hard.'

'Yes,' Edward said, and met the young man's eyes. He saw, with distant shock, how like Jamie he was. He's grown handsome, too, he thought, the way these things are measured; and he has Mary Loveday's quiet dignity. He remembered the day old Skelwith had come up to Morland Place to demand reparation and punishment for James. The scandal of this young man's birth had, Edward thought, broken their mother's heart and, he believed, shortened their father's life. One of James's many youthful indiscretions. Oh, the conversations he and his mother had had about Jamie over the years! She had always loved James best. Edward could hear her voice now, saying 'Dear Ned, you never give me a moment's unease: best of my children!' And he had tried not to; but in her heart it was Jamie, wicked Jamie, who held first place.

Now Mother was dead, and Chetwyn was dead, and Edward's life held nothing any longer of colour or warmth or joy. He filled his grey days with work, just to make himself tired enough to sleep; while Jamie had a new wife, his life's love, and his children. Where was the justice in that? And young John Skelwith was standing here in the yard of Morland Place, looking like a taller, younger James — that was extraordinary! What would Mother have thought, he wondered? The boy had grown up well, a pleasant, steady-looking young man, the sort you would instinctively trust.

'Would you like me to help you bury him, sir?' Skelwith said, and Edward realised he had been staring him out of countenance for some minutes. Not polite! And with this young man's quickness of mind, not safe!

'Thanks, but the grooms can do that. No need to trouble you with it. You've been more than kind already.'

'It was nothing, sir.' Still he stood, regarding Edward steadily, like a good soldier waiting for orders.

Edward felt suddenly lost, wanted to reach out to this young man in some way, make contact with him. 'I knew your mother, of course,' he blurted out, and it sounded foolish, even open to misinterpretation. 'I mean, we were all the same age, you know. She came to dances here — and the Fussell girls, and the Ansteys. My friend, the Earl of Aylesbury, danced with her once. Before she was married, of course.'

He stumbled to a halt, feeling astonished at his own stupid-ity, and suddenly John Skelwith smiled, a wide, friendly smile that made everything seem all right, and which held the ghost of that sidelong, enmeshing charm that had made Jamie so irresistible when he was one-and-twenty.

'I know,' he said. 'My mother was very handsome, I believe. Everyone was in love with her, so my Uncle Tom used to say. Well, if there's nothing more I can do, sir, I'd better be on my way.'

'Thank you again for all your help,' Edward said. Skelwith began to turn away, and suddenly he added, 'It's Mathilde's — Miss Nordubois' birthday next week. We're having a dance here on Tuesday for her — nothing grand, just a few young people, and a supper. I know Lady Morland would be delighted if you would come.'

It was a worse piece of clumsiness than the last, but Skelwith smiled again, and looked genuinely pleased.

'Thank you, sir, I should be honoured.'

'Good. Good,' Edward said helplessly, and Skelwith bowed and turned away to mount his stolid horse. He had Jamie's hands, too, Edward thought watching them firm and sensitive on the rein as he turned the horse towards the barbican.

41

Jamie's hands and Jamie's face, and I asked him to Mathilde's ball. Lord, what have I done?

By the time Héloïse reached home, Fanny had been quietened at last by a dose of laudanum which had sent her into a troubled sleep, but the atmosphere in the house was no easier for that. James was upset by his daughter's grief and pain, disturbed by the unexpected meeting with John Skelwith, and angry with Edward for having invited the boy to the ball.

'What the devil did you do it for?' he demanded, and Edward could not adequately explain it. The invitation could not now be withdrawn without explaining to everyone why contact between that particular young man and Morland Place ought to be avoided at all costs.

Edward was puzzled by his own stupidity; but pointed out angrily that it was James's fault the situation had arisen in the first place. 'It's always the same with you,' he said, all the old resentments seething in his heart. 'You blame everyone but yourself when something goes wrong, and it's always someone else that has to pick up the pieces. I told you from the beginning that you ought to train Puppy properly, but you never listened to me. An now he gets himself run over, and it's me that has to shoot him. And you've spoiled Fanny to the point where —'

'Oh shut up! You're always complaining about Fanny! I'm sick of it!'

'Yes, and Mother spoiled you, too. The number of times you broke her heart —'

'Don't start talking about Mother! I warn you, Ned, I won't stand it! You gave her plenty of grey hairs too —'

Edward and James had hardly ever quarrelled in their lives, one brother too industrious, the other too indolent ever to begin; but this quarrel, born of two sore hearts, escalated foolishly to the point where each was too hurt to continue, and they stumped away to brood at opposite ends of the house. By the time Héloïse came home, they were treating each other with wounded dignity.

James told her the story of the mishap and Puppy's death in a voice so racked with guilt that she wanted only to comfort him, and said gently that it was a great pity, but that

42

nothing so very bad had happened after all, and that the shock might even do Fanny good in the long term. Then Edward explained stumblingly that he had invited John Skelwith to the ball in gratitude for his help; and Héloïse took pity on him and said he was quite right to do so, and that she would write out the invitation the following day. She left them both more comfortable than she had found them, and they were too glad to have been eased to notice her unusual preoccupation.

At dinner there was still too much silence, so to make conversation she mentioned the rumour of the defeat of Bonaparte. Father Aislaby, fortunately, had more details to offer.

'Yes, it's true Bonaparte has been beaten. It's the first setback he's suffered on land since he was forced to flee from Egypt, and that was eight years ago.'

'I remember. Everyone thought he was finished then, but he came back,' Héloïse sighed. 'But what happened this time?'

'You remember that business at Putulsk in December? The Russians and French fought, and both sides got pretty badly mauled, but couldn't claim a victory. Well, it seems Boney had taken his army into winter quarters at a place called Preuss-Eylau, somewhere in the north of Prussia, and the Russians attacked them actually in camp. They fought in a snowstorm all through the streets of the town, and there was a great deal of confusion. Casualties were heavy on both sides, but the French came off rather the worse, and when they retreated, it turned into a rout.'

'And what will happen now?' Héloïse asked.

Aislaby shrugged. 'Not much, I imagine. The Russians will be anxious to press home their advantage, of course, and as we are their allies, they will look to us for support. But even if the Government had an army available to send to Prussia, I doubt whether it would. Grenville and his friends have never been keen on getting involved in Europe itself. Don't forget they came to power through an upsurge of anti-war feeling.'

'Grenville will soon be gone, you mark my words,' Edward said. 'Then we'll see something start to happen. We'll get some ministers who really believe in the war, and who'll fight it whole-heartedly. That's the only way to beat Boney.'

★ ★ ★

Later that night, Héloïse sat at her dressing-table while Marie brushed out her hair, making her ready for bed. James came through from the dressing-room, and Héloïse, noting his preoccupied air, took the brush from Marie and dismissed her with a nod. She observed James's reflection in the mirror as he walked aimlessly up and down the room, and continued to brush her hair with slow, thoughtful strokes.

'Well,' she said at last, when it was obvious he was not going to initiate the conversation. 'It has been quite a day for both of us.'

'Yes,' he said absently. 'Shall we go to bed?'

'Not yet, my James,' she said. 'We should talk a little. I think that something is disturbing you.'

He paused in his pacing, and gave her a rueful smile. 'Are you surprised? That business with Fanny and the dog —' He came over to stand behind her, took the brush from her, and began to brush her hair.

She bent her head to his strokes and half-closed her eyes in bliss, like a cat. 'It was very lucky,' she said casually, 'that John Skelwith came along. He seems a very good sort of young man, from what Edward says. He was right to ask him to Mathilde's ball. Have you known him long?'

'I've known *of* him all his life,' James said shortly, 'but I can't say I know him. He hasn't happened to have come in my way.'

'I think I had better call on his mother, before I send the invitation. It would be polite. You knew her, I believe?'

James looked at her sharply. 'What do you mean by that?' Her eyes met his in the glass, and she continued to look at him steadily, serenely; saying nothing, waiting for him to speak. 'Yes,' he said at last. 'I knew his mother. Well, we all did. We grew up together.' He hesitated, and Héloïse smiled.

'Go on, my James. Tell me the story. And go on brushing my hair, too. It feels so nice.'

The action, she knew, would help him talk. 'Well,' he began, 'there was Edward's friend, John Anstey, who was in love with my sister Mary, and Tom Loveday, who was Anstey's friend, and his sister Mary Loveday, who was my sister Mary's friend. We were all meeting for ever at balls and parties. Mary Loveday was a few years older than me. She was quiet and clever. I suppose that's why I liked her.'

He stopped again, and this time Héloïse just waited, knowing that it was coming. 'In fact, Marmoset, I have a confession — I more than liked her, I was in love with her. Oh, I was only a green boy then, and I don't suppose she thought me anything but a vague nuisance. But she was kind to me — I think it amused her to have me pursuing her so hard, when the other young women were all after me. It makes me sound like a coxcomb, I know, but so it was.'

'Yes, my love,' she prompted gently. 'What then?'

James's mouth turned down bitterly. 'The Lovedays weren't well-to-do. They were an old family, and respectable, but the father speculated unwisely, and the long and short of it was that when Mary was twenty, he arranged a marriage for her which was to repair his fortunes. The chosen man was old John Skelwith, a builder, very rich, with enterprises all over Yorkshire. A coming man, you might say. The trouble was, he was thirty years older than she.'

Héloïse nodded gravely. 'Such marriages are less common now than they were. No doubt her father had her best interests at heart; but I can see how it would appear to you.'

'Appear to me?' He looked at her over her shoulder, amazed. 'Don't tell me that you would approve of such a match! A girl of twenty and a bow-legged old man of fifty?'

'And you were — how old? Eighteen?'

'Seventeen.'

Her eyes twinkled. 'Yes, my James, seventeen, and hot-blooded, and handsome, and in love with this Mary Loveday. It must have seemed very bad to you. But she did not refuse the marriage, did she?'

'How could she? I told you it was arranged for her —'

'Ah yes, so you said. But you know, women are not always so romantic as men. Sometimes they may put practical matters first; and a kind, wealthy, older man may make a very good husband for a woman who is still unwed at twenty.'

'You know nothing about the case,' James said stiffly.

Héloïse reached behind her and put her hand over his. 'Perhaps not. But I know you, my James. You thought she had been forced into the marriage, and wanted to rescue her, like the *chevalier sans peur et sans reproche*! And perhaps also

45

your pride did not want to believe that she preferred this old man to you for a husband?'

He put the brush down hard on the dressing-table and tugged his hand free from hers; and then met her amused but sympathetic eyes in the glass, and gave a reluctant half-smile.

'Well, you may be right. Perhaps I was rather a coxcomb, and there was some hurt pride in the case. But I really loved her, Marmoset — that I do know. She was intelligent and fine, and I hated to see her sold like a horse for the sake of her fool of a father.'

'Well, *mon âme*, so what did you do?'

'Do?' James looked rather startled.

'You said you had a confession,' Héloïse reminded him. 'You have confessed nothing yet.'

He reddened. 'Ah — yes. I don't know quite how to tell you.'

'Go on from where you stopped — that is the best way. You loved this Mary Loveday. She married Mr Skelwith. *Et puis?*'

He looked away. 'He was away a great deal, her husband, attending to his business. I met her by chance one day in the street. I was miserable and she was lonely, and one thing led to another —' His eye returned to hers reluctantly. 'I became her lover. I know it was wrong, but I felt that she had been wrong to marry him, and that her father was wrong to force her to, and that —'

'Everyone was wrong, so one more wrong did not matter?' Héloïse offered.

'Don't make fun of me,' he said.

'You mistake me, my James,' she said gravely. 'There is no fun in the story, only sadness.'

'Yes,' he said, still hurt, 'and you don't yet know it all. Mary conceived, and because her husband had been away so long, it was obvious that the child could not be his. There was the devil of a to-do. He came up to Morland Place to demand that I be horse-whipped, and Mary came after him to plead for me. My father furious, my mother in tears, me in disgrace — everything as bad as it could be! Well, they calmed the old man down, and persuaded him to forgive Mary, and I was packed off to Court to get me out of the way, and everything was hushed up. I would have stood by her and looked after her and the child, but no-one wanted that, not even Mary. Especially not Mary.'

She turned and put her arms around him, feeling him rigid with the memory of his old anger. 'Come,' she said, 'come to bed.' He resisted. 'It is enough now,' she said. 'Come, my own love.'

In bed, when the candle was out, she felt him begin to relax in her arms. Some things were easier said into the darkness.

'So the young man, John Skelwith, is your son?' she said.

James grunted.

'Does he know it?'

He roused himself. 'I don't know. I hope not. Mary always said not. She said that was why she —'

'Why she would not see you any more? Well, my James, she was right. You were angry with her for refusing to leave her husband, weren't you?' He grunted again. 'But to compound the fault could not have cured it, don't you see? She had already agreed to marry another man, instead of you. It would be both weakness and folly to take you now, on worse terms than she had rejected you for. She had to make the best of it, and do the best for the child.'

'You think she was right?' he said, but his indignation was already less.

'I think she did the only thing possible. And if this John Skelwith does not know you are his father, then she has done well, and you would not put all her trouble at nothing, would you, love?'

'I wouldn't tell him, if that's what you mean. What kind of a fool do you take me for? It would hurt him, to no purpose.'

'Is that how you see it? You are in the right, of course,' she said, and there was a silence. She felt him gradually relaxing, his breathing slowing and steadying towards sleep, his body growing heavier. 'And now I have a confession to make also, my heart's love,' she said, choosing her moment.

'Mmm?' he enquired sleepily.

'I knew already that this young man was your child.'

'What?' he struggled up from the edge of sleep. 'You knew? Then why —?'

'I found it out today by accident; but I had to let you tell me yourself. How would you have thought if I had come to you, asking, like an accusation? It would have come between

47

us — now, it is nothing.'

'You —! You are —' he was at a loss for words.

'Very clever: I know,' she smiled into the dark. 'One of us must be clever, my James, for it is certain you are not.'

'No? But there is something I am good for, isn't there?' he enquired dangerously.

'Many things, *mon amant*,' she concurred, allowing herself to be engulfed. '*Mais surtout —*'

'*Surtout*,' he finished for her, 'to love you. As I do, Marmoset. This will not come between us, then, this business?'

'Nothing can come between us, love,' she said. 'It is good that Edward has asked John Skelwith to the ball. We shall make him welcome, and treat him just like anyone else. He will never suspect anything, and it will make up a little for the past.'

'How can it, if he never knows?' James said, kissing her ear.

'Not for him: for you,' she said into his hair.

48

CHAPTER THREE

Héloïse lost no time in calling on Mrs Skelwith. The following day, as soon as she had completed her morning tasks, she ordered the carriage to be brought to the door in half an hour, and went upstairs to dress, with Kithra and Marie at her heels.

'What shall it be, Marie?' she asked, staring at her reflection in the glass, while Kithra sat helpfully on the shoes she had just taken off. 'I must be smart, but not threatening. She will wonder how much I know, and what I intend. We are not rivals, but she may feel so. I must make just the right impression. It is a delicate business.'

'Yes, madame,' Marie said reflectively.

Their eyes met. Héloïse thought suddenly of all this woman had been through with her, of fear and betrayal and death and exile, of poverty and privation and sorrow. There had been days in Paris when the air was heavy with the smell of blood; when if you walked abroad, you were careful to meet no-one's eye; when you did not know from hour to hour which friendly neighbour or faithful servant might betray you to your death. Their King and Queen had been murdered, and their country was taken from them for ever; and beside all these things, any present preoccupation with the feelings of a Yorkshire housewife must seem absurdly trivial.

Kithra, sensing an atmosphere, edged forward a little and thumped his tail on the ground. Héloïse said suddenly, 'Marie, do you remember my little dog Bluette? I wish I knew what happened to her when we fled from France.'

'Oh madame,' Marie said, and suddenly their arms were around each other and they were both in tears, while Kithra whined and pressed his cold, wet nose between them. It was a good and cleansing thing to do, to weep, and when they had done, they dried each other's faces and felt restored.

'After all, James was not locked up in a box until I met

49

him,' Héloïse said briskly, and chose the new cherry-red pelisse trimmed with grey fur, and the velvet mameluk hat with the jaunty tassel, and her big grey fur muff. There now, she addressed her reflection, do your worst, Mary Loveday. You have his son; but he is mine now. You cannot hurt me.

Her phaeton was being repaired, so it was in her predecessor's *vis-à-vis* that she was driven into York. There was the usual crush of coaches and carts queueing to get over the Ouse Bridge, and she had plenty of time while they waited their turn to observe that the river was very high, and that King's Staith was flooded again. A band of workmen was labouring with grapples to rescue bales of wool from the warehouse there, and some barelegged children were gathering driftwood from the murky waters.

It took a long time to manoeuvre round the junction of Ousegate and Spurriergate, where the four streams of traffic had jammed themselves almost solid, but then they were trotting along Coney Street, and Héloïse caught a glimpse of the tangle of hovels and filthy yards and tenements which lay between the main street and the river. It was just like the Paris of her childhood, she thought, where behind the rows of great houses lay another teeming world of poverty, of ragged children and dunghills and foraging pigs and chickens; and the thought was somehow comforting, as if her world were not, after all, completely lost to her.

They crossed St Helen's Square, and now they were in Stonegate. There on the corner of Little Stonegate was the Maccabbees club, the heavy red velvet curtains at the upper windows promising comfort and seclusion to men who wished to escape from their wives, their duns, their responsibilities, or their sorrows. She thought of James drinking himself to forgetfulness there once a week during the years of his marriage to Mary Ann, and was sad at the waste of it all.

She remembered the terrible anguish she had suffered when she first heard that James and Mary Ann had a son. Well, Mary Ann was dead, and the boy was dead; and now she was going to visit another woman who had borne James a son.

The carriage halted outside the imposing stone frontage of Skelwith House. Like so many York houses, it was an old building with a modern façade, added not only to improve the look of the property, but to comply with the new fire

50

regulations: inside, she knew, it would present the crooked, humane proportions of a mediæval frame house. Now that the carriage was halted, Héloïse could hear the cathedral bells rocking the air above the roofs, the top layer in a cacophany of sounds which astonished her anew every time she came into the city.

The footman stepped down and rapped at the door, and when the servant answered, came to open the carriage door for his mistress, and let down the step.

'Come back for me in a quarter of an hour,' Héloïse said. The Skelwith servant was waiting, holding the house door open for her. She thrust her hands into her muff, took a deep breath, and stepped forward, inwardly rehearsing her opening speech.

A few moments later she was being shewn into a parlour on the first floor. It was a low-ceilinged room at the back of the house, whose small casement windows let in little light; but there was a bright fire burning in a modern hearth, and Mrs Skelwith rose from a chair pulled up beside it to meet her.

'I hope you will forgive me for calling on you without leaving my card first,' Héloïse said at once, 'but as I believe you are an old friend of the family, I hoped you would not think it an impertinence.'

'Not at all, Lady Morland. I'm very glad you did call,' Mrs Skelwith said. The words were hospitable, but the tone was unemphatic. 'Indeed, I should have called on you after your wedding, but I'm afraid I'm a sad invalid now, and rarely go out, except to church, so I hope you will forgive me. Won't you sit down?'

Héloïse sat down in the chair opposite and looked at her properly for the first time. *Why, she's quite old,* was the first thought that occurred. The former Mary Loveday was a thin woman in whose face any youthful beauty she may have possessed had been extinguished by years and unhappiness. There were unbecoming shadows around her eyes, two lines of discontent drew down her mouth corners, and her skin had the dry and unnourished look of a woman without a lover. Her hair was hidden by a cap whose lack of trimming was almost defiant; her gown was of good material, but of a sober brown, and plain except for some narrow black velvet edging; and she wore a fine cashmere shawl round her shoulders as if for warmth, rather than for ornament.

Was this the woman James had loved? Héloïse thought in astonishment. And yet, perhaps she might once have been pretty. Why was she so sad? Had she really loved James so much? But no, surely no-one could waste their whole life in regretting something they could never have. She thought guiltily about her own long exile from his arms, all the years when he was married to Mary Ann, and felt a brief kinship with Mrs Skelwith. But then, she thought, I never mourned and brooded and shut myself away like this. I tried to live my life and love God, and I almost married. The room was comfortably furnished with many signs of wealth; and a wealthy widow could always marry, if she had a mind.

But that only brought her back to the unhappy suspicion that perhaps this woman was in permanent mourning for James. The silence was beginning to be uncomfortable to Héloïse, and since Mrs Skelwith did not seem to feel obliged to initiate conversation, she said, 'I have not had the pleasure of meeting your son, but he did my husband and step-daughter a great service yesterday.'

Mary Skelwith looked at her with a leaden eye, but said nothing.

'Indeed,' Héloïse went on determinedly, 'if it were not for him, I believe my husband might have had a sad accident, so I am most grateful to him, as you can imagine.' Still no response. 'He must be a great comfort to you?'

She injected enough interrogative into the statement to force Mrs Skelwith to answer.

'He is a good son,' she replied. Her voice was light, but toneless, like a tired wind murmuring. 'He has never given me a day's unease in his life.'

'I suppose he mentioned what happened yesterday?' Héloïse said, thinking it best to stick to direct questions.

'Yes,' said Mrs Skelwith, defeating the ploy.

The sun came out for a moment, and in the briefly improved light, Héloïse saw that she was being studied closely with a suspicious and perhaps hostile eye. How much, she suddenly wondered, did Mary Skelwith know about her? Did she know about the time James ran away from his wife to live with her? Did she know, or at least guess, whence Sophie came? She suddenly saw herself from the other woman's point

52

of view — like her, a former mistress, and mother of an unintentional child; but fifteen years younger, and now possessed of the prize. Did she think it unfair? If indeed she did still love James, it must be a bitter thing for her to comtemplate, and Héloïse's ready sympathy rose up.

She leaned forward a little and said warmly, 'Well, as I said, we are all very grateful to your son, and I am glad that it gives me the opportunity to make your acquaintance. We are having a little ball next week, for my ward's birthday, who is eighteen, and I hope so much that he will be able to come to it. I believe that your son and my ward have many acquaintances in common, so it will be pleasant for the young people to be together. And perhaps you —'

'You refine upon it too much, madam,' Mrs Skelwith interrupted suddenly. 'It was no very great service that John rendered your husband. There is no need to reciprocate in any way, or to build on the acquaintance, as you seem, for reasons I cannot understand, eager to do.'

It was the most direct snub Héloïse had ever received in her life, and it so surprised her that for a moment she felt neither hurt nor anger; and she was still staring at Mrs Skelwith, trying to assemble her wits, when the door opened, and a tall young man came in. He was in riding clothes, and a faint smell of outdoors and stables clinging to him suggested he had just arrived home. Mrs Skelwith looked annoyed at his appearance, but she could have been no more agitated than Héloïse at this first sight of John Skelwith.

He looks like James, she thought, and it went through her like a hot needle into her heart. It was one thing to know with the mind that Mary Skelwith had borne a son to James; but to meet with the reality of it, to see the flesh and blood of it standing before her, was quite another. Her hands were cold in her lap, and she felt the blood leave her head, so that for a moment the room went dark, and she heard him speaking through a roaring mist.

'Mama — Betty told me Lady Morland had called. I'm so glad I wasn't too late. Lady Morland, how do you do? Forgive me for coming in in all my dirt, as you see me, but I did not want to miss the opportunity of making your acquaintance.'

Héloïse could not speak. Her lips felt numb as she offered her hand to the young man, who grasped it warmly, and

53

smiled down at her with James's elusive smile. The brown hand which held hers was James's too, the shape of the nails, the fine, long-jointed fingers, the texture of the skin. Across the room she caught sight of Mary Skelwith's face, and thought in a brief access of pity, *Dear God, she has lived with this ghost for twenty-one years — half her life! No wonder she looks so weary.*

'I am pleased to meet my husband's rescuer,' she managed to say at last, 'and to make formal the invitation my brother Edward gave you yesterday. We will all be very pleased if you will come to Mathilde's ball on Tuesday. I was speaking of it to your mother when you arrived.'

'I shall be delighted to come,' John said quickly. 'In fact, by coincidence, I had the pleasure of meeting Miss Nordubois yesterday afternoon. When I got back into town, I met her walking with Miss Keating and Tom in High Petergate, and as the Keatings are old friends of mine, they were able to make me known to her.'

'Well, then that is settled. I am so glad. You will find it quite an informal dance, just ten other couples, but all friends, I think.' She removed her fascinated gaze from John's face and looked a little defiantly at Mary Skelwith. 'I thought it only proper to call on your mama,' she added, 'as it seems by some chance we have never met before.'

'That was good of you,' John said warmly. 'I'm afraid my mother goes out very little, and as I am so much from home, life is sometimes very dull for her.' He smiled from his mother to Héloïse, and essayed a little joke. 'She must be eager for me to marry at last, so that I may bring home a daughter for her to love.'

'Nonsense! I have never said anything of the sort, John,' Mary Skelwith snapped. 'And as to the ball, I have already told Lady Morland that there is no need at all —'

Héloïse held her breath, but John only leaned down and silenced his mother with a kiss on the cheek. 'None at all,' he said cheerfully. 'That is why it is so kind, and why I am *very glad to accept*, Mama.'

The emphasis he placed on the words shewed Héloïse that they had already discussed the matter, and she wondered, rather troubled, what reason Mary had given him for not wishing to further the acquaintance. She could hardly have told him the truth. What must he imagine? Oh, what a tangled web, she thought wearily, and suddenly wanted to be out and away from here, away from this claustrophobic atmosphere of secrets and choked passions. How had John Skelwith managed to grow up so straight and fair in such inhospitable soil? She hoped he really would enjoy the dance: she doubted if he had had much simple pleasure so far in his life.

'I must take my leave of you now,' she said, rising. 'I am so glad to have met you both.'

'And I am honoured to have met you, ma'am,' John said. 'I look forward very much to Tuesday.'

Mary Skelwith said nothing, only watched Héloïse across the room with a gaze of burning resentment.

The addition of John Skelwith's name to the list of guests for Mathilde's ball caused certain problems. To make the numbers even, another suitable young female had to be found. Héloïse applied to Mrs Micklethwaite, the attorney's wife, who knew everyone, for intelligence. She was a comfortable woman of the old-fashioned sort, mother of a large and hopeful family, pillar of society, and staunch minder of everyone's business; and after careful thought, she suggested Miss Cowey of Beverley House, or Miss Chubb of Bootham Park. Miss Chubb was already on the list, and as Miss Cowey would never go to any kind of evening party without her next sister, Miss Pansy Cowey, that left the numbers uneven again.

Mrs Micklethwaite could offer no more help. 'You seem to have asked all the best young men already,' she complained. 'You have my Joe and my Ned, and you might have my Horace too, and welcome, but he's only just sixteen, and the likes of Miss Chubb and Miss Williams won't care to dance with a boy younger than themselves. I hardly know what to suggest.'

'I suppose I must look further afield,' Héloïse sighed. 'But I did so want all the guests to be friends — apart from the officers, of course.'

'Officers?' Mrs Micklethwaite asked, a little sharply.

'Three young officers from Fulford,' Héloïse explained. 'Very gentlemanly, I am assured, and recommended by their colonel, who is a friend of James's, and by the colonel's wife, who inspected them on purpose.'

Mrs Micklethwaite laughed. 'Then there's your problem solved,' she said. 'Ask the officers to bring a friend. Depend upon it, they will have no difficulty in recruiting someone, and the girls will be delighted to have the choice of four red coats instead of three.'

'But the mamas,' Héloïse asked anxiously. 'How will they like it? I do not wish them to think I am bringing their daughters to meet strangers.'

'If they're gentlemen, unwed, and possessed of anything resembling a fortune, the mamas will be as meek as pussycats, I promise you,' Mrs Micklethwaite said. 'Particularly Lady Grey, with her seven daughters to shift off her hands. I presume you must be having one Grey girl at least to the dance? Nothing ever happens within twenty miles of York without a Grey girl turning up.'

'Actually, there are three invited,' Héloïse said guiltily. 'Lady Grey was so pressing —'

'Three! The impudence of that woman knows no bounds! Well, my dear, you ask the officers to bring a friend. The Grey girls will dance with anything male and over eighteen.'

On the evening of the ball, everything looked set fair: it was dry and mild, and the full moon sailed clear between a few small clouds, so there was no reason for anyone to cry off. The family dined early to allow time to dress, and to give the servants the chance to clear the dining-room and lay out the supper. The floor of the long saloon had been chalked and tested, the flowers had been arranged and the chairs set out, and the musicians had already arrived and were being entertained in the servants' hall under Ottershaw's watchful eye.

The only problem, apart from Mathilde's extreme nervousness, which Héloïse hoped and trusted would go away of its own accord as soon as the fun began, seemed to be Fanny. She had always regarded Mathilde with too much contempt to wish to torment her, but the thought of a ball being given in *her* house for that ugly, freckled thing was too much to be borne in silence; especially when she discovered that she, Fanny, was to take no part in it.

'But Fanny, love, you're only eleven. You're much too young to go to balls. When your turn comes, when you're

56

older —' James coaxed again and again.

'I don't care! It's my house, and she shan't have a ball if I can't go! It's not fair! I'm nearly eleven-and-a-half, and it is old enough, it is!'

Fanny raged, and then sobbed, and then threatened. 'I'll spoil it. I'll *do* something, and then you'll be sorry.' And finally, her most pointed weapon, 'You don't love me any more. Ever since that woman came, you love everybody better than me. Everybody has things, except me. You killed my dog, and now I haven't got *anything*!'

Héloïse retired early in the altercation, knowing her presence would not help. Edward, rolling his eyes expressively, left the room the moment it began and went down to the kennels to shut up the house dogs, and managed to stay there settling them until the storm had passed. After long negotiation, James finally persuaded Fanny to go to bed and not to spoil the ball on condition that she would be allowed to watch the arrivals from the upper hall, and that James would personally bring her a tray of supper, and sit with her while she ate it.

Meanwhile, Héloïse and Marie had attended Mathilde in the Red Room to help her dress. Her gown was a present from James for her birthday, fine white jaconet muslin, embroidered with tiny flowers.

'It is very pretty, mademoiselle,' Marie observed, hooking up the pearl buttons down the back. 'And it fits you to perfection. But you will need to tuck a little lace,' she added approvingly. Mathilde had filled out a little since her come-out last year, and now, in Marie's opinion, had a very adequate figure.

'I wonder what my poor Flon would have said about it,' Héloïse sighed. 'I wish she could have lived to see you dancing at Morland Place!'

'She'd have found some fault, to be sure, madame,' Marie said with a small smile. 'The seams, or the set of the sleeve. Once a mantuamaker, always a mantuamaker.'

Héloïse had lent from her own wardrobe a spangled gauze shawl, and said as she arranged it, 'You wear a shawl so nicely, *chérie*. Some girls can, and some girls can't. It makes you look very elegant.'

Mathilde gave her a nervous but grateful smile. 'I'm sure I

shall trip over or drop my fan or something,' she said.

'Nonsense, why should you? You had a whole Season in London, and your come-out ball in Chelmsford House, and you didn't fall over once. Have some sense of proportion, *ma petite*. This is a small affair.'

'I know, I'm sorry. I don't know why I'm being so silly,' Mathilde said contritely, and Héloïse put an arm round her and kissed her heartily.

'You're not silly, you're a good girl; and you look lovely.'

'Madame, please!' Marie protested, dropping her comb. '*Attention aux cheveux, s'il vous plaît!*'

'Now, what have you for ornament?' Héloïse asked, when Marie had finished with the head. Mathilde's hair was the burnished, surprising colour of a marmalade cat, and she had arranged it in a cluster of shining Greek curls, threaded with narrow silver ribbon. 'The crystal beads that Lady Chelmsford bought you in Brighton, perhaps?'

'No, Madame, if you please,' Mathilde said hesitantly, her cheeks colouring. 'I have something else, if you think it is suitable — a present. Look — it was from Mr Edward Morland.'

'Oh, but how pretty!' Héloïse said, as Mathilde brought forward a small white jeweller's box and, opening it, revealed a necklace of gold filagree interspersed with small gold beads: very simple, delicate and pretty. 'When did he give you this?'

'This morning, after chapel,' Mathilde said. 'For my birthday, he said, but he wanted me to have it in time for the ball. May I wear it?'

'Of course, love. It is the very thing. How kind of him to think of it!' Héloïse said. She had thought Edward too preoccupied with the estate, and too wrapped up in his sadness, to notice Mathilde's existence.

'But he is kind,' Mathilde said, surprised, giving the necklace to Marie to fasten for her. 'Whenever I speak to him, he always listens so kindly, even when he is busy.'

'I am glad to hear it. Well, then,' Héloïse said, 'are you ready? Shall we go down?'

'Quite ready, Madame.' Mathilde gathered up her train, picked up her fan, and made her way downstairs. James and Edward were waiting in the great hall, warming their tails at the fire, and Héloïse thought how very handsome James looked in black and white, and just for a moment wished that it was not exclusively a young people's ball, and that she might dance with him. Edward had graced the occasion by powdering; the contrast with his brown skin made him look younger, and rather handsome.

'It is an elegant custom,' she told him approvingly. 'It is only a pity you men don't power more often.'

'I've never powdered in my life,' James said in horror at the thought. 'Not voluntarily, that is. God forbid! Of course, Ned doesn't crop either. He's the old-fashioned sort.'

'We're not here to discuss our appearance,' Edward said sternly. 'This is Mathilde's evening. Miss Nordubois, I should call you now, shouldn't I?' he said, smiling at her. 'May I say you look quite lovely tonight?'

Mathilde returned the smile shyly. 'Thank you sir. And thank you again for the necklace. It was very kind of you.'

'You compliment me by wearing it, my dear,' Edward said.

James caught Héloïse's eye and raised his eyebrows mockingly, and putting his mouth to her ear murmured, 'A very pretty scene — and a credit to all concerned.'

Héloïse frowned him down. 'James, behave yourself,' she said firmly. 'Is that a carriage I hear?'

The first arrival had come the furthest: Mathilde's old friend Lizzie Spencer from Coxwold, who was to stay at Morland Place for a few days. Then a clutch of coaches arrived one after the other, and for the next half-hour the great hall was filled with the noise and movement of arrival. The young women clustered together, light and pretty in their pale, delicate muslins, their heads, like flowers atop long stems, bound with beads or ribbons or tall plumes, nodding together as they chattered excitedly and admired each other's toilettes.

The young men were strange and suddenly dignified in their evening-dress and on their best behaviour, remembering not to bellow with laughter or jostle each other as they normally did on meeting. They smirked and pulled down their upper lips, anxiously comparing their own calf muscles, hairstyle and neckcloth with those of their friends. One or two had shaved rather too enthusiastically; some found the constriction of their collars unfamiliar. Only Tom Keating and John Skelwith seemed perfectly at ease, the former having too good a conceit of himself, the latter being too mature and sensible to be nervous.

The officers from Fulford arrived last, and at their entrance the chatter died down, as the young women eyed them admiringly and the young men bristled with resentment. The red coats were so distinctive and becoming, and the officers themselves seemed so sophisticated, bringing with them the scent of a larger world, of brighter lights and more dashing music. The three originally invited were two young cornets, Brunton and Fenwick, who had the downy faces and charming manners of someone's favourite nephews, and a Lieutenant Finucane, who was tall and had red hair and a hint of Irish in his voice.

They presented themselves most properly to James and Héloïse, and Finucane then brought forward the fourth officer, on whom all female eyes had been secretly fixed since they entered the great hall.

'May I present Lieutenant Fitzherbert Hawker, ma'am?' Finucane said. 'A friend and distant cousin of mine, who when he heard of my fortune in being invited here tonight, was ready to kidnap me, steal my invitation, and impersonate me, for the chance of clapping his eyes on you!'

Hawker was tall — not as tall as Finucane, but better proportioned — with an elegant figure, and a head of dark wavy hair any woman would have envied. His lean, handsome features were lit by a pair of smiling blue eyes, and his clothes appeared to have been moulded on him. Héloïse did not quite like Finucane's nonsense, and Hawker appeared to perceive this, for as he bowed over her hand, he gave a charming, boyish smile and said, 'I must apologise for my friend, ma'am. His Irish blood makes him a little high-spirited sometimes, but he means no impertinence, I promise you.'

He made his bow very respectfully to James and Edward, and accepted his introduction to Mathilde with just the right degree of polite friendliness to suit the informality of the occasion, and the fact that he was several years her senior. Héloïse was puzzled to guess exactly how old Hawker was. He seemed older in his manner than any of them except John Skelwith, but his physiognomy suggested that he was no more than twenty-one or -two.

'Have you been long at Fulford, Mr Hawker?' she asked, hoping to calculate something from his answer.

'Not long, ma'am; in fact, I came up from Brighton only a

month ago. I was with the Sussex.'

'Brighton — oh, I have been to Brighton,' Mathilde exclaimed. 'I was there last summer.'

Hawker bowed to her. 'I am only sorry I did not have the opportunity of making your acquaintance there,' he said, 'but I joined the Sussex only in October.'

'Brighton is a delightful place, isn't it?' Mathilde said enthusiastically.

'Very,' Hawker said, with a slight, conspiratorial smile at Héloïse. 'Did you attend any of the evening parties at the Pavilion?'

'Yes, several.'

'And how did you like His Highness?' Hawker asked, and the tone of his voice was satirical enough even to alert Mathilde.

'He was very — affable,' she said uneasily, glancing at Héloïse for help. From above the sounds of music revealed that the band had warmed up and were ready to play; glancing up, Héloïse saw a flash of white behind the balustrade, which she assumed was Fanny watching the arrivals. James and Edward were chatting to the older people and chaperones who had accompanied the girls.

'I think perhaps we might go up,' she said loudly, to catch everyone's attention. 'I think it is time to begin.'

Hawker bowed to Mathilde and said, 'Might I have the inestimable honour of your hand for the first dance, Miss Nordubois?'

He pronounced her name perfectly, which pleased and confused her. 'Oh, thank you — I should — but I am engaged already, to Mr Skelwith.'

John Skelwith, who had drifted up to them, nodded gravely at Hawker, and offered his arm to Mathilde. Hawker gave a charming, rueful smile.

'I am bested,' he said, and as they walked away, he turned to Héloïse. 'In that case, ma'am, may I solicit the even higher honour of your hand? *Voulez-vous danser avec moi, madame la comtesse?*'

Héloïse raised her eyebrows at him. 'You speak French with a French accent, Mr Hawker,' she observed. 'And how did you know my title?'

'I have lived abroad a great deal, ma'am,' he replied. 'And

61

as to your title, it would be simple of me to accept an invitation and not discover by whom I had been invited. So then, may I?' He crooked his arm insistently for her.

Héloïse couldn't help smiling, though she tried to speak sternly. 'This is a dance for the young people, Mr Hawker. I do not dance. You must apply to one of the young ladies. That,' she added pointedly, 'is what you are here for.'

He still held his arm for her. 'I am rebuked. But may I escort you upstairs to the saloon? Grant me that, at least.'

Everyone was following Mathilde and John Skelwith up the stairs, and Hawker's nonsense would leave a young woman without a partner, if they all paired off before they reached the saloon. Héloïse gave a distracted glance about her; but Hawker was smiling down at her, and met her eyes with a mixture of such admiration, amusement, intelligence, and conspiracy that she could not prevent herself from placing her hand on his arm and allowing him to lead her to the stairs. This is a dangerous man, she thought, and determined that she would keep an eye on him, and make sure he did his duty and danced every dance, even if it were with the youngest Miss Grey.

Mathilde, at the head of the set for the first dance, eyed John Skelwith obliquely. Apart from the two lieutenants, who were frankly terrifying, John Skelwith was the oldest of the young men present, and his gravity and air of maturity made her feel nervous and rather shy. She had been pleased that he had asked her for the first dance; she felt it a distinction; and as the rest of the set formed below them, she decided that despite his lack of dash and nonsense, she had much the best partner. His necktie and hairstyle might be sober and unadventurous, but his breadth of shoulder and strength of calf needed no help from buckram padding, like Ned Micklethwaite's; and if he did not speak much, at least he did not require constant admiration, like Tom Keating.

Finding that he was looking at her, she met his eyes hesitantly, and he smiled so pleasantly that she forgot that she had known him such a little time. It was a confident, friendly, unchallenging smile, such as, for instance, Mr Edward Morland might give her, and she smiled back unaffectedly.

'How pleasant this is,' he said. 'I think we shall have a

delightful evening, don't you?'

'Oh yes,' she said. 'And private balls are so much pleasanter than public ones, aren't they?'

'I'm sorry to say I have been to so few of either, I can hardly have an opinion,' he replied.

'Oh,' she said, disappointed. 'Don't you like to dance?'

He laughed. 'Whenever I have had the chance, I have liked it very much. But I have been kept busy ever since I left school, learning my father's business and taking care of it. I have had little time for pleasure — too little.'

'That is a great pity,' Mathilde said feelingly.

'The kindness of your heart makes you feel more sympathy for me than I am accustomed to feel for myself,' he smiled, making her blush a little. 'But standing here, in this pleasant place, and with such pleasant company, I believe you are right, and that it is a pity.'

She felt the implied compliment too deeply at once to reply; but then, remembering Héloïse's words, that it was a small occasion beside many others she had experienced, she summoned her confidence to say, 'Perhaps now you have begun, you may find it easier to go on.'

'To go on with what, Miss Nordubois?' he asked. She raised her eyes, and found him looking at her in a way that made her feel breathless and witless.

'Why — with dancing and — and balls — and so on,' she managed to say.

He took her hand at the demand of the dance, and she liked the gentle strength of his grasp, and the firm way he supported her.

'Perhaps it is a little early to ask,' he said, 'but I imagine I may not have another chance if I miss this one: so may I take you down to supper, Miss Nordubois?'

'Yes, please,' she said simply, and then wondered if she ought to have said 'thank you' instead.

Lieutenant Hawker was frankly bored. Finucane had been eager to come to this ball because the wealthy Miss Chubb would be here, and he was hoping for the opportunity to advance what seemed to Hawker a very hopeless cause. When the colonel had relayed the request for another officer to Finucane, he had put up Hawker's name without consulting

63

him; and when Hawker had later protested, Finucane had said, 'Oh don't be such a wet blanket, Fitz! There will be a dozen pretty girls there, and a decent supper. What more can you want?'

'A great deal more,' Hawker had said disagreeably. 'Country girls with thick ankles and red faces, and nothing to drink, I'll wager, but orgeat and lemonade! What the devil did you give Brunton my name for?'

Finucane laughed. 'Nonsense! York girls are the prettiest in the country, and quite as smart and sophisticated as your London girls. As to drink, you don't know, there might be champagne or anything. And you can take your own flask, can't you? Damnit, Fitz, you've nothing better to do, after all. Why not take the chance of seeing the inside of Morland Place? It's a fine old castle, you know, and the Morlands are one of the oldest families about here.'

'Stiff and fusty-faced, and full of their own importance, I suppose. Who's the girl?' Hawker asked indifferently.

'What, Miss Nordubois? Ward of Lady Morland, some kind of cousin-twice-removed, I think. She's French, you know.'

'So I imagined from the name,' Hawker said with a curl of the lip.

'No, I mean Lady Morland,' Finucane laughed good-naturedly. 'She's a countess in her own right — Papist, of course — descended from James II, but with a few bends in the line. From what I hear, she's had quite a life! Fled the revolution and — well, there have been some scandals along the way.'

Hawker's interest was slightly stirred. 'Is she a beauty? Rich?'

'What, Lady M? Has her own fortune. As to beauty — I couldn't say, never having seen her. Her marriage to Morland was a love-match, so I dare say she is. Why, what's it to you?'

'A wealthy married woman with a highly-coloured past, and French at that, might just amuse me sufficiently to make it worth going to this dreary ball of yours,' Hawker said. 'God knows, there's nothing else to do in this place! Why did I ever come to the North? Why did I ever leave Brighton?'

'You know why you left Brighton,' Finucane said disobligingly. 'It was because —'

'For God's sake, don't remind me,' Hawker snapped.

'So you'll come to Morland Place with me, then?' Finucane

64

pressed home his advantage.

'I suppose so,' Hawker sighed.

He had come; and it was as bad as he had expected. Orgeat, lemonade, and a harmless punch to drink; girls only just out, and flanked by chaperones like thorn-hedges to see they didn't flirt. Lady Morland turned out to be an ugly little thing, interesting because of the Stuart blood, which shewed clearly enough in her features and colouring, but too sharp-witted, and too obviously in love with her husband to offer any chance of an intrigue. Every time he tried to slip away from the dancing to refresh himself from his flask, she pounced on him and led him up to some giggling girl, and though he admired her strength of character, his boredom became more and more acute. She even obliged him — with, he could swear, a malicious gleam in her eye — to escort down to supper Miss Lydia Grey, who was the worst giggler of them all, and who had been schooled by her mama to do her best to get married to any man who so much as spoke to her.

At last, towards the end of the supper break, he managed to slip away on the pretext of fetching Miss Grey an ice, and as soon as he was outside the dining-room, hurried round the nearest dark corner to get out his flask and give himself a much-needed bracer. Almost immediately, however, he heard the sound of footsteps coming towards him. He had no wish to be discovered thus with a flask in his hand, and cursing inwardly, looked about him for escape. There were only two doors: one, by the size of it and the smell of incense, evidently led to the chapel, which he had no desire to enter. He tried the other door, swore as he found it locked, and took the only other available way, up the spiral stairs.

The stairs were unlit, and as soon as he rounded the first turn he was in complete darkness, which he disliked so much that he hurried on upwards, clutching the hand-rope. Another turn, and he could see the light from the upper landing, which was enough to reassure him. He stopped, leaned against the wall, unscrewed the flask, and renewed his acquaintance with the only good thing, in his opinion, ever to come out of the country north of Oxford.

He was so preoccupied that when the voice spoke he almost spilt the precious liquid.

'What's that you're drinking? Can I have some?'

It was a female child, rather oddly dressed in a yellow muslin gown much too big for her, tied unsuccessfully round the middle with a blue sash, and with a very expensive lace scarf draped about her shoulders. Her dark hair was a mass of tangled curls, but she had three feathers and an artificial rose stuck in it.

'You startled me,' he said, repressing the desire to smack the little brute and send it on its way. Any uproar — and this child, one look told him, was an uproarer — would reflect more to his discredit than the child's. 'Where did you come from?'

'I live here,' she said logically. She looked at him with evident hostility. 'Who are you?'

It would be better, he thought, to keep the child sweet. He made an attempt to amuse and disarm her. 'Lieutenant Fitzherbert Hawker at your service, my lady,' he said with a flourishing bow. 'And who are you?'

'I'm not a my lady,' she said scornfully, 'I'm Fanny Morland.' She looked at him to see if he were impressed.

'Miss Morland — your servant, ma'am,' he said with another bow. 'I should have known.'

'I could be a my lady, though. I'm very rich, you know.'

'You are?' His interest was engaged, as it always was at the mention of money.

'Well of course. Don't you know *anything*? I'm Miss Morland of Morland Place. All this is mine — this house, and all the land, and the farms and everything.' He managed to look impressed, and she drew a step closer. 'Down in the cellar,' she said confidentially, 'there's a room with an iron door, and it's *absolutely full* of treasure. Silver and gold and jewels. Really there is!'

'And it's all yours?' he asked, beginning to warm to his role.

'Yes,' she said emphatically. 'Well, it sort of is. It will be really mine when I'm twenty-one. It's in — something.'

'In trust,' he suggested. She nodded. 'And how old are you now?'

'I'm twelve,' Fanny said, looking to see if he would believe her. His interest had waned. Nine years was an eternity to a man in debt. He glanced towards the more accessible comfort of his flask again, and Fanny intercepted the look. 'What was that you were drinking?' she asked again.

'Whisky,' he said shortly, and took another gulp.

'I want some,' Fanny said firmly.

'It's not for little girls,' Hawker said unwisely, wishing she would go away. Fanny's eyes narrowed.

'If you don't give me some, I'll scream. I can scream louder than you've ever heard in your life, and someone will come, and you'll get into trouble.'

Hawker acknowledged the truth of this, shrugged, and handed her the flask. 'Be careful,' he said. 'You won't like it.'

Fanny gulped, choked, screwed up her face, and handed it back to him, panting a little and smacking her lips as a cat does at a bad smell. 'It's nasty,' she admitted, handing it back. 'Nastier than Uncle Ned's. His is brandy. I've tried that, too.'

'I warned you you wouldn't like it,' Hawker said, taking a mouthful himself.

'Well, grown-ups drink it, and I want to be grown up, so I'm going to keep trying. Give me some more.'

Hawker admired her spirit, misguided though it was, but doubted that giving whisky to a child would be considered correct behaviour on the part of a guest, if it were discovered. 'Young ladies don't drink ardent spirits,' he extemporised, 'so there's no point in getting used to it.'

'Don't they?' Fanny said doubtfully.

'Ladies never drink spirits at all, except sometimes very old women with whiskers and red noses that everybody laughs at.'

'Oh,' Fanny said, frowning. Hawker put the flask away, preparing to make his escape, but she went on, 'Have you come for the ball?'

'Yes,' he said.

'I'm not allowed to go. Papa says I'm too young,' she added disgustedly. 'I hate being too young! I wish I were grown up! If I were grown up, I'd shew them all! I'd do just what I want all the time, and wear what I want, and have the best horses, and go to dances — and drink whisky if I wanted to.' She glared defiantly at Hawker. 'When I'm grown up, and all this is mine, I'll send them all away!'

Hawker understood the odd clothes now. She had been

sent to bed, probably, and had got herself up and borrowed an older sister's dress, to pretend she was at the ball. No, not an older sister, if she really were the heiress. Perhaps one of Miss Nordubois' gowns. He felt a sneaking admiration for Miss Fanny, and experienced a rare impulse to be kind simply for kindness' sake.

'You look grown up already in that gown,' he said. 'I'll bet if you had gone to the ball, everyone would have danced with you.'

'Do you think so?' Fanny said. She looked at him intently, to detect any possible spirit of irony. 'Would you have danced with me?'

'I'd have been the first to ask you. One day, when you have a ball of your own, I will ask you.'

'Oh,' Fanny said, and seemed rather overcome. She inspected him minutely. 'P'raps when I'm grown up, I'll marry you,' she offered generously.

He smiled. 'You'll have forgotten me long before that.'

'No I won't,' Fanny said decidedly. She cocked her head, listening. 'They're coming back. I've got to go.' Papa would be bringing her supper, and she must be back in her room for that. 'Goodbye,' she said abruptly, and ran away up the stairs.

'I think it's gone very well, don't you, my love?' James said to Héloïse much later as they stood together at one end of the long saloon. 'Everyone seems to have enjoyed it.'

'Except the lieutenant from the world of fashion,' Héloïse said drily. 'He has walked here and walked there, looking so bored with the children's games! And did you hear him asking Miss Micklethwaite if she had tried the new dance, where the man puts his arm around the lady's waist? She did not know where to look, poor thing! She thought he was making an indecent proposition to her.'

James laughed. 'My love, he was only talking about the waltz.'

'Of course, I know that,' Héloïse said sternly, 'but Miss Micklethwaite did not. How should he expect such a child, who has never been further away than Scarborough, to have heard about the waltz?'

'If he'd asked Mathilde, he'd have got a different answer.

She saw it done at Brighton — I suppose that's where he's seen it.'

'Well, I don't trust him,' Héloïse said with decision. 'He smiles too much.'

'Oh, there's no harm in him,' James said lazily. 'He can't get up to any mischief at a private ball.'

'Mathilde evidently found another partner more to her taste,' Héloïse said thoughtfully, nodding to the set where her ward was once again partnering John Skelwith. 'I like that young man. I'm glad we asked him.'

James frowned. 'I hope he doesn't mean anything serious by his attentions. It would complicate matters horribly to have him hanging about Morland Place.'

'I suppose it might,' Héloïse said. 'But one must be careful how to discourage him. I would not wish him hurt.'

James pressed her hand gratefully. 'Damn Edward for asking him! I would not have had you meet him for the world, far less be obliged to entertain him.'

'It can't be helped,' she said quietly. 'It was not your fault.'

'I think the next ought to be the last dance, don't you think?' he said after a moment. 'It's getting late.'

'The young people don't even begin to be tired,' Héloïse pointed out.

'No, damnit, but I am,' James laughed. 'Enough is enough, Marmoset. I want to go to bed with you.'

She put her fingers against his lips. 'James! It is not proper to say such things aloud.'

'Not *comme il faut?*' he teased her. 'Give the nod to Ottershaw, love, and I'll go and tell the musicians. And — Héloïse?' She turned back. 'Will you honour me with your hand for the last dance?'

Her eyes widened. 'But I cannot dance at Mathilde's ball!'

He grinned. 'You can do anything you like. I warn you, if you won't dance with me, I'll ask Lizzie Spencer!'

Edward was standing next to Mathilde, who was fanning herself vigorously at one end of the room. 'Are you enjoying it?' he asked her with a smile.

'Oh yes!' she said emphatically. 'It's the best ball I was ever at, even including all the London ones! I suppose it's because everyone here knows each other. It's pleasant to be among

69

friends, isn't it, sir?'

'It is,' he agreed gravely.

'And dancing is such a pleasant occupation, don't you think?'

Her innocent enthusiasm touched him, made him want to smile and cry at the same time. He remembered all the balls he and Chetwyn had attended perforce, and the stratagems they had used to get out of the hated business of partnering young women. It all seemed so long ago, now. How his dislike of silly young women had plagued Mother! But if they had been nice, sensible girls like Mathilde, it might have been different. She never giggled or languished, and she listened when one spoke with such flattering attention, and really tried to understand.

'Yes,' he said, 'dancing is a very pleasant exercise. It is rather a pity this should be the last.'

'Oh, is it?' Mathilde said, her face falling. 'I didn't know.'

'I just saw my brother speak to the band-master. And look, he is leading Madame into the set.'

Mathilde looked pleased. 'Oh, I am glad she should dance! I wish everyone in the world could dance!'

'Do you?' He looked down affectionately at her happy face. 'Would you dance with me?' She looked surprised, and he felt at once extremely foolish, and tried to retract. 'But no, I have shocked you. You would not like to dance with an old man like me.'

She put out an impulsive hand, upset to think she had hurt him. 'Oh no, please, I would, indeed I would! I was only surprised that you should ask me. I should like it of all things!'

'Really?' he asked. She nodded earnestly, and after a little hesitation, he held his arm out to her and bowed, clowning a little to make it easier. 'Then, shall we, Miss Nordubois?'

She laughed and gave a little curtsey. 'If you please, Mr Morland.'

'No, no,' he protested. 'If we are to dance together, I think you should call me Cousin Edward. We are cousins, of a sort, I suppose. And may I call you Mathilde?'

'Yes, Cousin Edward.' She put her hand gladly on his, and he led her to the set which was forming behind James and Héloïse.

CHAPTER FOUR

Lucy, Lady Aylesbury, driving her curricle along Bond Street with her groom Parslow up beside her, was amused to see John Anstey and George Brummell standing on a corner deep in conversation. They presented quite a contrast: tall Anstey in his easy-fitting green coat, with comfortable breeches and top-boots suggesting he had only just arrived in Town; and small, slender Brummell looking as if he had been poured into his snugly-cut frock-coat, his starched neckcloth arranged to perfection, his fawn pantaloons a miracle of creaselessness, owing to the patent strap he and his tailor had recently devised, which passed under the foot and held the garment taut.

'Look at that *tableau vivant*,' Lucy murmured to Parslow, feeling the mouths of her famous chestnuts to slow them. 'You might call it "Town meets Country" perhaps. Hoa, there! Good morning, John. Just arrived?'

The two men turned as she pulled up her team beside them. Brummell exchanged a smile and a nod with her, and John Anstey came up to the side of the curricle to take her hand and kiss her.

'Lucy, my dear, I didn't know you were here. I thought you were still at Wolvercote, or I would have called immediately. When I passed through Upper Grosvenor Street, the knocker was off your door.'

'Ah, then you didn't know I have given up number ten and taken number twelve instead?'

'No, how should I?' Anstey laughed. 'You didn't tell me.'

'It was in *The Times* yesterday,' Lucy said reproachfully. 'Number twelve is bigger, so there's room for the children.'

'But I only arrived late last night, as I was telling Mr Brummell. I was travelling all day yesterday and didn't see the papers. So you've brought the children up with you? That's an innovation!'

Lucy shrugged. 'Trot insists that they ought not to spend all their lives in the country, but ought to have some experience of Town, too. I suspect, however, its because *she* wants to have some experience of Town herself.'

'Dear ma'am, can you blame her?' Brummell said with a delicate shudder. 'The thought of being incarcerated in the country for twelve months of every year is too dreadful!'

One of the chestnuts sneezed, and Parslow gave an admonitory cough to remind Lucy about the inadvisability of keeping horses standing at this time of the year, though it was warm for April. She glanced at him, and then handed the reins over. 'Take them round, will you, Parslow? I shall walk a little with the gentlemen.'

John Anstey jumped her down from her carriage, and frowned, and as Parslow drove the chestnuts away he said, 'But my dear Lucy, you are much too thin! This won't do, you know.'

'Oh, don't talk about me,' Lucy said with a hint of irritability, as she released herself from his grasp. 'Tell me what you two were discussing so seriously when I drove up.'

'Why, the war, of course,' Brummell said promptly, and Anstey followed his cue.

'I was saying we shall see something positive done at last, now that the Whigs are out and the Tories in again. The Whigs lost nearly two hundred seats in the general election. They must have been mad to press that Catholic Militia Bill.'

'Sheridan said he had heard of people knocking their heads against a wall,' said Brummell, 'but he had never known anyone who collected the bricks and built the wall for the express purpose.'

'Your majority was improved, I suppose, dear John,' Lucy suggested.

'My seat has never been contested in living memory,' Anstey said with dignity. 'But that "No Popery" election was just what we needed. The mood of the country's behind us now, and Portland may not be the most exciting of men to lead a government, but his heart's in the right place.'

'His interest, you mean,' Brummell smiled. 'What do you care for his heart?'

'Well, if you like,' Anstey admitted. 'But we've got a lot of sound men in office now. Chatham's at the Ordnance,

72

Perceval at the Exchequer, Mulgrave at the Admiralty —'

'All Mr Pitt's friends, in fact, without Mr Pitt,' Brummell murmured.

'Castlereagh's in the War Office,' Anstey went on, ignoring him, 'and he's the hardest worker I know. What can be achieved by application, he will achieve. And your friend Canning's the new Foreign Secretary, Brummell. He's an able man, you must admit.'

'He's not Mr Brummell's friend,' Lucy said. 'Much too rough and ready. Everyone says he's clever, of course, but he's no gentleman.'

'Nonsense. He was at Eton and The House — what more do they want?' Anstey said indignantly. 'Just because he's ambitious! There's always this absurd prejudice about anyone who's "too clever".'

'Quite,' Brummell nodded. 'Everyone prefers an amiable fool. You always know where you are with them. And Canning, you must admit, is an intriguer.'

'And a friend of the Princess of Wales,' Lucy said.

Anstey's drawn brow relaxed, and he gave a rueful laugh. 'Oh well, that damns him utterly, of course! But at all events, we'll be able to get on with making a new agreement with Russia and Prussia, and crushing Boney while we've got him on the run. The Cabinet's promised an early expedition to the Baltic. If only we could get our men back from the Mediterranean!'

'I never understood what they were doing there in the first place,' Lucy said. 'Why in the world should we attack Turkey?'

'Because Russia is our ally, of course,' Anstey said impatiently. 'We offered them help in their war against the Turk as part of the last treaty, but the whole thing's been a nonsense. However, I believe Canning's sending Sir Arthur Paget out there. If anyone can talk us free from that imbroglio, it's Paget.'

Brummell gave a theatrical sigh. 'Whatever did we talk about before we had the war? Imagine how dull we would be if it were ever to end!'

Anstey laughed. 'You would talk nonsense, just as you do now, and do it charmingly, of course! But I must take my leave of you. Lucy, now I know you are in Town, I'll call, if I may, and tell you all the home news.'

'Yes, do. Come and dine with me,' Lucy said cordially. Anstey took his leave, and Brummell offered Lucy his arm, and they strolled along together in the tenuous sunshine.

'Now, my dear Lady Aylesbury, I must talk to you very seriously,' he said after a while. 'I am doing you a great favour by allowing you to be seen on my arm in Bond Street, for really, you know, you are in very sad looks. I tell you this as an old friend, you understand, upon privilege.'

'Privilege to insult me, you mean?'

'Nonsense! How can the truth be an insult? You were never a beauty like your poor sister, Mrs Haworth —'

'Oh heaven! Am I never to emerge from her shadow?' Lucy struck her brow, and Brummell looked reprovingly at her.

'Hush! I am serious. You were never a beauty like her, but you were used to be almost handsome, and quite a pleasure to walk with, for I always admired your straight back and your elegant carriage, you know. Of course you have been in mourning, which one understands and forgives —'

'You are too kind,' Lucy murmured.

'But you are out of your blacks now,' he went on, undeflected, 'and I really cannot endure to see you so *mal soignée*. Even Lord Anstey noticed you are too thin, and heaven knows, he is not a man of fashion: only look at his coats!'

Lucy sighed. 'To tell you the truth, I find it difficult to care about anything at all since — since Weston died.' Tears sprang to her eyes simply with the conjunction of the words, and she shook them away, not wishing to embarrass her friend. He pressed her captive hand against his ribs in sympathy, and she drew a steadying breath. 'Sometimes it isn't so bad — when I'm actually doing something, riding to a fast point out hunting, for instance, or talking to a friend, like you — sometimes I can even forget for a moment or two. But then it all comes back in a rush. And in the morning when I wake up, that's the worst of all. Docwra brings me my chocolate and asks me what she should lay out for me to put on, and —' She stopped, looking down at the pavement.

'And what?' he prompted gently.

'And I think, what does it matter? What does it matter whether I get up at all? Without Weston, there doesn't seem any point to anything.'

Her eyes filled, and Brummell halted and turned her to face the nearest shop window while he drew his handkerchief from his sleeve. 'Here, have this, and pretend to be admiring the display in the window. A pity it should be nothing more fascinating than brushes, but perhaps I might be explaining to you the essential differences between badger and hog. My dear ma'am, what are you thinking of? You really cannot cry in public! And particularly not when I have been giving you my arm the whole length of Bond Street! What would people think? A woman on my arm is supposed to be enjoying the most uplifting experience polite society can offer. You will utterly ruin my reputation, you know.'

While he chattered to protect her, she pressed his handkerchief to her eyes, and blew her nose as discreetly as possible. The handkerchief was of spotless white linen edged with lace, and was subtly scented with the same elusive fragrance which hung about the Beau himself; and a surge of affection for him warmed her, and helped to dry the tears at source. Seeing her more herself, he went on in more serious vein.

'You have had a very poor run of luck, dear ma'am, and you know you have my every sympathy. But you must not give way to self-pity, which besides being unhelpful to oneself and tiresome to one's friends, also has the effect of introducing disagreeable lines to one's face.' She gave a watery laugh. 'That's better! Consider, dear Lady Aylesbury, how many friends you have, who are being deprived of the twin pleasures of talking *to* you, and *about* you behind your back! We need you to brace us and scandalise us again!'

'I never did,' Lucy said indignantly.

'You have been doing nothing but since you first came to Town! Don't forget, you are the woman who beat the Prince's driving time from London to Brighton; and your record, by the by, has never yet been broken! I think you should set yourself another challenge of the same sort. We are all dying for something new to wager upon. Alvanley, you know, is to make another attempt to run a mile in less than six minutes. One would never take him for an athlete, by the look of him, would one?' He sketched a circle in the air with one exquisite hand.

'You cannot mean me to challenge Lord Alvanley to a running race,' Lucy said amused. Brummell noted the new

75

life in her eyes, and smiled with inward satisfaction.

'I would not put even that past you, when you are in your normal spirits! But I think something in the riding or driving line might be more suitable. You still have that man-eating horse of yours, haven't you?'

'You mean Minstrel? Yes, of course.'

'Well, then, why not challenge somebody to a point-to-point race? It will amuse us all, and even if you don't win, it will give you something to do to keep your mind occupied.'

'If I do it, I will certainly win,' Lucy said with spirit, and at that moment a hesitant voice from behind them interrupted her.

'Lady Aylesbury?'

They both turned, to see Robert Knaresborough standing poised as if to flee, evidently deeply uncertain of his reception. The scandal of his relationship with Lucy's husband had broken so immediately before the latter's death that there were those who believed Lord Aylesbury had taken his own life. The scandal had been hushed up, Robert had departed the capital for the far North, and Lucy, at that time in a state of shock over the death of Captain Weston, had never understood all the details; but it took a great deal of courage for Robert to accost her at all, and particularly when she was in the company of George Brummell.

Knaresborough was wearing the bands of half-mourning, and in the time since Lucy had seen him last, he seemed to have grown taller and heavier, and aged five years.

'Why — Robert,' she said cautiously, and then on an impulse held out her hand. 'How do you do?'

His shoulders relaxed, and he took it gratefully. 'It's very good of you to ask,' he said. 'Mr Brummell, sir.' He bowed almost reverently to Brummell, who, for Lucy's sake gave him a civil nod, but did not smile.

'I see you are in mourning,' Lucy said.

'My mother died in January,' he said, and a shadow crossed his face.

'Good heavens! I had no idea she was ill,' Lucy said unguardedly.

Robert looked a little reproachful. 'She often complained of her delicate health, but I think many people believed it was only her imagination. I know Lord Ballincrea tried to hint as much last year when Mama was taken badly just before the Carlisle meeting, and I had to stay and look after her.'

Lucy coughed, and exchanged a fleeting glance with Brummell. 'But what happened, Robert? Was it her old trouble? Did the physicians find out what was wrong with her?

Robert shook his head sadly. 'They were always baffled by Mama's symptoms, and so it was at the end. It was very sudden. She had been upset during the evening because I was going away for a few days on business to a small estate of mine about fifty miles off. She didn't come down to breakfast, but sent a message saying she felt too tired, and that I need not come up to say goodbye, as she knew I was in a hurry to get away. I —' He hesitated, his cheeks reddening. 'I'm afraid I took her at her word, and didn't disturb her. I set off on horseback for Headsham, and I was only half-way there when I was overtaken by a servant. She'd been taken ill as soon as I left. I turned back with him at once, but it was too late.' He swallowed. 'She was dead before I arrived.'

Lucy looked at him with pity. 'Oh poor Robert!' she said. She had never had much imagination, but she could read between the lines of this story easily enough. The suspicion that his mother was a *malade imaginaire* must at last have begun to impinge on him, as it had long ago occurred to the rest of the world. For once in his life he had taken a stand and refused to give in to her velvet-gloved blackmail; and she had died, and he was riven by remorse and guilt.

It was entirely possible, Lucy thought with loathing, that the old witch had died of rage, or simply to spite him, but of course one could not say that to Robert. Lucy had always hated bullying, and her indignation on his behalf made her speak to him more kindly than she might otherwise have done.

'So you have come to London? Well, that was sensible. No-one can be dull in London. Do you make a long stay?'

'I was thinking of living here permanently,' he said shyly. 'I have nothing now to keep me in the North, apart from my estates, and they run themselves with only occasional supervision from me. I thought I might take a house, and settle down. I might get married, even, if anyone will have me.'

Brummell looked more approving, and said, 'You will have no difficulty there, Mr Knaresborough. You have only to murmur your income in the right ear, and you will find all the mamas consider you most eligible.'

Knaresborough smiled a little ruefully. 'Yes, I suppose that is all that matters.'

'It matters most, but not exclusively,' Brummell said. 'You need also to belong to the right clubs. I believe you once had a desire to join Watiers? If you are still of the same mind, I should be happy to put you up for membership.'

Lucy glanced approvingly at her friend and squeezed his arm in gratitude. Robert, astonished and pleased, stammered his thanks.

'It's most awfully good of you, sir,' he said.

'Yes, it is, isn't it?' Brummell agreed. 'And perhaps Lady Aylesbury might advise you on which young women to bestow your attentions.'

'Me? No, nonsense! My children are all too young for me to have that sort of interest,' Lucy said.

'How are the children, ma'am?' Robert asked eagerly.

'They are very well. I have them in Town with me. Why don't you call some time and see them? They were very fond of you; and Roland in particular often asks after you.'

'Does he? Oh, I should like it above all things. I missed them dreadfully when I — went away. Thank you, Lady Aylesbury, thank you indeed!' They exchanged a few more words, and then he took his leave, walking away down the street with a lighter tread.

Lucy and Brummell watched him go, and then turned the other way.

'Well, that was a good deed on our part,' Brummell remarked. 'I wonder why we should both have been seized with the desire to be kind to that young man?'

'Oh, there's no harm to him really,' Lucy said. 'It was his ogre of a mother who ruined his life.'

'Hmm,' Brummell said, as if unconvinced. 'I wonder. It's true that the particular manner of her death made me feel quite sorry for him, but when I tell you that I almost offered to walk to the end of the street with him —'

'Really?' Lucy said, startled.

'I managed to restrain myself,' Brummell nodded, 'but the impulse quite unnerved me. And if I put him up for Watiers after having made a point of refusing him, everyone will think I have run mad.'

'No-one will remember that; and if they do, they will only think you are being capricious, as usual.'

'I am never capricious,' Brummell corrected her sternly. 'I am interesting.'

Lucy grunted. 'But why did you refuse him, when my husband put him up?' she asked. 'I never did understand.'

Brummell looked at her affectionately. 'No, you never did. And you never would. That is one of the things I love about you, dear Lady Aylesbury, so please don't try. One cannot always predict the outcome of one's actions,' he added thoughtfully, as though to himself. 'Suffice it to say that if there is any peace to be found in making reparation, I am not one to spurn it.'

'I don't understand you,' Lucy frowned. 'What reparation?'

He kissed her hand. 'Nothing in the world,' he said. 'Here are your horses again, and the good Parslow, so I will take my leave. You are looking happier than you did ten minutes ago. I believe you haven't thought about yourself for the past fifty yards at least.'

'You're right,' she discovered.

'Of course I am. It is the beginning of your cure. Come and share my box at the theatre tomorrow. I will get together a little party of old friends — Mildmay and Alvanley and Wiske. Do you like Charlotte Bouverie? I might ask you to invite her, for Mildmay's sake, for he's most fearfully in love with her! And we'll have supper afterwards at the White Horse, and eat the last oysters of the year, with a great deal of champagne.'

'Thank you — I'd like that.'

He smiled. 'You have the rest of today and tomorrow to consider what you will wear. I wish you to dazzle, Lady Aylesbury. Nothing less will do.'

He helped her into the curricle, and she waved her whip to him as she drove away.

'I wonder if there is time to have something new made up?' she said aloud.

'My lady?' Parslow enquired.

'I think I'll drive to Grafton House, and see what new muslins they have in. I'm bound to have to wait at this time of day, so you can take the horses home, and send Docwra for

79

me; for if I find anything I like, I shall walk round to Madame Genoux's afterwards, and come home in a hackney.'

'Yes, my lady,' Parslow said impassively, but with a hidden smile of satisfaction. It was a long time since his mistress had shewn any interest in clothes, and the change could only be for the better. Inwardly he blessed Mr Brummell not only for a kind and loyal, but an intelligent friend.

At the beginning of June, Héloïse arrived at Chelmsford House in Pall Mall and found it covered in scaffolding and thronging with workmen, inside and out. Her old friend Roberta, the widowed Lady Chelmsford, was no less hospitable on that account.

'You have come to stay, I hope? We can make you comfortable, never fear, in spite of all this turmoil. Did you come straight here?'

'I called at Upper Grosvenor Street, but Lucy was not there, so I left my card and then came here. Dear Roberta, you are looking very well! What is it you are doing to this handsome house?'

'The roof to begin with — it was in a sad state. Athersuch tells me some of the lead was stolen during the time we lived in Ebury Street, and the thieves must have loosened some of the slates. And then the outside is to be repainted, and we are having all the principal rooms redecorated, too. Mr. Firth's idea is that if we confine the decorators to one end of the house at a time, we may manage to survive without being driven to distraction, but already I wonder if he is right. The smell of paint gets into one's food so.'

'Does all this work mean something special?'

'No, it was what was needed, that's all. I can't let Bobbie's inheritance go to rack and ruin during his minority. This is a fine old house, and I want it to be fit for him to inherit when he comes of age.'

'Well, it means at least that the war is not pressing on your finances,' Héloïse said practically. 'I am glad to hear it. James tells me that Bonaparte's embargo on our ships is already beginning to cause bankruptcies.'

'Oh, the Berlin Decrees! Mr Firth explained it all to me,' Roberta said. 'But the Chelmsford fortune is very widely invested. The fifth Earl — my late husband's father — had interests all over the world. I think we even own a munitions factory in Russia! So Mr Firth thinks the embargo isn't likely to affect us seriously.'

'James says it is the iron and textile trades which will suffer the most, for they export a great deal to Europe. I know Fanny's grandpapa, Mr Hobsbawn, says the demand for his cotton has fallen in the last few months. He writes to Edward about it.'

'Not to James?'

Héloïse shrugged. 'He still finds it hard to forgive James for marrying me so soon after his daughter's death. But it could not be helped — we could not have waited any longer, not for anything in the world! And he will probably be even more vexed with James when he learns of my condition.'

Roberta stared. 'Héloïse, my dear — you don't mean —!'

Héloïse laughed, her eyes shining. 'Yes, I do mean,' she laughed. 'Dear Roberta, I know you will rejoice with me when I tell you that I am with child.'

'You sly thing, why didn't you say so at once? Oh my dear! I am so happy for you! But when?'

'In January. I am only just sure about it.'

'Does James know? And he let you travel all this way alone, the villain!'

'I wasn't alone, I had Marie with me. He would have come too, but he is very busy at the moment, and I told him I did not need him. It would not quite have suited me to have him here, because apart from wanting to buy things for the baby, I wanted to consult you and your wise Mr Firth about Fanny.'

'Ah yes, Fanny!' Roberta said thoughtfully. 'I must say I did wonder when you and James got married, whether you would have trouble with her. Has she settled down at all?'

Héloïse made a face. 'I wish I could say she has, but I believe she hates me more than ever. Is that a terrible thing to say about a child?'

'I expect she's jealous,' Roberta said briskly. 'She was always allowed too much freedom, and James spoiled her. She needs to be taken in hand, that's all.'

'*Bien sûr*, that is what she needs — but I cannot do it, *ça se voit.*'

'Of course not — nor should you have to. She needs a governess.'

'So I thought,' Héloïse nodded, 'and I persuaded James at last of the same thing. But Fanny did not like the idea.'

'Fanny should not be given the choice,' Roberta said firmly.

'She was not, I assure you. I found a suitable woman and James engaged her — a Miss Pinckus. She was with us a week.'

'You found she wasn't suitable after all?'

'But she was! She spoke German and Italian, and played the pianoforte, and had very good references. James liked her, and I thought her a genteel sort of person.'

'Then what happened?' Roberta asked, but with a suspicion that she already knew the answer.

'She came after a week and said she would not stay. We asked her why, but she only cried and went away. So we looked again and found Miss Leggat. She was younger — James thought too young, but I thought Fanny would like better someone more lively. She sang very prettily, and played the harp, which made her more expensive.'

'And?'

'She was made of sterner stuff — she stayed a month, and only left when someone — we do not know who — cut the strings from her harp one night. It cost a great deal to have it restrung, but James felt it was only right, even though —'

'Héloïse, you can't mean that Fanny —?'

'Who can say? It must have taken a long time, even with a hacksaw, which was missing from the blacksmith's shop in the village. Miss Leggat was a sound sleeper, and would not have noticed, perhaps, if Fanny crept out in the night. The dogs in the hall did not bark, as they would for an intruder. But nothing could be proved, even if one really wanted to; which, dear Roberta, you must see one did not.'

'No, I can see that,' Roberta said thoughtfully. 'But Héloïse, if it was Fanny — it is all worse than I imagined!'

Héloïse nodded. 'Miss Bantry said that Fanny was a monster.'

'Miss Bantry? Was she another one?'

'Three in three months — quite an achievement, is it not? Miss Bantry had Irish blood, which made her more outspoken — or perhaps Fanny was less cautious. She endured the frog in her reticule, and the chicken's pluck in her bed, but it was

82

the eye that upset her.'

Roberta's cheek muscles twitched. 'The eye?' she managed to say.

Héloïse's face was likewise rigid. 'The poor woman had an accident in her extreme youth, and lost an eye, and to replace it she had a glass one. It was a very nice one made by a craftsman, and I must say that one did not at once notice the difference. She was not unpleasant to look at. But at night she kept her false eye in a glass of water by the bed, and one night Fanny stole it and replaced it with a sheep's eye.'

Roberta moaned. 'Where —'

'I cannot begin to guess.' Héloïse put her hands over her face and shook with laughter. 'Oh it is too bad of me,' she said at last reproachfully. 'Poor Miss Bantry shrieked and shrieked! The whole house came running. We thought she had been murdered in her bed; but there she was in her nightgown and curling-papers, and the eye on her bed where she had dropped it, staring at her, and her staring at the eye —'

'She's right, Fanny is a monster,' Roberta said at last, drying her eyes. 'But in all seriousness, Héloïse,' she added, sobering rapidly, 'that sort of thing cannot be allowed to go on.'

'I know — and that is why I have come to consult. I thought that you and Mr Firth between you might be able to advise me how to find a woman strong enough to stop Fanny.'

'Who is looking after her at the moment?'

'Oh, she is spending her days with James, which of course makes her happy and good. I told you in a letter how her dog was run over, did I not? James wanted to give her another, but she refused to have one, so he has decided instead to give her a new horse, instead of Tempest. A proper, lady's horse. He has let her choose one of the young mares, and they are training it together. Of course there is nothing she could like better. It keeps her occupied, and she had her father's company all day long. So while I am sure she will not do any harm, I have taken the chance to come here.'

'Does she know about your expectations?' Roberta asked thoughtfully.

'No. I asked James not to tell her yet. I don't know what it might provoke her to do.' Héloïse bit her lip. 'It is dreadful to have to say it,' she added in a low voice, 'but I am afraid for Sophie and Thomas, too.'

Roberta became brisk. 'Don't worry any more, dearest Héloïse. Peter — Mr Firth and I will do everything we can to help you. We'll find the right person, never fear. And don't forget, it's early days yet. Fanny will settle down in time, provided she has the right guidance. She's only a little girl, after all.'

Héloïse gave a pallid smile. 'That is what I tell myself.'

'Good. And now, tell me, what of my friend Mathilde? Bobbie will be so sorry you did not bring her with you. He quite doted on her.'

'Do you come to York for race-week? Then he can see her there. I told you in my letter about her ball, did I not?'

'Yes. I'm glad it was a success.'

'And she is enjoying herself so much in York. She is a modest girl, you know, and sensible, and though the London Season she spent with you is something she will never forget, she knows that without a dowry she must not look so high again.'

'Does she have any admirers?'

'She makes friends easily, and she always has enough partners at dances, which you know counts for everything at that age. As to admirers, there is one —'

She paused, thinking of John Skelwith. She liked him so much, and he gave her so much unwitting pain, that she wished his friendship with Mathilde were not developing so promisingly. At the moment, his attentions were not pointed enough to arouse talk about them. They met always in the company of other young people, most often the Keatings, and their cousins the Somers's. Mathilde accepted his attentions calmly, but there was sometimes something in John Skelwith's eye which made Héloïse suspect he felt more strongly than mere friendship.

'But nothing may come of it, after all. She is still very young. Oh, I am not anxious. The right man will come for her sooner or later.'

'Her first love, your friend the Duc de Vesine-d'Estienne, is in Town, you know. I believe he is to go out to the Baltic with this German Legion the Government is sending to join with the Swedes. He is sure to visit when he knows you are here.'

'I shall be glad to see him again. But he was not Mathilde's first love — that was a certain *curé*, a Mr Antrobus. He had a long neck like a chicken, and a very large —' She tapped her throat. '*Comment s'appelle-t'il, celui-ci?*'

'Adam's apple,' Roberta supplied with a smile. 'What strange men young girls fall in love with, to be sure! I remember when I was eleven I had a grand, unrequited passion for the molecatcher! I suppose he must have been forty, and he had a red face and hands like planks, and he wore leather breeches, and nether-stocks tied with string. But I used to dream of running away with him and living in a cottage in a wood and having nineteen children.'

Héloïse laughed. 'It is ridiculous, *n'est-ce pas?* But I suppose it is practising to love, as kittens practise killing dead leaves or pieces of string. Everything has its purpose.'

Hawkins, the Chelmsford House butler, appeared. 'Lady Aylesbury and Major Wiske, my lady,' he announced, stepping aside.

Lucy came in, dressed in a lilac walking dress and a very pretty cambric muslin bonnet, followed by Danby Wiske in uniform, but looking unusually soberly-dressed. Gone were the bright yellow boots, the gold-fringed breeches, and the red and yellow mirliton cap by which the Prince of Wales' Own had been recognised — and, by some, stigmatised as 'organ-grinder's monkeys'. Instead, he wore white breeches and black boots which were modesty itself; the yellow collar and cuffs of his tunic peeked out from under a handsome dark blue, silver-braided pelisse trimmed with grey fur; and under his arm he carried a tall, grey fur cap, rather like an elongated muff.

'Héloïse, here you are! I'm sorry I wasn't at home,' Lucy said, hurrying to hug her cousin with a warmth Héloïse was more than glad to see. 'I'd gone walking with Danby to shew off his new uniform, but as soon as I got back and found your card, I guessed where you would be and came straight here. Roberta, how do you do? Isn't Danby splendid?'

Danby Wiske smirked self-consciously. 'New idea,' he offered. 'We've been converted to Hussars — not being called Hussars, however. Still called the Tenth Dragoons. But we had to have a new uniform. New caps, too.' He drew the grey fur from under his arm and looked at it sadly, as though it were a dead cat. 'Not very useful. Falls off when you gallop,

85

you know. Still,' he brightened, 'only the Tenth have grey ones — makes us sort of distinctive. All the others have black or brown.'

'That means he won't lose his own regiment in joint manoeuvres,' Lucy said affectionately. 'I think it's a lovely uniform, Danby, much better than the old one. It makes you look quite handsome.'

Wiske had nothing to say to that, only looked embarrassed and drew out his snuff-box for something to do. It was one Lucy had had made and enscribed for him after he had rescued her from footpads — an act of courage which had surprised no-one but himself — and he was very proud of it and liked to flourish it, though he rarely actually inhaled the contents.

'But how are you, Héloïse? How are James and Edward, and the children? What are you doing in London?' Lucy asked. 'I haven't seen you since your wedding. You look well.'

'Indeed, so do you, Cousin Lucy. I am glad of it, for when I last saw you, you looked so uncomfortable.'

She nodded. 'I was — but I try to keep myself busy now, and that helps. Brummell put me on the right track. Don't give yourself time to think, that's the way. And Trot makes sure that the children plague me as much as possible. She has made me bring them to London, can you imagine it? I can't say I'm very fond of them yet, but I keep trying.'

Héloïse could not imagine not being fond of one's own children, but said only, 'You are so lucky in your Miss Trotton, I must tell you, Cousin Lucy, that James plots to bribe her away from you, for we need a good governess for Fanny and Sophie. That's why I am come to London.'

'I'll ask Trot if she knows of anyone. She might have a relation tucked away somewhere. But you may tell James that he could not drag Trot away from her children, even if I would let her go. She's devoted to them.' She paused a moment, and asked diffidently, 'And how is Thomas?'

'He thrives,' Héloïse said. 'He is rather shy, but he has the sweetest nature, and he learns very quickly. Sophie teaches him everything she knows, and he goes in with her and the chapel boys to Father Aislaby for an hour a day, so that he should get used to the idea. He likes to draw, too. James thinks he will draw very nicely when he is older.'

She watched Lucy carefully as she spoke, hoping to see some sign of maternal interest, but Lucy averted her face slightly, and her expression was rigidly schooled. 'I must do something about changing his name,' was all she said. 'I'll consult my man of business about it. It will be as well to have a legal document drawn up, so that there shall be no difficulty about his inheriting his father's fortune.' Then she changed the subject determinedly. 'Do you mean to go down to Brighton, Roberta? It's so hot, I'm sure London is emptying already.'

'I had no plans for it this year. I'm not so very fond of Brighton, and Bobbie seems to prefer the country to the seaside.'

'Well, if it doesn't get any cooler by the end of the week, I mean to go down to Wolvercote early. Why don't you come too, and bring Bobbie? It will be good for Roland to have another boy to play with.'

'Thank you, I should like it; but it depends on Héloïse's plans.'

'Oh, of course I want you to come too, Héloïse.'

'Thank you, but as soon as my business is done here, I mean to go home. I hate to be away from James and the children.'

'Just as you please. But you must come anyway, Roberta, and place a wager on my race next week. Didn't I tell you about it? From Red Barn Farm to the Swan at Osney across country: a distance of three miles. I've said that Minstrel can do it in less than fifteen minutes.'

'Lucy, you mad creature, what is this?' Roberta asked, startled.

'It was George Brummell's idea,' she said, 'to give me something to keep me busy. He's making a book, and Sudbury's giving odds, he's so sure I can't do it! Well, a fool and his money are soon parted! The only thing is,' she added with a frown, 'I don't know how it will affect Minstrel, if it is as hot as this. We shall have to run it early in the morning, that's all.'

'How could you think of such a thing? You will hurt yourself! Lucy, you must not be so reckless,' Roberta said with concern.

'Hurt myself? Don't be simple,' Lucy said with a laugh. 'It's easy country, and Minstrel knows every foot of it. He's never so much as stumbled in all the years I've had him. And I shall ride cross-saddle, so where's the danger?'

'It's most improper,' Roberta said with a worried frown.

'Never mind that — when have I worried about proper behaviour? Cousin Héloïse, are you shocked too?'

Héloïse sought for tactful words. 'Queen Marie Antoinette used to ride cross-saddle when she was young, but only on her own estates. It will be talked about — but I imagine that is what you want. Perhaps you should go, Roberta, and give her your countenance, since we shall hardly persuade her not to do it.'

'Never do that,' Danby Wiske said sadly. 'Tried myself.'

'Danby is going to pace me on his new grey — for as long as he can keep up, that is,' Lucy said with a teasing smile at her friend. 'Do come, Roberta! Bobbie will like it of all things!'

'Very well — but I shall still try to dissuade you from the attempt.'

'Oh, you may try, and welcome. Well, we must go. Come, Danby. Héloïse, do call on me before you go back!'

When they had gone, Roberta looked helplessly at Héloïse, who shrugged. 'She is a very good rider, after all. And she seems so much happier. If it helps her, should one mind that it will be talked about?'

'I wish she could be happy in a more conventional way,' Roberta said. 'She should marry again — that would keep her busy.'

'You have not married again,' Héloïse pointed out.

Roberta looked a little pink. 'That's different,' she said, but declined to elaborate. 'Well, now, would you like to go up to the schoolroom and see Bobbie? And then we can ask Peter — Mr Firth if he knows of a suitable young woman to be Fanny's governess.'

CHAPTER FIVE

When Lucy reached Upper Grosvenor Street, Danby Wiske left her, promising to call for her later to escort her to Mrs Edgecumbe's ball, and Lucy climbed to her own room, and dismissed her maid with an absent wave of the hand. Alone at last, she sat down at her writing-desk, leaned her elbows upon it and dropped her face in her hands.

She felt so tired all the time. Things had been easier to bear since she had followed Brummell's advice. She kept herself busy, put on an air of lively amusement, and sometimes it even worked, insofar as it stopped her actively grieving for a while. But at the end of it, she felt empty and worn. When the whirligig of activity stopped and she fell to earth again like a leaf that has been caught up briefly by a breeze, all the sorrow came back to her unabated, and she stared at her life as at some enormous exhausting task that she could never finish.

Nothing fed her. In Weston's arms, she had given and received some vital nourishment of the soul which she could get nowhere else. It was no use to tell her she was fortunate to have friends and family who cared about her; she knew that with her mind, but it assuaged nothing in her heart. Useless also to tell her that time would heal her. If healing meant forgetting him, she did not want to be healed. In bed at night, in the long, drifting time before sleep claimed her, she would seek him out, rifle through her treasured store of memories for his face, his voice, for the touch and the smell of him, for what it had felt like to be with him; and already he was becoming harder to find. Her love for him was the only thing by which she could make sense of her life. If she lost that, she lost herself.

Restlessly she got up and paced about the room, and then, on an impulse, reached into her desk-drawer and drew out a small key. Her fingers found it without looking: she had handled it many times before. She looked at it for a long time, as though it were something dangerous lying on her palm; and then, coming to a decision, she closed her fingers about it, and went out of the room.

She walked briskly along the drugget towards the back-stairs, past a startled housemaid with an armful of sheets, who pressed herself against the wall to give her mistress way, and climbed to the top of the house. A daytime quiet hung over everything; the sounds of the house were muffled by distance, and not even the ticking of a clock penetrated this remote place. Here, on a small landing, there were three doors leading to the attics: in two the junior servants had their sleeping-quarters; the third was a box-room. She opened the third door and went in.

It was hot and airless under the slates. Sunshine poured in through the skylight, illuminating the dust-motes which hung motionless in the undisturbed air. The room smelled dry and unused, and there was no sound except for a blue-black fly which buzzed and bumped monotonously against the window-glass. Boxes were stacked neatly around the sides — Hicks was too good a butler to allow disorder even in an unfrequented attic — and it took her a while to find the one she wanted. When she located it, she set her hands to the rings and dragged it clear, into the middle of the floor space.

It was a heavy oak sea-chest, strongly bound, and with the name burned deep into the lid: CAPT.J.R.WESTON. Lucy stood and looked down at it for a long time, the key pressed painfully into her palm by her clenched fingers. A story from her childhood came back to her, of some inquisitive female who had opened a box and let out all the troubles of the world. Of course, one part of her mind mused, it would be a female who was blamed for that!

The buzzing of the fly attracted her attention, and she glanced up. How had it come to be up here in the first place? Suddenly she could not bear its imprisonment, its hopeless frustration, as it butted itself interminably against the glass. The window-pole was by the door, and she grasped it irritably, caught the ring in the hook, and jerked the window open. At once cooler air seemed to flood the room, shaking the still dust into movement, and the fly shot upwards through the gap and disappeared into the baked blue sky above.

His sea-chest. It had been brought to her, along with his cabin furniture, by her brother-in-law, Captain Haworth, when he had returned after Trafalgar. The cabin furniture she had sold, placing the money so realised with the rest of his small fortune in the Funds for his son. The chest she had ordered to be put in the attic, and there it had been ever since, moving from number ten to number twelve with the rest of the boxes, without her ever having set eyes on it, let alone examined its contents.

She was doubtful now if it were the right thing to do. How could it help her? Would it make things worse? But then, how could they be worse? Perhaps inside there was something that would remind her of him permanently and vividly, so that she should never lose him, so that he would not dislimn and slip away from her stubbornly-alive mind. Life drew her on, like a resistless tide, further and further from the place where he had stopped for ever. Perhaps in the chest there was something that would carry her back to that place, to be with him.

With abrupt decision, she knelt on the dusty, bare boards, and pushed the key into the lock. The ward caught, the tumbler resisted for a moment, and then fell with a heavy click, which sounded too loud in the stillness. She paused and listened a moment, as if guiltily; and then set her hands to the lid and lifted it.

On top lay his best uniform coat; the dark blue cloth was stained from sea-water, but the lace and epaulettes were bright and untarnished, for they were real bullion. Weston, with no-one but himself to support, had allowed himself to enjoy a modest luxury, and spent all his pay on his food, his clothes, and his comfort. No second-best for him; no pinchbeck or poor-man's gilt. She stroked the heavy fringe with a finger, and it felt warm to the touch; then she lifted the coat in both arms — it was heavy — and held it to her chest, and closed her eyes, trying to imagine him inside it, his arms going round her, holding her warm and safe.

It was no use. The coat smelled musty — it had been put away damp, probably, for it was notoriously difficult to dry clothes which had been impregnated with salt spray. He was not there. She put it aside.

His dress-sword, and sword-belt. Lucy laid the scabbard across her knees and drew the sword half-way out. In her

91

mind she heard Weston's words: *Never draw steel under deck or roof — it's bad luck.* It was a handsome weapon, made by Roberts and Parfitt of Jermyn Street; fine dark blue steel, with a scrolled line inlaid in gold down the spine. There were seed-pearls set in the guard, and the hilt and pommel were of fine blue enamel inlaid with gold in the pattern of a medusa-head, commemorating the fact that the first ship into which he had been commissioned as lieutenant had been the *Medusa*.

A sword was a valuable thing, a personal thing to pass on to a man's son. She began to rock a little back and forth, without being aware that she was doing it. One day Thomas would be glad to have it; perhaps to wear it, though gentlemen wore swords less and less now, in these civilised times. Still, there were some formal occasions, and a sword was a sword. Weston's sword for Weston's son. She laid it aside, and reached into the box again.

His books — navigation manuals, historical works, a few essays and novels, collections of poetry; his cabin silver — candlesticks, vases, comfit dishes, a silver cigar-box she had given him, the Christmas of 1802, engraved with his name. She lifted them out, handled them, held them to her, looking for him, not finding him. A miniature of her, a copy of a portrait done at the time of her marriage, made by some artist unknown. She hadn't known he had that. It had been handsomely framed in silver, but the glass was cracked. She laid it aside, and rocked a little more.

A flat pokerwork box when opened revealed a collection of her letters to him, worn and dirty along the folds from frequent handling. A sailor far from home, even a busy captain, reads his letters again and again for comfort. Poor, cold letters, these were: she was no correspondent. Where were the words of love and longing he had a right to expect? The letter she had sent announcing Thomas's birth — how slight, how formal, how lacking in everything she wanted to say to him! She whimpered, putting them aside.

Shirts, silk shirts — this one neatly darned by his servant. A nightgown with embroidery round the yoke — where had that come from? Silk stockings, white china silk discoloured at the toe and heel from use, some darned by the same, neat hand. His hairbrushes, his manicure set and scissors, his silver-handled toothbrush and silver pot of tooth powder, the crystal bottle of bay rum with the silver stopper. His Bible and Prayer Book with the matching binding, and the double gold clasps to keep the sea-damp from the pages. A white silk scarf, her first gift to him, so long ago.

Almost done now. Her hands, groping blindly in the depths, came up with a pair of shoes. Good black leather, well-worn but well-dressed, with gold buckles, heavy and solid. She held them one in each hand, appalled, and the tears began to pour from her eyes. These were no virgin shoes: they were worn to the shape of his feet, softened and moulded by the living flesh which had thrust unthinkingly into them morning after morning, and tramped the holystoned deck, bearing him about his business. They were infinitely pathetic, those shoes. She turned them round and round in her hands, and the tears flowed unchecked, for here was the essence of his death, in this reminder of the frail and fallible flesh which had housed the man she loved, and which had perished, leaving her utterly bereft. She clutched them against her chest, sobbing now, pressed them absurdly to her cheek, as the pain of it welled up in her, and she knew her loss, absolute and eternal. He was gone for ever. She would never see him again.

'My lady?'

Docwra had come for her, stood in the doorway hesitantly. Lucy turned her head, hardly seeing her through the tears, made an inarticulate sound, and Docwra was across the room, kneeling beside her mistress, holding her. Lucy's hands stretched out, still clutching the shoes, and now sobs tore at her throat, a terrible, deranged, ugly sound. She was beyond restraint; she was unaware of anything but the terrible pain of loss.

'Go get Mr Parslow,' Docwra said urgently to the frightened housemaid who had alerted her. 'And tell Mr Hicks to send for the physician. Run!'

The maid disappeared, and Docwra, knowing there was nothing else to do, held the thin, rigid body of her mistress as it heaved and jerked, and the tears flowed in an unstaunchable flood. She said nothing, made no sounds of sympathy, knowing they would not help. This was beyond her to understand or heal. When Parslow came, hurrying in from the stables, she handed Lucy over to him. She was as rigid and unwieldy as a wooden doll, but she went to Parslow's arms

93

with an inarticulate, childlike cry, and he picked her up and carried her downstairs to her room. There he would have put her down, but she would not let him go, so he sat on a chair with her on his lap, while she wept and wept against his chest. She cried as though she were bleeding to death, and Docwra stood by, twisting her fingers in anxiety, fearing that the tears would never stop.

But nothing goes on for ever. In the end, she stopped from sheer exhaustion, and Parslow laid her down on the bed, and sat holding her hand quietly until the doctor came, and gave her a draught. After a time she began to be drowsy, and Parslow tried to withdraw his hand to leave her to sleep, but her fingers tightened on his, and she murmured, 'Don't go.'

He sat again, her small, calloused hand engulfed in his large, leathery one. The depth and tenderness of his feelings for her made it impossible for him to speak, even had there been anything he could conceivably say. He hoped she would fall asleep. At last she drew a long, hitching breath and opened her drowned eyes, and said, 'Thank you.'

He shook his head, meaning, there's no need.

'It's over now,' she said. Something in her had broken in that terrible paroxysm of grief. She would never feel like that or cry like that again.

'Yes, my lady,' said Parslow. He wanted to say more, but only squeezed her hand. They were very close at this moment; but she was his mistress, and the wrong words would destroy their unspoken and improbable friendship.

'What am I to do?' she asked after a while, in a small voice, near the edge of sleep. 'Where do I go now?'

'The way you were going, my lady. That was right. But it'll be easier now,' he said.

'Will it?'

'Oh yes. You were swimming upstream. Now you'll go with the current.'

'But what shall I do?' she asked again. Her eyes were closed, but her hand was still alive in his; she was listening. He searched his mind frantically for the right answer; but when he spoke, it was not from intellect but from an animal sense of rightness.

'P'raps you should bring the little boy home, my lady. The Captain's son.'

94

'The Captain's son,' Lucy repeated, and though her eyes were closed and sleep was fast overtaking her, she smiled, and to Parslow that smile seemed the most beautiful thing he had ever seen. 'How nice that sounds. The Captain's son —' She was asleep.

Parslow withdrew his hand carefully and got, a little stiffly, to his feet. At the door Docwra was waiting, looking enquiringly at him. Parslow looked down at his broad hands with the broken fingernails, the palms calloused from a lifetime of handling leather; at his leather breeches and coarse stockings, and his stable shoes to which a thread of dirty straw still adhered; and then he looked up at the lady's maid again.

'You're right, Bessie,' he said. 'It isn't my job.'

Tears jumped to her eyes, and she put out a hand and touched his arm. 'No, John, I wasn't thinking that.'

'Only I love her, you see,' he said. They were words open to misinterpretation, spoken only because of the depth to which his emotions had been stirred; but Docwra, who had lived closely with both of them for twelve years now, understood.

'I know,' she said. 'She loves you too. You did right, John.'

'Ah,' he said. He looked down at his hands again and sighed. 'I've got four horses to strap and bed down. That's where I'll be, if you want me.'

Miss Rosedale looked like a young woman, though a second, closer look revealed that she was well past the first flush of youth. Her face was smooth, open, cheerful, her eyes merry, her mouth curving upwards at the corners, as though she kept it in readiness for smiling; but there was a mesh of fine lines about her eyes, and one or two silver hairs caught the light amongst the brown when she turned her head. She might be five- or six-and-thirty, Héloïse decided; it was the brightness of her brown eyes that made her look younger.

Roberta's Mr Firth had found her in only a few days, through diligent enquiry. He had followed a trail which began with Roberta's father, Colonel Taske, led him through a number of military families of his acquaintance, and ended only just around the corner in Audley Street. Here in a decent, dignified, old-fashioned house, Colonel Barclay had lived for twenty years with his large and happy family; and for sixteen of those years, Miss Rosedale had been governess to his children.

Héloïse met her one morning in the Barclay's breakfast parlour, in the company of Mrs Colonel Barclay, and Miss Albinia Barclay, the last of her charges. At the table, which was covered in cards, boxes, straw, string and paper, Mrs Barclay and a maid were engaged in unpacking wedding gifts.

'You won't mind, I hope, Lady Morland, if we carry on with this while we talk? But there is so much to do, and so little time to do it, with the wedding on Friday.'

She smiled at her daughter, and Albinia blushed a little and looked conscious. Héloïse said what was polite.

'Quite a whirlwind romance it has been too!' Mrs Barclay went on. 'Married at sixteen! Not but what she has known young Glaisford practically since they were in their cots, but we never had any more idea that they would get married! And then they up and fall in love with each other, and since he is to go overseas at any moment with his regiment — well, you know what young people are! They would not wait, and as I said to the Colonel, 'My dear,' I said, 'as I remember, you and I were just as eager when we were their age!' You would be quite shocked, Lady Morland, if I were to tell you how little time elapsed between my dancing with the Colonel for the first time, and his asking me to marry him! Not that he was a colonel then, of course, only an ensign; but I always loved a red coat! We are all the same at heart, we women, aren't we?'

'Oh Mama!' Miss Albinia exclaimed in embarrassment. Her mother looked at her fondly.

'Why, love, you are blushing! She is all sensibility, Lady Morland, as you see, and that is all because of her education, for I tell you frankly that I had none! My Papa was a military man, too, you know, and he did not believe in too much education for females. But times have changed, and I am all for keeping up with the world, and I said to the Colonel when our first daughter — that was Sophy, who is now Mrs Andrews — was born, 'My dear,' I said, 'what was good enough for me may not be good enough for our girls'. And the Colonel agreed with me. So we got a governess — that was Miss Atkins — for Sophy, and for Mary and Jane when they came along. Then when Miss Atkins left to start a school of her own in Salisbury, along with her mother, because her mother had just come into a little fortune — such a charming woman, and she had the smallest feet I've ever seen! — well, then we found Miss Rosedale, and she has been with us ever since, and taken care of all our girls. We had six, you know.'

'Indeed, ma'am,' Héloïse said, noting out of the corner of her eye the affectionate amusement with which Miss Rosedale listened to the stream of inconsequence.

'Oh yes. Well, they are all gone now, all married, and Albinia is the last; and I always say it was the best day's work we ever did, employing Miss Rosedale, for every one of our girls has turned out just as we would have wished.'

'You are very kind to say so, ma'am,' Miss Rosedale said with a quirk of her lips.

'It's no more than the truth, my dear. I don't know what we should have done without you, and that's a fact! And I shall be very sorry to see you leave, but if it is a case of bettering yourself — and then, now that Albinia is to be married, there will be nothing for you to do, and I know how you like to keep occupied. She is such a worker, Lady Morland! I never knew her take her ease, for when she had finished her own duties, she would come to me and say, 'Mrs Barclay, is there anything I can do for you?' Well, I keep servants to do servants' work, and as I always said to the Colonel, we pay a governess to take care of the children, not to run about doing errands for me, so I can tell you, Lady Morland, that there was none of *that* sort of thing in this house, such as you see even in some of the best families! And besides, dear Miss Rosedale is quite one of the family. I'm sure I shall miss her as much as I miss the dear girls.' A tear brightened her eye, and was carefully dabbed away. 'But then, they have all married so well! And all because of dear Miss Rosedale's influence, and the excellent way she taught them. She is kind enough to say that I set them a good example, and so I hope I do, but it is a fact that though I can read and write with the best of them, I take no pleasure from it; and as to all the other things, like geography and history and French, they are like foreign languages to me.'

'Oh, Mama!' Miss Albinia said again.

Mrs Barclay nodded to Héloïse. 'You will find she has all the accomplishments, too, Lady Morland, not just book-learning. Needlework and singing and sketching and so forth.

97

You play the pianoforte too, don't you, my dear?'

'Yes, ma'am, a little,' Miss Rosedale said imperturbably.

'More than a little! You should hear her, Lady Morland, when we have had a little impromptu dance for the young ones sometimes, and Miss Rosedale plays reels for them on the piano by the hour! How her little fingers fly about! But I am sure you will want to talk privately to Miss Rosedale, without me listening. Albinia, love, just come with me into the next room and help Soames and me unpack the dinner service your uncle Waldegrave sent, for that's one thing we must have on display, though to be sure it would be more sensible to leave it in the box, seeing as it only has to be packed up again, to be sent over to the other house on Saturday. But your uncle Waldegrave would be sure to take offence — We'll come back in a quarter of an hour, Lady Morland, and then perhaps you'll take a glass of something with us before you go?'

'Thank you, ma'am,' Héloïse said.

'And don't you be too modest, Miss Rosedale,' Mrs Barclay admonished from the doorway. 'If you don't tell Lady Morland how good you are, I shall be obliged to do it for you, and you know that will embarrass you — aye, and you too, Albinia, I know! You think me too plain, but that is one of the advantages of reaching my age — you don't have to mind what you say.' And with a good-humoured nod to Héloïse and Miss Rosedale, she took her daughter out.

Miss Rosedale turned to face Héloïse. 'Well, your ladyship, what would you like to ask me?'

'I think all my questions have been answered before I ask them,' Héloïse said, amused.

Miss Rosedale's open, pleasant face broke into a smile that set all her fine lines in motion, and she said, 'Mrs Barclay is the kindest of employers. Indeed, it is hardly more than the truth when she says I am like one of the family, for in their generosity that is how they have always treated me.'

'I can see that you have given satisfaction, and so I am satisfied,' Héloïse said. 'But let me tell you about the child, my stepdaughter, for whom I wish a governess. I will tell you everything quite frankly, and then you may say if you think you can help, or if you even wish to try. For truly, it will not be easy.'

98

Miss Rosedale listened attentively as Héloïse described Fanny, and told her history and the tale of her wrongdoings. Then she asked a few short, pertinent questions, and lapsed into a thoughtful silence.

'Well?' Héloïse prompted at last. 'Have I frightened you with this terrible tale? Do you think, like Miss Bantry, that Fanny is a monster?'

'No, indeed, ma'am!' Miss Rosedale said quickly, raising her eyes. 'Poor little girl! I am so sorry for her! She must be lonely and unhappy.'

'Oh, you see it in that light, do you? I am glad. But you do not give me an answer.'

'If I am thoughtful, it is only because I am wondering what would be the best way to tackle the problem.'

'You wish to try?' Héloïse said hopefully.

Miss Rosedale met her eyes. 'That depends on one thing. May I ask you something frankly?'

'It is the best way to ask,' Héloïse smiled.

'Forgive me, but you said Fanny has been spoilt — may I ask by whom?'

'By her father, mainly, and by some of the servants.'

'I see. And — frankly again — how much authority will I have over the child? If she appeals against my judgement, will I be overruled? May I count on your support, and that of Fanny's father, whatever I do? I beg you will not think me impertinent, but it is of the utmost importance. If the case is as extreme as you say, I may have to resort to some unusual tactics; and if Fanny knows that she can run to you or her papa every time I cross her, it will all be in vain.'

'I understand. I do not think you impertinent, Miss Rosedale. It is very sensible of you to ask. And I promise you, if you think you can help Fanny, you will have my complete support.'

'And her father's?'

'Leave me alone for that. We both want Fanny to grow up into a happy, useful, sensible child. Indulgence has not answered, nor punishment. I don't know what more there is to try — but I dare say you do.'

Miss Rosedale smiled her pleasant smile. 'I wonder, has anyone ever tried love?'

Héloïse considered. 'I really think they have not. Poor Fanny!'

99

'Poor Fanny indeed! Well, ma'am, if you are satisfied, I am too.'

'Then you will come? I am so glad. Oh, but we must discuss your salary and other things before you decide.'

'No, no, Lady Morland, I have decided already.' Her smile almost became a grin. 'Life here has become almost too easy in recent years. I cannot tell you how much I am looking forward to the challenge! I feel most stimulated already!'

Héloïse travelled post back to Yorkshire, and as the weather was fine and the moon near-full, and as she was aware of a stronger need every moment to be at Morland Place, she chose to sleep on the road to be home the sooner. She woke when the chaise finally stopped at the Hare and Heather early in the morning. It was that still time between first light and sunrise, and as she stepped down stiffly from the carriage and snuffed the clean air, she was seized with the desire to walk to Morland Place across the fields.

'You shall wait here with the luggage,' she told Marie. 'Rest, have some coffee, some breakfast if you like. I'll send someone to collect you as soon as I get home.'

'But madame, you don't mean to walk over the fields alone?' Marie protested.

'Why not? It's my home, Marie! What harm could come to me?'

She crossed the road and climbed the stile, and stepped out on the footpath that led across Holgate Stray and over the beck onto Morland land. Everything was quiet. It was going to be another hot day. The sky was pale with the promise of it, the air unmoving and already warm, but still fresh and dewy. There was no sound except for the birds — past the dawn chorus now, and already about the business of the day. The trees were fat with the full leaf of June, the grass silver with dew, marked here and there with dark tracks, where some animal had passed, dog or vixen perhaps, trotting home after a night's hunting.

She had the world to herself, new and unused, delicate and perfect, as if it had just that moment been created. She walked briskly, shaking out the cramps and stiffness of a night in a carriage, feeling the blood running vigorously under her skin, breathing deeply of the clean, cool air. It was so good to be alive! To go home to James and Sophie, Thomas and Mathilde, brother Edward — yes, even poor Fanny! How those two words came together in her head! But Miss Rosedale would make everything right again. Héloïse liked her instinctively, trusted her already.

She reached the top of the long, slight slope, and there at last was Morland Place, square and serene, unchangeable and immoveable, floating like an island in the moat. The water reflected the serene sky, and the swans were drifting casually towards the window where they rang a bell to be fed in the morning. The still-invisible sun was tinting the air with gold and blushing the bricks to rosy, and now the upper windows began to flash with the sun's light, as though welcoming it back into the world. The house had stood there, just so, for more than three hundred years, and generations of Morlands must have come upon it just as she did now, returning from work and travel and school, from pleasure, from war, from success and disappointment, and had looked down gratefully at the citadel of the family, the resting-place the place of safety. Home!

She thought of Jemima, her aunt, and past mistress of Morland Place, who had so wanted it to belong to Héloïse. Well, Maman, she addressed her inwardly, things belong in truth to those who really appreciate them; and so Morland Place is mine. I will guard your kingdom well, and try to make Fanny worthy of your trust. She hoped and believed that sooner or later Fanny would be claimed by history and her blood. Who could be born a Morland, and not respond?

She set off again down the hill, past the little copse of birch and hazel which was all that was left of the larger wood that had once surrounded the house. As she came clear of the trees, she saw Fanny only a little way from her, standing on the bottom rail of the home-paddock fence. She had her back to her, and was talking to a chestnut filly in the paddock, the new youngster that she had chosen for her own. The filly was eyeing her suspiciously, flirting her ears back and forth, while Fanny held out her hand steadily, trying to wheedle her into coming nearer.

Héloïse stood still to watch, and marvelled at Fanny's patience with the young horse.

'Come, Honey, come. Come little lady. Come then,' she

crooned over and over, her hand held out quite still, and a piece snipped off the sugar loaf white and inviting on her palm. But Honey lifted her muzzle and flared her nostrils, and the dark eyes in the golden face eyed the gift warily, almost knowingly.

'Come, Honey. Come then,' Fanny crooned; but Honey knew of the hand which accompanied the gift, which would catch her headcollar as she bent her head, and lead her away from the green field and freedom. She kept her distance, and watched, poised to dart away.

Héloïse remembered something that James had told her long ago.

'Salt is better,' she said very quietly.

Fanny jerked round at the sound of her voice, and Honey startled at the movement, whirled and dashed away. At once Fanny's face contracted into a fierce scowl. 'No wonder she wouldn't come to me,' she said resentfully. 'And now you've scared her away.'

'I didn't scare her,' Héloïse said reasonably. 'She was facing me. She knew I was here all along.'

Fanny jumped down from the fence and stood sullenly kicking the bottom rail. Her feet were bare under her brown cambric dress, and wet from the dew. 'Spying on me,' she said almost inaudibly, refusing to look at her stepmother.

Héloïse ignored the words and the pose. 'When I arrived at the inn the day seemed too good to waste, so I decided to walk home across the fields. Everything is especially lovely at this time of morning, isn't it?'

Fanny looked at her suspiciously, so exactly as Honey had watched Fanny that Héloïse wanted to laugh; and yet her heart was tugged towards the wild, ungoverned little girl. Who, indeed, had ever loved Fanny? Of course James doted on her, but did he know her? Did he even really see her, or was she rather some image of perfection to him, some symbol of unattainable happiness? Fanny's mother had abandoned her at birth, the servants either flattered her or complained about her. She had no brother or sister, no friend — she hardly saw other children, except the children of servants whom the servants had taught her to despise. She lived all alone in her lofty dignity as heiress, waiting for the wealth and the power and the responsibility which would one day cut her off even more completely from the rest of the world.

Suddenly Héloïse smiled. 'Will you walk back to the house with me?'

'What for?' Fanny said rebelliously.

'Just for the company,' Héloïse said unemphatically. 'Look, the sun's coming up! Oh, I never get tired of seeing that!' She stared towards the horizon and began to walk, as if assuming Fanny would follow; and after a brief hesitation, she did. 'How is Honey coming along?' she asked after a moment.

Fanny kept her eyes on the ground, which she kicked now and then as she walked; but she answered. 'We backed her the day before yesterday, and we've had the saddle on her every day. She doesn't like it. Papa says she has a cold back, but I don't think so. I think she just doesn't want to be ridden.'

'Why not?' Héloïse asked with interest.

'Why should she? Until she's broken, she runs free. She can do what she likes. Why should she carry me? I wouldn't want to, if I was her.'

'Then, why do you make her?'

'Because she's *mine*,' Fanny said fiercely, looking up. 'Anyway, she'll like it once she knows. We'll go everywhere together. One day we'll —' She stopped abruptly, realising she was saying too much.

Héloïse pretended not to notice. 'When I was a girl,' she said dreamily, 'I had a chestnut horse called Prestance. He was so beautiful, and I loved him so! But I had to leave him behind when we ran away from France.'

'What happened to him?' Fanny asked gruffly, unwilling to allow her interest to show.

'I wish I knew! Of course, no-one would hurt a horse; but I wish I knew that he went to a kind person, who would talk to him and stroke him. They need to be petted and loved.'

Fanny said nothing, only walked along kicking the silver dew from the grass with her bare feet, enjoying making her mark on the new morning world. At last she said, 'Why is salt better?'

Héloïse rejoiced inside. 'They will stand longer for salt. With sugar they crunch it up and then it's done; but with salt they'll lick and lick at your hand, as long as there's the least taste of it left.'

'How do you know that?'

103

'Someone told me,' Héloïse said, avoiding the mention of James between them. She went on, 'I used to ride Prestance in the woods near Paris, and if ever I was unhappy, I used to think I would just gallop away on him, and never come back. But I didn't, of course. It wouldn't have worked.'

'Why not?' Fanny said, feigning indifference.

'Because you can't run away from unhappiness. It can run faster than you.'

They were nearing the house. Héloïse stopped and turned to face her, and for once, Fanny stood her ground and met her look. Fanny's eyes were hazel, a light, golden brown flecked with shifting lights of gold and green, and fringed with dark lashes which somehow gave the impression of being tangled, like her dark bushy curls. Her face had grown thinner lately, not with ill-health, but with the shedding of childhood's rounded contours, and Héloïse realised for the first time that those eyes, that face, were not those of an absolute child. Fanny was growing up. Héloïse looked for James's likeness, but there was none there, except perhaps for something indefinable about the shape of the mouth. She must look like her mother. It was a strong-featured face, not pretty, but very much itself, and unforgettable.

The eyes were wary and hostile, but there was something else there, too — a woman's vulnerability. Héloïse wanted suddenly to give her something, but she had nothing Fanny would accept. Yet there was something in the air, some tenuous breath of contact between them; delicate as the first laboriously woven strand of a spider's web, and as fragile.

'I have something to tell you, some news,' she said suddenly. Fanny only looked. She wanted to tell her about Miss Rosedale, but there were no words which would not arouse Fanny's hostility, and telling her now would only arm her against the new governess ahead of time. So she said instead, 'I hope you will think it good news, Fanny. I am to have a baby — a new brother or sister for you. Isn't that wonderful?'

She almost held her breath; and for a moment, the words did not seem to make any impact on Fanny. The wild, shy eyes only looked uncomprehendingly, neither with interest nor dislike. But the moment passed, and Fanny's face seemed suddenly to grow thinner, her eyes narrowed, her mouth pinched.

'No it isn't!' she cried shrilly. 'It's *disgusting*!' And she turned on her heel and began running, back the way she had come, veering across the grass, her bare brown feet twinkling under the hem of her plain linen gown. But there was something different about the way she ran. It was not the long, free, child's lope Héloïse had seen before. She ran from the knees, as a woman does; and clumsily; and when she flung a hand up across her face, Héloïse realised that she must be crying as she ran.

The main gate was still closed, but the postern stood open, and Héloïse stepped through into the cold shadow of the barbican, and out into the sunlit courtyard. From the stables came cheerful morning noises, the swish of a broom, the scrape of shovel on cobble, the clank of a bucket, the rustle of horses moving about in their deep straw beds, pulling at their hay-racks, sneezing as the hay-dust tickled their nostrils. On the stable roof a young peacock with a juvenile tail was shrieking dolefully in answer to a distant and more senior companion. A sparrow flew up into the gutter with a piece of bread, and was instantly set upon by a brown and bickering mob.

The house door was also closed, but the kitchen door in the corner of the yard was open, and the cook, Monsieur Barnard, sat on a wooden stool just outside it, his back to the wall, his legs stretched out into the sunshine, and a thin cigar sending a wreath of smoke up into the still, blue air. There was nothing unusual in this: Héloïse knew that he liked to have his moment to himself before beginning the frantic daily round of cooking. What surprised her was that he was not alone. Thomas, barefoot and still in his nightshirt, was standing beside him, his hands on Barnard's knees, talking to him.

Barnard had seen her, but Héloïse made a quick negative gesture, not wishing to disturb the scene. 'And what happened when you got on the ship?' Thomas had just asked. 'Was it a big ship?'

'No, no, it was a very little ship, and it went up and down on the water, and I was very ill,' the cook replied genially. 'There was a storm, which nearly sank us, and we all would have died; but a ship of the King's navy came along, and rescued us. So I met Mr William Morland, the master's brother, who brought me here.'

Thomas had asked in English, and Barnard replied in French, but now when Thomas spoke again, it was in French, as if it made no difference to him which language was used.

'My father was a captain in a King's ship,' he said proudly. 'He was very brave. He's dead now.'

'Yes, I know, little one,' Barnard said, clearing his throat. He touched Thomas's head very lightly, and evidently decided it was a good moment to terminate the interview, for he looked beyond the child towards Héloïse, and Thomas, alerted, turned and saw her. His face broke into a flattering smile, and he came running to her, and she caught him and lifted him up, to receive a wet and hearty kiss on the cheek.

'*Cher petit*, I am so glad to see you!' Héloïse said. 'But what are you doing out here in your nightgown?'

'I woke up. Sarah was still asleep, so I came to see M'sieur Barnard,' Thomas explained as if it were an obvious consequence.

'Well, you had better go and get dressed now, or you'll be late for breakfast. Run, *mon étoile*; I'll come and see you later.'

She set him down, and he tugged her down by the neck to kiss her again, and scampered off. Héloïse turned to her cook, who had risen to his feet and was looking rather embarrassed. 'Does this often happen?'

'Just lately, yes, my lady;' Barnard answered. 'The sun wakes him early.'

'And what do you speak of?'

'I tell him stories of France, and he tells me about himself.' He met Héloïse's eyes. 'I saw no harm in it.'

'Oh, no, no, I am not angry, only surprised. I did not think you had a taste for the prattle of children.'

'I like the little fellow, my lady,' Barnard said unemphatically.

'And does he understand everything you say?' she asked curiously. No-one had ever heard Barnard speak English. Their present conversation was, of course, in French.

'Certainly, my lady,' Barnard said. 'He speaks French and English equally, just like Miss Sophie.'

'I suppose she has taught him,' Héloïse mused, and caught a look which flickered in her cook's eye, which suggested that

106

there had been more and longer conversations between him and Thomas than she knew about. From Barnard rather than from Sophie, had he learned his French? The thought of such tenderness nestling in the tough old heart of the Tyrant of the Kitchen both touched and amused her. 'Well, as long as he doesn't annoy you —'

'Not at all, my lady.' He looked as though he were about to say more, perhaps embark on some confession he might later regret; but they were interrupted. There was a sound of bolts being drawn, the great door opened, and a large grey figure came bounding out to fling itself on Héloïse in frantic, tail-thrashing, silent joy.

'Kithra, you fool! Get down! *Zut, alors*, you will knock me over!'

Kithra's rapture at having her back, however, was beyond the confines of discipline, and while his mistress was attempting to remain upright under the onslaught of love, Barnard, with a small smile, put out his cigar and made his escape back into the kitchen.

CHAPTER SIX

On 30 June, news reached England of a crushing defeat inflicted by Bonaparte on the Russians at Friedland. Far from being overcome by his set-back at Preuss-Eylau, Bonaparte had rallied, somehow raised a new army of conscription, and marched back into Prussia, to meet the Russians on 14 June, while the English reinforcements were still waiting to embark. The Russians were utterly defeated; Prussia had instantly capitulated; thousands had been slain; and the Csar, who had led the battle in person, was said to have sat down amongst the Russian dead and wept.

Within days further news arrived, of a new treaty between France and Russia. Bonaparte had sought out his vanquished foe and offered peace on his own terms. The two emperors had met on a raft tethered in the middle of the river Nieman — the Russian frontier — and sworn eternal friendship. The world henceforth was to be divided between them, and ruled by these 'natural brothers', Russia holding the north and east, France the south and west. England now stood alone, the last country which still resisted the world's most successful soldier.

London was stifling hot, but because of the news, people were delaying going down to the country. Lucy left the children at Wolvercote and came back to Town. Calling at Chelmsford House, she found Colonel Taske giving a lecture, with globes, on the current situation, to an audience of Roberta, Mr Firth, Bobbie, and his cousin Marcus Morland.

'What do you suppose will happen next?' Lucy asked. 'I have never heard so many rumours in one day.'

'Most of them false, I dare say,' the Colonel replied. 'No layman understands the military mind. I could have told 'em Boney would move this summer. He had enough of the Prussian snows last year; didn't mean to leave anything to do next winter.'

'I imagine France will help Russia to overrun the Turks and the Swedes,' Mr Firth suggested more helpfully, 'and Russia will help Boney expand his empire in the other direction.'

'What other direction?' Colonel Taske said sharply.

'Spain and Portugal — the Iberian peninsula, sir,' Firth said.

'What? Cross the Pyrénées? Nonsense! Boney may be a rogue, but he's a soldier, and he's got more sense than that.'

'But he is unfailingly ambitious, sir, and that is the obvious next move,' Firth said apologetically. 'He's conquered everything else.'

'Except England,' Bobbie put in proudly, 'and he knows he can't beat us, not while our navy rules the seas.'

'Certainly not; but can we beat him?' Lucy put in. 'As Cousin Héloïse says, there'll be no peace in the world until we do.'

Firth exchanged a glance with Roberta, and said, 'That's enough of Boney for today, I think. If you will excuse us, ma'am, sir, we had better be off, or we shan't get a good place at the front.'

'Are you sure you don't want to come, Mother?' Bobbie asked. 'They say it is *amazingly* lifelike!'

'You can tell me all about it,' Roberta laughed. 'I don't think I could bear to be jostled in all this heat.'

'I shall leave you too, m'dear, and walk down to my club,' Colonel Taske said. 'Your servant, ma'am!'

When they were alone, Lucy asked her, 'Where are they going, to be jostled?'

'To see the new panorama of the battle of Trafalgar,' Roberta said. 'Mr Firth thought it would be a good way to keep Marcus's mind off things: he's very worried about his papa.'

'Why? What's happened to Horatio?'

'He was with Lord Cathcart's expeditionary force, the advance guard to Rugen. Of course they set off before the news arrived about Friedland, and no-one knows yet what has happened to them. If they have landed, they are very exposed.'

'And that's why Marcus is here?' Lucy asked.

'Well, not entirely,' Roberta said, a little awkwardly. 'The fact is, Lady Barbara suggested again that it would be nice for Marcus and Bobbie to do their lessons together, and of course she's right —'

'Fustian!' Lucy snorted. 'You mean she wants to save herself the expense of keeping and educating her own son, and she's managed to foist him onto you. Confess, now — it isn't just lessons, is it? You've taken him in.'

'Well, yes, he is living here at the moment. It seemed silly for him to go back and forth each day, and Bobbie does like having company.'

'Lord, you make things easy for Lady Barbara!' Lucy said. 'And are you to be saddled with Barbarina, too?'

'No, she stays with her mother. But really, Lucy, I don't mind having Marcus here. The expense is nothing to me, and it helps Bobbie to have someone to share his lessons. And they get on so well together. Besides, you are in no position to criticise — you look after Hippolyta for Captain Haworth, and you've offered to have Bobbie often enough.'

'That's different. You know that Lady Barbara's one ambition — beyond saving money of course — is to have Marcus inherit the title. This plan of hers is just the first foothold.'

Roberta looked ruffled. 'Goodness knows what harm you think it can do to have him here! Do you suppose she's instructed Marcus to poison Bobbie?'

'I wouldn't put it past her. But Marcus, to do him credit, seems a nice enough boy, though he and his sister always remind me of two white mice. Well, as long as you're a willing victim — for you know you'll never get rid of him, don't you? Now tell me — do your papa and your Mr Firth really not know what's going on? I came for instruction, for everyone I know who has a minister's ear has suddenly become tight-lipped and refuses to gossip — which is suspicious in itself.'

'I wish you wouldn't keep calling him "my Mr Firth". And I don't know what you think he could have learned that you wouldn't have heard first,' Roberta said, still a little ruffled. 'He doesn't hob-nob with admirals and Members of Parliament like you.'

'No, but he knows a lot of senior military men,' Lucy said with a grin, 'and everyone knows that soldiers are much worse gossips than sailors. Come, Roberta, don't be cross with me. Has your revered papa not told you anything? Where are all these soldiers off to, who are assembling at Yarmouth?'

'Papa doesn't know. Castlereagh's orders were issued in complete confidence,' Roberta said, relenting, 'and there's a strict embargo on all ships, too, in case it should leak out that way. All Papa knows is that Sir Arthur Wellesley's to be put in charge of the expedition. Whatever is happening, no word of it must be allowed to reach France.'

'Well, that will be a novelty, at all events,' Lucy said. 'Usually they know our plans before we do.'

Two days later, Lucy had just returned from exercising her team in the park, when Hicks announced a visitor, and her brother-in-law, Captain Haworth, walked in.

'Lucy, my dear!' They exchanged an embrace, and he stepped back to look at her critically. 'You are looking better. How are things with you?'

'Oh, I go along pretty well,' she said cautiously.

'I heard about your race. You madcap! And cross-saddle, I understand? How can I make a lady of Africa, with her aunt's example always before her?'

'I won two thousand guineas on it,' Lucy pointed out. 'But how on earth did you hear about that, all the way down in Southsea?'

'News travels, particularly news about you. Tales about Lady Aylesbury are meat and drink to the senior service, don't you know that? Africa boasts far more about having you for an aunt than having me for a father.'

'What nonsense,' Lucy said. 'When were sailors ever interested in horse races?'

'Actually, it was young Morpurgo who told us,' Haworth admitted. 'He'd been staying with relatives in Oxfordshire, and he called on us on his way to Portsmouth to join his new ship. I like that young man enormously: if the war only goes on long enough, he will make a fine admiral one day.'

'Judging from the news, there is every chance it will,' Lucy said.

Haworth smiled. 'At all events, I wish he could have delayed a few days more, then I could have taken him with me.'

'You have a new command? You sly thing! But I thought you had decided to come ashore for good.'

111

He shrugged. 'You can't refuse, when the admiral asks for you in person. Even if it is Dismal Jimmy.'

'Admiral Gambier asked for you personally?' Lucy's face lit. 'Haworth! It's the secret campaign — you are to be part of it!'

'Not so secret, if you know all about it,' he said ruefully.

'But I don't. Oh, everyone knows there are transports and troops at Yarmouth, but no-one knows where they are going. I've never known the Government keep such secrecy.'

'It's vitally important that the whole exercise is kept secret,' Haworth said. 'All I can tell you is that we sail on the twenty-sixth. I'm hoisting my pennant as Commodore in the *Rochester*.'

'Commodore! A promotion! Dear Haworth, I'm so pleased for you! Is that what you came out of your way to tell me?'

'Not so far out of my way. The *Rochester*'s lying at London Pool, so naturally, as I was so near, I felt I must call on you. Dipton has taken Africa direct to the ship.'

'Africa goes with you, then?'

'It might be my last command, her last chance to go to sea. I couldn't deny her that. You know how she feels — how you would have felt in her position.'

'Your last command? But surely now you won't come ashore, now they've given you your pennant?'

'I'm not so very ambitious, you know. I know that if I go on serving long enough, I'll become an admiral; but I'm fifty-four, Lucy, and I keep thinking of poor Collingwood, and how he hasn't seen his daughters since the war began. He hasn't watched them grow up, and I don't want to end that way myself. Of course, I've had Africa with me, but I want her to have a normal life ashore. And I'd like to see more of Hippolyta too — though I shouldn't think of trying to take her away from you now.'

'Well, I suppose you know your own mind,' Lucy said doubtfully, 'though if it were me —'

'If you were me, you'd feel the same. Hicks told me you'd had the children staying with you all this year. You're softening with age, Lucy.'

She opened her mouth to make a retort, and then closed it. She walked over to the window and stared out at the dusty street, baking under the strong sunlight, and said quietly, 'I think you may be right, Haworth; though I don't know that it's age that's done it.' She remembered the day she had gone through Weston's chest; something had altered in her that day, but it was not a thing she could explain to Haworth.

'That was just a joke, my dear,' Haworth said gently.

She looked at him a little bleakly. 'I have changed. Despite the race and — and everything, I can't go back to being the way I was. I feel as if there's nothing more to expect for myself. I must live for the children now. Their lives are all before them.'

'Well, don't sound as though it were a sentence of death! You must learn to enjoy your children. Lucy dear. It can be very pleasant, you know, being with them.'

'For you, perhaps.'

'Well, when this expedition's over, I shall come back and teach you the trick of it.'

Her face brightened. 'Would you? If anyone could teach me, it would be you.'

He looked at her affectionately. 'If you would like it, of course I will.'

Fanny received with gloom the news that Lucy's three children and Hippolyta Haworth were to descend on Morland Place for race-week. They would sleep in the nursery with Sophie and Thomas, of course, but she had no doubt that some disruption to her life was on its way. Since Miss Rosedale had arrived, she had been living in a state of constant confusion and mild shock, so that she never knew from day to day what was going to happen to her. Fanny was not stupid, and it had taken her very little time to suspect that confusion and shock were a deliberate ploy on Miss Rosedale's part, but she didn't yet see what she could do about it.

Miss Rosedale had remained with the Barclays for Albinia's wedding, and for a few days afterwards, to help Mrs Barclay recover from the event; and then she had packed her trunks and travelled by the mail to Yorkshire. Héloïse had advised James not to tell Fanny that a new governess had been hired, so the first Fanny knew about it was when Jenny came rather earlier than usual one morning to fetch her down to the dining-room.

The adults were still at breakfast, and there, opposite the

113

door, next to Madame, was a stranger in a dark blue dress eating smoked mackerel and buttered eggs with the calm concentration of one whose health and digestion have never given her a moment's worry.

'Fanny, darling, I want to present you to your new governess, Miss Rosedale,' James said, sounding distinctly nervous. 'Miss Rosedale, this is our dear Fanny.'

Miss Rosedale lifted her smooth, smiling face and regarded Fanny with a bright, brown eye, like an inquisitive bird. 'Good morning, Fanny,' she said cheerfully. 'Have you had breakfast? Do you eat here or in the nursery?' Fanny merely scowled, and Miss Rosedale went on, 'In the nursery? I think you ought to take your meals in the dining-room from now on. I'm sure twelve is old enough, wouldn't you agree, Mr Morland? Won't you come and sit by me, Fanny? I expect you've already eaten this morning, but you won't mind chatting to me while I continue, will you?'

Fanny turned her stunned eyes on Uncle Ned's stricken face — he had often said that if he couldn't get away from Fanny at meal times, he would have to go and live in the stables with the horses — and then walked numbly, like a sleepwalker, to the seat beside Miss Rosedale which was being offered her. As she sat down, Miss Rosedale, crunching unconcernedly through fish-bones with her large white teeth, met her gaze with what was indisputably the ghost of a wink.

The invitation had been to chat, but even had Fanny wished to, she would have had little opportunity. Miss Rosedale, while continuing to make a hearty breakfast, managed to talk almost non-stop, asked a great many questions, and answered most of them herself. Fanny could only stare at the newcomer in horrified fascination. Miss Rosedale's overt good nature and unquenchable spirits were a shock when she hadn't been expecting anyone at all; added to that, she was so appallingly healthy and full of energy, and had begun her campaign by acquiring for Fanny with apparent effortlessness the privilege of eating with the adults, something she had been pleading for fruitlessly for months.

That was the beginning of it. Miss Rosedale had been at Morland Place a month now, and Fanny felt as though her feet hadn't touched the ground for an instant. She never knew what was going to happen next. She was quite likely to be woken by her governess early in the morning and taken out to watch for badgers in Harewood Whin, or for a long ride over the moor to look for curlews' nests. On one occasion, Miss Rosedale even rousted Fanny from her bed in the middle of the night, to go up on the leads and look at the stars.

'Pointless trying to learn astronomy from books,' she had said. 'And clear nights like this are all too rare. Take the blanket from your bed, Fanny, and put it round your shoulders. It'll be cold on the roof.'

Lessons became a mixture of the astonishing and the exhausting. There was no regular curriculum or timetable. Miss Rosedale seemed to teach Fanny whatever she felt like teaching, in any order, and at any time. She might start off one morning with geography, and in the middle of drawing a map, suddenly drag Fanny off to the blacksmith's shop to persuade him to shew them how to shoe a horse. A lesson on the Civil War ended up with their riding out to Marston Moor and re-enacting the battle with the help of some village children, two farm labourers, and the shepherd. The latter shook his head sadly and tapped it significantly behind Miss Rosedale's back, but was nevertheless so flattered to be asked to represent Prince Rupert that he was soon galloping up and down as fast as his legs would carry him, and uttering blood-thirsty war cries, to the astonishment of his dogs.

Fanny had laughed herself nearly sick on that occasion, and afterwards had been surprised to realise how much she was enjoying herself. She resented it, and tried hard to stay aloof from Miss Rosedale, to be sullen with her, simply to refuse to co-operate; but it was difficult. To begin with, Miss Rosedale was so energetic she simply rolled over resistance like a tide; and then the things she did were interesting, and life was never dull if Fanny went along with her.

And again, she always seemed to assume that she and Fanny were on the same side, against the rest of the world. She seemed a complete hoyden, rode as well as Fanny, was just as ready to take off her stockings and stand in the stream catching guppies in her hands to teach Fanny icthyology; or to climb the oak tree looking for emperor caterpillars as part of an entymology lesson. The notion of having a henchman was tempting to one who had always been a solitary sinner; and to remove herself from Miss Rosedale's camp was to put

115

herself on the side of those she had always regarded as the enemy. Fanny's thunder had been stolen, and she knew it. She would strike back, she promised herself, as soon as she was able to draw breath.

Héloïse viewed the campaign with amusement, James with apprehension. 'But don't you see what she's doing?' Héloïse said. 'She's forstalling Fanny, thinking of everything before Fanny does, and diverting her energies from malicious pranks to harmless ones.'

'But where will it stop?' James said. 'I'm afraid she's putting ideas into Fanny's head; and she's hardly teaching her to be ladylike.'

'No, my James, not yet. She must get Fanny to like and trust her before she can teach the things Fanny does not want to learn. I think we should not interfere. I'm sure she knows what she's doing.'

'I can't stand the suspense of wondering what dreadful thing she's going to do next. Was she like this with the Barclays? How did they survive sixteen years of it?'

Héloïse laughed. 'Oh, I like it! She amuses me.'

Later Héloïse spoke alone to Miss Rosedale about her progress. 'Mr Morland is worried that you are putting ideas in Fanny's head. He wonders how long this phase of the battle will continue.'

'Until Fanny surrenders,' Miss Rosedale said with a wry smile. 'She hasn't yet.'

'She has been very quiet since you came, and Mr Edward Morland is surprised at how well she behaves at the table. She looks a little like a *somnanbuliste, enfin*. Is not this surrender?'

'I fear not. She is waiting, thinking. She goes along with me at the moment because it suits her to, because I make life interesting for her, but she has not yielded one inch of her position. She may strike back at any time.'

'Well, it is at all events better for everyone as it is,' Héloïse concluded. 'You must go on as you think right; and for the moment, continue to teach Fanny alone. Marie and I can take care of Sophie at present.'

Lucy arrived at Morland Place for race-week, accompanied by her children and their household of governess and nursery-maids, and apologised to Héloïse for the invasion.

'But Lady Barbara has attached herself to Roberta for the trip, and I cannot endure to be in the same house as that woman.'

'I am glad to have you, and the dear children,' Héloïse protested. 'I love the house to be full. I should not mind if you brought twice as many people.'

'I almost did, for Danby Wiske came up with me, and Robert Knaresborough, but I did not think you would have room for them, so they are to stay at Shawes, too.'

'Oh, but there is good room for them in the bachelor wing,' Héloïse said. 'I shall write Roberta a note to say she should send them here.'

'No, don't do that — the house will be quite crowded enough without them. I know your notions of hospitality! I shall never forget the four months I spent with you at Plaisir: you don't think you have enough guests until they are falling over each other.'

Though Héloïse felt the house could never be full enough, the arrival of the race-week parties brought certain tensions. The children settled in to the nurseries, and Miss Trotton and Miss Rosedale eyed each other with evident approval and the promise of long tête-à-têtes to come; but Fanny held herself aloof from her cousins and, demanding a holiday from lessons and Miss Rosedale, attached herself to her father with an air of triumph.

James accepted her presence with an air of distraction. He was feeling uneasy because John Skelwith seemed all too often at the house: Mathilde was to attend the races each day with a party of young people, the Keatings and Somers's and one or two others, and since John Skelwith was making all the arrangements, it seemed to necessitate his calling frequently on Mathilde, sometimes in company, but more often alone. James could not object without some reason, and he cursed the unlucky accident which had brought them together. The more Skelwith and Morland Place were exposed to each other, he feared, the more likely he was to discover the truth.

Edward was feeling uneasy because Robert Knaresborough, though staying at Shawes, could not absent himself from Lucy's children, and seemed to run tame about Morland Place. The sight of him reminded Edward painfully of the last time he had seen Chetwyn, and the circumstances of Chetwyn's death. Certainly there was nothing to complain about in Knaresborough's manner or behaviour, but Edward still wished him at the bottom of the sea, or some warmer place.

'It's the outside of enough for Lucy to have asked him,' he complained bitterly to Héloïse. 'Why does she let him hang about her children?'

'He is very good with them, and they are fond of him,' Héloïse said distractedly, 'and you must remember, Lucy never understood about the scandal. I, for one, should not like to try to explain it to her.'

Ned took the point, but reluctantly. 'Well then, why doesn't he spend his time at Shawes? It's an insult to Roberta that he's here all day long.'

'Roberta does not mind,' Héloïse said, detaching her mind with a sigh from the guest-list for the grand dinner they were giving on Wednesday. With limited space, the question of who to include and who to leave out was a delicate one.

'Roberta is altogether too easy-going. It does no-one any good to be allowed to do what they like.'

'It is not going to be easy to tell Fanny that she is not to be present at the dinner,' Héloïse murmured, unable to keep her mind from her own problem.

'And that's another thing,' Edward said. 'That new governess is making Fanny worse than ever. It's time you sent her packing.'

'Oh, but she has kept Fanny out of mischief so far. And at least she stays, not like the others,' Héloïse said placatingly, and offered a counter-irritant. 'I wonder should we ask John Skelwith? It might seem a slight if we do not — and yet we can hardly ask him without asking his mother too.'

Edward's eyebrows shot up. 'Ask his —! I should think not! What are you thinking of? It's bad enough having him haunt the place, without having to endure his mother as well.' He looked around him with a frustrated air. 'Tiger — here! Sometimes I think everyone in this house has gone mad,' he complained, and stumped off to the stables.

As well as all the arrangements for entertaining, and her worries on behalf of the rest of the family, Héloïse had quite another source of unease, and one to which she could not very well own. Lucy, since her arrival, had been paying unusual attention to Thomas, and Héloïse began to suspect that she was thinking of taking the boy away with her. This was entirely as it should be, and Héloïse had often regretted that Lucy had shewn so little interest in her child before; but the fact remained that she loved Thomas very much, just as if he were her own, and she knew that she would be very unhappy if he were taken away. Not only that, but Sophie would break her heart, and she rather suspected that Thomas would not take kindly to the idea either.

Added to that, Héloïse was about to enter the fifth month of her pregnancy, and was suffering from continuous indigestion, which was wearying, and the frequent desire to pass water, which was tiresome; and she was obliged to be hospitable to guests, patient with children, and to express a keen interest in the horses Edward and James were running, when all she wanted was to go off on her own and find somewhere cool to lie down, with her feet propped up on several pillows.

But her early training stood her in good stead, and she bore every minor irritation with patience, though she sometimes felt that one more interruption would break her heart. When the last straw was added, it came from the expected source — Fanny.

Fanny had rejoiced when her plea to be let off lessons had been admitted, and she had looked forward to glorious days of being with her father, like the days when they were breaking Honey together. Honey's training had been suspended for the moment, with the imminence of race-week, and she had been turned out with the other young horses. James spent most of every day at Twelvetrees, working on the horses who would be racing, and to Fanny's surprise and dismay, he didn't seem to have time for her.

When she had first made her request, he had said, 'Yes, of course you can come, Fan, but you mustn't get in the way.' This was slightly less welcoming than she might have expected, but she put it from her mind. When she presented herself the first day, ready to drive with him in the gig up to Twelvetrees, he had smiled and ruffled her hair rather absently, and once at the stables he had seemed to forget her existence.

She trailed round after him as he busied himself with all

119

the last-minute details and decisions, but he seemed to find her in the way, and did not consult her, or invite her to help, or even talk to her, except to say, 'Mind, Fan, watch yourself,' or 'Stand over there, out of the way, that's a good girl.' If she did not look sharp, he was likely to walk off without her, and once or twice he did disappear, leaving her feeling unwanted, conspicuous, left out.

Finally there came the dreadful day when they were in the box of the promising four-year-old, Nimrod, and James and Salton, the rough-rider, and Nimrod's groom were anxiously examining a slight cut on his hock.

'It doesn't look too serious,' James said, 'but we can't afford to take any chances. I'm not sure if this is swelling or not.' He passed his hand down Nimrod's stifle and the horse lifted its foot warningly. 'You'd better bathe it every couple of hours, Harry, and let me know at once if it seems any worse.'

'Yessir,' said the groom.

'And he'd better have plenty of gentle exercise,' James added to Salton, 'to make sure it doesn't get stiff. He'd better be walked about the paddock for ten minutes every hour. See to it yourself.'

'I've got four others to ride, sir,' Salton reminded him. 'Anyone could walk this one round, I haven't got time.'

'I'll do it, Papa,' Fanny said eagerly from behind him, but no-one even seemed to hear.

James frowned. 'Make time,' he said, a little irritably. 'Nimrod's more important than the rest put together.'

'Very good, sir,' Salton said sulkily, and at that tense moment James stepped back from the horse and bumped into Fanny. In staggering to regain his balance, he kicked the water-bucket, which clanged against the wall, and Nimrod, startled, laid back his ears and fly-kicked, catching Harry in the meaty part of the thigh.

The groom stifled a curse and stepped back, hugging his leg, and James rounded on Fanny in a fury. 'If you can't keep out of the way,' he snapped, 'you'll have to go home!'

Fanny paled. 'But I want to help,' she cried.

'You're being nothing but a nuisance at the moment,' James said angrily, and turned his back on her. 'Are you all right, Harry? Hoa, there, boy, stand still! I hope to God that cut hasn't opened up any further —'

Fanny pressed herself into the corner of the box, biting her lip in mortification, while the three men inspected the cut and agreed at length that it was no worse. Then they filed out, James waiting pointedly at the door of the box to see Fanny out, and then walking off with Salton without a word to her.

Fanny was desolated. He had never spoken so sharply to her before, never said that she was a nuisance or suggested that he did not want her with him. She was not to know of the various anxieties which were making him tense and irritable; she only knew that she had angered him, and that he had rebuffed her. Somehow she must mend matters, make him look at her lovingly again, shew him she was useful, that he needed her, that he could not manage without her.

The idea was already in her head. Nimrod needed to be walked round every hour, and Salton had said he was too busy. She, Fanny, had offered to do it, but Papa had not heard her. She would take on the task, walk Nimrod so carefully and regularly that his leg would be healed up in no time, and then everyone would be grateful to her.

She went back to his box and looked at him over the half-door. Nimrod turned his head to look at her, and laid back his ears unwelcomingly. He was a big horse, nearly sixteen hands, looking massive and strong in comparison with Honey's narrow body and slender legs. But Fanny had no fears. To control him from the ground with only a headcollar might present problems, she thought, but she had been in the saddle since before she could walk, and she firmly believed there was no horse she couldn't ride.

His bridle and training-saddle were on the rack inside his box. Fanny looked around, but there was no-one nearby, so she unbolted the door and slipped inside the box, pulling the door to behind her so that she could simply push it open when she had Nimrod tacked-up and ready. He watched her with a sidelong eye, and as she approached him, he swung his hindquarters round towards her and laid his ears back. He had had enough attention for one day, and wanted to be left alone with his hay-rack. Fanny spoke to him and tried to come round the other way, but he moved over, his eye shewing white, and lifted a foot suggestively.

She paused for a moment in thought, and then put her hand into her pocket slit and fumbled for a titbit. Nimrod's

121

ears came forward, and he watched her calculatingly. She drew out a piece of carrot and held it out on her hand, and took a careful step towards him. He did not move, and foot by foot she approached him while he watched her over his shoulder. Then at the very last moment, when she was about to take the last step and catch hold of his headcollar, he laid his ears back, whirled around, and dashed past her, knocking her aside. She stumbled back against the wall, and stared in horror as the big horse butted the half-door with his nose, and feeling it give, shouldered it open and clattered out into the rotunda.

Instinct started her after him, and even as she ran for the door, she heard the sounds from outside, the clatter and skid of Nimrod's shoes on the bricks, the sound of a bucket being dropped, the shout of 'Loose horse!', the confusion of voices giving each other directions. She reached the door in time to see Nimrod veer away from a groom's outstretched hand and canter away, head up, nostrils wide, enjoying his moment of freedom. He skirted the central fountain-bowl, heading for the doorway to the outside, but, thank God, there was a groom there with a pitchfork, who waved it threateningly, making the horse breenge and slip a little on the bricks. More people and more shouts, and Nimrod, wildly excited now, was circling the fountain for the third time, when James appeared at last.

'What the devil — ! Silence! Everybody stand still! Still, I said!'

At his ringing command, all movement ceased, and Nimrod, finding no-one was pursuing him, slowed from a canter to a trot, looking about him for someone to continue the game. Round he went a fourth time, and embarked on a fifth, and then grew bored with the solitary occupation, and slithered to a halt, snorting, turning his head this way and that.

'Everybody stand still,' James said again, and pulling out an apple from his pocket, he held it out visibly in his hand, and walked steadily towards the horse. Nimrod snorted and stamped his forefoot, but his nostrils fluttered as he caught the scent of the apple, and his ears came abruptly forward as James covered the last few feet and stood right beside him.

Fanny's nails dug into her palm with tension, expecting every

122

moment that the horse would leap away again, wondering why her father did not make sure of his capture, grab the headcollar at once. But James, apparently confident, took time to bite the apple in half, while Nimrod, eager for the treat, nudged at him with his muzzle, and finally made a little whickering noise of impatience. James slid the first half of the apple under the enquiring lips, and only as he gave Nimrod the second half, did he finally, gently, take hold of the headcollar.

As if released from a spell by the gesture, everyone began moving and speaking at once; except for Fanny who stood her ground miserably at the open door of Nimrod's box as her father led the horse back towards her. She stepped aside as James led the horse in, and when he came out again, carefully bolting the door, she kept her gaze on the ground, unable to meet his eyes, feeling her face hot with shame.

His feet came into her view. 'What the *devil* did you think you were doing?' he asked quietly, but his voice was quivering with anger. Fanny could not speak. 'Are you quite mad, Fanny? Do you know what it would mean if he'd slipped and come down? He might have broken his knees, or his leg, and that would have been the end of him. Don't you know we're running him in the Gold Cup? Were you deliberately trying to ruin his chances?'

Tears began to course down Fanny's cheeks, but she lifted her head at last, driven to speak in her own defence. 'I was trying to help!' she cried. 'You said you wanted him walked round, and S-Salton was too busy —'

James was not listening. 'Help! You call it helping to let a valuable horse loose out of its box two days before the most important race of the year? Ned was right — this is no place for children! I'm packing you off home this minute. You've been in the way all day, but I never thought —'

'But Papa, *please* listen —'

'Be quiet, Fanny. I won't have any arguments. You're going straight home, where you belong. I suppose I'll have to send someone with you, and that will be another pair of hands lost to me! Here, you, Alton, put Missy to in the gig, and drive Miss Fanny back to Morland Place. See she's handed over to her ladyship or the governess, and then come back as quickly as you can. There's enough for everyone to

123

do, without having you driving about the country all day. Jump to it, man!'

Brought home in disgrace by a very embarrassed and reluctant groom, Fanny wished as she had never wished before that the earth would open and swallow her, that a thunderbolt would descend and blast Morland Place and everyone in it to smithereens, or that she could go instantly into a decline so rapid and unmistakable that nothing would lie before her but an affecting death-bed scene, where her tearful father would beg forgiveness for being so unkind to her.

None of these interesting possibilities intervened, however. Alton drove the gig into the yard, and was preparing to wind the reins and escort Fanny into the house, but she was determined to avoid *that* at least. She jumped from the gig as soon as it stopped, and ignoring his shouts, ran into the house and up the stairs as fast as her legs would carry her; and along the passage to her room, where she slammed the door behind her and flung herself across her bed to weep the hot tears of passion and humiliation.

For a while she knew nothing but the soreness of her heart; but as the storm began to abate she realised that she would not be left alone for long. Alton would tell, and soon everyone in the house would know. Uncle Ned would say 'I told you so', and her smug cousin Hippolyta would look shocked and pious because *she* would never do anything bad like that; and worst of all that little beast Sophie would be Papa's favourite, and Fanny would simply die of grief. Any minute now one of the maids would come in and summon her downstairs for a sermon, and she couldn't bear it; she *wouldn't* bear it!

She began to grope for a handkerchief; and sure enough, the door opened behind her.

'Go away!' She cried out hoarsely, her face still buried in the bedclothes. 'I won't come down. You can tell them that! I don't care!'

There was no reply; but quiet footsteps crossed the room, and a large, dry handkerchief was pushed into her fingers, smelling of the lavender-water Miss Rosedale always used. The bed creaked and Fanny felt the mattress tilt under her as her governess sat on the edge of it, and she flung herself over resentfully, turning her face away from the unwelcome intrusion. She still couldn't find her handkerchief, and was forced, reluctantly, to make use of the one she had been given. 'I wish you'd go away,' she said bitterly.

Miss Rosedale drew breath. Now comes the sermon, Fanny thought.

But 'Poor Fanny!' Miss Rosedale said with cheerful sympathy. 'That was bad luck. The groom told me what happened — and when you only meant to help, too! I know how you must feel — it happened to me once.'

The sympathy was harder to bear than a rebuke. 'I don't believe you,' Fanny said rudely, her head still turned away. 'Your father didn't have racehorses.'

'No, it wasn't horses, and it wasn't my father, but it was the same sort of thing,' Miss Rosedale replied in an everyday tone. 'It was my mother that I upset. She had some beautiful hand-painted china which she really loved — her most treasured possession, in fact. My father had bought it for her years before, when they first got married. One day I overheard her saying that it was a pity it had got so dirty, and that the white background was quite grey. I thought I'd wash it for her, as a surprise, so I got a bucket of hot water and soda and stood on a chair in front of the chimney-piece and started lifting the pieces down, putting them into the bucket so carefully, because I didn't want to chip them.'

Fanny was listening now, despite herself, and when Miss Rosedale paused, she only just managed not to prompt her.

Miss Rosedale continued unasked. 'Well, what I didn't know was that the china hadn't been reglazed after painting, so all the delicate birds and flowers and butterflies simply came off in the water. That was why it hadn't been washed before, of course — but that had never occurred to me. And as the last straw, just as I was lifting down the last piece — a particularly fine vase, the jewel of the collection, my mother came in and saw what I was doing, and let out such a shriek that I dropped it, and it shattered on the hearth into a thousand pieces.'

Miss Rosedale's voice was sadly reflective. 'I loved my mother so much. Of course I realised later that she wouldn't have said all those things had she not been upset, but at the time I wanted the floor to open up and swallow me.'

There was a pause, and then the bed bent as the governess

125

stood up. 'I was thinking, Fanny,' she said cheerfully, 'that it's much too nice a day to eat indoors. I think we should excuse ourselves from dinner, and ride out to Bur Field, and see if we can find those Roman footings we were reading about the other day. We can take some bread and meat and have an *al fresco* meal, and come back over Low Moor and through the Whin, and have a good gallop. I've brought up some hot water, so wash your face and put on your habit, and I'll order the horses for half an hour's time.'

The footsteps crossed the room again, and the door clicked softly closed. Fanny rolled over and opened her eyes, and finding herself alone, sat up. The jug on her wash-stand was steaming gently. Her eyes felt prickly, and her nose swollen, and her hair was damp at the temples, and the thought of hot water was tempting. She contemplated the offer which had been made to her. A ride and a picnic meal were always attractive, but especially so was the thought of not having to go in to dinner, not having to speak to anyone, nor endure their pitying looks.

Fanny swung her legs over the side of the bed and got to her feet. Miss Rosedale was making everything easy for her, and Fanny saw it, and resented it. She didn't want to like her; but the fact remained that things already looked less black; and when she examined her heart, she found that, inexplicably, it was less sore than it had been a quarter of an hour ago.

CHAPTER SEVEN

Lucy was still at Morland Place when the news broke in September about the secret expedition. It had been to Copenhagen, where the Danes had a fleet of fifteen of the line and thirty smaller vessels at anchor in a harbour protected by the guns of the fortified city. Sir Arthur Wellesley had landed with the troops he had embarked at Yarmouth, and was joined by the detachment from Rugen under Lord Cathcart. Lord Gambier's fleet of seventeen of the line had closed in from the seaward, and after offering the Danes the chance to surrender, they had opened fire on the city with Congreve rockets from the bomb-vessels, while the army pounded it with hot shells. After two days and three nights, the Danes had surrendered, and the Danish fleet had been confiscated and was being sailed safely to England.

James had brought the news-sheet in from his club, and read the details to Lucy, Edward and Héloïse in the drawing-room.

'It was the most complete success! Our casualties were less than two hundred! Listen to this: "There never was an expedition of such magnitude so quickly got up, so secretly sent off, and which was conducted from the beginning to its termination with greater ability or success".'

'Well, that's true, at all events,' Lucy said. 'No-one had any idea what they were up to beforehand. Try as I might, I couldn't get anyone to break confidence.'

'But surely the Danes are neutral?' Edward said, frowning. 'How can we attack them and seize their ships like that?'

'Oh, the Opposition's up in arms about it, of course,' James said, 'and even Sidmouth's spoken out against it. But from what I gathered at the club, it seems that the Government received intelligence months ago about a secret pact between Boney and the Csar, signed at the same time as Tilsit. Apparently they meant to force the neutrals, like Denmark, to join

Russia and France in a great expedition against us. There was to be a massive Baltic fleet assembled, and Boney was all ready to march into Copenhagen by land and confiscate the Danish ships to use against us. So really, you know, what could we do? It may seem high-handed, but Castlereagh couldn't very well sit back and let Boney have 'em, could he?'

'I suppose if the Government was not blamed for doing it, they would be blamed for not doing it,' Héloïse remarked, 'but it does seem a little hard on the Danes.'

'They were given ample chance to surrender,' James pointed out, 'and Boney would have given them just as bad a time, or worse.'

'Well, so that's where Haworth has been,' Lucy observed. 'Is there any mention of him in the paper, Jamie?'

'Only that he was in command of a detachment of ships. There isn't much detail in this edition. You'll have to wait for tomorrow's paper for that. He's not on the casualty list, at any rate, so you may be easy. Nor Colonel Horatio, either.'

'I wonder if they know about it at Shawes?' Héloïse said. 'Perhaps you should ride over, James, and see, for Roberta told me poor little Marcus was very anxious about his papa. I would go myself, but I am not feeling quite so well.'

James was up in an instant. 'What is it, love? Have you a pain anywhere?'

'No, mon âme, don't worry,' she said, managing a smile. 'I feel rather tired, that's all, and I have a little of the headache.'

'It's no wonder — you have been doing far too much. You should go upstairs and rest,' James said, with a sternness which inadequately masked his anxiety.

She smiled at him. 'Well, I will,' she said reasonably. 'But I think you should go to Shawes all the same.'

'Yes, do, Jamie,' Lucy said briskly. 'I'll see that Héloïse goes upstairs, and you can bring Danby back here to dine with us, and he can tell us what everyone has been saying about it. He's very good for that,' she observed dispassionately. 'He hasn't much of a brain, but he does have an excellent memory.'

James grinned at her. 'You are so cruel to the poor man! Wiske has been dangling after you ever since you were fifteen, looking like a lovesick spaniel. Isn't it about time you put him out of his misery, and married him?'

'Stuff!' Lucy said shortly. 'Don't talk such nonsense, Jamie. Danby would have fourteen fits if I so much as hinted at marriage. He's a confirmed bachelor, and he likes 'dangling after me', as you call it, because it stops him having to make up to other women. You know nothing about men,' she finished with dignity, which made James roar with laughter. 'Oh do stop making that dreadful noise, and go and ride over to Shawes. Come on, Héloïse, let's put you to bed.'

When they reached the great bedchamber, they found Marie, alerted by some mysterious sixth sense that good servants seem to possess, already there, and looking anxious.

'Are you ill, madame?' she cried, hurrying to Héloïse's other side. 'I was afraid of this. I begged and begged her to rest, milady,' she said to Lucy, 'but she would not. She is not strong, you know, though she pretends to be, and she has such spirit that she will never own to feeling unwell.'

'Peace, Marie,' Héloïse said, trying gently to push her away. 'I am not ill, and there is no need for all this fuss.'

'It isn't fuss to ask you to take proper care of yourself, and the little one to be,' Marie said indignantly.

'Well, I am, I shall. Don't annoy me, dear friend. It is nothing but a headache,' Héloïse said. Marie stepped back, and Héloïse began to walk towards the bed, and was betrayed by a stagger which brought both women to her side again.

'Dizzy?' Lucy said briskly. 'Yes, I'm not surprised. Just lie down and close your eyes, and we'll do everything else. Marie, help me lift her legs. That's right. No, Héloïse, don't try to help. Just lie still.'

Héloïse was glad to obey, for Lucy was the very best person to have around if one was feeling not quite well. Calmly and efficiently, and without fussing or talking, she helped Marie to unhook Héloïse's gown, unlaced her stays, removed her shoes and stockings and propped her feet on two cushions.

'See how swollen your ankles are,' Lucy observed, massaging them with a firm hand.

'Oh, that is heaven!' Héloïse murmured, closing her eyes. 'You are a good nurse, dear Lucy. You have such kind hands.'

'I've never heard them called that before,' Lucy said with a small smile. 'Now, Marie, never mind those smelling salts: your mistress isn't having a fit of the vapours. Run and fetch some wine for her — good wine. Ask Ottershaw for a pint of the best claret. That will do her more good than all the vinaigrettes in the world. And find my maid and send her to me.'

Marie looked doubtful, but receiving a confirmatory nod from her mistress, she went away to do as she was bid. When they were alone again, Lucy remarked, 'These elderly virgins are all alike — and the more so when they're servants. They grow hysterical at the slightest sign of illness, especially anything to do with pregnancy. I'm lucky with Docwra, really — she may be unmarried, but she came from a large family, and she had to nurse her mother through childbed a good few times. How are you feeling now?'

'Better,' Héloïse said. 'The dizziness has gone, and the headache isn't so bad as it was.'

'Well, just lie still and keep your feet up for a while, and you'll be right as a trivet,' Lucy said briskly. 'I wanted to talk to you privately, anyway. It's about Thomas.'

Héloïse opened her eyes in dismay. This was the moment she had been dreading; but she controlled her features, and tried not to betray her feelings. 'Yes, Cousin Lucy? What of Thomas?'

Lucy continued absently to massage Héloïse's ankles. 'I was thinking that perhaps it's time I took him back to live with me. I want him to grow up to be a gentleman, and to be proud of his father's name. He'll have a small fortune to inherit, and there's no reason why he shouldn't enter one of the professions later on, if he wants to.

'Are you displeased with the way I have looked after him?' Héloïse asked hesitantly.

Lucy looked at her with raised eyebrows. 'Good God, no! No-one could have given him better care than you, Cousin. Don't think I'm not grateful. What I mean is that it's time I established him properly, and gave him his identity, instead of leaving him here like a kind of waif with no name, to scramble into life anyhow. He must have an education fitting to his station, and meet and mix with the right people. That's especially important, given the circumstances of his birth.'

Héloïse nodded, unable to speak.

'And besides, it would be nice for Roland to have another boy to play with. They could do their lessons together, until Thomas is old enough to go to school. Roberta says it helps

130

Bobbie to do his lessons with Marcus, so perhaps Thomas can help Roland. After all,' she said as a thought struck her, 'they are —' She broke off just in time. She had kept the secret so determinedly that it hardly ever even occurred to her that Thomas and Roland were brothers; it was the surprise of remembering it that had almost betrayed her. 'They are almost the same age,' she finished lamely. 'So I think when I go back this time, I'll take him with me. What do you think?'

'I shall miss him very much,' Héloïse said, but she seemed distracted, as though her mind was no longer on the subject of the child. 'Sophie will too. But it's right that he should go to you.'

'Well, that's what I thought. I should have taken him before,' Lucy said, 'but I haven't felt able to — Héloïse, what's wrong?'

Héloïse's eyes were blank and fixed, and her face was drawn. Her hand groped out blindly for Lucy's and gripped it like a bird's talon. 'Lucy,' she whispered , and stopped.

'What is it? For God's sake, Héloïse, tell me!'

'Lucy,' she began again, and her voice sunk almost to soundlessness, 'I think I'm bleeding.'

Edward went out at the same time as James, and having seen his brother off to Shawes on Nez Carré, decided to walk up to the coppice paddock to check on a couple of in-foal mares which had been isolated because they had ben losing condition. He mixed a bucket of feed and collected a hemp halter, and started off with Tiger at his heels; but he had only just crossed the moat when he saw Mathilde come out of the archway into the rose garden in the company of John Skelwith.

Edward stopped and frowned. He didn't like the Skelwith business to begin with, but this looked rather too much like a secret assignation, not the sort of thing he would have expected from a strictly-brought-up girl like Mathilde. As he watched they paused and exchanged a few words, and then Skelwith bowed over Mathilde's hand (*conceited dog!*), raised it to his lips (*impudent puppy!*), and then walked away in the direction of Holgate.

Mathilde watched him go for a moment, and then turned towards the house, carrying a flat basket of roses on one arm, and walking with a light step which somehow only made

Edward feel more irritable. She saw him, and gave a light-hearted little wave, and Edward stood his ground and waited for her. Tiger bounded over to her, and she stooped to caress him, and then walked on, while the brindled hound ran back and forth across the diminishing distance between them, lashing his tail with pleasure.

By the time she reached Edward, Mathilde had noticed the expression on his face, and her smile faltered. 'Is something the matter?' she asked.

'I hope not,' Edward said sternly. 'I have just seen you come out of the rose garden with John Skelwith. Why wasn't he announced at the house? And how did you know he was here, to come and meet him in this — informal way?'

Mathilde coloured. 'Why, Cousin Edward, do you think I have done something wrong?'

'I should be very loath to think that. I know you have been brought up as a young lady should, but I feel it is my duty as someone considerably older than you to point out that it does have a very peculiar appearance. To be blunt, it looked like a secret assignation.'

Still blushing, but with vexation rather than shame, Mathilde said, 'I did not make an assignation with Mr Skelwith. He was coming up to the house to deliver a message to me from Patience Keating, and he arrived just as I was going into the rose garden to pick some roses for Madame's bedroom. So naturally he came with me while I cut the roses and gave him the reply to take back to Patience. We were there only for as long as it took me to cut these,' she finished, gesturing with her basket, and raising her pink face to meet his eye with a clear look.

Edward felt ashamed, annoyed, prickly, out-of-sorts. 'I'm sorry if I have offended you,' he said gruffly, 'but please believe I spoke only for your own good. That young man is too often here, and his attentions to you are too particular for you to be in any way careless about what liberties you allow him.'

'Liberties?' Mathilde was clearly angry now.

'I saw him kiss your hand,' Edward said.

'You consider that a liberty? Forgive me, Cousin Edward, but I thought it was customary in polite society,' she said in a resentful voice.

132

Edward was at a loss what to say next. Why had he been angry? He looked at the sky and the ground; Tiger nudged him, hoping to be off, and then seeing it was going to be a long conversation, sighed heavily and lay down at his feet.

Finally Edward cleared his throat, and said, 'I'm sorry. I spoke clumsily. But I couldn't help wondering how things stand between you and Skelwith. You see, he has made it obvious that he is — well, fond of you, and if you feel the same way about him —' He coughed nervously. 'I only have your good at heart, you know. There are reasons why a marriage between you and him would be — inadvisable.'

'What reasons?' she asked with dangerous quietness.

Edward spread his hands. 'I'm not at liberty to say. Oh, I know how that must sound, Mathilde, and I'm sorry, but it's a matter of a confidence which I'm not able to break. All I can say is that a connection between you and John Skelwith would be unwelcome in certain circles.'

Mathilde looked down and bit her lip, and then said, 'Cousin Edward, may I talk to you?'

'Of course,' he said in surprise.

'No, I mean — can I speak to you in confidence? There is something I need advice on, and I don't know who else to turn to.'

All Edward's irritability disappeared in an instant. 'Of course, my dear,' he said. 'I should be glad to be able to help you, in any way I can. Would you like to walk with me up to the paddock?'

He switched the bucket to the other hand and offered her his arm, and she put down the basket of roses and took it gladly. They began to walk, with Tiger frisking ahead of them, delighted to be on the move again.

'Well then, what did you want to ask?'

'It's about John Skelwith,' Mathilde said, frowning a little. 'You see, although he is perfectly proper in his manner towards me, and though nothing has been said, I can't help knowing that he is very fond of me, and I have reason to believe that he does mean to make me an offer.'

'I see,' Edward said.

Mathilde glanced at him anxiously. 'He hasn't spoken yet, but I think he will soon, and I don't know what to say if he does. Especially if there is some reason I don't know about why I should refuse him.'

Edward shook his head. 'I was wrong to mention it. It is no impediment, I assure you. If you love this young man, you may accept his offer without reference to what I have said. I spoke only because — because I thought you were not in love with him, and I wanted to put you on your guard.'

'But I'm not in love with him,' Mathilde said. 'That's the problem. If I were, things would be easy. Oh, I like him very much, and he is very kind and pleasant, and everything he should be, but — that's all.'

Edward smiled. 'Then, my dear Mathilde, what is your problem?'

'Well, sir, Madame has spent a lot of time and money on me so that I may make a good match, and be settled for life; and John — Mr Skelwith is certainly a good match. He is very well-to-do, with his father's business, which is a very good one; he is educated and refined, and in every way the kind of suitor a girl like me ought to be proud of. I *am* proud that he loves me; and if he makes me an offer, I feel that I ought to accept it. It is likely to be the best I shall ever have; it may be the only one I ever have; and it would be the greatest ingratitude to Madame to refuse him. Don't you think so?'

Edward cleared his throat. 'It might appear that way,' he said cautiously.

'I'm sure everyone would say so,' Mathilde said unhappily. 'And I do like him, and I'm sure he would make a good husband, because he is so kind to his mother; but I'm not in love with him.' She glanced at Edward anxiously. 'I suppose that sounds a very missish thing to say, doesn't it? I oughtn't to be so nice, ought I, about something that doesn't matter?'

She stopped, looking to Edward for his reply, and he could not immediately give her one. On the one hand, she was perfectly right that it was her duty to marry as well as she could, where there was no positive dislike in the case; but on the other hand, he, Edward, had always with him the memory of his own mother and father, which made it hard for him to dismiss love as unimportant.

The children of lovers, he thought, have a difficult row to hoe. Always before them lies an example which is hard to match and impossible to better. Was that why they had all been so reluctant to marry? He was still single, a greying

134

bachelor wed to his horses and his duty; William had married the sea, and wed only late in life, to an utterly unsuitable woman; James's and Lucy's matrimonial problems were now legendary; Harry was a bachelor and a sailor, and looking like to remain both. They had all grown up in the shadow of their parents' love for each other, excluded from that glowing radiance which surrounded each of them for the other. The children of lovers, he thought, are waifs and orphans; and yet they can't help always hoping to enter that shining land.

'What should I do, Cousin Edward?' Mathilde prompted him.

He pressed her hand against his ribs. 'You are still very young, Mathilde, and there's no reason to suppose there won't be other offers. I wouldn't recommend you to accept the first offer you ever receive, unless you're quite sure about it.'

She looked at him with relief and gratitude. 'Then you don't think I'm being missish?'

'Not at all. Love is as important as you think it is. For some people, it doesn't seem to matter; but if it matters to you, then you ignore it at your peril,' he told her from the heart.

'Oh, thank you, Cousin Edward! You've taken such a weight off my mind,' Mathilde said.

They had reached the paddock. Mathilde slipped her hand out from under his arm and went to stand at the rails, looking at the horses. Tiger found an interesting patch of grass and got down to roll in it, twitching his hind-quarters back and forth ridiculously, rubbing his muzzle with his forepaws and sneezing like a cat. Edward rapped the bucket with his knuckles to attract the mares' attention, and they lifted their heads from grazing, and began to drift casually towards him, swishing through the tawny, sun-dried grass, their eyes bright and soft, their flanks rounded with fecundity. The heat of the day lay over everything like a gentling hand.

'The thing is,' Mathilde went on, her eyes still on the horses, 'that quite apart from not being in love with John, I don't really want to get married at all — not yet, I mean. I love the balls and the parties and the picnics: it's all such fun. And I love it so much here at Morland Place, just as if it were my real home.'

'It is your home,' Edward said, stirring the feed in the

bucket. The lead mare heard the dry rustle of the silky oats through his fingers, and quickened her pace.

'Oh, yes, I know, but I mean as if it had always been my home. I feel as if I belonged here; and I should like so much just to go on as I am.'

'But eventually,' Edward said cautiously, 'eventually you will want to marry?'

'I suppose so,' Mathilde sighed. 'If only there were a way to be married and not to have to leave Morland Place! But perhaps I could learn to be useful to you and Mr James with the horses, and then I could earn my keep, and not have to get married at all?'

Edward smiled. 'Do you know, you sounded just like my sister Lucy then! But if you really want to be useful, you can hold this mare for me while I examine her.'

'Of course, gladly,' Mathilde said, preparing to climb the rail, ready to sacrifice both gown and sandals in a good cause.

'No need for that: you can hold her through the rails. I shouldn't like you to get dirty.' He climbed into the paddock and caught the first mare by the forelock and slipped on the halter, and passing the rope's end to Mathilde, he added, 'You are doing just as you ought, my dear. Enjoy the dancing and the parties. Enjoy being young. It passes all too soon.'

When James returned from Shawes, the crisis had passed, but the sensation of it was still in the house. Kithra came running to him as soon as he arrived, and pressed his muzzle anxiously into his palm. Fanny reached him next, big-eyed with the news that Madame had been taken ill and the physician had been sent for. James was too shocked at the news to hear the glee in her voice, and since he left her instantly to run up the stairs as fast as he could, she had no opportunity further to expose herself.

In the great bedchamber all was peaceful, and Lucy met him as he burst in at the door to clap a hand over his mouth and hiss, 'Don't wake her! She's sleeping, and everything's all right now, but she mustn't be disturbed or upset, do you understand?'

James gripped her wrist and firmly removed her hand from his mouth. In the background, Docwra was folding fresh linen strips, while Marie sat by the bedside gently fanning Héloïse.

She was lying with her feet propped up and her eyes closed. She looked pale, and there were shadows under her eyes.

'Tell me what happened. Did the physician come? What did he say?'

'He came and went away again,' Lucy said. 'He was no use to anyone. All he wanted to do was to bleed her — as if she hadn't already lost enough! — and burn pastilles in the room to choke her, the old imbecile! I sent him packing. It's all right, Jamie, don't look so blue. She's all right now, but she'll have to be more careful from now on.'

'For God's sake, Lucy, *tell me what happened*!'

'She had a haemorrhage, not long after you'd left.'

'A haem — bleeding? Oh God, you mean — the child?'

'Hush! Don't make a noise. She hasn't lost the child,' Lucy said, 'and there's a chance she'll carry it to term, if she's careful.'

James buried his face in his hands and groaned. 'If anything happens to her, I'll never forgive myself!'

Lucy looked at him with understanding, though without sympathy. 'There's no need for you to make a fuss. She isn't going to die. She's very strong, you know, for all that she looks so small and thin. She may lose this baby, but you can always have another, can't you? For goodness sake, Jamie, pull yourself together, and think of her for a change. She mustn't be upset. It's up to you to keep her calm and happy, and make sure she rests properly, and doesn't exert herself.'

'James?' came Héloïse's voice. James gave Lucy a meaningful look and went past her to the bed, flung himself down beside it, and took Héloïse's hand in a crushing grip.

'Oh my love, I'm sorry I wasn't here.'

'There was nothing you could have done,' she said. 'I'm all right now, only sleepy. But I didn't want to go to sleep until you came back. I knew you'd fret if I didn't tell you myself that I was all right.'

'Have they given you a draught?'

'No; only rather a lot of wine. I think I am a little drunk, James,' she smiled. Her eyelids were drooping. 'Lucy says we haven't lost the baby.'

'No, darling, it's all right.'

'I'm so glad. I didn't want to let you down,' she murmured drowsily.

'You could never do that, Marmoset. Don't worry about anything. Just sleep.'

'So glad Lucy was here. Thank her, James.'

'Yes, I will.'

James waited until her breathing was deep and regular, and then got up quietly and went back to where Lucy was standing near the door watching them. She met his eyes, and he gave a crooked smile. 'Thank you, Lucy. I'm glad you were here, too. I'm very grateful to you.'

'Don't be silly. All I did was apply common sense, and keep that fool of a doctor from her,' Lucy said briskly. 'But, look here, Jamie, if anything like this happens again, you've got to know what to do. I'll write you some notes.'

'Me?'

'Well, notes for Marie, if you like — but someone will have to supervise her or she'll just cluck and run about like a hen.'

'All right, I'll see to it. Anything else?'

'I hope not, not if Héloïse uses some common sense. But I think perhaps I had better try to be on hand when her time comes, just in case.'

'Would you really do that? I know she'd feel much happier about it.'

'That's all right. I've brought enough foals into the world to know what's what; and I've read all of Smellie's works, which is more than can be said for that fool of a doctor!'

Thomas didn't seem to understand that he was going away with the other children for good. Héloïse, still confined to bed, explained it to him as clearly as she could and he nodded solemnly and seemed to accept it; and he watched Jenny pack his box without comment; but when the Aylesbury children assembled in the day-nursery to put on their coats and go down to the waiting carriage, Thomas stood with Sophie and watched as if it were nothing to do with him.

'Come, Thomas, put on your coat now,' Jenny said, and he looked bewildered, though he obeyed from old habit. But when Miss Trotton took his hand and began to lead him away, he suddenly grew frightened and pulled back, looking towards Sophie questioningly. Miss Rosedale reached for Sophie's hand, and as Thomas was led away and she stayed where she was, he suddenly understood that they were parting, and began to cry. He was too well-behaved to struggle or resist, but he looked back over his shoulder all the way, his mouth shapeless with grief.

When he was gone, Sophie, who had tried to contain herself for his sake, broke at last, and flung herself against Miss Rosedale's comfortable brown cambric front and sobbed. Her life had suddenly been turned upside down. Her mother stayed in bed, and though everyone kept saying she was all right, she looked pale and tired and worried, and Sophie knew all was not as it should be; and now Thomas had been taken away from her, and who would button his buttons and tell him bedtime stories? Who would know that he liked all the fat cut off his mutton, or that he had to have his left shoe put on before his right? Who would make it all right for him when he was afraid of the dark, and sing him the French song about the rabbits and the fox to make him laugh?

'There, my poor little dear,' Miss Rosedale said, stroking Sophie's dark head, while her tears soaked through to Miss Rosedale's stomach. 'I know it's hard, but things usually happen for the best. Remember, he will have every advantage where he's going, and grow up to be a gentleman.'

'But he won't have me,' Sophie said unanswerably. 'And I shan't have him.'

Fanny watched the scene with mixed feelings. Her hated rival had been wounded, and that was good; and Madame was ill in bed, and she had heard the servants whispering that she would probably lose the baby, which was better. Perhaps Madame might even die, which would be best of all. But these things, oddly enough, didn't make her feel as happy as she expected. She was conscious that the nursery was very quiet without the Aylesbury children, and that no-one would cry for her if she were taken away, as Sophie was crying for Thomas.

She looked at Miss Rosedale petting Sophie's head, and frowned. Miss Rosedale was *her* governess: she ought to be paying attention to *her*. Well, if Miss Rosedale was so busy caring for Sophie that she had no time for Fanny, Fanny would just go off on her own, as she had used to in the old days. She'd go out riding, and see what adventure came her way. With a final glare at Miss Rosedale's back, she slipped out of the room.

When Miss Rosedale had comforted Sophie, dried her face and brushed her hair, she told her to go out into the fresh air for a little while before dinner. 'Go and ask for some bread to feed the swans, dear,' she advised her. 'There's something very soothing about feeding animals.'

Sophie wandered downstairs and out into the courtyard, feeling light-headed as one does after crying. She felt the sun hot on her head, and the cobbles burning through the thin soles of her sandals, while inside her everything felt loose and weak and lethargic. She didn't want to feed the swans. She wanted her mother, and she wanted Thomas. She didn't know what to do with herself.

It was the quiet time of the day when the servants had their dinner, and the yard was deserted. Sophie stood staring at her own short shadow under her feet, until a movement in the corner of the yard made her turn her head, to see Monsieur Barnard coming out of the kitchen door. He stopped when he saw her, and Sophie saw that his face was drawn with tragedy, and that his eyes were red. It occurred to her that, in some way she didn't understand, his grown-up sorrow was harder to bear than her child-grief. For a long moment they regarded each other, and then Sophie ran to him and put her arms round him, glad to have someone to comfort.

He hugged her hard, and she pressed her face into his apron, smelling the clean-laundry smell of starch, and a faint, delicious aroma of fried onions which always seemed to hang about him. Finally he released her, gave her a watery smile, and reaching into the long pocket of his apron, drew out a twist of paper which he held out to her.

'Treacle toffee. I made it for him, for the journey, but they left before I could give it to him,' he said in French.

Sophie took it and undid the paper, selected a lump and put it in her mouth, and offered some to Barnard. He took a piece, and then thrust the paper back at her, nodding for her to keep it. They sucked in silence for a while.

'Why did they have to take him away?' Sophie asked at length.

Barnard shook his head, as though the ways of the world were too complex for him to understand. 'You'll miss him, too,' he observed. Sophie's eyes filled inexorably with tears. 'Do you like treacle toffee?' She nodded. 'It's a Yorkshire recipe.' He sighed. 'I've been here so long, I can hardly remember France. Les Landes! — I cooked for a Duc there. I used to do a dish — *poulet aux gousses d'ail* — with tarragon — But you can't grow tarragon here. It's too cold.'

Sophie looked up at him, understanding what was unspoken. 'I've never been to France,' she said.

Though most of his life had been spent isolated in kitchens amid mountains of food not for his own consumption, he recognised love when it was offered. His rare smile lit his face, and he returned it, with interest, in his own coin. 'Do you like honeycomb?' he said. 'I'll make you some honeycomb tomorrow.'

Fanny would have liked to take Honey out, but that would have involved co-operation from one of the grooms, for she could not abstract Honey's tack without being noticed, so she turned instead to her old friend Tempest. He was enjoying a semi-retirement in the orchard, in the company of the donkey who turned the water-wheel for the American Garden, but he came at once when Fanny called him, glad of the company, and eager to go out. Fanny fashioned a halter for him out of a piece of rope she had taken from the laundry-room, led him out of the orchard gate, and scrambled on to him bareback. They had known each other so long, that she could almost guide him with her thoughts alone.

Riding towards Shawes or Twelvetrees was likely to bring her to someone's attention, so she turned Tempest instead towards Hob Moor. If she rode as far as Chaloner's Whin, there was an outlying cottage there where the weaver would be bound to give her something to eat. She knew all the houses out that way. There was Marsh Farm; and Eastfield Farm – although she was not very well liked at Eastfield since she let the pig out into the vegetable garden; but that was long ago, before Miss Rosedale came, and they'd probably have forgotten about it by now; and the Quaker's cottage at Dringfield; and best of all, at the edge of Acomb Wood, there was the gamekeeper's cottage. Black Tom had all sorts of interesting things to drink, and he had promised once, long ago, to teach her how to cure a skin. He had a gamekeeper's gibbet in his garden, and if there were enough moleskins, he might shew her how to make a pair of gloves. She bet even

Miss Rosedale didn't know how to make a pair of gloves out of moleskins.

On the whole, she thought she had better go straight there. She cantered Tempest across Hob Moor, and took the Acombmoor track which eventually came out on the road to Askham Bryan. She skirted Acombmoor Cottage, and beyond it the thick, dark woods came right up to the track. This was supposed to be a bad place — footpads and poachers and bad men were said to hang about here — but Fanny had no fear. She was Miss Morland of Morland Place, and the world belonged to her. Besides, if anyone came near her she would gallop away on Tempest too fast for them to catch her.

Nevertheless, it did give her a start when someone came out of the woods onto the track in front of her; just for a moment, until she saw that whoever it was, it was a gentleman, not a ruffian. He was driving a dog-cart, and the horse that drew it might not be, to Fanny's critical eye, up to Morland standards, but it was a road-horse, not a farm-horse. The gentleman himself was dressed in a double-breasted, square-cut blue coat, tight Hussar boots, and a *demi-bateau* hat, under whose upturned sides could be seen the glossy locks of his fashionable Brutus crop.

Reassured, Fanny now rode on. She saw the gentleman looking at her, reining-in his horse, putting his hand politely to his hat, and recognised the man she had spoken to at Mathilde's ball; and she suddenly became aware of how she must look, and wished she had been riding Honey, and properly clad in riding-habit. Fanny's vanities were many and various, but this was a new one. The man, though driving what appeared to be a job horse in an undistinguished vehicle, and though undoubtedly less thrilling out of his red coat, was still very handsome, and the fashionableness of his attire impressed Fanny.

For his part, Hawker had been equally taken aback to find anyone on the path when he emerged from the wood; seeing that it was a child, had determined to cuff it for its impudence in scaring him; and then at the last moment recognised the little hoyden of the staircase. What was her name? Heiress of Morland Place, she had claimed to be, and his subsequent enquiries had confirmed her story: everything had been left in trust for her by the old lady, the last owner. Miss Morland, he supposed she must be. Well, there was no harm in exercising a little of his charm, just on the off-chance that it might one day be useful.

Then another thought occurred to him. What the devil was the child doing riding about the countryside unattended, and particularly in such a place as this? It might do him more immediate good if he were to escort her back home, and claim the credit for having saved her from who-knew-what danger. There might even be a little material gratitude in it for him, and God knew he could do with that. He touched his hat, and fixed an ingratiating smirk on his face.

'Miss Morland!' It had to be Miss Morland, didn't it? Yes, the Morlands of Morland Place, now he remembered, were spoken of as an ancient family. 'Well met indeed! I trust you remember me, ma'am?' In his experience, children of that age were flattered by being spoken to as if they were adults. 'Lieutenant Hawker, at your service. I had the pleasure of making your acquaintance at the ball.'

Fanny checked Tempest, and looked at him doubtfully. 'Yes, I remember you. You had a flask.'

He gave a rueful smile. 'Is that the only thing I am remembered for? Too cruel, Miss Morland! Did I leave so little impression on you?'

Fanny felt puzzled, but vaguely excited. She had never been flirted with before, and though she recognised it instinctively for what it was, and knew she ought to like it, she couldn't yet see why she should. 'What else should I remember?' she said, and then feeling that some kinder return was expected of her, she added, 'You had a red coat on then.'

'The clothes make the man, so the saying goes,' Hawker said with a theatrical sigh. 'Well, that seems to have been true in my case. But Miss Morland, what are you doing in this dangerous place all alone? Is no-one with you? This is not right, ma'am.'

Fanny frowned. 'It's all right. Everyone knows me. I was going to Black Tom's cottage.' Hawker flinched, but Fanny didn't notice it. 'I'm going to make him teach me how to make moleskin gloves.'

Hawker gathered himself together. 'Why, there's a coincidence,' he said with a light laugh. 'I have just come from there myself. But you will waste your labour, ma'am, for he was going out as I left to — to look round his traps. He won't be back for hours.'

'What did you go there for?' Fanny asked bluntly. She stared at the dog-cart, noticing that the flap to the underseat compartment was not properly fastened, and that there was something inside. Black Tom had a terrier bitch that was a famous ratter. 'Did he give you a puppy? Is it in there?'

'No — no, not a puppy,' Hawker said, glancing down nervously. He kicked the flap closed with his heel, and cursed inwardly at the faint musical clink which followed. 'No, I was commissioned by my mess-mates to get some pheasants for our dinner. Black Tom has the best-hung birds in the country.'

It was the first thing he could think of, and a pretty frail story, but Fanny, fortunately, was not interested enough to pick holes in it. Hawker hastened to distract her attention, and to press on with the rest of his plan. 'I do think, though, ma'am, that you ought not to ride alone, even if you are well-known. In fact, that in itself could be a danger. Suppose you were kidnapped and held to ransome? Miss Morland of Morland Place would fetch a handsome price, I imagine.'

Fanny considered this intriguing possibility. 'They'd have to catch me first,' she objected. 'And Tempest is very fast.'

'They might leap out from the trees and overpower you,' he said, and then felt it was a ridiculous conversation. He hurried on, 'Won't you let me escort you home? Allow me to offer you a seat in this humble conveyance. We can tie your pony to the back of the cart.'

Fanny thought of the thrill of driving alongside this handsome, fashionable man, and weighed it against the disadvantage of being returned to the fold of respectability. She was still only twelve, and fashion lost.

'No thank you,' she said, and added on an inspiration, 'you might be a kidnapper yourself,' and was away down the path before Hawker could protest.

CHAPTER EIGHT

Thomas, now invested with the full dignity of the name of Thomas Rivers Weston and an official, if dead, father, was installed in the Aylesbury nursery along with his unacknowledged full-brother Roland, and his half-sisters and his cousin. He had acquired at a blow a large family, but for the moment was unable to appreciate it, longing only for the family he had lost, his 'Maman' and his Sophie and the familiar servants with whom he had spent all his short life so far.

Lucy was concerned with more practical matters. 'It's time we thought about a tutor for the boys,' she said to Miss Trotton. 'You have enough to do with teaching the girls, and Roland ought to have a proper governor, don't you think?'

'Yes, my lady, indeed. If his lordship were of a more robust character, I would recommend sending him to school; but as it is, I don't think he would benefit much from exposure to Eton. A governor is certainly the best idea, at least for the time being — and that will answer for Thomas, too.'

'Good, I'm glad you agree. That only leaves the problem of finding the right person. I shall make enquiries.'

'Yes, my lady.'

Lucy turned to go, and then asked as an afterthought. 'How is Thomas settling in?'

Trotton thought of the endless sobbing at night, the languor during the day, the depressed appetite at meals; but what use to tell her ladyship of these things! She would not reverse her decision and send Thomas home. Indeed, since this must now be his home, the sooner he got used to it, the better. His homesickness was simply something he had to come to terms with.

'I think he'll be happier now his pony has arrived, my lady. He's very fond of it.'

'Yes, it's a nice little beast. My brother chose well,' Lucy said, pleased with the answer. She had so little experience in

145

giving and receiving love that she hardly knew how to begin with Thomas; Miss Trotton's words had given her an idea. 'I think I'll take him out on his pony this afternoon and see how well he rides. I suppose I'd better take Roland too. Parslow can come along and look after him. If Thomas has a reasonably good seat, I might start teaching him to jump, and then he can come out hunting with me this winter. Oh, only for an hour or so at first,' she added, seeing Trotton's face. 'Don't worry. After all, I went out for the first time when I was about his age, and I've lived to tell the tale.'

At least she would be paying attention to him, Trotton thought, as aware as anyone in the household could be of how little attention she had ever paid to her other children. 'Yes, my lady,' she said.

In October the whole household moved back to Town, and Thomas, who was just beginning to get used to Wolvercote, was uprooted again. Since not only Miss Trotton, but Parslow too, advised Lucy that the child would be very unhappy if separated from his pony, Cobnut was brought up to Town, along with Roland's pony Misty, and Lucy's mounts. The riding expeditions, which had so far proved successful, could therefore continue, though the park through which they now rode was a public one, and they were now under continuous public scrutiny.

Lucy chose to take them out in the morning, before the Park got crowded, and thus discovered a whole separate world of children and their attendants, which had always existed alongside the real, grown-up world, but which had never impinged on her notice before. She had always before used the Park very early when it was empty, for serious exercise, or at the fashionable hour, to be seen. In between, she now discovered, was a time when the nursery-maids and governesses and grooms brought the little misses and masters and lordships for their sedate exercise, some in perambulators, some walking, and a few on horseback.

As in the world of grown-ups, there was a hierarchy of children, and tremendous rivalry between their attendants, who were fiercely proud of their charges. Lucy was amused to note that Roland was highly placed in public regard, not only because he was already an Earl, and heir to a large and ancient estate, but because he exercised on horseback, and because Misty was such a fine animal. Thomas, however, was also much admired. He was a handsome little boy, and his father's having been a Hero of Trafalgar went down very well in certain circles, just as his association with the Earl of Aylesbury did in others.

Lucy was well accustomed to being talked about, less so to being copied. After a few days, the *ton* decided to approve of her eccentricity in accompanying the children to the Park: Society was always wild for new sensations, and it was early in the Season. By the end of a week, other parents began to appear, parading their children in a variety of attitudes and costumes. Some brought them on horseback, others in carriages; some really fashionable people saw an hour of the day they had previously only heard about, and spent more time with their offspring than in the whole of their lives before. Lord Hardcastle met two younger sons he had no means of recognising, since he had not clapped eyes on them since their christening; and Mrs Edgecumbe caused a small but gratifying sensation by appearing with her five-year-old daughter dressed in an exact replica of her riding-habit, and mounted on a pony which was an almost exact miniature of her horse. The charming tableau was rather marred when Philomena fell off, and firmly refused to get back on the 'nasty thing' until bribed with quantities of sweetmeats.

Lucy viewed it all with distant amusement. It was a nuisance to be accosted by people with whom she had only the slightest acquaintance, and who, under the guise of admiring her children, were actually begging, like dogs for sugar, for compliments on their own. But even the determinedly fashionable soon found getting up so early an intolerable drudge, and turned to other, newer and less strenuous fads. Only those who genuinely enjoyed an early ride and the company of their children continued to appear, and peace and order were soon restored to the Park.

One morning Lucy was riding along the tan with Thomas at her side, and Roland and Parslow behind, when she saw Captain Haworth and Africa walking towards her.

'Haworth! You're back! How lovely to see you!' she cried. She swung her leg free and jumped down before Haworth could help her, and shook his hand heartily. 'What are you doing here? Did you come looking for me, or is this a chance meeting?'

'A lucky chance. I was coming to see you, but I didn't know you would be here. I've just walked from the Admiralty.'

'I read about your daring deeds in the *Chronicle*,' Lucy went on. 'You must be very proud of your papa, Africa.'

'Yes, ma'am, I am,' Africa said. With her brown face and black curly crop, she looked like a gypsy's child, except that the bold, frank eyes were heavenly blue.

'And this is Thomas, I take it?' Haworth said.

'Yes, I brought him back with me in September. He's quite settled in now, haven't you, Thomas?'

Thomas could only whisper, 'Yes, ma'am,' for his eyes were rivetted on Africa, who reminded him painfully of his Sophie, whom he missed so dreadfully. She was the same age and much the same colouring, though bigger and stronger than Sophie; but the resemblance was enough to make him long to talk to her.

'He's the image of his father already,' Haworth was saying. 'Africa, my love, you remember Captain Weston, don't you? Well, this is his son, Thomas. And here's your cousin Roland, of course. Parslow, how do you do?'

'But Haworth,' Lucy interrupted the social amenities, 'you haven't told me yet what you're doing here.'

'I have a few days' leave before I go to join my new command: a squadron under Sir Sidney Smith, in the western approaches,' Haworth said.

'So you're not coming ashore after all. I knew you'd succumb!'

'There's a new crisis brewing,' Haworth said with a shrug. 'Their Lordships were flatteringly insistent that I was needed.'

'Tell me everything,' Lucy said, slipping Mimosa's rein over one elbow and taking Haworth's arm to walk along with him. Africa, seeing that her papa wished for private conversation, fell back between Thomas and Roland.

'You must have heard, of course, about the French army that's been gathering at Bayonne,' Haworth said.

'Yes, under the command of Junot,' Lucy said. 'But what does it mean, Haworth? Bonaparte can't really mean to try to take Spain and Portugal, can he? Roberta's Mr Firth has been saying all along that he will, but after all, it's nothing but a trackless waste! Even if he could conquer it, why should he want to?'

'Because it's the last corner of Europe he doesn't control, and where our merchants have a foothold. He was furious over the business at Copenhagen —'

'You must tell me all about that, by the way,' Lucy interrupted. 'Can you dine with me tomorrow? I must have all the details. People keep asking me, thinking that I of all people must know, and it's intolerable not to.'

Haworth laughed. 'With pleasure, my dear Lucy. Though there's not much to tell. But it put a flea under Boney's shirt and set him scratching! He was furious! The word is that he had one of his famous outbursts of temper and swore that he would not tolerate an English ambassador anywhere in Europe, and that he would declare war on any power who received one.'

'Insolent man!'

'And he claimed that with three hundred thousand Russians at his disposal, he was in a position to make his threat good.'

'Has he really so many?'

'Yes. Strangford, our Ambassador there, is trying to persuade the poor devil to defy Boney, so our fleet is being sent he's caught between the devil and the deep blue sea. No-one can resist Boney on land. If he marches his massive army across Spain and attacks Portugal that way, the Regent has no hope of stopping him. On the other hand, our navy can paralyse Portuguese trade, not only in Portugal itself, but in her colonies.'

'Something of a quandary!' Lucy remarked.

'Yes. Strangford, our Ambassador there, is trying to persuade the poor devil to defy Boney, so our fleet is being sent off to shew its teeth as an added inducement! At least we may persuade him to transfer his court to South America and his fleet to us, so that Boney shan't be able to claim a complete victory. Between us,' he added, 'I think there is also some question of trying to persuade him to lease us Madeira, which would be of great benefit to our merchants.'

'But surely —' Lucy began with a frown.

'The island, simpleton!'

'Oh, I see. But the situation seems rather hopeless, doesn't it? It looks as though Boney has everything his own way.'

'Things are bad,' Haworth admitted. 'Denmark has gone

149

over, and now Russia's closed her ports to us, though she hasn't actually declared war yet. All our markets in northern Europe are lost to us, and you know what that means.'

'I've heard enough from John Anstey about it,' Lucy nodded. 'Warehouses bursting with goods we can't sell, mills closing, merchants going bankrupt. John says he used to sell his coal to Russia and the other Baltic countries; now he has to sell it to America, and that means extra cost transporting it right across the country to Liverpool, and then across the Atlantic.'

'All the same,' Haworth went on, 'Boney hasn't had it all his own way. We've had reports from American travellers who've been in France recently, that this trade war he's started has affected France even more than us. No traffic on the main highways, commercial towns half deserted, beggars swarming the streets. They've no outlet for their goods either, remember; and then there's all the things they used to import from us, or from our colonies, that they can't get any more — coffee and tobacco and spices and sugar, to say nothing of cotton and wool. The embargo is crippling Europe. I've even heard,' he added with a grin, 'that Boney himself had to authorise the smuggling of Yorkshire cloth last winter to make uniforms for his army in Prussia!'

'Oh nonsense! That would be foolish in the extreme,' Lucy laughed.

'War is foolish, my dear,' Haworth said, glad to have brought a smile to her face. 'But since someone else has started it, I'm afraid I shall have to do my part to end it, so I'm off to the Tagus in a few days' time. Oh, and here's a piece of news for you — I'm to give passage to an old friend of yours, who's going out to join Strangford. Can you guess?'

'I haven't an idea,' Lucy said. 'What old friend have I got in the Foreign Office?'

'John Anstey's younger brother, Ben! I hear that Canning thinks highly of his powers of oratory.'

'I don't know where he learnt it. He was always the quiet one of the family. Well, you'll have good company on the voyage, at any rate.'

'So it seems. But I'll be here long enough to dine with you, and escort you to the theatre, if Major Wiske will make room for me.'

150

'I shall like that,' Lucy said.

'And I've something to ask you — a sort of favour,' he went on.

'Yes? Anything at all!'

'Don't say that until you know what it is! The fact is, Africa has long had a deep desire to go to the circus, and I should like to gratify it while I'm here. Would you make it tolerable for me by coming with me? If you like, we could take your children, too, and make a regular party of it. What do you think?'

'Go to Astley's? Haworth, you can't be serious!'

'Oh dear, is it too unsophisticated for Lady Aylesbury?' He made a wry face.

Lucy grinned. 'Not in the least! Don't you know I've wanted to go all my life, only when I was younger, I was never allowed, and since I've grown up, I haven't dared. But taking the children makes it all above-board, doesn't it?'

'That's what I hoped you'd think,' Haworth grinned.

The expedition to Astley's Amphitheatre took place two days later.

'Numbers are everything in a party like this,' Haworth observed as they waited in the drawing-room at Upper Grosvenor Street for the carriages to be announced. As well as the six children, the party included Midshipman Morpurgo, a last-minute addition at Haworth's request. 'I've managed to steal him away from Manby to join me in my new command,' Haworth explained. 'I've said he can travel down to Portsmouth with Africa and me, so he's at a loose end at the moment. I hope you won't object, Lucy? He is one of Africa's oldest friends.'

Morpurgo was a handsome, fair-haired youth with exquisite manners, and the self-possession which came from long service at sea from an early age. He attempted to make himself useful by attaching himself to Hippolyta, and Lucy was amused to note how Africa quickly scotched the plan, and intruded herself firmly between the young man and her sister, with a look that said quite clearly, 'Morpurgo is *my* friend'.

As Miss Trotton, and Lucy's maid Docwra — who could control a group of children with the ease of one brought up amongst a plethora of brothers and sisters in a tiny one-roomed cottage in Wicklow — also accompanied them, Lucy had nothing to do but look elegant, accept Haworth's arm, and prepare to enjoy herself.

The circus had been performing on the site in the Westminster Bridge Road for thirty years, but the amphitheatre itself was a new building, and very impressive. It had a proscenium stage and orchestra pit as well as the circus ring, and four tiers of seats finished in the first style with gilded scrollwork and red velvet curtains, and a veritable galaxy of candles. Haworth had procured a large private box near the stage at ring-level, and Lucy was interested to see that some of the other boxes were occupied by people of fashion, and not just by rustics and newcomers to Town. Evidently since the new amphitheatre had been built it had become an acceptable venue.

The programme was lengthy, and included a whole Chinese shadow-play, interspersed with comic songs and dances, which Lucy found rather tedious, although the displays of fireworks between the acts were very beautiful. The play ended with a hornpipe by two men who had obviously never been nearer to the sea than the fish-pond in Vauxhall Gardens. It was advertised as being 'Performed in a Most Extraordinary Manner'.

'Extraordinary's the word,' Haworth murmured to Lucy, while Morpurgo repressed a smile as Africa remarked in a piercingly audible whisper that any of the tars on her ship could do better than that, even dead drunk and in the middle of a broadside-to-broadside engagement.

The circus acts in the ring, however, were fascinating. There was a team of slack-rope dancers, who also did pole-balancing, and two tumblers who seemed able to contort their bodies into the most curious attitudes. There was a troupe of dwarves who tumbled and juggled and threw each other around the ring like cork balls, walked on their hands, and finished with a tableau entitled 'Men piled on Men, or the Egyptian Pyramid'.

But best of all, in Lucy's estimation, which evidently coincided with that of the children, were the horse-acts. There were displays of horsemanship and agility on one, two and three horses; a clown who 'burlesqued the various parts of horsemanship in a manner most diverting'; a horse which had been taught to dance to music, and to answer questions by stamping its hoof once for 'yes' and twice for 'no'; and some costume tableaux on horseback and various scenes from history.

Finally the orchestra played a resounding fanfare, and into the ring came a broad-backed dapple-grey horse, which cantered round slowly under the direction of the ring-master with his long whip. Another fanfare, and a small, slender figure in tight pantaloons and swallow-tail coat ran in, and vaulting lightly onto the horse as it passed, stood up on the broad rump, balancing with arms outstretched as easily as if on the solid earth.

Africa leaned forward with a gasp of astonishment. 'Papa! It's a girl!'

'So it is, chick.' Haworth smiled. The Equestrienne, as she was called, had become moderately famous in London. Africa leaned as far forward as she could without falling out of the box, her eyes rivetted on the slim, supple figure as the Equestrienne balanced on one leg, reversed herself and stood on her hands, and performed somersaults on horseback, while the placid grey cantered endlessly round. Then a hoop was brought in and held by an assistant, for the Equestrienne to jump through as she passed. It was an exhibition of great skill, but the fact that it was given by a female somehow made it seem even more impressive.

'I bet I could do that,' Rosamund hissed to her sister. 'If only I could train one of the horses to canter in a circle —'

'Training the horse might be the hardest part of it,' Hippolyta remarked sensibly, while Flaminia merely looked faintly surprised that anyone should *want* to do anything so energetic and dangerous. Thomas, who was finding the performance too long for his attention, was dozing and waking against Docwra's plump shoulder; while Roland was gazing at the display with minute and dazzled attention, and planning to ask the Equestrienne to marry him as soon as he was old enough. He could make her a countess, and she could dance on horseback for him every day.

The Equestrienne cantered out of the ring, there was a final set-piece, and it was all over. Outside in the ante-room there was the usual delay while they waited for the carriages to be called. The crush was dreadful, and though the children

153

didn't seem to mind it, chattering excitedly about everything they had seen, Lucy stirred restively, pressing close to Haworth to avoid contact with strangers. Then to her surprise, she heard her name called. She looked around, and saw Roberta squeezing her way through the crowds towards her.

'Hello Lucy. It was a good show, wasn't it? I saw you from my box, and waved to you, but you didn't see me.'

'What on earth are you doing here?' Lucy asked. 'Of all the places in London to meet you!'

'I could say the same,' Roberta smiled, 'except that I see you are on the same errand as me.' And she nodded towards the children, and then gestured behind her to where Lucy now saw Bobbie and Marcus waiting, in the company of Mr Firth.

'Captain Haworth promised to take the children, and asked me to come to make it tolerable for him,' Lucy explained. 'Don't tell me your Mr Firth couldn't bear it without your company?'

Lucy had spoken idly, but to her surprise, Roberta suddenly blushed, and turned away. Lucy took her arm, and since their turned backs gave them privacy in that crowd, she said, 'You're blushing: what is it?'

'Lucy, please, you embarrass me,' Roberta said, distressed.

'But what have I said? Not simply calling him your Mr Firth again?' Lucy said, puzzled. She had never been noted for being sensitive to other people's feelings, but looking towards Mr Firth, she intercepted a glance he cast towards his employer. It was a look which mingled tender concern with faint amusement, and something else — a sort of confidence or accustomedness, the sort of look which might pass between a husband and his wife of several years' standing. Illumination spread over her features. 'You're in love with him!' she discovered.

Roberta looked up, and then away again, unable to hold her gaze, and gave a small nod. 'You're not shocked, are you? I made sure you had guessed many times, from the things you said.'

'Lord, no,' Lucy said, 'though I hadn't thought about it, truly! But if he feels the same way for you, then I hope you will be very happy together. He's a splendid fellow! And it's no-one's business but yours, after all.'

154

'Oh, I knew people would be shocked, and blame us, and talk about inequality of rank and such things. That's why I've been at such pains to hide it, even from myself,' Roberta said in a low voice. 'And Peter — Mr Firth — tried hard to disguise his feelings, too. He talked about *abusing his position* — as if he had ever done anything, *anything*! But, oh Lucy, people will gossip and disapprove, and it's so unfair! I'm a colonel's daughter, though I married an earl, and Peter's father was Papa's old friend, and how can that be unequal or wrong or —?'

'Hush, Roberta. I'm not arguing with you, or accusing you. I'm sure you're suited to each other in every way,' Lucy said, patting her arm vaguely. 'Besides, even if people do talk, it will blow over. These things always do. Good God, look at me! People forget even the worst scandals soon enough. When do you think of marrying?'

Now Roberta lifted her eyes. 'Oh, not until Bobbie has come of age, of course.'

'What? But that's ten — eleven years away! You can't mean to wait so long!'

Roberta looked surprised. 'But how could I do otherwise? Bobbie's welfare must come first, and I couldn't marry his tutor, or deprive him of him. We must continue to hide our feelings from Bobbie and from the world; only — only I needed to speak of it to someone, and I hoped you wouldn't mind. You will keep my confidence, Lucy dear?'

Lucy smiled. '*I'll* keep it; but *you* won't. All Lombard Street to an orange you give in and wed each other within two years!'

'Never! I couldn't,' Roberta exclaimed, and Lucy merely smiled and shook her head. From seeing them together, she thought they were admirably suited, and Bobbie evidently loved and respected his tutor; but she could see Roberta's dilemma. The talk would undoubtedly be very upsetting if they were to marry. For her own part, she had always rather do what she wanted, and brave the scandal, but she knew Roberta was made of more delicate stuff. Still, someone was bound to guess sooner or later, and then there would be no point in having the name without the game.

'We'll see,' she said, and they turned back to join Captain Haworth and the children.

On the first Sunday in December, 1807, Mary Skelwith accompanied her son to the service at the Minster with a familiar reluctance. She preferred to perform her devotions in the quiet and privacy of St Helen's, a small church dedicated to the guild of glass-painters, and not particularly popular with people of fashion; but several times a year, on the important festivals — Easter, Whitsunday, All Saints', and all through Christmastide — it was so much expected that everyone would attend the Minster service, that even Mary Skelwith baulked at behaviour so particular as to miss it.

It was not that she disliked the service there. She was orthodox in her religious views, regarding any kind of Enthusiasm as suspiciously papist, and preferring one minister's delivery to another's would have looked uncommonly like Enthusiasm of the most reprehensible sort; but she disliked the social aspects of an attendance at the Minster. Hurry as she might when the service was over, she had never managed to avoid speaking to some at least of her neighbours. John, who had a sociable nature, was inclined to linger and encourage the contact.

On this particular occasion she was more anxious than ever to escape, for during the service she had glanced towards the enormous Anstey pew, and seen that the former Miss Celia Anstey, now Mrs Philip Masters, was paying a rare visit to her family. Celia and Mary had been friends in their girlhood — close friends, Celia would have said, for she had been very pretty and popular, and since Mary had been neither, it had suited Celia to claim her as a bosom-bow.

But Celia had fallen in love with James Morland, and had pursued him determinedly with, in many peoples' view, a good chance of success. When James rejected her, and what was worse, rejected her because of his hopeless passion for Mary Loveday, Celia's jealousy had known no reason. She had spied on Mary and on James so diligently that she alone had discovered the secret of their guilty liaison. She had used the knowledge to try to blackmail James into marrying her; and when he had refused, contemptuously, she had retaliated by telling old Skelwith himself what was going on.

Things had not gone quite as Celia had planned; for

though Mary and James had suffered in the resultant storm, Celia had also come off badly. She had been mocked as a jealous spinster, and things had been made so uncomfortable that her father had been forced to send her away to an aunt in Harrogate, and to keep her there until a marriage could be arranged for her with a very dull and respectable business associate.

All those things were far in the past. Celia Masters rarely visited York, even after her marriage, and probably no-one now remembered anything about her part in the old scandal. But that she remembered, and still resented, was clear from the lowering look she gave Mary when their eyes met during the sermon, and Mary was eager, even desperate, to avoid any contact with her.

It was not so easy, however. When the service was over, John gave her his arm down the aisle, but at the door, when she tried to draw him away for the short walk home, he resisted, scanning the emerging crowd for friendly faces and bowing happily this way and that.

'There's Lady Mickelthwaite nodding — do nod back, Mama, she's so good-natured! There's Mrs Cowey and the Miss Coweys, inseparable as usual. And over there, look, the Pobgees — I must find a moment to see young Pobgee about that lease in St Leonard's Place. Not now, however — here are the Morlands coming out. We must go and speak to them. Do come, Mama!'

The Morland party consisted of Edward Morland, Miss Nordubois, Fanny Morland and her governess, and Miss Sophie Morland. Lady Henrietta was a papist, as was well known, and in any case had been much confined to bed lately; and evidently Mr James Morland had decided to keep her company that day. As Edward Morland immediately joined his party with the Pobgees, and engaged Mr Pobgee senior in conversation, John Skelwith approached them with plenty of excuse, though it would not have escaped the attention of some observers that it was to Miss Nordubois that he really wanted to speak.

But Mary hung back, allowing the press of people emerging to separate her hand from her son's arm, and once free of him, turned and began to inch her way through the crowd, bent on escape down High Petergate to Stonegate and safety.

But it was hard to cross the current of outward-flowing humanity, and in her determination she thrust herself directly into the path of the emerging Anstey party.

It was impossible to ignore them. John Anstey was amongst her oldest acquaintances, dear friend of her brother Tom who had died of despair when the Loveday business finally foundered during the panic caused by the Invasion Scare of 1803. Mary stood, angry and alarmed, defeated and at bay, making a last attempt to avoid Celia's malicious attentions by asking after John Anstey's numerous children — another was due at any moment, explaining his wife Louisa's absence — and for news of the youngest Anstey brother, Benjamin, of whom the whole family was extravagantly proud.

John Anstey, everyone's friend, and a lifelong defender of Mary Skelwith, fell to work with vigour, giving her all manner of details about Louisa's pregnancy that Mary would not normally have wished to hear, and discussing the political situation just as if she knew what he was talking about.

'Ben's doing very well at the moment — he's quite one of Canning's pets, you know. We had a letter from him just last Thursday. Canning sent him out to Portugal with Lord Strangford — I expect you know all about that mission.'

Mary, who paid little attention to events outside her own house, and none at all to the events outside England, nodded dumbly. Celia was trying to edge nearer, her expression grimly determined.

'The Regent always was a weak man, but the news that Junot and his army had actually entered Spain and were marching on Lisbon put him quite in despair. It was all Strangford could do to persuade him not to lie down there and then. But our fleet, thank God, arrived before Junot! Once the Regent saw the warships, Strangford persuaded him to escape for Rio, with his family, his treasury, and his ships. So when Junot gets there, he'll find the bird has flown! Ben has gone with the Regent as Liaison Officer, with a squadron of our ships as escort. Our old friend Haworth is Commodore commanding. I expect your son is getting all the details from Ned Morland this very minute.'

'Yes — really — how interesting,' Mary had been murmuring. Now she glanced across, and saw that not only was John talking to Ned Morland, but that he was making a serious attempt to bring the Morland party across to join the Ansteys. At that moment John Anstey's attention was resolutely claimed by old Sir Thomas Chubb, whom he could not ignore; and as Mary turned away sharply to escape, Celia took her chance and intruded herself between Mary and freedom.

'Mary, my dear, how lovely to see you again! Ever since I saw you were at the service, I have been promising myself a good, long talk with you. What an age it is since we had a comfortable chat! Were you about to leave? Do let me walk with you, and we can be private, and have a coze, like we did in the old days.'

'Yes — that is, no, I must wait for John. I will walk with John, thank you, Celia,' Mary muttered in confusion.

Celia's eyes bloomed with malice. 'Oh yes, dear John! What a comfort he must be to you, Mary dear! Such a fine, upright young man, and so like his father!'

The words, overheard by a third party who knew nothing of the affair, would sound quite innocent; and Celia plainly thought the presence of so many people within earshot would allow her to torment Mary with impunity; but Mary, already overwrought, flared up at the covert cruelty.

'How dare you say that? How dare you?'

'How dare I? Why, Mary dear, what can you mean? Why shouldn't I say your son is like his father? That would be thought a compliment by most people! And what a pity it is that he's not here to see him now, when he must be making you so happy!'

'You know very well he is dead! John's father is dead!' Mary said wildly.

'That's just what I said. What a pity he won't see John bring home a bride at last! Has the day been named? When may we expect the happy announcement?'

Mary pulled herself together. 'I don't know what you're talking about, Celia. Is this more of your vile plotting? If so —'

Celia's eyes widened. 'Why, Mary dear, don't get so upset! It's only what everyone has been saying ever since I got here. And you only have to see them together to know the truth of it! Your John is planning to marry the Morland ward, and a very fine bride I'm sure she'll make him! You must be so fond

159

of her already! And of course, as I understand it, she's a sort of distant relation, too — if anyone were able to be completely sure of her ancestry.'

She looked pointedly towards the other group, where John Skelwith was stationed at Mathilde's side, between her and Edward Morland, the three of them chatting with every appearance of intimacy. Mary turned back toward Celia, her eyes burning with anger in her pale face. 'You poisonous bitch!' she hissed, and her hand came up, hooked, ready in her desperation to claw Celia's face — Celia who had done her so much damage already, and who would do far more, given any opportunity.

But John Anstey intervened. Freeing himself at that instant from Sir Thomas, he turned just in time to catch Mary by the wrist, and say, 'No, no, you mustn't! Everyone will see. Celia, what have you been doing?'

'I? Nothing! Why should you think —?'

'Because I know you, Cely. I know all about your mischief-making, don't forget. Now go over there and talk to Lizzie, and behave yourself. Don't argue with me! You've never yet seen me angry, but I promise you, if you do, you'll regret it!'

Celia glared a moment, and then flounced away, nose in the air. John Anstey's hand moved from Mary's wrist to her upper arm, and he began steering her quickly and firmly through the crowds. 'You'd better go home, Mary. I'll get a quiet word to John and send him after you — I'll say you weren't feeling well, or something like that. Go on, now. And try not to mind what Celia says. She's a disappointed woman.'

Mary was still too shaken to speak, but she cast him a look of gratitude, and hurried away down the street. It was almost half an hour before John joined her, running up the stairs two at a time, and into her sitting-room, his face flushed with some excitement, though his eyes sought her with concern.

'Mama, what is it? What happened? I looked around for you, and you'd gone, and then Lord Anstey sent me word you were ill.'

Mary regarded his face carefully. 'I felt — a little unwell. It was nothing. I'm all right now, John.'

'Are you sure? You look — well, strange.'

'I'm all right,' she said again. 'The crowd pressed too close,

160

that's all. You know I hate crowds.'

He looked at her shrewdly. 'Are you angry with me because we got separated? I'm sorry, Mama. I wanted you to come and speak to the Morlands for a particular reason. I wonder if you can guess what it is?'

'I'm not interested in the Morlands! I've told you before! May we have dinner, now that you've returned? You know it disagrees with me to eat late.'

'But Mama, there is something particular I wish to say to you,' John said holding out his hands and smiling. 'Won't you come and sit here, by me?'

She withheld her hands from him. 'I don't want to hear it,' she said sharply. 'Ring the bell, I must have my dinner.'

'No, Mama — this is something you must hear — and something you'll like, I promise you! The reason I wanted you to come and talk to the Morlands is that I wanted you to meet Lady Morland's ward, Miss Nordubois. You know that I've been seeing her quite often lately? Yes you do, for I've told you so, though you pretended not to be listening! Well, I've quite lost my heart to her! She is the dearest girl, and I'm going to ask her to marry me. So naturally I wanted you to meet her first. Of course, I'll ask her here formally — or rather, you will — but for the very first meeting, I thought it would be better —'

'Marry her?' Mary's face was white. 'No, John. I absolutely forbid it.'

John cocked his head, uncertain how serious she was. 'Mama? What is it? You cannot have heard any ill of her, for apart from the fact that you see no-one, I'm certain she hasn't an enemy in the world. She has the kindest nature —'

'I won't hear any more! I forbid you to talk about her!'

'But I must! Mama, what is it? This is not like you. You cannot condemn the girl before you've met her. To be sure, she hasn't a portion, but that can't signify. I have more than enough for us all, and I would sooner have a poor woman of good character and sweet temper for a wife, than the richest heiress in the world. Besides, I am in love with her, and you wouldn't want me to marry a woman I didn't love, would you?'

'Don't talk to me about love! You don't know what you're saying! In any case, I forbid you to marry this girl, and I don't

161

want to hear any more about it.'

Now John was growing angry, though he controlled himself from long habit. 'No, Mama, that isn't good enough. I have behaved exactly as I should in this matter. I've spoken to you before declaring myself to Miss Nordubois, before even asking her guardian for permission to address her. I am over twenty-one, and I can marry anyone I please.'

'Oh, can you? And break your mother's heart, I suppose! I mean nothing to you now!'

'Mama, stop it! You're being unreasonable. You can't simply forbid me to marry without telling me why.'

'I can do as I please,' she flared, and his temper broke. He seized her hands to stop her turning away from him, and glared down into her face.

'You shall tell me! You shall name your objections, or — or go to the devil!'

Mary gasped. 'How dare you! How dare you speak to me like that!'

He gripped her harder. 'Name them!'

'I won't have you associate yourself with the Morlands,' Mary gasped. 'I won't have you hanging around Morland Place. I told you often enough not to go there, but you ignored me. You always ignore me, when it's a matter of your own selfish pleasure.'

This was the grossest of calumnies, and John released her hands and stood staring at her, still angry, but puzzled. 'There is something here,' he said slowly, scanning her face. 'Surely it cannot be that old business of you and James Morland?' His mother said nothing, but her eyes were wary. 'But that would be too foolish. I've heard it said that you were in love with him once when you were a girl — well, that all the young women were. It can't simply be that. There's something more here — something more to cause all this anger. What is it, Mother. What makes you hate the Morlands so?'

'That's my business,' Mary snapped, but her anger was now tempered by fear.

'Mine too. Oh yes! You have made it mine. Do you hate James Morland? Is that it? But why should you? What has he ever done to make you hate him?' She began to turn away, and he caught her back, his fingers digging into the soft flesh of her arms. 'You shall tell me.'

'Let me go,' she hissed.

'You shall tell me, or I shall find out elsewhere. I'll ask questions — do you want me to find out from someone else? I'll ask at the club. I'll bet Sir Arthur Fussell knows something.' She glared at him mutely. 'Or how about Mrs Masters? I know you and she were old friends. I'll ask her.'

'No!'

'Then tell me,' he said, shaking her. 'Why must I have nothing to do with James Morland?'

Mary tried to wrench herself away from him, and the biting of his fingers hurt her, making her temper flare again. 'Because James Morland is your father!' she shouted. 'There, are you satisfied now?'

He stared at her. 'I don't believe you,' he said. She only glared at him, her mouth set, and his face slowly whitened. 'I don't believe you! You're lying! I don't believe you!'

He released her arms, and she sighed, rubbing them slowly, all the anger and excitement draining from her, leaving her feeling tired and old. 'You're a fool,' she said. 'You would meddle in what didn't concern you. I've protected you all my life, but you would go courting that girl, when you could have anyone, anyone! James Morland for a father-in-law! That's what you wanted! Well now you know, and I hope you're satisfied!'

He looked at her in slowly-dawning pain. 'You hate me, too, don't you? What did I do, Mother? Did I ruin your life for you, was that it? Is that why you're trying to stop me being happy?'

'I don't hate you, John,' she said wearily. 'You're the only person in my life I have ever loved, apart from Tom.'

'Then why are you telling me this lie about James Morland? My father was John Skelwith. Your husband, for God's sake! sake!'

She turned away. 'Have it your own way. Marry who you like. I don't care any more. Just don't bring that girl anywhere near me. And don't ever mention the name of Morland to me again.'

He watched her in disbelief as she walked towards the door, expecting her every moment to turn back and speak to him gently, apologise, take back the cruel, intolerable words. But she didn't stop. Her hand was on the door-knob, she was leaving him without a look.

'I don't believe it!' he cried as she went out; but she didn't look back.

He didn't remember afterwards exactly where he had been. When his mother left him, he ran downstairs and out of the house, through the alley to the stables in Grape Lane where he kept his horse, saddled up, and rode away. He left York the nearest way, through Bootham Bar, and rode across the fields, galloped until poor Trooper was blown and sweaty; but he had no clear recollection of where he had been. He only knew that he came eventually to the track leading from Morland Place to Twelvetrees, and there he halted Trooper, and sat waiting. Eventually, even on a Sunday, he was sure James Morland would come by. He didn't believe any day passed without his visiting the stables.

In the end, it was not James, but Edward who found him as he returned from Twelvetrees. It was growing cold. The wind had changed, and the sky was darkening with clouds that foretold snow. The short day was closing, and Edward's mind was on home and a glowing fire and toasted muffins, and perhaps a game of chess with Mathilde, who was getting quite good at it, since he had begun to teach her six weeks ago.

He was not best pleased, therefore, when Tiger, who was trotting ahead, halted on the track and turned to look back at him, drawing his attention to the solitary horseman. John Skelwith, waiting for him! Edward thought crossly. He supposed the wretched youth would be hoping for an invitation to the house. Well, he could go on hoping! But as he drew nearer, he could see that all was not well. Skelwith looked like a man who had suffered a severe shock, and he was shaking with the cold, inadequately dressed in what looked like the same clothes he had worn to church that morning.

Edward was not usually quick at putting two and two together, but as he halted before him, he couldn't help remembering that Celia Masters was paying a rare visit home, and feeling some foreboding.

'Hullo!' he said. 'What's the matter? You look as though you're in trouble.'

John Skelwith looked at him like a man slowly waking up. 'Oh — it's you, sir. I — I've had a bit of a blow. The fact is —'

He stopped, and didn't seem to be able to go on.

'You're shivering with cold, man!' Edward said, glad of his silence. 'You'd better get off home as quick as you can. It's getting dark, and there'll be no moon tonight, by the look of these clouds. I wouldn't be surprised if it snowed soon.'

'Home? No — no I can't,' Skelwith said dazedly. 'The fact is, I've had words with my mother. Well, she told me something —'

'Oh, I expect that will all have blown over by the time you get back,' Edward said, determinedly cheerful. 'Women have their little moods you know, but they don't last long. She'll be worried about you by now, glad to have you back in one piece. You'll see.'

'No, you don't understand.' John was equally determined, and Ned's heart sank. 'She told me something — something incredible. I have to find out if it's true. I meant to ask — but you've come along now. Sir, is it true —' He stopped again, but Edward's wits were not quick enough to think of another diversion. John began again. 'You see, sir, I told her that I was planning to marry Miss Nordubois —'

Edward drew a sharp breath. 'You've spoken to her? To Mathilde, I mean? She's accepted you?'

Skelwith hadn't been expecting the question, and looked distracted. 'What? Oh, no, I haven't declared myself, not yet. It wouldn't be proper for me to ask her until I'd spoken to my mother and her guardian. I know how these things should be done, sir, I promise you. No, I thought I'd speak to Mother first, and ask if I could present Miss Nordubois to her, because she'd never met her —'

'Just a minute, young man,' Edward said drily. 'What makes you think that Mathilde would welcome a proposal from you? Don't you think you ought to have — ah — tested the water first?'

Skelwith looked dumbfounded, working his way painfully through the sequence of thoughts. 'Do you mean — do you think she wouldn't? I hadn't — I mean, she has always seemed fond of me, and I —'

'I don't think Miss Nordubois has any thoughts of marriage at the moment,' Edward said kindly. 'She's still very young, you know.'

Had all this, then, been for nothing? John thought. 'Forgive

165

me, sir, but are you in her confidence?'

'To an extent, yes. Enough to vouch for what I have just said.'

'Oh God,' John said, putting his face in his hands. 'Oh God.'

Edward looked at him with impatient sympathy, noticing that Skelwith's horse looked foundered, and was shivering too. 'You'd better get off home, young man, before that horse of yours gets pneumonia.'

Skelwith lifted his head sharply, and the blood began to run more swiftly under his skin. 'Home? No, I can't, not after what Mother said. Not until I know the truth of it. I was waiting here for your brother, sir, but I dare say you know all there is to know.'

Edward braced himself for unpleasantness, but at that instant John saw how utterly impossible it was to ask what he had to ask. If it were not true, how dreadfully the question would expose both him and his mother, shame them both for ever. He could only ask if he were absolutely certain that it *was* true, and to admit to any third party that he was certain of the truth of something so unbelievable and shocking as that his mother had cuckolded his father, was something it would shame him to do. What kind of a son would believe that of his mother? How would that make him appear?

He stared at Edward, his mouth working soundlessly, two red spots of distress high on his cheekbones. He would have to live forever with the doubt. He would have to live with his mother, knowing that either she had committed adultery with James Morland all those years ago, or that she hated him enough to want to make him think she had. He would spend his life wondering if it were true, wondering how many people in York knew it, and looked at him behind his back with secret, pitying knowledge.

And then he met Edward's eyes, and saw his answer in them, in the older man's fear of what he might be asked. The moment extended itself, and Ned saw Skelwith's mouth turn down bitterly, saw that he would not now ask the dreaded question. In his relief, he felt warm towards the young man.

'Go on home, John,' he said gently. 'You're worn out.'

Skelwith gathered his horse's reins, and the shattered pieces of his life. 'You're right, sir,' he said with harsh dignity.

'I'm sorry I made a fool of myself. I hope you'll forgive me, and forget anything I may have said.'

'I never saw you at all,' Edward assured him cheerfully. 'Go on, before it gets completely dark.'

Skelwith turned and rode away across the field, and Edward watched him a moment before setting off for home. The danger was averted. What had that stupid woman said to her son? Well, whatever it was, it looked as though it would end his unwelcome visits to Morland Place. Mathilde might be a little sorry to lose her most attentive beau, he considered; but then, she had plenty of others. There was safety in numbers. And she was so young, she oughtn't to be thinking seriously of anyone yet. It might be years, he thought happily, before she felt any serious desire to get married.

shere was ...

CHAPTER NINE

The snow came; winter set in, and was bitter. The temperature went down and down, at first exhilarating, then frightening. The Christmas season was interrupted by expeditions, whenever the snow stopped falling, to find and dig out trapped sheep, and to cut paths through to stables and stock-shelters — work which called upon every able man, whatever his rank, to help.

Héloïse did her best to make the season within doors cheerful, though she conducted the festivities from a sopha. The baby was due in mid-January. She had got through her pregnancy so far by the skin of her teeth, since that dreadful day back in the summer when she had begun to bleed. She had expected and feared every moment that she would lose the baby, but it was still there inside her, and still alive, and as she passed into the ninth month, she began to feel the cautious hope that it would be all right after all.

Lucy was spending Christmas at Belvoir, where the Rutlands were entertaining a large party, including the Prince of Wales, and George Brummell and his immediate set — Mildmay, Wiske, Alvanley and the rest. She had promised to come up to Yorkshire immediately after Twelfth Night and to stay with Héloïse until the baby was born. There was no party at Shawes, but the Morlands had the usual Christmas festivities, the fetching of the Yule log, the St Stephen's Day meet, with the traditional ball in the evening, and a Twelfth Night masquerade, which James and Mathilde organised between them.

Large numbers of young people were invited, as well as friends of James's and Edward's generation. Mathilde, along with the Keatings, arranged a special game of 'The Witch is Dead' for the young people in the dining-room after the table had been cleared. Everyone sat around the table, all the candles but one were doused, and 'horrors' were handed round in the semi-darkness.

'The witch is dead, this is her head!' Tom Keating intoned, and passed a carved turnip to his sister, the first person in the chain. It went from hand to hand with a succession of muffled shrieks and giggles. The reaction grew more noisy as the game progressed and the items grew more grisly.

The culmination, 'The witch is dead, these are her eyes!' heralded a pair of skinned grapes, which passed extremely rapidly down the line, accompanied by screams of excited disgust. In her haste to be rid of them, Antonia Somers threw them at Miss Chubb who, clutching at them instinctively, knocked one down the neckline of her dress, where it lodged between her breasts, sending her into violent hysterics. She had to be led away by Marie and the housekeeper to a quiet room with plenty of candles, and restored with a vinaigrette and a glass of port. Since she was basically a sensible girl, she soon revived enough to return to the party, which was playing a very sober game of speculation while it waited for her.

The arrival of the mummers gathered both generations into the hall to watch the traditional play; after which, since the fiddlers were lingering with hopeful expressions, the young people begged to be allowed some dancing. Mathilde seconded the request to James, and receiving a nod from Héloïse, he agreed. Joe Micklethwaite almost ruined everything by suggesting with a worldly-wise smile that they should have some waltzing, at which the stricter mamas flung up their hands in horror, and one or two betrayed their ignorance of fashion by not understanding the nature of the threat. But Valentine Somers and Tom Keating hastily quashed the suggestion, silenced their friend by main force, and clamoured loudly for country-dances.

Most of the older people went back to their cards and conversations, but some stayed to watch the dancing, Edward among them. Héloïse had been amused earlier in the season to see him trying to comfort Mathilde for John Skelwith's defection, though it was plain to Héloïse at least that she needed no comforting, and had not cared more for Skelwith than for any other of the young men. Héloïse was glad that it had come to nothing, and that Skelwith no longer haunted Morland Place. He had troubled her, and his ghostly look of James, reminder of the past, of all the years James had not been hers. She tried not to be jealous, but she sometimes wished, guiltily, that he had had no children except with her. She hoped the new baby would be a boy. Marie swore that it would be, and prayed to Our Lady every night for a male child, safely delivered at the right time. Sophie, too, prayed for a boy, a new brother to ease the ache of losing Thomas.

What Fanny hoped was hard to tell. She had settled down so well with Miss Rosedale that for the last month Sophie had been allowed to join her lessons as well, relieving Father Aislaby of the strain. A sort of resilient tension had built up between Fanny and her governess, half reluctant admiration, half resentment. Miss Rosedale actually liked Fanny, and Fanny was not used to that, and suspected it as a trick. She didn't want to like her in return: liking people made you vulnerable, meant that you had to do things to please them instead of yourself, made you think about what you did, in case it upset them. Fanny still, as regularly as she could make herself, did things to upset Miss Rosedale, just to shew her independence, but the occasions were growing less frequent and more reluctant all the time. It was far better to go along with her and enjoy what came, and revel in the luxury of having someone who treated her not as a child, or a nuisance, or a threat, or an idol, but as a person.

Fanny had come to mind much less about her father and Madame since she had Miss Rosedale, and had managed to ignore the whole question of the approaching baby. She even viewed Sophie with something approaching tolerance, especially since Thomas had been removed, and Sophie so evidently missed him. Sophie's lessons with Miss Rosedale were much less advanced than Fanny's, and even when they learnt something together, like history or geography, Fanny's grasp of the facts was much quicker. Only in French did Sophie excel, and that, Fanny observed to herself, was only because she had been speaking it since birth.

The Christmas season had passed pleasantly for Fanny. On Christmas Eve, when the weather cleared after a prolonged snowstorm, Fanny had been anxious to go out and see that Tempest was all right. The nursery-maids had thrown up their hands in horror at the idea, but Miss Rosedale had taken Fanny's part, and said that it was perfectly proper for Fanny to feel responsible towards her animal.

'Miss Fanny can't go out in that wilderness alone, and

that's the fact of it,' Jenny had said firmly. 'And the mistress would say the same if you asked her, which you can't, Miss Fanny, because she's resting and mustn't be disturbed,' she added triumphantly.

Fanny scowled, but Miss Rosedale intervened. 'There's no question of Fanny's going out alone,' she said pleasantly, 'I shall go with her.'

'You, Miss? Out there?' Jenny looked astonished, and then shrugged, remembering Héloïse's instructions that the governess was to have full support in her decisions, however odd they seemed. 'Just as you say, Miss, I'm sure I don't care. I just hope you don't both fall in a drift, and have to be dug out by the men afterwards, with a deal of trouble and pain to everyone, like the sheep.'

But Miss Rosedale knew more of country matters than that. Since the snow had stopped it was freezing hard, so she borrowed two pairs of snow-shoes from the steward, and accompanied Fanny out into the dazzling, sunlit world of crystal. Everything was different and unfamiliar in its muffling shroud, rails and hedges almost buried, trees fantastically decorated and hung with icy spars. The short walk to the home paddock was hard work despite the snow-shoes, and Fanny felt like an intrepid explorer by the time they reached the three-sided shelter at the far end, where they found Tempest, along with the other rough horses, comfortably crunching hay and looking perfectly snug. On the way back, they met up with the men bringing in the Yule log, and walked the rest of the way with them, singing the jolly, pagan songs, whose mediaeval tunes always seemed so pleasantly disjointed, with the stresses in the wrong place, as though they were in a foreign language.

On Christmas day itself, quarter-day, the tenants came up to the house to pay their rents, and by Miss Rosedale's advice, Fanny was allowed to play a prominent part in the proceedings. It was time, Miss Rosedale suggested to James and Edward, that Fanny began to learn something about the business of the estate that would one day be hers. She stood with her father and Uncle Ned behind the table which had been dragged out into the centre of the great hall, watching Compton, the steward, record the payments in the estate ledger. Following her father's example, she shook hands with each man and wished him a happy Christmas, learning their names, in some cases, for the first time, and enjoying the consequence, and the respectful admiration of 'her people'. James was delighted that she seemed ready to take a responsible interest in the estate, though Edward remarked a little sourly that Fanny simply liked being at the centre of the stage, whatever the play happened to be.

On St Stephen's day the servants received their gifts, and Fanny stood behind Madame's chair in the great hall to perform the ceremony; though this was not quite so satisfying, as the servants all knew her very well, and there was nothing like the adulation she received from the tenants, to most of whom she was a distant goddess. Still, she quite enjoyed it; and then there was the hunt, and she was allowed to take Honey out for the first time. Durban however, advised her only to shew the mare to hounds and ride her as far as the first draw, for he suspected she would get too excited. Fanny stuck out her lip rebelliously, but in the event was glad to change onto Tempest, whom one of the grooms had brought to the covert on Durban's instructions.

The family's exchange of New Year gifts almost spoilt the harmonious atmosphere, for James and Héloïse gave Sophie a very beautiful china baby with real silk clothes, and real hair on her head, and Fanny came close to believing that it was better and more expensive than her own china baby, which she had been given years ago, when Mama was still alive. But Miss Rosedale managed to put things into better perspective by observing that it was a very suitable present for such a *little* girl as Sophie, and asking to be shewn Fanny's present again.

Fanny's present from James was a new bridle for Honey, and Fanny came as close as she ever had to being grateful to Madame when she opened *her* present, for in a neat little box was the pair of coral and gold bridle ornaments which had always decorated the headpieces of Madame's cream ponies, and which Fanny knew were an heirloom of great antiquity.

'Your grandmama gave them to me, Fanny, and now I give them to you. It is right that you should have them. They belong in the Morland family. They are over two hundred years old, so you will know how to value them, I'm sure. They will look so pretty on Honey's bridle.'

Fanny was wild to try them out, along with the new bridle, at once, but the weather had thickened alarmingly, and there was no possibility of stirring out of doors. Miss Rosedale kept Fanny amused in the nursery with a mixture of lessons and games, and just when Fanny's good behaviour began to wear thin, she won her approval by persuading James to allow her to attend the Twelfth Night masquerade in its entirety.

Jenny and Sarah fell in with the plan and helped Fanny devise her costume, and Mathilde and the Keatings good-naturedly let her help assemble the 'horrors' for the game, and even went so far as to allow that her suggestion of shelled hazelnuts for teeth was a good one. Then, although it was not a formal ball, Fanny was present when the fiddlers struck up, and was able to feel that she had attended her first dance. Several of the young men good-naturedly asked her to dance with them, and she enjoyed herself so much that she did not even make much of a fuss when Miss Rosedale came to sweep her off to bed before the end.

The following day, Christmas was really over; and perhaps it was a reaction to the flatness after all the gaiety that made Fanny feel cross and out of sorts. She felt strangely restless, and had a perilous feeling that everything had been going too well: she had been being too good, and Miss Rosedale was having everything her own way. Fanny feared that she was in danger of being tamed, and by an unremarkable woman with undeniably thick ankles.

The day began badly, with Fanny upsetting the milk at the breakfast table, which caused Uncle Ned, who perhaps was also suffering from a deranged liver after twelve days of high living, to remark that the proper place for children was in the nursery, and that if Fanny meant to turn the breakfast table into a quagmire, he would go and have his breakfast in peace in the steward's room. He then suited his actions to the words, taking his plate and stumping out of the room with Tiger at his heels. Fanny felt the force of the rebuke deeply: her pride was touched, and she brooded silently on it for the rest of the meal.

After breakfast Sophie had to go to Marie to have a gown refitted, and Miss Rosedale and Fanny had the nursery to themselves. Miss Rosedale, perhaps feeling that hard work was the best remedy for over-indulgence, proposed some

173

exercise in mathematics, at which Fanny baulked.

'I don't want to. It's dull.'

'It isn't,' countered Miss Rosedale infuriatingly. 'Come, we'll imagine you are Compton, and receiving the rents from the tenants. Now, this is your book and this your pen: let's suppose three of your tenants come in at once, and one gives you —'

'I don't want to do mathematics,' Fanny said, throwing down her slate pencil with a fearsome scowl. Under her lowered eyebrows she regarded Miss Rosedale rather dubiously. There ought to be some kind of quarrel between them, she felt; but on the whole she hoped that Miss Rosedale would find a way round it, and manage to restore her to good humour.

'Exercising your mind will make the time pass more quickly,' Miss Rosedale said understandingly. 'I tell you this from experience. Besides, you will need to be good at mathematics, if you are going to make sure your stewards don't cheat you, when you are mistress of Morland Place.'

Usually any reference to Fanny's status worked wonders with her vanity; but this time Fanny only stuck out her lip. 'I don't want to. Why should I do anything I don't want? You can't make me.'

'We often have to do things we don't want. It's a part of being grown-up. Sometimes I don't want to teach you, but I do, because it's my duty. No-one can make me do it — I have to make myself. That's being grown-up, too.'

Fanny stared at her in hurt and amazement. Not want to teach her? But it was she who conferred the favour by *letting* Miss Rosedale teach her!

'If you don't want to teach me, you can go away,' she said furiously. 'I don't want you here. I never asked to have you here. I can look after myself. Just go away — see if I care!'

'Very well,' said Miss Rosedale, and went.

Fanny was staggered. 'You come back!' she shouted, but Miss Rosedale closed the door behind her and didn't reappear.

Fanny sat and brooded. The ideas fermenting in her mind were new and unpleasant. She came to the realisation that she liked Miss Rosedale, enjoyed her lessons, wanted her to approve of her, even love her; and the fear that she might not

174

made Fanny very angry. The more she thought the more she feared and the angrier she got. She wanted to strike back in some way. She must shew Miss Rosedale she didn't care, make her suffer, make her sorry she had ever thought of crossing Miss Morland of Morland Place.

Fanny got up and marched out, along the corridor to Miss Rosedale's bedroom, and there hesitated at the door. The voice of better sense intruded. This was all wrong. Why not find Miss Rosedale, apologise, and continue the lesson? The days would be very long if she were left to her own devices, unable to go out of doors, and with only Sophie to play with. But Fanny had never apologised for anything in her life, and it would be hard to begin now, when she was hurt and angry into the bargain. She squashed down the voice of reason, tapped on the door, and receiving no answer, opened it cautiously.

Miss Rosedale was not in the room. It was clean and tidy, and there was little evidence of the occupier's personality there, except in the very sparseness of personal possessions. There were a few books on a little mahogany stand on the chimney-piece; a polished wooden box — locked — on the dressing-table, containing, one must suppose, personal effects such as letters, since Miss Rosedale never wore jewellery. There was also, in pride of place in the centre of the chest of drawers, a vase.

Fanny had been told a little about the vase. It was Miss Rosedale's one great treasure. She took it with her wherever she went, always seeing to its packing and unpacking herself, and asking the housemaids wherever she stayed not to touch it even to dust it, since it was both fragile and very precious.

Fanny stared at it critically. She thought it hideous, with its black background and snaky green and yellow flowers. *Famille Noir* Miss Rosedale called it. It was over a hundred years old, Chinese and very valuable, she said, but its value to her was much greater, because it had been given to her by her grandmother, whom she had loved very much, and who was now dead.

The notion stole into Fanny's head to break it. She picked it up, and held it, and her fingers tingled from the contact, as though the vase itself were infested with the idea which was so terrible it was also wonderful. She held her breath. To break the vase would be an act of such enormity that her mind circled the idea in fascinated horror, almost unable to look at it directly. Miss Rosedale would be heartbroken — she would be furious — she would be shocked and shaken. It would prove Fanny didn't care a jot for her. Once she'd done it, they could do what they liked to her, nothing would put the vase back together again. It would prove her power, deny Miss Rosedale's power. It would be terrible.

She let out her breath in a sigh. She couldn't do it, of course. Quite apart from the reverence which had been instilled in her from birth for things old and valuable, she couldn't do anything so bad to Miss Rosedale whom — she admitted reluctantly — she loved and wished to please. Yet thinking of it, handling the vase and imagining the deed, had eased something in her. Perhaps just thinking about doing something so wicked was power enough: you didn't actually need to do it. She reached up her hands and began carefully to replace the vase on the chest of drawers.

What happened? Was some demon, released into the air by her wicked thoughts, hovering in the room, looking for some mischief to do? As she reached out to do something so simple — merely replace the vase on the level surface from which she had just taken it — somehow her hand shook, or her judgement was faulty, and instead of lifing it clear, she struck the edge of the chest with the base of the vase, which let out a musical chime. Fear like an icy knife contracted her stomach as she thought it would break. It didn't break, and relief flushed through her, making her knees feel weak. And then in the instant in which the door behind her opened and Miss Rosedale came in, Fanny's hands somehow lost their power, released their grip, and the vase fell from them, hit the polished wooden floorboards, and shattered.

Fanny was numb with shock. Her eyes met Miss Rosedale's in the mirror, and she whirled round, her mouth open, her face drained of colour. Her mind babbled uselessly with horror: *That wasn't meant to happen. I didn't mean it. I was putting it back. Oh please* — but nothing came out. Miss Rosedale's face was grim, grim. She said nothing, only crouched down on her haunches over the shattered ruins of her precious vase.

Fanny stood where she was, rooted to the spot, her hands

thrust behind her as if to hide their infamy. Miss Rosedale looked at the pieces in silence for a long time. Then she picked up a fragment, and then another, and stared at them, as though disbelieving. Fanny waited numbly for the outburst. Whatever Miss Rosedale said or did, Fanny swore to herself she would bear it in silence. She could *kill* her if she liked. No anger could be great enough to burn out the guilt from Fanny's mind at that moment.

But nothing happened. The silence went on, Miss Rosedale did not rise up like an avenging angel and smite Fanny down. And suddenly Fanny realised to her unspeakable horror that Miss Rosedale was crying. Her head was bent over the fragments of her vase, and tears were seeping out from her eyes and running down her adult, unassailable cheeks.

Fanny's paralysis was broken. 'Oh no!' she cried out. 'No, no, I didn't mean it! Oh please don't, please! I didn't mean to. I didn't, I promise I didn't!' She threw herself down beside her dear, kind Miss Rosedale, and flung her arms round her shoulders in a clumsy embrace. The shoulders were stiff and unyielding. Fanny was pierced with rejection.

'Oh I didn't, I didn't!' she moaned. 'Oh please — I never meant to break it. I was putting it back! Oh please —'

Her incoherent plea was that Miss Rosedale should understand that it was an accident, that the moment when she might have performed such a wicked, unspeakable act had passed and gone as if it had never been; but with despair in her heart, Fanny knew she could never be believed, that she had lost for ever the trust and esteem of the only person who had ever really liked her. Tears broke from her, and she sobbed with desperate grief.

And then, to her astonishment, Miss Rosedale dropped the two broken pieces she held, sat down with a bump, and drew Fanny into her arms. Fanny fell against her shoulder, her sobs intensifying in sheer relief, Miss Rosedale crying jerkily through her own tears, 'Oh poor Fanny! Oh my poor vase! Oh dear!'

It was several minutes before they were able to stop, and disentangle themselves rather shyly from each other.

'Here, have my handkerchief,' said Miss Rosedale, always practical. 'I've got another.'

Fanny blew her nose and pushed her hair out of her eyes,

and then looked around her at the shattered fragments of the vase. Her heart seemed to grow cold at the extent of the damage she had caused.

'Could it perhaps be mended?' she asked in a small voice.

Miss Rosedale raised her head from the contemplation of the ruin and held Fanny's gaze. Fanny longed for reassurance, and for a moment Miss Rosedale almost gave it. But then she shook her head. 'No, I'm afraid not. It's too badly broken; and some of the pieces have splintered.'

'I really didn't mean to do it,' said Fanny urgently. 'You do believe me, don't you?'

'Yes, I believe you,' Miss Rosedale said sadly. 'But the vase stays broken, you see.'

Fanny returned the regard steadily, understanding. This, then, was the beginning of being grown-up, accepting that sometimes things were done that couldn't be undone, and bearing the guilt of them, that no amount of saying sorry could ever take away from you. A weight seemed to descend on her, and she almost felt her soul stretch under it, and then steady to take the strain. She looked at Miss Rosedale with different eyes, seeing her for the first time not as a figure put in authority over her, a shape with the label 'governess' attached to it, but as a separate human person, for whom she must have care, as she had care for herself. When you hurt someone, she discovered, even when you didn't mean to, in a way you take responsibility for them.

During that day — 7 January — the temperature dropped again, and by the next morning it was seventeen degrees below freezing. No more snow fell, and with the freezing hard of the surface, the men were able to go out on snow-shoes and with sledges to fetch in firewood and take hay to the beasts. But for those in the house there was no possibility of remaining warm at that temperature. No fire could combat it, no walls keep it out.

Héloïse stayed in the steward's room, because it was smaller and easier to heat. The fire in the grate was stacked high with logs and coal, and Héloïse lay on the chaise-longue, brought in from the drawing-room and pulled up close to it. She was bundled up in several layers of clothes, with her heavy cloak over the top, and with her hands stuffed into her muff, and Kithra lying across her feet, but still the cold seemed to penetrate. Beyond the circle of the fire, the air struck chill and damp, and it seemed to creep and creep into her body, making her lethargic, as though her blood were gradually congealing in her veins.

Everyone sat with her when they were not otherwise occupied, partly because it was the warmest place in the house — Tiger lay on the hearth so close to the fire that the hair on his belly began to singe, filling the air with the smell of burning wool — and partly because they knew how anxious she was. Marie and Mathilde sat with her most of the time, sewing and chatting, or reading aloud to her to while away the hours.

Edward came in from his trips about the estate to give her news of the animals and the state of the snow, to ask how she felt, and look uncomfortable at the answer, since there was nothing he could do to help. Héloïse tried to persuade Mathilde to go out for a while, even if it was only around the courtyard, to keep her circulation moving, and Edward at once offered to teach her to use snow-shoes; but Mathilde would not leave her side.

She and Marie had the notes that Lucy had left, and Mathilde knew them off by heart now. She intended to be as useful as possible to dear Madame, to repay her for all her kindness and, she felt obscurely, for her failure to marry John Skelwith, who had evidently abandoned Morland Place because of her lack of encouragement. She was sure that Marie would not be of much use when the baby came, although she claimed to have delivered Madame of Sophie. But from what Mathilde remembered of that occasion, Marie and Flon had spent all their time arguing about procedure, and precious little help either of them had been to Madame. If the baby should start before her ladyship arrived, Mathilde would see to everything. So she would not leave Madame's side for a moment, and every time she moved or even coughed, Mathilde was half out of her chair on the instant.

Héloïse was unaware of the effect she was having on her ward. She was too uncomfortable to be aware of anything much outside her own body. The baby was very low in her belly, making any movement difficult and every position uncomfortable. She was afraid that her time was near. She didn't think she was going to last another week, and thought

179

of Lucy, still travelling up from Belvoir. She longed for her to arrive, and prayed that she would not be delayed by the condition of the roads, or by more bad weather.

James came in with a fresh hot-water-bottle which dear Barnard had filled for her, and tucked it under the crook of her knees. His cheeks were bright, and he smelled freshly of outdoors. He had just been as far as the Hare and Heather, more for the sake of the exercise than for any prime purpose, for the snow made him restless, and he couldn't settle indoors.

He asked how she was, and sat down beside her, holding her hand inside her muff. 'Well, I've brought you the news from the great wide world,' he said. 'Or perhaps I should say the great white world! It's so cold that a barrel of beer froze solid in the taproom of the Hare and Heather. Though judging by the number of people huddled together in there, I'm surprised it had a chance to freeze.'

Héloïse smiled at him, grateful for the cheering up. 'More,' she said simply, and he laughed.

'Some good news I gathered there — Louisa Anstey's had her baby. Another boy, born this morning, and they're calling it Henry, after its maternal grandfather. Louisa is said to have had an easy birth, and is comfortable, so that's a good omen for you, isn't it, my love?'

'Yes, my James, if you say so. What else?'

'Let me see — oh yes, that family of gypsies that were living down by Askham Bogs was found frozen to death — the whole family, right down to the dogs. Blackie from Marsh Farm found them when he was out looking for sheep. It seems they just ran out of firewood.'

'Oh, les pauvres!' Héloïse cried in distress, and Marie glared at him over her stitching. James saw that he had chosen his news badly, and looked awkward. Héloïse shifted her position uneasily and said, 'What was the road like, James? The great road, to the south?'

'It's hard to say,' James said. 'It looked passable as far as I could see, and some riders had come in from Tadcaster, but no coaches so far today.' He looked at her anxiously. 'Do you feel anything, love? Is it starting?'

'I don't know. I think it may be soon,' Héloïse said. 'I wish Lucy were here. Do you think she will get through?'

'If I know Lucy, she'll come even if she has to walk. But the road into York is all right, and if the worst comes to the worst, we can call in a midwife or a physician — both, if you like. Two physicians. You shall have anything you want.'

Héloïse smiled and squeezed his hand. 'I know. But what I want is Lucy.'

The pain began in the late afternoon, so gradually that by the time Héloïse became conscious of it, she had no knowledge of how long it had been going on. She had been waiting for the normal pains of birth, the strong, tightening pain that came suddenly, held on a while, and then faded. This pain was different: it did not fluctuate and it did not go away. Once started, the grinding ache went on and on.

'What is it, madame? Is it the baby?' Marie asked when Héloïse finally admitted to it.

'I don't know. It isn't like labour pains — just a long ache, like backache. It isn't very bad yet. Perhaps it will go away.'

'Perhaps it's indigestion,' Marie said hopefully. The short day was closing into night, and it would be in all ways better if the baby didn't come until the morning.

'Yes, perhaps,' Héloïse said. 'We'll wait a while, and see what happens.'

Mathilde listened to all this in silence, and then got up and slipped out of the room, and went to find the housekeeper. Mrs Scaggs had left shortly after Madame came to Morland Place — or rather, shortly after Barnard came to the Morland Place kitchens — and the new incumbent, Mrs Thomson, a ripely handsome local woman, was in all ways more pleasant and friendly.

'I don't know if it is the baby or not,' Mathilde explained, 'but at all events, Madame's room ought to be prepared.'

'You're right, Miss,' said Mrs Thomson. 'It would never do to have to do it at the last minute. I'll see to it straight away. I've kept the childbed linen handy this week past, and it only needs putting 'fore the fire a moment or two to air it. You leave all that to me. But I think you had better tell Mr James, Miss — not to worry him, but a message did ought to be sent for the midwife right away, for it'll take time for her to get here, and somebody ought to be on hand, in case her ladyship don't turn up. Which,' she added with a knowing look, 'it would be a miracle if she did with the roads the way they are,

181

if you'll pardon my frankness, Miss.'

'Lady Aylesbury left instructions what to do,' Mathilde said with dignity. 'I have them here. There's no need for a midwife. In any case, Madame is very much against having one.'

'Aye, I know all about them instructions, Miss, but believe you me, it doesn't look the same in real life as what it does on paper. To begin with, a piece of paper doesn't groan, nor yet it doesn't bleed. As for the mistress, she'll want a midwife right enough when the time comes. It's all very well for her ladyship: aside of having four — three children of her own,' she corrected herself hastily, 'she's brought all manner of creeturs into this world, which it's not what I would want for a lass o' mine, but there's no denying she does know what she's at. Which is more than you do, begging your pardon, Miss, but truth is truth, and there's lives at stake in this business. What would you do, Miss, if aught was to go wrong? Your piece of paper wouldn't help you then.'

Mathilde had paled at the first mention of groans and blood, and the thought of lives being at stake made the whole business look very different. 'Yes, you're right. Someone ought to be sent for,' she said when Thomson paused. 'I'll go and speak to Mr James at once.'

By the time the bedchamber was prepared and Héloïse had been helped into bed, she no longer had anything to say against the calling of a midwife. Despite the huge fire in the grate and the heavy curtains drawn across every door and window, the great bedchamber was bitterly cold, and James, coming in to see how Héloïse was, said, 'This is ridiculous! You'll freeze to death in this great barn of a room. Why didn't you have them make up the bed in the dressing-room? Or better still, we can make up a bed in the steward's room, which is already warm.'

But Héloïse wanted to have the baby in the Butts Bed. 'He will be a Morland, and I want him to be born in the Morlands' bed,' she said anxiously.

'It might be a girl,' James said, anxiety for her making him irritable. 'In any case, our child can't inherit. You know that. Morland Place goes to Fanny.'

'I know. But it's what Maman would have wanted. Please James.'

'Oh, if you're determined, I've nothing more to say,' he

said and went out. Héloïse bit her lip, but the continuous pain prevented her from feeling his ill-temper very much. And a short while later he returned, followed by two footmen carrying braziers. 'They may make the room smell a bit, but they'll take off some of the chill,' he said, leaning over the bed to kiss her contritely. 'And I know you didn't really want it, but I've sent for the midwife and the physician. I'm afraid it looks as though Lucy won't be here in time, Marmoset. You'll have to make up your mind to it.'

'Yes, I know. You were right to send for them, James,' she said wearily. 'Oh, please don't leave me. Stay and hold my hand. I feel better so.'

'Of course, darling,' he said, but looked so alarmed that she almost laughed.

'Oh, don't worry, nothing will happen for a long time yet.'

'I'll stay as long as you like,' he said, smiling. 'I was only thinking of your modesty. And how shocked the world would be if I were to witness my own child's birth.'

They didn't talk much. Each was desperately worried, and afraid of communicating that worry to the other. All through the pregnancy, James had thought longingly of the child, and had been horribly afraid that Héloïse would lose it; but now, seeing her in pain, he cared nothing about the baby, and would have sacrificed it cheerfully for Héloïse's sake. He wanted her whole and well: nothing else now mattered.

For Héloïse, very soon nothing mattered at all. The pain gradually filled her so that she was unable to think, or to be aware of anything else. She knew James was there, holding her hand, and was dimly aware of other people coming and going; but when James left her, she had no strength to protest, or even, really, to mind. The midwife had come and had dismissed him from this solely female province. Her face swam across Héloïse's vision, and her hand came down and rested on Héloïse's forehead.

'Naught doing yet, m'lady? By God, it's warmer in here, I can tell you, than anywhere else in Yorkshire this night! But don't you worry — you're in safe hands now. I delivered a babby yesterday, a fine little boy, quick as you like. We'll do well enough when the time comes.'

Héloïse was grateful for the reassurance, and wanted to know whose child it was, but hadn't the strength to ask.

183

Time ceased to exist. The room was cold and stuffy, dark, lit with candles. The physician came, examined her with hands both cold and rough, and pronounced that there was nothing for him to do here until the waters broke. They should call him again, he said, at the proper time. They gave her bread and milk to keep up her strength, but she brought it up again a little while later; easily, like a dog.

'Thirsty,' she said later. The midwife leaned over to look into her face. Her breath smelled of gin; but after all, it was very cold, and the night was very long. 'Thirsty.' The midwife gave her a drink of water, which tasted of tiredness and sickness and aching, but she soon brought it up again. Would the night never end?

No, it wasn't night any more. There was daylight in the far end of the room, though the candles still burned near the bed. The day was a dark one.

'Is it snowing?' Héloïse asked.

'No, Madame.' That was Mathilde beside her. 'It's a little milder outside.'

She dozed, and woke in alarm. 'James!'

'My lady?' Marie leaned over her. Beyond her, the midwife dozed in a chair. It was dark again.

'Is the baby born?'

'No, my lady.'

'What time is it?'

'Just after six, my lady. Could you eat a little broth?'

Héloïse turned her head away fretfully. 'I feel sick.' Marie fetched the basin, but nothing happened, and the nausea gradually passed. The pain was everywhere now, filling the room, pressing the walls out of shape.

'This'll never do: we're getting nowhere. It's high time we broke them waters to hasten things along,' the midwife said. She got to work, dilating the external parts to insert her hand and rupture the membrane. It was painful, a different kind of pain from the one Héloïse had got used to, and she resented it, and wept a little. Then she felt a tremendous warm rush, and she cried out in terror, thinking she was bleeding again.

'No, m'lady, it's only the waters,' the midwife said. 'Now we shall have some movement. You'll get relief soon, m'lady.

It's been a tedious long labour for us all.'

But nothing happened for a long time; the candles burnt down and were replaced. 'What time is it?' Héloïse asked. Her lips were dry and when she tried to wet them, the tip of her tongue stuck to the skin.

'Nearly eight o'clock, Madame,' said Mathilde. Héloïse wondered if it were eight in the morning, or eight in the evening.

'Which day?'

'It's Tuesday, Madame, Tuesday morning.' She had been in labour since Sunday afternoon.

'Is it snowing?'

'Not now, Madame.'

Did that mean it had been snowing, she wondered? Lucy would never get through. But suddenly the pain was gone, and in its place a contraction; a strong, normal contraction. Héloïse's eyes flew open. Oh, thank God! The baby was coming at last.

'It's coming!' she cried, but the midwife was already there.

'Right you are, m'lady. Told you so, didn't I? Out of the way, please, Miss. Let t'dog see the rabbit.'

'Shouldn't we send for the physician?'

'Lord, no, Miss, I know well enough what to do. We'll soon have the babby out and in its cot now.'

But something was wrong. The contractions came, but nothing moved. Héloïse knew it, and her fear made her sweat, despite the cold, despite her thirst.

'What's wrong?' she asked, but no-one heard her. Then she heard Mathilde's voice.

'What's that?'

'It's a hand, Miss.' The midwife, grim, displeased. 'Bloody thing's put an arm down. Now we've our work cut out.'

Oh, it was an agony. The midwife cajoled, bullied, encouraged, and whenever Héloïse bore down as instructed, she pulled on the offending arm, but the baby wouldn't come. Héloïse was growing weaker, she knew, worn out with pain and effort, and soon she wouldn't be able to push any more. For the first time, she knew she was going to die, and she felt a terrible despair. She didn't want to die like this, not like this, leaving James, failing him.

'Oh God, help me. Oh Lady Mother, help me,' she prayed.

185

Later again, and the thought of death no longer alarmed her. She was sinking into darkness, and in the darkness there was relief from the pain and exhaustion. If only they would leave her alone. If only James would come.

'Marie,' she whispered. 'Bring James. Bring Father Aislaby.' But no-one heard her.

A long time later. They had sent for the physician: she heard his voice. 'That arm will have to come off, then the head. Then we can deliver the rest.' Someone said something inaudible. 'No, no, it's dead of course. I doubt whether we can even save the mother, but we must try.'

The baby — she had killed the baby. Even that comfort would be denied James when she died. She turned her head on the pillow, and weak tears broke from her eyes — only two, for she had no moisture left in her body.

'Father, help me,' she prayed inwardly. 'Oh James, I'm sorry.'

And then the miracle happened. Into the dim and smoky room, blood-smelling, filled with despair and pain and death, where the physician was already preparing his grisly tools to deliver not a warm, living child, but a heap of bloody pieces, came a gust of cold, clean air, and a strong, wild voice cried out, 'What the devil is going on here!'

Héloïse knew that voice. She opened her eyes, turned her head gladly towards it.

'Lucy! Oh Lucy!'

'Dear God alive, what a mess! Where's James? I told him not to let them — for God's sake, why did he let this butcher in here? Yes, sir, I said butcher! You look exactly like one, with your crotchets and knives! Get out this instant! And you, you hag! Parslow, escort the good doctor and his moll out of the house. Docwra, look to her ladyship. You, Mathilde, go and tell James he's not to let any more of these quacks in. Here, take my cloak. Marie, bring me soap and water, and some kind of salve — pomatum, goose-grease, anything.'

The strong voice, pouring strength into her; movement and voices; relief, a sense of oppression passing away. Lucy was here! She was leaning over the bed now, saying, 'Dear God, Héloïse, what have they been doing to you?'

'Dear Lucy! You've come! Now I can die in peace,' she whispered.

CHAPTER TEN

'Stuff! You're not going to die, now I've got here,' Lucy said briskly. 'You'll never know what a terrible journey I've had! I had to do the last half on horseback — I've been in the saddle for ten hours today. I almost turned back a dozen times, but I had a feeling somehow — Well, anyway, I've arrived, and if you die now, you'll make me look nohow, so I won't allow it. Let's have a look at you. It's all right,' as Héloïse flinched, 'I won't hurt you any more.'

Héloïse felt the hands on her — small hands this time, icy cold, but gentle.

Lucy grunted. 'It's a shoulder present. Some fool has been pulling on this arm, trying to deliver the baby that way.'

'The midwife,' said Docwra, looking over her shoulder. 'I had it out o' her on the stairs. Hours and hours she's been pullin' away at it, like a sailor on a rope. What do you think, my lady?'

It looked bad enough, Lucy thought. The baby's arm, protruding from the vulva, was swollen and misshapen; and the tissues of the vulva itself were engorged and painful-looking.

'The ignorance of these people,' she muttered angrily. 'Docwra, give me a pin, or a needle or something.' Docwra passed her a needle, and she stuck it into one of the baby's fingers, and saw, to her relief, the starfish reaction of the hand.

'Thank God for that,' she said. She leaned over Héloïse, smoothing the damp hair from the cold forehead. Héloïse opened her eyes, and Lucy spoke slowly and clearly, holding her attention. 'Listen, Héloïse, I'm going to turn the baby inside you and bring it out by the feet. I'd like to give you time to rest first, but I'm afraid the baby might not be able to stand any more delay.'

'The baby — alive?'

'Yes, it's alive.'

187

Héloïse closed her eyes with relief. 'The doctor said it was dead.'

'Much he knows! Everything's going to be all right now. The baby's still alive, and there's a chance it will survive, if we work quickly. You must help me all you can by pushing when I tell you to.'

Héloïse nodded slightly, gathering herself for the effort.

'Right, Docwra, let's get these covers off, so that I can see what I'm doing,' said Lucy, but as she and her maid took the folded-back mass of sheets and blankets, Marie intervened with a cry of distress.

'No, what are you doing? You must not!'

Lucy straightened and fixed the maid with a steely eye. 'Listen, Marie, you can take your provincial prudery and leave, or you can stay and help, I don't care which. But I'm not going to work groping about under blankets because you have some misplaced sense of modesty about my seeing your mistress's body. Do you think she cares now?'

Not tactful, Docwra thought, as Marie mottled up with anger. She intervened placatingly. 'Don't mind my lady,' she whispered, putting a hand on Marie's arm. 'She's had a hard day. Would you like to keep Miss Mathilde out of the way? I don't think she ought to be seeing this sort o' thing. You could get the linen ready between you. It's best if I help my lady — I know her ways.'

She edged Marie gently but firmly out of the way, winked conspiratorially at Mathilde, and then returned, her expression grim, to her mistress's side. She knew both the gravity of the situation, and how much hard work was ahead of Lucy — and when she was already exhausted from her five-day journey across snow-bound England. Had it not been freezing hard, they would not have made it at all. Many times Lucy urged Docwra to stay behind — she not being much of a horsewoman, and not the shape for it either — but Docwra wouldn't leave her. Her behind felt like brawn now; she was glad to be standing up, and not to have icicles hanging from her nose. That was about the sum of what she had to be thankful for: that, and the fact that they had arrived before her poor ladyship and the infant were dead.

'Ready now, my lady,' she said.

'At least,' Lucy said with oblique humour, 'it's easier with humans than with horses.'

It was a long and gruelling task. Firstly she took up the pomatum Marie had brought. The waters must have come away long ago, she thought: everything was both dry and swollen. The infant's engorged arm, the surrounding tissues, her own hand and arm, must all be lubricated, and then, seating herself on the low stool the midwife had been using, she began to insert her hand, working it inch by inch past the prolapsed arm towards the cervix. There was no thought of embarrassment in her mind, or that what she was doing was both unnatural and wrong. Héloïse was no longer Héloïse: she was a medical case, more interesting than one in a book, but as academic.

'Lord, you'd have made a fine doctor, if only you'd been a man,' Docwra breathed. It had taken some getting used to, to see her mistress behave so far out of her sex, but in the last thirteen years Docwra had helped her sew up wounds, draw teeth, deliver babies, and God knew what else, and she had come at last to feel pride in her skills, rather than horror at her shamelessness.

Despite Héloïse's exhaustion, her muscular contractions were still strong — sign of the human body's astonishing resilience, Lucy thought. Her job was now to repel the baby against those contractions, turning it in the womb far enough to be able to draw the feet down. Despite the bitter cold in the room, she was soon sweating with the exertion, and again and again Docwra reached over to wipe her face with a napkin. There was a complete silence now, apart from the sounds of breathing, and even Marie and Mathilde, overcoming their distaste, had drawn near to watch the tense battle with nature. Mathilde alone had a thought to spare for the men waiting below for news, ignorant of everything that was happening. She did think of slipping down to reassure them, but could not quite bring herself to leave the scene. Everything seemed so perilously poised, that she felt superstitiously as though any change might cause a disaster.

Then, at long last, Lucy gave a long groan of accomplishment. 'That's it!'

'My lady?'

'It's round. I've got the feet. Now, Héloïse, we're almost done. Can you hear me?'

'Yes.' It was no more than a whisper.

'When you're ready, bear down as hard as you can. I'll help you. Two or three good pushes should do it.'

Marie hastened to take her mistress's hand, and gripping it with astonishing strength, Héloïse pushed, while Lucy drew firmly on the baby's feet.

'Again, Héloïse.' The tiny purple feet emerged from the vulva, and Lucy paused to wind a strip of linen round them, to give herself better purchase, and to save damage to the fragile extremities. 'And again. And once more!'

The long body slithered free, the pulsing cord rising up from the centre like some exotic jungle creeper. With her fingers under the infant's neck Lucy waited, until at last Héloïse strained again, and she finally guided the head out in a rush of blood. Docwra regarded the baby anxiously. It was a bad colour, and apart from the still-swollen arm, it looked misshapen. Lucy examined it quickly. She cleared the mouth of mucus with a finger, and it gave a little crowing gasp. She tied and cut the cord, and passed it over to Docwra.

'No dislocation, at least. Here. Keep it warm.'

Héloïse was trying to lift her head. 'Lucy — the baby — is it all right?'

'Yes,' Lucy said tersely. 'A boy.'

'A boy!' Héloïse whispered. She let her head fall back on the pillow, and smiled. To Marie, her face seemed transfigured. 'Can I see him?'

'In a minute,' Lucy said. 'Let me attend to you first.'

'A boy, Marie! I'm so glad. James will be glad. A son!'

Ten minutes later the placenta was delivered, and Lucy was able to get up at last, grunting with the pain in her muscles. Apart from the saddle-soreness and stiffness from crouching so long in a cold room, her arms and shoulders were aching abominably, and the fingers of her right hand were stiff and painful. She knew that by tomorrow they would be swollen up like an old woman's, and she'd have no use of them for a day or two.

She crossd the room, and looked down at the long, purplish baby on Docwra's lap. It looked small and frail; it was a wonder it had survived the long ordeal. 'How is it?'

'All right now,' Docwra said with some pride. 'He stopped breathing a while back, but I foxed him! I turned him upside

190

down and gave him a little shake and a skelp, and he's back with us now.'

'We'd better shew it to Héloïse, or she'll think we're hiding something from her,' Lucy said. 'She's already worried that it hasn't cried.'

'Ah, sure God, the poor little creature's exhausted. He hasn't the strength to cry, till he's had a sleep,' Docwra said, getting up. They took the baby back to Héloïse, who had sunk into an exhausted doze; but she woke when they approached, and took the baby into her arms with the look of unearthly joy which Lucy never saw on a human face except at such a moment. It made it all seem worthwhile, just for a moment.

'He's lovely,' Héloïse whispered. 'My son!' She kissed the mottled face reverently, and then said, 'Tell James! He must be so worried.'

'Yes. I'll tell him,' Lucy said.

'We'll get you cleaned up, my lady,' Docwra said, 'and give the little fellow a bit of a wash, and then Mr James can come up and tell you himself what he thinks of it all. Here now, Miss, would you like to take the baby and sponge him over, while Marie and me see to her ladyship?'

Lucy went downstairs. On her way to the steward's room she halted, and turned back and went into the drawing-room where there were always several decanters on the side-table. She had thought of wine, but seeing the brandy, decided she needed something a little more stiffening, poured herself a generous measure into a glass, and raised it to the empty air. She thought of Morgan Proom, the old horse-doctor who had been her mentor and teacher when she was a little girl longing to be a doctor. He had always celebrated after a difficult case with a large quantity of smuggled brandy — in his case, usually a bottle or two.

'To you, Morgan, wherever you are,' she said with a quirky grin. 'You taught me well. May your instruments never rust!'

She swallowed, coughed a little, and then headed for the steward's room.

The scene within might have made her laugh, had she been less tired. The three men were crouched miserably over the fire, their feet under the two dogs, and as she came in, five pairs of melancholy eyes rolled up at her. Of course, not having heard the baby cry, they would think the worst. Father

Aislaby's hand reached automatically for the cross hanging against his chest, Edward looked as though he might cry at any moment, and James looked exhausted beyond fear or grief.

'It's all right,' she said, and Father Aislaby, quicker witted than the other two, closed his eyes with relief, crossed himself, amd mouthed a short prayer. The other two simply stared at her. 'It's a boy,' Lucy said. 'They're both all right. James, do you hear me?'

'Héloïse — she's alive?' he said blankly.

'Yes — no thanks to that quack you brought in! I warned you, Jamie.'

'You weren't here — what could I do?' he cried in distress. 'Someone had to be with her. The midwife's got a good reputation.'

'Oh well,' Lucy shrugged, seeing there was no point in berating him, 'I got here in time, that's the main thing.'

'And the baby?'

'It's had a hard time of it, but there's no reason why it shouldn't survive — no more reason than usual. You can go up and see them both in a minute, when Docwra's cleaned them up a bit.'

'We must drink their health,' Edward said, reviving slowly as the news sank in. He rang the bell by the fireplace. 'A boy! That's wonderful. Congratulations, Jamie. Mother would be so pleased.'

'I'll make arrangements for the baptism,' Aislaby said. 'It had better be done immediately, I suppose? Is the child strong enough to be brought down to the chapel?'

Lucy shrugged. 'In an hour or so, yes.'

The door opened, and Ottershaw stood there, a little out of breath from hurrying, his face twitching with the effort not to ask for news.

Edward took pity on him. 'Ottershaw, her ladyship has been delivered of a boy. You may tell the other servants — and bring a bottle of the Clicquot, please. We want to drink the baby's health.'

'Oh, thank God, sir! My congratulations, sir, on behalf of all the servants, sir.' Ottershaw looked genuinely delighted. 'May I ask how it is with her ladyship?'

'She's well enough,' Lucy answered for him. 'Tired. You

might ask Barnard to prepare something light for her. And something more substantial for me — I don't remember when I last ate, and I feel as limp as a bootlace.'

'Of course, your ladyship. With pleasure. At once,' Ottershaw said, unusually effusive.

'And you may wet the baby's head in the servants' hall too, Ottershaw,' Edward added as he turned to go. 'Open something suitable. I leave it to you.'

'Thank you, sir.'

'There'll be some smiling faces in the servants' quarters,' Aislaby commented when the butler had gone. 'They all love her ladyship very much.'

'I just hope Barnard doesn't collapse with joy before making me some supper,' Lucy said dourly. 'Jamie, will you step outside — I have to talk to you privately for a moment.'

Outside in the hallway, she faced her brother, seeing by the light of the sconce beside the chapel door how drawn he looked. He had aged in the last few days. His eyes were meshed round with fine lines, and there was a glitter of silver here and there in the chestnut hair which she'd never noticed before. I keep forgetting, she thought, that we're none of us children any more.

'What is it?' he asked. 'Is she really all right? Don't hide anything from me, Luce.'

'She's had a hard time of it,' Lucy said. She paused a moment. There was no way of telling a man, other than an *accoucheur*, how hard it had been. 'She's exhausted, but there's no reason why she shouldn't recover.'

'And the baby?'

Lucy shrugged. 'I don't know. It's always touch and go after a hard delivery. It's not very robust, but it's got a good chance, if it's nursed properly. But that's not what I wanted to say to you.'

'Well, then?' he said impatiently.

'You understand that to deliver the baby I had to pass my hand into the womb?' James looked away in embarrassment. 'I discovered that it's abnormal. This may be because of something that happened when Sophie was born, or it may have always been like that. You see, her pelvis is very small and narrow, and the lowest three vertebrae project —'

James interrupted, his face still averted. 'I don't understand

193

your medical talk. What are you trying to tell me?'

'She may not be able to conceive again. If she does, she may not carry to term. I'm only surprised that she's had two children already.'

James was silent a while. Then, 'Have you told her this?'

'Not yet. I thought you might want to tell her yourself.' He nodded, biting his lip, beginning to turn away. 'But Jamie — wait. I haven't finished.' He met her eyes reluctantly. 'She may or may not be able to conceive — I don't know. But I'm quite sure she *ought* not to.'

'You mean —?'

'I had the deuce of a job bringing the child round. Another time I might not be here — or the child might be bigger — or she might be weaker. Do you understand what I'm telling you? She ought not to have another baby. She's not formed for it. It might kill her.'

James nodded, looking very old. 'Yes, I understand.'

'Will you tell her, or do you want me to?'

'I'll talk to her. Thanks, Lucy.'

Footsteps across the hall heralded Ottershaw with champagne and glasses on a tray, and a broad smile on his face, followed by a footman with a tray of food.

'Your supper, my lady. Everyone in the servant's hall is delighted with the news, sir. When you see her ladyship, sir, would it be too much trouble to convey to her our respectful congratulations?'

'Yes. Very well, Ottershaw,' James said shortly.

And as he spoke, the house bell began to ring: the quick double strokes for a birth. They were muffled here in the hall, but outside they would be ringing clearly in the dark icy air across the white fields, to tell the villagers and tenants and estate workers the glad news, that another Morland had been born at Morland Place.

The baby was frail; so frail that, once he had seen it, James felt despairingly that there was no point in giving it a name. Aislaby performed an immediate baptism — in the bedchamber after all, so that Héloïse could witness it — and James thought that there would probably never be a christening. The child had breathing problems, and had to be revived several times in the first two days. Lucy, having no pipette,

194

used her wits and sent to the kitchen for a piece of macaroni, and shewed Sarah how to pull the infant's tongue forward, and blow through the tube down its throat until it began breathing again.

The cold was also a problem for a child so weak. There was no place warm enough for it to be left, so Héloïse kept it in bed with her in the crook of her arm, except when she handed it over to Sarah to change. Though she was the junior nursery-maid, it was Sarah who took charge of the baby, for Jenny had an aversion to it, thinking it ugly and malformed. It's right arm was still grotesquely swollen, and its face was misshapen, though Lucy assured them that its features would straighten out of their own accord in a few days.

Héloïse loved holding her child, but she was too weak to feed him, so a wet-nurse had to be found, one who was willing to live in. After two days of fruitless enquiries, Mrs Thomson produced a girl from Huntsham Farm, out near Harewood Whin. How she had come to hear of her was a mystery, but the girl was a dairymaid of fifteen who had become pregnant and refused to name her seducer. The farmer and his wife, finding her useful, had allowed her to stay on, and she had recently given birth to a male infant, which had died soon afterwards. They were now only too glad to be rid of her, since in her delicate condition so soon after childbirth, she was no longer able to go out and tend the cows.

The girl's name was Matty, and once Héloïse had seen what beautiful, clear skin she had, she was quite willing for her to take over the feeding of the baby. Sarah was happy also to yield up the business of changing it, though she still watched over it jealously, not believing the ex-dairymaid would not have the sense to tell whether it was breathing normally or not.

Matty did not seem to find her new charge ugly or deformed. She had been desperately miserable when her own baby died, and had feared that the farmer's wife would turn her out into the snow at any moment. Morland Place seemed a haven of luxury to her, and understanding that her remaining there depended on the baby's survival, she lavished as much care on it as Héloïse would have herself.

'Hasn't he got a name, my lady?' she asked on her second day when she brought him in to shew to Héloïse.

James, who was sitting on the edge of the bed holding his wife's hand in a way that Matty thought truly pretty, mused that the dairymaid had cleaned up quite well. With her plain blue nursemaid's dress and white apron and cap, she looked rather fetching. 'Not yet, Matty,' he said kindly. 'We weren't sure if he was going to stay with us, you see.'

Matty's mouth made an 'o' of distress. 'Oh, never say that, sir! He's coming on right well now, the little daystar! Look what a pretty colour he's getting! He's going to grow into a big, strong man, aren't you, my precious, my baby lamb?'

She bowed her head over the baby, smiling, and the wavering eyes looked back at her. Dark blue, they were. She proffered the baby to Héloïse. 'See, my lady, he's going to have black eyes, just like yours,' she said beguilingly. 'He did ought to have a name, my lady.'

'Yes, you're right,' Héloïse smiled. Looking at the baby still gave her almost as much pain as pleasure, for he looked so pathetic and frail, and he never cried, as though even that effort were beyond him. 'But what name?'

'We could call him Henry, after your father, if you like,' James said — a little tactlessly, since his son by his first wife had been called Henry, though he had forgotten that for the moment. But Matty saved Héloïse from replying.

'Oh no, sir,' she exclaimed, her adoration of the child making her bold. 'Begging your pardon, sir, he doesn't look anything like a Henry.'

'What does he look like?' James asked indulgently.

Matty touched the tiny mauve cheek with one fingertip. 'He's a Nicholas, sir, sure as I'm a Christian. It's writ on his face. Only look at him, sir! He's a little Nicholas for sure!'

James caught Héloïse's eye, and she smiled. 'Well, my James, it is a good saint's name. A winter saint.'

'As you please, my love,' James said, still unsure that it was going to make any difference in the long run. 'Nicholas it is.'

When the baby was a fortnight old, Héloïse got up for the first time. The bitter cold had loosened its grip on the land at last, and the thaw had come, transforming the glittering, frightening world of ice into a more familiar and tedious scene of grey skies, fog, dripping trees and gutters, and oceans of mud. Coughs and colds replaced chilblains and frostbite as the universal ills, and the servants who had complained that they couldn't keep the house warm now complained that they couldn't keep it clean.

Héloïse, however, was brimming over with good spirits. She had recovered very well from the ordeal of childbirth, and since baby Nicholas had also survived his hazardous first fortnight, and was looking both more healthy and more pretty, she felt that all was well with the world.

She got up after breakfast, and insisted on having a proper bath and washing her hair for the first time since she went into labour. Marie was doubtful of the wisdom of it, and Héloïse did find it more tiring than she had expected, but the fatigue was more than compensated for by the feeling of freshness.

James came up to see her, and found her being dressed in a very becoming gown of fine wool the colour of holly-leaves

'My love, you've got up! Did Lucy say you could?' he exclaimed.

Héloïse laughed. 'I am not a child, James, to be told when I can get out of bed!'

He examined her critically. 'You look rested. Are you sure you feel strong enough?'

'I feel wonderful!' she said. 'Oh James, let us have the christening tonight. I feel so well and hopeful. Can it be arranged in time, do you think?'

'Of course it can, though we shan't be able to have many guests. There are fifteen fathoms of mud outside. But I'm sure the Ansteys will come. Shall we ask John Anstey to be godfather?'

'Oh yes! He is such a good, kind man. And Lucy for godmother, don't you think?'

'Yes, of course,' James said, but his mind was no longer on the christening. He bit his lip. 'Listen, Marmoset, there's something I have to tell you.' He took her hands and led her to the sopha at the foot of the bed, and sat down with her.

Héloïse cocked her head at him questioningly. 'But what a serious face! What is it, *mon âme*? Do you fear for my health? Do not, I beg you. I am very well. Quite well.'

'It is your health I want to talk to you about.' He paused, drawing his courage together, holding her gaze with his. 'You had a very hard time of it with the new baby. Lucy tells me that it is a miracle you had him at all. You are not formed for childbearing, my love — that's what Lucy says.'

'But James —!'

'I don't understand the details of it,' he went on determinedly. 'I know nothing of these things. But Lucy knows what she's talking about; and she says there must never be another.'

Her eyes were stricken. 'No, James. No. Don't say it.'

'I must say it. We have two children, Marmoset, and that must be enough for us.'

'But James, I love you so —'

'I love you too. For God's sake, don't you see? How could I risk your health — your life, even — by allowing you to have another child? It mustn't be. I couldn't live without you. God knows —'

Héloïse pressed his hands comfortingly. 'Yes, yes, you are right. He knows. So we will leave it to God, James. Let it be His decision.'

He drew his hands away, anxiety making him irritable, and said impatiently, 'God gave us minds of our own! He gave us the intelligence to choose for ourselves and take care of ourselves.'

'Some things we can't choose about,' she said stubbornly.

He stared at her, frustrated. 'Not true,' he cried. 'Our lives are in our own hands. You can't just sit down and let things happen to you, like some dumb beast of the field. Where's your spirit?'

'Where is your faith?' she countered resentfully. There was a silence, and they looked at each other, shocked. It was the nearest they had ever come to quarrelling. Héloïse began again, but quietly. 'James, do you want for us never to make love again?'

'No, of course not. What a question. You know how I feel about you.'

'And I feel the same way about you. Do you think we can lie together every night and never act our love again? I don't think so.'

'We must, if it's a matter of your safety,' he said doggedly. But she smiled at him, her eyes glowing, and he found himself once more up against that shining, transparent, impenetrable barrier of faith which had separated him from his mother,

198

and from time to time separated him from her. It was unreasonable and beautiful, sustaining and frustrating; it was an endless strength and a terrible weakness, and there was no arguing against it.

'I am not afraid, my James,' she said. 'God sees us: He knows best. We will just have to let Him decide the issue.' Her smile became mischievous. 'And that is a joke in English, is it not?'

During the day the wind got up and changed direction, clearing away the fog and grey clouds. The temperature dropped again, but the brisk breeze dried out the land most satisfactorily, promising the invited guests a better journey to Morland Place, and moonlight to go home by.

Monsieur Barnard had laboured all day to prepare a feast which would not utterly shame him. It was fortunate that, expecting the summons from moment to moment, he had made the cake over a week ago, so he had only to cover and decorate it. It was maturing nicely. He had been feeding it daily with brandy from a dropper, brooding over it as though it were some orphaned fledgeling he had determined to raise by hand.

Héloïse, aware of the notorious sensitivity of cooks, had gone herself to the kitchen to tell Barnard that the christening was to be that day.

'It is short notice, I know,' she said apologetically, 'but there will not be many guests: Lord and Lady Anstey, Mr and Mrs Pobgee, and Sir Arthur and Lady Fussell — and ourselves. Fourteen in all, for the children will dine with us today.'

Barnard drew himself up to his full five-feet-four and expanded his noble chest. 'For you, my lady,' he said fiercely, 'everything is possible. Invite twenty — forty — I shall not fail you!'

Héloïse smiled. 'I know you won't. Thank you, Monsieur Barnard, from my heart. Is there anything I can do to help you? If you wish anything brought from the city, someone shall be sent at once.'

'I need nothing,' he said sternly. 'For such an occasion, I make everything myself. I have been waiting only for the word.'

He stood proudly to attention until she had left, and waited until the swing door between the kitchen and the buttery passage had come completely to rest before flying to his receipt books and screaming for the kitchen-maids.

When everyone sat down to dinner at five o'clock, the two full courses set before them would have defied anyone to guess it was a last-minute affair. There was chestnut soup and oyster stew removed with a handsome chicken pie and a cod's head, to which Barnard knew Mr Pobgee had a partiality; there was carp in fennel sauce, pigeons with peas, a smoked saddle of venison with high sauce, roasted sweetbreads — Edward's favourites — buttered oranges, and apricot pudding. Then for the second course there was a veal galantine, a roast capon, a dish of creamed celery, mutton with redcurrant sauce, a pistachio cream, curd tarts, and Lucy's favourite cheesecakes.

James felt much more cheerful when he saw with what good appetite Héloïse ate; and he applied himself to be charming to Mrs Pobgee, the lawyer's wife, who was on his right. On his left was Louisa Anstey, who was practically a sister to him: it was no effort to talk to her. She was looking remarkably well after her own recent delivery, and she ate everything that came her way, while defying elegance by chatting comfortably across the table with Miss Rosedale about child-rearing.

Arthur Fussell drank deeply of the claret, and talked to Edward about hunting.

'There's never been a season with so few outings,' he said. 'Even my heavyweight has been out only twice, and my youngster's never even seen hounds. How the deuce have you kept your pack exercised, Morland?'

'It's been difficult,' Edward admitted. 'We've had to walk them whenever we could. But the ground's drying out so well, I think we shall be able to hunt tomorrow at last. It may be rather muddy, but not impossible.'

Father Aislaby said, 'You could do worse than draw the copse out at Turn Mire. I hear Mr Rodwell of Acomb Grange has been complaining about a big dog-fox. It's been taking his ducks with impunity these four weeks.'

'The horses won't be fit. Still you have to start somewhere,' Edward said. 'You'll come out, won't you, Lucy?'

'If you can find me something to ride,' Lucy said. 'I might as well have one outing before I go home.'

'Oh, are you going back to London?' Lizzie Fussell said, disappointed. 'I was hoping we might have the pleasure of your company at Fussell Manor for dinner next week.'

'I'll come out, Uncle Ned, on Honey,' Fanny said eagerly.

'Well, if you want her laid up for the rest of the season with a sprained shoulder, so be it,' Ned said unkindly.

John Anstey and Mr Pobgee were discussing politics.

'You can tell by that report in the *Moniteur* — you must have seen it? — that Spain is Boney's next object,' Pobgee said. 'He openly attacks the Queen of Spain and her lover — what's his name — Godoy? All his usual rhetoric, the unrestrained language. He means to enter Spain as a deliverer, welcomed by the populace. You mark my words — it's Poland all over again.'

'You're right, of course,' Anstey said, 'but Canning thinks — and I agree with him — that Spain is only a step in a greater plan. The East is his real object: he believes it's the true source of our power. I believe he means to make a two-pronged attack, round the two sides of the Mediterranean. Spain is Boney's doorway to Africa, and from there he can march through Egypt to India, while attacking from the other direction through Turkey and the Levant.'

'Oh can he, by God?'

'That's what he believes, anyway. Of course, he has to get past our navy.'

'Your son is with Collingwood in the Mediterranean, I believe?'

Lucy caught the name and looked across at John. 'Have you had news from Little John? How is it with Coll?'

'Not well,' Anstey answered down the table. 'He's been ill again, and he's very tired. He wrote asking to be relieved, but of course we can't spare him. There's too much movement in Sicily and Corfu.'

'Where is your brother Harry at the moment?' Mrs Pobgee asked James. 'The last I heard he was on detached duty at Gibraltar.'

Silver clinked against china; candlelight winked in the prism of cut glass. Ottershaw stood massive and watchful at the serving-table, directing the ballet of service with imperceptible

201

gestures. The footmen in their white gloves removed dishes and changed plates so deftly they were almost invisible. Héloïse watched it all while chatting to her neighbours, noting how well the training of the servants was paying off, her senses stretched for the 'feel' of the party. Was it a success? Was everyone happy? Was Arthur Fussell drinking too much?

'They have silk stockings at Remington's at twelve shillings the pair,' Lady Fussell was saying to Héloïse. 'I do think it's shocking, the price they are these days. I suppose it's the war,' she added vaguely.

'Enderby's had cotton ones at three and elevenpence, the last time I was there,' Mathilde offered. 'Miss Keating thought them a great bargain, and bought three pairs. She said they were very well-knit.'

'Oh, but I do prefer silk. I had sooner have only two pairs of silk stockings, than half a dozen of cotton.'

Past the barrier of the vast silver epergne in the centre of the table — Mr Hobsbawn's gift for Fanny's christening long ago — James caught Héloïse's eye and winked, and she smiled her sudden smile. All was well.

'Four of mine are down at once with epidemic colds,' Louisa was saying to Mrs Pobgee, 'and I suppose the baby will have it next, for my nursery-maid was sneezing over him this morning.'

'I sometimes think, though, that it's best for them to get whatever is about, and get it over with,' Mrs Pobgee said comfortably. 'I remember my poor husband coming down with the chickenpox a few years back, because he had never had them as a child; and very uncomfortable they were for him, too, poor creature!' She smiled affectionately at her husband, who caught the look and smiled back without interrupting his flow.

'But the Crown Prince, Ferdinand, is very popular with the Spanish people,' he was saying. 'If Boney removes the King and Queen and helps Ferdinand onto the throne, I doubt if anyone will resist him.'

'Another puppet king, and not just Spain, but Spanish South America too, in Boney's pocket,' Aislaby remarked. 'Things can hardly get any worse, can they?'

'He'll over-stretch himself one day; he's bound to,' Anstey said, though without much hope in his voice. 'Until then, we must just go on resisting. Our new Orders in Council are going to bite Boney, and bite him hard. We're automatically blockading every port he's banned us from, and any neutral ship that touches them will have to pay a freight duty to us, or else have its cargo contrabanded. As long as we hold the seas, we won't give in. Collingwood says the Mediterranean's virtually empty of trading ships. He says the waters have become a desert.'

Stephen drifted up to refill Héloïse's glass, and a silent query and reassurance passed between them through the telepathy shared by a good servant and mistress. By leaving a calculated space at the top of Sir Arthur Fussell's glass, and by being always at the other end of the table when it was empty, he was slowing down his rate of drinking considerably.

'But it's so important that they should learn good, plain needlework,' Louisa said earnestly to Miss Rosedale. 'I know I learned astronomy along with my brother Jack when we were young, and I don't remember the name of a single star; but I hem every one of John's shirts myself. I wouldn't trust them to anyone else.'

'Astronomy and needlework both have their value,' Miss Rosedale said diplomatically. 'I don't believe any knowledge is ever wasted: I would recommend everyone to learn everything they can.'

When dinner was over, Louisa and Lizzie and Héloïse went up to the nursery to see the baby got ready, while Father Aislaby prepared the chapel, and at eight o'clock the ceremony began. Nicholas was brought down in the lace-trimmed robe and embroidered shawl in which his father, his aunt Lucy, and his half-sister Fanny had all been christened, and on his behalf John Anstey, Mr Pobgee and Lucy renounced the Devil and all his works. Father Aislaby scooped the holy water over Nicholas's bony forehead, and Nicholas frowned and clenched his fists, but did not cry. Matty, hovering anxiously in the background, twitched with anxiety to take him back, and when allowed at last to have him, hurried him away before the female guests had had half enough chance to coo over him.

Then everyone returned to the drawing-room, and the cake was brought in on a wheeled table, since it was too heavy conveniently to be carried. Héloïse cut it, and champagne was poured, and everyone drank the health of the newest Morland – except for Fanny who, restricted like Sophie to lemonade, merely drank.

James caught her eye across the room, and lifted his glass to her with a particularly loving smile. He was remembering his own feelings when Fanny had been born, and later, when she had been christened. He had been the outsider then; it had been him and Fanny against the world; and though he now had the woman of his heart for a wife, and two other darling children, nothing could quite erase the memory of that particular closeness.

'Here's another toast,' he said abruptly, arresting the murmur of conversation which had broken out. 'To Miss Fanny Morland, of Morland Place. May she prove a worthy mistress of her inheritance.'

Fanny's cheeks glowed and her eyes shone with pleasure as everyone drank the toast; though Edward at least deplored James's judgement in proposing it, and Miss Rosedale watched her charge closely for any sign of over-excitement. But Fanny, for a wonder, only smiled, and looked almost modest. Héloïse was glad, and inwardly praised Miss Rosedale for the good effect she had had on Fanny; and then discovered Mr Pobgee watching her with a strange and thoughtful expression. His gaze was removed as soon as he saw she had noticed, but it disturbed her for a long time afterwards, while she tried to determine precisely what the look might have meant.

It was a pleasant party, and everyone had plenty to say, and it wasn't until quite late that Mrs Pobgee asked if their carriage might be called for, and the guests all took their leave. Only when they had gone did Jenny come into the drawing-room and approach Héloïse.

'I beg your pardon, my lady, but I think perhaps you had better come up to the nursery and have a look at Baby. I don't think he's quite well.'

BOOK TWO

The Young Princesses

And on that cheek, and o'er that brow,
So soft, so calm, yet eloquent,
The smiles that win, the tints that glow,
But tell of days in goodness spent,
A mind at peace with all below,
A heart whose love is innocent!

Lord Byron: *She Walks in Beauty*

CHAPTER ELEVEN

January 1811

Having taken a stroll in the Park to clear his head after a long session in the House, John Anstey walked to Upper Grosvenor Street to call on Lucy. He arrived just as she got back from a drive, and was about to enter the front door, with Thomas at her heels like a faithful hound.

'Is that your new team?' Anstey asked, looking with interest at the four handsome black horses harnessed to the curricle standing at the kerb. 'I haven't seen them before, though Tonbridge was talking about them at the club last night.'

'Yes,' said Lucy. 'I mean to race them against Carlyon's greys in a few weeks' time, when I've got the measure of them. Carlyon's been having it all his own way of late. It's time someone cut him down to size.'

Anstey grinned at this manly statement, so at odds with her small size and fashionable appearance. In her smart driving-coat with the Hussar frogging, and a very saucy *demi-bateau* hat, with a green hackle in the ribbon, she looked every inch a leader of the *ton*, and not more than five-and-twenty years old.

'If anyone can do it, you can,' he said, taking another critical look at the team as Parslow drove off towards the mews. 'I may have a few guineas on the race myself. They're certainly well-matched.'

'That's because they're all Morland bred,' Lucy replied. 'The wheelers came straight from home — I bought them from Edward a fortnight ago — but the leaders are the pair he sold to Robert Knaresborough last year.'

'And why has Knaresborough sold them to you? Don't say he's another one gone bankrupt! There've been so many failures this past year.'

'Lord, no! He'll be as rich as a nabob, now he's married the Fletcher fortune.'

'I thought it was a love-match? It was talked of as one.'

'Well, I don't say he isn't fond of Julia, but I hardly think he'd have married her without her fortune. A lot of the Knaresborough money was bound up in sugar, and you know how Boney's embargo has ruined the West India trade. The Fletcher fortune's very safe. Planters may fail; manufacturers may fail, for the matter of that; but brewers just go on getting richer and richer.'

John laughed. 'How caustic you are, dear Lucy! Don't you like the new Lady Knaresborough?'

Lucy looked surprised. 'I neither like her nor dislike her — she's just the sort of goose-brained, feather-witted, missish female I never think about at all.'

'You mean she's perfectly feminine?'

'If you say so,' Lucy said indifferently. 'Do you mean to stand here on the doorstep for ever, or are you going to come in?'

'Since you ask me so nicely, how can I refuse?' he said, and followed her in. Hicks and Ollett took their outdoor things, and Lucy led the way up to the drawing-room on the first floor.

'Will you take a glass of sherry, or madeira?' Lucy asked.

'Sherry, thank you.' Anstey was intrigued to note the automatic way that little Thomas went to pour the drinks and hand them, and then took his place on a low stool by Lucy's chair. Not so little Thomas now, of course. At seven he was tall for his age, and had grown into a handsome boy, rather grave and reserved, which made him seem older than his years. Lucy took him everywhere with her — riding, driving, walking, on morning calls — and at home, although he was supposed to share lessons with Roland under Roland's tutor, he was more likely to be found at Lucy's elbow, attending her like a page, or running small errands for her.

Of course, there had been other great ladies with pet children: Mrs Fitzherbert, for instance, had her Minney Seymour, and the Princess of Wales her William Austin; but these were childless women. Some people thought it odd in Lucy to prefer Thomas Weston to her own children; and though he had been trained to address her as 'ma'am', there were plenty of gossips to suggest that Captain Weston's son was not as complete an orphan as he appeared. Lucy, as always, was oblivious to gossip, and no-one was quite brassy enough to ask her questions directly; and as Thomas had exquisite manners and an enchanting, though rare, smile, he was generally judged to be quite acceptable in the morning-rooms of the fashionable.

'So,' Anstey said when they were settled, 'again, why has Knaresborough sold you his pair? I thought he was so pleased with them? I saw him driving them for ever last summer.'

'So he was; but now Julia's in the family way, she's full of green fancies, and believes they're going to bolt with him, or turn him over, so she's persuaded him to get rid of them. He was going to send them to Tatt's, but I stepped in and bought them privately.'

'At a good price, I imagine, if I know my Lucy,' Anstey said.

She shrugged. 'If he wants to be fool enough to give in to that kind of nonsense —' she said. 'But in any case, I don't suppose he'd have much use for a pair like them, now he's gone into the country for good.'

'Where is it, again, that he's going to live?'

'Some dismal place one's never heard of — oh yes, Mansfield,' Lucy said vaguely.

'I've heard of Mansfield,' Anstey said indignantly, and she grinned.

'Well, yes — I believe it's all coal-mines and manufactories, so you would have! God knows what Robert will find to do there.'

'He'll do what all gentlemen do in the country: hunt, shoot, and raise a parcel of brats.'

'Ah yes, I've heard there's good hunting around there,' Lucy said betraying her knowledge, 'and I suppose even brewers must have horses. I wonder how he'll like living with his father-in-law?'

'I expect he'll keep him in order. At any rate, your Mr Brummel will be glad that Knaresborough's married at last, and gone from London. That's one young man he never liked. I believe it tried him sorely to have to admit him to Watier's.'

Lucy frowned. 'I don't know what everyone's got against Robert. He seems to me perfectly harmless — even rather pathetic.'

'I expect that's what everyone has against him. People like him tend to give others a great deal of trouble in keeping them out of it. I think Mr Brummell only countenanced him at all for your sake.'

'Did you hear what Brummell said yesterday?' Lucy said with an obvious effort to change the subject. 'Fred Byng went past us, driving those new greys of his — Siddington's breakdowns, you know. Much too good for him, by the way. I'd have had them myself if I hadn't been committed to this pair. I had a real fancy to them — but I dare say Parslow's glad I didn't get them, after all. Greys are so much hard work to keep clean.' She faltered. 'What was I talking of?'

'The wit and wisdom of George Bryan Brummell, I think,' Anstey said with a grin.

'Oh yes! Well, Fred Byng had just had his hair cut, and of course his poodle was sitting up beside him in his phaeton, as usual. Well, with that short curly crop, you could hardly tell them apart. Brummell pointed at them and said, "Ah, a family vehicle, I see!" Byng heard him, of course, and he was furious — you know how vain he is of his hair! And lots of other people were close enough to hear. I don't suppose he'll ever live it down.'

'You at least should be kind to Byng's foibles — you have a mascot yourself,' Anstey pointed out.

She stared a moment, and then caught his drift. 'Oh, you mean Thomas? But I never worry what people say, you know that. Besides, after all this time I don't suppose people even notice him, any more than they notice Parslow. And at least I can't be nicknamed for him, like poor Poodle Byng. Really, Brummell will go too far one day! But he's very fond of Thomas,' she added inconsequentially, looking down at her son, who gazed up at her intently, almost reverently. Adoration of her was what he had put into the emptiness inside him, where Maman and Sophie and home had been. He had not seen them for over three years — half his lifetime — and their memory was growing dim now.

'But I didn't mean to be talking nonsense to you, John,' Lucy said, rousing herself from her reverie. 'I want to hear about the Regency Bill. Have you been in the House today? Are the amendments going to go through? Is it to be a full Regency, or a conditional?'

'The final vote isn't until tomorrow,' John said. 'I think it's going to be a close-run thing. There's a lot of sympathy for the Prince. After all, a conditional Regency might have been appropriate in 1788, when he was only twenty-six, and wild —'

'He's wild now,' Lucy interrupted.

'He's fifty years old,' John countered, 'and he's behaved very well since the King went mad again: perfectly correct, dignified, and restrained.'

'Yes, that's true,' Lucy admitted. 'MacMahon says he's given no audience of any sort to any politician; no intrigue or jobbery; and he's behaved perfectly properly towards the Queen. But I hear that the King is already much better. If it was really only Princess Amelia's death that sent him mad, he might recover at any time, mightn't he?'

John shook his head. 'I wouldn't count on it. The doctors are divided in their opinion; but the fact remains that the King had been growing strange for some time, and the Princess's death only precipitated the crisis. He's a very old man now, remember, and almost blind, and growing deaf. I don't believe he'll ever be fit to rule again.'

'Well, in that case, surely —'

'Oh, I'm sure the Bill will go through unamended. It will be a conditional Regency for the first twelve months. Spencer Perceval will talk them round. You should have heard him in the House today! Such fire and conviction! Sam Whitbread called him 'as bold as brass' — of course, he believes Perceval is simply trying to make sure that government remains in his hands.'

'It's so strange to think of that funny little man as Prime Minister,' Lucy said. 'If anyone had predicted it five years ago, everyone would have laughed.'

'I've a great respect for him,' John Anstey said firmly. 'He may not be a man of great qualities, but he's a good politician, and he's held things together through a very difficult time.'

'What can you mean by a good politician?' Lucy asked, wrinkling her nose at the term.

'He's a good orator, he's immensely brave, and he has an instinct not only for what's important, but also for what's possible. I tell you, Lucy, we could do a lot worse than him.'

'Once we have a Regency, we probably will,' Lucy said with grim humour. 'No doubt the Prince will have the Tories out and the Whigs in — Grenville and Sheridan and Moira and the rest. A shabby crowd, to my mind.'

'Yes, I suppose so. It will hardly be a strong administration; though I have heard that Grenville has spoken of asking Canning to come in with them, which would be all to the good. He may rub people up the wrong way, but he's talented, and he's been sorely missed in the Foreign Office. If only he and Castlereagh hadn't fought that disastrous duel!'

'That was a perfectly foolish affair,' Lucy agreed. 'But the Prince would never accept Canning — he's been too closely associated with the Princess of Wales.'

John shrugged. 'That remains to be seen.'

'At any rate, will you come and tell me tomorrow, as soon as you know which way the vote goes?'

'Of course. I'll see you get your news fresh and hot,' Anstey said good-naturedly.

'Come to dinner, if you'd care to. The children will be glad to see you. Did you know I had Bobbie Chelmsford and Marcus staying with me, while Roberta's in the country?'

'No, I didn't. I'm surprised she didn't stay in Town for Christmas like everyone else, with the Regency crisis undecided.'

'She hasn't gone away for pleasure. There were apparently family problems to be sorted out, caused by her father's death. You did know the old Colonel died in November?'

'Yes, of course I did. But I didn't know she had any family, apart from him.'

'No close family — only some elderly cousins. But apparently there's some sort of legal wrangle over a house, and she's gone to sort it out, and taken Mr Firth with her, for the sake of his fine legal mind. So I have her boys.'

'You're lucky. I've missed my own children dreadfully. It was hard not to be with them over the Christmas season.'

'Hard on Louisa, too, I should think, especially after that last confinement of hers. Really, John, you'll have to stop increasing your family! Ten children in fifteen years — no wonder poor Louisa's worn out. Isn't it enough, in all reason?'

Though he had known Lucy since she was a little girl, it still made him blush to hear her talk so freely of such things;

but he tried to make light of it. 'Ah, yes, but of course reason doesn't come into it much, when you're in love, as Louisa and I are.'

'If you love her,' Lucy said sternly, undeflected, 'you had better make your mind up to leaving her alone. Let this new baby be the last. What was it you called it, again?'

'Aglaea,' John said defiantly. 'Louisa chose it. Well, it's the fashion to give Greek names.'

Lucy grinned. 'I know. Billy Tonbridge's wife has called their latest daughter Psyche! Still, with a Hippolyta and a Flaminia under my own roof, I suppose I can't complain.'

As Anstey had predicted, the vote was close; but the amendment was defeated and a restricted Regency for the period of a year was accepted by both Houses of Parliament.

'Now the fun begins,' he told Lucy with a shake of the head. 'Lord Grey has come posting down from Northumberland to Carlton House to confer with the Prince and Grenville about forming a Whig government; but I don't believe they have an idea how difficult it's going to be. The Whigs have been in opposition so long, they all have long lists of promises to fulfil, apart from their own personal ambitions, which are bound to conflict.'

'Grenville, I suppose, will be First Lord of the Treasury — that's traditional for the Prime Minister,' Lucy said.

'Yes, but he says he can't afford to give up his sinecure as Auditor of the Exchequer, which brings him a large part of his income; and Grey is adamant that he can't hold both posts together. And then Grenville wants his brother to be First Lord of the Admiralty, which Grey has already promised to Whitbread; and Buckingham says that if Whitbread goes to the Admiralty, he won't support the Whigs at all.'

'The Prince will have some suggestions of his own to make, I imagine,' Lucy said. 'He has friends to please and debts to pay like everyone else.'

Anstey smiled. 'Oh yes! That's another problem. He's promised Norfolk he can be Lord Privy Seal, and Grenville won't work with Norfolk; and he wants Northumberland in the Cabinet, and Grey hates Northumberland worse than he hates Canning. It's going to be the deuce of a job satisfying everybody. Winning the war will be simple by comparison.'

The discussions and speculations went on for days. London seethed with place-seekers, and the clubs throbbed uneasily with faction and jobbery, ancient debts recalled and old slights revived. Lucy was greatly diverted by the reports brought to her every day on the latest state of the negotiations, and said to John Anstey that the Whigs went through more contortions than the famous Flexible Man at Astley's Circus. But even when the Whigs had decided amongst themselves who should have what place, they had great difficulty in persuading the Prince to commit himself.

'He's afraid the King is going to recover, that's what it is,' Danby Wiske said, warming his tails at Lucy's morning-room fire. He and George Brummell had called to take Lucy out riding in the Park. 'Wouldn't look good, you know, if he'd dismissed his pa's ministers the first minute. Filial piety and so on,' he added vaguely.

'Filial piety?' Brummell said, raising one perfectly-arched eyebrow. 'Stuff and fustian! The fact of the matter is that he's never had the least loyalty to anyone or anything but himself. His career is littered with broken promises and betrayed friendships.'

'Now, George —' Wiske protested uneasily.

'I think there may be more to it than that,' John Anstey said judiciously. 'The Prince knows as well as anyone how little the Whigs agree amongst themselves, and he must also be aware how important it is at the moment to have a united government.'

'I don't believe he has any real sympathy with the Whigs at all,' Lucy put in. 'It's my belief he only pretended to be a Whig to annoy his father; and now he's come to realise that he's a Tory at heart, like the rest of us. It's all very well to have revolutionary ideas when there's no chance of putting them into action, but when you actually find yourself in power, things look very different.'

There was a brief silence, and then Anstey said, 'That's very profound, Lucy. You could be right.'

'Well, don't look so surprised,' she snorted. 'I'm not a complete simpleton, you know.'

The door opened, and Bobbie and Marcus came in.

'Oh, I beg your pardon, ma'am,' Marcus said. 'I didn't know you were engaged.'

'It's all right — come in,' said Lucy. 'We were just discussing the possibility of a Whig government. It's a pity your tutor isn't here to put us all right. But perhaps after so many years under his influence, you can tell us what he would say?'

Marcus looked around hesitantly, not sure whether or not he was being roasted. 'I shouldn't like to speak for him, ma'am; but for myself, I think it would be a bad thing.'

The years under Firth had improved Marcus enormously, John Anstey thought, remembering the timid, pale, oppressed creature he had been years ago. He had grown up into a pleasant, thoughtful young man, and though with his father's rather protruberant eyes and pale eyelashes he would never be precisely handsome, he had a manly dignity which did him very well instead. Lucy's younger daughter, Rosamund, had a crush on him, and quoted everything he said as if it were Holy Writ, while Bobbie, at fourteen, two years younger than Marcus, evidently both loved and admired him. Marcus was kind and patient with Rosamund, and was very protective of Bobbie, which would have annoyed Lady Barbara greatly had she been aware of it.

'Why so? Let's hear your opinion, my boy,' Anstey said encouragingly. 'I should have thought all you young people would be wild for a change of government.'

'Well, sir, I don't think the Whigs have ever been in favour of the war,' Marcus said, glancing round shyly at the illustrious company, 'and it seems to me that we need a government that will prosecute it vigorously.'

'Prosecute it vigorously? That sounds like Mr Firth's phraseology,' Lucy said, and Marcus blushed with embarrassment. Since his skin was very fair, he blushed easily, and Danby Wiske felt sorry for him.

'I'm sure you're right,' he said. 'And I think there will be one change which you'll approve, Mr Morland — the Prince is determined to reinstate his brother at the Horseguards.'

Marcus turned to him gratefully. 'The Duke of York to be Commander-in-Chief again? That would be beyond anything great! Do you really think so, sir?'

'Sure of it — don't you say so, Geroge? You're closer to the Yorks than anyone.'

'It certainly looks that way,' Brummell said. 'Have you military ambitions yourself, Mr Morland? I know your father's serving in the Peninsula. Have you a mind to follow him?'

'Yes, sir, Papa's in Portugal with Lord Hill. It's the one thing I really want, to go out there too.'

'If it's what you really want, you probably will,' Brummell said kindly.

But Marcus knew the expense of a pair of colours, and his mother's dedication to economy seemed unlikely soon to change. 'I'm afraid the war may be over before I have the chance,' he said sadly.

'I doubt it. It's going to be a long business — no quick and easy victories in the Peninsula, you know,' Wiske said, shaking his head. The Tenth Dragoons — so long nicknamed "The China Tenth" because it had been looked after like something fragile and precious — had seen action there in the winter of 1808-9. The war had been going on so long, now, that even the most fashionable of regiments was not safe from getting its uniform dirty. 'There'll be enough fighting for all of us before it's over.'

'You were at Corunna, sir, weren't you?' Marcus said eagerly. 'I've always wanted to ask —'

'Not now, Marcus,' Lucy interrupted, feeling he had been encouraged enough. 'What was it you came in for?'

'I beg your pardon, ma'am,' he said, shrinking. 'I came to ask if Bobbie and I might go up to Hatchard's, and whether there was anything we could do for you while we were out.'

'No, thank you — Miss Trotton is out at the moment, and has my errands in hand. What do you want at Hatchard's?'

He and Bobbie exchanged a look. 'It's Mr Firth's birthday next month, ma'am, and we wanted to buy a book for him,' he said.

'And we thought we'd better do it before he comes back from the country, because of wanting it to be a surprise,' Bobbie added.

'I see. Yes, well, run along then,' Lucy said.

'They seem very fond of their tutor,' John Anstey said when the boys had gone. 'To be spending all their pocket-money on a book for him is a great thing.'

'If I know anything about it, it will be Bobbie's money, for I never knew Marcus to have any,' Lucy said.

* * *

As the boys hurried along Curzon Street together, Bobbie, who had been quiet since they left the house, suddenly said, 'Do you really want to go to the war?'

Marcus glanced down at him in surprise. 'Of course I do. I thought you knew that. Why, what's wrong?'

'Nothing,' said Bobbie.

'Well, don't you?' Marcus countered. 'I mean, I know your papa wasn't a military man like mine, but — just think of it, Bobbie!'

'I do,' Bobbie said. 'All the time. When Mr Firth shews us the maps, and we work out the routes Lord Wellington must have taken.'

'And the names — Badajoz and Almeida and Cuidad Rodrigo —'

'Yes, but it's all very well for you,' Bobbie complained. 'You know I should never be allowed to go, because of the title and everything, and having no brother.'

'I can't see that being an earl makes any difference,' Marcus said. 'I mean, once you're of age, you can do as you like. No-one can stop you — and at least you'd have enough money to choose.'

'But that's years and years away. The war will be over by then.'

'Well, I'm no better off than you,' Marcus sighed. 'My mother would never buy me my colours. To begin with, she'd say we couldn't afford it; and then she wouldn't want me to risk my life, because I'm your heir.'

Bobbie grinned. 'Maybe your mother would buy *me* a pair of colours, in the hope that I'd get killed, and then you'd be the Earl!'

Marcus stopped suddenly and looked down at his cousin. 'You know *I* wouldn't want that, don't you, Bob? You know *I* don't want your title?'

'Of course I do, stupid!' Bobbie said. 'We're friends. I'd *give* you the title, if I could.'

'No you wouldn't,' Marcus said seriously. 'You were born to it. Even if you don't realise it, you're an earl through and through. You'd never give it up.'

Blue eyes looked thoughtfully into grey, and Bobbie regarded his own life objectively for an instant. He felt suddenly very lonely, burdened with responsibility, and reached for warmth. 'We'll always be friends, won't we, Marcus? Whatever happens?'

'Of course,' Marcus said.

The moment was too solemn to be extended, and they both felt the need to be brisk.

'Come on, I'll race you to the end of the street!' said Marcus.

Piccadilly was crowded — the second most fashionable lounge, after Bond Street — and it was hard work to make progress against the tide of humanity. The air reeked of horses, sweat, perfume, and cabbage-leaves; the road was crammed with traffic, and the path from each shop to the kerb was made hazardous by liveried footmen carrying parcels and forcing a passage for their ladies to the waiting carriages. Bobbie kept close to Marcus, and kept his hand over his purse, keenly aware of the danger of pickpockets; but in fact it was Marcus who was accosted, by a very heavily-painted young woman with a hoarse voice who invited him to 'have a bit of fun'. Marcus blushed with vexation, but Bobbie went into fits of giggles, which at least had the effect of sending the young woman off with an offended toss of the head.

As they reached Hatchard's, they almost bumped into two men coming out. The elder of the two looked haughty and flicked an imaginary affront from his sleeve, but the younger stopped and smiled genially.

'Hullo! It's Bobbie Chelmsford! I say, George, stop a minute — here's young Chelmsford, and Marcus Morland.'

George, Earl of Wyndham, turned back with a sigh. He was a heavily-built, self-important young man of twenty-six, heir to the Marquis of Penrith, and fully aware of the honour he would do the title by inheriting it. But he had firm ideas about Blood being Thicker than Water, and the importance of Family Ties. As his great-grandfather had been the third Earl of Chelmsford, the present Earl and his heir presumptive were both his cousins, and must be noticed.

His younger brother, Lord Harvey Sale, was tall, handsome, and easy-going, and by his appearance was a devoted disciple of Mr George 'Beau' Brummell. Bobbie could hardly help staring a little, for Lord Harvey was wearing trousers, only about the sixth pair Bobbie had ever seen. His blue coat was exquisitely cut, his white waistcoat and shirt-frill immaculate, his neckcloth a snowy miracle of intricacy, his glossy black hair was delicately dishevelled à la Titus.

Wyndham greeted the boys with perfunctory courtesy, but Lord Harvey engaged them in easy conversation.

'Any news from your papa, Marcus? Are the French still sitting about in front of Lisbon? They must be getting damned cold and hungry by now. They could hardly fare worse if they dined at Limmers!'

'It's about time Wellington drove them off,' Wyndham grumbled. 'This war's devilish expensive to keep up, and there's nothing to shew for it.'

'I've heard nothing since before Christmas, sir,' Marcus said circumspectly. He and Bobbie knew from their regular lessons with Mr Firth exactly what Wellington was doing — how he had retreated across Portugal, burning everything behind him, and lured the French army under Massena into the siege of the impregnable Lisbon. Wellington's army was spending the winter snug and safe, supplied from England by sea, while Massena's troops were forced to live off the scorched land, growing weaker and more discouraged every day, and learning the bitter lesson that they could not take Portugal by superiority of numbers.

But he would not attempt to explain that to Lord Wyndham, who had a short way with halflings, and cared only that the war had put up his taxes and ruined his West India income.

Lord Harvey perfectly understood his reticence, and changed the subject. 'How is Lady Aylesbury getting on with those blacks she bought from my cousin Knaresborough?' he asked instead. 'I think it was clever of her to take them from under Alvanley's nose. He'd had his eye on them ever since Knaresborough first brought them to Town.'

'She's bringing them on, sir. They're beginning to look very good,' Marcus said. 'I believe Lord Carlyon will lose the race.'

'Very loyal of you, I'm sure,' Wyndham said, looking loftily amused. 'But you haven't had the advantage of seeing Carlyon's greys in action. They're the finest team in England.'

'Ah, but the blacks will have the advantage of being driven by an expert,' Lord Harvey said with a wicked grin. 'Have you taken that into account, George?'

'Enough said, I think,' Lord Wyndham remonstrated sternly It was not his way to encourage the young entry by admitting them to his opinions, particularly about contemporaries.

'Carlyon deserves no quarter,' Lord Harvey said, refusing to be snubbed. 'Not only does he have hands like stone, but he beats his cattle unmercifully. My money will be on Lady Aylesbury — and yours too, Morland, I'll warrant.'

'Oh yes, sir! That is, if I had any, it would be,' Marcus said, and then added boldly, 'But I'll tell her what you've said, sir. I'm sure she'll be obliged to you.'

Lord Harvey grinned, but Lord Wyndham looked disapproving. This is what came of encouraging halflings to speak up: impertinence and intolerable freedom.

'We must be going, Harvey, or we'll be late,' he said pointedly, 'and that would be ill-mannered indeed! Good day to you, Chelmsford, Morland. *Do come on*, Harvey!'

Lord Harvey tipped the boys a sidelong wink, and walked off in his brother's wake.

The following day, while Docwra was dressing Lucy for her morning visits, a note came by the hand of one of the Chelmsford House servants.

'It's from Lady Chelmsford — she's back at last! What a time her business has taken!'

'I hope it was successful, my lady,' Docwra said, tweaking at the gathers on a sleeve.

'She doesn't say. She says she will call on me later today, but there's no need for that.' Lucy pulled herself impatiently free, and ran a hand over her short, hay-coloured crop by way of arranging it. 'I shall go and see her at once. I only had duty calls this morning anyway. The green jockey-cap, I think, Docwra, and my beaver muff.'

The carriage was waiting when she went downstairs, and Thomas was sitting on one of the little hard hall-chairs, ready to go with her. He looked up as his mother came towards him. He thought her as beautiful as an angel.

'Are you ready, my dear?' Lucy asked. She paused, cocking her head enquiringly at the gaze of the brown eyes under the delicately arched eyebrows. 'Why do you stare at me?'

'I think your hat is very pretty, ma'am,' he said frankly,

with his sudden smile. Something inside her turned over: he looked so like Weston when he smiled.

'Thank you,' she said gravely. 'I'm glad you think so.' She held out her hand to him. He jumped down from the chair and took it and they walked towards the door.

'I think you are very pretty, too,' he added with an air of mature judgement, which made Hicks, who was holding open the door for them, bite his lip to keep his countenance.

At Chelmsford House, they were met in the vast, black-and-white-tiled hall by Hawkins, who looked unaccountably agitated.

'Have I taken you unawares, Hawkins?' Lucy said cheerfully, thrusting her muff and gloves into his unready arms. 'I'm not expected, but I'm sure her ladyship will see me.'

'Oh, my lady! Of course, my lady,' he said, made even more flustered by Lucy's apologising to him. He had always held her in the greatest respect, even when she was a new young bride of fifteen. 'I beg you won't think — allow me to shew you up, my lady. Her ladyship is in the small saloon —'

As this was where the Chelmsford ladies had always sat in the morning, Lucy positively grinned at the idea of being shewn where it was. 'Don't trouble, Hawkins. I ought to know my way by now,' she said, and, leading Thomas, started briskly up the stairs before the slow-moving Hawkins could prevent her. The butler's unusual lack of self-possession she put down to Roberta's return being sudden and unexpected; but as she opened the door to the small saloon, she heard a small muffled cry and the rustle of hurried movement. When she stepped over the threshold, she saw Roberta sitting on the very edge of a sopha, looking ruffled and holding up a newspaper defensively, while Mr Firth was standing by the chimney-piece with his back to her, industriously poking the fire.

'Lucy!' Roberta cried in a mixture of relief and embarrassment. 'Oh, I wasn't expecting you! But how lovely to see you! Please come in. And Thomas too. Do sit down. You received my message, then? I was going to call on you later.'

Lucy raised an eyebrow at this unnatural garrulity. 'What *is* the matter, Rob? I thought Hawkins was behaving oddly, and now you start to chatter like a lunatic, too.' She looked from Roberta's pink face and downcast eyes to Mr Firth's inhospitably turned back, and a slow smile began to spread

221

over her face. 'You will surely ruin that fire, Mr Firth, if you don't put down the poker,' she said in amusement.

He straightened up and turned to her, giving her a look half defiant, half conspiratorial. 'How delightful to see you again, Lady Aylesbury,' he said, laughter quivering just under the surface.

'I was going to call on you the first moment,' Roberta went on, still valiantly trying to keep everything on a normal, social footing. 'How are the boys? It was so kind of you to —'

'It's no good,' Mr Firth said, catching her eye. 'We can't deceive Lady Aylesbury's sharp eye. You've guessed, haven't you, ma'am?'

Lucy hadn't, entirely, but looking from him to Roberta and back again, it came to her in a sudden illumination. 'You're married!' she exclaimed.

Roberta blushed the more deeply, but Mr Firth grinned and came forward to take Lucy's offered hand. 'Guilty!' he laughed. 'We discovered while we were marooned in the depths of Sussex, surrounded by mud and hens and ancient cousins, that we simply couldn't bear to wait any longer. Roberta has done me the inestimable honour of becoming my wife, and I do hope you will forgive us, and wish us joy.'

'Forgive you? What is there to forgive?' Lucy said, turning from wringing his hand to embrace Roberta, and kiss her hot cheek. 'I'm only astonished you waited so long.'

'I'm sorry we couldn't let you know, Lucy dear,' Roberta said, beginning to look happier now that the secret was out. 'I would have liked you to be at the wedding, but the whole thing was so sudden — and then, we didn't quite know how to tell the boys. I was going to come and see you today, and tell you about it, and ask your advice. It will be such a shock to them — and I'm afraid a lot of people will disapprove.'

'Let 'em!' Lucy said robustly. 'I told you before, it's no-one's business but yours. Besides, why should anyone disapprove? You're both over twenty-one, and free to choose for yourselves.'

'That's what Peter says.' Roberta's tongue betrayed how familiar, and how dear, the name was to it. 'He insisted on telling Hawkins the moment we arrived —'

'My wife thought she could keep it from the servants,' Firth said, giving her a delighted look. 'As if anyone ever kept

222

anything from the servants! Far better to tell Hawkins, and give him the official task of enlightenment.'

'But I wanted to keep it a secret for the time being,' Roberta said. 'Just until Bobbie's older.'

'Then, my darling,' Firth pointed out, 'there would have been no point in our getting married in the first place. Do you really think I could go on calling you "my lady", and sleeping in the nursery wing, and stealing kisses from you in dark corners like some sneaking dog —'

'Oh don't!' Roberta begged. 'I don't know what I thought! Only I'm afraid —'

'I know you are,' he said gently, 'but don't be. We'll face them out together.'

'I should have thought,' Lucy said, 'that the only person who mattered was Bobbie; and that he'll be delighted.'

'Do you really think so?' Roberta asked doubtfully.

'Of course. He admires Mr Firth more than anyone — except possibly Parslow,' she added thoughtfully.

Thomas had been sitting quietly on the sopha beside Roberta all this time, listening, his head turning from one speaker to the next like someone at a play. Now he suddenly said, 'Bobbie knows.'

Lucy stared at him. 'Knows what, my dear?' Thomas looked confused. 'He can't know about Lady Chelmsford and Mr Firth getting married, because it's only just happened,' she pointed out.

'But he knows they were going to,' Thomas said. 'He told Marcus when we were out riding that Mr Firth would be his step-papa one day, and Marcus told Bobbie he was a lucky dog.'

Lucy and Firth exchanged a glance. 'Are you sure about this, my love?' Lucy asked. 'When was it?'

Thomas nodded firmly. 'It was ages ago.'

'When?' Lucy insisted.

Thomas screwed up his face. 'When they went away,' he said at last. Before Christmas was ages ago as far as he was concerned.

Roberta gave him a short, fierce hug by way of thanks for the reassurance.

Firth caught her eye and said, 'That should make you feel happier, love. Perhaps it won't be so hard to tell him after all.'

'I'm glad he guessed. But it will still be hard,' Roberta said.

Lucy held out her hand to Thomas, and said, 'I think we had better leave you two to settle in. I'll send the boys over to you this afternoon, Roberta, and you can tell them everything. I shan't say anything myself beforehand, so you may do it whatever way you think best. And be sure to let me know when it's no longer a secret. I shall hold a special dinner for you.'

'We will. Thank you, Lucy, for being so understanding,' Roberta said.

'There's nothing to understand,' Lucy said. 'I'm very happy for you. Come, Thomas. No, don't bother to ring. I'll see myself out.'

She had other calls to make, but when she reached the carriage, she ordered it to drive home. She needed time and silence to assimilate the news and understand her feelings about it — in particular the pang of jealousy which she had felt when Firth looked at Roberta in that particular way, and called her 'love'.

It was not that she had any desire for Mr Firth to look at her that way; but it reminded her of her own relationship with Weston, and how much she missed him, and how empty her life was without him. She held Thomas's hand absently as the carriage jerked its way through the traffic in Pall Mall, her thoughts far away; and Thomas, feeling her absence, looked up into her stern face sadly, longing for her to come back to him.

Two days later, on 4 February, the Prince of Wales wrote to Perceval to say that he did not intend to remove 'His Majesty's official servants' from office.

'So we are back exactly where we were,' John Anstey said, calling on Lucy directly from Carlton House. 'The letter, apparently, says that the Prince is afraid lest any action of his delays the King's recovery — the doctors have been hinting that His Majesty might be well again within three months. But I shouldn't be surprised if Lady Hertford's recommendation hadn't more to do with it than filial duty. She and Hertford never had any time for the Whigs.'

'I agree with Brummell,' Lucy said. 'I don't believe he ever meant to dismiss the Tories. I dare say the Whigs are furious?'

'They're saying at the club that Grenville is rather relieved than otherwise!' he said with a smile. 'But certainly the rest are very upset. Pall Mall this morning was thronged with shoals of angry Whigs, all muttering together and crying calamity. I heard that Sheridan told the Prince that his character is wholly gone, and Thanet said it was the worst disaster to befall the country since the death of Fox.'

'You must be glad at the way things have fallen out, though?'

'I think most people will be,' Anstey said. 'There may not be any brilliant men in the Cabinet, but they are united in their desire to win the war, and not to compromise with Boney. And at least they know their limitations — they'll leave expert decisions to the experts.'

Lucy nodded. 'And what happens now?'

'The swearing-in is to be tomorrow, at Carlton House. I believe they mean to make something of an occasion of it, with bands and banners and so on. You ought to drive past there at around noon: you might find it diverting. And then the serious business of the Regency will begin,' he added with a suppressed smile.

'What's that?' Lucy asked guardedly, seeing that he was in a frivolous mood.

'The Prince will give the most enormous party!'

'It's a serious matter, the beginning of a Regency,' Lucy said reprovingly. 'Even if it is only a conditional one.'

'It is indeed,' he said, 'though I doubt whether it will be conditional this time next year. I can't believe the King will ever recover. Don't worry Lucy, I feel the solemnity of the occasion just as I should; though you must forgive me if I don't believe it's going to make a jot of difference to any of us.'

CHAPTER TWELVE

The first day in March when the wind came easterly was the signal to begin the great wash at Morland Place. It was an event which lasted several days, turned the whole house upside down, and involved every member of the household — except for Ned and James, who disappeared to the stables at the first glimpse of a wash-tub, returning at intervals only to consume such picnic meals as Barnard had found time to prepare in between the spring-cleaning of his own kitchens and pantries.

All the curtains and hangings were taken down and washed, upholstery was cleaned, and every scrap of household linen dragged out from every cupboard to be inspected, laundered and counted. Furniture had to be moved so that the carpets could be taken up and beaten, and cleaned with a vile-smelling compound which was made according to an ancient Morland recipe, mixed up in a huge tub outside the house, and downwind. The air was full of the smell of soap and soda and bran and starch; no-one and nothing was in its accustomed place; extraordinary meals were consumed in unexpected places; and the house took on the air of a mediæval tournament tent, every window and baluster hung with banners.

Lost needles, beads and buttons appeared from the creases in upholstery and from behind sopha-cushions, and Héloïse's good scissors turned up at last, wedged between the lowboy and the wall beside the fire, where they must have slipped months ago. There were a few casualties, only to be expected, James said, in a campaign of such magnitude: Monsieur Barnard found a decaying *blancmanger* at the back of a shelf in one of the pantries, and bellowed so savagely at the nearest kitchen-maid that she stepped back hastily and cut her shin on a bucket; and one of the men slipped while taking down the curtains from the Butts Bed and pulled the rail half off and sprained his wrist.

The dogs did what they could to add to the chaos by racing round the house in a pack, eyes gleaming, tongues lolling, up the great staircase, along the passage, down the backstairs, across the hall, and round again; with Héloïse's spaniel Castor, which James had bought her for her last birthday, bringing up the rear, one long ear turned foolishly inside-out over his curly head. Only grey-muzzled Kithra refused to join in the game. He was always to be found near Héloïse and Nicholas, lying down with his head on his paws, but keeping an eye on the boy in case he should wander into danger. The old dog took almost as much interest in the youngest Morland as his parents did.

At the moment Héloïse and Mathilde were in one of the bachelor rooms, which had been turned into a temporary linen-closet, examining sheets for signs of wear, and dividing them into piles: wash, mend, and past all help.

'I do not think it will be worth mending this one,' Héloïse said, gazing down a white slope towards Mathilde. 'It is worn so thin in the middle.'

'The rag pile, then?' Mathilde said hopefully. Héloïse sometimes found it difficult to forget habits of thrift learned long ago, in harder times.

'But I wonder,' she hesitated now. 'Perhaps if we turned it sides-to-middle and hemmed it —'

'Mrs Thomson is very short of cleaning-rags, Madame,' Mathilde said helpfully. 'Here, let me fold it for the rag pile.' And she took it away before her guardian could change her mind again.

Héloïse smiled at her indulgently. 'The mending pile is now smaller than the rag pile,' she observed.

'Just as well,' Mathilde said briskly. 'The servants have plenty to do, without mending sheets as well.' She had just had her twenty-second birthday, and Héloïse thought she had grown very handsome, with her fine, upright figure, and her burnished hair twisted in a soft coil at the back of her head. It was a pity, she thought, that she had not found anyone she liked well enough to marry. It was not that she had lacked suitors. After John Skelwith had quit the scene, Ned Micklethwaite had been disposed to pay her attention for a while;

then there had been that nice young officer, Nicholson, who had seemed very smitten indeed; and lately Tom Keating had been more than merely polite, though that was an attachment Héloïse would not have wished to encourage.

But though Mathilde accepted attention with every appearance of pleasure, it was evident that she was not more attached to one beau than another, and they soon fell away for lack of encouragement. It began to look as though she meant to stay single, and Héloïse was sorry for it, though there was no doubt that she made herself very useful about the house, and was a pleasant companion, too. Héloïse wondered sometimes whether she had been mistaken about Mathilde's feelings for John Skelwith. Perhaps she really had favoured him, and was still heart-sore at losing him. Héloïse had asked Edward what he thought — for he spent a good deal of time with Mathilde, one way and another, and Héloïse thought she might have unburdened her heart to him on the subject — but he had only shaken his head and said he didn't think so, though afterwards he looked thoughtful.

Mathilde, however, didn't seem unhappy. On the contrary, she sang about her work, looked cheerful, and did whatever she did with energy, whether it was shopping with Patience Keating, dancing at the Assembly Rooms with the officers from Fulford, riding out with Edward or playing chess with him in the evenings.

Héloïse had had plenty of other things to worry about in the past three years. One of them was sitting on the floor beside Kithra at this moment, playing patiently and absorbedly with two toy soldiers which James had carved for him out of beech-wood. Nicholas had a great capacity for amusing himself, and could play for hours with one simple thing, even a stone or a leaf which had interested him. Héloïse remembered Jemima saying that James had been like that when he was a little boy — but as the middle one of the family, separated by a number of years from his siblings on either side, he had been obliged to find his own company sufficient.

Every few moments Héloïse glanced up from her work at the child she had had such labour to bring into the world, and felt the familiar pang of love and anxiety. He had been frail from the beginning, of course. She remembered the day of his christening, when Jenny had run in to announce that Baby was ill: that moment had heralded an endless series of ailments. In the early months of his life he had had difficulties with his breathing and with his digestion. There had been one dreadful period when everything he ate came straight back, and Héloïse held him on her lap hour after hour, his legs drawn up to his belly, his face purple, and his mouth open in a soundless wail, because he couldn't draw enough breath to scream protest at his hunger and pain.

He passed out of that phase at last, but he was still prone to catch any illness that was about. The whooping-cough almost killed him when he was eighteen months old, and the chicken pox when he was two-and-a-half; intermittent bouts of sickness and diarrhoea kept his mother and nurse from relaxing in between times, and if nothing else happened, he was as likely as not to be suffering from a cold.

Lucy, in her occasional, terse letters, tried to comfort Héloïse by pointing out that he must be extremely tough to have survived all these illnesses, but they were not words to calm a mother's anxieties. She rather feared that sooner or later one ailment would prove to be the last straw for Nicholas's frail constitution. She knew that James, though he never spoke of it, believed they would not raise him. He was everything that was tender and affectionate to the boy, but there was something in the way he hugged him sometimes, something guarded in the way he talked of future plans, which told Héloïse that he didn't expect Nicholas to be there to share them.

The boy still looked rather odd. His limbs were spindly and weak, and his head seemed too large for his body, and too long for itself, giving him a high, bony forehead that made him look like a worried old man. His hair was still very thin, hardly more than a sparse auburn down over the fragile skull, and his face looked curiously unfinished, as though the clay of him were still wet and waiting to be moulded. There was nothing you could put your finger on, she thought, but he looked in some indefinable way misshapen — not grossly so, simply a little odd.

Physically, Héloïse thought with an aching heart, he was not very prepossessing, poor little boy; but he had a loving nature, and when he came to Héloïse's knee and held up his arms to be hugged, the smile he gave her made her love him more even than she had loved Sophie. He adored his father, too: the first word he had learned to say was 'Papa', and he would sometimes sit with Kithra under the table in the great hall for hours on end, waiting for his father to come home. Kithra was his close companion and nursemaid. When he was at the crawling stage, the hound prevented him from straying very far, fetching him back like a gun-dog retrieving a pheasant; and it was by pulling on Kithra's tail that Nicholas had first learnt to stand up, and to walk.

Sophie adored him, too, and would not allow anyone to say that he was unattractive, seeing qualities in him that no-one else could see. Héloïse understood her possessiveness: she had always wanted a little brother, and having had Thomas taken from her, she was more than ever delighted with Nicholas, whom no-one could take away, except God. Whenever Nicholas was ill, Sophie prayed long and earnestly to God to let him stay, and undertook all sorts of penances in return for his recovery. She had been very reluctant to go to school, because it meant leaving Nicholas, and Mathilde had promised to write to her every week with a bulletin on his health. On her return home, the first thing she did, even before hugging her mother, was to ask how he was.

Sending Sophie to school had been hard for Héloïse to do, for she not only loved her daughter, but enjoyed her company, too. By a kind of irony, it was because of Nicholas that the necessity arose. Once the first few weeks were past, and it appeared that his death, though likely, was not imminent, Fanny began to be jealous of him. She had never been jealous of her brother Henry, for it had been plain to her from the beginning that her father cared nothing about him, and that he was the exclusive province of her mother.

But James brooded over Nicholas, worried about him, evidently cared deeply for him, and worst of all, shared these concerns intimately with That Woman; and all the jealous pangs which had died away since Miss Rosedale came began to revive. Fanny had tried at first to gain her father's attention by normal means, but he, like everyone else, was too preoccupied with Héloïse's and the baby's health to respond.

She began to hope very hard that the baby would die, and the idea took such a hold on her, that one day Sarah had found her hanging over Nicholas's crib, red in the face from holding her breath with the force of wishing for his to stop. Fortunately, there was no chance that Fanny might translate her thoughts into action, for the baby was too well guarded by Matty, who would not leave it for an instant unless it was in the charge of someone else. The occasion when Fanny had found him alone had been a freak chance, and unlikely to be repeated.

Miss Rosedale, aware of her charge's turbulent feelings, kept Fanny as busy as possible, and after a week or two began to hope the jealousy had dispersed. Then it erupted again in a series of attacks on Sophie, who, in the warped logic of Fanny's passions, was the next obvious target. At first she had merely picked quarrels with Sophie, provoking her to the point where she could not help retaliating; then the warfare progressed to the physical plane, and she had slapped and pinched Sophie, pulled her hair, torn her dresses, and broken her toys in the course of their quarrels.

No-one could have guessed, however, that it would go farther. One day — Héloïse could never forget it — Edward and James, Mathilde, Fanny and Sophie all went out hunting. Sophie's pony had seemed a little uneasy and skittish, but as it was the first time he had been shewn to hounds, it was thought that he was merely excited. Durban, leading James's second horse, undertook to ride at the back with Sophie, and stay close and keep an eye on them. Nothing much had happened until they went over the first jump of the day; then, as they had landed, the pony seemed to go mad, bucking like a crazy thing, and Sophie had been violently thrown.

It might have been a very serious accident. Sophie was lucky to escape with bruises and a shaking-up, for the ground was hard; had she landed worse, she might have broken bones, or even her neck. Fortunately they were not far from Morland Place across the fields, and there had been plenty of followers on foot to carry the little mistress home. Durban caught her pony and led it back, and it seemed so quiet that he was more than ever curious about what had caused its strange behaviour. In the courtyard at Morland Place, he waved away the groom who came forward, took the pony into an empty stall, and untacked it himself; and in lifting off the saddle, pricked his finger badly on something.

It was a needle — the heavy-duty sort used for saddlery

repairs — embedded in the underside of the cantle. An examination of the pony's back revealed a puncture wound, with a spot of congealed blood, just to the side of the spine. All was now clear. The needle would have been pricking the whole time, just enough to make the pony uneasy; but when Sophie's weight came down in the saddle on landing over the jump, it must have driven the needle hard into the poor beast's back.

Thoughtfully, Durban removed the needle from the tack, dressed the pony's wound, and mulled the business over in his mind. It was possible that the needle had come there by chance, even though the saddle shewed no evidence of repair. Left lying about somewhere, it might have embedded itself into the saddle in just that way. But there was another possibility, a more sinister one. If it had not been chance, it was a cold-blooded attempt to harm Sophie, and whoever had devised it had calculated very carefully the effect it would have: a fall over a jump was the most likely way for any rider to break his neck. But who in the world would want to harm Sophie? He could think of only one person.

Durban said nothing to anyone, until his master returned from the hunt, and Durban was undressing him for his bath. Then he shewed him the needle, and explained how he had found it. James listened in silence, his face paling as the implications became clear to him.

'Who else knows of this?' he asked tersely.

'No-one, sir. I thought it best no-one should know until I had spoken to you. As Miss Sophie came out of it all right —'

'Yes, you were right. Say nothing to anyone,' James said. 'I must speak to Madame about it. Of course, it might have been an accident.' Then his legs began to tremble and he sat down abruptly, putting his hands over his face. He felt sick. 'Thank God she's all right!' he groaned through his hands. 'If she had been hurt —'

He hastened through his dressing and then went in search of his wife. The house was quiet: everyone was at their baths. James hurried past the closed door of Fanny's room, not daring to think, to wonder —

Héloïse was with Sophie, who had been put into the old night-nursery for ease of nursing. The little girl, looking astonishingly unmarked, had been bathed, her bruises dressed with arnica and witch-hazel, given a draught, and was now drifting off to sleep, holding her mother's hand. James bent over her to kiss her smooth, hot cheek. She looked so small and so fragile in the big white bed, and he thought, shudderingly, how nearly he had lost her. Worrying about Nicholas had been part of Nicholas's life from the beginning, but he had never for an instant contemplated life without Sophie.

When she was finally asleep, James took Héloïse through into the deserted schoolroom for privacy, and in as few and as calm words as possible, told her what Durban had told him. She listened in silence, and when he stopped speaking, put herself wordlessly into his arms. They held each other for a long time, each thinking they were comforting the other.

At last she said, 'Oh, James, it can't be possible.' And yet, he thought with dull resentment, she did not sound as surprised as she ought to be. Shocked, but not surprised.

'We know nothing,' he said in a hard voice. 'We don't know that it got there by design. It might have been the merest chance.'

Héloïse straightened up, and looked at him steadily. 'No, we don't know. And there can be no investigation. You see that?'

'Yes,' he said miserably. 'It might have been an accident, as Durban says, but if it wasn't —' He couldn't believe that Fanny would do such a thing; and yet if she had —

'Who else knows of it?'

'Only Durban. He's very discreet. And he's undertaken to see to Sophie's pony himself from now on, whenever she goes riding.'

Héloïse looked up at him with frightened eyes, suddenly realising the full implications. 'Oh, my poor Sophie! Suppose —'

'Don't,' he said, gripping her hands. 'Don't think about it. I can't bear it.'

'But what shall we do? James, it is not just a matter of her pony. If — someone — wishes to harm her, they will find a way, some other way. It is intolerable to go on, risking her safety, not knowing; and yet how can we find out?'

'It's only a passing phase. It won't last for ever,' he said miserably. 'We'll watch over her carefully —'

Héloïse's face was white and set. 'No,' she said. 'I won't

233

sacrifice my child for yours. That is no bargain.'

'Héloïse, you must understand, I can't face Fanny with this. How could I ask her if she tried to kill her sister? Put yourself in my place. Could you ask such a thing? Supposing she didn't — think how it would shock her!'

'Supposing she did,' she said stubbornly.

He shook his head, a gesture as much of pain as negation. 'No, not my Fanny. Not my little Fanny. You don't know her —'

'Then Sophie must be sent away. It is the only way. She must go away to school, where she will be out of reach of harm.'

There was a silence. James stared, unable to speak as his mind twisted uselessly this way and that. Finally he said, 'If one of them must be sent away, in fairness, it should be Fanny.'

Héloïse pressed his hand, aware of how much it had cost him to say that. Though he loved Sophie dearly, his feelings for Fanny were of a different order entirely. She caused him so much pain, yet he would give his life for her, if he could.

'Thank you' she said. 'I shall not forget that. But Fanny belongs here. She must stay with her inheritance, and learn how to govern it. She is Miss Morland of Morland Place. It is Sophie who must go. Oh James — !' And the tears she had been holding back until then broke through her self-control. James held her close, resting his cheek on her hair, and staring blankly at the wall behind her, wondering how things could have gone so wrong, and how it would all end, and how they could ever explain it to Sophie.

The choice of school was made unexpectedly easy. By chance, a letter came the next day from Lucy, and one of the items of news it contained was that Captain Haworth had at last yielded to her advice that Africa should have a proper education.

'Haworth gives her up as reluctantly as an opium-smoker his pipe, and how Africa will settle down I cannot guess. I offered to have her myself, but he said Miss Trotton had enough to do, and that Africa's was a special case, in which he speaks some truth, for she is the oddest creature. At all events, he has got a place for her in the school of a Mrs

234

Touchstone, in Queen Square in Bath. It is a fashionable place, he assures me, though I believe he chose it rather because there are several other sea-officers' children there, and Bath, as you know, is very popular with the navy. At all events, Africa is with me now, and I am to take her down there in a few days' time, when she has some new clothes fit to be at school in.'

Bath was a long way off; but for Sophie to be with her cousin, instead of all alone among strangers, was a great advantage. James and Héloïse discussed it together, and agreed. Letters were sent off to Mrs Touchstone, to Lucy, and to Captain Haworth. The business was concluded rapidly, as it must be, and it remained only to tell Sophie.

Sophie was too well-brought-up to resist her fate. She listened in obedient silence, but her eyes filled with tears even while she tried to understand the necessity, and to be good and do as she was told. It was the harder because they could not tell her the real reason, to lessen her inevitable feelings of rejection. The time between the accident and Sophie's departure was difficult for Héloïse, such as she hoped she would never have to endure again. It had been hard for her to be in the same room with Fanny, to meet her eye, or to speak civilly to her; and once when she expressed a polite concern for Sophie's recovery, Héloïse was close to taking her by the neck and choking her.

James and Héloïse had agreed that no-one else must know what they suspected; but it seemed likely that Miss Rosedale guessed what was behind the fraught atmosphere in the house, and the sudden sending of Sophie to school. At all events, she kept Fanny as much out of the way as possible, and kept her occupied from morning to night, and found reasons for them to have several of their meals separately from the rest of the family. It was impossible to tell what Fanny thought about it all. She shewed no evidence of guilt, nor of indecent triumph at the vanquishing of her enemy. She had expressed surprise and shock when first she heard of the accident — since she had been up with the first flight during the hunt, she had not witnessed it — but if she had indeed been calculating enough to plan the business, she must also have been cool enough not to give herself away.

The parting from home had been a dreadful wrench for

Sophie, and her first letters were hard to read, full of home-sickness; but it had answered well in the long run. She had come to like the school, and the other girls, and Bath itself; and she and Africa had become firm friends, so much so that Africa had spent the school holidays at Morland Place, rather than with her sister at Aunt Lucy's.

The house had seemed very empty without Sophie; but Fanny had settled down again, and having Miss Rosedale to herself had improved her to such an extent that James began to assert with more and more certainty that the business with the needle had been pure accident, and nothing to do with Fanny. Héloïse at least no longer had any fears that she harboured dark thoughts about Nicholas. Even her manner towards Héloïse had improved, and she conversed at the dinner table like a rational young woman. It did become harder to believe that she was capable of such an act, or to remember accurately the emotions and fears which had been so vivid at the time. In all, it promised to remain as much of a mystery as ever, and all anyone could do was to try to put it out of their minds.

'Madame?' said Mathilde, recalling Héloïse from her reverie to find another sheet being offered her for opening up and inspection. 'Are you tired? I could finish this on my own, if you wanted to go and rest.'

Héloïse smiled and shook her head. Since Nicholas's birth, everyone seemed to think that she was frail and in need of continuous cosseting. 'No, my dear, I'm not tired at all. But I was just thinking that you ought to go out and get some fresh air. It is such a nice day, you should not be shut up inside.'

Mathilde opened her mouth to protest, and at that oppor-tune moment, the door opened half-way and Tiger thrust in, his claws clattering busily on the polished floorboards, to be followed by the upper part of Edward's body, politely intruded.

'Ah, here you are!' he said, looking from Héloïse to Mathilde. 'I wondered if you were feeling in need of a little refreshment after your labours? I'm just going to ride over to Healaugh, to the Manor Farm, to see that breeding-ram I've been talking about. I thought you might like to come too, just for the ride.'

Héloïse was perfectly well aware to whom this was

236

addressed. It was not with her that he had been discussing livestock. 'Why, thank you, Edward, but I have too much to do,' she said. 'Mathilde will come with you. I was just telling her she should not stay indoors all day when the weather is so good.'

'I have to help you,' Mathilde said. 'There's so much to be done.'

'I have all the help I need,' Héloïse said firmly. 'It is not for you to be worrying about it, my dear. Go and have your ride — Matty shall help me finish this.'

'Matty is doing the nursery linen,' Mathilde said stubbornly. 'And if I must not be shut up all day, then nor must you.'

Héloïse laughed. 'I shall have a walk later, I promise. Go on, now, before Edward loses patience and goes without you! Have a good, long ride, and put the colour back in your cheeks, for I'm sure you are getting as pale as these sheets, with bending over them all day.'

By the time Mathilde came downstairs after changing into her habit, Edward had the horses tacked-up and ready at the door: his own black Thunderer, and the little chestnut mare Vanity, who was kept up for the use of Héloïse when she cared to ride instead of drive, but was more often Mathilde's mount. Mathilde had sufficient vanity of her own to be glad the mare was a chestnut, for her shining coat only drew attention to her rider's burnished head. Mathilde was very well aware that if one had the misfortune to be born red-haired, one must make the most of it, and her new riding-habit of fine broadcloth was black, for the most effective contrast, and cut very tight and trim across the bodice to shew off her neat figure. Her hat was a small black tricorn which she wore tilted forward, with the great mass of her copper hair coiled behind, and a half-veil of black net over her eyes.

If she had any doubts about the effect she made, they would have been dispelled by the haste with which Edward forestalled the groom, who meant to lead Vanity to the mounting-block, and came forward to link his hands for her boot and throw her into the saddle. He held Vanity's head — quite unnecessarily — while Mathilde settled herself, found her stirrup, and arranged her skirts, all the time looking up at her with so much quiet pleasure in his face that it was as well for her modesty that her eyes were engaged elsewhere.

It was a bright, chill day, the sky a faint, dusty blue scudded with clouds, grey-edged but moving too fast for rain. The two riders crossed the drawbridge and turned left onto the track towards Acomb Moor. As soon as they were clear of the West Fields, where there were breeding ewes which must not be disturbed, they had a good, long gallop to settle the horses. It soon developed into a light-hearted race, for the fresh breeze excited the horses and 'got under their tails' as Edward put it, making them skittish.

Though her troubled childhood had afforded Mathilde no opportunity to learn to ride, it was in her blood. Her mother had been a notable and fearless horsewoman, and Mathilde had taken to it from the first time she mounted, and now handled Vanity with confidence. Edward had checked Thunderer a little, for he would soon have outstripped the smaller mare, but as he was taking a wide path to avoid the soft ground at the head of the Foss Dike, Mathilde turned a bright face to him and laughed, and boldly drove the mare on, swerving away to the right to take the short route, jumping the Dike neatly and pulling up at the gate of Hagg Farm the clear winner.

'I win! I win!' she called mockingly as he rode up. 'You will have to do better than that to beat us, Cousin Edward!'

'Ah, but you cheated,' he returned cheerfully. 'You did not keep to the course. There'll be a steward's enquiry, mark my words.'

'In a cross-country race, I believe one may choose one's own line,' she said, smiling. They rode on together, skirting the farm and taking the track into Askham woods. It was a pleasant change, now, to be out of the wind, and the horses walked almost soundlessly on a thick layer of leaf-mould. It was too early yet for bluebells, though in a few weeks' time there would be a vivid carpet of them in every direction, but there were bright yellow aconites and frail white wood-anemones thrusting through last year's dead leaves, and there, where a break in the leaf-canopy let in enough sunlight, patches of primroses, pale and delicate as eggs in their nests of tough green leaves.

'It's so lovely here,' Mathilde said after a while. 'There's always something new to be seen. I wish —' She broke off, looking pensive, and Edward was about to prompt her when she resumed again. 'Oh look, a squirrel! There, in the birch tree! Doesn't his tail ripple beautifully, like shot silk?'

Leaving the woods, they were in arable fields, and had to keep to the paths around the edges. 'This was all grazing land once, when I was a boy,' Edward said. 'It wasn't worth draining and fencing; but of course the war has put up the price of corn so much it's a different story. Every bit of land possible is being put under the plough. Squire Podworth of Hessay's even beginning to plough up the edges of Marston Moor, so I've heard.'

They had three more dikes to jump before they reached Healaugh, and rode up the track to the Manor Farm, which stood on a slight rise. There the steward was waiting to shew Edward the breeding-ram he hoped to sell him.

'Now then, Maister Morland,' he said respectfully, squinting up at Edward, framed by the bright, windy sky. 'Ah've the tup shut in t'barn all ready. Jed, coom and tek maister's hoss!' He took hold of Vanity's bridle, and said, 'Now, Miss, if you'd like to step into th' house, missus'll give you a sup o' something, and a clean place to sit down until maister's ready.'

'By no means,' Mathilde said quickly, swinging her leg free and jumping down, much to the steward's dismay. 'I want to see the tup as well.'

The steward looked embarrassed at her use of the word, and said hastily, 'Nay, Miss, tha'll get dirty for naught. Sure tha's not interested in sheep!'

'Indeed I am,' she said, smiling mischievously. 'I've read all about Bakewell's methods in Mr Young's new book, which I'm sure you've read — *The Husbandry of Three Famous Farmers* — have you come across it? I quite long to see your ram — I've never seen a pure-bred merino before.'

The steward had no more to say, only stared at her open-mouthed for a moment, before gesturing to the man Jed to take her horse as well, and leading the way to the barn. Edward offered her his arm, and as she caught up the long end of her habit over her arm — for indeed it was very muddy — he murmured, 'That was very unkind of you! You've shocked the poor man with your unwomanliness. But

239

you haven't really read Arthur Young's book, have you?'

'Oh yes! Well, I've been listening to you and Mr James talking about improving the flock night after night, and then I saw the book lying on the table in the drawing-room — I haven't read it all, but I've looked at the pictures,' she admitted.

Edward laughed. 'That's more than I could get James to do! He hates anything more serious than the *Gentleman's Magazine*! So have you understood, then, why I'm interested in this tup — ram?' he corrected himself hastily.

'Because Bakewell's methods produce bigger sheep with coarser wool — very good for mutton, but not so good for wool,' she said promptly.

'That's right. It's all right for long-staple weaving, but our Morland Fancy needs fine, short-staple wool.'

'And the merino is a little sheep with fine wool, isn't it? They come from Spain, don't they?'

Edward looked impressed. 'Quite correct. My dear Mathilde, what a farmer's wife you would make!' A blush spread over her cheeks, and it was fortunate at that moment that she really did have to look down to see where she was treading.

When they had looked at the ram, and Edward and the steward had discussed it at a length even Mathilde began to find excessive, they resolutely refused all offers of hospitality within the farmhouse, remounted, and set off for home again.

'It's a fine little animal, don't you think?' Edward said enthusiastically as they trotted the eager horses down the track. 'The wool is so soft and short, I could hardly believe it! It's one thing to read about it, and quite another to handle it.'

'And you mean to cross it with our ewes, to make their wool finer?' Mathilde asked.

'That's right. I might even produce a new breed, and have it named after me — the Morland Merino, you know — like the Gresley Longhorn!'

'But will one ram be enough to make all that difference?' Mathilde asked. They reached the end of the track, and she halted Vanity as she contemplated the problem with a frown. 'Won't its blood be very diluted, mixed with so many hundreds of ewes?'

Edward checked Thunderer and looked at her with delight.

'Oh my dear Mathilde, it's a peculiar sort of comfort to discover that you don't understand everything about stock improvement after all!'

Mathilde turned her head to smile at him. 'I told you I only looked at the pictures!' she said. 'But I'd like to learn. You could teach me, couldn't you, Cousin Edward?'

The sunlight, broken by the fast-scudding clouds, was illuminating her hair, and shining through her golden eyelashes, and Edward looked at her, suddenly heart-in-mouth, realising how much he had come to love her over the last few years; not just as his young cousin and a pleasant companion, but as a beautiful and desirable woman. She *is* beautiful, he thought to himself fiercely, realising how far into his heart she had burrowed, and how very, very painful it would be to root her out. But she was a young woman, with all of her life before her, and he was almost fifty, more than twice her age. What right did a grey old man have to fall in love with a golden girl?

And there were other considerations, he reflected grimly. Though he lived in every comfort at Morland Place, was Fanny's trustee and sole arbiter of everything to do with the house, the estate, and all its incomes, he possessed nothing of his own. When the trust ended, he would inherit the sum of six thousand pounds which, invested in the Funds, would bring him an income of three hundred pounds a year. That, of course, would be ample for his needs, as long as he remained at Morland Place, which, under the terms of his mother's will, he was entitled to do as long as he remained unmarried. But on three hundred pounds a year he could not marry and support a woman with no fortune whatever; he could not even contemplate it as a possibility.

For the first time he thought bitterly of his mother, and saw how monstrous it was for her to have left everything to Fanny, making no provision for her other children. William and Harry were all right, of course, because they had their careers, and Lucy and James were well-married, but Edward — what thought had she taken for Edward? He had worked all his life on and for the Morland estate. He had given up the chance to go to university and have a career in order to learn about the estate to which, everyone had assumed at that time, he would be the heir. He had given his life to drudgery, had grown grey in the service of the ancient house and the broad, green acres, and now he was left the merest pensioner, unpaid steward to a spoilt brat not even of his fathering.

Of course, another part of his mind might offer in expiation, it was by his own choice that he had not married and produced a family long ago. If he had done so, Morland Place would have been left to him and his offspring: his mother's monstrous will was the result of his long and chosen celibacy. But that was no comfort now, and he thrust the excuse away angrily. His mother had no right to place him in this intolerable position. He was no better than a farm-hand, a beggar, a poor relation!

And he had no right to think of Mathilde; sweet, lovely Mathilde, who was smiling at him now, waiting for an answer as these thoughts rushed through his head in a bare few seconds.

'Teach you?' he said harshly. 'No, I don't think I could. It's a complicated subject; not suitable for a female, in any case.'

He had spoken more abruptly than he meant, and saw that he had wounded her. Her mouth trembled, and she lowered her eyes, bewildered and hurt, and he wanted to cry out and comfort her, tell her everything, how much he loved her, how he would die to defend her from the least pain. But he stopped himself, knowing that it was better so. Better if the warmth were allowed to seep out of their relationship. Better if there were no more rides together or games of chess. Better if she came — oh God! — just a little to dislike him. If he must root her out of his heart, let it be as soon and as completely as possible.

They rode on in silence for a while, Edward keeping his eyes away from her, his brow drawn, his mouth turned down as he brooded over his troubles. Mathilde looked at him covertly from under her lashes, as much puzzled as hurt by his abrupt change of mood, and the sharp way he had spoken to her. They had been such good friends that she could not bear to be at outs with him, and after a while plucked up courage to ask timidly, 'Cousin Edward, have I said something to offend you?' He neither replied nor looked at her, and after a moment she went on, unconsciously turning a knife in his heart, 'Pray, pray forgive me if I have. I didn't mean to, for the world.'

His arms ached with the longing to take her in them, but

242

he schooled his voice to cool politeness. 'Offended me? No, not at all. There is nothing to forgive, I assure you.'

'But there is, I'm sure of it,' she cried eagerly, encouraged by the fact of his answering, if not by the words. 'We had been so comfortable before, and now you won't look at me.'

He turned his eyes painfully on her, and forced a brief, and he hoped avuncular, smile. 'Not look at you? Nonsense! You're imagining things. But I think we'd better hurry — I'm sure it's going to rain.' He kicked Thunderer into a trot, and thence to a canter, taking him ahead of Mathilde where she wouldn't be able to see his face. She followed, puzzled and unhappy, and as he kept up a fast pace all the way home, there was no opportunity for further conversation. It was all she could do on Vanity to keep up with him; but at least, she thought, if there were tears in her eyes, they might be put down to the rush of cold air in her face.

The great wash was finished at last, and everything was put back in its place, and the house was comfortable again. As she looked about the drawing-room with pride and pleasure on the first day afterwards, Héloïse, noticing her ward's pale face, was seized with guilt.

'Ma pauvre, I have kept you indoors in all the dust, except for that one ride you had, and you have wilted like a cut daisy! I shall tell you what, though, my Mathilde: I shall have the ponies put-to in the phaeton, and you and I and Nicholas will drive into York, and do a little shopping. We shall call at Enderby's, and see if they have any new muslins for a gown for you, how would that be? For you have worked so hard these last few days, you deserve at least a new gown.'

'Thank you, Madame,' Mathilde said listlessly, 'but I have no need of a new gown. I have the one Mr James bought me for my birthday which I've hardly worn yet.'

Héloïse bore the astonishing reply bravely, realising there was more to Mathilde's pallor than merely being confined indoors. For a young woman to refuse a new gown was evidence of some deep malaise. 'Well, we shall go to York anyway,' she said calmly. 'I need some new gloves, for my white ones are quite grey; and I wish to speak to Mr Pobgee; and I have some cards to leave. But,' she added with a smile, 'you need not fear I shall drag you with me to be bored! I shall drop you off at the Keatings' house on my way to Davygate, and collect you on my way back. I am sure you haven't spoken to poor Patience this age.'

Mathilde brightened a little. 'Thank you, Madame. I should like that,' she said.

The Keatings lived in a new house in Blake Street, and Héloïse meant to drop Mathilde at the door; but when she reached the corner of St Helen's Square, where it made a junction with Blake Street to the left, Davygate to the right, and Stonegate straight ahead, she found the way blocked. A brewer's dray coming out of Stonegate had collided with a vegetable cart on the way to the market, and the entrance to Blake Street was a tangled mess of empty barrels, apples, cabbages, splintered wood, altercations, vociferous chairmen, pigs, children, gawpers and trapped traffic, and it was plain there was no getting through.

'It doesn't matter, Madame,' Mathilde said quickly. 'Let me jump down. It's only a step from here — I can walk the rest.'

'Very well,' Héloïse said, looking at the seething crowd doubtfully, 'but do be careful, *chérie*, and hold tight to your reticule. Go straight there; and if they should not be at home, ask for a servant to walk with you to Mr Pobgee's, where I shall be for the next half-hour at least. Don't think of walking alone.'

'No, Madame. I shall be all right,' Mathilde said, and jumped down with a lighter heart, for there was nothing like a little noise and bustle for blowing away gloom. She crossed the street with difficulty, and worked her way through the crowd, listening appreciatively to the rapidly-escalating quarrel between the two carters as to whose fault it was, interspersed with fierce cries from the vegetable man as he saw his wares being gathered up quietly from the road by passers-by and removed to places of concealment.

The Keatings' house was half-way along the street, and she had just cleared the fringes of the gathering when she saw a tall figure she knew very well come out of the front door and turn along the street towards her.

He paused in front of her and raised his hat. 'Miss Nordubois! How do you do? What a pleasant chance! Are you going to visit Miss Keating? How comes it that you are alone?'

'How do you do, Mr Skelwith,' Mathilde said, and explained the circumstances. Since he had stopped coming to Morland Place, they had met tolerably often on neutral ground, at balls and other peoples' houses, and any awkwardness there might have been between them had passed long ago. They had even danced together once or twice, and chatted pleasantly like any slight acquaintance.

As she spoke, Mathilde eyed him with interest. She hadn't happened to see him for several weeks, and she thought now how well he was looking. His usually grave face seemed lighter; there was something like a sparkle in his eyes, and a hint of a smile lurking on his lips, and his carriage spoke of a man at ease with the world. Really, she thought, he is almost handsome — certainly a very attractive man! She had always liked him, had been deeply flattered in the beginning by his preference; and seeing him now, it came to her what an excellent suitor she had lost in him. How foolish she had been not to encourage him more! How arrogant, to assume that she could have her choice! How profligate, to throw away what was to hand, in the hope of better to come!

She would be glad now, she thought more humbly, to receive a renewal of his attentions. A kind, personable, gentle man of large fortune: she must have been wandering in her wits to let him go. As for that other folly — she shuddered inwardly to think of it. How could she ever have supposed that he cared for her in *that* way? It was plain to her now that he had viewed her only in the light of a younger relation, almost like a niece, and she had deeply offended him by being too bold, by allowing her preference to shew; embarrassing him, perhaps even shocking him.

'You have just been to see the Keatings yourself, Mr Skelwith?' she said now. 'Then I suppose they are at home?'

'Oh yes, very much at home,' he said with a grin. 'I am sure you will be the most welcome sight in the world to Miss Keating — she will have such a lot of things to tell you! I wish I might walk back there with you, but I must be on my way. I have several very urgent things to do.' He suddenly took her hand and pressed it, something between a handshake and a friendly embrace, and smiled down at her. 'Dear Miss Nordubois, I am so very glad to see you! And Patience will be too! Pray, go up at once, and let her think I sent you on purpose.'

Mathilde didn't quite understand him, but he was certainly behaving in a very warm manner towards her, and she wondered if perhaps all was not lost, and that he had a heart returning to her after all. Well, if it were so, this time she would know better how to value it! She returned the handshake cordially, and before tracing her steps to the Keatings' front door, turned to watch him as he strode away along Blake Street, looking, had she not known better, every bit like a man in love.

Héloïse often thought that the offices of Pobgee and Micklethwaite in Daveygate were one of those places in the world where, if you sat still long enough, you would one day meet everyone you had ever known. Everyone in York — everyone who mattered, that was — seemed to entrust their legal business to the old-established firm, and sitting in the comfortable ante-room for an hour or two, one might save oneself all the trouble of going calling on one's acquaintance.

Héloïse did not rush her business, partly because she liked Mr Pobgee senior, who always saw her personally, and chatted to her more like a friend than her man of business; and partly because she was installed in a very comfortable chair, with Nicholas beside her, Castor on her lap, and a glass of madeira in her hand; and partly to give Mathilde time to reach her, if the Keatings should be from home.

When at last she did rise up to leave, and was shewn to the door by Mr Pobgee senior, she entered the ante-room at the same moment as John Skelwith emerged into it from the room of Mr Pobgee Junior, and they came face to face with each other. Neither of them precisely blushed, but a strong consciousness overspread them both. To Héloïse, nothing could be more productive of pain equally mixed with pleasure than to come upon this young man with his haunting look of James. She liked him very much, and wished with all her heart that there were something she could do for him, or that it were possible for them all to be comfortable and friendly together.

'Mr Skelwith,' she said now, holding out her hand cordially. 'What a pleasant coincidence. You have had business with the Pobgees too, it seems?'

It was only said for something to say, and she didn't really expect a specific answer, but he smiled his pleasant, poignant smile and said, 'Yes, ma'am, indeed! I have had a very particular sort of business — the best sort! I met Miss Nordubois in the street a while ago, on her way to visit Miss Keating. No doubt she will know all about it by now.'

'Will she, Mr Skelwith?' Héloïse said, rather mystified by his cheerfulness.

'Yes, ma'am. Can't you guess? I have been consulting Pobgee about marriage settlements!' For the fraction of a second, Héloïse's heart jumped, before he continued, 'Miss Keating has done me the honour of accepting my hand. We are to be married in four weeks' time.'

Héloïse said what was proper, thinking that Patience Keating was a nice, sensible girl, and would make him a good wife, though Mathilde was worth six of her. What had happened to his evident preference for her ward? Had he simply realised that Mathilde was indifferent to him? It had taken him a long time to choose another. No inconstant heart, his! Had Mathilde really been indifferent? She hoped so, now, or there would be an awkward interview going on at this moment in the Keatings' house.

'I wish you very happy, Mr Skelwith,' Héloïse said, and then, cautiously, 'Is your mother pleased, also?'

He actually grinned. 'Oh yes, Mother likes Patience very much. She can't wait to have her as a daughter.' This, Héloïse thought, was certainly an exaggeration. 'There's only one thing she may not like — but no, I'm speaking like a fool,' he stopped himself with a look of vexation.

'What, then?' Héloïse asked. 'Come now, you have intrigued me. You must finish what you were saying.'

He looked uncomfortable. 'Well, ma'am, you know that Mother was against my marrying Miss Nordubois?' he said awkwardly.

'No, I didn't,' Héloïse said. Ah, she thought, so that was it, was it? Mary Loveday put her foot down and said no, and so the good son took up his pride and left!

Skelwith looked as though he wished he had never mentioned it. 'It was nothing really, ma'am — I mean, she had nothing against Miss Nordubois herself, of course. It was — I can't explain really. It was old history.' Héloïse nodded kindly. 'Well, Mother's very pleased about me and Patience,

247

but I happen to know that she — Patience, that is — means to ask Miss Nordubois to be her bridesmaid, and I'm only afraid Mother might —'

Héloïse smiled at him. 'I think you will find that you are worrying for nothing, Mr Skelwith. I am sure your mother will be quite happy with the arrangement. And now I must be on my way. Come, Nicholas. Once again, my best wishes, Mr Skelwith. I'm sure you will be very happy.'

Out in the street, she hesitated, and then decided to go straight to Blake Street. She ought to offer her felicitations to Miss Keating; and she wanted to be sure all was well with Mathilde.

'So she will need that new gown after all,' she murmured aloud, with a private smile.

CHAPTER THIRTEEN

Everyone said afterwards that Patience Keating's wedding was one of the nicest they had ever been to. Though Mrs Keating had wanted to to take place in the fashionable St Michael-le Belfry, she eventually gave in to Mary Skelwith's desire that her son should be married at St Helen's — largely because Mary Skelwith threatened otherwise not to attend the wedding at all.

This slight unpleasantness having been got over, there was nothing else to mar the pleasure of the happy couple or the guests. The Keatings were extremely glad to see their daughter well-married, especially when, at twenty-two, she had looked likely to be left on their hands. John Skelwith was a fine young man, and his fortune was even finer, and the Keatings were not so high themselves as to object that it came from Trade.

Patience had accepted John's proposal with pleasure not unmixed with relief, and though she might have some doubts as to the congeniality of her future mother-in-law, her prospects of comfort and happiness as John's wife were so bright that she began to look almost beautiful, especially when dressed in her wedding finery. Mr Keating was glad to spare no expense on such a unique occasion, and Patience was arrayed in the first style, white satin with a lace veil and her mother's pearls, just as if it had been a London wedding.

Mathilde was her bridesmaid, in pale yellow jaconet embroidered all over with tiny white daisies, which became her excellently; and John Anstey's eldest daughter Louisa, aged ten, preceeded them up the aisle scattering flower petals in their path from a basket, which everyone thought a very pretty conceit. John Skelwith looked pale and serious in a new blue coat and a white waistcoat embroidered with silver threads, his fox-brown hair newly cropped and brushed into a shining pelt. He was attended by Tom Keating, who was red-faced and merry, and whose wedding-favour was on upside-down. He had been pressing John all morning to bolster his courage with brandy, and tormenting him by pretending to have mislaid the ring. When the moment came in the ceremony, he found he really had mislaid it, but after a frantic few minutes' search, it was discovered nestling in the bottom of Tom's tortuously tight fob-pocket, where he'd put it because 'he was sure it couldn't fall out from there'.

After the ceremony, the couple were seen off in a ribbon-bedecked post-chaise for Scarborough, where they were to stay for a month at the house of Patience's paternal aunt, who had a fortune to leave and no-one to leave it to. Every-one else retired to the Keatings' house in Blake Street, where the wine flowed, an excellent cold feast was spread on a buffet, and there was a promise of dancing later, and cards for the gentlemen.

Mathilde found herself at the centre of one group of young people, some of whom were anxious to know whether she now regretted having rejected John Skelwith, as she was popularly thought to have done. No-one, of course, was bold enough to put the question quite like that, but Mathilde knew what they were thinking, and by her cheerful demeanour hoped to make it plain that she was very happy for her friend, and regretted nothing. It was inevitable, however, on such an occasion that she should wonder a little about her future. She was amongst the oldest of the young women still unwed, and she had no fortune; she was not precisely worried, but she would have been glad to know that she would be addressed by a man in respectable circumstances within a twelvemonth.

Fanny was at the centre of another group, the younger generation of unmarried girls, some of whom were out, and others, like Fanny, who were not. Not being out did not stop Fanny from feeling superior to them all, and behaving as the leader of their society. Who, after all, was there to come before her? She had birth, beauty, and fortune, all three; and she hoped Roxane Grey and Edys Cowey noticed how Tom Keating — who was absolutely twenty-five years old — drifted away from the group of older girls in order to hang about Fanny's elbow and offer to fetch her lemonade.

Though she was not out, and could not therefore attend formal balls or assemblies, Fanny had already collected a court of fervent admirers, most of whom were too young to be anything but contemptible in her eyes, even though they were necessary to her. It was already becoming the fashion amongst the younger males like Horace Micklethwaite, Jack Appleby, and Edmund Somers to worship Fanny Morland, and she was happy that they should do so; but in company with her female contemporaries she referred to them loftily as 'scrubby boys', and asserted that only older men were interesting to her. Tom Keating was no great catch, and a notorious flirt, but he was indisputably older, and it was a matter of intense satisfaction to Fanny that the man who had so recently been paying marked attentions to Mathilde was now disposed to pay them to her.

James had joined a group of his former cronies in front of one of the fireplaces. It amused him to watch Fanny, across the other side of the room, queening it over her contemporaries, and half his mind was occupied in the perennially fascinating speculation of a future match for her. He was therefore listening only half-heartedly to the conversation about the frame-breakers who were causing trouble in Nottingham.

'In my view, they ought to call out the military, before things get out of hand,' Edgar Somers was saying. 'It's a damn' disgrace that these rioters should be allowed to get away with it scot-free. The penalties aren't by half severe enough, that's the truth of it.'

'Fourteen years' transportation for frame-breaking, isn't it?' said Isiah Keating easily. 'Hardly scot-free, old fellow.'

'You wouldn't say that if it were your livelihood at stake,' said his brother-in-law crossly. 'A man ties up all his capital in expensive machinery, and these damn Luddites, or whatever they call themselves, come along and smash them to flinders! It should be made a capital offence. The rope's what they need!'

'*On a diablement peur de la corde*,' James murmured. The others ignored him. There was a time and a place for speaking French, they thought; and besides, they didn't have French wives to keep them in practice.

'You'd still have to catch them first,' Arthur Fussell said with the detachment of a man two generations distant from the origins of his fortune. 'I've heard these Luddites hang out

251

in Sherwood Forest. You'd never find them in there!'

'If frame-breaking were made a capital offence, the militia could shoot them on sight,' Somers said fiercely.

'Wouldn't it be better to capture them alive? Then you could torture them, to find out who their leader is,' James said, straight-faced. 'This "King Ludd" they talk about.'

'I don't believe there is a "King Ludd",' Keating said. 'He sounds like a mythical character to me. Like Robin Hood — why else would they say he lives in Sherwood Forest? Fairy tales!'

'Enough of the labouring poor believe he exists,' said Henry Bayliss, the newspaper proprietor, quietly. 'It really doesn't matter whether he does or not.'

'But I don't understand why these people smash the frames in the first place,' said Keating indifferently. 'What do they hope to gain?'

'The lower orders don't reason,' Somers said sharply, 'they simply destroy. There are always enough ignorant brutes ready to act against their own interests, once they're whipped up by a few fanatics. Catch the ringleaders and hang 'em, that's what I say.'

'Very well, but why do the ringleaders want to smash the frames?' Keating insisted.

'They don't need a reason,' Somers snorted.

'In this case, they have a very good one,' said Bayliss. He was often better-informed than the rest of the Maccabbees club members, and always more reasonable.

'I'd like to know what could be a good reason for wanton destruction,' Somers began, but James, tired of his fulminating, interrupted.

'Do you know something about this, Bayliss? Let's hear it, man.'

'Yes, as it happens, I do. My brother, you know, is a stocking manufacturer in Nottingham, so I hear about it from him.'

'And has he your liberal tendencies, too?' Arthur Fussel asked, hoping to stir up an argument, but Bayliss ignored him.

'It's the stocking-knitters who are rioting, because their livelihood's being destroyed. Stockings, as you probably know, are knitted on narrow frames. The cloth knitted on wide frames was mostly made into pantaloons, and the Continent was the biggest market for them. Well, now the war and Boney's embargo have closed the market, the wide-frame manufacturers are in trouble. So to keep their looms busy, some of 'em are cutting up the cloth and sewing it into stockings and gloves. These cut-ups, as they call 'em, fall to pieces in no time, but they're cheap, and they're ruining the market. The narrow frames are idle, and the stockingers are out of work; so they strike back by smashing the wide frames.'

'And what good do they think that will do them?' Somers said contemptuously.

'It's hard to see what else they can do,' Bayliss observed. 'Would you stand by and see your wife and children starve, and do nothing?'

Somers coloured dangerously. 'Are you suggesting there's some similarity between me and a member of the lower orders?'

'The lower orders are still sentient beings,' Bayliss argued. 'Like us they feel hunger, despair, paternal love —'

'You talk like a damn' Jacobin!' Somers said angrily. 'Sympathising with rioters and revolutionaries! What are you — some kind of Reformer?'

'I say, steady on, Somers,' Keating murmured. 'Only a friendly discussion, old fellow. No call for abuse.'

'There's a good deal of sympathy for the stockingers in the county,' Bayliss went on, unmoved. 'Yes, even amongst the manufacturers! Oh, not for their methods, of course; but the cut-ups are ruining master and man, and there are enough narrow-frame owners in and around Nottingham who would turn a blind eye to frame-breaking if the cut-up trade could be stopped.'

'These are troubled times,' Colonel Brunton pronounced sagely, with a wag of the head. 'I don't know what we're coming to. Country's goin' to rack and ruin. Decent brandy costs the earth these days. And talkin' to young Skelwith the other day about m' new house — says he can't get hold of good building timber for love nor money. Boney's embargo — import duties — and now this trouble with the Americans —' He sighed heavily.

'We shall have a crisis before long,' said Dykes, the banker, 'if we keep pouring money into the Peninsula — and gold,

253

too, not this wretched paper currency we're cursed with. Two bad harvests pushing the price of corn beyond reason, exports almost vanished — there'll be more bankruptcies soon, you mark my words. How's your father-in-law managing, Morland? Now the Americans have refused to send us any more raw cotton, he must be feeling the pinch, what?'

Isiah Keating was looking as though he wished they would remember it was a wedding-party, so James said lightly, 'Why, you know, he never tells me anything about his business — knows I wouldn't understand a word of it if he did! But he's a canny old brute, and I'd back him to come out ahead in any situation, just as I'd back our new chestnut colt to win the steeplechase at Easter.' An instant clamour of disagreement rose up from the sporting gentlemen in the group, and having successfully changed the subject, James gave Keating a solemn wink, and strolled away, saying 'But I must go and see how Fanny is doing. I'm afraid she's being obliged to hold an intellectual conversation, and needs rescuing.'

Far from feeling the need for rescue, Fanny was at that moment triumphantly routing her closest enemy, Roxane Grey. The Grey girls, though unluckily numerous and notoriously lapped in poverty, felt themselves superior because their papa was a peer, and their mama had been a Miss Parr, and related to the Percys of Northumberland. Roxane, the nearest in age to Fanny, was a quick-tongued, lively girl who particularly resented her family's poverty, and hated Fanny, who had everything, and was insensitive enough to boast about it.

Fanny felt that one so plain as Roxane, who had crooked teeth and sometimes even appeared to squint, had nothing to be proud about, and ought not to give herself airs in Fanny's presence, simply on the strength of a viscountcy of relatively recent date. Roxane Grey, however, had a close friend in Miss Edys Cowey, who, on account of the early marriage of her two elder sisters, had been out since she was fifteen, and therefore had all the rights of superiority over a Fanny Morland who was still in the schoolroom. Whatever Miss Grey proposed, Miss Cowey supported, and between them they were almost a match for Miss Morland.

It happened that the three of them found themselves in a

group with no young men nearby to impress, so there was nothing for them to do but quarrel. The present conflict had begun through a remark of Miss Grey's.

'Of course, John Skelwith is well enough,' she said with a kind and pitying smile, 'but I wonder Patience Keating should want to marry Trade. I should not care for it myself.'

'Oh, but the Keatings are not obliged to be so high,' Miss Cowey said languidly. 'They may be genteel now, but the family is not an old one, you know.'

'Yes, and the mama was an Anstey, wasn't she?' Miss Grey added eagerly. 'They're in Coal, for all that he's a peer now.'

'Blood will out, dear,' Miss Cowey said with a superior smile, 'And though I dote on Patience Keating —'

'Oh, so do I! She's the dearest creature!'

'Yes, but Tom Keating, you know, is not quite the thing. Don't you agree, Miss Morland?'

Fanny had been listening with scant interest, caring little for Keatings or Ansteys or anyone else she thought beneath her; but the final remark was addressed so pointedly, and attacked Fanny's proudest conquest so blatantly, that she felt obliged to retaliate.

'Agree with what?' she asked coolly. 'I was not attending.'

'Don't you agree that the Keatings are not quite genteel — particularly Tom Keating? Roxane and I were agreeing that we should not care to associate too closely with them.'

'Perhaps *you* might not,' Fanny said, raising an eyebrow in unconscious imitation of her governess's style, 'but then I have not so much need as you to be careful who I talk to.'

'Why, what can you mean?' Miss Grey asked, exchanging a glance with her friend, feeling that they had Fanny wrong-footed.

'I mean that the Morlands are such an old and well-connected family, my credit must be better than yours,' Fanny said with unconcealed triumph. 'My family was granted its coat of arms three hundred and fifty years ago, you know.' She smiled maliciously at Miss Grey. 'But I believe your papa is only the *third* viscount, isn't he? And the Coweys, I understand, were graziers a few generations back. Isn't that where the name comes from — cowherd?'

Miss Cowey went scarlet with rage, and Miss Grey hissed, 'You think yourself so high, Fanny Morland, but everyone knows your family's had more scandals than rooks in a rookery! And your grandpa's a mill-owner, so you needn't be so top-lofty about your fortune, neither!'

Fanny, however, felt herself to be unassailable. 'Pooh! Every old family has its scandals. We don't regard them, the way the middling sort of people are obliged to do.' Miss Grey almost choked at hearing herself thus classed with 'the middling sort', and Fanny went on blithely, 'As to my grandpapa's mills, I don't mind in the least if *half* my fortune comes from manufacturing. It's the modern way for old money to marry new money, and make it respectable. It just makes me richer than ever, rich enough to buy both of you *and* your papas ten times over, if I wanted.'

'You're a vulgar, spiteful little cat, Fanny Morland!'

'And you're just eaten up with jealousy, because your pa makes you wear cotton stockings!'

It was at this interesting moment that James strolled up to the group, and by his adult presence stopped the battle in mid-bombardment.

'Hullo, Fanny! Are you having an agreeable time? And your friends — it's Miss Cowey, isn't it, and Miss Grey — though deuced if I know which one,' he said with his most charming smile. ' You Grey girls are all so pretty, it's a day's work telling you apart! Do you all enjoy yourselves? The Keatings have put on a splendid feast, haven't they? Those lobster patties must be the best I've tasted!'

There was no being rude to Fanny's father, who apart from being a grown-up, smiled in such a way as to make a half-grown girl feel like a pretty woman. Both young ladies, though longing to rend Fanny limb from limb, were obliged to swallow their fury and murmur something socially acceptable.

'What was it you were talking about when I came up?' James went on pleasantly. 'You all looked so serious, I made sure it must be Lord Wellington's campaign you were discussing.'

For a moment they were all too taken aback to answer. Miss Cowey recovered herself first. 'We were talking about Fanny's grandpapa, sir,' she said, with a sweet, grim smile at Fanny, 'and how lucky she is to have such a fortune coming to her from his *manufactories*.'

256

'Were you indeed? We have just been discussing much the same thing over by the fireplace,' said James. 'But if things go on the way they are, poor Fanny may have to fall back on Morland Place for her fortune, for the cotton kings are feeling the pinch of the times, you know.'

'But Papa,' Fanny said urgently, not wishing her position to be eroded, 'surely Grandpapa's mills are too big to be troubled by the war?'

'These are hard times for all the mill-masters, big and small,' James said. 'I'm sure your grandpapa will come through, however. He's a very clever man. But you know, you don't inherit the mills, Fan — only a capital sum: your grandpapa always felt mills ought not to be left to a female.' Fanny blinked. 'But come,' James went on with a smile, 'this is too grave a subject for a wedding-day — even someone else's! Should you girls — young ladies, I should say — like some ices? Since your beaux have all deserted you, I will place myself at your service.'

Before they could answer, however, Tom Keating had appeared at Fanny's elbow again, with the information that Mrs Keating had engaged a fiddler, and dancing was about to begin in the saloon.

'I hope my reward for bringing you this intelligence may be your hand for the two first dances, Miss Morland?' he concluded.

James had never much approved of Tom Keating, largely because of his poor seat and heavy hands on a horse, but he was also a notorious flirt, and judging by his red face and moist eye, had been indulging himself fairly heavily in liquor. He was not the partner he would best like to see Fanny stand up with, even at an informal dance like this one; but he knew enough of Fanny's pride not to wish to intervene in front of her friends; and Fanny accepted the offer so regally, as a deserved but commonplace tribute, that he felt she was in no danger from him.

The next day after breakfast, Fanny followed her father into the great hall and accosted him as he was putting on his gloves to go out to the stables.

'Papa, may I speak to you?'

'What is it, Fan? Be quick, love — I want to lunge Comet,

257

and if I don't get to Twelvetrees soon, Salton will have taken him out.'

'It's about Grandpapa's mills — what you said yesterday at the Keatings',' she said anxiously. 'It isn't true, is it?'

'What isn't true?' James asked absently, searching around in the heap of hats, gloves, whips and miscellaneous bits of tack on the marble side-table for his crop. 'Deuce take it, I laid it here only last night!'

'About Grandpapa not wanting to leave the mills to a female,' Fanny said, and then with an exasperated movement unearthed the crop, which was protruding from under a pile of spurs and boot-straps, and thrusting it at him. '*Here's* your crop! Now do attend to me, Papa. It's important.'

'Yes, Fan, sorry Fan. What is it?' James said, making a comical face.

Fanny sighed. Sometimes it was a great trial to have a father who was so little serious. 'I always thought I was Grandpapa Hobsbawn's only heir, and that I would get everything of his when he dies. Isn't that so?'

'Well, love, I don't exactly know,' James said. 'As I told you yesterday, Grandpapa felt the mills ought to be left to a male heir. In his old will, you were to have twenty thousand pounds, and the house, and all his personal effects, and the mills were to go to your brother Henry. After Henry died, the only other male Hobsbawn was your grandpapa's cousin Jasper, who was his heir before you were born. But whether or not he's made a new will and left the mills to Jasper, I can't say, for he's never mentioned it.'

'But can't you ask him?' Fanny said urgently.

'No I can't,' James said promptly. 'What an idea! You know your grandpapa don't care for me. Anyway, why are you so interested? What do you care about cotton-mills? Twenty thousand pounds is a vast fortune, you know, besides the Morland estate.'

'But I want the mills as well!' Fanny cried passionately. 'Why should cousin Jasper have them? I am Grandpapa's heiress. They should come to me!'

James laughed and pressed the tip of her nose with his finger-tip. 'Little avarice! I wonder if any fortune would be enough for you? But don't forget you are Fanny Morland, not Fanny Hobsbawn. The twenty thousand pounds will be very useful to improve the estate, Fan, but the mills — leave them to those who understand them, that's my advice. We're gentlemen farmers, not mill-masters! And now I must be off. Shouldn't you be at your lessons? What is it this morning? Drawing? Didn't I see the drawing-master cross the hall just now?'

'He teaches Nicholas first today. I have pianoforte with Miss Rosedale,' Fanny said absently: she was evidently deep in thought about something far removed from lessons.

On a glorious May day, Héloïse was sitting out in the rose-garden, with Nicholas, Kithra and Castor at her feet, and a basket of sewing in her lap. It was Marie's day off, and she had been taken out for a drive by Kexby, the carrier from Thirsk, who had been asking her to marry him twice a year for the last five years at least. Marie always refused his offers, not wishing to leave Héloïse's service, and Héloïse wished she could think of a way to persuade Marie to accept. Not that she wished to be without her dear friend and servant, but she felt very guilty at depriving her, however involuntarily, of the establishment and happiness she deserved.

Kithra lifted his head and thumped his tail on the ground, and a moment later Castor gave a single bark of greeting as Mathilde came through the archway into the arbour where Héloïse was sitting.

'The letters have come, Madame,' she said, 'and there's one for you from Lady Aylesbury. I thought you might like to have it out here.'

'Thank you, my dear. That was a kind thought,' Héloïse said, and put aside the sewing, which had been occupying her with little enthusiasm, to break the seal and unfold the letter. Though Lucy had not visited Yorkshire since Nicholas was born, they had kept up a regular correspondence, and Héloïse looked forward to her letters. Mathilde sat down beside her, and talked to Nicholas, so as not to seem unwarrantably curious.

'Dear Lucy is growing a better correspondent of late,' Héloïse remarked. 'It is only a single sheet, to be sure, but she has written it quite close and crossed half of it! I remember when she would not have been able to fill half so much space.' She began to read, passing on the news to Mathilde as she went. 'She has been to Oatlands with Mr Wiske and Mr Brummell. There has been a special gathering there, to celebrate the Duke of York's reinstatement as Commander-in-Chief. Also the Duchess's birthday, which fell during the week. Hmm — hmm — hmm. There is a great deal about that. And about a bow-window — how is that?'

Mathilde gave a brief description, with gestures.

'Ah yes — a bow-window which has been built at White's club, and Mr Brummell and his friends sit in it all day and look out of the window and make remarks about the passers-by. This is important news in London? Tiens! Hmm — hmm. And Mr Nash has been given the job of drawing plans for a grand scheme of building between Marylebone and Carlton House. There are to be whole new streets, an ornamental park, a canal, houses and shops.' She laughed. 'Listen to this, Mathilde! Lucy says, "It is all in honour of the Regency, so I dare say we shall have a Regent's Street and a Regent's Park, to say nothing of Regent's Villas by the score. What no-one seems to know is, who shall pay for it? By my guess, it will not be Regent's Purse." Oh, that is like her!'

Mathilde smiled. 'Yes, Madame.'

'And that is all, but the crossed part.' She turned the page sideways. 'Oh, mes yeux, but Lucy's handwriting is difficult! Hmm — hmm — hmm — and here is the real news: Captain Haworth had written to say he will be in England by the autumn, and means to stay a six-month. "I shall make him stay with me, at Wolvercote or here, to save expense. I don't believe sailors are paid half enough." Oh, but she is an original, that one! And that is all. Should you like to read it, Mathilde?'

'Thank you, Madame, I should. But I have something to ask. I received a letter of my own this morning,' Mathilde said, proffering the folded sheet she had been holding in her lap. 'It's from Lizzie Spencer.'

'Tell me it, chérie,' Héloïse said good-naturedly. 'I'm sure she has written many things she meant only for you to read.'

'Oh, there are no secrets in it — well, not really,' Mathilde said with a smile. 'The thing is, Lizzie is to be married, and she asks me to be her bridesmaid, and to go away with them afterwards on their bridal tour. Do read it, Madame, and tell me what you think.'

Héloïse read the letter. 'I cannot tell from the way she writes — will she be happy? She says so little about this Mr Wickfield. Have you heard of him before? Is he agreeable?'

'Yes, very, I believe, Madame. She has written about him in other letters. He's a friend of her papa's, and a great deal older than she, but she likes him excessively, and he's very wealthy and respectable. He has a large house in Thirkleby, which you know is very close to Coxwold, so she won't be far from home. She'll be able to visit every day if she wants.'

'That is a great thing indeed,' Héloïse agreed solemnly. 'And the wedding tour is to go to the Lakes, and then to the Peak District, if time permits. Ah, if it weren't for the war, I dare say they would go to Paris and Vienna and Florence and Rome! That would have been a great thing for you, Mathilde, to see Europe! The churches, the piazzas, the art galleries! It is very sad, that there are whole generations of young people who have never set foot outside England.'

'You forget, Madame,' Mathilde said with a smile, 'that like you, I was born outside England — though to be sure I don't remember much about it.'

'Well, that is true,' Héloïse agreed. 'And so, should you like to go on this tour? Would it amuse you?'

'Very much indeed, Madame. I should like it above anything, if you can spare me.'

'Oh, as to that, I shall manage somehow, with only a butler and housekeeper and a score of servants to help me,' Héloïse said solemnly. 'Well, then, you shall write and say yes and thank you to Lizzie Spencer.' She cocked her head at her ward. 'Now you will have been twice a bridesmaid. I hope it does not make you unhappy?'

Mathilde remained composed, but she did not meet Héloïse's eye. 'Not at all, Madame,' she said calmly. 'I have no wish to marry.'

'But you should wish it, *ma chère*, Héloïse said indignantly. 'You are a very handsome and clever young woman, much too good to waste on spinsterhood.'

'Perhaps I haven't met the right man yet, Madame,' Mathilde said, trying to make light of it. Héloïse eyed her thoughtfully, seeing the slight blush that stained her cheek. Oh, you have met the right man, she thought, but perhaps at the wrong time. But who is it? Not the Skelwith, I think? No, I

261

don't believe so. I wonder — no, that was too foolish! And yet —

'Mathilde, I meant to ask you,' Héloïse said casually, 'have you quarrelled with your cousin Edward? Well, no, not quarrelled — that is the wrong word — but, forgive me, *chérie*, for noticing that you don't play chess with him in the evenings any more. He is such a lonely man, I'm sure he must miss your company very much. I feel very sorry for him.'

'It is by his own choice that we do not play chess, Madame,' Mathilde said quietly. 'I have not refused to play — it is simply that he hasn't asked me.'

Her tone was not quite as non-committal as she evidently intended it to be, but Héloïse did not feel she could press the matter any further. She continued to look at Mathilde in a puzzled way, however, until Mathilde was roused to ask, 'Well, Madame, I have your permission, then, to go with Lizzie? I shall be away for a month at least, perhaps six weeks, for you see Lizzie says they will not hurry back if there is something particularly worth seeing.'

'Of course you may go, and with my blessing!' Héloïse said quickly. 'I hope you will amuse yourself very well. It is kind of Lizzie to ask you — though perhaps,' she added thoughtfully, 'she anticipates more good to herself in securing an agreeable companion. It will be a great thing for her to have you there, if this Mr Wickfield should prove to have inconvenient interests, and wants to tramp about in the rain, and look at mountains when there are shops to be visited.'

'But Madame!' Mathilde began, shocked and ready to defend the School of the Picturesque; and then she saw the laughter in Héloïse's eye, and realised she was being teased.

Only a day or two later, when Mathilde was still spending hours locked up in the Red Room with Marie, going through her clothes and deciding what to take and what new gowns she would need to have made, Edward came to James with a puzzled look and a letter in his hand.

'It's from Papa Hobsbawn,' he said, waving it distractedly. 'He says he wants Fanny to go and stay with him, for six weeks or two months. I think he's taken leave of his senses.'

'What, because he wants Fanny to stay with him?' James said indignantly.

'No — though as to that — but however, I mean his letter sounds very odd. Listen to this: "I think your plan an excellent one" he says. My plan? And this: "As previously discussed — at my expense I may add —". What can he mean by that? What do you make of it?'

James perused the letter, frowning, and then said, 'I believe we must apply to Fanny for the answer. I always find, wherever there is a mystery, Fanny knows more about it than anyone in the house. Shall we go and ask her? Where is she this morning?'

'You should know better than I,' Ned said shortly. 'You're her father.'

They found her in the day-nursery with Miss Rosedale, reading a book of Italian essays in a listless manner, and it would be hard to say which of them looked the more relieved at the interruption.

'Fanny, we've had a letter from your grandpapa which rather puzzles us, and we wondered if you could shed any light on it,' James said, thinking how pretty Fanny looked, now she had begun to turn up her hair. Her schoolroom dress of dark green cambric became her very well, its very plainness setting off her prettiness, and shewing up the green lights in her wide hazel eyes. She would be a killing little witch in a year or two, he thought, not without wistfulness.

'I, Papa?' she said now, looking up, but a faint flush betrayed her.

'Yes, chick, you. Don't look at me like that, all dewy innocence! Your grandpapa asks for you to go and visit him, and seems to think that *we* have already proposed the matter to *him*, so either he has taken leave of his senses, or —'

'Well, yes, Papa, I did write to him,' Fanny said. She looked quickly round the adult faces gauging their reactions. 'But it was Miss Rosedale's idea.'

'Mine?' Miss Rosedale exclaimed, astonished.

'Yes, ma'am, don't you remember? You told me to compose a letter framing "a Delicate Request to an Older Person of Uncertain Temper",' Fanny said brightly. 'In our English composition lesson. So I wrote a letter to my grandpapa asking if I might come and visit him. Well, I didn't precisely ask him that. In the first letter I asked if he remembered the last time I visited, and what he promised then.'

263

Miss Rosedale looked at her askance. 'I remember setting you some such task, though I don't precisely remember what you wrote. But that was just an exercise, Fanny. Do you mean to say you sent it off?'

Fanny looked ever more innocent. 'Didn't you mean me to? It seemed a waste to throw it away, especially when you'd ruled the lines for me.'

'Just a minute, what do you mean by the *first* letter?' James said suspiciously.

'Well, Grandpapa wrote back to me, so I had to reply, didn't I?' Fanny said. 'It would have been impolite not to.'

'And so you wrote and he wrote — Fanny, you're impossible!'

'He seemed to like it very much,' Fanny said judiciously, 'only he did ask why the devil I couldn't get Uncle Ned to frank for me, and save him having to pay for my letters. Well,' she said defensively to Miss Rosedale, 'those were his words.'

Ned looked at James. 'That accounts for the bit about his expense. Well, go on, Fanny.'

'That's all, really. In my last letter I said that I'd like to come and visit him, and I suppose he thought it best to write to Uncle Ned about it.'

'That isn't quite all, is it?' James said quietly. 'Did you let him think we had put you up to it?'

Fanny looked down at her hands. 'Well, I don't know that I mightn't have said that you would like me to get to know him better.' She looked up. 'But that was true, wasn't it? You've said so to me sometimes.'

Ned, however, was pursuing a different line of thought. 'I just don't understand how you could get letters delivered into your own hand without anyone knowing about it. It's always William who goes down for the letters, and he gives them to Ottershaw. I can't believe either of them would so far forget his duty as to —'

'No, I don't believe that either,' James said. 'Come on, Fanny, own up. How did you get the letters?'

Fanny met his eyes fearlessly, even with a glint of humour. 'It wasn't William's fault, Papa. It was Mr Pecky at the post-office. He put them aside for me, and Foster fetched them while he was exercising the carriage horses, and gave them to me when I went out riding.'

'Well, I know Foster is your faithful lieutenant; but how on earth did you bribe the good Pecky into such a dereliction of duty?'

Fanny lowered the fans of her lashes over her bright eyes. 'Oh, I didn't bribe him,' she said modestly. 'He did it for me. I think he must like me.'

James roared with laughter, but Ned looked angry. 'He had no right to do such a thing. Whatever possessed him? I shall have to have him removed from his position. He can't be trusted, that's plain to see.'

Fanny's eyes flew open. 'Oh no, please Uncle Ned! He didn't do anything wrong!' she exclaimed. 'The letters were addressed to me, after all. And he wouldn't agree to do it at all, until I told him they were from my grandfather, so you mustn't blame him.'

'No, you mustn't blame him, Ned. What could he do? She gave him a melting look, and he couldn't help himself, poor idiot. No, it's Miss Minx here who has made fools of us all.'

'Well, I didn't think you'd ask Grandpapa for me, so I had to ask him for myself,' Fanny said frankly. 'And how he has said he wants me, I may go, mayn't I, Papa?'

'Shameless,' Ned growled. 'If she were mine, I'd lock her up.'

James ignored him. 'Why do you want to go, chick?' he asked curiously. 'I should have thought you'd find it dull.'

Fanny put on her pious look. 'I think I ought to get to know my grandpapa better. I think he's lonely, and it would cheer him up to have me there, because he loved poor Mama so much, and I am her only child.'

James cocked his head at her, and she met his look unflinchingly. He began to have a shrewd idea what was behind it all, and if he was right, he had no intention of shewing her up in front of Ned. Indeed, why should he try to prevent her, or spoil her plan? There was nothing wrong or immoral about it. If anyone was going to inherit the mills, why not Fanny? If she could get round the old tortoise, then good for her.

'Well, I see no reason why you shouldn't go, if you really want to,' he said. 'What does Miss Rosedale think?'

Miss Rosedale had been looking very thoughtful all this while. 'I wonder, sir, if the invitation mightn't have come at

265

exactly the right time. Fanny's grandfather — forgive my asking, but is he a very strict man, a man of regular habits and serious disposition!'

James grinned. 'Yes to all of those! When I tell you he heartily disapproves of me, you will have the measure of the man! But why do you ask?'

'Well sir, I, too, have received a letter recently. It's from my brother-in-law who lives in Derbyshire. My sister is increasing, but she has been very unwell recently, and she's finding things rather too much for her to manage, with the other five children to care for as well. It had occurred to me to ask if I might have leave of absence to go and take care of her and the children until after her confinement, but I put it reluctantly from my mind. How could I leave Fanny? But if Fanny is to go and visit her grandfather, perhaps my request might not be impossible to grant after all?'

Fanny was trying hard to suppress a gleam of joy in her eyes, and had either her father or her uncle looked at her at that moment, they might have vetoed the scheme at once. But they were looking at Miss Rosedale, who glanced appealingly from one to the other.

'You want this very much?' James asked.

'I wouldn't ask it otherwise, sir. Reading between the lines of my brother-in-law's letter, things are very bad, and my sister in great anxiety. As I said, I wouldn't normally think of leaving Fanny, but at her grandfather's house, in his charge, and perhaps better amused than she is here at home —'

A great deal, necessarily, had to be left unsaid, but the three adults visualised Fanny, on her best behaviour as a visitor, and under the stern eye of her grandfather, enjoying all the novelty and consequence of being shewn off around the neighbourhood and being no trouble at all. The picture in Fanny's mind's eye was a little different, but they were not to know that.

'I'll talk it over with Madame,' James said.

Héloïse was eager to be able to grant Miss Rosedale's request. 'She has worked so hard, and has never had a holiday since she first came to us. But will Fanny behave herself at her grandfather's?'

'Oh, I think so, Marmoset,' James said with an airiness

which was meant to disguise his feeling of hurt that Fanny was always so much mistrusted. 'She is different now, so much more grown-up. Miss Rosedale has done wonders with her, you must admit. And why should she want to misbehave? Going on this visit was her own idea; it's something she wants. She'll go round the neighbours, and everyone will fête her, and her grandather will pet her. She'll purr like a cat, believe me. Nothing will be further from her thoughts than getting into trouble.'

'Very well, James, I have nothing to say against it. But someone must go with her. She must have a chaperone — a maid at least.'

'She shall. She can have one of the housemaids go with her, one of the steady ones. And we'll send her in our own carriage, with our own coachman and a footman to make sure she gets there safely.'

They talked a little more over the details of the arrangements, and then Héloïse said, 'You know my James, with Mathilde away, Sophie at school, and Fanny going to Manchester, it occurs to me that it might be a good time for us to go away as well.'

'Go away?' James said. 'What on earth for?'

'Oh, it is the new thing amongst people of fashion, didn't you know? To go away from home for a month in the summer is *de rigeur*. They go to the seaside, you know.'

'Oh, do they? Well, I'm not going to Scarborough, if that's your plan,' James said quickly. Scarborough was increasingly fashionable, but it had bitter memories for him.

'No, love,' Héloïse said with a soft smile. 'I thought we might just take a few servants and go and stay at Plaisir for a little while, all on our own.'

'At Plaisir?' His face brightened.

'Just as if it were our honeymoon. For we never had one, did we, my James?' She looked up at him with shining eyes.

'No, Marmoset, we didn't,' James said, folding his arms round her. He thought of the little cottage in the tiny village at the foot of the North York Moors; of living with her in the intimacy of a small house, and the simplicity of few servants; of recapturing the delight of the magical time they had once spent together there, stolen out of the main flow of life, and the sweeter for it. He felt younger just thinking about it.

He kissed the crown of her dark head. 'We'll do it,' he said decisively.

Fanny set off for Manchester in high spirits, with all the bustle and consequence she could hope for. She had a smart new bonnet and pelisse, which she was sure made her look at least seventeen, and a waiting-woman of her own, even if it was Letty the housemaid upgraded into lady's maid. Letty had been given strict instructions, amounting almost to threats, from both Ottershaw and Mrs Thomson, as to the responsibilities of a lady's maid, and Miss Fanny's maid in particular; and she sat rigidly beside her new mistress with her hands clenched in her lap, trying simultaneously to look dignified and calm, and to rehearse mentally the list of her new duties.

Fanny would rather have liked to travel post, but was soon reconciled to travelling in the family coach, and convinced herself that there was even more consequence in having your own coachman and footman, to say nothing of a couple of outriders, who had been added to the scheme at the last minute by James's paternal solicitude. The times were hard, and there were such things as footpads and highwaymen, after all. Edward had nothing to say against it, though he felt that the outrider's task would be rather to keep Fanny in than robbers out.

With two trunks strapped on behind, a purse of guineas in her reticule for present expenses, and a promise of more whenever she wanted them, Fanny had nothing more to wish for, and she leaned out of the carriage window and waved goodbye as the coach drew out of the courtyard, and laughed in sheer high spirits.

When the last waving hand was out of sight, she settled back against the squabs with a sigh of contentment, and observed to Letty, 'Now the fun begins!'

'Yes, Miss,' Letty said, believing her, but unsure whether to be pleased or apprehensive at the prospect.

The following day, with much less ceremony, Héloïse and James set off for Plaisir. Stephen and Marie had gone on ahead with luggage and provisions, to open the cottage and air it; and apart from them, they were taking only Durban. Barnard had been almost tearful at the idea of Héloïse's cooking for herself, or relying on Marie's help at best.

'You will starve, madame!' he cried tragically. 'It must not be!'

'But you forget, dear Monsieur Barnard, that Marie and I cooked for ourselves for many months, years ago. We are quite capable of preparing meals for such a small household. You are needed here.'

Barnard remained unconvinced. 'Only send word, and I shall come at a moment's notice,' he promised with a moist eye. 'I shall walk if necessary.' And he consoled himself by packing a hamper for Stephen to take with him which, he calculated, would keep them going for three days at least — long enough for them to realise the folly of their decision, and either send for him, or better still, come back home. This desire for the rustic life was unnatural and unhealthy, he thought. Queen Marie Antoinette used to like to pretend to be a dairymaid and milk her own specially-washed cows, and look what happened to her!

James and Héloïse set off early in the morning in the phaeton, with Héloïse driving her bay ponies, the pair which replaced the now retired cream arabs. Kithra sat at her feet, and Castor on the seat between them, grinning his wide spaniel grin and waving his plumy tail like a banner. Durban rode behind, leading Nez Carré and Vanity. Nez Carré was twenty-five now, a great age for a horse, and Héloïse had been surprised that James wished to take him instead of his usual road-horse. James was surprised at her surprise.

'I don't suppose we'll be doing much riding — nothing strenuous, anyway,' he said. 'I couldn't go away with you on our honeymoon without old Nez Carré, could I?'

Matty waved goodbye to them from the steps, with Nicholas in her arms, and Héloïse had to bite her lip at the thought of not seeing her little boy for two or three weeks. She had felt from the beginning that it would not be a proper honeymoon unless they were quite alone, but parting from him was harder than she expected.

'But you can come back any time it gets too much for you,' James had pointed out. 'We'll only be twenty miles away,'

Edward stood beside Matty to see them off.

'Old Ned's getting as grey as a badger,' James remarked cheerfully as they started off. 'I feel rather bad about leaving him all alone; but then, he works so hard, he probably won't notice we're gone. And it's only for a few weeks, after all.'

They crossed the drawbridge, and Héloïse turned the ponies onto the track. James looked back and waved, and Ned lifted his hand briefly in salute, before turning to go back into the quiet house to collect his hat and gloves and set off about his day's business.

CHAPTER FOURTEEN

On 18 June 1811, the Prince Regent was to give a lavish dinner and ball which was expected to be one of the most spectacular entertainments ever witnessed.

There was a great deal of argument about what the occasion was meant to celebrate. Some said that it was in honour of the French Royal Family, in exile in England; others that it was for the poor mad King's birthday, though what pleasure, even vicariously, he might be expected to gain from it was not explained. The Prince himself was reported to have said that it was meant to benefit 'those artists who by the illness of their sovereign and the discontinuance of the accustomed splendour of the Court had been deprived of many advantages in their respective pursuits'. Since, however, the Prince's inability to pay the bills of either tradesmen or 'artists' was legendary, this was held to be a piece of frivolous invention.

Most people concluded that the real reason for the party was to celebrate the beginning of the Regency. The Queen certainly thought so, and holding it to be in bad taste, refused to attend. The Princess of Wales was not invited, though most of her household was; and Mrs Fitzherbert sent back her invitation when she was informed that she would not be given her usual seat at the top table.

Lucy attended with her accustomed cicisbeo, Danby Wiske. Two thousand guests had been invited, and simply to get everyone into the house was a difficult and time-consuming business. The first coaches began to arrive early in the morning, and by eight o'clock the queue reached from Carlton House to St James's Street. To avoid lengthy delays, everyone had been told at what time to arrive, but inevitably, the instructions were ignored by some. By nine o'clock, when the gates were opened and the carriages began to crawl forward at last, the queue stretched all the way to Bond Street. The

271

heat was intense, and the smell of horse-sweat and dung made it inadvisable to open the carriage windows. The streets were lined with spectators, who had ample opportunity to gawp at and discuss the occupants of the carriages, who were often trapped stationary at one point for fifteen minutes.

'If it weren't for the crowds, I'd get out and walk,' Lucy said at one point. 'It would be heaven to stretch my legs. What do you suppose would be said of me in the *Chronicle* tomorrow, if I arrived for a State reception on foot?'

'Lady Aylesbury displayed her usual propensity to shock and dismay,' Danby quoted with a quirk of the lips.

Lucy looked at him critically. 'You look very handsome in your Hussar rig, Danby. Much more distinguished than in an ordinary suit of clothes. I'm glad it's formal and you can go in uniform.'

Danby blushed a little and looked away. 'The Prince is sure to be in uniform,' he said.

'As Colonel of the China Tenth?'

'Field Marshal, I've heard,' Danby said shortly.

Lucy snorted at that. 'Damn these feathers,' she said after a while. 'They keep catching on the roof. It would be almost worth having Prinny king at last, to leave off wearing feathers to every State reception.'

Danby turned to look at her with a softened expression. 'Always think you look so well in them. Takes a certain sort of woman to wear feathers. Most of 'em just look like moulting chickens.'

Lucy grinned. 'I believe you're flirting with me, Danby!'

'Could be,' he smiled.

'Well, it's too hot to be wearing satin and all the family jewels, at any rate,' she said. 'This tiara scratches my head. And the Chetwyn diamonds are particularly hideous — the worst sort of Jacobean settings. I shan't be sorry to resign them to Roland's wife, when he comes to marry.'

Wiske tried to think of something to say to amuse her. 'Know what I read somewhere? Goin' to be 14 dukes, 15 duchesses, 15 marquesses, and 16 marchionesses at this reception.'

Lucy was intrigued. 'Who could have counted them? Some petty secretary in the Prince's household I suppose. How clever of you to remember the numbers, Danby.'

'Good at figures,' he said modestly. 'Shall I tell you the rest? 98 earls, 85 countesses, 39 viscounts, and 214 lords and ladies. Can't remember all the rest — admirals and generals and such. Cost Prinny a bit,' he remarked thoughtfully.

'If he pays,' Lucy said succinctly.

'Has to pay for the food, at least. Can't get any more credit on that,' Danby observed. 'Buckingham says it's in bad taste, considerin' the weavers are starving in Lancashire.'

'What on earth have the weavers to do with it?' Lucy asked, mystified.

The last-comers did not enter the gates until after one o'clock, and even by then it was plain that more people must have come than were officially invited. The Prince, enormously fat again now that he had recovered from his illness of last winter, was dressed in the scarlet uniform of a field marshal, his huge chest decorated with stars and ribbons, badges and aigrettes. He smiled and bowed and was charming, dividing his attentions in the most accomplished way.

'He's wearing as many diamonds as I am,' Lucy said, but with a smile. She had a little of a soft spot for the Prince, who had always been kind to her.

He received the French royalty in a room lined with blue silk, ornamented with gold *fleurs-de-lys*.

'A pretty shabby lot, these Bourbons,' said Lucy. 'All except the Duchess of Angoulême — she looks as though she had some spirit.'

Danby regarded her with interest. 'She looks sad, poor creature.'

'Wouldn't you?' said Lucy. The Duchess was the daughter of the murdered Louis XVI and Marie Antoinette. She had been married to her cousin, the Duc d'Artois, the stolid, pudding-faced son of her father's younger brother. Though she was now thirty-three, she was still attractive, having a great deal of her mother's fabled beauty: petite, auburn, bright-eyed. What must it be like, Lucy wondered, to have your father, mother, brother and aunt murdered by revolutionaries, and to be sent begging round Europe, when you had been brought up a princess at the richest court in the world?

The interior of Carlton House was always a little overpowering, but today it looked even more extraordinary, with great masses of flowers, multicoloured geraniums and roses, stacked everywhere amongst the lavish decorations and ornaments, the bronze horses and ormolu clocks, the red porphyry dragons and ebony elephants, the japanned cabinets and Chinese enamel vases, the marble columns, gold friezes and crystal chandeliers.

From the top table across the end of the great hall, where those of the rank of marquis and above would be seated for dinner, other tables ran in all directions, down the hall, through the library, across the vaulted, Gothic-cathedral conservatory, and out into the gardens under coloured awnings. Two thousand place-settings of silver and crystal had been laid, but only those, like Lucy, who were seated at the tables in the main hall, had a glimpse of the most extraordinary feature of the decorations. In front of the place where the Prince was to sit was a tiny temple containing a silver fountain, from which water gushed, forming a cascade, and ran in rivulets down the centres of the tables, in specially-devised channels lined and edged with living moss, spangled with tiny flowers. Here and there it ran under fantastic bridges in the Chinese style; and in the miniature rivers swam gold and silver fish.

'Prinny's outdone himself this time,' Wiske remarked to Lucy as they took their places behind their chairs, waiting for the royal party to come to the top table. Lucy only grunted, occupied in looking about her, at the rows of magnificently dressed women, the flashing of jewels on white bosoms, the army of liveried servants lining the walls. I must remember this, she thought. One day, when I'm old, I may tell my grandchildren about it, for who knows what the world will be like then? Even amongst the grand receptions I've attended, this one is remarkable, and such things may not go on for ever.

Dinner took four hours, and after it there was dancing, which went on until six the next morning. There were four bands, and floors had been laid out in the gardens, some in the open air, some under marquees, as well as in the house itself. Two suppers were served in the continental style, and as soon as dusk fell, lamps were lit in such profusion that it was impossible to tell when it got dark.

Lucy did not stay to the end, for after midnight things began to get a little rough, and she was tired of all the noise and movement. Wiske called for her coach, and by a quarter after midnight they were on their way, jolting over cobbles into the dark, warm night, away from the blaze of lights which lifted Carlton House out of its black surroundings, so that it seemed to float in the sky like a dream-palace.

Lucy let down the window on her side of the carriage, and rested her head on her forearm, enjoying the rush of tepid air on her face. Danby Wiske, sitting back against the squabs, watched her with pleasure as the light from the newly-installed gas-lamps along Pall Mall illuminated and eclipsed her alternately.

'What a strange evening,' she said at last, her voice quiet, almost bemused. 'Don't you feel it was strange, Danby? There we were, guests of the Prince, Regent of England, as secure in his place as anyone could be. And there were the French Royal Family, exiled in our country while Boney sits on their throne and calls himself Emperor, with a new son he calls the King of Rome to come after him. And out there in the wide world, armies march and fight, and ships patrol the seas, and men bleed and die, all to try to oust the Emperor and put that fat old man in the powdered wig on the throne in his place. And we all wore our feathers and ate a dinner and danced and flirted and talked about each other, and — and it suddenly all seems so strange to me. Why did we do it? What was it for?'

She raised her head and looked towards the place where he sat, for in the darkness she couldn't see him. 'Don't you feel that, Danby?'

His voice came back to her, calm and sensible. 'No.'

She smiled a little. 'Then why do I?'

The answer was longer coming this time, but just as assured.

'Indigestion,' he said.

Lucy slept late, and was sitting alone at her breakfast at noon the next day, sorting her way through the usual pile of letters and invitations in the intervals between consuming cold beef and game pie, hot sausages and wheaten bread and coffee. The sun poured in almost vertically through the tall windows, and the small breakfast-table had been drawn back into the middle of the room to avoid its rays; but Jeffrey was curled up on the window-seat in full sunshine, enjoying the heat. He slept almost all the time now. He was an old cat after all — fourteen — and Lucy closed her mind to the knowledge that she would be lucky to keep him another winter.

The knocker on the street door had been busy all morning, and Lucy was noticing it only subconsciously, for she had told Hicks she was not receiving visitors. She looked up in surprise, therefore, when the butler came in, and with an apologetic cough, mentioned that Major Wiske was below.

'Has he bribed you to ignore my instructions?' Lucy asked, but smilingly. Danby Wiske was a privileged caller, and Hicks knew it. 'Yes, let him come up. And ask him if he has breakfasted, and if not, send up another cover.'

'Yes, my lady.'

A few moments later Danby Wiske came in, looking somehow smaller and slighter in civilian clothes, like a peacock bereft of its tail. His neat blue coat, white waistcoat, creaseless fawn pantaloons, gleaming Hessian boots, and starched white neckcloth were all immaculate, unimpeachable, and in the best style laid down by George Brummell; but out of his uniform, Lucy thought, he was indistinguishable from any other gentleman of fashion. He might be anyone.

He advanced across the carpet towards her, and then, finding himself stared at, halted, a little puzzled, in the streaming sunlight. No, Lucy thought, that wasn't entirely fair. There were a great many men in London who thought of themselves as men of fashion, who would give a good deal to look as entirely well-dressed as Danby. She had known him so long, and was so used to his being there to serve her, that she had grown out of the habit of seeing him; but the introspective mood of last night had lingered a little into today, and she looked at him with new eyes.

Why, he's quite handsome, she thought with faint surprise. His short, wavy hair was light brown, and in the sunlight she saw there was a hint of reddish-gold to it, which went with his fair skin and blue eyes. His nose was short and straight, his chin strong with a slight, rather attractive cleft, and since she had last really looked at him, however many years ago that was, his face had grown in the maturity and dignity which came with the command of men. Though he was not tall, he was neatly, compactly built, and he had the naturally upright carriage of a cavalryman, along with the broad chest and strong thighs. Any woman would be proud to be seen walking along Bond Street on his arm, she thought.

Fair and foolish, she had always considered him, her faithful hound; but he was a man, and suddenly, in that instant, strange to her, so that she felt disturbed, almost shy, at his presence.

Danby, meanwhile, had decided that if he didn't speak, they would be trapped like that for ever. 'Something wrong?' he asked, and glanced down at himself. 'Haven't forgotten anythin' vital? Dreamt once I walked into Lady Tewkesbury's drawing-room without m' small-clothes. Feel a bit like that now.'

Lucy smiled. 'No, you haven't forgotten anything. You look as immaculate as ever. Come and sit down, Danby. Have you breakfasted?'

He blinked a little at the warmth of her greeting, and took the seat she offered him. 'Had a bite early, thanks. I'll have some coffee, though, if I may.'

'Of course.' Lucy poured it, and passed the cup to him, and then addressed the last of her game pie. 'I can't think why I'm so hungry this morning, after that banquet last night, but I feel as though I could eat for ever. Do you know what I suddenly have a fancy for? Strawberries! Roberta's bound to have plenty. They grow wonderful strawberries at Chelmsford House. When I've finished breakfast and changed my gown, we'll go and visit her, and make her invite us to go out and pick them. They always taste better when you eat them off the plant.'

Danby shook his head. 'I'd love to, but I'm afraid I can't. I'm wanted at the Horseguards in an hour. Just came to tell you so, and apologise for not riding with you this afternoon.'

'Oh, that's all right, don't worry about it,' Lucy said lightly. 'I shall only ride around the Park. You can't refuse a summons to the Horseguards, after all. Is it something important?'

He didn't answer at once, looking down and fiddling with his cup and saucer as though unsure what to say. Lucy cocked her head at him. This was not just his usual self-effacement. There was something different about him today.

'Danby?'

He looked up. 'Well, yes, it is important,' he said. 'Really, quite.' He stopped again, and began rolling a crumb of bread into a pellet between his finger and thumb. 'Fact is, we're going abroad. The regiment, I mean. We're being brigaded with the fifteenth and eighteenth Hussars, and sent to the Peninsula, to reinforce Wellington.'

'You're going to fight?' Lucy said, with a hollow feeling in her stomach, at odds with the large breakfast she had just eaten.

'Wellington's planning a big offensive this winter. So far he's only been able to keep the French at the Portuguese border, but now the supply lines have been set up, and the natives trained and so on, it's time to attack. Recapture the frontier posts, advance into Spain, take the war to them. New phase beginning, and so on. So it's our turn at last.'

'The Tenth?' Lucy said teasingly.

He didn't smile. 'Now the Prince is Regent, he can't be expected to lead us personally, so there's no difficulty about letting us go into active service.'

'You needn't go. You could sell out: I believe you could get four thousand pounds or so for your commission these days.' She looked at him carefully. 'Or do you want to go?'

He smiled suddenly. 'Lord, yes! Sick of parades and civil duties! Longing to put all that drill into action. We all are, you know — there isn't an officer or man who'd give up his place now. We didn't like bein' called the China Tenth. No man likes to be labelled a coward.'

'No-one who knows you would ever call you a coward, Danby.' Lucy said warmly. 'You'll make your name out there, I'm sure of it.'

'Thank you,' he said, and hesitated again, looking down at the third bread-pellet, and then up at Lucy, his blue eyes suddenly bluer than ever. 'Only one thing I regret — leavin' you. It's been my privilege to escort you these last few years. Don't know why me — always felt you did me too much honour.'

'Don't be too modest, Danby,' Lucy said flippantly, to cover her growing embarrassment, 'or I'll think you're hanging out for a compliment.'

'No,' he said seriously, 'I mean it. I'm not special in any way. Younger son — no title or anything — no particular talents. Family always thought me a bit of a fool. That's why

278

they bought me m' colours. Put him in a fashionable regiment, they said, where he can't do any harm. Lucky having been to school with George — he took me around, introduced me to the right people. Made me acceptable.'

'Nonsense! You would always have been acceptable, with or without Brummell,' Lucy said firmly.

The interruption seemed to have made Danby lose his thread. He looked at her for some moments in silence, and then said, 'Thing is, Lucy, I've grown to love you over the years. I suppose you might think it's impudence on my part. But I know you very well — bound to, after all this time. Sixteen years, is it?'

'Seventeen,' she corrected him absently.

He nodded. 'I've seen you happy and I've seen you sad. Weston was a good fellow — he was right for you. I was glad you had him. And then when he died —'

'Don't, Danby,' Lucy said, turning her head away. 'Don't say any more.'

But he was curiously determined, a quiet, unregarded man who had found his moment to speak. 'I can't tell you how it hurts me to see you suffer. I'm not an imaginative chap — no brains at all, really — but it was as if everything you felt, I felt. You've been so brave, and anyone who didn't know you would think you're all right now. But you're not.'

Lucy could bear no more. She stood up abruptly and walked to the window, keeping her back to him. Danby stood automatically as she did, and turned towards her.

'You're lonely — I've seen that,' he went on relentlessly. 'You were never meant to live alone. Oh, I know you have your children, and lots of friends, and even me, God help us, for what use that is. But you need more than that. You need a husband.'

She turned in desperation. 'Danby —'

'I love you Lucy,' he said. 'I came here today to ask you to marry me. I've been thinking about it for a long time, but when I heard we were going abroad, I decided I'd better speak up before it was too late. The war won't last for ever. One good campaign, and we'll drive Boney out of Spain, and then we'll drive him back into France, and then we'll corner him like a fox, and have him. Two years, three perhaps, then it will be over, and I'll be back for good.'

He paused, and she said nothing, backed up by the flood of his words, wide-eyed, rather like a cornered fox herself. 'Well,' he said, suddenly nervous, 'what do you think?'

She looked at him, amazed, perplexed, touched, terrified. What was it she had kept by her all these years and never recognised? The Danby she had thought she knew could not have spoken so much and so eloquently. He looked far from fair and foolish now, his eyes burning with intensity, his face firm with decision. She realised he had said nothing about the disparity in their rank or fortune, and she saw that it was from some inner sureness, a pride without vanity, which told him that such things did not matter. How many men, in fashionable, nervous, money-grubbing London society, could have thought like that? There was a strength in him, unsuspected by her, that could woo a woman more wealthy than himself, and not feel in any way threatened or diminished by it.

'Danby — I don't know what to say,' she said at last. 'I never thought — I didn't expect —'

'Don't suppose you did,' he said frankly. 'Got used to me — part of the furniture. Furniture don't propose. Fireside chair suddenly ups and asks you to marry it — disconcertin'.' She smiled unwillingly. 'I don't want an answer now. That would be unreasonable. You need time to think.'

'How much time am I allowed?' she asked in a small voice. 'You're going abroad.'

He shrugged. 'Abroad or not, I won't press you. You've all the time in the world. Give me your answer when you're ready — I won't ask you for it. But think about it seriously, Lucy. We could be comfortable together. I know I'm not an exciting sort of chap, but I know you very well, and I could make you happy.'

She looked at him doubtfully. 'But what about you? It shouldn't be just me. You ought to want to be happy too.'

He smiled suddenly, and something in her turned over disconcertingly, as though he were not her safe, familiar Danby, but someone strange and exciting. 'I'm always happy with you. Don't you know that? And now,' pulling his watch out from his fob, 'I must be going. Theatre tonight, isn't it? I'll call for you as usual. Servant, ma'am.'

He bowed and took his leave in his usual manner, as if

nothing untoward had been said between them; and Lucy sat down abruptly on the window-seat and stared into space, deep in thought, absently stroking Jeffrey, who purred rustily in his sleep, his paws and tail-tip twitching as each stroke intruded into his dreams.

Fanny felt her campaign had opened well. The servants at Hobsbawn House had been suitably impressed by the grandeur of her arrival, which had made them treat her from the beginning with respect, so that she was able to be gracious and pleasant to them. The housekeeper, Mrs Murray, had curtseyed all the way to the ground, and had begged Miss to let her know if the slightest thing was wanted in the arrangements in her room.

'I've been accustomed to decide the meals myself, Miss, the Master not caring to be bothered with such things,' she said, 'but if you was wanting to take over the ordering, Miss, I'd be happy to attend you at any hour you like each morning.' She smiled obsequiously, a smile which intensified when Fanny indicated that she had no desire to take over the pains of Mistress of the house along with the consequence.

Fanny found her grandfather much aged in appearance since she had last seen him, but his voice and his spirit were as vigorous as ever. He met her on the steps when she got down from the carriage, and folded her in his arms in a fierce hug, which she did not quite like, but endured with a good will. Then he put her back from him, and gazed at her with tear-filled eyes.

'Eh, my little Fanny! Let your old Grandpa look at you. Why, you've grown into quite a young lady! And so pretty — ain't she pretty, Mrs M?'

'Indeed, sir, it's not for me to say, sir, but I'd say Miss was beautiful, rather.'

'Beautiful! You're right, Mrs M. Beautiful's the word — and the image of your mother, Fanny, God rest her poor soul.'

'Mrs Morland was always known as a beauty, sir, and Miss Fanny's just like her,' Mrs Murray agreed with a smirk; and Fanny found herself wondering at the familiarity with which Grandpapa addressed the housekeeper, and the freedom with which she expressed her opinions. Fanny didn't like servants to be encroaching, and she slipped her hand through her grandfather's arm and turned him pointedly away from Mrs Murray, and into the house.

'I'm glad you think so, Grandpapa,' she said sweetly. 'My greatest wish is to be as like Mama as possible, though I fear I can never match her. But she has been my guiding inspiration all my life.'

This seemed to go down very well with Grandpapa, who sighed and pressed her arm, and squeezed out another tear. Inside the hall, the rest of the servants were assembled, all of them new to her except the old butler, Bowles, and her father's ancient manservant, Simon. Both of them were presented to her as old friends, and they sighed and remembered her dear late mother and brother, and Simon's wrinkled old cheeks trembled, and Bowles's eyes grew moist. Really, Fanny thought, if everyone in Manchester is going to weep over me all the time, it will be very tedious.

The house seemed dark and over-furnished to her; everything was richly coloured and elaborately decorated, and every available surface was covered with clocks and statues and ornaments and bowls and vases, many of them Chinese or Indian or otherwise fantastic, and all, to Fanny, quite hideous. Her bedroom, however, was very comfortable, larger than her room at home, and with a vast quantity of mirrors, of which Miss Rosedale would have disapproved. Every comfort had been supplied for her, and little as she trusted Mrs Murray already, Fanny had to admit that she was a good housekeeper, and that everything was very clean and well cared for.

Dinner that day was served at five, in recognition of the fact that Fanny had been travelling and must be weary. She sat at one end of the table, and her grandfather sat at the other, and Bowles and the footman, Peter, served them. There was only one course, and the food was plain and nourishing rather than elegant: a soup, a cold joint, a hot joint, a currant pudding, and a raised pie in cut. It was much the sort of food she had had in the schoolroom, and she was disappointed that her first day here was not offering her more in the way of elegancies. Mr Hobsbawn looked down the table at her, and guessed her feelings.

'I'm afraid our dinner is rather plain for you, Fanny,' he

said apologetically. 'I'm used to dining alone, you see, and when I come back hungry from the mills, I don't care much about sauces and kickshaws. But you must tell Bowles and Mrs Murray what you like, and you shall have it. I want you to be happy here, love.'

Fanny smiled at him. 'I *am* happy, Grandpapa. And anything that you like must be good enough for me.'

He beamed. 'Nay, love, you're a young lady, and you're used to dainty meats, I know that. I shall like it too, if I have your pretty, smiling face to look at. You tell Mrs Murray what things you fancy, and we'll eat like fashionable folk. Now, what do you like to drink? Bowles here has brought up some claret for me — do you drink claret? Or will you want lemonade or something of that class?'

Fanny's eyes gleamed. She did not have wine at home, but evidently Grandpapa didn't know that. 'Oh, I'll drink whatever you're having. Claret will do very well, if you please.'

Mr Hobsbawn gestured Bowles to fill Fanny's glass, and then lifted his own to her. 'A toast to you, Fanny. It's grand to have you here at last! I hope we can make you so happy, you don't want to go away again!'

'I'm sure you will, Grandpapa,' Fanny said, and tasted her first wine. It was exceedingly nasty, and she wondered if perhaps this particular bottle had gone off. It looked so pretty and red in the glass, like raspberry syrup, and she had expected it to taste sweet and fruity. However, Grandpapa was drinking it with every sign of relish, so she concealed her distaste and sipped again, and smiled as though it were what she was used to. After a few more attempts, it began to taste better, and she thought she might get used to it quite soon. After all, she had got used to Uncle Ned's brandy.

'Your mother always shared a bottle of claret with me when she sat at the head of my table,' Hobsbawn said, pleased. 'She was a rare one for knowing a good wine. I'm glad to see you've inherited her taste, Fanny.'

'Oh yes,' Fanny said, swallowing bravely. 'I'm excessively fond of a good claret.'

After dinner, Mr Hobsbawn outlined his plans.

'Tomorrow I shall take you out calling, and introduce you to some of my old friends, the ladies who lead our society here. Some of them have young ones of about your age, and I daresay you will soon make enough friends to keep you happy. I shall have to spend some time at the mills, though I'll try to be with you as much as possible. But when I can't — well, you can order the carriage just as you like, and go driving, and visiting, and there are shops here in Manchester as good as anywhere in England. Has your father given you money for your necessaries?'

'Yes, Grandpapa — twenty guineas in a purse, and I'm to ask for more when I need it.'

Hobsbawn squared his shoulders. 'Twenty guineas won't last you long, if I know anything about young ladies. Once you see the shops, you'll have spent it in no time. But no need to trouble your father, love — you just have what you want, and tell them to send the bills to me. I'll see that the principal traders all know my granddaughter is in town.'

Fanny lowered her eyelashes modestly. 'Thank you, Grandpapa, but I don't know if I ought —'

'If you ought?' Hobsbawn growled with mock severity. 'If I can't spend my own money on my own granddaughter, what's the world coming to?'

The next day, Fanny dressed for morning calls, and went with her grandfather in his shabby old chariot to visit the senior matrons about the town. They called first on Mrs Pendlebury, widow of an old business partner of Hobsbawn's, who considered herself the leader of Manchester society.

'So this is Mary Ann's daughter?' she said. 'How do you do, Fanny? You don't look very much like your poor mother, though you have her eyes. How old are you, child? Fifteen? And when do you have your come-out?'

'Next Season, I hope, ma'am,' Fanny said unwillingly. She disliked being asked questions as though she were a child.

Mrs Pendlebury sniffed. 'Don't scowl at me, child, you'll mark your brow. Well, sixteen is young to be coming out these days, but I suppose in your case, it is just as well. And after all, many of the girls of my generation were married at sixteen. Well, these are my daughters at home, Prudence and Agnes — their sister is married, of course. Come forward, girls, and say how do you do to Miss Morland.'

Prudence, a tall, thin, colourless girl a year or so older than Fanny, stepped forward and curtseyed and murmured a polite how-do-you-do. Agnes was a snub-nosed, merry-looking girl of about fourteen, who greeted her cheerfully, and with a look of frank curiosity.

'Can you ride? Do you have your own pony?' she asked, giving Fanny no time to answer. 'Prudence don't care for horses. She thinks about clothes *all the time*!'

'I can see you girls will be great friends,' Mrs Pendlebury said determinedly. 'And now, Fanny, this is my son Frederick.'

'How do you do, Miss Morland,' he said sullenly. Frederick was nineteen, also tall and pale, but stoutish, with moist hands and a great deal of self-importance. He had resented his mother's obliging him to remain in the house that morning, simply to do the pretty to a chit of a girl not yet out. His mother had retorted sharply that Fanny Morland was the richest heiress ever likely to come in Frederick's way, and that it was never too early to make a good impression on such a valuable acquaintance.

Having made his leg, he now moved away and half-lounged, half-sulked against the sopha's end, while Mrs Pendlebury chatted to Mr Hobsbawn, and occasionally interrupted the half-hearted conversation which began between Fanny and her daughters.

'What do you mean to do in Manchester?' Agnes asked. 'If I were you, I'd have stayed at home. I'm sure York must be vastly smart. We hear about it for ever from Miss Imber — she's our governess, or she was, only we're too old for a governess now. She don't teach us, but she goes about with us when Mama's busy. Have you got a governess?'

'More a sort of chaperone,' Fanny said grandly, 'only she's not with me at present. I have a maid to attend to me instead.'

'What, a real lady's maid?' Agnes said, wide-eyed with wonder. Fanny began rather to like her. 'You are lucky! But what do you mean to do here? If you're not out, you can't go to balls and assemblies. I wish I were out! I shall die having to wait another three whole years. Even Pru isn't coming out until next year. Mama thinks it ain't smart for girls to come out too young, but you told her, didn't you, Miss Morland? I wish she may change her mind, now you've said that.'

'Don't rattle on so, Annie,' Prudence reproved faintly.

'Still, there are always at-homes, and suppers, and so on, and there's usually dancing of some sort. We're allowed to dance, if it ain't formal, though it's only with *boys*, of course. Still, I expect the young men will want to dance with you, Miss Morland, for you look quite eighteen, and everyone knows you're an heiress.'

'Annie!' Prudence whispered.

'Oh hush, calling me and calling me! Miss Morland don't mind, do you, Miss Morland?'

'Not at all,' Fanny said, thinking that anyone who thought she looked eighteen must be a very good sort of girl.

'There, you see? And you only had to hear how Mama went on at Freddy this morning, telling him he must come and be polite to her, only he's such a stick, he made a mull of it! Do you like round games, Miss Morland?'

Mrs Pendlebury caught the last words. 'Round games I think a very innocent sort of amusement for young girls. You play, I dare say, Miss Morland? Speculation, and Lottery Tickets, and the like? We must arrange for you to meet some other girls of your age, here in my drawing-room, and play. A little supper-party, perhaps.'

'That'd be right nice of you, ma'am, to introduce my little Fanny to some other nice girls,' said Mr Hobsbawn, beaming. 'I shouldn't want her to be lonely, stopping with an old man like me.'

'Do you care for clothes, Miss Morland?' Prudence asked faintly, when the adults had turned their attention away.

Agnes snorted, but Fanny didn't wish to be classed entirely with the children, so she said rather loftily, 'Oh yes, we have all the principal ladies' journals at home. I'm told the shops in Manchester are very good — almost as good as at home.'

Prudence, unnerved by mention of ladies' journals, had nothing to say, so Agnes answered for her. 'We think the shops very good, but I don't know what you will think of them, Miss Morland. What did you want to buy, in particular?'

'Oh, one never knows, until one sees it, what one wants to buy,' Fanny said grandly. 'I like just to walk about the shops and buy what takes my fancy.'

Prudence rallied a little. 'Oh yes, I like shopping a vast deal.'

'But what sort of things?' Agnes insisted. 'Do you mean gowns and hats?'

'Well, I really do need a new gown made, if I'm to attend anything like a dance, for I haven't brought anything suitable with me,' Fanny said. 'Perhaps you can tell me who is the best mantuamaker in town?'

'Oh, certainly dear,' Mrs Pendlebury cried, appropriating the question to herself. 'Madame Renée is out of question the best. She's quite French, you know — used to make for all the court-people over there, before the Revolution, of course. Don't you think so, Frederick?' she said sharply, in an attempt to make him shew himself to better advantage.

He jerked out of his reverie, and almost slipped off the end of the sopha, and was obliged to look more than ever languid and superior in compensation. 'What do you say, Mama? I did not attend.'

'Wouldn't you say Madame Renée is the best mantua-maker?' his mother repeated impatiently.

'Oh yes, without a doubt, famous good,' he drawled, half-closing his eyes with an air of world-weariness, 'but everything she makes is amazing ugly. She made that hideous purple thing for you, didn't she, Mama? Puts me out of all patience to hear people praise her, for she never makes anything fit to be seen in. But she is out of question the best. A woman might go to her with every confidence. On the whole, I don't know but what she makes better than anyone in the world, and vastly fashionable, quite like a London mantua-maker, let me die!'

Fanny listened to him with astonishment and growing bewilderment, for she had never come across this sort of affectation before. She thought he looked as though he were about to fall asleep, and his contradictions seemed to her utterly fatuous.

His mother, however, merely said, 'I think you will find she makes as well as anyone in York, Fanny, only she's very expensive. Still,' eyeing her speculatively, 'I don't suppose that is an object, with you. You can't do better than go to Renée. But who goes with you? You can't expect poor Mr Hobsbawn to hang around a mantuamaker's parlour hour after hour, and it is quite impossible for a young woman of your degree to go about the town alone.'

'I have a maid to attend me, ma'am,' Fanny said with dignity, and a hint of triumph.

Mrs Pendlebury would not be bested. 'Yes dear, a maid is all very well, but it is not the same as a chaperone. Besides, young girls need an older, steadier female to advise them, particularly when choosing anything as important as a gown.' Fanny began to fear Mrs Pendlebury meant to propose herself, but she went on, 'I think it would be best if you make use of our Miss Imber — my girls' governess. Mr Hobsbawn, you have seen her with them, I am sure. While Fanny is staying with you, I shall be happy for her to be chaperoned by Miss Imber. It will be nice for the dear girls all to be together.'

'Why, that's very kind of you, ma'am,' Mr Hobsbawn said, smiling. 'Isn't it, Fanny? It will be much nicer for you to go shopping and such with friends.'

Fanny was dismayed, thinking she had got rid of one governess, only to be shackled to another, but she could do nothing but smile and agree. But a moment later Agnes, guessing her problem, winked at her, and whispered, 'Don't worry, Miss Morland, Miss Imber is the very best sort of governess, as timid as a mouse, and short-sighted, too. Pru and me can do anything with her. It's as good as being out on your own, nearly. She won't stop us having our fun, I promise you.'

After dinner that evening, Fanny offered to play backgammon with her grandfather, having discovered by a little judicious questioning that he liked the game very much, and sometimes had the housekeeper in of an evening to play with him. She began to fear that the housekeeper nursed a secret plan to elevate her relationship with her employer onto a more intimate plane, and felt it incumbent on her to scotch it.

Mr Hobsbawn was pleased and flattered at the suggestion, and soon had the board set up, and chairs placed to either side. 'It's very good of you to indulge me like this, Fanny,' he said. 'I like a game of backgammon more than anything. You're a good-natured little thing, aren't you?'

Having put him into a pliant mood, Fanny felt it was a good moment as any to advance her campaign.

'I shall play with you every evening, if you like, Grandpapa. I suppose I shall not see you very often during the day, for indeed, you must not neglect your business for me. The mills are very important, not just to you, and to me, but to the whole country.'

Hobsbawn looked surprised and pleased. 'I'm glad you think so.'

'Grandpapa,' Fanny pursued. 'I know I am only a female, but I do so want to understand about cotton-spinning, and how the mills work.'

Hobsbawn looked doubtful. 'Do you, love? But that's a man's business.'

'At home I often go about the estate with Uncle Ned and Papa,' Fanny pursued, 'and I look over the books with the steward, and talk to the bailiff, so that I may understand how it is run. One day I will come into my inheritance, you see, and I feel I ought to know the business, so that I can make sure everything is done properly.'

'Nay, but Fanny, love, you'll have a husband one day —'

'Yes, Grandpapa, to be sure: but Morland Place will be *mine*, not his,' Fanny said firmly.

A gleam of admiration came to Hobsbawn's eye. 'Eh, love, but you've got Hobsbawn spirit in you!'

Fanny hastened to make profit. 'I have *your* blood in me, Grandpapa, and though my name is Fanny Morland and not Fanny Hobsbawn, it doesn't change what I feel inside. What interests you must interest me, and I want to understand your business. Won't you please tell me about it?' She put on her most appealing look, and Hobsbawn visibly weakened. 'If *you* were to explain everything, I'm sure I should understand in no time.'

Hobsbawn thought of the times he had taken little Henry, Fanny's brother, to the mills, to shew him his inheritance. They had been proud times, happy times! Little Fanny was his only grandchild now, his only living descendant — the last of the Hobsbawns.

'Well, after all,' he said, 'I suppose there's no harm in talking to you, if you think you can understand it. But I hardly know where to start. What is it you want to know?'

Fanny racked her brain for something to say that would convince him of her interest. What had she heard her father and Uncle Ned talking about?

'Well, sir,' she said, 'I have heard that the Americans won't send us any more cotton. Do you know why that is? And is it very bad for you?'

'Bad? It's as bad as can be!' Hobsbawn growled. 'It's all a lot of damned nonsense, anyway. The Americans complain that our anti-contraband patrols are always stopping their ships and seizing their cargoes — well, they shouldn't ship contraband, then it wouldn't happen!' Fanny nodded wisely, not understanding a word. 'So now they've struck back at us with this damned silly Non-Intercourse Act, and the upshot of it is, they won't send us any raw cotton. As if times aren't hard enough anyway, with cloth lying about in warehouses, because we can't sell it in Europe; and what we sell in South America we might as well have given away, for they promise plenty, and never pay up! Damn dagos! I never trusted 'em!'

He paused, and Fanny recaptured her wandering mind, and tried to think of another question.

'I'm sorry you should be so worried, Grandpapa,' she said, marking time.

'Don't let it trouble you, love. I've been through hard times before, and when they come, I just pull in my horns like an old snail, and sit it out. Oh, this war won't last for ever, and then we'll be back on full-time working, and you'll see what will happen!'

'Full time working?'

'Aye, lass, didn't you know we are on a three-day week now? We just haven't got the raw cotton to spin.'

This was more concrete, more understandable. 'So on the other three days, the mills are closed? No-one goes to work?'

'There's always some work, for the likes of me, and the managers, and the mechanics; but the spinners and piecers and so on are idle, yes.'

'You don't pay them, I suppose, when they're not working?'

His brow contracted. 'Pay them when they're not working? What kind of talk is that? I was beginning to think you had some brains, Fanny, but you're talking like a simpleton now.'

'I was just wondering how they manage,' Fanny said hastily. 'It isn't important.'

'Well, it's hard for them, of course,' Hobsbawn said grudgingly. 'Especially with the price of bread what it is these days. I'm sorry for them, but there's nothing I can do about it. And now, is there anything else you want to know, or can we get on with the game?'

She saw she had angered him, and tried to think of something flattering to say. She remembered her father's words. 'Well, I'm sure you won't go bankrupt, Grandpapa, because everyone says you're much too clever.'

He looked at her sidelong. 'You little puss, are you hoaxing me? Of course I won't go bankrupt! In fact, I've got a scheme in hand at this very minute to put me ahead of all my competitors and make myself another fortune.'

'Oh, do tell me, Grandpapa! What is it?' She injected eagerness into her voice, leaning forward a little and clasping her hands to her breast.

Fortunately, Hobsbawn was not very critical of female behaviour, having had so little experience of it. He took her interest at face value, and chuckled, pleased with himself. 'Well, Fanny, it's like this. Practically next-door to my number two mill, another mill-master I know has built a weaving-shed, a big one, for mechanical looms, driven by steam-power. He's a spinner, like me, and this American business has hit him hard. He'd a finger in a lot of pies, and they've all failed, and now the pieman has come along asking for his reckoning.'

Fanny nodded. 'He's gone bankrupt.'

'Not gone, but going. He's all to pieces — deep in debt, and no hope of getting free. Now this weaving-mill of his, he'd only just finished building it, but never started it running. If I step in now and offer him a price for it on the quiet, he'll sell it to me to get the cash in his hand, for if he's declared bankrupt, it's all up, and the creditors'll get everything.'

Fanny frowned. 'But why do you want a weaving-shed?' she asked.

'Why, to weave in, of course. Use your sense, Fanny. In normal times, our spinning mills produce more spun thread than all the weavers in Lancashire can handle. That's why Monkton — that's his name — went in for these mechanical looms, but the times caught up with him. We're on a three-day-week now, but that won't last for ever. Once the spinning mills are back to normal, I'll have all the thread I need, and I can have five hundred looms spinning my own thread into my own cloth! Do both processes, and take both lots of profit — that's progress!'

Fanny nodded, thinking it through. 'That's what this Mr Monkton meant to do, but he ran out of money. And now you can take advantage of his mistakes.'

'That's right. I've been canny, and I'm able to hold on, so I can buy a weaving-shed at a tenth of what it would cost me to build it, sit out the bad times, and be ready to start the moment the cotton's there again.'

Her eyes shone with approval. 'Oh Grandpapa, you are clever! If I were a mill-master, I should want to be like you! You'll be richer than all of them!'

He looked at her with such a similar expression, that if there had been a third party present, they might have noted a marked family resemblance between them at that moment. 'That's what business is all about, Fanny!' he said. 'By God, you're a Hobsbawn all right! I tell you what, I'll teach you about the business before I'm through! And one day soon, you shall put on your bonnet, and I'll take you down to Water Street with me, and shew the mills to you, and you to the mills!'

'Oh, yes please, Grandpapa,' said Fanny, as though it were the greatest treat in the world.

CHAPTER FIFTEEN

'It's finished,' James said, putting aside his brush. Héloïse looked up from her work enquiringly. 'Don't you want to see it?'

'But of course,' she said.

'No, don't get up — I'll bring it to you. You make too pretty a picture to be disturbed.'

It was a small piece of board on which he had been working, about eight inches by twelve. Stephen had found it and was proposing to use it for firewood, but James had first taken a fancy to it for its smoothness and grain, and then decided it would be perfect for the portrait he wanted to make of Héloïse. He always worked best on a small area.

'There now — what do you think?' he said, holding the painting so that the light was right for her. Héloïse could tell by his voice, before she looked at the painting, that he was pleased with it. 'I shall call it *Love in a Cottage*. Before now, I would not have thought such a thing possible, but the School of the Picturesque has won another disciple!'

The picture shewed her sitting in the window of the tiny parlour, in profile, facing right, her head slightly bent over the muslin handkerchief in her lap on which she was embroidering. At her feet James had painted Kithra, asleep, head on paws, and Castor, sitting up and looking up at her. Because of the darkness of the interior of the room, and the brightness of the summer light shining in through the window, she appeared to have a nimbus all around her, and particularly around her head.

She glanced up at him, wonderingly, and then gazed irresistibly at the painting again. She knew that her neck was not so long and swan-like, nor her piled and curled hair so glossy, nor her hands so long and slender; and besides all that, she was almost thirty-four years old, and she had never been handsome. Yet the woman in the painting was unmistakably

293

her, and unquestionably beautiful.

'It is so good, James,' she said. 'I think it is the best thing you have done.'

'Yes, I thought so, too,' he said cheerfully. 'I don't usually do so well in oils as in water-colour — my style is too meticulous — but somehow everything came right this time. It all flowed together, vision and medium and execution, all right for each other.'

She smiled at him, the particular smile which, even now, made his heart turn over. 'You have made me too beautiful, as always. How many times have you taken my likeness? Fifty? A hundred? And always you make me too beautiful.'

'No, Marmoset. There you display your ignorance,' he said, leaning over and nibbling the edge of her ear, so that his next words were breathed warm and damp into it. 'God has made you beautiful — I simply record the fact.'

She moved her head just enough to put her lips to his, and a satisfactory moment later he straightened up and said, 'Now I must put this somewhere safe to dry, and then we can go out.'

'Yes, I must walk a little, for I am stiff with sitting still so long.'

He laughed. 'How many times, foolish one, have I told you you don't need to keep absolutely still? You have no faith in my skills, have you?'

She put her work aside and stood up, and Castor gave a single, glad bark which woke Kithra, who stood up too, stretching and yawning and lashing his tail against the panelling like a drumbeat.

'Shall we walk in the garden?' she suggested. 'The roses need cutting.'

'Walk, not work,' he said firmly. 'I want your attention to myself. Let Stephen or Marie cut the roses.'

She was glad enough to comply. Their time here at Plaisir had been utterly peaceful, and almost perfectly happy. Héloïse found it easy and delightful to slip back into the simple life, sleeping long, eating simple meals, walking, driving or riding with James in the day, reading, working or talking with him in the evenings, retiring early to sleep the profound and nourishing sleep of contentment.

The only hint she had had that James was not completely

happy was her instinctive feeling for him, and the fact that he had taken to drawing her over and over again. She remembered the time they had lived here together, while he was married to Mary Ann, and he had made sketch after sketch of her, as though trying to catch hold of something that was fading from him. It was not quite like that this time; he did not draw with that frantic hunger, and this latest painting seemed to have pleased him in the execution and satisfied him in the completion. Yet it made her a little uneasy. He had painted the fleshly Héloïse with whom he lived, but the image that had emerged was unearthly, rimmed in light, like a saintly memory of someone loved and lost.

But how had he lost her? He was a complex and difficult man, whom she understood only instinctively. She knew that he fought against a kind of chronic discontent which seemed to have entered him early in life, and which from time to time threatened to destroy him. He was like a crippled child who had learned as he grew up to compensate for his deformity, so that he appeared to the casual eye to be perfectly normal; yet study him closely for a while, live with him and care for him, and you could see that he was somehow, minutely, not quite straight.

It tore at her heart, this maiming of his inner self, for she did not know what to do for him. At night sometimes, when she held him in her arms, he would burrow and burrow against her, as if trying to get closer, when he was already as close as flesh could be to flesh. He had somehow lost touch, not with her, but with himself. It had something to do with Nicholas, she thought. It pained him to look at the child, though he loved him dearly. Well, it hurt her too, but with a natural outpouring of love and pity; but with James, the hurt went inwards, like blame, and healed nothing.

Since Nicholas was born, James had not made love to her fully. She knew that with the front part of his mind he believed he was following Lucy's advice, and protecting Héloïse's well-being; but she also knew, probably better than James did himself, that in the back of his mind, he was punishing himself for what he believed he had done to her and the child. There seemed to be nothing she could do about that. They held and caressed and kissed each other lovingly, but no matter what she did, or how aroused he became, he never lost control, or let her entice him into the conjunction they both wanted and needed so much.

Well, she must count her blessings, she thought as they stepped out of the house into the sunshine. Today he seemed almost completely happy: the painting had eased something in him. He took her hand and tucked it through his arm, and matched his step to hers, and they strolled along the old, soft brick paths between the banks of flowers, dazzling and almost colourless in the strong sunlight. Kithra padded contentedly behind, enjoying the warmth. Castor frisked ahead of them, burying his nose in a lavender bush and startling himself with a bee, chasing butterflies with a happy lack of determination.

'Fool!' James apostrophised him kindly as he ran back and laughed up at them. 'Perhaps he's meant as an example for us, Marmoset — what do you think? Perhaps chasing butterflies is all we can ever do.' She knew he didn't expect an answer, which was as well. He seemed to realise he was being unfair, and said instead, 'Mathilde seems to be enjoying her trip — more that I thought she would, certainly. Didn't it strike you as odd, though, how little this Mr Wickfield was mentioned in her letter?'

'I imagine him to be comprehended in some of the *we*'s' Héloïse said unconcernedly. 'After all, it was not she but Lizzie who married him. And he seems to have been very kind, buying her a new bonnet.'

'I dare say we shall have a small mountain of sketching-books to look through when she comes back,' James said with a sigh. 'Lake Windermere looking south. Lake Windermere looking east. Ambleside, from a fishing-boat. A fishing-boat, from Ambleside. And a curious squiggle and three smudges entitled *Blasted Thorn and Rocky Outcrop*.'

'Don't be so cruel,' Héloïse said peacefully. 'It is a very proper, ladylike occupation.'

'So is getting married. Do you suppose she'll meet someone on one of these genteel sketching-parties? At least this Wickfield seems to be fixed in one place for a week or so — enough time, surely, for Mathilde to fall in love? Hard to do, I grant you, in a carriage travelling from place to place, but nothing could be more conducive to love than a large stretch of still water and a young woman's face under the shadow of a lacy parasol.'

'Perhaps Mathilde does not want to get married,' Héloïse suggested.

'She had better,' James growled.

'Why, love? May she not live with us? She makes herself very useful.'

For answer he put his head under the brim of her sunbonnet and kissed the end of her nose. 'I like having you to myself.'

'Fanny seems to be enjoying herself, too,' Héloïse said as they resumed walking. 'This Mrs Pendlebury seems to be taking a great deal of trouble to make her happy. She must be a good-natured woman.'

'I'll give you odds,' James said with a smile, 'that she has an unmarried son.'

'Oh, James!'

'Don't sound so reproachful. It's human nature — Fanny's a great heiress.'

'Well, I'm glad at least that she has lent her governess to Fanny. It makes me feel more comfortable.'

'Does it? Doesn't it strike you that if Fanny writes so complacently about being saddled with a governess, there must be something wrong with her? I suspect she's some poor, downtrodden drudge whom Fanny has already wound completely round her thumb.'

'You are in a destructive mood today, my James,' Héloïse said severely. 'There is no pleasing you.'

He stopped and took her in his arms. '*You* please me,' he said, kissing her eyes and nose and mouth. 'Marmoset — little monkey-face — my black, black princess —'

Kithra whined a warning an instant before Durban's hesitant cough. They broke hastily apart as he appeared very slowly around the corner of the butterfly bush.

'Yes, Durban, what is it?' James asked the ex-trooper in a dangerous voice.

But Durban was too good a servant to have interrupted them for nothing. His usually well-schooled face held a hint of concern. 'It's the old horse, sir,' he said. 'I think perhaps you ought to come and have a look at him. He was off his feed this morning, and I think maybe he's got a touch of colic.'

The horses had been stabled at the Fauconburg Arms in the

village, a few minutes walk from the cottage, and though the cost of stabling included the services of the ostler, Durban did everything except the mucking-out himself, partly to keep himself occupied, and partly because he didn't trust anyone he hadn't trained himself.

Besides, a horse as old as Nez Carré needed his routines. He had always been fit and healthy, never ailing a thing, except lately a slight stiffness first thing in the morning, which was only to be expected in old age, for man or beast.

'He's always been a good doer, sir, you know that,' Durban said, unbolting the door of the stall, 'and usually he's kicking the door for his feed as soon as he hears me coming. But this morning he seemed listless, and when I put it in front of him, he sniffed at it, and wouldn't eat.'

James went in, and Nez Carré turned his head and whickered softly in greeting. The cold hand unclenched from his heart for an instant — he's all right, he's calling to me — and then closed down again as his horseman's eye told him all was not well. There was that slightly tucked-up look to the big bay body, the preoccupied look in the great brown eyes, the patches of sweat dulling the coat which Durban groomed so thoroughly every day of his life that a white glove passed over it stayed white.

'Hullo, old man, what's up with you?' James said, going up to Nez Carré's head, stroking the square nose and pulling the long ears. Nez Carré nuzzled his hands, nudged him in the chest, and then turned his head away, resuming that inward-looking, preoccupied stare. 'His ears are cold,' James said to Durban, who was standing inside the door, turning his hat round anxiously in his hands as he studied the horse from a different angle.

'I think it is colic, sir,' he said quietly a moment later. 'Do you see that spasm?'

James laid his hands against the horse's smooth, barrel of a flank, and a moment later felt the slight muscular contraction. At the same time, Nez Carré grunted softly.

James bit his lip. Colic was always worrying, though nine times out of ten a dose of medicine cured it in an hour or so. 'What's he been eating?'

'His usual feed,' Durban said. 'I mixed it myself.'

'No-one else could have given him anything?'

298

Durban shrugged. 'I don't see why they should, sir.'

'And the oats — they weren't musty?'

'I looked over all the feed bins here, sir. They all seemed perfectly sound and dry to me, otherwise I wouldn't have used them.'

'No, of course not. Well, perhaps it's just a touch of the gripes. We'll give him a drench. I'll do it myself, Durban. You get the rugs on him, will you? And rub his ears until I get back.'

James mixed his and Durban's favourite recipe of turpentine and linseed oil, epsom salts and whisky, and the familiar, comforting smell rose up to him as he poured it into the slim-necked bottle that was always to be found somewhere in every tack-room. Nez Carré had always disliked being drenched, and he resisted this time with a vigour which heartened James. He couldn't be feeling so very bad if he attempted his usual trick of holding the drench in his cheek in the hope of spitting it out at the other side as soon as his head was released. Durban pushed his head further up, and James tapped the old horse lightly on the throat, and Nez Carré gave the involuntary gulp which sent the medicine down where it was needed.

'That'll fix you, old man,' James said, rubbing the long ears consolingly. Nez Carré nudged him again, and then sighed and raised his tail hopefully, but passed only a little wind.

'Still, that's a good sign in itself,' James said.

'I think he looks better already,' said Durban.

But by dinner-time, Durban was forced to call James back again. The drench hadn't worked, nor the second dose he had administered on his own authority.

'He's paining now, sir, every few minutes,' he said. James looked at the damp coat, the distressed eyes. Nez Carré was groaning, too, at each spasm, a low groan ending in an involuntary grunt, which frightened James; and as he looked, the horse turned to stare along his side, and raised a hind foot to paw at it.

'Has he passed anything?' Durban shook his head. 'We'll try one more drench,' James said helplessly.

Nez Carré hardly struggled this time, too preoccupied with his internal discomfort. 'We've got to walk him round,' James said. 'Get an extra rug, will you. He's sweating, and the last

299

thing we want now is for him to catch cold.'

They took him out into the stable yard and began to walk him round. The other ostlers and grooms had all heard the story, and from time to time a head would pop out from a doorway to give a look of anxious sympathy. Nez Carré walked round quietly after his master, groaning now and then, and occasionally stopping to try to paw his side.

The long summer afternoon drew towards dusk. The two men were weary now, taking turns in keeping the horse moving, as he grew more and more reluctant. The sweat had creamed on his neck, and his ears and face were dark with it. As the light began to fade they took him into the loose box which the head ostler had cleared for them, and continued to walk him round it on a thick bed of straw.

At seven o'clock James sent Durban off to get some dinner, and Durban knew better than to argue. He walked back to the cottage to give a bulletin to the waiting household, and brought back a packet of food for James, cold meat and bread. James thanked him, but put it aside, trudging round and round with the horse as though to save his soul.

Even in the half-hour he had been away, Durban could see that the horse had worsened. He was groaning all the time now, stumbling a little as he walked, following his master in blind trust, trying to walk away from the pain that always came with him. James talked as he walked, leading Nez Carré with the sound of his voice, encouraging him, rousing him when he tried to lie down.

'No, no, old man, keep walking. You mustn't lie down. Come on, Nez Carré, come on, boy. Walk on.'

But Durban looked at the shivering, sweating animal stumbling past him, and knew it was no good.

'Sir,' he said gently, urgently, 'sir, he's suffering.'

James rounded on him furiously. 'He'll get better!' he cried. 'Don't you look at me like that! He's going to get better!'

'Sir, it isn't fair on him.'

'Fair on him? What the hell are you talking about? What do you want to do, condemn him? Give him a chance. He'll get better. He's strong, he's a fighter. Come *on*, boy!' as Nez Carré trembled and tried again to lie down. 'Walk on, Nez Carré. Walk on!'

Durban let it be. 'All right, sir. But let me take him for a bit, while you eat your supper.'

'Go to hell!'

'You won't help him by starving yourself. Ten minutes, to eat your supper.'

'You go to hell! You don't care about him. Get away from me, butcher!'

He looked almost wild. Durban retired to the corner of the box. There was nothing he could do now but wait.

It was almost ten o'clock when Nez Carré went off his legs. He had tried more and more often to lie down; now at last he gave a long groan, and went slowly down, like a great cathedral collapsing, while James tugged helplessly at his headstall, tears of anguish and frustration running down his cheeks.

'No, oh no! Oh don't! Up, Nez Carré! Up, boy!'

But the horse was beyond obeying him, even though he wanted to. James dropped to his knees beside him, stroking the damp head, holding the great, troubled eyes with his own, his tears dropping onto Nez Carré's forehead. 'Oh please, Nez Carré,' he whimpered, stroking and stroking, 'please don't, please don't, oh please don't.'

Nez Carré tried to get up again, lifting his head and neck and straining, but the effort was too much for him, and he lay down again with a groan. James took the great, heavy head onto his lap. He cupped one long ear in his hand and put his mouth to it, licking his dry lips and tasting his tears salt on them. 'Don't die,' he whispered. 'Please don't die.'

He sat in the straw, stroking the face and neck and ears over and over, trying to pour his strength into the old horse, willing him to live. Time crawled on. At half-past ten, an ostler brought a lantern, driving the darkness which had crept in back to the corners of the box. Outside the sky was a luminous turquoise and the evening star shone low and pure; and inside, in the yellow lamplight, Nez Carré quivered, and died.

It was a long time before Durban could coax him away. James sat, numbed with disbelief, still stroking Nez Carré's head and damp neck, long after he had heard the sigh of the last breath leaving him. It couldn't be true. He would get up again. If only he stayed here and didn't move, he would get up again, and it would be all right.

He struggled when Durban touched him, but when the head ostler came and took an arm too, he could not resist them both. He let them help him to his feet and lead him towards the door.

'Don't you touch him,' he cried to the ostler. 'No-one's to touch him.'

'Nay, maister, I'll see to it,' the ostler said soothingly. 'No-one s'l coom near 'im, I promise. He were a good old 'oss, and he s'l be respected.'

Even so, as he closed the door and bolted it with his own hand, James looked back before closing the top half, still expecting the big bay horse to struggle to his feet in that ungainly way horses had, and come to him, ears cocked and greedy muzzle outstretched to see what he had. But the dark shape was motionless in the straw. He closed the door tenderly, as though not to waken him, and stood staring at it, his hands hanging helplessly by his sides.

'Come, sir,' said Durban gently. 'Come on home.'

They had taken a message to Héloïse, and she was waiting to receive him. He stumbled into her arms like a child, and she nodded to Durban over his shoulder that she should be left alone with him. She didn't speak, knowing there were no words that would help, only coaxed him upstairs, undressed him with her own hands, and put him to bed.

'Come here,' he said desperately as she pulled the covers over him. 'I must have you here.'

He began to shiver. She dragged off her clothes quickly, and when she was naked, he caught her arm and tugged at her. Seeing his desperate need, she did not wait to put on her night-gown, but turned back the sheet and climbed into the bed beside him as she was. He pulled her against him fiercely, pressing her small body close, folding his arms across her, even locking one leg over her hip, as if he expected someone to try to snatch her away. He was shaking all over, and after a while, he began to whimper. Then at last he spoke.

'I can't bear it,' he said. 'I can't bear it.'

'James, my James,' she said, stroking his neck and shoulder, all she could reach.

'Oh God, it isn't fair!' he said, and then with a terrible, broken cry which seemed to be dragged up from somewhere deep inside him, he thrust her over onto her back and buried his face in her neck, kissing and nuzzling. His hands were locked about her wrists, holding her still, as his mouth tracked down her throat, across her fragile collar-bone, found her breast, nipping and tugging at her nipple until she gasped and wriggled. He lifted his head. 'Héloïse,' he said clearly, and then with one swift movement, he was inside her.

He made love to her so hard and powerfully, as though he were in the grip of some force outside him. Crushed beneath his weight, she could only go with him, meeting his thrusts at first of her will, and then, as her own feelings changed, helplessly, gripped with a purely physical desire that she had never experienced before. It was fierce, thrilling, dangerous. She gasped, pulling at him, greedy for him, aware of his body and hers as never before, feeling, as if they had only one sense between them, that their bodies were utterly in tune. They reached the same point at the same instant, cried out in the same voice, and were done.

She lay in the tenuous summer dark, dragging her breath in against his crushing weight, hearing her blood thudding in her ears, her physical self tingling and singing with fulfilled pleasure. Her mind lay separate and calm, cradled in the cool night, seeing and knowing. They had been given this. It was not sinful. Only those who had loved each other long and unselfishly could have such a moment, such a complete loving of the flesh, when the mind was wounded beyond help. She knew why he had said her name; it was the moment when his mind stepped aside, but he had called her, to make her know that it was to her, and to no other, that he could have gone at that moment.

He was hers, completely hers. Her pulse slowed to normal, and she felt her blood flow sweetly through her body, felt her life lie warm and easy in her, singing with the pleasure of its own existence, in tune with everything that had life from earth up to heaven. She felt him inside her, small and gentle now, possessed by her as she had been possessed. She felt the wetness, his ultimate gift to her, and smiled secretly into the silvery darkness.

God knew! It was by His will that the stars moved in their eternal dance, and everything that lived touched and grew and intermeshed in a pattern of His devising. He had taken the old horse back to Him, to be young again in the Elysian fields; everything that lived must die; but in taking, He had given. James would not know it yet, but he would come to understand.

She stroked his head and kissed him, and he sighed and withdrew from her, but moved away only enough to slide down so that his head was on her shoulder, drawing his legs up like a child and curling into her. She wrapped her arms round him and he sighed again, but with comfort this time, and slept. She lay still, unsleeping, through the short summer night, listening to the infinitesimal sounds of life all around her, inside and out, feeling it unfolding like a flower in the warm darkness.

The weather being hot enough to make London unpleasant, Lucy had gone down to Wolvercote for a couple of weeks, and had persuaded Roberta and Firth to come with her, together with Bobbie and Marcus. At the end of the week Danby Wiske was to join them for a few days with a group of friends — Brummell, Alvanley, Mildmay, and the Manners brothers, Robert and Charles — for what Brummell described as a 'farewell party' before Wiske went overseas with his regiment. Though he had not referred to his proposal again, Lucy could not help feeling that he ought to have her answer before he left, whether he actually expected it or not.

It perplexed her to know why she found it so difficult to decide what her answer should be. At no time in their long friendship had she even considered the possibility of marrying him, so why now did she not simply, kindly, refuse him? It had never been in her nature or her experience to seek a confidante, but seeing Roberta so glowingly happy with her Mr Firth, she decided at last to ask her help, and invited her to come out with her alone for a ride.

Roberta, who was no great horsewoman, detached her mind from her love, observed Lucy's furrowed brow, and accepted the invitation meekly. Parslow, to whom nothing seemed to be a secret, provided her with a quiet horse, fielded Thomas with a significant look which kept the boy at his side, helped both ladies mount, and let them ride off alone without him. Lucy seemed oblivious of all this. She rode beside Roberta in deep thought, controlling Hotspur's light-hearted

304

attempts to buck automatically, and it was not until they were some way into the park that she roused herself to speak.

'I wanted to ask your advice about something,' she said with characteristic abruptness.

'So I imagined,' Roberta smiled, leaning forward to pat the neck of the kindly plodder Parslow had found for her. 'I'm not the person you would usually choose for a riding companion.'

'Oh, that's all right. I can have a good gallop later,' Lucy said vaguely, and lapsed into thought again. After a while Roberta prompted her.

'Well, Lucy. What was it you wanted to ask? You seem worried.'

Lucy looked up, and her furrowed brow cleared. She laughed a little self-consciously. 'Oh, it's nothing bad. In fact, I ought to feel happy about it, I suppose. The thing is, Rob, I need to confide. I don't know what to do, and I don't know why I don't know.'

'Lucy dear, start at the beginning. It makes it much easier to follow,' Roberta said patiently.

Lucy smiled a little. 'Very well, I'll try. It's Danby Wiske, you see — he's asked me to marry him, and since he's going abroad with the regiment very soon, I feel I ought to give him his answer.' Whatever surprise Roberta felt at the news, she displayed none. She merely nodded encouragingly. 'The difficulty is, I don't know what to say to him.' She looked hopefully at Roberta.

'You mean you don't know how to frame your answer? You must know whether you want to accept him or not.'

'That's just what I don't know. Rob, you must advise me.'

'Lucy, I can't,' Roberta said with an exasperated smile. 'How can anyone tell you what to do in such a case? You must make up your own mind. What is your problem?'

Lucy stared ahead of her, trying to assemble words. 'It was such a shock when he asked me,' she said at last. 'I'd never thought of him in that way. I never supposed he thought of me that way. But when he asked — suddenly I felt as though he was a stranger. It frightened me —' She paused, and then didn't seem able to go on.

'But it was a pleasant sort of fear?' Roberta offered after a while.

Lucy glanced at her, a little pink, relieved and ashamed. 'Yes! Dear Rob, you know! You *do* understand.'

Roberta smiled. 'Yes, I understand. That was the most natural feeling in the world, and it proves that you are not indifferent to Major Wiske. You felt suddenly strange, because he is a man, and you were responding to him as a man. That's all.'

Lucy frowned. 'But I never felt like that with Weston.'

'Didn't you?' Roberta was doubtful.

'No!' Lucy said certainly. 'With Weston I felt — oh, excited, and happy, and restless sometimes, but never strange! He was — I *knew* him, you see. And yet I've known Danby much longer.'

'But you've never thought of him as a man, perhaps,' Roberta said, feeling she was getting out of her depth.

'Well of course I haven't — not like that. The first thing I felt when he asked me to marry him was panic — why was that? And if the idea frightens me, why didn't I refuse him at once? Why don't I know what to do?'

'Lucy, if you don't know, how should I?' Roberta said, and yet she did know, in a way. Lucy's relationships with her husband and her lover had been those of a child with an adult — parent or older brother. But in Danby Wiske she had suddenly met someone on her own level. He had surprised her out of her extended childhood, and made her feel a woman's feelings. Her fear of the idea of marrying Danby was because she knew subconsciously that it was possible.

But how to say such things to Lucy? How to make her understand herself, when she had no more self-awareness than a fox?

'If you didn't refuse him at once, it must be because the idea was not wholly repugnant to you,' she said carefully. 'You didn't burst into laughter or cry "Ridiculous!", did you?'

'No, of course not! I like Danby. I'm very fond of him.'

'Well, then, start from there. You like him, you are fond of him, the idea of marriage does not fill you with horror. You enjoy his company?'

'I suppose so. I go everywhere with him, after all.'

A deep blush began under Roberta's collar. 'Does — does the physical side of things trouble you?' she asked bravely.

Lucy had not particularly contemplated it. She thought

306

about it now, conjuring Danby's face before her, and a faint blush troubled her, too. 'It doesn't — doesn't *repel* me,' she said faintly.

'Well, then,' Roberta said briskly, 'you have a good beginning. There's no reason why you shouldn't marry him, is there?'

Lucy thought. 'Wouldn't it be, well, disloyal? After Weston, how *could* I marry anyone else?'

Roberta smiled. 'Life doesn't work like that. I loved Charles dearly; nothing can change that, or lessen it. Now I love Peter, and it's quite different.'

'I see,' said Lucy doubtfully. It didn't seem to her that she had got much further along. She had hoped Roberta would give her a clear answer, tell her what to say and how to think. Roberta looked at her with sympathy, having a pretty clear idea what was in her mind.

'Lucy, dear, would the idea of never seeing Major Wiske again upset you? Suppose he should be killed in the war —'

'No! Don't say it,' Lucy said quickly, and looked around for some wood to touch.

With a private smile, Roberta offered the handle of her whip, and Lucy touched it with a guilty blush.

'I think you perhaps like Major Wiske a great deal more than you know.' Roberta said.

The Misses Pendlebury and their governess called for Fanny at Hobsbawn House one morning in the family barouche, complete with a footman and an elderly coachman in a cauliflower wig. Miss Imber, a small, retiring creature with frightened, fieldmouse eyes, who always looked somehow dusty, as though she had been standing in a corner neglected for a long time, removed to the backward seat with the air of one who deserves no better of life. The barouche having been built on a grand scale, like most new things in Manchester, there was sufficient room for even Fanny not to think herself ill-used in sitting three across.

The day was cool, and it looked as though it might rain later, so a trip to the new bazaar in the Exchange Hall, where they sold gloves, stockings, ribbons, purses and other delightful nothings, was exactly what was wanted.

'If we have time, we might go to the library afterwards,

too,' Prudence suggested.

Agnes bounced. 'Oh yes, they have ices there! Oh excellent creature, Pru!'

'I meant to look at books. But you may do as you please.'

'What did you think of the supper-party last night, Fanny?' Agnes asked. The girls had all been on first-name terms for some time now. 'Wasn't Percy Droylsden a perfect fiend at Lottery Tickets? He cares for nothing but winning! And that monster Jack Withington came straight from ogling you in that ridiculous manner, and put on a sentimental face and told me he had writ me a verse for my album!'

Fanny laughed. 'Was it a verse about your fine eyes? Yes, I thought so! He had just that minute told me the same thing!'

'Had he? The impudent scrub! And I'll bet my hair that he never wrote it at all. It will have been his sister's work, for he can hardly write his own name. Libertine was mad in love with a poet last year — or fancied herself so.'

'Oh Agnes, Miss Withington's name is Albertine,' Miss Imber protested in a faint voice, her brow furrowing with distress. 'Libertine means — well, it means something quite inappropriate, for Miss Withington is a very nice young lady indeed.'

'She's a languishing ninny!' Agnes retorted smartly.

Prudence said wisely, 'She knows what libertine means, Imby, you may depend on it. Annie, don't talk so shocking, it isn't becoming.'

Fanny was only half attending, engaged in looking about her. It was still strange to her to be in a new town, where building was going on everywhere, and everything had an unfinished look, but it was oddly invigorating, as though there were more possibilities for things to happen here than in an ancient city like York. All around there were new, fine buildings going up, while between and behind them, one could catch glimpses of the other world, the dank, dirty, and odorous lanes and courts where the mill-hands lived.

It occurred to her that there seemed to be more of the inhabitants of that half-world on view than was usual. Of course, as Grandpapa had said, most of the mills were on three-day working, and the mill-hands were idle, but even so, the ragged and dirty people seemed more visible than usual. She found herself remembering the time at home when the new stables were being built at Twelvetrees, and a derelict barn had to be pulled down to make space. Hooks had been set into the ancient and pitted stone walls, and the horses harnessed up; and just as they were about to be set in motion, to pull the structure down, suddenly there had been a flood of rats come boldly into the daylight, frightened out of their usual hiding places in the walls by some foreknowledge of destruction.

The barouche was held up at a crossroads by the press of traffic making turns, and while they were stationary, Fanny found herself within feet of a member of the lower orders, who was standing at the side of the road, waiting to cross.

They were about the same age, Fanny thought, and the same height, but otherwise there was no similarity between them. The mill-girl was thin, so thin that the cords were visible in her neck, and in the claw-like hand which clutched the edges of her shawl — a dirty bit of blanket — together at her neck. Her skin was pale, but not with the clear pallor of a lady. It had a greyish, cloudy look, like brackish water. From under the blanket-shawl, a rough brown dress hung to her ankles, below which her dirty feet were thrust into crude wooden clogs. She wore no hat, and her hair was a sour and matted brown rat's nest.

And yet, Fanny could see, she was not absolutely ugly. If she had been clean and well-fed, she might even have been tolerable to look at. Why doesn't she at least wash herself? Fanny thought in disgust, noting the black grime under the fingernails and the mud-splashes on the legs. And she might wash her clothes, and brush her hair.

The road ahead cleared, and the carriage jerked as the horses threw themselves against their collars; and in that instant Fanny's eyes and those of the mill-girl met. The girl's eyes were tawny, like Fanny's, bright and long-lashed: they, and they alone about her, were beautiful. A strange, unwilling sensation of sympathy passed between them. If we ever met again, Fanny thought, we should know each other, however many years had passed.

The girl's lips parted, as if she began to say something. One hand released the blanket-shawl, and moved towards Fanny, turning palm upwards and uncurling like a sea-anemone; and with a sensation of disgusted horror, Fanny saw that the

309

other hand, clinging to the girl's throat like a maimed animal, had only three fingers.

The carriage moved forward, the contact was broken, the girl was left behind. The incident had lasted only seconds, and yet Fanny felt deeply disturbed. The image of the girl was impressed on her brain like a brand. She had never been so close to a member of the labouring poor. Of course, she knew all their labourers and servants at home, but they were decent, clean, prosperous people. That thin, dirty, maimed creature was something quite different. Fanny felt as though she wanted to retch; wanted to find soap and water and scrub her own hands, as though the dirt had been transferred to her by that instant of sympathy. She put one dainty, gloved hand in the other, and felt them over and over, to make sure they were whole and unblemished and beautiful.

'Fanny?'

Prudence was wanting her attention. She looked round a little wildly.

'Are you all right? You look quite pale. I was asking if you would prefer to go to the library first, and the bazaar afterwards, but you didn't seem to hear me.'

'Oh — I did not attend. Yes — whatever you like. I don't care,' Fanny answered at random.

'Do you feel quite well, Fanny?' Prudence persisted. 'You do look strange.'

'Quite well, thank you. Don't fuss,' Fanny said, the colour beginning to come back into her face. Dirty, nasty creature, with her disgusting wounded hand! But the image was receding. 'It was very hot when the carriage stopped, that's all.'

'Perhaps we ought to go the library first, as we are just passing it,' Miss Imber suggested, and the coachman, hearing her, drew rein. 'It would be quieter than the bazaar, if Miss Morland feels faint.'

Fanny's brow drew down in irritation, but just at that moment her name was spoken from the other side of the carriage, averting the storm.

'Miss Morland! What a curious chance — and a very happy one, might I add! How do you do, ma'am?'

A militia patrol was marching down the street towards them — a common enough sight in Manchester these days to rouse no particular interest — but the officer had brought his

310

horse alongside the barouche, and raised his hand to his cap.

'I fear you have forgotten me, ma'am,' he said with a teasing smile as Fanny did not answer.

Fanny looked up at the strongly handsome face with the dark, cavalry moustache which was such a surprising contrast to the white teeth, and recognised belatedly the officer of Mathilde's ball, and of the woodland path.

'Why, yes, of course, it's Lieutenant — Lieutenant —' she racked her brain for the name.

'Hawker, ma'am, Fitzherbert Hawker, completely at your service,' he said, taking the hand which Fanny extended hastily to him, and bowing over it quite correctly. The horse waltzed back and then forward, breaking the contact, and Fanny noted with approval how quickly with heel and hand he checked it and brought it back to stand beside the carriage. The other two girls were staring at him in awed fascination, while Miss Imber seemed to have shrunk up into herself in terror.

Their reaction made Fanny feel instantly older, more self-assured, the young lady of fashion amid the country clowns.

'How do you do, Lieutenant Hawker. What brings you to Manchester?' she said in her most polished manner.

'I am here on duty, Miss Morland, as you see,' he gestured towards his patrol, marching on under the command of their sergeant. 'There have been threats of frame-breaking, and we have been sent here to prevent any trouble.'

'Frame-breaking? Here in Manchester?' Fanny said in surprise. 'Surely not? You see for yourself how quiet everything is.' Then she remembered the flood of rats again, and felt a shiver of nervousness run down her spine.

'Yes, it is quiet, and we hope to keep it that way. But you must have heard that the Luddites have been moving north. There was an outbreak last week in Macclesfield. Our presence here, I hope, will prevent its moving any further north.'

Agnes was almost bursting with excitement at the presence of this real, grown-up, handsome man, who was looking at Fanny as though she were absolutely *out*. 'Fanny's grandpa is a mill-master,' she blurted at last, unable to hold her tongue a moment longer. Miss Imber looked shocked, and Prudence pinched her reprovingly, but Lieutenant Hawker only smiled kindly.

'Is he indeed? Then we must make sure he is not inconvenienced.'

Fanny hastened to repair the situation. 'I am staying with my grandfather for a few weeks. He is Mr Hobsbawn of Hobsbawn Mills — perhaps you may have heard of him? But pray allow me to present you to Miss Pendlebury, and Miss Agnes Pendlebury. And this is Miss Imber.'

Hawker touched his cap. 'Ladies, how do you do? I'm honoured to make your acquaintance. Miss Morland, I must hasten after my men; but may I do myself the honour of calling on you in a day or two, when my duties permit?'

Fanny was delighted, excited, taken aback. She did not know how her grandfather would take to a gentleman calling on her, when she was not even out. Miss Imber was looking as disapproving as a fieldmouse can.

'I think, sir —' Fanny began hesitantly, and Hawker saw his mistake.

'I mean, of course, to leave my card with your grandfather as soon as I can. We are members of the same club, I believe, and I'm sure we have met at the Exchange on several occasions.

Fanny's brow cleared. 'We should be pleased to see you, sir,' she said.

Hawker saluted again, bestowed one last smile, and rode on down the street. By God, he thought, the little heiress had grown up a regular beauty! And a bold one, he thought, from her eyes. How old was she now? She looked seventeen or so, but on the other hand, she hadn't behaved as though she were out, and he hadn't seen her at the ball the other night. No matter — she remembered him all right, and not unkindly! He had been looked at by enough women to recognise admiration when he saw it, however veiled it was meant to be.

Now he had the task of finding some way to scrape up an acquaintance with the old gentleman within the next twenty-four hours. How the devil was he to convince a mill-master that they had anything in common? But poverty, they say, he reminded himself grimly, makes strange bedfellows.

CHAPTER SIXTEEN

Lucy and Thomas were just mounting up for their early morning ride when Major Wiske appeared at the door, drawing on his gloves and looking about him at the fresh, lovely morning.

'Hullo! You're up early,' Lucy said. 'I didn't think any of the Bow-window Set would be astir before noon today, after your late night last night.'

'Doubt if they will. But I'm not really one of the Set,' Wiske said. 'Not a full member — not obliged to keep up appearances.'

'Or non-appearances,' Lucy suggested.

'Thought I might come out with you, if you've no objection? Think you can find me something to ride, Parslow?'

'Yes indeed, sir,' Parslow said quickly. 'Feather's going very well at the moment, sir. I'll have her round for you in five minutes.'

'Good fellow. I'll help her ladyship to mount,' Wiske said, taking Hotspur's head as Parslow hurried away.

'You've plainly made an impression on Parslow,' Lucy said, throwing the long end of her skirt over her arm, and lifting her left foot for Danby's linked hands. 'He won't let anyone but me ride Feather usually; and I don't think he'd let me take her out if he could stop me.' Wiske threw her up, and the instant Hotspur felt her on his back he whipped his head free and tried to leap away. Lucy was ready for him, however, and turned him in tight circles, while she unconcernedly found her stirrup and settled her skirts.

'Don't know why you ride horses like that,' Wiske complained, trying to catch Hotspur's head as he passed.

'Oh, he always does that,' Lucy said. 'It's only his fun. He doesn't mean anything by it.'

Hotspur champed his bit and gave the Major a speculative look.

313

'If he were in my squadron, I'd send him to the rough-rider,' Wiske said.

'He's just a baby. He'll settle down,' Lucy said.

'Mimosa was just the same, and she didn't settle down,' Wiske pointed out. 'And Minstrel was wicked to the end. You like difficult horses, that's the truth.'

'Mimosa had a cold back,' Lucy said firmly, 'and Minstrel had been spoilt before I got him. Really, Danby —' She had been about to say, 'You lecture me like a husband,' but thought better of it.

A few moments later Parslow returned with Feather, the Major mounted up, and the four of them set off into the park. The horses were all fresh, and when they had walked the prescribed half-mile to settle them down, Lucy glanced round to see that they were all ready, and put Hotspur into a canter. He sprang away, and Feather after him. The speed was too much for Cobnut's short legs. Parslow held his horse back to stay with Thomas, and Lucy and Wiske were soon well ahead, and out of sight.

The track went up a long, slow incline, and the horses began to slow and to labour for breath, and at the top Lucy and Wiske pulled up, and jumped down to breathe the horses.

'What do you think of Feather?' she asked. 'I think she's a bit light in the neck, don't you?'

'She'll make a lady's horse,' Danby said politely, patting the mare.

'That's a damning compliment,' Lucy observed. 'Don't let Parslow hear you say that.'

'Depends on the lady, doesn't it?' Danby said. He studied Lucy appreciatively. She always appeared to her best in riding-clothes. The tight-fitting jacket of dark blue superfine, relieved at the neck with a white stock, the voluminous skirt, the small, neat tricorne with the net veil — they made her look very young and girlish. Hotspur put his head down to graze, and Lucy slipped the rein over his head and sat down on the grass, hugging her updrawn knees as she gazed out over the park.

She glanced up at Danby, and then patted the ground beside her. 'Come. Sit. The grass isn't wet.' He obeyed her, and resumed his contemplation of her profile. Lucy found being stared at unexpectedly confusing, and searched for something to say. 'Well, Danby, what did rouse you from your bed so early this morning?'

'I rather wanted to ride out with you once more, before I go abroad,' he said.

She was taken aback. 'Oh. It is soon, then?'

'Yes, very soon. We embark on Thursday. So I'll have to leave Town on Tuesday.' She continued to look at him, and he could not fathom her expression. 'What are you thinking?'

She bit her lip. 'I was thinking,' she said with difficulty, 'that I ought to give you your answer before you leave.'

He felt a little panic. If she was going to refuse him, he would sooner not know. 'No hurry. I told you I wouldn't press you.'

'Yes, but it isn't fair to you,' she said.

Oh God, it was a refusal, then. 'You need time to think,' he suggested.

'I've been thinking,' she said. 'Danby, can I ask you something. Why do you want to marry me?'

'Should have thought it was obvious,' he said, twiddling with a blade of grass. 'I love you. I want to live with you.'

'You don't mind that I have more money than you?'

'Best for one of us to have money,' he said reasonably. 'Bit awkward otherwise.'

'But won't you mind that people will say you are marrying me for my money?'

'They won't,' he said simply, and waited for the next thing.

'I have thought about it,' she said eventually. 'I thought about you going away to the war, and —'

'And?'

'And I don't want never to see you again,' she said unhappily.

'Lucy, I don't mean to blackmail you,' he said. 'If you don't want to marry me, we'll go on as we are, that's all. Just say no, and that will be the end of it.'

'I don't want to say no,' she said in a small voice.

His heart leapt. 'Then — you mean —?'

She looked at him, disturbed and confused, not knowing what to say, not knowing how to answer him. He didn't know how to help her, though he had an idea what her trouble was; and then, simply because her dear face was so close, and because he longed to take her in his arms and cherish and

315

protect her, he leaned over and kissed her.

Lucy felt a shock like a blow to the pit of the stomach; and then everything inside her seemed to tremble and disintegrate. Danby's mouth on hers was exotically strange, and yet familiar. It was long, very long, since a man had kissed her, but her body remembered, and inclined towards him like a flower turning to the sun. Despite herself, her hands lifted to touch him, and instantly his arms were around her, crushing her to him, and she felt all the terrible power of his love and desire, held in check for God knew how long. It excited and attracted her, and she was afraid.

It lasted only a second: Danby was too much a gentleman to forget himself for longer. He released her gently, though his face was flushed and he breathed as though he had been running. Then he touched her cheek tenderly with his finger-tips.

'Thank you,' he said. 'I shall remember that when I'm riding along some desolate track in the Serra da Estrela, cold and wet and tired and hungry. I'll remember you just as you look at this moment. And when I come back, dear Lucy, we'll take up where we left off.'

Lucy said nothing, since nothing more seemed to be required of her. He seemed to feel she had given him his answer, and that was such a relief that she had no desire to inquire more deeply into what had been implicitly asked or promised. Time enough for that when he came back again; by then, perhaps she would understand her own feelings better. His absence, she thought, might clarify them for her.

By dint of urgent enquiries, Hawker discovered that Mr Hobsbawn belonged to Sackville's, the club at the corner of Cross Street and King Street; but on presenting his card to the doorman and enquiring after the old gentleman, he learned that Mr Hobsbawn hardly ever used the club, and hadn't been in, to the doorman's memory, since last March. A half-crown appeared and disappeared, and the doorman remembered that a couple of years back, Mr Hobsbawn had used to come in several times a week to play whist; powerful fond of whist he had been; but recently he didn't seem to go out much at all, except if there was a concert on at the Corn-market. Never missed a concert, didn't Mr Hobsbawn.

Thus armed, Hawker waylaid the old man as he left his factory, gave a creditable start of surprise, and stepped forward, hand to hat. Hobsbawn frowned, looked puzzled, but seeing the uniform, reined-in his horse.

'Mr Hobsbawn, sir! How good to see you again. I was wondering, as I was in these parts, if I should happen to bump into you.'

'Have I had the honour, sir?' Hobsbawn said gruffly. 'I don't think I remember you.'

'Hawker, sir. We met some time ago, at the Sackville. I partnered you at whist one evening. Of course, I wasn't in uniform then. We were introduced by your great friend, the magistrate — oh, his name escapes me just this instant. My wretched memory! Distinguished, grey-haired gentleman.' This was a venture — a man of Hobsbawn's influence, he reasoned, must know at least one magistrate, and a grey-haired one was most likely.

'Sir John Legge, do you mean?' Hobsbawn asked doubtfully.

'That's the very name! Sir John Legge, of course.'

'Well, he's no great friend of mine,' Hobsbawn said. 'Acquaintance, more like. So he introduced us, did he? I don't remember you, young man, and that's a fact.'

'It was a long time ago,' Hawker said hastily. 'Though I did see you at the concert recently, and would have stepped across to pay my respects, but unfortunately I lost sight of you in the crowds.'

'The concert, hey? Fond of music are you, Mr Hawker?'

'Extremely, sir. I never miss any opportunity of listening.'

'You'll be at the concert on Monday, then?'

'I wouldn't miss it for the world,' Hawker said, and went on hastily, 'but I am glad to have met you like this, sir, for I am acquainted with a relative of yours — a relative by marriage, I should say — and was charged with his respects to you, only he forgot to mention where you live, so I was unable to acquit myself of his request. Mr James Morland, sir — he's a close friend of Colonel Brunton, my commanding officer. We were meeting for ever at mess dinners.'

Hawker had thought this line rather good, implying that he was on close social terms with the Colonel, and that he had frequent communication with James Morland, who was not only Hobsbawn's son-in-law, but Fanny's father. What could be neater? But Hobsbawn did not respond as planned, looking, indeed, rather cool.

'Oh, Morland sent his respects, did he? I see. And I suppose you didn't know his daughter Fanny was staying with me at the moment?'

Hawker allowed his face to light up. 'Miss Morland, staying with you? Why, no, sir, I had no idea. I had the great pleasure and honour of making Miss Morland's acquaintance on a visit to Morland Place some time ago. I hope she is well?'

'She is,' Hobsbawn said succinctly.

'Pray convey my compliments to her, sir. But I must not delay you any further. Your servant, Mr Hobsbawn.' He bowed and touched his cap.

'Good day to you, Mr Hawker. Doubtless we'll meet again,' said Hobsbawn. He bestowed one more thoughtful look, and then rode on.

At home that evening, over dinner, he said, 'I met an acquaintance of yours, Fanny — or so he claims. Do you know a Mr Hawker? Officer in the militia, handsome fellow with whiskers?'

Fanny tried not to blush. 'Yes, Grandpapa, I have met him once or twice.'

'Claims to have met me at my club, though I can't say I remember him. Knows your father, too.' There was a hint of a question in the statement. Fanny wished she knew exactly what Hawker had said.

'Yes, Grandpapa. It was at home that I met him. Papa invited him to the ball for Mathilde's birthday.'

'Aye, so he says,' Hobsbawn said, softening. 'Well, he seemed a pleasant enough fellow. Laying himself out to be polite. Amazing fond of music, so he said. That's a coincidence, isn't it, since I'm fond of music myself?' Fanny kept her eyes on her plate, thinking furiously. 'I asked him if he'd be at the concert on Monday, and he said he wouldn't miss it for the world.'

Fanny's cheeks burned. 'But —' She stopped herself.

Hobsbawn chuckled. 'Aye, that's what I thought. Concerts are on Tuesday's, aren't they, Puss?'

Fanny had nothing to say.

'Well, well, he had a valiant try at scraping an acquaintance

318

with me, I'll say that for him,' Hobsbawn went on, pleased with himself, 'and I don't like a man less for trying. If he really knows your pa, there can be no harm in the acquaintance. If he calls here, I shall receive him.'

Fanny kept her eyes down. 'Thank you, Grandpapa,' she said.

'And now, Fan, I hope you haven't any engagements planned for tomorrow morning, for I want to take you down to the mills with me. I promised to shew you them; and there's someone I want you to meet, too. It's about time, since he's a relative.'

'Yes, Grandpapa?'

'My cousin Jasper. Well, he's more of a second-cousin really, so what that makes him to you I don't know. But blood is thicker than water, they say, and you ought at least to be acquainted with him. He acts as my manager, and there's precious little he doesn't know about cotton and spinning and machinery. He went into the mills when he was six as a doffer and piecer, and he worked his way up over the years to foreman-overseer. There's not a job in the mills he couldn't do, if he had to put his hand to it. I made him mill-manager when he was twenty-one. Well, it's best to have someone you've some hold over, for its a position easy to abuse.' Hobsbawn chuckled again. 'There's a very good reason why I know I can trust him. He won't cross me, Fanny, I can be sure of that!'

'What reason, Grandpapa?' Fanny asked, in a voice that shook a little with repressed fury. Fortunately Hobsbawn was too pleased with himself to notice.

'Why, Fanny, because if he crosses me, I'll cut him out of my Will, that's why!'

Fanny drew a deep breath and controlled herself. 'Have you left him a great deal?' she asked.

Now Hobsbawn looked up, and narrowed his eyes shrewdly at her. 'Why, Fanny, what's it to you? I may leave my fortune where I please, mayn't I?'

Fanny managed a smile of both sweetness and innocence. 'Of course, Grandpapa,' she said gaily. 'I only thought that if he had a great deal to lose, he would be even more loyal to you.'

'Oh, you thought that, did you?' He inspected her smile minutely, and apparently found it flawless. 'Well, the fact is,

Jasper don't know what he's getting, for I haven't made a new Will since your mother and brother died. Old Spicer keeps nagging at me, and I keep meaning to get round to it; but as long as I haven't, it gives Jasper every reason to toe the line, don't it?'

'Yes, Grandpapa,' Fanny said thoughtfully.

The next morning Fanny put on her smart pelisse and hat, and went with her grandfather to Water Lane in the carriage. Mr Hobsbawn gave instructions for his horse to be led down to the mill, so that Fanny could come back in the carriage when her visit was over.

'I don't want you to stay there for long — it isn't the place for a young lady. Coachman can bring you back — you'll be quite safe with him. And that maid of yours better come with us. She can wait in the carriage.'

Fanny had never been to that part of Manchester before, and as they drew near to the river, she shrank back involuntarily against the squabs. The River Irwell was lined on both sides with factories and mills, and behind them lay a tangled mess of mean tenements and squalid courts, foetid in the summer heat with the waste, human and animal, which lay exposed in the streets. The river itself was turgid with rubbish and the outfall from various factories and private houses, and the air was filled with smoke, and with other effluvia from tanneries and glue factories and soap factories.

Her grandfather did not seem to notice the unpleasant atmosphere, so Fanny declined to shew herself less stoical than he, and sat up straight, clasping her hands in her lap and breathing as shallowly as possible. Here again, she noticed that the poor people were very much in evidence, and many of them were simply standing about at the corners of the streets and lanes, talking together. They stared sullenly as the carriage passed, and Fanny kept her eyes averted, not wishing to see them.

'There you are, Fanny,' Hobsbawn said suddenly, his voice ringing with pride. 'Ain't it a grand sight? Hobsbawn Mills — built up from nothing by the labour of these hands and the sweat of this brow. What do you say? Did you ever see anything that warms the heart more?'

Fanny looked at the two high, square buildings, many-windowed, tall-chimneyed, grimy with the soot-laden precipitate. Number Two Mill was taller than the old Number One, and had the name HOBSBAWN painted along the parapet at the top in huge black letters. It thrilled her to see that name there, and to know she was part of the power and the pride. There and then she swore to herself that the mills should be hers, whatever it took to get them.

'Never, Grandpapa,' she said, turning her shining eyes to him, and he felt a lump in his throat at her unmistakable enthusiasm.

'Eh, you're a creature after my own heart, Fanny, and that's the truth! What a crying pity you shouldn't have been born a boy,' he said.

Fanny managed to hold her tongue. The carriage turned into the yard of Number Two, through the high iron gate which was held open by the gatekeeper. He had recognised the carriage from a distance; and when it had passed, he closed and locked the gate again. A moment later Fanny stepped down into the yard and looked about her with keen interest.

'It's an idle day today,' Hobsbawn explained, following her. 'If the mill was working there'd have been such a noise as would amaze you, Fanny. Smoke, too, enough to blot out the sun! It's a fine sight! Come into the office, now, and meet your cousin Jasper.'

The office was very dark, though Fanny realised that it was only because of the grime which coated the windows and kept the light out. Three men were there, leaning over a plan spread on the table, and all three straightened up as Hobsbawn and Fanny came in, and favoured Fanny with a stare which not even the most optimistic person could have called welcoming. Fanny was at a loss to guess which one was Cousin Jasper, for all three were thin, undersized men with the greyish pallor of poverty about their skins, lank, mouse-coloured hair, and coarse clothing. None of the three looked like a gentleman; perhaps he was not here after all.

But the man in the middle stepped forward and gave them an impartial bow to divide between them, and said, 'Good morning, sir. I've got the plans of the weaving-shed here, as you see. Bates, Delaney, you can go.'

'No, just a minute,' Hobsbawn said. 'Fanny, these are two

321

of my overseers, been with me for fifteen years, isn't that right, Bates?'

'Yessir! Fifteen years and three months, sir!'

'My granddaughter, Miss Fanny Morland. Very well, off you go. I'll speak to you later. And this, Fanny,' as the two men left the office, 'is your cousin Jasper, my mill-manager.'

Jasper gave her the slightest inclination of the head which could be construed as a bow. 'Your servant, Miss Morland,' he said. His voice was even, his expression inscrutable, though his pale eyes glittered with some suppressed emotion. Fanny could guess what it was, and was not displeased that he should be jealous of her.

'How do you do, Mr Hobsbawn?' she said sweetly. 'Grandpapa has told me so much about you.' She extended her gloved hand, and he placed his fingertips under it reluctantly. His hand, she noticed, was coarse and rough, with broken fingernails, and a line of ingrained dirt along the forefinger. What a clown! she thought, and met his eyes to see the realisation of her contempt smouldering in them for an instant before it was veiled. She smiled ever more sweetly. I'll beat you, she thought; and I'll have the mills.

'It's a pleasure to meet you, Miss Morland,' he said, withdrawing his hand and dropping it out of sight at his side. 'Though a mill isn't the place for a lady, as I know Mr Hobsbawn agrees. Still, as we are not working today, there can be no harm in your making a short visit.'

'Aye, I wanted her to meet you, Jasper, and I thought I might just shew her the machines.'

'I think, sir, that it would be inadvisable for Miss Morland to remain here long,' Jasper said. '*This* was delivered last night — thrown over the gate wrapped in a half-brick.'

He handed Hobsbawn a crumpled piece of paper. Hobsbawn flattened it out, and Fanny saw over his arm that it was lettered in crude capitals:

BEWAR HOBSBORN I SHALL VISIT YOU TO-MORROW!

I SHALL BREAK UP YOUR DEVIL'S FRAMES AND BRING YOU SORROW!

SINED - GENERAL LUDD

Hobsbawn crumpled it again in his hand and threw it contemptuously on the floor.

'Stuff and fustian! By God, I should like to get hold of the creatures that wrote this! And I shall! They'll get no mercy from me, or from the magistrates neither. We had enough of this back in '98. We'll crack down on 'em as hard as the law allows. It's about time they made frame-breaking a capital offence. Have you done anything about this, Jasper?'

'All the gatekeepers are armed. I've put on six extra men for now, and more are coming at dusk. They aren't likely to attack in broad daylight, when they can be recognised, of course, but there have been one or two cases of flaming rags being thrown through windows, so I think it would be wise if Miss Morland didn't linger today.' He turned to Fanny with a rather rigid smile. 'Any other time, ma'am, I should be delighted to shew you everything myself.'

Liar, she thought. Two years ago she would have told her grandfather that she meant to stay and fight the frame-breakers alongside him; but she had learned better now. 'Whatever you think best, Grandpapa,' she said meekly, but with a disappointed sigh.

He weakened. 'Eh, well there's no harm in just shewing you a floor or two before you go. Jasper can come along and tell you how it all works. He's better at explaining things than me.'

Jasper, Fanny saw, also knew better than to argue. Without another word, he led the way through the inner door and across an ante-room, unlocked a further door, and preceded Fanny and Hobsbawn into the silent factory. Fanny saw a huge, long room, filled with row upon row of machines. Even silent and motionless they were an awesome sight. She had expected to be bored, but as Jasper began to explain the processes carried out here, she became more and more interested, and began to ask questions. Jasper answered her at first aloofly, and then with growing enthusiasm as he warmed to his subject. He really loves cotton, Fanny thought in faint surprise; he really loves the factories. It isn't just because he wants to own them: he really *cares*.

Hobsbawn remained a step to the rear, listening to it all, and watching them with a faint smile, delighted that Fanny was so evidently interested in the mill. The visit extended itself naturally, and they had walked to the end of one floor, and were about to mount to the next when they heard a voice, echoing strangely in the silent hall, calling them urgently.

Jasper turned back. 'Over here!' he called, and added, 'It's Wendell, the gateman at Number Three. What the deuce is he doing here?'

'Oh, Mr Jasper, sir, there's terrible trouble a-coming!' the man cried as he hurried up to them between the row of jennies. Then he stopped abruptly as he saw Fanny and Hobsbawn behind Jasper, and his mouth hung open in surprise and fright.

'What is it, Wendell?' Jasper prompted.

'Go on, man, speak up,' Hobsbawn added, seeing Wendell was still overcome at the unexpected presence of his master. 'Don't be afraid. What is it you've got to tell?'

'Luddites, sir!' Wendell managed at last. 'A-coming to break the frames and burn us down, sir! Thousands of 'em! There's a sojer come to warn us, so I come here to find Mr Jasper, sir.'

'A soldier? Where? Who?' Hobsbawn asked sharply.

'Here, sir.' Lieutenant Hawker came striding down the aisle between the machines. He looked taken aback as he saw Fanny. 'Good God, Miss Morland! What are you doing here? Sir, Miss Morland must leave at once, before the mob gets here.'

'What mob?' Hobsbawn demanded. 'Tell me what you know, and quick about it.'

'We received information a few hours ago that an army of frame-breakers plans to attack your Number Three Mill this morning, sir,' Hawker said succinctly. 'They are —'

'Number Three? What the deuce —? Nay, lad you must be wrong there. Number Three isn't in operation — never has been. No-one knows about it.'

'I only know what I have been told, sir,' Hawker said patiently. 'Is your Number Three a weaving-factory?'

Hobsbawn looked troubled. 'Aye — but no-one knows that, bar Jasper here, and my overseers. All trustworthy men.'

'Well, sir, you know best about that. All I know is that it is the hand-loom weavers who are marching, with help from the spinners who have been laid off, and they have sworn to break every weaving-frame in Manchester. Somehow the information about your Number Three must have got out. At all events, they are on their way there now, and I have come —'

Hobsbawn interrupted again. 'But they will not attack in daylight, surely?'

Hawker looked grim. 'These Luddites have grown bolder since the spring. They are also armed, sir, with muskets and pistols. This is no rag-tag mob of unorganised labourers: this is an army under discipline, with officers and a plan of attack. I am deploying my men around your mill to meet them, but I came on ahead to warn you to take yourself off to a place of safety.'

Hobsbawn looked grim. 'Thankee, sir, but I'm going to Number Three this minute to see for myself. Jasper, get every man you can, that we can trust —' His eye came round to Fanny, whom for a moment he had forgotten. 'Fanny, you must go home at once, and stay there until I come.'

Hawker looked astonished. 'Sir, you cannot mean Miss Morland to go home alone? It is much too dangerous! Surely you mean to go with her?'

'I cannot leave my mills!' Hobsbawn cried, distracted. He looked from Hawker to Fanny. 'I cannot. You understand, don't you Fanny, love?'

'Of course, Grandpapa,' Fanny said. 'I'm not afraid.' But the thought of that flood of rats came unbidden to her mind, and her cheeks were pale.

Hawker stepped in. 'Sir, if you will permit me, I will escort Miss Morland home. But it must be now. I cannot answer for the consequences if we delay any further.'

Hobsbawn's face lit with relief and gratitude. 'Aye, go!' he cried. 'And God bless you, young man! Fanny, go on, now. I'll come home when I can. Hurry!'

Fanny hurried along beside Hawker, her mind reeling. As soon as they were out of sight of her grandfather, she said, 'Is there really so much danger? Or was it a ruse?'

Hawker grinned down at her. 'Do you think I would invent a whole riot, just for the sake of seeing you again, Miss Morland?'

'Yes,' Fanny said boldly. 'Grandpapa told me what you said to him outside the factory yesterday, about liking concerts and so on.'

'Ah yes, that was unfortunate. How was I to know he would try to trap me? But on this occasion, Miss Morland, I had no idea you were here. How could I? Had I known it — but however, we really must hurry. There is a mob on its way here, but I shall get you safe away before it arrives. I exaggerated the urgency, not the nature of the danger, in order to make your grandfather the more grateful for my intervention.'

'You are utterly unscrupulous, Mr Hawker,' Fanny said severely.

He smiled at her in a way that made her heart beat faster. 'Miss Morland, I rather suspect that you are too! Might I ask what you were doing at the factory at all?'

'You may not,' Fanny said repressively.

'It is hardly the place for a woman,' Hawker mused, unrepentant. 'Perhaps you felt you ought to shew an interest? Wheedling your way into your grandpapa's heart, eh?'

Fanny blushed. 'Mr Hawker, you may shew me to my carriage. I shall not need your escort — or your ungentlemanly remarks — any further.'

Hawker grinned. 'Do I come too near home? I beg your pardon — my manners are disgraceful, I know. But I shall escort you all the way home nevertheless — for two very good reasons.'

'Name them,' Fanny said haughtily.

'With pleasure,' he said promptly. 'First, that there really is a mob, and I believe some considerable danger, and second —' he paused teasingly.

'Well?' she prompted at last.

'Second, because I do not know when I may have another chance to win your gratitude, Miss Morland, and a soft look from those heavenly eyes of yours. Ah, here we are. Allow me to help you into the carriage, then I'll have a word with old Coachman.'

Fanny could think of nothing witty or cutting to say, and had to content herself with a dignified silence as he helped her into the carriage. Her maid had evidently been talking to the gatekeeper in her absence, for she greeted Fanny with, 'Oh, Miss Morland, whatever is to come of us? They say there's a thousand rebels coming, armed with pistols, to burn down the mills, and we will be killed for sure. Oh Miss Morland, I'm so afraid!'

Fanny pushed away the clutching hands. 'Oh, hush, Letty,

don't you see Lieutenant Hawker is going to escort us home? We shall be quite safe. Now hold your tongue, I want to hear what's said.'

Hawker came to the window on Fanny's side of the carriage. 'I shall ride alongside you, Miss Morland, in case of any trouble, but I don't anticipate any. Coachman knows the best way to go.'

A moment later the gatekeeper opened the gate, the carriage passed through, and with Hawker riding alongside, turned into Water Street. Fanny was feeling rather a sense of anticlimax, and began to plan how to tell the story to Agnes Pendlebury to make it sound more exciting, when the carriage suddenly lurched and stopped, and Letty gave an involuntary shriek.

'Hush!' Fanny said sharply, slapping her hand. She heard the men's voices outside, Hawker's and the coachman's, and leaning out of the window, saw with a cold sensation that the street was inordinately full of people.

'Go on,' she heard Hawker say. 'Turn right at the next junction. We'll try and cut across to Deansgate.'

'Mr Hawker, what is it?' Fanny called. He reined his horse and fell back beside her.

'A crowd up ahead. They don't look dangerous, but it's best if we avoid them. We don't want trouble if we can help it.'

They turned down Grape Lane, and the carriage jolted violently over the rutted surface of the unmade road. There were more people, mostly just standing about, as she had seen them before; but now their silence and immobility seemed somehow menacing. She told herself that it was just imagination, and that she was being as silly as Letty, who was crooning her fear under her breath in a kind of lament for past sins and a promise of doing better in the future if she were spared.

The carriage was moving more slowly, and Fanny heard the coachman's whip cracking more often, together with shouts from him for the way to be cleared. The people seemed to be clustering more thickly. Hawker shouted too; and then suddenly a clod of mud hit the side of the carriage, making the women jump. Another hit the window-frame, and a spattering of dry crumbs hit Fanny's cheek and shoulder. She

327

gave an involuntary cry and drew back, reaching for the strap to pull up the window.

At the same instant she saw in the crowds, now pressing all too close, the same young woman that she had seen in Piccadilly. Their eyes met, but this time there was no sense of sympathy between them. The mill-girl's face was twisted with rage and hatred. She stooped in one swift movement to pick up a broken piece of wood and ran at the carriage with it raised above her head, shouting something incoherently. Fanny pulled the window up just as the girl brought her makeshift weapon down in a violent blow. It hit the glass, but fortunately did not break it, bouncing off harmlessly.

Fanny stared in fright for an instant at the girl's dirty, contorted face, only inches from her; she doubted whether the girl even recognised her, and it was dreadful to be the object of so unreasoning an attack. Then Hawker's hand appeared in her line of sight. Holding his pistol by the barrel, he struck the girl on the side of the head. Fanny screamed; the girl's face froze in an expression of shock; and then she seemed to crumple, and disappeared out of sight.

It had all happened in an instant; but when the girl collapsed, there was a cry from the crowd like a composite animal moan, the sound of one beast with a hundred mouths, and like one beast they surged forward to surround the coach. Fanny heard shouts from Coachman, a furious cracking of his whip, thumps and thuds as the crowd beat on the side of the carriage. One of the horses whinneyed in shrill fear. A horrible face, toothless and with only one eye leered in at the window, and Letty screamed abandonedly.

'Hold the door shut,' Fanny snapped at her, seizing the handle on the door her side only just in time. It was tugged violently, but she held on grimly, aware that if she were pulled from the coach, she would very likely be killed. 'Get away!' she screamed, in furious defiance. The door tugged again, her hands were slipping. More faces pressed in behind the toothless one. The door was jerked half open, and with a sob of fear and anger she just managed to pull it shut again. 'Get away from me!' she screamed.

With a despairing cry Letty abandoned the struggle with the door on her side, and it flew back, knocking over the woman who had been pulling at it. Her place was taken by another, a thin, unspeakably dirty man, whose face was inhuman with a mob-inspired desire for rapine, glassy-eyed with hatred and blood-lust. He set his hands to the door-frame to pull himself into the carriage, and Fanny, almost with detachment, knew that the game was up and she was going to die. When she let go of the door handle to fight him off, they would drag her out from this side. Well, by God, she would go down fighting! She would rip their faces, she would bite and claw for her life!

His foot was up on the step, he was pulling himself in; Fanny could smell him, and her teeth were bared in an involuntary snarl. And then there was a sharp report from outside the carriage, and at the same instant the centre of the thin man's face disintegrated. Letty shrieked in abandoned horror as fragments of bone and blood spattered her. The grimy hands flew upwards towards the shattered mess where his nose and eyes had been, even as his lifeless body tumbled backwards into the street. Fanny had a glimpse of him lying on his back in a space which had miraculously appeared in the crowd. There was a composite gasp from the crowd; the pressure on her door eased; the people fell back on both sides of the carriage, stunned by what had happened.

In the silence Fanny heard Hawker's voice shouting, 'Now stand back, all of you! Make way, there!'

The carriage jerked forward. They were moving again! Letty was pressed back against the squabs as though she had been nailed there, so Fanny leaned across her and grabbed the door, and dragged it closed, upon which Letty began sobbing with fear and relief and horror. The carriage was picking up speed. Fanny heard Hawker fire again, but guessed from the sound of the report that he had fired into the air, to frighten rather than wound. Now they were lurching along at a great lick, and she could only hope they didn't overturn, or crash into something in the narrow lane. And then, oh thank God, the lane widened out, and with a final sickening lurch they turned into Deansgate, and civilisation was around them, shops and pavements and decent-looking people.

Fanny leaned back against the squabs and felt that she was trembling all over. Letty had passed into full-fledged hysterics, but Fanny hardly heard her. Her mind was raw with the images, the hatred in the faces, the girl crumpling, the thin man's face smashed to a bloody cave. But we survived, she thought triumphantly, and felt a fierce excitement running through her veins. I wish he had killed more of them! I wish he had killed them all!

They didn't stop until they reached Hobsbawn House, and then Hawker himself jumped down from his horse and flung open the carriage door.

'Are you all right, Miss Morland?' he cried.

'Yes,' she said. She had wanted to make a dignified speech, but she found that she was trembling all over, and had to clench her jaw to stop it chattering.

'I'm so sorry you were not spared such a terrible experience,' he said, holding out his hand to help her down. 'It must have been shocking beyond anything for you.'

She took his hand and met his eyes. 'I'm glad you shot that man,' she said fiercely. 'He deserved it. I'm not shocked — well, only a bit. I wish you had shot more of them. I hate them!'

He stared at her, a little taken aback, and then smiled a grim sort of smile. 'It is probably best for you to see it that way. But let me recommend you to take a glass of brandy when you are indoors. As I remember, you do not dislike it, and it will guard against any belated spasm of the nerves.'

Fanny looked up at him, her eyes bright. 'You saved my life,' she said. 'I shan't forget it, Lieutenant Hawker.'

'I am only glad I was on hand. And now, ma'am, if you're sure you are all right, I had better get back to my men. I will try to persuade your grandfather to come home, if there is still time.'

'Good God, yes!' Fanny said. 'I had forgotten Grandpapa! Oh, please hurry back, and make sure he's safe! Pray, Mr Hawker, pray look after him!'

The urgency in her voice was unmistakable, and Hawker was surprised, not having expected her to have so much affection for the old man. Her heart, he thought, was warmer than anyone could have guessed; and it made her more intriguing than ever, and infinitely more attractive.

Within the house, there was the story to tell, and her hysterical maid to attend to, to keep Fanny from any immediate reaction

330

to her adventure. But when Letty had been put to bed with a dose of laudanum, Fanny found herself almost in a state of collapse. Mrs Murray proved unexpectedly sympathetic, led Fanny to a chair in the drawing-room, and administered a glass of brandy.

'You drink it up, miss, and never mind the taste,' she said. 'It's medicine, and not meant to taste nice.'

Fanny gulped it back without a grimace and held out the glass for more.

'Well,' said Mrs Murray under her breath, 'you're a cool one, and no mistake.'

'I'm all right now,' Fanny said. 'I was more angry than afraid, although it was horrid when that man — when Mr Hawker shot that man.' She shuddered involuntarily at the memory of the shattered face.

'You've your grandfather's spirit, miss, and that's a fact,' said Mrs Murray.

Fanny bit her lip. 'I hope Grandpapa will be all right. I hope Mr Hawker gets back in time to make him come home.'

'Your grandad won't leave the mills until they're safe, miss, and there's nothing anyone can do to make him,' Mrs Murray said. 'Now, shall I bring you in a nuncheon? You must be starved, for it's after two o'clock.'

'Mr Hawker was wonderful,' Fanny said, not hearing her. 'He wasn't the least bit afraid of the mob. Grandpapa must be grateful to him now.'

'I daresay we'll be seeing more of him, then, miss,' Mrs Murray said drily, and went away to fetch her something to eat.

It was a long, weary time before news came to reassure Fanny that her grandfather was unharmed, and the mills had been saved, and the servants, seeing how much she worried, liked her for it, thinking it shewed a very proper, feeling heart in her, that she cared so much for her grandpapa. Only Mrs Murray was unmoved, privately believing that if Miss Fanny had been assured that her grandfather had made a Will leaving everything to her, she wouldn't have worried about the old gentleman's safety at all.

CHAPTER SEVENTEEN

Morland Place was alive again; it was full; there was sound and movement and company. Edward had endured two months of loneliness relieved only by the presence of Father Aislaby. Certainly his hours of work were long, and gave him little leisure for brooding, but it was a sad thing to come home to an empty house, to have no-one with whom to share his glass of sherry before dinner, no-one to ask him how things had gone, or to argue with him, tease him, approve him, sympathise with him.

At first he took dinner, largely out of habit, at the vast table in the dining-room, he in his usual place at one end, and Father Aislaby seated cater-corner to him, with Ottershaw and William in white gloves solemnly serving them. Barnard was sulking because Héloïse had not taken him to Plaisir with her, and there was never any knowing what they would be served for their dinner. Sometimes it would be a meal of savage elaboration, dainties vying with each other for attention on a hopelessly overloaded board; at others it would be cold cuts, gloomy vegetables and sad puddings. Sometimes the meal would take on an hysterical air, and Edward would be obliged for the sake of his own pride to send back a curdled sauce or an uncooked fowl; knowing that as a result, the next meal might well resemble the footings of a Roman villa, burned down in the second century AD and recently but carelessly excavated.

After braving dinner, Edward and Father Aislaby dutifully retired to the drawing-room, and there evinced good will at each other for an hour or two from either side of the fireplace. Aislaby was a man who could find complete satisfaction in his own company, and he appeared in the evening only for Edward's sake; Edward needed, longed for, company, but could not initiate conversation unless encouraged. After ten days of perilous meals and awkward silences, Aislaby decided to take his dinner in his own room and remain there, and Edward's isolation was complete.

He abandoned the dining-room, to everyone's relief, and had an ample but unrefined meal sent in on a tray to the steward's room each evening, where he shared it with Tiger. He tried playing patience and unapposed chess, but found it unrewarding, and took instead to staring into the fire for half an hour, with Tiger's head on his knee and a glass of brandy in his hand, before retiring early to bed. It was a dismal sort of life, and his joy and relief when he came home from Twelvetrees to find Héloïse and James in residence again was enormous.

With Héloïse home, the house seemed to vibrate with life. Servants walked briskly and sang about their work; mirrors and table-tops gleamed, the sun shone in brightly at the windows, and everything seemed to smell nice. Wherever Edward turned, in the few hours he was ever awake and within doors, Héloïse seemed to be somewhere near, smiling at him like a little household goddess, small and dark and idiosyncratic, but exuding warmth and safety; James argued with him over everything and anything, but always understood exactly what he was talking about; and meals became again delicious and surprising, hot, on time, and vibrant with conversation.

At the end of July, Sophie and Africa came home, and the house echoed with the sound of running feet and high, happy voices. Sophie ran up and down the stairs, chattering in English and singing in French, followed everywhere by Nicholas, who trotted after her with a determined expression on his face, while Kithra padded after him as though he were on a string. Sophie had brought home presents for her favourite people, hugs and kisses for everyone, stories of her adventures and new songs and the names of new friends.

'Oh, it's so good to be home!' she cried a dozen times, hugging her mother round the waist. '*Chère petite Maman*, it's been a hundred years! Now I must go and see Monsieur Barnard, and give him the picture I drew for him. Look, Maman, don't you think he'll like it? It's the view from our window in Queen Square. Come on, Nicholas, hurry up! All right, I'll tell you the story about the three little pigs as we go.'

Africa was just as glad to be home, but for different reasons. 'I wish I never had to go back there, Aunt Héloïse,' she said as soon as she arrived. 'It's awful. I was punished for climbing a tree — can you imagine? They shut you up all day, and make you recite the dates of battles and play the piano and paint silly vases of dried flowers. Why, my tars could paint the most amazing things on tiny pieces of bone, and they'd actually fought in the battles, and they taught me a hundred and seven songs before I was eight years old. And Miss Brabant said it was unladylike to dance the hornpipe and the sword-dance. Unladylike!'

'Oh dear,' Héloïse said anxiously, 'I know it is difficult, dear Africa, but it is necessary for you to learn to be a lady. You will have to live all your life on shore, you know, and it is best that you get used to it as soon as possible. Does Sophie hate it too?'

'Oh no,' said Africa frankly. 'She likes it. But then she'd like anything, she's so good-natured. Only she does get homesick, Aunt Héloïse. Couldn't we both stay home here, after all? I shouldn't mind so much, if I could be out in the fields, and not in a town, with all those other mimsy girls; and Sophie wouldn't mind anything, if only she could be here.'

'I wish you might, chérie. I will see what can be done,' Héloïse said anxiously. 'In the meantime, perhaps you had better go out and climb every tree in the orchard, just to make you feel better. I promise I shan't mind.'

Africa grinned. 'That's all right, Aunt. Before I left school, I climbed up the flagpole on the roof and hoisted a signal — well, a chemise, actually, but I think everyone will understand what it meant.'

'The flagpole?' Héloïse said faintly.

'On the roof,' Africa said mercilessly. 'There was such a nice breeze up there.'

'Oh dear,' said Héloïse.

Then Fanny came home, fetched by her father from Manchester, and arriving in style, demanding all the consequence of the young mistress returning home. Héloïse found her improved during her stay in Manchester beyond expectation: she had gone away a child on the brink of womanhood; she came back every inch a young lady. Though Miss Rosedale was not due to return until September, Héloïse for once anticipated no trouble from Fanny in the meantime. She did not quarrel with Sophie or Africa, or throw tantrums, or demand unreasonable privileges. Even Edward found himself, quite against his own wishes, enjoying her company at dinner, and listening to her conversation with pleasure.

'The next thing, I suppose, will be her come-out,' Edward said to James one evening when the three girls were out of the room.

James looked taken aback. 'Oh, not yet, surely.'

'She'll be sixteen in October,' Héloïse reminded him over her sewing.

'Sixteen's too young to come out,' James said, more with hope than conviction. 'She's still only a child.'

'But you've only got to listen to her conversation, Jamie,' said Edward. 'All about the people she's met and the parties she's been to. You'll never keep her in the schoolroom now. It wouldn't be reasonable to try. You've given her a taste of grown-up life, and now she'll want the rest.'

James looked rueful. 'It isn't that I mind the idea of her going to parties. But as soon as she's out, the fortune-hunters will come buzzing around her. I was hoping not to have to fight off suitors for a few years yet.'

'Keeping her in the schoolroom won't stop her having suitors,' Edward said. 'You heard her talk. What was all that about a militia officer? And from what she said, this Cousin Jasper was pretty jealous of him.'

'Fanny exaggerates,' Héloïse said peaceably.

'That's right,' James said. 'She likes the idea of having suitors, but I'm sure they weren't really interested in her. Besides, she won't be in the way of seeing them again. Hawker's been posted to Nottingham, and Cousin Jasper's firmly tied to the factories.'

Edward shrugged. 'I don't see that it matters. The point is, as you said yourself, she likes having admirers. She likes going to parties. You can't expect her to go back to wearing pinafores and reciting the kings and queens of England all day.'

The girls re-entering the room closed the conversation. It was Héloïse who brought it up again, when she and James were alone together in their bedchamber. The servants had just gone, leaving them to linger over a last glass of wine before getting into bed.

'James, I was thinking about Fanny's come-out. Edward is quite right, you know.'

'I'm not bringing her out at sixteen,' James said, with all the firmness of an uncertain man.

'Sixteen is very young,' Héloïse agreed, 'but I was married when I was fourteen.'

'And was it a happy experience?'

'You know that it was not. But Fanny is old for her age; and letting her come out does not mean that you are obliged to let her marry. I think it is better for her to come out while she is still young enough to be influenced by you. Let her meet all the fortune-hunters and bad men now, while you can still chase them away; then, in a year or two, when all the excitement over her has died down, you may find her a real, true man, whom she will love. But if she does not come out until she is eighteen, she will be all the more likely to fall in love with the first man she sees, and he will be, as likely as not, unsuitable.'

James listened in silence, turning his wine glass in his hand and watching the reflection of the candle-flame deep in its red heart.

'I don't want my little girl to grow up,' he said at last.

'I know,' Héloïse said gently, 'but she will do that anyway, my James. She *is* doing it. And one day there will be a man who means more to her than you. That is something you have to accept.'

After a moment, without taking his eyes from the candle's reflected flame, he stretched out a hand to her, and she came and knelt beside him in the circle of his arm, resting her head against his chest.

'Yes, I know,' he sighed. 'I just didn't want it to be yet. What do you suggest, then? That we bring her out as soon as she's sixteen?'

'I think you might have a birthday dinner and ball here, and let her have the Little Season in York, to give her experience,' Héloïse said. 'And then she could have her first proper Season in London next year.'

'A London Season?' James said, without enthusiasm. 'I suppose that means taking a house and spending three interminable months there.'

Héloïse laughed. 'Here is your real reason for not wanting

to bring Fanny out! But I think you may be spared it. Flaminia will be sixteen in March, and I know Lucy means to bring her and Hippolyta out together. I think if you ask she will agree to take on Fanny as well. The three girls can have a joint ball, and then they will be able to go everywhere together, which will be more pleasant for them, and safer.'

'And you mean I won't have to do anything?' James brightened.

'Only pay for Fanny's Court dress, share the cost of the ball, and attend it, of course. After that, you may come home and let Lucy do all the work and worry for you.'

'That seems most unfair,' he said happily. 'And what about you? Will you have to stay in London with Fanny? For if you do, I shan't want to come home alone.'

Héloïse smiled at him. 'I shall have other things to think about in March, my heart's darling. I shall have the best excuse in the world to stay home.'

He grunted absently, his mind busy elsewhere; and then as the import of her words struck him, he screwed his head round to look down at her. 'What? Héloïse, you don't mean —?'

She laughed. 'Oh yes, I do. Hadn't you guessed? Sometimes, *mon âme*, you are not very noticing.'

'But how —?' He thought furiously. 'The night Nez Carré died?' She nodded, her eyes brimming with laughter, 'Oh my darling! So it will be due — when?'

'The beginning of March. Our new baby will come with the new lambs.'

'Our new baby!' He tried the words, and laughed aloud, and held her against him. 'Oh Marmoset, I do love you!'

'I love you too, my James.'

'I hope it's a boy.' He kissed her brow. 'Or a girl. I don't mind really. Oh my darling!' She turned her lips up for his kisses, and then watched as the first astonished, grateful joy faded from his face, to be replaced with apprehension.

'No, don't,' she begged him. 'Don't look like that.'

'I can't help it. Marmoset, this is all wrong. You shouldn't be pregnant. You know what Lucy said. I shouldn't have — oh, it was all my fault! My selfish, selfish folly!'

'Don't James,' she said with tears in her eyes. 'I can't bear it. You must be glad about the baby. It was meant to be —

you must see that, remembering how it came about. God meant it, and God will take care of us. You must be glad from the beginning — the child deserves it.'

'Glad that you are risking your life? Glad that you must run the gauntlet for seven months, and then —'

She pulled back from him abruptly and stood up. 'Stop it! I shall become very angry.' She bit her lip and turned away from him, hiding her face. James was stricken with a double guilt — that he had made her pregnant, and now that he was making her unhappy. He drew his breath, assembled his thoughts, held out his hand to her again.

'I'm sorry, my darling. Of course I'm happy about the baby — how could I be anything else? I wish we could have a dozen children. It's only your health I'm worried about. If anything happened to you —'

She turned back to him, and he saw that there were tears on her cheeks.

'Don't you think I have been worried too? But we must trust in God, *mon âme*. He wants our child to have existence. One cannot be niggardly with life. Everything will be all right, my own love. I'm sure of it. Be happy — please be happy.'

'I am happy,' he said, and drew her to him again to sit on his lap. He folded his arms round her, and she rested her head against his. Under his hands, within her narrow body, his child grew, the seed of life that would not be denied, growing in the darkness, struggling towards the light. It was nothing to him yet, only an idea; but she, she was the warmth of the sun to him. If he should lose her —!

She pressed her cheek against him, knowing his thoughts, as she so often did. 'I love you too, James,' she said.

Last to come home was Mathilde, delivered to the door by the Wickfields in their handsome new travelling-chariot. There were affectionate farewells, promises of letters and future visits, and the carriage drove away, leaving Mathilde to walk into the house, feeling a little flat and rather low-spirited in reaction.

In the hall, Ottershaw was waiting to greet her with a quiet smile. 'It's good to have you back, miss,' he said, and Mathilde's heart was warmed.

'Where is everybody?' she began to ask, when with a clattering of claws on the marble floor, Tiger flew at her in silent joy, tail revolving frantically, wolf-eyes shining; and there was Edward, hurrying out from the direction of the steward's room. His face was alight with pleasure, and he advanced with both hands out, to take hers and press them warmly.

'I thought I heard the carriage! My dear Mathilde, how good it is to see you!'

'I'm glad to be home, Cousin Edward,' she said, feeling her cheeks to be a little pink. Don't be foolish, she told herself sharply. That is all in the past, all over.

Edward released her hands, but continued to stand before her, smiling as though he had forgotten how to leave off. 'You're looking well,' he said at last. 'Is that a new hat?'

'Yes: Mr Wickfield bought it for me.'

'That was kind of him. It becomes you. You look very well.'

'You said that before, Cousin Edward,' she said.

'Did I?' He continued to smile. 'You've done your hair differently, too.' She didn't think that needed an answer. 'Well, so you're back,' he said foolishly. 'Everyone thought you would come back married, or engaged to be married at least.'

'Is that what you thought?' she asked, trying to resist a delightful idea that was attempting to make its way into her head.

He didn't answer that. 'You didn't meet anyone agreeable, then, on your travels?'

'I met lots of agreeable people, thank you, Cousin Edward,' she said, 'but no-one I wanted to marry.'

'And so you're back,' he said with an air of satisfaction. 'Well, the others will be wondering what's happened to you. We'd better go and find them. Will you take my arm?'

She tucked her hand under his elbow, and it seemed dangerously comfortable. They crossed the hall together, circled by Tiger, bent on tripping them up.

'I was wondering,' Edward said diffidently, 'whether, if you're not too tired from your journey, you might like to play chess with me tonight.'

'Gladly,' she said. 'And you can tell me how the Morland Merino is coming along.'

Fanny was delighted with the plans for her come-out. It

seemed to her doubly delightful, for she would be officially out as soon as she was sixteen, which had been her ambition, and would have all the glory of a grand ball at Morland Place, and the chance to go to formal assemblies in and around York; and then she would have it all again in London, with an even grander ball, and all the excitements of the Season.

She would have preferred not to have to share her London *début* with her cousins, but there seemed to be no help for that. It was plain that Madame could not bring her out in her present condition, and it was unthinkable to wait for another year. She comforted herself that Hippolyta, though pretty, was no-one, without rank or fortune; and though Flaminia was *Lady* Flaminia, which was annoying, she was quite plain, and not an heiress in the same way that Fanny was. Flaminia would have twenty thousand pounds, but Fanny would have Morland Place *and* Hobsbawn Mills.

Everyone at Morland Place seemed to be happy that autumn. Héloïse was particularly happy because, from her own observations, and after consultation with the returning Miss Rosedale, she had decided that there was no need to send Sophie back to school. Miss Rosedale had agreed with her that Fanny no longer posed any threat to Sophie — if, indeed, she ever had, for the incident so long ago had never been proved to be anything to do with Fanny — and that, with all the excitement of her come-out ahead of her, she would be too busy and happy to make trouble for anyone.

Miss Rosedale was happy to take on the teaching of Sophie. She had been sorry to think that her time at Morland Place was coming to an end, for once Fanny was launched on the world, she would no longer need a governess; Sophie would give her a few more years' grace. Sophie, of course, was deliriously happy at the news that she might stay at home with Maman and Nicholas and all her friends in the servants' hall.

'But what about Africa?' she asked anxiously. 'Her papa wanted her to go to school. Will she have to go back on her own?'

Héloïse didn't know. 'We shall have to ask him, of course, and if he says she must go, then I'm afraid we shall have to send her. He will be coming to England in November, according to your Aunt Lucy, so I think for the moment she can stay here and take her lessons with you and Miss Rosedale, and he can make a decision when he comes home. But I think if I tell him that she is not happy at school, he will not insist.'

The preparations for the ball fell mostly on Héloïse, and she and Fanny were naturally thrown together for long periods. Héloïse was amazed at how she had changed and grown up, how sensibly she could talk, how excellent her air and manner had become. She remembered the brooding, sulking child she had met on first coming to Morland Place as James's bride, and all the tantrums and storms and escapades they had endured since then. She remembered the torn dresses, the lost shoes, the muddy feet, the tangled hair, the hoydenish tricks. This Fanny was a different person.

A tentative friendship began to build up between them, as they pored over ladies' journals together, visited warehouses, fingered materials, drew up lists of guests, planned decorations and menus. Héloïse, remembering Fanny's bitter resentment of herself, was as surprised as pleased that they were now able to have calm, pleasant conversations, even occasional little jokes, and that Fanny seemed sensible of Héloïse's good will, even of the worth of her advice.

James noticed them getting on together, and was delighted. 'My two favourite women,' he said one day, putting an arm round each of them and kissing their cheeks, as they pored over dress-designs. 'You look so lovely together — you might almost be sisters.' It was a remark to gratify neither of them, and they glanced at each other with identical expressions of distaste, and then both laughed.

'It is fortunate that Fanny accepts me now,' Héloïse said afterwards to James, 'for I shall have to chaperone her until Christmas at least, and it would be dreadful for both of us if she hated me still.'

'Fanny never hated you,' he said, wrapped in his new euphoria. 'You never understood her properly.'

The plans were complete. There was to be a dinner first for forty people, two full courses plus dessert; a supper later, halfway through the ball, with a decorated cake, and champagne; and for those who survived to the very end, white soup and oyster patties. Monsieur Barnard went into a prolonged frenzy, which only just exceeded those of Mrs Thomson and Ottershaw, whose preoccupation with linen, silver, crystal, servants, liveries, and the etiquette of receiving, seating and serving all the guests, left them no time to worry about decorating the house. Mathilde was glad to take over that task, and pottered happily about the gardens with a gardener anxiously in tow, and even walked over to Shawes, to see if she could inveigle some hot-house blooms out of old Morton.

Héloïse and Fanny between them drew up the guests lists and sent out the cards of invitation, and determined the placings for dinner. They walked about the house and decided that the long saloon simply wasn't big enough, and that the dancing should take place in the great hall, with the musicians playing upstairs to save room. The card tables could then be set up in the drawing-room, the steward's room could serve as a smoking-room, and the great bedchamber and its closet could be made available to the ladies for their toilette.

The children were fascinated by the whole business, and made themselves useful by remembering details such as the need for a pin-cushion and a sewing-maid in the ladies' room; pencils and paper as well as new packs of cards for the card-room; and Sophie suggested sensibly that supper should be laid out in the long saloon — 'Otherwise the servants will have to walk through the hall where everyone's dancing with trays of food and things.' Fanny, listening, was aware of a delightful glow inside her at the thought that now at last she would be part of the ball, and not, like Sophie and Africa, confined to watching the arrivals through the balusters, before going to bed.

Not only that, but she would be the most important person there, and would lead the first dance. It was a matter of considerable interest to her to know with whom she would open the ball. Every eligible young man in the neighbourhood was invited, along with all the respectable families, but when she contemplated the Micklethwaites and Applebys and even Tom Keating, she couldn't help feeling they were a poor bunch. Of course, now she was coming out, she would not be confined for choice to the younger set, but still she wished that Lieutenant Hawker was going to be there. To open the ball with him would be distinction enough for her; but he was still in Nottingham, as far as she knew. She knew that Papa had dined again with Colonel Brunton, and hoped that there would be some officers present. A ball with no red-coats at all would be in danger of being stigmatised a dull affair.

The mantuamaker called with her gown, and there was a last fitting, and last-minute alterations. It was of the finest, softest muslin, of a pale apricot colour, with raised, glossy spots woven into the material. Tiny silk rosebuds decorated the neckline, and the little cap-sleeves had a deep inverted pleat, also held by rosebuds. It was so soft and clinging that there was no room under it for a petticoat, and a flesh-coloured all-in-one undergarment came with it, which Marie thought indecent, and Fanny thought delightful.

The hairdresser came on the day itself to cut and curl and arrange Fanny's hair; and though she complained afterwards that he had almost pulled her hair off her head, and scorched her scalp with the curling-irons, the result was certainly worth the pain. Her luxuriant but rather coarse hair had never looked so glossy and well-kempt. The front hair was cut short and curled into a mass of feathery fronds which framed her face, while the rest was drawn up to the top of her head, formed into a Grecian knot woven with silver ribbons, and tumbled down behind in glossy ringlets.

Fanny would have liked to impress her contemporaries with some of the family jewels which were, after all, hers; but James joined Héloïse in deprecating the idea, and she accepted, without believing it, the dictum that a girl should be simply dressed at her come-out. Her mother's pearls were decreed suitable, but she wore them without enthusiasm, not feeling that they were very good ones — not good enough, at all events, for Miss Morland of Morland Place. Héloïse lent a pair of pearl earrings, and Papa gave her long white gloves as a birthday present, and a new fan with ivory sticks and a gold clasp.

So on 4 October 1811, the day after her sixteenth birthday, Fanny Morland was presented to the county. The most important and influential people were the dinner-guests, and they applauded genially as Fanny walked, very dignified, to her place at the table, and drank a toast to her; and Fanny stood with cheeks glowing and eyes modestly downcast, enjoying the moment enormously. James watched her with a heart bursting with pride, and looked across at Héloïse with a tender smile, forgetting in the emotion of the moment that she was not Fanny's mother.

The dinner was a great success, Barnard having excelled

himself; and despite the stringencies of the war, there were some very good things to drink, for James had been buying and hoarding for some time in anticipation of this very occasion. Afterwards there was a hiatus, as everyone gathered in the drawing-room, and waited for the carriages to bring the evening-guests for the ball.

James came across to Fanny, who was conversing politely with Lord Grey. He smelled of mothballs and old cigars, and she was very glad to be rescued from him.

'I've been trying to decide who should open the ball with you, Fanny,' he said.

'Yes, Papa?' she said meekly, as though the same consideration had not been occupying her for the last fortnight.

'I know there are lots of old friends here — and even some old admirers of yours, Fan, low let it be said! — but I think it should either be Mr Howick, or Richard Lambert who leads off with you. They are the highest-ranking of the unmarried young men we've invited for you. Have you any preference?'

Fanny gave a dutiful smile. Piers Howick, son of a Scottish viscount, or the Hon. Richard Lambert, son of Lord Lambert of Baldersby — there was nothing to choose between them from her point of view. Neither was handsome, rich or, as yet, titled, and the man must be all three who was good enough for Fanny Morland. She knew that, and Papa knew that. But he was quite right, there was a deference due to rank.

'Perhaps it should be Mr Howick first, and then Mr Lambert?' she suggested, her eyelashes fanning her pink cheek.

'Very well, then, my darling,' James said. 'I'll send Howick to you.'

How gentle and modest she had become, he thought happily, as Howick led her to the first set amid polite applause.

That will make the Micklethwaites and Keatings smart! she thought triumphantly.

At ten to three in the morning, a handful of diehard young people were still dancing. Fanny had danced every dance, working her way through the young, and even some of the not-so-young men with a studied impartiality, and winning herself admiration for betraying no greater pleasure in dancing with the Hon. Richard Lambert than with young Jack Appleby. She had gone up to supper on the arm of Mr Bayliss, but he had been forced to share her attention at supper with Edmund Somers, Tom Keating, and Captain Fordyce, the two latter being the only gentlemen with whom she danced more than once in the evening.

Mathilde had danced as many sets as she wanted to, and could have danced a great many more, had she not refused. Now, as it became plain that the last dance would be called at any moment, she was standing near the door to the buttery passage, ready to slip through and give the word for the soup and patties to be brought; and suddenly she found Edward standing beside her.

'It's been a great success, hasn't it?' he said. 'I'm glad, for everyone's sake. Fanny's position demands it; and you've all worked so hard.'

'I haven't done very much,' Mathilde said in faint surprise.

'The flowers look lovely,' Edward smiled. 'And I know in how many little ways you make things run smoothly in this house. I hope it hasn't been all work for you? I hope you've enjoyed it too?'

'Oh yes,' she said neutrally.

'But I haven't seen you dance this past half-hour. Are you tired?'

She looked at him carefully. 'A little. No, not really. I haven't wanted to dance.'

He looked at her quizzically. 'Do you remember your birthday ball? That was the first time I ever danced with you.'

'I remember it very well,' she said. It had also been the last time, she thought. Dancing did not very often come in their way.

'I wonder —' he hesitated, and she held her breath. 'Would it be too much to ask? Would you dance with me again?'

'I should like it very much,' she said gravely, but her heart was singing. She laid her hand on his arm, and he led her to the set.

Looking around him, Edward became very conscious of his age, and of Mathilde's youth and beauty. 'It's very kind of you to indulge me,' he said awkwardly. 'There must be lots of young men who want to dance with you. Perhaps —'

'It isn't kind of me at all,' Mathilde said quickly. 'And I don't want to dance with any of the young men. I don't want to dance with anyone but you.'

345

The sentence, begun boldly out of desperation, faded almost to inaudibility towards the end, and she felt herself blushing at her own daring, and could not meet Edward's eyes. When at last she felt able to steal a glance, she saw that he was looking around him with pleasure, smiling, and humming a snatch of the music. She thought perhaps he had not heard what she said, but a moment later, when she gave him her hand at the demand of the dance, he pressed it and said, 'Dear Mathilde!'

No more words passed between them during the dance, but Mathilde's heart was as light as her feet, and Edward never stopped smiling until the music stopped. Then as he bowed over her hand, he murmured, 'I must speak to you. Come out into the herb garden with me.'

'Oh, but I must order the soup,' she said foolishly, panicking now that it seemed the moment she had longed for so hopelessly had arrived.

'Someone else will do that. Please, Mathilde — or do you think you would do wrong in being alone with me? I assure you, I mean you no harm.'

She could not let him think she thought that. She put her hand on his arm and said, 'I will go anywhere with you, Cousin Edward.'

'Well,' he said looking pleased, 'the garden will do for the moment.'

They slipped out through the little door by the chapel into the garden which formed the inner court of the house. It had been a herb garden long ago, and still bore the name, out of habit; but the herbs had never grown well there, getting too little light, and now it had been paved, with spaces left amongst the stones for such hardy plants as would thrive there. The air struck chill after the ballroom, and she shivered a little in reaction.

He stopped in the darkness beyond the oblongs of light falling from the window and turned to her, but for a while did not speak. She began to feel a little awkward, standing here in the darkness with him. What if a servant should come? Sometimes they used the court as a short-cut between the servants' hall and the nursery stair.

'Well, Cousin?' she prompted him at last.

He took a step nearer. 'Mathilde,' he said, 'this is very

346

difficult for me to say. I have to ask you something which may embarrass you.' He cleared his throat. 'I have noticed sometimes — I have thought —' He stopped, evidently deeply confused. Then he began again. 'No, I'm doing it all wrong. Why should I ask you to expose yourself? I will tell you plainly, and trust to your kindness. Mathilde, you may think it impertinent, forward, even foolish of me, but — I have been in love with you for a very long time. I hardly know when it began, but for longer than I can remember you have been the dearest object of my heart.'

Mathilde drew a breath to answer — though she hardly knew what she would say — but he went on quickly, 'It has seemed to me lately that you are perhaps not indifferent to me? Forgive me if I have misunderstood you. Perhaps you regard me only in a friendly light. I know I am a great deal older than you —'

'Cousin Edward,' she said breathlessly, anxious to say something before he talked himself out of love again. 'I — I don't feel just a friendship for you. I hoped you knew that.'

He stepped closer again, and took her hands, holding them so hard he hurt her, though she didn't notice it at once. 'Do you mean — can you mean — can you possibly love me?'

This time she needed only to nod, and he gave a small sigh of relief and took her in his arms. At last, she thought, at last. She leaned against his strong chest, and closed her eyes, and felt safe and loved and warm. It was the most exquisite moment of her life, and she savoured it, old enough to know that such moments must be enjoyed to the full while they last.

'Mathilde, my beautiful, my lovely Mathilde,' Edward murmured against her ear.

'Dear Edward,' she whispered.

Then he released her, and the light from the upper windows illuminated his worried expression.

'Dear Mathilde, I wanted to ask you to marry me before you went away on your tour. Do you remember the day we went to look at the ram? I thought then that you might love me. I wanted to declare myself.'

'I wanted you to,' she said shyly. 'Why didn't you?'

The last of his smile faded. 'Because — for the same reason that still exists. I am not in a position to marry. Oh God, I am in the most devilish fix.'

Mathilde felt the blood leave her head. She clutched his forearm faintly. 'You can't mean — that you have a wife already?'

He looked startled. 'Good God, no! My dearest girl, what are you thinking of? No, what I mean is that I am not in a position to support a wife. I have no money of my own. I live here, at Morland Place, free of charge, by the terms of my mother's will. When Fanny comes of age, I shall receive a small sum — six thousand pounds — and I may continue to live here while I remain unmarried. But six thousand pounds is not enough to support myself and a wife, if I leave Morland Place.'

'But why should you leave?' she asked. 'I don't want to go. I love it here — I regard it as my home. And it *is* your home.'

'Only until Fanny comes of age. My dear, you don't think that imp will hesitate to throw us all out of doors, as soon as the trust is terminated, do you? James and Héloïse and their children will be obliged to go, you may be sure, and you with them. That's why they have always kept Plaisir, so that they would have a home to go to. Well, Héloïse has money of her own, and James will have his six thousand pounds like me. They will manage. But as for me —'

'Fanny would never throw you out of doors,' Mathilde said angrily. 'With all the work you do — why, you run the estate almost single-handed! She wouldn't be so ungrateful! She could never manage without you.'

'She may well want me to stay as her manager — though I don't know that I would want to — but she would never accept a wife of mine,' he said sadly. 'And when she marries, her husband may have other ideas about how to run the estate. My dear, I am the last person in the world to think of money in connection with marriage, but you have no fortune, and we could not live on three hundred a year.'

'We could! I'm sure we could! Lots of people live on less than that,' Mathilde said, fighting back the tears.

He touched her hand. 'You don't know what you're saying. You don't know what it would mean. And do you think I would let you condemn yourself to poverty for my sake? No, my dear, it's impossible.'

She was silent a moment, and then anger broke through, the anger of frustration. 'Then, if you don't want to marry me, why have you brought me out here? Why have you declared yourself? Was it just to torment me?'

'Do you think that of me? Oh Mathilde, I do want to marry you, more than anything in the world! If things were only different — but it's foolish to talk like that. I'll tell you why I had to speak to you: though it was arrogant and foolish of me, lately I had begun to think that perhaps you felt the same way about me as I felt about you. I wondered if perhaps that was why you hadn't married, or formed a connection with any of the young men I saw dangling after you. I couldn't bear to think you were waiting, uselessly, for me, wasting your life, losing your chance of happiness. No, let me speak! I love you, Mathilde, more than I ever thought I could love anyone. I'm unspeakably glad and grateful that you have said you love me. And knowing that, I can let you go with a quiet heart. You must marry some young, wealthy man, who can support you and give you the establishment you deserve. I want you to be happy.'

'Have you finished?' Mathilde said evenly. 'Well, then it is my turn to speak. I have told you before, and I will tell you again, that I don't want to be married, unless it's to you. You can't get rid of me so easily! You have declared yourself, and you can't take back your words. I think we could live on three hundred a year; I'm willing to try, anyway. But if you aren't — well, something will happen, I know it will! We must be together. That's all that matters.'

'But what could happen?' he said despairingly.

'I don't know,' she said with the fierce carelessness of youth. 'Maybe Fanny won't send us away. Maybe someone will die and leave you some money. Maybe Madame will give me a dowry. Something will happen, if only you don't give up hope.'

He took her hands again. 'Do you mean you would be willing to wait, in the hope that we might be able to marry some time in the future? I can't believe it.'

'Believe it,' she said. 'What have I to lose? This is my home. I shall be here anyway, until Fanny throws *me* out. We'll just go on as we have done, working, being together, and wait to see what happens.'

He drew her towards him and kissed her brow. 'Bless you, dearest Mathilde. If that's what you want, then so be it. I

349

can't believe I'm so lucky. But remember, no promise binds you. If at any time you receive an offer of marriage you feel is to your advantage, you mustn't hesitate —'

'Oh hush!' she said. 'I told you, Cousin Edward, that I don't want to marry anyone else.'

'We must keep this a secret for the time being,' he said. 'In public we must be as we have been until now. You see the necessity.'

'Yes, I see the necessity. But in private —?'

'You will be my dear love,' he said happily. 'And now, we had better go in, before we're missed.'

'Yes,' she said dutifully, and led the way.

CHAPTER EIGHTEEN

Captain Haworth did not come home in the autumn as he had planned. He had applied for leave, but like Collingwood before him, had been denied it on the grounds that he could not be spared. He was commanding a squadron in the western Mediterranean, and depending on the winds, letters could take up to three months in either direction. His letter explaining that he would not be coming home arrived with Lucy at the end of January, 1812.

'It is a great pity,' he wrote, 'but it cannot be helped. The situation here is delicate, and though there are signs that Bonaparte may soon be forced to lighten the embargo and grant some licences, we cannot afford to loosen our grip now. We begin to see a little hope for a conclusion, if not soon, then at least in the foreseeable future. We have hints that Boney may be spoiling for a fight with Russia, and if they are true, then he may find he has bitten off more than he can chew. It is hard for anyone who has not been there to imagine how large Russia is, and Boney has never been very good at judging distances!

'So for the moment, I believe it is best that Africa remains with Mrs Touchstone. I think it is important for her both to get a good education, and to be with other girls in her situation; and Bath, you know, is conveniently placed to visit if I should come home unexpectedly. I have made arrangements with the paymaster for the school fees and Africa's allowance to be continued.'

Lucy brought the letter with her when she came to Morland Place in February to stay with Héloïse until the baby was born. Nothing less would satisfy James, though Héloïse's pregnancy had so far been without incident.

'But it is very good of you to come, dear Lucy,' Héloïse said when she arrived.

'It certainly is,' Lucy agreed. 'You've timed this very ill,

351

you know. The restrictions on the Regency end on February the eighteenth, and everyone thinks the Prince will have a change of government and bring in the Whigs. Well, almost everyone — Brummell thinks, and I agree with him, that caution will prevail again. But it's a very interesting time to be in Town, at all events, and I shall miss it.'

Héloïse gave a small smile. 'I was not thinking of the Regency when I began this baby,' she confessed.

'You weren't thinking at all,' Lucy said severely, 'but there's no helping it now.'

There was a very painful reunion for Héloïse with Thomas, whom Lucy had brought with her, as automatically as she brought Docwra and Parslow. He had had his eighth birthday in December, had grown into a sturdy handsome boy, very like his father, but with enough of Lucy in him to make their relationship obvious to anyone seeing them together. It was plain that he didn't really remember Héloïse, and though it was sad for her, she was glad for his sake that there was nothing to tug his heart away from his mother, for whom he had evidently developed a very strong affection.

Sophie, however, was overjoyed to see 'her' Thomas again. He had spent much more time in his early life with her than with Héloïse, and remembered her more clearly, and though he was shy with her at first, he gradually warmed to her. With Nicholas in tow, she took him first of all to Monsieur Barnard, who dropped a few tears on Thomas's embarrassed head, and promised to make them all peppermint creams, and then on a tour of the house and yard, to introduce him to every servant and animal at Morland Place. Her frequent cries of 'do you remember?', met at first with bewilderment, after the first couple of days began to elicit a response.

It was hard for Africa to join in her cousin's euphoria, for the news that she was to go back to school was extremely unwelcome to her.

'But Aunt,' she protested, 'that letter was written months ago! Papa didn't know when he wrote that, that Sophie had left Mrs Touchstone's. He wouldn't mind me staying here if he knew.'

'Yes, but he doesn't know,' Lucy said. 'It's his wish that you should go back to school, and there's nothing more to be said.'

Africa plainly thought there was a great deal to be said,

and Héloïse intervened on her behalf. 'I think perhaps if we write to Captain Haworth, Cousin Lucy, he may change his mind.'

'Oh certainly — write by all means. In fact, I'll do it myself, and get Yorke to put it in the first bag going out to Gibraltar. I've no objection to your staying here, child, but until your father sends his permission, to Bath you must go.'

Africa looked stricken. 'But it might be six months before we can get a letter from him!'

'Oh dear,' said Héloïse, 'I know it is hard, ma pauvre, but the time will soon pass. If you work hard and attend to your lessons, you will find it goes quicker than you imagine.'

Africa knew better than to argue any further, but her mouth set grimly, and her agile mind began to revolve plans in her head, mostly impractical ones to do with hiding aboard a ship and making her way to the Mediterranean to find her father. Aunt Lucy ran away to sea dressed as a boy, she thought resentfully; but her common sense told her that, well-grown at thirteen-and-a-half, she looked less like a boy than Aunt Lucy did even now.

'I'll take her to London with me when I go back,' Lucy said to Héloïse later, 'and send her on from there. There's no great hurry, I suppose, to be rid of her?'

'None at all; I wish she might stay here,' Héloïse said.

'How is Fanny behaving? You've been chaperoning her, I suppose? Has she been difficult?'

'Oh no,' Héloïse said. 'I've been much pleased at how well she behaves. Of course, she loves being out at last, and having all the young men flock round her — as they do, Lucy, for really, she is very pretty! Not precisely beautiful, I suppose, but she has a certain something all her own which is very attractive.' Héloïse sighed. 'I'm afraid she flirts dreadfully, but she does it so prettily one must be amused. To see her play off one poor stuttering beau against another!'

'It will do her good to be in London,' Lucy said, 'where she's of less consequence. Once she sees how many other pretty girls there are, and with good fortunes, she'll settle down and find her place. It's probably just as well to give her a London Season before she gets too high an idea of herself.'

'I think Fanny was born with a high idea of herself,' Héloïse said.

'Where is she now, by the way?'

'Hunting,' Héloïse said succinctly. 'She goes out three or four times a week, which is a good thing, for it uses up her energy. I have not been able to take her about since Christmas, but as long as she can hunt, she gets up to no mischief. Edward takes her out. It is astonishing how well they get on, considering how he has always criticised her. But she always was a good horsewoman.'

'Hmm. Well I shall see for myself, I suppose, for I mean to get a little hunting in, while I'm here. I must have some compensation for waiting around for you to give birth, when I ought to be in Town with my finger on the pulse. Great things may happen without me!'

'Have you heard from Major Wiske recently?' Héloïse asked.

'Oh yes, he writes regularly. He makes the most surprisingly good correspondent.'

'Why surprisingly?' Héloïse asked.

'Oh, I don't know,' Lucy said vaguely. 'Somehow I never expected him to be; I suppose because he was never a great talker. But he wrote most amusingly about the siege of Cuidad Rodrigo. Wellington took the French completely by surprise, marching in the middle of winter like that, and in such terrible weather. The way Danby described it, you could almost have been there — all about how it was so cold their wet uniforms frozen on them, and how the ground was so hard they could hardly dig the trenches around the walls. But they took the fortress, as you know, and with the loss of only a thousand men, which considering the conditions was not a bad butcher's bill at all. Danby came out without a scratch, though they lost Craufurd, which was a blow. He was well-liked. The last I heard from Danby, they were marching straight away to take Badajoz. Once they have that, the border is secure, and they can start pushing into Spain.'

'Does he enjoy campaigning, do you think?'

'Oh, beyond anything,' Lucy said with a rueful laugh. 'The hardships are nothing to him, which when you consider the sort of life he used to lead — a downy bed, hot water at ten, hot rolls and coffee while his man laid his clothes out — is astonishing!'

'But Lucy, you always said he was brave,' Héloïse reminded her.

'Brave, yes, I grant you — but who would have thought he could bear dirt and discomfort? I always though him another George Brummell — now it's impossible to imagine *him* being happy in a place with no mirrors or curling-tongs!'

'I suppose it must be the adventure Major Wiske likes. Men are all the same. Even James sometimes speaks wistfully of his soldiering days.'

'James is humbugging,' Lucy said firmly. 'I remember very clearly that he sold out the instant war was declared. Mother was relieved, but as I remember, Papa pursed his lips a little. Not all men are born soldiers, you know.'

'It is lucky, then, that we have people like Lord Wellington. What does Major Wiske think of him?'

'Oh, Danby speaks very highly of him. He says he has made a wonderful change in the men under his command. You know what common soldiers are usually like — the sweepings of the world — but Wellington has them drilled and disciplined like machines, and they adore him for it. Perverse creatures, men! They call him Old Hookey, because of his big nose, but they'd die for him just the same. No-one out there, according to Danby, would give credit for the progress they're making to anyone else.'

'It is heartening to have some good news at last,' Héloïse said. 'There is so much trouble here in the North, with manufacturers failing, and all this dreadful frame-breaking, and poor people starving because the price of bread is so high.'

Lucy shrugged. 'These things can't be helped. We must win the war first — that comes before everything. But the good news strengthens Perceval's hand, at least, when he has to ask for another vote of money for the war. Grey and Grenville say the manufacturers have been complaining about the cost of keeping two armies in Portugal. It's lucky most of the mill-towns don't have a Member. God help us if they ever get the vote! They'd have us make peace with Boney, for the sake of their looms and steam-engines.'

'Peace! It is impossible to remember what it was like,' Héloïse said. 'I sometimes think the war will go on for ever. Unless — do you think there is anything in what Captain Haworth says?'

'About Russia? Oh yes, it looks as though Boney's thinking of it. He's taken men out of the Peninsula, and moved an army of twenty thousand right up to the Russian border. Official reports say he claims that Russia's broken the agreement to ban trade with our ships, but of course that's only an excuse. He wants to be master of the world. He was bound to want to conquer Russia sooner or later.'

'But will he succeed?'

'It's hard to say. The Csar can certainly put more men into the field than Boney, but they're not experienced soldiers, and they won't have the leadership. Everyone agrees that Boney can work miracles on the battlefield. If anyone can conquer Russia, it's him.'

Héloïse was silent. Lucy eyed her. 'I think we've talked enough about the war,' she said briskly. 'This is not the time for you to worry about things you can't help. Your business is to have a healthy baby, and to have it quickly so that I can get back to Town in time to plan the coming-out ball.'

'You'll take Fanny with you when you go?'

'Of course. It will take time to have her Court dress made, and I shall want to introduce her to some of the leading hostesses beforehand, to be sure of getting the right invitations for her. James does know he must be there for the ball itself, doesn't he?' she added suspiciously.

Héloïse smiled. 'Yes, he understands that. I think underneath he is not at all unwilling. He pretends to be for the sake of being manly, but really he longs to see Fanny take London by storm. I don't think he would miss the ball for worlds.'

'Good,' Lucy nodded, 'because I must have someone. It's very tiresome of Danby to go away to the war just as I have three girls to bring out.'

'You must miss him very much,' Héloïse said, meaning only to be polite, and was surprised that Lucy looked put out.

'He was useful,' she said briefly, looking away.

Héloïse went into labour late in the evening of the last day of February. Lucy, Docwra and Marie shut themselves into the great bedchamber with her, leaving Mathilde downstairs to comfort the waiting men and to act as messenger between them. Fanny and the children had already gone to bed, but some sixth sense woke Sophie, and she got out of bed and went padding along to the bedchamber, where she found Castor and Kithra, also banished, sitting with their noses glued to the closed door. Here Mathilde found her when she came upstairs for news.

'What are you doing out of bed?' she asked, but gently, seeing Sophie's anxious eyes turned up to her.

'Is Maman all right? She won't die, will she?' Sophie asked abruptly.

'I'm just going in to see how things are going,' Mathilde said. 'But you mustn't wait here. Go back to bed, and I'll come and tell you in a little while how she is.'

Sophie shook her head in dumb fright. A low moan sounded from inside the room, and her eyes widened. 'Maman!' she whispered.

Mathilde took her by her bony shoulders and turned her firmly round. 'Sophie, go downstairs to Papa. He's waiting in the drawing-room. Go on, now, or I won't tell you anything. I'll come down in a few minutes.'

Sophie went reluctantly. In the drawing-room she found her father pacing up and down, his face drawn with anxiety. Uncle Edward sat by the fire, staring hard into the flames. They both looked up as the door opened. Sophie ran to her father, and for the first time in years he picked her up and held her against his shoulder.

'Papa!' she said, her thin arms going round his neck.

'Yes, I know, chick. It's all right. She'll be all right,' he said without conviction. He didn't try to send her to bed, even when Mathilde came down a little later to report no progress. She sat on his lap all through the long night, dozing and waking, living through a nightmare sense of unreality, a feeling of impending doom which she could never afterwards forget, and which came back to her at moments of unhappiness or anxiety. She and Papa and Uncle Edward were the constants. Mathilde and Father Aislaby came and went through the night, and early in the morning Miss Rosedale joined them, unable to sleep, wanting news.

At eight o'clock a hollow-eyed Ottershaw appeared to ask about breakfast, and while he was standing at the open door of the drawing-room, faint but clear from upstairs came the sound of a new baby's wail. James and Edward stood up as though pulled by the same string, and Mathilde, her face pale, thrust out of the room and ran up the stairs.

A deathly silence fell over the room as every ear was strained for some sound that might convey news, but there was nothing to be heard. The baby did not cry again, and Sophie, her hand crushed in her father's, looked up into his face and saw death written there. Her lip began to tremble.

The minutes dragged by. The great bronze and marble clock — a gift of Mr Hobsbawn to James on his wedding day so long ago — gave a preparatory click which made everyone jump, and then solemnly struck the quarter-hour; and as the vibration of its chime died away, there was the sound of a door upstairs opening, and then of descending footsteps. Mathilde appeared in the doorway.

'It's all right,' she said, and they could hear her voice shaking. 'She's all right. It's a boy.'

James sat down abruptly; Edward said, 'Oh, thank God!' and Father Aislaby crossed himself and whispered 'Benedictus Deus'. Sophie looked from face to face, and wondered why nobody spoke or smiled. Maman's alive, she thought. It's all right. She suddenly felt very tired, and very hungry, as though she had been walking all night.

'Ottershaw,' said Mathilde, 'I think we all need some breakfast.'

'Yes, miss. Right away, miss!' said Ottershaw fervently.

Later, Lucy came down to tell James he could go up and see Héloïse. 'But only for a few minutes. She's very tired, and needs to sleep, but she won't settle until she's seen you.'

'Is she really all right?'

'Yes. She's had a hard time of it, but she's come through it very well. You're luckier than you deserve, the pair of you.'

'And the baby?'

'I had to help him along a bit, with forceps, but he's strong and healthy, though he's a bit sleepy at the moment.' She gave a tired smile. 'He's certainly better looking than the last one.'

It wasn't until James saw her for himself that he could really believe Héloïse was all right; but as soon as he saw her, he could see that this was a different case altogether. She looked very tired, but not unnaturally so, as if she had been working very hard, rather than suffering. She gave him the

358

transfiguring smile he remembered from last time, and offered him the sleeping baby to be admired.

'Isn't he beautiful?' she said. 'The most beautiful, perfect baby in the world!'

As Lucy had said, he was better looking than Nicholas had been. He was small, but compact, and his skin was smooth and glowing, and he had a considerable thatch of dark hair. James caressed the velvet cheek with one finger, and the baby frowned and pursed his lips, but continued busily to sleep.

'Yes,' James said, 'he's beautiful.'

Héloïse closed her eyes. 'I told you so, my James. I told you God knew what he was doing. Our beautiful baby is a gift from Him.'

James smiled. 'The first thing Aislaby said when he heard the news was *Benedictus Deus*.'

Héloïse smiled too, through encroaching sleep. 'That is a very good name for him, don't you think?'

'What, Aislaby?' James said, startled.

'Benedict,' she murmured. 'Our blessing.' She was asleep.

Héloïse recovered rapidly, and baby Benedict throve, and when he was three weeks old, James and Lucy went to London, taking Africa and Fanny with them. Africa was sent off to Bath on the mail, accompanied by a maid to see her safe, and Lucy began preparations for the *début* of the three girls.

James confessed himself taken aback when she revealed that she would be hiring another house for the Season, at considerable expense.

'I don't know what you expected,' she said crossly. 'There's no ballroom at Upper Grosvenor Street. Where did you think we were going to hold a coming-out ball for four hundred guests?'

'I hadn't thought about it,' he confessed. 'But really, the expense of this business is more than I compounded for!'

'I'll pay for the house,' she said shortly. 'It's really Flaminia's ball, after all. If I weren't bringing her out, none of this would be happening. All you have to pay for is your share of the expenses of the ball, and Fanny's Court dress.'

'Only!' he said with a groan. 'Are you sure a Court dress will cost three hundred and fifty pounds?'

'Guineas,' Lucy said mercilessly.

'For something she'll only wear once?'

'Do you want her presented or not? Really, Jamie, this is not the time to be paltry about money. Anyway, it can come out of the estate, can't it? Surely Edward has discretion over the income?'

'The Court dress will have to,' James said, 'but I said I'd pay for the other expenses myself. How many gowns is she likely to need for the Season?'

'I've no idea. We'll buy them as we go along. But you want her well launched, don't you? And that means morning dresses, afternoon dresses, carriage dresses, walking dresses, at least two riding habits, ball gowns; and then there are hats and pelisses, shawls, gloves —'

'You are deliberately teasing me,' James said coldly.

'— to say nothing of silk stockings,' Lucy finished. 'You'll just have to hope she makes it worth your while by getting a really good husband.'

'I don't want her getting a husband of any sort, thank you,' James said quickly.

'Then why on earth are you going to all this trouble?' Lucy asked. 'You don't think I'd do it for Flaminia, except to get her married?'

'Well, obviously she has to marry eventually, but she's much too young yet.'

'Then you shouldn't be bringing her out,' Lucy said, with the air of one ending the argument.

'You're very hard, Lucy,' James complained.

'Life is hard,' she retorted.

London that April was restless with change. The Prince had again disappointed the Whigs of power, and though he tried to placate his old friends by attempting to bring one or two of them into the Government, they refused the compromise. Grenville, Grey and Canning were condemned, it seemed, to eternal Opposition. They were soon joined by Lord Wellesley — Wellington's brother — who, seeing he would never be able to fulfil his ambition of leading a new administration, resigned in a fit of pique, which allowed Castlereagh to take over his office of Foreign Secretary.

The Prince had been unwell, ever since the approach of the end of restrictions to the Regency presented him with the problem of what to do about the Whigs. His hands had become gouty and palsied; a horse had trodden on his foot, breaking a tendon, which was slow to heal; his stomach troubled him on and off, as did his debts. He took to his bed as an escape from his problems, complained of pains in his head, snapped at his friends, and had fits of weeping. His brother, the Duke of Cambridge, was heard to say hopefully that the Regent was going the same way as his father.

The news from the Peninsula was of another victory: Wellington had taken the third of the frontier fortresses, Badajoz, though it had not been as easy as at Cuidad Rodrigo. Five thousand men had been lost in the frontal attack, and the fortress fell at last, almost by accident, to a flank attack which had been intended only as a diversionary tactic. Wiske's letter to Lucy gave darker details of the affair, which took the shine out of the victory: after the battle, the English soldiers had disgraced themselves, breaking out for once from Wellington's iron discipline, rampaging through the town, looting, burning, and butchering the inhabitants.

News came also that Bonaparte had sent a formal letter of complaint to the Csar of Russia, about the breaking of the Treaty of Tilsit by allowing English goods to be imported into Russia in neutral ships. Bonaparte was still assembling men and supplies in northern Prussia and Poland, which looked like preparations for war, and it was hoped that if he really did declare war on Russia, Russia would then make peace with England, and re-open the Baltic to trade.

Events seemed to be justifying the dogged policy of Spencer Perceval's Government, and never had Perceval himself been more popular than that April. He even managed to get a Bill through the House of Commons for the increasing of the Regent's income: no mean feat, considering the high cost of the war and the Prince's legendary extravagance. Then on the evening of 11 May at about five o'clock, when Perceval was passing through the lobby of the House of Commons, a man walked up to him, pulled out a pistol, and shot him dead through the heart.

The man, Bellingham, was a commercial agent, whose business had been ruined by the embargo and the Orders in Council. For weeks he had been trying to obtain recompense from various government offices, and now it seemed that his troubles had turned his head, and he had taken an insane act of revenge against the Prime Minister. Perceval's murder threw the Government, the whole of Parliament, into disarray. Lord Liverpool, the Secretary for War, took over the administration on a temporary basis; but the Whigs, sure that their moment had come at last, attacked the Government so violently that the entire administration was forced to resign.

Then there followed the familiar dance of ambition, through lobby and club and private house, as the great men of the day grouped and regrouped, bickered and postulated, made and unmade alliances, bargained and betrayed; until at last, when all possible combinations had been tried and failed, there was nothing left but for the Regent to step in and ask Lord Liverpool to take office again, with the same ministers as before.

Little of this impinged on the three young women in the large, hired house in Grosvenor Square. The coming-out ball had been a great success. Three hundred and sixty of the four hundred invitations had been accepted, and well over four hundred people came, making it certain that it would receive the final accolade of being voted 'a sad crush'. James had looked on in amazement at the preparations beforehand. He had thought Fanny's ball at Morland Place grand enough, but it was nothing to Lucy's.

A striped awning was erected over the pavement to the road, and under it a red carpet led up the steps into the hall, sure sign to passers-by that something worth watching was to happen. From quite early in the day, idlers gathered on the flagway, to watch footmen staggering up the steps with huge pots of plants and greenery for the decoration of the ballroom, cases of champagne and baskets of delicacies. As the time for arrivals approached, footmen were stationed at intervals around the square to direct the coaches, and to divert any traffic not meant for the ball; while a dozen link-boys had been hired to attend at the door after dark.

The dinner beforehand was set for forty people, and James was able to appreciate how Lucy's high connections would make a difference to the way Fanny was launched. As well as members of the *ton* and the nobility, they sat down to dinner with highly-placed Members of Parliament, representatives of the diplomatic service, senior army officers, and two admirals.

Not only that, but Lord Melville and the Rutlands were coming to the ball, having been already engaged to dine elsewhere, and the Duke of York had promised to look in at some point in the evening, giving the ball a royal seal of approval.

After dinner came the moment that James had long been anticipating. He and Lucy stood at the top of the stairs leading to the ballroom, with the three girls at their side, receiving the guests who flowed upward in a flood of jewels and distinction. His own partiality aside, he could not help thinking that Fanny looked the best of the three. On Lucy's advice she was dressed all in white — white spider-gauze over a plain satin slip, with her mother's pearls round her throat, and another string wound in the knot of her hair. She carried her birthday fan, and a reticule sewn all over with spars, which glinted and caught the light. Her long, tawny eyes glowed with excitement, and the fresh colour in her face made her look vibrantly alive. His little girl, he thought, had grown up into a beautiful young woman; his eyes were a little misty, and no compliment directed towards him could have been too extravagant for him to believe.

Flaminia, small and plump, with her reddish hair and green eyes, could never outshine either of her companions; but she was too good-natured to wish to. Whatever happened, her future was secure, for with her title and her dowry, there was not a doubt of her marrying well. Hippolyta, on the other hand, standing beside Fanny, would have outshone any girl but her. James had to admit that Polly was beautiful, as her mother had been. Her alabaster skin, her perfect features, her vivid blue eyes, and her shining black hair, combined with a tall and graceful figure, and a complete composure, made her seem like an exquisite Greek statue. But perhaps she was rather too like a statue, he thought. She had always, even as a little child, been grave and mature for her years; now her upbringing, her dependency, and her knowledge of how small her dowry was likely to be, had made her even more reserved.

Lady Flaminia Chetwyn might have the title, and Miss Haworth the classical beauty, James thought, but of the three young women, there was no doubt in his mind as to who was going to make the splash that Season. Bright-eyed, smiling, energetic Miss Morland of Morland Place would have been his choice of partner if he had been a single young man at that ball; and before the evening was out, he was to have the pleasure of seeing that young men nowadays were not so different from him in their judgement.

Having been launched into society, the three young women were bent on enjoying the Season to the full. There was a succession of private balls and routs, and public assemblies to attend; there was the theatre, the opera, the ballet, the concerts of Ancient Music, and the exhibitions at Somerset House. There was Almacks, where they must make their mark, and where, thanks to Lucy's friendship with Mr Brummell, they were sure of acceptance; and later on there would be presentation at the Queen's Drawing-Room, with all the absurd glories of satin, hoops and tall feathers. There was walking and riding and driving in the Park to be fitted in; and above and beyond all, there was shopping. Fanny's taste of its joys in Manchester had not prepared her for the exquisite delights of London. She found herself, rather like the despised Miss Prudence Pendlebury, thinking about clothes *all the time.*

One day in June, the three young women were in the morning room, waiting for Lucy to come back from her ride so that they could go out. Rosamund was also present, hanging over the back of a chair and kicking its rail idly, waiting to be collected by Miss Trotton, who was busy writing a letter.

'What are you going to wear to Lady Tewkesbury's tonight?' Hippolyta asked Flaminia.

'I don't know,' Minnie answered predictably. 'What do you think?'

'If you wear your lavender silk, could I borrow your gauze scarf?'

Before Minnie could answer, Fanny said, 'You can't wear the lavender silk, because I'm going to wear blue, and we'll be too much alike. You'd better wear your green crape, Minnie.'

Minnie nodded, perfectly happy to do what she was told, as long as she didn't have to think for herself, but Hippolyta said, 'Don't be so unkind, Fanny. She can't wear green — you know it doesn't suit her.'

'Nonsense, redheads always wear green,' Fanny said firmly, with a hint in her voice of the contempt with which she had always regarded red hair. 'Petersfield said to me the

364

other day that he thought you ought to wear green.'

Minnie grew pinker. Though she regarded most people in her life in the same vague and woolly way, she had actually managed to achieve a slight partiality for Viscount Petersfield. 'Did he really?'

'Certainly. When we were going down the set at the Assembly the other night. "I do think Lady Flaminia ought to wear green," he said. "Really, Lord Petersfield?" I said. "Oh certainly," he said. "Pomona green crape, with ruched velvet trim, would look vastly well on her," he said.'

'How strange,' Minnie said with a gasp. 'Pomona green, with velvet trim — but that exactly describes my gown!'

'Fanny, stop it,' Polly said crossly, and Fanny burst into laughter.

'Oh you goose, Minnie! Don't you know when you're being roasted?'

Minnie looked from one to the other. 'Well, if Lord Petersfield likes green, I'm sure I don't see why I shouldn't wear it,' she said. 'It's very good-natured of Fanny to tell me.'

Rosamund snorted. 'I don't know which of you is the sillier!' she said energetically. 'All you can do is talk of gowns and men! Anyone would think you didn't know there was a war on.'

'Don't kick the chair, Ros,' Hippolyta said in automatic reproof.

'Well, I can tell you, Minnie, it don't matter what gown you wear, you won't be marrying Fred Petersfield. He's as good as engaged to Lady Mary Fleetwood.'

'How do you know that?' Fanny said sharply. It sometimes annoyed her that Rosamund knew things she didn't, but she was always willing to make use of any source of information.

'Because I heard Mr Brummel tell Mama so the other day. She was asking him if Petersfield would "do", and Mr Brummell said that Petersfield was hanging out for Lady Mary, because Fleetwood was worth four votes in the commons. So you may as well wear the lavender, Minnie, for you look hideous in green.'

'Little cat,' Fanny muttered.

Rosamund stuck out her tongue.

'Don't do that,' Hippolyta said with a frown. 'It isn't lady-like.'

'I don't care if it isn't. I don't want to be a lady. I'd far rather be a soldier,' Rosamund said promptly.

'Don't be silly,' Hippolyta said. 'You can't be a soldier.'

'Well, Mama was a sailor when she was my age. I don't see why I shouldn't run away to the war. If Marcus gets his colours, I'll cut my hair and go with him as his servant.'

'Oh, don't talk so shocking, Rosamund!' Minnie said, wide-eyed.

'Marcus wouldn't want you anyway,' Fanny said contemptuously. 'What use would you be? He'd want a proper servant.'

Rosamund's cheeks were pink with anger. 'He would want me! He said the other day that I was a regular little trump, and I sewed his shirt for him, and he said it was the best sewing he'd ever seen, so there! *And* Ollett's shewn me how to bone and polish boots, which is more than you know, Fanny Morland!'

Fanny shrugged. 'Marcus won't get his colours, anyway. Everyone knows his mother doesn't want him to go to the war.'

'He will get them, I know he will,' Rosamund says. 'I heard him talking about it to Bobbie yesterday when we were watching the steam-engine in St James's Park, and Bobbie said —'

'Rosamund, you really must stop this dreadful habit of listening to other people's conversations,' Hippolyta said. 'It's very bad of you. Aunt Lucy would be shocked if she knew.'

'Well, how else am I to find things out?' Rosamund said reasonably. 'I'm the only one stuck away in the nursery, and no-one tells me anything, and you two are so hateful you never let me join in anything. Anyway, if you're so pious about it, Pol, I shan't tell you what I heard Mother saying to Hicks this morning about the dinner-guests for Saturday.'

'I don't want to hear,' Polly said firmly. 'I don't want to know what you've learned by such methods.'

Rosamund was not deterred. 'Oh yes you do! She said that as the Knaresboroughs were coming, she was going to invite the Sales, too — Lord Wyndham, and Lord Harvey Sale. And as you're nutty on Lord Harvey, I should think you'd be very interested.'

Hippolyta looked vexed. 'I am not nutty on him. Don't be

so vulgar. And stop kicking the chair-rail.'

Rosamund grinned. 'Nutty on him! Marcus says Georgy Wyndham's a conceited ass, but Lord Harvey's a trump card; so I wish you might get him, Pol! He has a capital bay horse, a right 'un, fit to go, Marcus says —'

'Marcus says, Marcus says,' Fanny mocked. 'How we do love those words!'

'— and Mr Brummell says he might get the reversion, so then you'd be a Marchioness one day,' Rosamund went on undeterred.

'Mr Brummell didn't say any such thing,' Fanny said shrewdly.

'Well, he said to Mama that Georgy Wyndham was the dullest young man in London, and the only unwed man in the country that even Lavinia Fauncett wouldn't marry. So that means he'll stay single, and *that* means Lord Harvey will get the title when his pa and his brother are both dead.'

Hippolyta's alabaster complexion was growing agitatedly pink, with a mixture of vexation at Rosamund's manners, and embarrassment at having her private feelings so ruthlessly handled; but at that moment Miss Trotton came in, having finished her letter, and looked around the room.

'I'm ready for you now, Rosamund. What have you been up to? Have you been annoying the young ladies? Really, you are an impossible child!'

'No I'm not, Trot — I'm quick and clever, and you love me best, you know you do,' Rosamund said, twining her arms round Miss Trotton's waist and giving her a sweet smile. 'You always felt you were wasted on Polly and Minnie, because Polly was born good and didn't need you, and Minnie is too stupid ever to learn anything.'

'Be silent, abominable girl,' Miss Trotton said sternly, but she did not rebuff the caress, 'Young ladies, Lady Aylesbury has come back, and will be up in a moment, so you will be able to take your drive very soon.'

Rosamund dashed to the window to see if she could see the horses being led away, and peering down into the street, saw instead a familiar cockaded hat pass below. 'Here's the postman! He's coming up our steps, too!'

Thus alerted, they could hear the double rap of his staff on the front door, which always annoyed Hicks, who would ostentatiously inspect the paintwork for damage before deigning to receive any letters from the bag. Still craning her neck, Rosamund said, 'There's Hicks come out now. Oh such fun! He's taken out his handkerchief and he's polishing the door, and the postman's as cross as two sticks! I wish I might hear what they're saying to each other. Hicks has taken the letter now. Oh, he's having to pay! I wonder who it's from?'

'Rosamund, come away from the window now. It's time we started our lessons,' said Miss Trotton.

The door opened and Lucy came in, and Rosamund moved extremely rapidly across the room to stand dutifully at her governess's side. Lucy favoured her with a frowning glance as she said, 'I shall be a quarter of an hour, girls, changing my clothes, and then we can go out. I heard the postman just now. I wonder if it might be a letter from your father, Polly?'

'Oh no, Mama, for I saw Hicks paying him, and Captain Haworth's letters would be franked,' Rosamund said.

Lucy looked at her coldly. 'Go to the schoolroom, Rosamund.'

'We were just leaving, your ladyship,' Miss Trotton said quickly, taking Rosamund's hand and heading for the door. She passed Hicks in the doorway, who had brought the letter on a tray. It was a single sheet of common paper, folded and crudely sealed.

'Thank you, Hicks. Have the barouche brought to the door in fifteen minutes, please.'

'Yes, my lady.'

Lucy broke the seal as she walked across to the window to get the better light. She unfolded the letter, read it through, and cried out, 'Good God, now what's to do?'

The three young women looked at her enquiringly. Lucy sat down on the window-seat and read the letter again, and then looked up at Hippolyta.

'It's from your sister,' she said. 'What the deuce has she done now?'

'Is she ill, ma'am?' Polly asked. For answer Lucy handed her the letter to read.

It was short and to the point. 'Dear Aunt,' it said, 'I cannot bear it here at school, so I am running away. Please do not worry about me, as I know where to go and what to do, and I shall be quite all right. I am sorry to be disobedient, but I know Papa would approve if he knew, because he always liked me to be independent. When he comes home I shall tell him everything. Your humble obedient niece, Africa Haworth.'

'Humble! Obedient!' Lucy said. 'What has the idiotic child done?'

'I expect she's run away to sea, Aunt Lucy,' Fanny said promptly. 'She was always talking about it at Morland Place. She wanted to be on a ship with her father.'

'Run away to sea?'

'Like you did, Aunt Lucy,' Fanny added sweetly.

Hippolyta frowned a warning at her, and said quickly, 'Aunt, is it certain she has gone? Perhaps she may have changed her mind, or been prevented; she may yet be at Queen Square.'

Lucy stood up, looking worried. 'Yes, that's the first thing to find out. I'll send Parslow to Bath at once with a letter —' She stopped, deep in thought. 'No, that's no good, it will waste time. If she has gone, a search must be made at once. I shall have to go myself.' She walked to the door and called back the butler, who had been walking very slowly down the passage in the hope of overhearing who the letter was from. 'Hicks! Send someone out to hire a chaise and the fastest horses they have. I am going at once to Bath. Tell Parslow he's coming with me, and send Docwra to my room to pack me a valise. I shall want to leave in fifteen minutes, no more.'

'Yes, my lady. And the barouche?'

'The barouche?' She glanced round at the expectant girls. 'Oh, I think you may still take your drive. There is no point in keeping you within doors. Moss shall go with you, and you may drive around the Park, but you must stay in the carriage. Polly, I look to you to see that you all behave exactly as if I were there.'

'Yes, Aunt Lucy,' Polly said, and prayed fervently that Fanny would hold her tongue and not say anything provocative until her aunt had gone. But Fanny, though her eyes were sparkling at the thought of an unsupervised outing, knew her own advantage, and said nothing.

Half an hour later the barouche was proceeding at the correctly sedate pace along the main carriageway in the Park, and the three girls were looking around them with a delight freshened by the fact of being out alone. Moss, the maid who attended to Minnie's and Polly's clothes, sat in the drop-seat very stiff and formal, her hands folded in her lap, her eyes gazing rigidly past the feather in Lady Flaminia's hat. Her presence was the official guarantee of propriety, but they all knew that there was nothing she could or would do to stop them enjoying themselves, provided they remained in the carriage.

'Now we shall have some fun!' Fanny said. 'I wish it weren't so deuced early — there's hardly anyone about!'

'Fanny, don't swear,' Polly said quietly. 'It isn't nice.'

'Aunt Lucy says "deuced" all the time,' Fanny pointed out.

'Anyway, there are lots of people about,' Polly said, realising the futility of that particular argument. 'Look, here comes Mrs Edgecumbe's carriage. Now do be proper, or she'll tell Aunt Lucy.'

'Oh, don't worry, Pol, I know how to behave to dowagers. Watch this.' And Fanny screwed up her mouth and fluttered her eyelashes, and when the carriage came opposite and Mrs Edgecumbe bowed, she placed a hand at her breast as though the honour was too overpowering, and she was about to faint away.

Despairingly, Polly tried to mask her with her body, and bowed politely and said, 'How do you do, Mrs Edgecumbe? How do you do, Miss Edgecumbe, Miss Tulvey? Isn't it a fine day, ma'am?'

'Miss Haworth,' Mrs Edgecumbe said grudgingly, casting her sharp eyes over the occupants of the carriage. 'How come you girls are out without a chaperone?'

'We have our maid with us, ma'am,' Polly said in her gentlest manner. 'Lady Aylesbury was called away on urgent business just as we set out, and did not want to deprive us of our fresh air.'

'Oh yes, she always was one for fresh air,' Mrs Edgecumbe said, 'All you Morlands are. You'll be at Lady Tewkesbury's tonight, I suppose? Miss Tulvey is to open the ball with Lord Somercott. It will be a match at last, you mark my words. Lady Flaminia, the button of your glove is undone. Attention to detail, child, that's the way to succeed in life. Good morning.'

The carriages parted.

'Hideous old witch,' Fanny said as soon as they were out of earshot. 'And why does Violet Edgecumbe always wear fawn and pink? It doesn't become her. It makes her look like a plate of brawn.'

'I suppose Miss Tulvey was with them to keep her out of her mother's way,' Polly said. 'Lady Tewkesbury must have a great deal to do before tonight.'

'Poor Corinna Tulvey! Does she really think her mama will get Somercott for her? Mousey thing! You watch tonight. I shall cut her out with him.'

'Oh Fanny, why do you say such things? Anyway, if she's to open the ball with Lord Somercott, that means it's all arranged.'

'Only the first dance. Watch me for the rest! Ah look, here come Mr Brummell and Sir Henry Mildmay! John, pull up here,' she called to the coachman.

The two gentlemen halted their horses beside the barouche, and chatted good-naturedly with Lucy's protégées. Fanny was at her best with Mr Brummell: fearing his sharp tongue and his vast influence, she spoke in a lively, witty, but perfectly proper way, making him smile once or twice, but never offending. Mildmay had an aesthetic admiration for Polly's beauty, and engaged her in conversation so that he could legitimately look at her. No-one could get more than a silent smile out of Minnie, who liked Polly to shine, but had no ambition to be noticed herself.

While they were still thus grouped, three other horsemen came up and touched their hats to the company, and after a few moments of general conversation, Brummell and Mildmay rode on, leaving the girls in the company of Lord Harvey Sale, Lord Somercott and Lord Petersfield.

Now Fanny became even brighter, and managed to sparkle in two directions at once. Petersfield would rather have liked to pay his compliments to Flaminia, who had almost achieved a dimple on seeing him approach, but he was allowed no more than a bow and a tentative smile in her direction before Fanny addressed a remark to him which drew him into conversation with her and Somercott.

Somercott was a lively, though commonplace young man, easily distracted, fond of making himself pleasant; Petersfield was tall, thin, rather serious and shy, and unused to being flattered by vibrant young women. He swallowed nervously once or twice, but as Fanny continually referred Somercott's remarks to him for his opinion, he began to enjoy himself. Fanny was in her element, playing the young men like musical instruments, working on their weaknesses: she praised Somercott's coat and his dancing, and admired Petersfield's intellect and propriety.

Lord Harvey, meanwhile, was being agreeable on the other side of the carriage, finding the silent Flaminia no barrier to his conversation with Hippolyta.

'Have you heard from your father recently, Miss Haworth? I hear great things of him from Melville. That engagement of his off Palermo was the completest thing of its kind! He took two prizes, I understand, and destroyed a battery. You must be very proud of him.'

'It's kind of you to say so, Lord Harvey. The pity of it is that his success means we do not see him at home. His request for leave last year was denied because he was needed in the Mediterranean, and now it seems less likely than ever that he will be spared.'

'Ah yes, that's the price our sailor heroes pay for keeping us all safe in our beds!' He smiled at her, loving the way her dark lashes brushed her perfect cheek; but hoping for a glimpse of the heavenly blue eyes, too, he said, 'I don't know if I'm speaking out of turn, Miss Haworth, but I have heard that there's some thought amongst Their Lordships of an honour for him, after Palermo. Scorton was very strong, I know, for a baronetcy.'

It worked. She looked up at him, and he saw a faint flush of colour enhance her cheeks. 'Is that true, sir?'

'I should not have mentioned it, ma'am, if it were not extremely likely. Sir George Haworth would sound vastly well, don't you think? It would be a delightful thing for you and your sister, though I'm sure the honour is less than he deserves.'

Her sister! Polly's thoughts turned to Africa, hoping again that she had been prevented from leaving the shelter of the school. Surely they must keep a close watch on the girls in their charge? Probably she was still there, thwarted but safe, doing her lessons. Polly had had very little to do with Africa in their lives, too little to have any deep affection for her, but she couldn't help worrying, all the same, about one so closely tied to her in blood.

'Have I said something to upset you, Miss Haworth?' Sale asked, watching her face.

'Oh — no, not at all! I beg your pardon. I was thinking of some news I had this morning — a little disturbing. It's nothing, really.'

'It will not prevent you from attending the ball tonight, I hope?' he asked.

Polly lifted her eyes to his again, and lowered them, feeling too much to be able to hold the glance. 'No, I'm sure — that is, I believe we shall be there.'

Sale smiled with satisfaction. 'Then, Miss Haworth, may I be so bold as to request your hand for the first two dances — if it has not already been bestowed elsewhere?' He watched her delightful confusion, thinking, damnit, she's the most beautiful creature I've ever seen — and all sensibility!

'No, it is not bestowed elsewhere, sir,' she murmured.

'Then — may I hope for the honour?'

Polly's answer was almost inaudible, but undeniably affirmative.

Sale smiled about him, and drew in a deep breath. 'What a perfectly beautiful day it is, don't you think? Somercott, Petersfield! Ladies, we must bid you adieu — until tonight, that is. Miss Morland, Lady Flaminia — Miss Haworth!'

He touched his hat and bowed to all three, but his eyes were on Hippolyta, and he was rewarded by a brief but feeling flash of blue from under the long lashes.

'Well,' said Fanny as the carriage moved on, 'that was very satisfactory, I must say. How did you get on, Polly? Did he ask you to dance? It's a great thing to have at least one dance spoken for beforehand. It makes the men more eager when you can refuse them and say you are already engaged, especially when they come up to you at the very beginning.'

'You don't mean that Lord Somercott asked you to dance?' Polly said, managing to avoid answering the first question.

'Certainly,' Fanny said promptly. 'I couldn't get him to give up the two first with Corinna Tulvey — I suppose he's too afraid of Lady Tewkesbury — but I'm engaged to him for the two second. That suits me well enough, for I mean to lead off with Freddy Petersfield.'

Hippolyta, aware of a movement of Flaminia's shoulders beside her, said quickly, 'Has he asked you to?'

'Oh, he's such a slow-top, I was obliged to ask him,' Fanny laughed.

'Fanny you couldn't have! It's most improper,' Polly said. Minnie was looking the other way, apparently studying a passing tree with close attention.

'Oh, not directly. Don't be such a goose, Polly. There are ways of doing these things you know. It is easy enough, once you know how, to twist the conversation around until a man pretty well has to say what you want him to, or appear damnably rude. Good manners in a man are a great thing! What are you staring at Moss? Keep your eyes — and your ears — to yourself, if you please.'

'Well, anyway,' Polly said, her own pleasure fading as she thought of it, 'we probably shan't be going to the ball. With Aunt Lucy in Bath, and all the worry over Africa —'

'Pho! Africa's all right,' Fanny said robustly. 'Ten to one she hasn't gone anywhere — and if she has, what of it? They'll find her all right. And as for Aunt Lucy's being away — what's that to us? Trotton can take us — that's perfectly respectable.'

'She wouldn't — not without Aunt Lucy's instructions.'

'I can persuade her. Or there's always Lady Chelmsford. Leave me alone for it, Polly — we'll go one way or another, you can be sure. I'm not staying at home just because your goose of a sister has made a fool of herself.'

CHAPTER NINETEEN

Lucy must have passed the express carrying a letter for her from Mrs Touchstone somewhere on the road, for when she arrived at Queen Square at about half-past six that evening, she found them expecting her, though not so soon.

'Upon my word, your ladyship must have flown here!' cried Mrs Touchstone.

'She is gone then?' Lucy said. 'I hoped it might be a false alarm, when I got her letter.'

'She wrote to you? Oh, I understand now how you come to be here so soon! Did she say where she was going, your ladyship?'

'If she had, do you think I would be here?' Lucy said impatiently. 'Tell me what happened.'

'Well, my lady, we discovered she was missing this morning. The maid, Betty, went up to wake the young ladies as usual, and Miss Haworth's bed was empty.'

'Had she taken anything with her?'

'It is difficult to say, your ladyship,' Mrs Touchstone said unhappily. 'Betty thinks she has taken some clothes, but certainly not all of them. Some of her personal possessions are gone, and her brushes and toilet things.'

'And what has been done?'

'Oh, we have all the other boarders confined in one room, with Miss Scully watching over them,' Mrs Touchstone began.

'Why, do you think them all so likely to escape? Upon my word, ma'am, there has been some mismanagement here! How did you come to let a child of fourteen walk out of the house with a bag in her hand, and not to try to stop her?'

'A bag, your ladyship?'

'If she had clothes and other possessions with her, she must have been carrying a bag,' Lucy pointed out.

'Your ladyship is such a clear thinker! But she must have

375

gone during the night, for she was here at supper-time; and indeed, at night there would be no-one to see her go.'

'Is not the street door kept locked?'

'No, my lady, only bolted on the inside. We have never before worried about keeping people in, only undesirables out. There was no reason to suppose any of our young ladies wished to leave us.'

'Or to get out of the house on mischief?' Lucy asked dangerously.

Mrs Touchstone coloured. 'We have never considered the need to lock them up like animals. These are well-born young ladies. I'm sure none of them would do anything so unprincipled. And if they wished to,' she added with more spirit, 'if they were determined on something of the sort, I doubt whether one locked door would stop them.'

Lucy considered herself at fourteen; she thought of Fanny; and was forced to the conclusion that Mrs Touchstone was right. She appreciated for the first time how her own mother must have felt when she ran away from home; she would not allow herself to consider at that juncture how much her own example had inspired her niece.

'Well, leaving that aside,' she said briskly, 'have you questioned the other girls? Someone must know when she left last night, and where she was going. Who was her particular friend? She probably confided in someone.'

'If your ladyship would care to question the young ladies, I shall be happy for you to make use of my sitting room,' Mrs Touchstone said faintly.

'Very well. Meanwhile enquiries had better be made at all the coaching inns, and of the Watch and the hackney-drivers, in case someone saw her. Have you footmen for the job? And find out who her closest friend was, and send her in to me, if you please.'

Mrs Touchstone, considerably cowed by the brisk way Lady Aylesbury handled the matter, went away to do her bidding. A little later she came back, escorting a shrinking girl into the Presence. 'This is Julia Johnson, your ladyship.'

Lucy waved Mrs Touchstone away, and gestured the child to a chair. Julia Johnson was small and fair, with large foolish eyes, and she perched on the edge of her seat looking terrified, wringing her hands in her lap.

'You are Africa's particular friend? Speak up, child, I'm not going to bite you.'

'Well, ma'am, I suppose so.'

'You suppose so?' Lucy snapped.

'She wasn't one to mix very much, ma'am,' Julia whispered. 'She kept herself to herself. Her cousin Sophie was her intimate friend while she was here, ma'am, but since she came back on her own, ma'am, she hasn't talked to anyone very much.'

'To you more than others?' Lucy asked, trying to soften her voice. 'Did she tell you anything about her plans?'

Julia looked as though she might cry. 'No, ma'am.'

'Come now, she must have said something.'

'No ma'am, truly. When she came back, she said she wasn't going to stay here, that's all.'

'She wasn't going to stay here? What do you mean? Tell me exactly what she said, if you please.'

'She said — she said she hated it here, and that no-one could make her stay. "I've got a plan," she said, ma'am, "and one day you'll wake up and find me gone".'

'And did you?'

'Ma'am?'

'Did you wake up and find her gone?'

'Oh no, ma'am. She never went to bed.'

Lucy stared. 'What?'

'She was the last one to use the closet, ma'am, and she was still in there when I went to bed. I fell asleep, but I woke up a while later, and her bed was still empty.'

'What time was that, do you know?'

'I heard the church clock strike twelve before I fell asleep again, ma'am,' Julia said after a hesitation.

Lucy looked grim. 'And you never thought to tell anyone that she had gone?'

Now Julia really did cry. 'I didn't know she'd gone! Really I didn't! I thought she was still in the closet!'

Lucy saw there was no more to be got out of her, and dismissed her. Questioning the other girls produced no more useful information than that Africa had been very quiet at supper, and had refused a game of spillikins, saying she had to write a letter. Since that letter was nowhere in evidence, it seemed likely that it had been an excuse to go to the dormitory and make her preparations.

The enquiries at the stage-coach office and the post-houses proving negative, Lucy consulted Parslow.

'If she left before midnight last night,' she said grimly, 'she has a good start on us. None of these fools seems to have done anything. She doesn't seem to have confided in anyone, so we must guess for ourselves as best we can.'

'Miss Africa would most likely head for the sea, my lady,' Parslow suggested.

'That was my thought. But where?'

'Portsmouth, my lady,' said Parslow, so promptly that Lucy knew he had been thinking about it already.

'Bristol is nearer — a great deal nearer,' Lucy said.

'Yes, my lady, but Miss Africa doesn't know Bristol. Besides, if she is trying to get to her father, my lady, Bristol would be no use to her. There's a good fast road direct from Bath to Portsmouth, which I reckon she would know. My guess is that she'd go that way. If she hasn't taken the stage or the mail, she'd probably walk and hope to beg a ride.'

'That's what I think, too. We must go in pursuit, Parslow. She's my responsibility.'

He didn't waste time arguing with her. 'We'll check at the turnpikes, my lady. If she went through, someone will have seen her.'

'Pray God we catch up with her before something happens,' Lucy said quietly.

At the end of a fortnight Lucy returned to London, leaving Parslow behind to continue the search, with the aid of agents hired for the purpose. She was reluctant to go, but as he pointed out to her, there was nothing she could do that he could not, and her presence was required in London, where her sudden disappearance, in the middle of the Season in which she was bringing out three protégées, was bound to cause speculation.

As soon as she was in residence again, she received a polite visit of enquiry from George Brummell.

'How the deuce did you know about it?' she asked, not pleased.

The Beau shrugged. 'My man told me. How does one ever find out anything? You found no trace of her, then?'

378

Lucy sat down and passed a hand across her brow. 'We enquired at every pike and inn on the Portsmouth road, at the Dockyard and at all the inns in Portsmouth. We spoke to every boatman and idler on the Hard. She seems to have vanished from the face of the earth.'

'Perhaps she didn't go to Portsmouth,' he said quietly.

'But where else would she go? She didn't go to Morland Place, that we know, and she hasn't come here. The only other thing she could do is to try to reach her father.' She paused, and then added in a low voice, 'It's the kind of mad-cap thing she would do — especially since I'm famous for having run away to sea when I was her age. With my example before her —'

'You mustn't blame yourself,' Brummell said.

'Give me one reason why I shouldn't,' she said bitterly.

'I can give you three — your daughters, and the elder Miss Haworth. If your example was all that was needed to make a girl run away, there'd be no girls at home.' He looked at her bent head compassionately. 'Don't despair — she'll be found.'

'The best we hope is that she's managed to stow away aboard some ship or other,' Lucy said after a moment. 'If she did, and it set sail before she was discovered, that would explain why we haven't heard anything. Aboard any King's ship — well, any English ship at all — she'd be quite safe.'

'Yes, and sooner or later, she'd be delivered safe and sound either to her father, or to you,' he said.

The worst to fear was that she was dead, by accident, starvation, or at the hands of some ruffian of the road. But that was a possibility Lucy had never voiced, being too horrible to be thought of.

Mr Brummell begged to be instructed, if there were any way in which he could be of service: his person, his intellect, and his influence were equally at her ladyship's service.

'There seems to be nothing to do, that isn't already being done,' Lucy said. 'But thank you for asking.'

He bowed. 'Then, if there is nothing to be done, dear ma'am, let us try not to think about it any more. Let me entertain you instead with the gossip.'

'I haven't seen a newspaper since I left London,' Lucy said, making an effort for his sake.

'Oh, you want the news first?' Brummell said, making a

moue. 'Very well, let us have it over with. You heard, I suppose, that we have revoked the Orders in Council, in an attempt to placate the Americans?'

Lucy grunted, hardly attending. 'We should have dropped them last year, when Boney began issuing licences again.'

'Ah yes, I forget that you have Lord Anstey to teach you about financial matters,' Brummell said politely. 'I never understood what it was all about. I rely on you, ma'am, to tell me anything I need to know.'

'Why do you like pretending to be a fool, George?' Lucy said with a reluctant smile. 'What else has happened?'

'Oh, Boney sent us an offer of peace in the Peninsula, that's all.'

'What!' She looked up, startled.

'Provided we accepted his brother Joseph as King of Spain.'

'A most reasonable condition.'

'Quite. Castlereagh had no hesitation in telling His Imperial Majesty what we thought of it. So it's back to the old, slow grind, which, we are assured, wears away mountains in time. I fear our friends will be a long time coming home,' he said, giving her a look askance. 'But Wiske will be due for some leave very soon. He has been out there a year. We may look forward to seeing him this summer, I expect.'

'So what was Boney up to?' Lucy said, ignoring the jibe. 'He must have known we'd refuse.'

'It was a vain hope, but he had nothing to lose. He was clearing the way for his invasion of Russia, it seems. The Csar won't come out and fight, so he has to go in. Boney himself was in Danzig three weeks ago, inspecting the troops, so it looks as though he means to lead the army in person. Let's hope he has started what he can't finish.'

'The Russians aren't the world's best soldiers,' Lucy said doubtfully. 'Look at Austerlitz. Look at Friedland.'

'It may be different when they're on their own ground, defending themselves against invasion,' Brummell said. 'A man naturally fights best when he has something he values to protect.'

Lucy smiled. 'You sounded quite sensible then, George.'

'My dear ma'am, it was the merest oversight. Let me instantly become properly frivolous again. What can I tell you of real moment? Ah yes, I am quite settled in my new lodgings, at Chapel Street, with all my pretty things about me; except for my favourite sweetmeat dish — you know the flower-encrusted one, with the entwined cupids on the stem — which a villainous brigand masquerading as a footman dropped on the stairs! Your enterprising cousin, Lady Greyshott, has begun a new intrigue with Sir Geoffrey Cavendish. He keeps a miniature portrait of her right eye in his breast-pocket — quite a horror, I assure you! Puts one in mind of a fishmonger's slab. And I have just had the most delicious new waistcoat delivered from Guthrie's — grey toilinette, with a remote-purple stripe — which I shall wear to Mrs Kirklington's crush tonight, so I hope you will be there to see it.'

'Oh — I don't know — I hadn't thought —' Lucy said vaguely.

'Dear ma'am, you must think! Now you are back in Town, you must escort your protégées, or there will be despair and probably suicide amongst the young men of the *ton*. It would be quite a crime to nip in the bud such a promising inclination as that between Lord Harvey Sale and Miss Haworth, and Miss Morland's admirers are legion.'

'Hippolyta and Harvey Sale?' Lucy said.

'He courts her assiduously,' Brummell nodded. 'It's quite pretty to see them, for she puts the rest of womanhood to shame for modesty and propriety, and Sale has aged fifty years in manner. He has become quite courtly — Versailles come to London, you know.'

'I feel as if I have been away a very long time,' Lucy said, shaking her head.

'You have,' said Brummell solemnly. 'Too long.'

June became July. No news was forthcoming of Africa's whereabouts, and Parslow returned to London, leaving the continued search in the hands of Lucy's agents. Through her friends in the Admiralty, enquiries were put in hand to discover if she had been found aboard any of the King's ships, but such enquiries would inevitably be long in answering. Meanwhile there was nothing to be done but to wait, and hope, and in Lucy's case, to feel wretchedly guilty and anxious. Mr Brummell, Miss Trotton and Parslow continued to try to convince her that Africa must be safe somewhere at sea;

but the image would haunt her mind of a body tumbled somewhere in a ditch.

The news came that Bonaparte had indeed invaded Russia, crossing the river Nieman on 23 June with the largest army ever assembled in Europe, over six hundred thousand men, more than half of whom where Prussians, Poles, Italians, and other allied troops. News also came that the Congress of America had declared war on England on 19 June, despite the fact that the Orders in Council, against which they were largely protesting, had already been revoked. It was a war without a point before it even began, but it meant that the American navy of sixteen large frigates and a hundred and sixty-five gunboats were now hostile vessels, and sufficient to prove a serious nuisance to the British merchant ships' carrying trade.

One afternoon in July, Harvey Sale waited on his brother in his house in Bond Street. Wyndham liked to keep up a certain ceremony in all his doings, which did not quite suit Lord Harvey, who lived in plain but convenient lodgings in Ryder Street. Wyndham kept him waiting just long enough to emphasise the difference in their rank, and then came bustling in, arrayed in a dressing-gown of startling design.

'Good God, George, what are you wearing?'

'What, this?' Wyndham feigned a casual surprise. 'Haven't you seen one like it before? It's Chinese, or Indian, or something of that sort. I believe Prinny has one something the same.'

'It's perfectly devilish. Don't tell me you put that on when you first get up in the morning? The colours are enough to drive your eyes back into your head.'

'Yes, well, I didn't ask you here to discuss my clothes,' Wyndham said hastily, 'I was talkin' to Fleetwood this morning, and he asked me about you and Miss Haworth.'

'Fleetwood talks too much,' Harvey said. 'And if he's so interested in my affairs, he might as well talk to me about them.'

'Well, naturally he didn't think there was any harm in asking me. Dammit, I am your brother!'

'So you are, George. And what did you want to see me about?'

'I've told you — Miss Haworth. Fleetwood asked me if it

382

was a case between you and her. Put me in a damned awkward position, I can tell you! I didn't know what to say!'

Harvey controlled his temper. 'You might have told him to mind his own business, I suppose. Or told him that it was none of yours.'

Wyndham mottled. 'It certainly is my business, if my brother is paying enough attention to a girl to make people think he means to marry her.'

'Perhaps I do mean to marry her,' Sale said, 'though what it's got to do with you I can't imagine.'

'You're my brother, damnit!'

'So you have said already.'

'And when the Guv'nor hangs up his tile, which won't be long, I shall be head of the family. It's very much my business when my brother and heir presumptive thinks of marrying and don't even consult me!'

'Consult you?'

'Look here, Harvey, this Miss Haworth — perfectly nice girl, and all that, but who is she? Nobody! Nothin' against her father — sailor hero and all that — but he ain't one of us, and neither is she.'

'What are you talking about? Her connections are more than good. She is first cousin to the Earl of Aylesbury.'

'Only on the distaff side.'

'Miss Haworth is a gentlewoman by birth and education, and I'll thank you to keep your tongue to yourself,' Sale said dangerously. His attentions to Hippolyta had not, until then, been made with any very serious intention. He thought her the prettiest girl in London, without necessarily intending more than to pass an agreeable Season flirting mildly with her; but his brother's interference set up his bristles, and made him begin to think that to marry Miss Haworth might not be a bad idea at all.

Wyndham breathed heavily through his nose. 'Don't get on your high ropes, old fellow. As I said, Miss Haworth's a perfectly decent sort of female —'

'She's the most beautiful girl in the world,' Sale said. 'And the most modest. Her gentleness, the excellence of her understanding —'

'Yes, yes, yes,' Wyndham said, waving all that away, 'but the fact remains she ain't out of the top drawer; and she's no dowry worth speakin' of. It won't do, Harvey, and that's what I asked you here to tell you. You can't marry her, and that's that.'

Sale reddened with anger. 'And how do you propose to stop me?'

Wyndham looked unhappy. 'Damnit, Harvey, I don't want to come to cuffs with you. Can't you see it's impossible? You could have anyone you want, any girl in London —'

'I don't want any girl in London. I want Miss Haworth.'

'What about the reversion? You know I ain't in the petticoat line. The Guv'nor's always looked to you for the son-and-heir bit, and damnit, I have too. Pick the right filly, and I'll back you all the way. But this Miss Haworth — you can't see her as Marchioness of Penrith, now can you?'

'Whether I can or whether I can't, I ask again, how do you propose to stop me from marrying the woman of my choice?' Sale said.

Wyndham's expression hardened. 'If you mean to make a fight of it, Harvey, you'll soon find out. I can get the Guv'nor to stop your allowance to begin with. You'd find that pretty damned uncomfortable. There are your debts of honour — you've been having some pretty deep doings lately at Watiers, so I hear, and if they are called in and you haven't a feather to fly with —'

'You may go to the devil,' Sale said ferociously, and stormed out, slamming the door behind him. Wyndham stared at the closed door for a while, deep in thought, and then called for his manservant.

'Have the carriage brought round, will you, Rundell? I'm goin' to pay a call on Lady Aylesbury.'

Lucy was not entirely surprised to receive a visit from the Earl of Wyndham. After Brummell's hint to her about Lord Harvey Sale, she had watched him and Hippolyta at various dances and assemblies, and had seen that he preferred her to any other girl of the Season. She was a little surprised at Sale's choice, for a young man in his position could have looked higher as far as rank was concerned; but she was ready to admit that Polly was an excellent young woman, and though her dowry would be small, she would make any man a fine wife. She thought it would not be very long, therefore, before his family wished to discuss the matter.

The Earl began in his usual way with formal compliments and heavy circumlocutions, and having endured as much of this as she could, Lucy cut through it all briskly.

'Had you something in particular you wished to speak to me about, Wyndham?'

He blinked, but managed to take it in his stride. 'Well, yes, ma'am, in fact I have. The best subject in the world, I believe,' he added with ponderous humour, 'to a mother with a daughter in the marriage-mart.'

Lucy raised an eyebrow. 'A daughter?'

'Yes, ma'am — Lady Flaminia has been enjoying her first Season, I hope?'

She looked at the stout young man, whose stiff shirt-points served to emphasise the fullness of his jowls. In his late twenties, he already looked ten years older, and he had long been supposed, from his way of life, to be indifferent to females; but his father, the Marquis, was known to be in poor health, so perhaps Wyndham had decided it was time to do his duty.

'You wish to marry my daughter?' she asked bluntly.

Wyndham's colour increased richly. 'Me? Good God, no, ma'am!' he spluttered, and then realised how rudely he had spoken, and hastened to say, 'That is, Lady Flaminia is all excellence, of course! A most modest — intelligent — ah, beautiful girl! But I'm not in the petticoat line, ma'am, as you know. Never have been! Despair of m' parents!' He gave a nervous laugh.

'Lord Wyndham, pray compose yourself and tell me what it is you wish to propose,' Lucy said with diminishing patience.

'Propose! Yes — that's the word. A proposition of marriage, ma'am, between your excellent daughter, and my brother, Lord Harvey Sale.'

Lucy stared. 'Lord Harvey? But I thought — that is, there is some misunderstanding here, surely? Lord Harvey has been paying attention to my niece, Miss Haworth. I was not aware that he had any inclination towards my daughter.'

Wyndham wriggled in his chair. 'Let us be frank with each other, ma'am! My brother is young and perhaps a little head-strong. Young people do not always know their own interest. A match between him and Lady Flaminia would be highly desirable, I believe, to all parties. It is by no means below Lady Flaminia's touch. I don't mean to marry myself, ma'am, so the reversion will come to my brother. He will be Marquis of Penrith when the Guv'nor and I are gone. And for his part, an earl's daughter with twenty thousand pounds is an excellent catch, leaving aside Lady Flaminia's many personal charms. It seems to me to be an arrangement of benefit to everyone — what do you say, ma'am?'

Lucy frowned. 'Let us be clear about this. Does your brother wish to marry Lady Flaminia?'

Wyndham looked cunning. 'As the acting head of the family, Lady Aylesbury, and soon to be head indeed, I can say that I take the keenest interest in Harvey's matrimonial arrangements. My approval is necessary for him to marry at all, for without my approval, he will find himself quite without income, and his wife without establishment. My approval would be most willingly bestowed upon a match between him and Lady Flaminia. Indeed, I am so very eager for it, that the thought of his marrying anyone else would make me very unhappy indeed. I trust I make myself clear?'

'Quite clear,' Lucy said. 'I must have time to consider this.'

'Of course, ma'am. The details of settlements, I'm sure, can be arranged to our common satisfaction.'

'Oh, I'm sure of that. That doesn't concern me.' She rose and pulled the bell, and Wyndham took his cue and rose too. 'Does Lord Harvey know his own happiness?' Lucy asked as Hicks opened the door.

'Not entirely, ma'am. That is, I have not told him how fortunate he is. Of the — shall we say — negative side of the affair, he is fully aware.'

He bowed and retreated, leaving Lucy with plenty to think about.

Fanny and Hippolyta, with the addition of Miss Trotton and Rosamund, were taking a little horseback exercise in the Park. Flaminia had stayed at home, for she disliked very much to ride, and her figure did not appear to advantage atop a horse. It was an arrangement very much to Fanny's taste, for Miss Trotton's attention was largely claimed by Rosamund, leaving the two elder girls much more liberty than if they rode alone with Lucy. Fanny was aware that Hippolyta looked very well on a horse, but she was learning to live with Polly's beauty, for as the Season advanced, she had seen just how much her cousin was admired — which was a great deal at a distance, and much less close up. Polly's cool, grave manners were not conciliating to young men on the flirt, and her lack of dowry repulsed those who were seriously seeking a wife. Only Lord Harvey Sale had remained a constant admirer, but Fanny had long believed he meant nothing by it; and indeed, for the last week, nothing had been seen of him.

Fanny, on the other hand, was everyone's favourite — except the mamas with daughters on their hands. She was pretty, lively, and very rich, and those who were not attracted to her of their own free will, she pursued and captivated of hers. It was the best game in the world, she decided, to make men in love with you; and her father, had he been in Town to witness it, would have been perfectly satisfied, for she was the most successful *débutante* of the Season, but had given her heart to no-one.

There was no-one, she felt, who was worthy of her. She had brought Lord Somercott to the brink of an offer, but she would not have taken him if he had offered, for he was only a baron, and she did not mean to wed below an earl. Other men had actually proposed, but they were mostly gazetted fortune-hunters, and she was shrewd enough to recognise those when they came in her way. She would be very rich when she finally came into her property, but she didn't intend to waste what was hers by paying off a husband's debts and mortgages.

The tributes she liked the best were the genuine sighs of passion from men who knew they had no chance with her, but could not help themselves. She actively encouraged one or two of them — like Mr Paston and Sir Henry Hope — partly for the pleasure of being adored, and partly to annoy her less smitten but more eligible suitors.

It was, however, sometimes just a *little* dull not to be in love. Occasionally she felt it, and just occasionally she admitted to herself that she envied Polly her interesting situation. She felt she would like to be a little in love: it would make the chase so much more interesting. Of course she quite saw that if one were very much in love, it could be inconvenient; and that if the love led to serious considerations of marriage, that was an end of the game. No, just a mild involvement of the heart — just enough to cause an interesting flutter when the object came into the room — was what she wanted.

Polly, she thought, was probably too far in. She glanced sideways at her cousin under the brim of her hat as they walked their horses along the tan beside the carriageway, and thought Polly was unusually silent, and looking a little pale. Fretting over the defection of her lover, Fanny thought impatiently.

'Is Harvey Sale out of Town, Polly?' she asked. 'I didn't see him at the assembly last night. Or at Mrs Fairfax's rout on Tuesday.'

'No, he wasn't there. I have no idea where he is,' she said evenly. 'Perhaps he may be in the country.'

'I should have thought he'd tell you if he was going away.' Fanny said with a private smile.

Polly raised her beautifully arched eyebrows. 'He is not obliged to account to me for his movements,' she said, and she turned her head away, but not quickly enough to prevent Fanny from seeing the vexed flush, or the bite of the lips. Much too far in! Fanny thought triumphantly; but then the distant view of some horsemen distracted her attention.

'Let's canter on a little, Pol — come,' she said, and before Polly could answer, sent her mare on. Hippolyta was obliged to follow suit, or Fanny would have been quite alone; as it was, the two young women were soon well ahead of Miss Trotton and Rosamund, though still within sight. Fanny pulled up just enough short of the gentlemen to avoid the charge of seeking them out, and a moment later they were touching their hats and gathering round. Fanny patted her mare's neck, pushed her curls back over her shoulder, turned her head this way and that, all in the most fetching manner. Her new habit had the fashionable Hussar frogging, which looked well on her womanly figure, and her hat was one of her own design, with a wide brim over which a long ostrich feather curled, and under which she could give soft bewitching glances at her admirers.

Two of them had red coats — Mr Beauchamp and Sir Harry Henderson, on leave from the Peninsula, and more than ready for a light flirtation with the delicious Miss Morland.

'We will see you at Vauxhall on Friday, won't we, Miss Morland?' Mr Beauchamp said. 'It is to be our last outing before we're recalled to duty, ain't it, Harry? We want a little fun and gig to remember when we are back on campaign, starving on the Tagus.'

Fanny glanced over her shoulder to see how far away Miss Trotton was, and gave them a dimpled smile. 'At Vauxhall? How can you think it? I am told it is a very vulgar place, and that the lower orders may enter it for a small sum and stare at their betters.'

'Vulgar! No, never say it!'

'It's the most delightful place in the world! You can't imagine if you've never been there.'

'There are lovely groves, and coloured lights in the trees, and one may stroll about and listen to music, and take a little supper in one of the pavilions.'

'And be as private as one pleases,' Sir Harry added, *sotto voce*, with a significant look.

Hippolyta, alarmed and disgusted, turned her head away. Fanny gave her an exasperated look, and said to Mr Beauchamp, 'Now, gentlemen, you see how you offend our modesty. I'm sure one could not be *seen* at Vauxhall and retain one's credit.'

Her slight emphasis made Beauchamp edge his horse nearer. 'Many ladies, of course, go masked,' he murmured. 'There is much more fun to be had in observing others, if one is oneself unobserved.'

Fanny gave him a glance under her eyelashes, and then said loudly, 'Ah, there is the good Miss Trotton and my cousin! We must be riding on, gentlemen. I'm sure —'

She broke off, her eyes widening in surprise, as a gentleman on foot paused on the path nearby and raised his hand to his hat. In civilian clothes he looked quite different; but she could not forget the glossy military whiskers, or the secretly-gleaming eyes which were watching her with amusement, as if they knew exactly what she was up to. The military gentlemen looked in astonishment as her cheeks first paled and then glowed, never having seen Miss Morland discomposed. She gave a graceful bow from the saddle, and was even more disconcerted when he bowed in return, and then resumed his stroll. Why did he not stop and speak? Piqued, Fanny stared

389

after him; and then straightened in the saddle, and as Miss Trotton and Rosamund joined them, bid the gentlemen a terse farewell and rode on, her eyes bright and her lips a little compressed.

'Who was that gentleman, Fanny? He seemed to know you,' Polly asked.

'It was a Mr Hawker — an acquaintance of my grandfather's. I met him in Manchester last year,' Fanny said abruptly. Polly looked at her sideways in surprise, but did not pursue the matter. She was not to know that Fanny had just felt the flutter she had been idly wishing for, and had found it more disturbing than she had bargained for.

The Earl of Wyndham sought out his brother at White's, and drawing him into a private room, flourished a letter, already opened, whose seal bore the Aylesbury coronet.

'Well, Harvey, I have here Lady Aylesbury's final answer. Shall I read it to you?'

Lord Harvey leaned against a high-backed armchair and picked idly at the trim. 'You may save yourself the effort. Just tell me what you have been deciding between you.'

Wyndham looked at him more kindly. 'I have only your best interests at heart, Harvey. I'm deuced fond of you. I wouldn't go to all this trouble on your behalf if I wasn't.'

'What trouble? The trouble of trying to separate me from the woman I love?'

'Come now, there's no need for that sort of talk. Miss Haworth is a nice girl, but there are plenty more fish in the sea.'

Harvey jerked his head irritably. 'Spare me your platitudes! I suppose you have enlisted Lady Aylesbury's help in parting us. You might as well have left it alone. I've neglected my dear girl so badly this last week, she probably hates me utterly.'

Wyndham looked startled at the choice of words. 'You haven't declared yourself to Miss Haworth? You haven't done anything foolish?'

'No, of course not. I couldn't ask her to marry me, until I know that I can support her as she ought to be supported. That's why I've been avoiding her — curse my cowardice! Until I've persuaded you to let me have her, I dare not let myself —'

Wyndham waved away the rest of the speech. 'You may forget all that, my dear brother, for Lady Aylesbury has said that she would categorically refuse your suit to Miss Haworth, should you be foolhardy enough to press it. She is in *loco parentis*, of course, while the good Captain is away — which is likely to be for a long time.'

'What? Refuse? You mean you've *persuaded* her to refuse!' Sale straightened up, his eyes glittering. 'Why, you unspeakable swine —'

'Oh do stop blethering, Harvey,' Wyndham said, looking pleased with himself. 'You haven't heard the all yet. Lady A. has agreed, on the most generous terms, for you to marry her daughter, the lovely Lady Flaminia. The settlements are all worked out, the Guv'nor approves, and all that's wanted now is to decide the date. You're a lucky man, Harvey, for she's one of the best catches of the Season, I can tell you!'

'You can tell me nothing about women! Lady Flaminia? How can you even mention her in the same breath as Miss Haworth? What is all this nonsense?'

'An earl's daughter — twenty thousand pounds, that's what I'm talking about. A generous allowance from the Guv'nor, and the Stainton estate for your own, absolutely your own, until you inherit the title. I repeat, you're a lucky man. Lady Flaminia's a sweet girl.'

'Your objections, then, don't cover the whole family?' Harvey said contemptuously. 'The blood is good enough now is it?'

'It's a different matter entirely,' Wyndham said, surprised. 'Surely you must see that? Lady Flaminia is the daughter of an earl. Well, I never liked Aylesbury — not the boy, I mean the late earl — but the Chetwyns are perfectly all right, and his mother was a Cavendish. Now I suggest that we visit Lady Aylesbury tomorrow morning, see the girl and all that sort of thing —'

'Oh no,' said Harvey, shaking his head and backing off. 'You may prevent me from marrying the woman of my choice, but you cannot force me to marry anyone else!'

Wyndham frowned. 'What are you talking about? Of course I can — in exactly the same way. The Guv'nor and I are agreed that this is a good match, and we want it concluded as quickly as possible. It's time there was an heir. It don't do to leave these things to chance.'

'An heir?' Sale said in disgust. 'My God, you talk as if I were breeding stock!'

'Well, so you are, in a way.'

'That's one thing you cannot force me to do.'

'Not force, exactly, but persuade. Your allowance will be doubled when the gal produces. I think that's an attractive offer, don't you?'

Sale's mouth twisted bitterly. 'My God, you think of everything, don't you?'

Wyndham smiled modestly. 'I try to. I think I have this time.' He looked at his brother kindly. 'Come, Harvey, be sensible! The girl's a perfectly nice little thing, no harm in her at all. You'll have a comfortable wife, a sufficient income, all the consequence you could wish for. Think of your duty, man! Think of the honour of the family. It ain't like you to be selfish and wilful. You were always Papa's favourite you know. It would break his heart if you were to go to the bad.'

Sale felt his stomach churning, as though he had physically eaten the horrible situation, which was violently disagreeing with him. Yet what could he do? A man could not live without money — certainly could not marry without money — and his was not a nature to thrive in poverty.

'Very well,' he said. 'You win — you and the power of money between you.'

'You mean — you'll marry Lady Flaminia?' Wyndham felt greatly relieved. He had not been sure, even though he pretended to be, how far his brother's passionate nature might drive him.

'Settle it how you please,' Sale said bitterly. 'I'll do my duty like a man. Just keep out of my way for a day or two, will you George?'

And he left the room without another word or a look.

Lucy came into the morning room where the three young ladies were sewing and talking over the previous evening's entertainment. They looked up as she came in — a little cautiously, for Lucy's temper had been uncertain since Africa's disappearance. Lucy surveyed them calmly and then said, 'Fanny, I would like you to take your work into the dining-parlour for a few minutes. I wish to talk to Polly and

Minnie alone. I will call you back when I have done.'

It was not a voice to be argued with. Fanny said, 'Yes Aunt,' meekly, picked up her work, and went into the next room, closing the double-doors behind her. It took no more than one second's battle with her conscience before she laid her ear to the join of the doors. One must fend for oneself in this world, she told herself firmly.

In the next room, Lucy began, 'This concerns you only indirectly, Polly, but I thought I might as well tell you together. I have arranged a match for you, Minnie — a most advantageous match, and I suppose I needn't tell you how lucky you are to be spoken for so handsomely in your first Season, when you are only sixteen?'

'I am to be married, Mama?' Minnie said, bewildered.

'Yes, married, and very soon. You will have an excellent establishment, a handsome allowance, and the very finest of prospects for the future. Your future husband's family want everything settled as quickly as possible, so I think I may safely say you will be married by the end of the summer.'

Minnie stared at her, too taken aback by the unexpected news to know what to think or say. Told that she was lucky, she tried to feel herself so, but the idea was too strange to her to be able to feel anything about it at all. Then she thought of Lord Petersfield, and a little flush of pleasure and trepidation passed through her. At last she managed to say, 'Who am I to marry, Mama?'

'Lord Harvey Sale,' Lucy said. Hippolyta gave a little gasp — as did the listening Fanny in the next room — but Lucy went on without heeding it. 'His brother, Lord Wyndham, has arranged everything with me in the handsomest manner. You will be Lady Harvey Sale, my dear, and at some time in the future, you will be the Marchioness of Penrith, for Wyndham doesn't mean to marry. As I said, Polly, this doesn't really concern you, except that I believe at the beginning of the Season, Sale was disposed to pay some attention to you, and you may have thought it more serious than it really was.'

Since giving that initial, betraying gasp, Polly had listened in silence, her hands clenched by her side, while a number of thoughts rushed through her head. He had not loved her, then! It had been nothing to him but a flirtation. Her own affections had been deeply engaged, and he had trifled with them. She was astonished he should be capable of it, for she had thought she knew him. But then as Lucy looked at her and uttered those last words, she understood what it was that had happened. She saw how she had been slighted, not by Lord Harvey, but by her own aunt and guardian! All the humiliations of her dependency suddenly surfaced, and her lifelong calm abandoned her.

'*You* have done this!' she cried out in a low voice. 'You have arranged it! I'll never forgive you.'

Lucy looked at her with hard eyes; and then, seeing how she shook, she said sharply, 'Flaminia, go into the next room.'

Minnie ran, startled, almost knocking over Fanny as she pushed the door open. When they were alone, Lucy said to Hippolyta, 'You must control yourself. This sort of passion will do you no good.'

'The whole world has seen how he behaved towards me. Everyone will know I am betrayed. You have humiliated me! I shall be laughed at, derided!'

'You are not the first woman to be deceived by a man's attentions, and you won't be the last,' Lucy said. 'Sale has changed his mind, that's all. It happens all the time.'

'He doesn't care a jot for Minnie, and you know it. It's me he loves! I wondered what had happened to him this last week, and now I know. You forced him to betray me, you and Wyndham. How did you bring him to it, between you?'

'Betray you — nonsense! There was no promise between you and Sale — therefore no betrayal. This is hysterical talk. I'm sorry you should have fancied yourself in love with him, but these things happen.'

'It didn't just happen. You made it happen, and all for your own advantage, to see your daughter well married!' she cried passionately.

'Hold your tongue,' Lucy said angrily.

'You've always hated me, haven't you? You were jealous of our mother, and you hated me and Africa, and you've done everything you can to ruin us. You sent her to school, though she begged you not to, and drove her to run away, probably to her death, and now —'

Lucy whitened, and stepping forward, struck Hippolyta on the cheek. Polly's words were cut off with a little cry, and she stood trembling, her eyes wide with shock.

394

Lucy was trembling too, but made herself speak softly. 'You're beside yourself, Polly. I think you had better go to your room and lie down until you are calm.'

Polly stared a moment longer, and then turned away.

'Think carefully before you speak again,' Lucy said quietly to her retreating back. 'Remember your cousin is very fond of you. You don't want to say anything to upset her, do you?'

Polly looked over her shoulder, a hard and bitter look. 'Upset her? Did you think of her feelings at any point, while you were selling her to Lord Wyndham?' she asked, '*Hypocrite!*'

The last word was hardly louder than a whisper, but it was feelingly spoken, and Lucy let her go in silence.

In the next room, Fanny removed her ear from the door, feeling a little shaken, and gave her cousin, seated at the table quietly sewing, a thoughtful look. Listening at doors was certainly entertaining, might even be essential, if you were ever to learn what was going on; but there were some things you might overhear which you could never repeat to anyone.

Fanny knew, better than Aunt Lucy, how devoted Minnie was to Hippolyta. Though Polly was fond of Minnie, she could have got on perfectly well without her — without anyone indeed. But if anything happened to shake Minnie's faith in her beloved cousin, it would be the end of the world for her. From the time she could walk, she had trotted after Polly, leaned on her, borrowed her opinions and sought her advice. Without her, she would pine away.

When Polly joined them an hour later, pale but composed, she had evidently been thinking the same things, for the first thing she did was to go quietly up to her cousin and kiss her, and congratulate her.

'I'm sure you will be very happy, Minnie dear,' she said, and if Fanny could detect a strain in the voice, it was evident Minnie did not. She beamed with pleasure.

'I'm so glad you like it after all, for when Mama told us, I thought you did not,' she said. 'Indeed, I thought Lord Harvey was *your* beau. He always asked you to dance before anyone else.'

'Oh, that was nothing,' Polly said calmly, resuming her seat and taking up her needlework again. 'We liked to dance together, but there was never anything between us. He wasn't

395

my beau, Minnie. It was a surprise to me, that's all.'

'It was to me, too,' Minnie said placidly, 'for I hadn't thought about getting married — well, only a little, at the beginning of the Season, but that was nothing. I suppose if Mama says it is right, and if you like it, then it is the best thing. After all, we have to get married some time, don't we?'

'I don't mean to get married for as long as possible,' Fanny said with a grin, 'but it will suit you prodigously, Min.'

'Will it? Yes, I'm sure it will, if you say so. And you like him too, don't you, Polly? Which will be pleasant, for we will all be together.'

Polly looked startled. 'What can you mean?'

Minnie looked up from her work. 'Well, you will be living with me still, won't you? I don't want to go away if you do not come.'

Fanny began to laugh quietly, and Polly glared at her, and said, 'No, Minnie dear, when you marry we shall be parted. You will live with your husband, and you won't need me. That is the way of it.'

Minnie's eyes filled with tears. 'But it needn't be!' she cried. 'Lots of married women have friends to live with them, and I'm sure you would rather be with me than with Mama, for you will have much more fun. I can't do without you, Polly, indeed I can't! Please say you'll come! Please don't make me go away without you!'

Fanny bit her lip and kept her face bent over her work, as Polly began the hopeless task of trying to persuade her cousin to give her up. Oh, it was the greatest fun! Fanny thought. Minnie was the stubbornest creature alive if ever she did decide on anything, and Polly would be obliged to give in at last, even if only to save her pride, and let people know she had not really cared for Sale at all. What a *ménage à trois* that would be, to be sure! Love, Fanny thought, makes such fools of people!

CHAPTER TWENTY

'Mama, may I speak to you, please?' Bobbie asked, coming into the blue saloon, where Roberta sat placidly sewing in the window-seat.

'Of course, darling.' She looked up and smiled at him. Bobbie thought that since she had married Mr Firth and taken to wearing prettier caps, she looked younger and more beautiful than ever. 'What is it?'

'It's about Marcus.'

Roberta laid her work aside and patted the seat beside her, and Bobbie sat down and fixed her with an earnest gaze. 'Oh dear, is it something serious?' she asked with mock alarm.

'Well, yes, it is, sort of,' Bobbie said, frowning. 'I wanted to ask you — Mama, have I got any money?'

'What an extraordinary question! What do you mean? Have you overspent your allowance? There's no need to look so worried, my dear — I can give you a shilling or two, if there's some little thing you want to buy.'

'No, Mama, it's not that. I mean, I know I'm the Earl of Chelmsford and all that, but does that mean I have any money? Or is it just the title?'

'No, darling, of course it isn't. There's lots of money, invested in all sorts of places — in the Funds, in forests and mines and factories and houses. It's all yours, although of course I am your trustee until you are twenty-one.'

Bobbie looked more than ever concerned. 'So I can't have any of it until I'm twenty-one?'

'I didn't say that, precisely.' Roberta looked at him shrewdly. 'Darling, what is all this? Perhaps you had better tell me from the beginning. And what has it to do with Marcus? Don't tell me you have lost some prodigious sum of money to him at macao? If it's more than a guinea, I shall have to stop you playing for pennies, for it's only meant to be fun between

397

you, you know. I shouldn't like to think you're developing a taste for gaming.'

Bobbie flushed. 'No, Mama, it's nothing like that. But it is more than a guinea I need.'

'How much more.'

'I'm not sure exactly, but I think it might be about two thousand pounds,' Bobbie said carefully. 'Would there be as much money as that in the estate?'

Roberta stared. 'You want two thousand pounds? For Marcus? Good God, has he been kidnapped?'

Bobbie laughed. 'Oh no, Mama, of course not! It's for his colours.' Illumination spread over Roberta's face, and Bobbie went on, 'You see, the one thing Marcus wants in the world is to be an officer like his papa, and to go to war, and he's so afraid it will be over before he's had a chance to fight. And his mother won't buy him a commission because — well, you know how she is, Mama.' Delicacy forbade Bobbie's naming her parsimony for what it was. 'So I thought that, as he is my cousin, and we are friends, and he lives with us, which makes him almost like my brother — well, I thought perhaps I might be able to buy his colours for him. If there's enough money.'

'Oh, there's enough money. There's twenty thousand in the Funds alone,' Roberta said. 'As sole trustee, I can authorise a release of capital, if I think the case is justified. But, darling, two thousand pounds is a great deal of money, just to be given away.'

'It doesn't seem a lot, when I have so very much,' Bobbie said tentatively.

'And it isn't only the capital, you know: there's the income that would be lost as well.'

His face fell. 'You mean I can't have it? Only if I wait until I'm twenty-one, it might be too late.'

She regarded him thoughtfully. 'Do you want this very much?' she asked.

His eyes lit. 'Oh yes, beyond anything! You see, Marcus has always been so good to me; and he is heir presumptive to the estate, isn't he, Mama? If anything happened to me, it would all be his anyway.'

'Nothing is going to happen to you,' she said quickly.

'Well, but if I didn't get married, or didn't have a son, Marcus would have everything, so it seems only fair to let him

398

have a bit now, when it's something he wants so much. And I don't mind about losing the income, because even if I have to go without new clothes or eat cabbage or anything like that, it will be worth it. Marcus is a trump card, you know, Mama!'

She smiled at the idea, and then added seriously, 'You love him very much, don't you?'

Bobbie looked cautious at the use of the word. 'I like him awfully. Don't you?'

'Yes, of course,' Roberta said absently. 'Well, darling, I can't give you my decision right away. I shall have to think about it, and ask Mr Firth for his opinion. And I shall have to consult the lawyers about it, too. That will all take time.'

'Yes, I understand. Only you will say yes after all, won't you Mama?' Bobbie said with a winning smile.

'I can't promise anything yet. Go along with you, now.' He got up to leave her, and she called to him as he reached the door, saying, 'Bobbie, did Marcus put you up to this?'

Bobbie turned, looking vexed and upset. 'Of course not!' he cried. 'He'd never ask me for anything. He doesn't even know I'm asking you.'

'No, of course not. I'm sorry, darling. I'll let you know my decision as soon as I can.'

The news came of another victory for Wellington's army on 22 July at Salamanca, where Marmont's army had been utterly defeated. Fourteen thousand of the French had died, and the remnant, thoroughly demoralised, had scattered and were said to be straggling back towards France.

John Anstey called to give Lucy the earliest news of it. 'So now the road is open to Madrid,' he said. 'It's the most marvellous victory! Shews how a compact force of ours can overthrow a great mass of Frenchmen. And the Spanish irregulars are picking away at the French in the south and wearing them down. If Wellington can hold Madrid and break the French supply-line, victory may be in sight at last.'

'Victory?' Lucy said. 'I can hardly believe it.'

'Victory in the Peninsula,' John explained. 'For the rest —' he shrugged. 'But for the moment, we're making as much of it as possible. The Opposition's been damned noisy lately about the cost of the war. Liverpool's seeing the Regent at the moment, about another title for Wellington. He's to be made

Marquis for Salamanca. I wish to God we could bring him home, to shew him to the mob, but of course he can't be spared.'

'How often have we heard those words,' Lucy said. 'Collingwood — Haworth —'

John looked at her with sympathy. 'Still no word about the little girl?'

Lucy shook her head. 'I still have four people looking for her, but after so long, I don't suppose they will find any tracks. I can only hope she's on a ship somewhere.'

'You've written to her father?'

'Oh yes. Now I dread receiving his reply.' She reached out a hand blindly for Thomas, stationed at her side, and drew him against her. 'Africa was the dearest to his heart. He hardly knows Hippolyta, though he loves her for Mary's sake, but he had Africa with him from birth. Losing her would be a dreadful blow.'

There was nothing John could say to comfort her, so after a moment he changed the subject. 'Have you set the date for Flaminia's wedding yet?'

Lucy roused herself from a deep reverie. 'What? Oh, yes, I meant to tell you — it's to be the fourteenth of September. You will come, of course? And bring Louisa — unless you've got her pregnant again?'

'Lucy!' John gave her a look of exasperated affection. 'I suppose, then, that you won't be going out of Town for the summer? You'll have too much to do, with a September wedding?'

'That's right. I've decided to keep this house on, and she can be married from here. There'll be too many guests for the other house, what with all the Chetwyns and Manverses and Cavendishes, to say nothing of the Sale side of the family. The Knaresboroughs will be staying, of course, and the Ballincreas, and I suppose I'll have to give the old Marquis a bed, if he's fit to make the journey. And out of courtesy I'll have to ask Cavendish, the children's other trustee, to stay, though I expect he'll prefer to stay in a hotel. Hicks keeps rubbing his hands at the thought of having the house full, but as far as I'm concerned, the whole thing is a nuisance — a necessary evil.'

'It's a good match for her,' Anstey mused. 'Of course,

400

Wyndham's a bit of a stick, but I meet young Sale at the club, and he seems a very decent sort of fellow.'

'He's of her rank; the family is all right, and the settlements are good,' Lucy said tersely.

'How hard you've become, Lucy,' Anstey said. He remembered the merry, passionate, tumble-haired child she had been, and was saddened. 'Is that all you care about?'

Lucy looked annoyed. 'Of course, I'm glad he's a pleasant, personable man as well; but I would hardly have been doing my duty if I hadn't settled her as well as possible, would I? I never thought you would be so romantic, John. You've a large family of your own — don't you want them to be established creditably?'

'Yes, I'm sorry. I was being unjust,' he said frankly. 'Forgive me.'

Lucy nodded. 'Minnie seems to like him well enough. He came courting and did it very nicely, paid her a compliment or two, bowed over her hand — attentive, but not fulsome. I must say I liked him better for it, and Minnie is half-way convinced she's in love with him. And she likes being the centre of attention for once in her life, opening wedding-presents, visiting silk-warehouses and so on.'

'Everyone loves a wedding,' Anstey smiled. 'I suppose Hippolyta's going to be a bridesmaid?'

'Yes, and Fanny and Rosamund; and Helena Greyshott's daughter, Thalia, is to be flower-girl. I think Fanny's enjoying herself most of all. I heard her say to Rosamund the other day that as a bridesmaid she gets all the glory and a new gown, without actually having to get married.' John laughed, and Lucy gave an unwilling smile. 'James is going to have trouble with that girl before he's done.'

'She's certainly set the town by the ears. Is James coming to the wedding?'

'Yes, he and Héloïse will travel down, and take Fanny back with them.'

'I expect half Fanny's pleasure in being a bridesmaid is that it means she can stay in Town longer,' Anstey said shrewdly. 'How she'll settle in York, after a London Season, I can't imagine. Are the happy couple to make a wedding-trip?'

'Sale's taken a house at Isleworth for six months. They'll be going straight there after the wedding, but after that, I don't know what's intended. Wyndham's signed over the cadet estate at Stainton to them, but I don't know if Sale will care to live there. It's in the Chilterns, rather far from London for a club man. I suppose he might leave Minnie there and live in London himself *en garçon*, or he might take a Town house. By that time, it won't be my problem.'

'By then you'll have Rosamund ready to bring out,' John said with a smile. 'If you can get her and Polly settled as well as Minnie, you'll have nothing to reproach yourself with.'

'Except having lost Africa,' she said quietly.

The news of the victory at Salamanca, and of Wellington's further ennoblement, was received in London with joy and excitement, which after dark spilled over into rioting. Gangs of drunken men roamed the streets carrying flaming torches, chanting and singing, and attacking anyone they didn't think was celebrating hard enough. They threw stones or poked poles through the windows of houses not shining lights for the victory. They overturned coaches and set light to them, and terrorised pedestrians, and all through the night woke up householders by firing pistols and muskets into the air, and then demanding to know if they had heard the news, and what they thought of it.

The following day, as the debris was swept from the thoroughfares, the rumours began to circulate that the gangs had not been genuine revellers, but had been mobs in the pay of the war party in Parliament. On that night and the subsequent one, the riots were repeated, two houses were set on fire, and eight people were killed, as well as numerous others being wounded.

After the first night, Lucy had ordered the shutters to be put up as soon as darkness fell, and had stationed servants with buckets of water in case of fire, and they had sat it out with nothing more harmful than a few alarms, though Fanny had complained bitterly at having to miss the assembly at Almacks.

The following day while Lucy was sitting in the morning-room with Docwra, Flaminia, and Thomas, opening the latest batch of letters of congratulation and replies to wedding-invitations, there was a rap at the street door.

Lucy looked at Docwra with raised eyebrows. 'Who can

that be? It's too early for visitors.'

'I didn't hear a carriage, m'lady,' Docwra said. 'Probably a messenger with another wedding-present.'

'At the front door?' Lucy queried.

'Some of 'em are told to deliver only by the front door, m'lady,' Docwra said wisely. 'So as to get the present noticed. Especially if it's a large parcel, and a messenger in livery.'

A few moments later, Hicks appeared at the door, his face wreathed in very unprofessional smiles.

'A visitor, my lady.'

'At this hour?' Lucy said. 'Send them away. And why are you smirking like that?'

Hicks stepped aside, and Major Wiske came in. His face was very thin and very brown and he had a partly-healed scar on his left temple, half-covered by his hair. His eyes went straight to Lucy, and he smiled in such a way that Docwra's throat tightened, and she caught Flaminia's eye and jerked her head significantly towards the door.

Lucy had stood up, her eyes wide, taking in everything, including the scar. 'Danby!' she said, and in her face surprise and pleasure struggled for supremacy. He stepped forward and held out his hands, and Lucy crossed the room to him, placed her own in his, and looked up into his face, astonished at her own feelings. 'Oh, I've missed you!' she said in a low voice.

'Can't be as much as I've missed you,' he said. Docwra hurried Minnie and Thomas out of the room, and as soon as the door closed behind them, he folded Lucy in his arms and held her tightly against him for a moment.

Released enough to look up at him, she asked, 'You're wounded?'

'What, that scratch? Just a bit of flying granite, surface wound, nothing.' He gave her a wry smile. 'Took a ball in the shoulder, though, at Salamanca. Terrible waste — due for leave anyway, no need to get m'self shot too.'

'A ball in the shoulder? Where? Which one? Did they get it out?'

'Now, now, steady! Of course they got it out, what do you think?'

'I know about army surgeons,' Lucy said fiercely. 'Butchers — and drunken butchers at that! Did it break the bone?

403

There may be splinters. You must let me look at it, Danby. You don't want it going septic.'

He patted her shoulder comfortingly. 'We have an excellent surgeon, thank you, ma'am, a skilled man, and as sober as a Methodist. And it didn't break the bone, and it's healing nicely, and as for shewing you — you must wait until we're married for that!'

Lucy coloured. 'Really, Danby! As if I couldn't look at your wound without —' She stopped in confusion.

'Pink suits you,' he said agreeably. 'Did you really miss me?'

'Never mind that. Are you sure you're all right?'

'Never better.'

'Campaigning seems to suit you,' Lucy said, 'though you're too thin.' As her arms were unaccountably still around him at that moment, she was in a position to judge.

'You can feed me up,' he offered unselfishly.

'How long can you stay?'

'I'm due for six weeks' leave, but Hookey told me not to come back until my shoulder's completely healed.'

'Then it is a serious wound,' Lucy concluded, paling a little.

'Don't fret, it ain't so bad. Can't use my sword properly, that's all, and wounds take longer to heal on campaign. I balked a bit, but it makes sense. No use to anyone if I can't use m' sword.'

Lucy privately resolved she would look at the wound, by hook or crook, but was wise enough to keep the resolution to herself. 'You didn't want to come home?'

'What do you think?' he asked, squeezing her a little. 'But I'd have liked to be there for the taking of Madrid. Joseph's there — Boney's brother — and quaking in his shoes already. We'll take it by the end of the month — would have liked to share in that, before I came on leave. However —' He shrugged, and winced, and seeing Lucy open her mouth hastened to put in a question. 'What're you doin' still in Town in August? Expected to have to go down to Wolvercote for you.'

'Didn't you get my last letter? Flaminia's to be married in September, to Harvey Sale.'

Wiske's brow wrinkled. 'I thought he was Hippolyta's beau? Seem to remember you said something in one of your letters —'

404

'No, that was nothing. I was mistaken. They danced together once or twice, and you know how rumour starts. It's all arranged, settlements, everything — very handsome. And,' she added with satisfaction, 'you'll be able to be here for it.'

The tone of her voice made him look down seriously into her face. 'You really did miss me, then?' he said softly.

Lucy felt absurdly shy, but forced herself to meet his gaze. 'Yes, I did,' she said. 'I didn't know that I would, but I did.'

'A handsome admission,' he said. He placed his hands one either side of her head and tilted her face up to him, and kissed her. Lucy quivered with an astonishing desire, a reaction that surprised and disturbed her. His male, muscular body, the faint smell about him of leather and fresh air; the thought of him commanding his men, fighting, being wounded; the strong, lean hands holding her face with such gentleness, the touch of his lips, the taste of him: he was strange and exciting, different, familiar — her own, hers to command, and yet still a male animal, unpredictable, under her control only because he wished to be.

She barely thought these things, only felt them wordlessly in a hot, exciting flood which made her press against him avidly. For an instant she felt his response, before he controlled himself and drew away a little, breathing hard. He stroked her cheek with a hand that trembled slightly, and then dropped it to his side.

'Any more of that sort of thing,' he said softly, 'and I might end by shewing you my wound after all.'

Marcus, standing in the entrance hall while Hicks went to enquire if my lady and the Major were at liberty, had his attention called by a hissing from above.

'Marcus! Up here!' Rosamund was hanging over the bannister.

'Hello, Rosy. What are you doing?'

'I saw you come up the steps, so I slipped out. Are you staying long? Will you come up and see me?'

'I don't know — I'll see. I'll come if there's time.'

'What do you want with Mother?'

Marcus smiled indulgently. 'None of your business.'

'She's with Major Wiske. I think they're going to get married. What do you think of that?'

'That's not your business either, Rosy-posy. Hadn't you better get back to your lessons?'

'Docwra says one wedding brings on another. I don't mind, really, if Mama wants to marry Major Wiske,' she said generously, 'but I think Lord Harvey's wasted on Minnie: she never rides. I don't think she even *likes* horses. I shall be fifteen next month — don't you think that's old enough to marry?' she added wistfully.

'You have to be brought out first,' Marcus pointed out.

'People marry from the schoolroom sometimes — I saw it in the novel Moss was reading the other day.'

'That's only a novel. It doesn't happen in real life. Anyway, why all the hurry to get married? I thought you didn't approve of that sort of thing.'

'Well, I'm only worried that you might get tired of waiting for me to grow up, and marry someone else,' she said.

Marcus looked up at her anxious freckled face floating above him, and the two long plaits hanging down like bell-ropes on either side. 'I'm not going to marry anyone for a long time yet,' he said. 'You concentrate on doing your lessons and learning how to be a lady. By the time you're grown-up, you won't want to marry me. You'll have met dozens of men you like much more.'

'I shall *never* want to marry anyone but you,' Rosamund said solemnly. She glanced over her shoulder. 'Here comes Hicks,' she said, and disappeared.

A few moments later, Marcus was ushered into the small drawing-room, where Major Wiske greeted him cordially, and proposed to withdraw.

'Oh, no sir, please don't go! I beg your pardon, ma'am,' he added to Lucy, 'but I wanted to consult Major Wiske as well as you.'

'Very well,' Lucy said, and gestured towards a chair. 'Please sit down, Marcus. What was it you wanted to ask?'

Marcus perched rather uneasily. 'I heard you were back, sir,' he said, 'and I thought you would be the very person to advise me. Mr Firth says you were at Salamanca?' Danby nodded genially. 'What was it like?' Marcus asked eagerly forgetting what he had come for. 'Is it true that it only lasted forty minutes? Did the French centre really collapse so quickly? I've read Lord Wellington's report in the *Chronicle*, but I dare say that doesn't tell the half of it.'

'Nor the quarter neither,' Danby said. 'That's a tale for some other time. Don't want to bore her ladyship with it,' he prompted.

'Of — of course! I beg your pardon. Well, sir — ma'am — I wanted your advice about something.'

'Fire away, then,' Wiske said.

'Well, you know that Papa is serving in the Peninsula? And for years and years I've wanted to follow him, but Mama — well, Mama wasn't keen on my becoming an officer. I think she was afraid I might get killed. And then,' he coloured as he came to a delicate matter, 'there's the expense of a pair of colours, and the horse and the uniform and everything.'

'Expensive business,' Wiske concurred. 'Not a poor man's sport, bein' a soldier. Mess bills — fodder — servants. All cost a ransom.'

Marcus nodded gratefully. 'Precisely, sir.'

Lucy looked from one to the other. 'Are you sure you need me here? Because if not, I have a thousand things to do.'

Marcus turned to her eagerly. 'Oh no, ma'am, please don't go. You see, the thing is, her ladyship — that's to say, Mrs Firth — called me in this morning to tell me that she would like to buy me my colours, and fit me out, all out of the estate. It was Bobbie's idea, apparently, and she and Mr Firth talked it over, and decided it could be done.'

Lucy raised an eyebrow. 'That's very generous. You're a fortunate young man.'

'The thing is, ma'am,' Marcus bit his lip, 'that I don't know whether I ought to accept.'

'Accept? Of course, why not?' Lucy said.

'Because — well, I've no claim on Bobbie or the estate. Perhaps it's too generous. He's such a good, kind fellow, it's just like him to think of this, because it's the one thing in the world I've always wanted, but how can I accept something so valuable from him, when I've already had so much — my keep and my education — at his hands?'

'That's silly,' Lucy said. 'If they don't mind, why should you? Accept it with a good grace, and say no more.'

But Danby Wiske looked at him with sympathy, understanding a young man's touchy pride better than Lucy ever could. 'If young Chelmsford wants to give you this out of

407

affection,' he said quietly, 'it would be churlish to refuse. Hurt his feelings. Nothin' worse than givin' somebody somethin' you've thought long and hard about, and havin' it thrown back in your face.'

Marcus looked doubtful. 'Do you think so, sir?'

'Sure of it. Makes you feel a fool.'

Lucy was catching up. 'You don't want to feel under an obligation, is that it? Well, I can tell you, if it makes you feel any better, that Roberta took on your education for Bobbie's sake, so that he would have someone to share lessons with.'

'Really, ma'am?' He reflected. 'Yes, that does make a difference.' His brow corrugated again. 'But then there's the question of my mother — might she not be offended if I accepted my colours from Bobbie, when she couldn't afford to buy them for me herself?'

Lucy opened her mouth to tell him that Lady Barbara could well afford to send him to the war twice over, only she was too clutch-fisted to part with a penny where there was no hope of profit; but Danby Wiske caught her eye and shook his head minutely. She closed her mouth, rearranged her words, and said with an effort, 'I shouldn't worry about that, Marcus. Roberta will know how to tell your mother so that it doesn't offend her. And she's bound to be glad of something that advances you, isn't she? Any mother would be.'

He looked relieved. 'I hadn't thought of that. Oh, thank you, ma'am! You've eased my mind a great deal. There's only one other thing,' he added, looking at Wiske again. 'Would anyone — I mean, the other officers, sir — would they think it — well, shabby of me? I couldn't bear it if anyone thought I was not quite the thing.'

Danby smiled inwardly, but kept his face perfectly grave. 'Nothin' to it, dear boy! Nine out of ten of us had our commissions bought for us. Don't matter a fig who it was. You'll do very well. Decided which regiment you fancy?'

Marcus's face was alight now. 'Not yet, sir, though of course my father's regiment was mentioned.'

'Heavy cavalry, eh? Well, there's plenty to do out there.'

'Oh, yes, sir! I read in the paper that at Salamanca, the French right flank —'

'Not now, Marcus,' Lucy said firmly. 'I'm sure that

another time the Major will be happy to tell you all you want to know.'

'I beg your pardon, ma'am. It was good of you to give me so much of your time,' Marcus said rising obediently. 'Please don't trouble to ring — I can see myself out. Might I go up and say hello to the children before I leave?'

He hadn't far to go to see Rosamund: she accosted him, wild-eyed, on the first flight of stairs.

'You're going away to the war!' she cried.

'Rosy, have you been listening at the door? Shame on you! That's not the sort of behaviour expected of a lady.'

'Oh, never mind that,' Rosamund said tragically. 'Is it true? Marcus, are you really going to go away?'

'I hope so. But you mustn't repeat it to anyone, not yet.'

'When will you go?'

'As soon as I can. It will take a few weeks to make the arrangements, I suppose. But I'll stay for Minnie's wedding, anyway,' he added, hoping to make her smile. 'I wouldn't miss seeing you as a bridesmaid.'

She ignored all that. 'Take me with you!' she begged passionately.

'Now, Rosy, don't be silly —' he began.

'I'm not being silly. Please, please Marcus, take me with you! I'll cut off my hair, and wear boy's clothes, and be your servant. No-one will know. I can wash your shirts and polish your boots, and cook for you. I'll do everything for you!'

'Rosy, you're talking nonsense,' Marcus said gently. 'I can't take you with me, and you know it.'

She clutched his arm. 'Then I'll run away! I'll follow you!'

'Stop it! Don't talk like that. Isn't there enough trouble in the house, with your cousin Africa?' She looked at him with resentful, tragic eyes, 'Listen to me, Rosy, if you run away, I'll send you straight back, I swear it! I won't take you with me, no matter what you say or do.'

Two large tears escaped her lashes and rolled down her cheeks. Marcus was moved as much as embarrassed. He had never seen Rosamund cry, not even the time she slipped and put her foot down a grating, and took all the skin off her shin.

'Don't do that. Please don't cry,' he said. 'You'll spoil everything if you cry.'

'You're going away, and I'll never see you again,' she

whimpered. 'You'll forget all about me, and marry a Spanish woman, like Lord Leith, and never come back.'

'Rosy, love, I promise I won't forget you, and I promise I'll come back — unmarried — as soon as the war's over. It won't last much longer, you'll see. Then I'll be home.'

She looked doubtful. 'You really promise?'

'I really promise. Come on, now, blow your nose, and we'll go upstairs and see Roland. And I suppose I'd better make it all right with Miss Trotton, since you seem to have left your lessons again.'

'It's all the same time,' she said more cheerfully. 'I never went back after Hicks took you up.'

'You are an abominable child, you know.'

'I know. That's what Miss Trotton calls me.'

James was greatly surprised to receive an invitation to meet Mr Hobsbawn, 'to discuss Fanny's future', as the letter proposed, but even more surprised that the meeting was to take place in Huddersfield. 'I shall be there on business on the sixteenth,' Hobsbawn's letter said, 'and shall stay overnight at the George in St George's Square. If you will do me the honour of dining with me at six o'clock, we can have our discussion in comfort. I shall bespeak a room for you, if I don't hear to the contrary.'

'I suppose,' he said to Edward, 'that the old fellow hates me so much he doesn't want me to cross his threshold. A year's ablutions would hardly serve to cleanse his house of my contamination.'

'Probably he thinks to save you half the journey,' Ned said sensibly. 'Are you going?'

'Of course. Does one ignore a summons from the King of Cotton?'

'Well, do try to act sensibly, then,' Ned advised. 'Don't be theatrical. And don't jump to the defence until you've heard him out. I know what you're like where Fanny's concerned.'

'Perhaps you ought to go with me,' James suggested evenly. 'You are Fanny's trustee, after all.'

'I've too much to do,' Ned said shortly. 'And it's you he asks for.'

'True,' James sighed. 'Perhaps he wants to advise me on being a parent. I ought to have some kind of moral support.

410

Perhaps I'll take Héloïse.'

'Don't be silly,' Edward said impatiently. 'I hate it when you're in this facetious mood.'

'I'll take Mathilde, then. She'd like a change of scene, I'm sure.'

Edward glared at him and stalked out in disgust.

Grandpapa Hobsbawn didn't precisely glare at him when he entered the private parlour at the George, but his expression wasn't exactly a smile of welcome either. 'Morland,' he said, with a brief nod. 'Sit ye down. I've ordered dinner ahead, or we'd be waiting all night, and I'm sharp-set after a day's work. I hope you don't mind?' The tone of voice that went with the words suggested that if James did mind, he might as well go to the devil for all the difference it would make to Hobsbawn.

'Not at all,' he drawled, with his most charming smile. 'An excellent idea. I'm sure whatever you've ordered will be good enough for me.'

Hobsbawn looked at him suspiciously, not sure how serious he was. 'Aye,' he said at last. 'Well, I've ordered a good one, and a pint of wine to go with it. Now, will you have a glass of sherry?' James looked enquiringly at the bottle, being rather particular about sherry. 'I brought my own with me,' Hobsbawn said shortly. 'You never know in coaching inns.'

'Thank you, sir.' He sat down, accepted a glass, sipped, and found it excellent; and since he had the sense to say so, sincerely, Hobsbawn thawed quite a bit during the next few exchanges. 'Well, sir,' James said at last, 'you wanted to discuss Fanny's future? You know that Edward is her trustee, not I?'

'Aye, I know that.'

'Of course you do,' James said smoothly, feeling nettled. 'It was you that arranged matters so with my mother.'

'And a good job we did, as things turned out,' Hobsbawn said. 'But I didn't ask you here to quarrel with you, young man. You're Fanny's father, and it's only right you should be the one I talk to, when it comes to matrimonial matters.'

'Ah,' James said, enlightened. 'Fanny's marriage.'

'Just so. It's a matter that can't be thought about too soon or too long. She's a considerable heiress — aye, and might be more so, if things go the way I want them to.' He looked

411

pleased with himself.

'Have you someone in mind for her?' James asked, genially sarcastic.

'Aye, I have,' Hobsbawn said promptly. 'Now listen to me, young man, and don't get all high and mighty with me, until you've learned what I propose. You know that when Fanny was born, I settled a large sum of money on her, but my mills I left to my cousin Jasper, my nearest male relative.'

'You didn't want to leave the mills to a female. I know that,' James said indifferently. He had never cared whether Fanny had anything from her mother's family, and cared less now.

'Just so. Of course, when little Henry was born —' Hobsbawn's face clouded at the memory of his lost child — 'I changed my will, and left the mills to him. That was only right. But my boy's dead now —' He took out a handkerchief and trumpeted briskly into it '— and life must go on.'

'What has all this to do with Fanny's marriage?' James asked impatiently.

'I'm coming to it, never fear! I've thought long and hard about it, and since I've come to know Fanny better, I don't feel right about leaving the mills away from her. She's a Hobsbawn all right, from her head to her toes — though she bears your name,' he added almost as an afterthought, '— and she ought to have what's hers by blood. She's my only grandchild — her mother's only child — and she ought to have everything.' He paused, but James did not interrupt.

'But there's two things against it,' Hobsbawn carried on. 'One is that I still don't think a woman knows how to manage a mill — let alone three, or four as it will be soon. Of course, she could employ an agent or a manager, but hirelings are prone to cheat you. The second thing is that I feel I owe something to Cousin Jasper. I've never told him that he had expectations, of course — that would be foolish, and I'm not a foolish man.'

'No, sir,' James said.

Hobsbawn shot him a hostile glance. 'You know, I've never liked you, Morland. You talk soft, and you've no sense when it comes to money. Just keep your mouth shut, will you, and remember it isn't your own advantage you're trifling with, but Fanny's. You've no right to play ducks and drakes with

412

her future, whatever you do about your own.'

James held his tongue with a great effort, by visualising himself dancing at Hobsbawn's funeral.

'Now then,' Hobsbawn went on, 'I was saying about Jasper — blood's thicker than water, and he's worked long and hard for me. He knows the mills inside out, better than anyone — aye, even better than me, though I don't like having to say that. He can run them as they should be run, and he knows the market, and he's got a good notion of investment and expansion.

'So what I propose is this — that I leave the mills to Fanny, but that she marries Cousin Jasper. That way, she gets a manager who knows what's what, and who'll not cheat her, or put the profit in his own pocket. And he'll get the benefit of all the work and study he's put in. There now, what do you think?'

James exerted self-control again, for the first words that jumped into his mouth were hardly complimentary. He remembered Edward's injunction, breathed deeply, and said in a voice that barely trembled, 'I would never arrange a marriage for Fanny on the grounds of pecuniary advantage.'

Hobsbawn frowned. 'Pecuniary — talk sense, man! What the devil's that?'

'Money,' James said tersely. 'I won't marry Fanny to anyone for financial reasons.'

'Then what the devil would you marry her for?' Hobsbawn exploded. 'What kind of talk is that? What sort of a father are you? If you don't arrange a marriage for her to her advantage who are you going to give her to? A passing gypsy?'

James reddened. 'I don't mean that.'

'Well what the devil do you mean?' Hobsbawn said angrily.

'The man Fanny marries — of course he must be able to support her, but that isn't all. I should want him to have birth and fortune — rank perhaps, though that isn't essential —'

'Jasper is a gentleman born; and what greater fortune do you want than Hobsbawn Mills?'

'But above all,' James continued firmly, 'he must be Fanny's choice. I want her to be happy —'

Hobsbawn looked disgusted. 'I thought you were a fool, and now you've proved me right. Why, Fanny has more sense in her little finger than you've got in your whole head!'

'It's foolish to want my daughter to be happy, is it?'

'No, but that's not what you're talking about,' Hobsbawn said shrewdly. 'You're talking about falling in love, and all that romantic nonsense, aren't you? Oh, aye, I know what's in your mind. I saw how you treated my daughter. You're all alike, you people! You'd sooner Fanny was dragged off to a hovel by a pauper and lived on boiled turnips, as long as she was *in love* with him, wouldn't you? A good, solid marriage, to a hard-working man, a house, a carriage, servants — a good settlement, and a handsome widow's portion for her old age — you'd scorn all those, wouldn't you, because they're not *romantic* enough for you.'

He poured scorn into the word, and James bristled. 'You seem to forget,' he said furiously, 'that Fanny has a fortune of her own! Whoever she marries, she won't be living in a hovel. Morland Place — the whole estate — is hers. She doesn't need to marry at all if she doesn't want to, and if she does marry, she can follow her inclination, and marry a man whom she loves. And she doesn't need your money, or your mills, Mr Hobsbawn. They are of small importance to her, or to any of us.'

'I sometimes wonder if you know your daughter at all,' Hobsbawn said. 'Do you think that's what Fanny thinks about it? Have you spoken to her? Small importance my eye! Fanny knows what the mills are worth. Since the first day of her visit, she was wheedling and working to get me to leave 'em to her!' He chuckled, pleased with himself again. 'Aye, that surprises you, don't it? I told you she was a Hobsbawn! There's not much of the soft Morland in my little girl! And before you make any more grand gestures, Morland, and throw away my proposal, you might ask Fanny what she thinks about it. She won't marry for love, not my Fanny! She'll marry where her best advantage lies. Give her her head, and she'll follow the scent all right, and it'll lead her to Hobsbawn Mills, and a greater fortune to come than anything Morland Place can offer. You despise me, I know — you think I'm a coarse, ignorant man with dirty hands. But I tell you, the future's mine! Your day is done. You may posture and preen, and ride your fine horses, and talk all you like, but it's me and my sort who'll shape this country from now on.'

In his eloquence he was almost impressive. James stared at

him, and for an instant was inclined to think that perhaps he knew more than James did, and had a window of his own on the future. And then he remembered the festering slums Edward had described, and the recent bankruptcies, and the fact that Manchester didn't even have a Member of Parliament, and his common sense returned.

'Say what you like,' he said, 'I would never marry Fanny against her will.'

'Do you think I would?' Hobsbawn said promptly. 'You just help me set things in train, and she'll see where her advantage lies. Jasper's a comely enough fellow, and I dare say he knows how to make love as well as the next man. Only let them be together enough, and she'll fall enough in love with him to make it all right in *your* eyes.'

James shrugged. 'If she chooses, of her own free will, to marry your cousin Jasper, I wouldn't stand in her way,' he began, and Hobsbawn cut him off.

'Good enough! That's all I want from you. Let Fanny visit me again, and we'll see what we see. And in the meantime, to shew you that I've confidence in my own judgement, I'll have a new will made out, leaving everything to Fanny. How about that?'

'That's very fair, sir,' James said. 'But there's to be no coercion, however subtle, on Fanny?'

'On no account. Here's my hand on it, sir!' said Hobsbawn grandly, and looked about him with a vast, satisfied smile. 'And now, where's that dinner? By God, I've an appetite on me! Sealing bargains always does that to me, especially when it's a good one for me. And this is, Morland. I shall have my way in the end, you know — without coercion.'

'The best man, I dare say, will win, sir,' James said smoothly.

'What?' Hobsbawn stared, and then smiled. 'Oh, aye, I follow you! Do you know, Morland, there are times when I almost like you.'

'Infrequent ones I hope, sir, for your peace of mind's sake,' said James.

415

CHAPTER TWENTY-ONE

The day of Flaminia's wedding dawned fine, with a slight, milky mist over the gardens which disappeared as the sun rose above the rooftops and lit the upper windows of the west side of Grosvenor Square.

Docwra came to see how Moss and Hill, the new, smart lady's maid who had been engaged to attend Minnie in her married state, were getting on, and found that no progress had been made, the bride being in a deplorable state of nerves.

'You really must stop bein' sick, Miss Minnie,' Docwra advised her at last. 'It's only makin' your stomach sore, for you've nothing in there to be sick with.'

Minnie turned a shade greener, and Hill said severely, 'I can manage Lady Flaminia, thank you, Mrs Docwra. We shan't need to trouble your kindness. Hadn't you better be seeing to your lady? We don't want any unfortunate last-moment rushes, do we?'

Docwra had been eating uppish maids for breakfast for the last fifteen years, and gave Hill a withering look. 'Ah, sure God, don't be puttin' on your airs with me, Miss Hill,' she said, abandoning the last of her London accent in the interests of effect. ''Twas me that brought Miss Minnie into the world, and I know the class of her stomach better than me own. And as for her ladyship, she's been dressed and gone this hour, and I can't change her until she comes back, can I?'

'Dressed and gone?' Hill deigned to query.

'You don't think a little thing like a weddin' would keep her from exercising her horses, do you?' Docwra said triumphantly.

Hill sniffed, and declined to give an opinion on the subject. 'To my view, it's all the noise and excitement that's making Lady Flaminia queasy. There are *too many people* in this room.'

'Now there I'm agreein' with you,' Docwra said cheerfully. 'Judy,' she said to Moss, 'why don't you go and see to Miss Polly and Miss Fanny? Hill an' me can manage now. And now, Miss Minnie,' she added as Moss scuttled away, 'just you take a little nip o' this, and it'll make you feel like a bird.'

Minnie, who was feeling like a bird already, but like one plucked and drawn and spitted rather than the singing variety, held out her hand obediently for the little silver flask which Docwra conjured out of her pocket, but snatched it back as though she had been stung when Hill screamed.

'Mrs Docwra! Are you suggesting that Lady Flaminia should go to her wedding with ardent spirits on her breath?'

Docwra looked indignant. 'I am not! Sure, d'you think I'd give a bride-to-be brandy at a moment like this? No, I came prepared all right: 'tis nothing more than a little drop o' port wine; and as for the smell, sure no-one's goin' to kiss her until after the ceremony, and then the Communion wine'll hide it.'

Hill shrieked again at the near-blasphemy, but Docwra winked at Minnie with the eye furthest from the scandalised lady's maid, and Minnie couldn't help giggling. 'That's better,' Docwra went on. 'Here now, have a little nip, and it'll settle your stomach and your nerves.' Flaminia obeyed, and as Docwra took back the flask, she gave the girl a quick hug and kiss, and said, 'You'll look a picture in your gown, don't you worry. And himself is as nice and pleasant a fellow as you'll meet in a long walk, so there's nothing to worry about, is there?'

'No,' Flaminia said, looking better. 'I'm sure there isn't. I'm all right now, Hill,' she said, assuming her dignity, which was hardly ever seen by anybody. 'You may begin.'

'That's my girl,' said Docwra, further annoying Hill, who swore privately to knock her ladyship into shape once she had her to herself. 'I'll send Miss Polly to you as soon as she's dressed. She'll do you more good even than my little flask.'

She left Hill to get on with the job, but saw to it that a steady stream of visitors to the bedchamber kept Flaminia's spirits up, and prevented Hill from bullying her. Lucy came in, still in her riding habit, her cheeks bright from a pleasant canter round the Park in Major Wiske's company, her curly crop tousled. Minnie was still in her underwear. Lucy surveyed her daughter with unusual benevolence.

'It's a lovely day, Minnie, and I'm sure everything will go well. You're marrying well, bringing credit to your family, so you've everything to be proud of. Hold your head up in church, and make the responses firmly, as though you mean them. There's nothing worse than a bride who mumbles.'

'Yes, Mama,' Minnie whispered.

'Your father would have been proud of you,' Lucy went on, and then couldn't think of anything else one ought to say to a daughter about to be married. She glanced at the maid. 'Don't draw Lady Flaminia's stays so tight, Hill. We don't want her fainting.'

'Yes, my lady. No, my lady.' Hill said meekly. She knew her match when she met it.

Miss Trotton, hinted in by Docwra a while later, kissed Minnie's cheek, and told her she was a credit to her. She chatted for a few moments, and was about to take her leave, when she paused doubtfully, for there had been something on her mind all day. 'Minnie dear, has your mother spoken to you about marriage?' she asked.

Minnie looked bewildered. 'What do you mean, Trot?'

Hill's eyes bulged, and Miss Trotton looked ever more hesitant.

'About being married, dear. About men, and what to expect.'

Minnie's round green eyes were innocent as young leaves. 'I don't understand,' she said, and then offered helpfully, 'Mama said I must speak up in church, and not mumble.'

'If you'll excuse me, Miss,' Hill said, trying to edge her away, with all the hostility lady's maids always feel for governesses, 'I must get my lady dressed. Now is not the time for such talk, if you don't mind.'

'You're quite right, Hill,' Miss Trotton said thoughtfully. 'Don't worry, Minnie dear, it was nothing important.'

Outside, Miss Trotton sought out Docwra and put the question to her. 'I quite thought her ladyship would have broached the subject, but it seems not. What do you think we ought to do, Docwra? Is it too late? It seems dreadful that she should approach the matter wholly unprepared. Should you perhaps have a little chat with her — though I suppose it ought really to be a married woman's task?'

Docwra raised an eyebrow at the thought that she, as a

spinster, didn't know enough to have a 'little chat' with Flaminia, but she said comfortably, 'No, no, miss, it's by far too late now. In any case, there are some creatures in the world that knowledge only confuses them. Miss Minnie'll be all right. She'll come out of her weddin' bed as innocent as she went in, and if I know men, which I do, that one'll know how to handle her so she doesn't break. It'll all seem like a dream to her, and she'll forget it from one occasion to the next.'

Miss Trotton was deeply tempted to ask how Docwra knew that, but the conversation was already making her cheeks warm, and she resisted. She considered that the maid's experiences since she had come into Lucy's service must have been as varied and pungent as those she had endured in famine-haunted Ireland beforehand. Nothing Miss Trotton had absorbed from the classics about the curious proclivities of gods and heroes could compare with that.

When she judged that Minnie would be at the stage of having her hair dressed, Docwra sent Polly in to visit her. Polly was already dressed in her bridesmaid's gown of pale prim-rose jaconet, and her exquisite, porcelain beauty seemed more breathtaking than ever. Minnie, looking at that perfect face in the mirror beside her own, felt humbled, dull, inadequate; and then when Polly smiled at her, she felt all her good fortune at having such a dear, good friend.

'Oh Polly,' she cried, 'I'm so glad you're going to be with me today. I couldn't bear it if you weren't here. And you will stay with me afterwards, won't you? Not just for the honey-moon, but after that as well?'

Polly didn't answer at once. Since the announcement of the engagement, Sale had treated her with perfect propriety. His calm, gentlemanly good manners, and nice blend of friendly affection, were such as any man might shew towards a girl he had danced with once or twice, and who was his bride-to-be's cousin. He had treated Minnie, too, as if she had been his own choice, and Polly was grateful for that, both on Minnie's behalf, and for herself, since it was essential that no-one should ever guess that she had thought him fond of her. His behaviour was so circumspect that she began now to doubt whether he had ever favoured her, or whether it had all been her imagination. Easier in many ways to believe it had. She couldn't now remember the look in his eyes which had made her feel so happy and confused; perhaps it had never existed.

Minnie, waiting anxiously for the answer, could not know the substance of her cousin's thoughts, and went on, 'It won't be dull for you, I promise. We'll go to all the balls and parties, and you'll soon be married too. I expect Lord Harvey has lots of friends, and if they visit us, they'll all fall in love with you, and you'll have your pick. I'm sure no-one,' she added innocently, 'could be in the same room with you and not fall in love. So you will stay with me, won't you, Polly?'

'Minnie, dear,' Polly began, and her tone so evidently preceded some kind of negative that Minnie's eyes filled with tears.

'I'm scared, Polly,' she whispered. 'I don't want to be married without you.'

'You won't be,' Polly said quickly, a shade impatiently. 'I'll be at your wedding, won't I? And I've promised to be your bride-guest on your honeymoon, haven't I? And I'll stay with you afterwards for a little while, but you won't want me by then.'

'I will!'

'No you won't, Minnie, believe me. Anyway, we'll see.'

Minnie clutched at that, as she so often had through her life. Putting things off was always best, in her view. Sometimes you never had to cope with them at all. 'Yes, we'll see,' she said.

At eleven o'clock a ribbon-bedecked carriage deposited Minnie and her second-cousin Mr Cavendish, who as her other trustee had the agreeable duty of giving her away, at the door of the Abbey. The bridal party was waiting there, three bridesmaids in pale primrose jaconet to walk behind the bride and carry her train, and little Thalia Hampton, Lady Greyshott's eight-year-old daughter, in pale pink, with a basket, to walk before the bride and scatter rose-petals in her path.

Inside, the Abbey was respectably populated, though nowhere near full, with around five hundred guests; an orchestra was tuning up, ready to augment the organ, half a dozen trumpeters were preparing to play the fanfares, and the choir was assembled in full voice for the anthem; and the archbishop was waiting at the altar, with his attendant satellites, to conduct the service.

420

In the front pew, Lucy sat with Major Wiske, Thomas, and Roland, feeling more than a little bemused. It seemed like only a few years ago that she had walked down the aisle to her own wedding: she didn't feel anywhere near old enough to be marrying off a daughter. Wiske, beside her, rather hoped Lucy would shew some proper feminine weakness and cry, so that he could offer her his handkerchief, but he rather doubted she would oblige him. He also hoped that the example of Flaminia's wedding would inspire her to agree to marry him before he went back to the Peninsula. It was becoming more difficult all the time to control himself when he was alone with her, and he felt sure she was feeling the same sort of needs herself. Of course, a gentleman never would lapse, but it was a strain on the nerves, as well as being, to his view, rather pointless.

The fanfare echoed brazenly around the fan-vaulted ceiling, everyone stood up, and nearly everyone turned round to look as the bridal procession entered the church. Minnie looked as beautiful as she was ever likely to, in a three-quarter slit tunic of ivory Mechlin lace over a gown of white satin, with a long train sewn all over with little silk knots. On her glossy auburn hair she wore a little satin cap sewn with pearls, from which hung a froth of gauze veiling; pearls trimmed the neckline of her gown, and there were pearls at her throat and in her ears. She carried a white doeskin prayer-book and a bouquet of orange-blossom and white and yellow roses; and on this one day, the happiest day — everyone had told her, and so she believed them — of her life, she walked proudly with her head up, and heard the murmur as she passed which told her she was as lovely as every bride had the right to be.

At the altar ahead of her stood Lord Harvey Sale with his brother beside him as groomsman. As she drew near, Lord Harvey, too, turned to look, and she saw he was surprised. I *am* beautiful, Minnie thought triumphantly, and gave him a smile which completed, though she didn't know it, the image the gown and the day had begun.

Even Lucy, seeing that smile, was almost in need of the assistance Danby Wiske so longed to give. As Flaminia came to rest beside him, Sale looked down at her and smiled in return, and Polly, seeing them together, felt that she had certainly been mistaken, that he didn't care for her and never

421

had, and that Flaminia was going to be truly happy with her new lord.

An hour later Minnie returned the way she came, now bearing a new name and a diamond-studded gold ring on her wedding-finger, leaning on the arm of the man who from now on had absolute power over her person, her body, and her fortune. The Abbey bells began to ring a long change, and the carriages were drawn up in order to take the guests back to Grosvenor Square for the wedding-breakfast. From there, in four hours time, a post-chaise would convey the happy couple and the bride-guest to Isleworth Spa, where tonight Minnie would pass through those mysterious portals of knowledge no-one had prepared her for, and keep her innocence if she could.

'It's a wonderful wedding, Lucy. You must feel very proud,' James said, on his fourth glass of Lucy's excellent champagne. 'I only hope I get Fanny off as well when the time comes.'

'Minnie quite surprised me,' Lucy said. 'She was so dignified, and she looked really quite pretty today.'

'I was trying to work out what relation Minnie and Sale are to each other,' James began, 'and I got as far —'

'Oh don't,' Lucy said. 'I've already had a lesson in genealogy from George Wyndham. If he tells me blood is thicker than water once more, I shall scream. Brummell says he's the dullest man in London, but I'm sure that's too great a compliment.'

'Is that Robert Knaresborough over there, talking to Roland? He's changed amazingly. I wouldn't have known him.'

'He's a husband and father now, and quite a local figure in Mansfield,' Lucy said, glancing that way. She grinned at her brother. 'You wouldn't believe it, but he actually organised a man-hunt, with dogs and beaters, to try to flush out some Luddites from their local bit of Sherwood Forest. He sounded quite bloodthirsty when he was telling me about it.'

Héloïse looked distressed. 'You mean they hunted men like animals?'

Lucy shrugged. 'These Luddites are animals, or worse. It's open season on 'em.' Danby Wiske joined them at that moment, and fortunately for Héloïse's peace of mind, the subject was changed.

'All the young people keep asking me if there's to be dancing later on,' he said. 'I suppose it wouldn't do any harm?'

'Oh no! What's a wedding without dancing?' James put in.

'Save your efforts, Jamie — there's an orchestra coming at three o'clock,' Lucy said. 'I suppose Sale will want to dance with his bride before they leave for Isleworth.'

'I shall certainly want to dance with mine,' James said, smiling down at Héloïse, while Wiske looked wistfully at Lucy and wished he could say the same. 'Ah, here's Fanny,' James added, brightening, as his daughter made her way through the crowds towards them. 'She looks wonderful, Lucy! You've done so well with her.'

'I've done nothing — it's London bronze, that's all,' Lucy said.

James didn't argue, only thought Fanny was certainly the prettiest girl in the room, and now that she had gained a little poise and sophistication, she was a match for anyone. She was certainly too good to be thrown away on any Cousin Jasper from Manchester: it must be an earl at least for Fanny Morland!

'Hello, my darling,' he said as she reached him. 'Are you having an agreeable time?'

'Yes, thank you, Papa,' Fanny said, 'only I came to ask if it's true there's to be dancing later, Aunt Lucy? Several of the men have asked me to stand up with them, and I don't know what to say.'

Lucy thought privately that there would never be a time when Fanny didn't know what to say, but she said only, 'Yes, there will be dancing. It's all arranged.'

'Oh, good,' Fanny said, smiling prettily, and dimpling at Major Wiske. 'It seems so long since I had any, I quite long for it.'

'You're enjoying London, then?' James said, a little wistfully.

Fanny looked at him under her eyelashes. It was fortunate that he had raised the subject, for she had been wondering how to do it. 'Oh yes, Papa, beyond anything! I love staying here with Aunt Lucy, and London is so interesting. I wish I might stay here for ever.'

'You don't long for the peace and quiet of home, then?'

James said. 'It seems very quiet without you.'

'Of course, I miss you dreadfully, Papa,' Fanny said carefully, 'but there is so much to do in London, and so many people to meet, that home is nothing to it. I can't imagine how people in York fill their days!'

There was a little silence, and then James said bravely to Lucy, 'I suppose there's no real reason why she must come home with us, is there? If you are willing to have her stay a little longer?'

Fanny held her breath, and looked appealingly at her aunt. Lucy felt annoyed with James — not because it was any trouble to have Fanny, but for putting the question to her in front of Fanny, and making it difficult for her to refuse.

'I should have thought you'd want her back home,' she said.

'I do,' James said, 'but a girl is only young once, and for such a short time. I should like Fanny to have all the fun and dancing she can. But if it's troublesome to you, Luce —'

'Oh it's no trouble,' Lucy said tersely, and Major Wiske intervened.

'You know, you might be glad of a companion, with your daughter and Miss Haworth gone away. The house will be very quiet — and I shall be gone soon, too.'

Lucy shrugged. 'As I said, it's no trouble. If you want Fanny to stay, she may, for the Little Season at least. I'll find some way to send her home at Christmas.'

'Oh thank you, Aunt Lucy!' Fanny said as prettily as she could. Her heart lifted at the thought of three more months in London; and after that, who knew what might happen? She might never have to go back to Yorkshire at all. 'What a wonderful party this is!'

'I'm sure there are more people here already than were invited,' Lucy said, gazing round at the company. 'Who's that young man in uniform over there, for instance? I don't remember receiving him.'

'I don't think you did,' Wiske said drily. 'He's a messenger.'

'Looking for you?' Lucy asked, trying to sound casual.

'I'll go and find out.'

Lucy watched him cross the floor, saw the messenger's roving eyes light on him with evident relief, saw them put their heads together in conversation. Fanny had excused herself, and James was saying something, but Lucy's attention was fixed on Danby's broad shoulders and bent head. At last he turned and walked back towards her, smiling broadly.

'Wellington's in Madrid!' he said. 'Joseph hardly put up a fight at all — took his men and retreated to Catalonia.'

'That's wonderful news!' James said enthusiastically. 'The capital of Spain in our hands! Now things are really beginning to move along.'

'What will happen now?' Héloïse asked.

'Wellington's leaving Hill and a garrison in Madrid, and pushing on up to Burgos. The remains of Marmont's army were heading that way, trying to get back to France. Once we hold Burgos, we can cut the French supply-line any time we like.'

'And leave the French to rot,' James said with satisfaction.

Wiske nodded. 'Soult down in Andalusia, Joseph in Catalonia, and the Spanish irregulars picking away at them all the time, wearing them down. Without reinforcements or supplies, they won't last long.'

Lucy went bluntly to the point that concerned her. 'Does this mean you will be going back?'

'I was going to have to go anyway,' Wiske said apologetically. 'Leave's almost over.'

'When?' she asked.

He met her eyes. 'I'm wanted at the Horseguards. That's what the messenger came for. Will you forgive me?'

'Of course,' Lucy said, turning her eyes away.

'I'll come straight back,' he said. 'I don't want to miss the dancing.'

Lucy kept her eyes averted. 'Duty must come first, of course. Now, if you will excuse me, I ought to go and speak to some of my other guests.'

After several energetic dances, Fanny had stepped out of the room for a moment into the quiet of a corridor to fan herself. There was the slight sound of a movement behind her, and before she could turn, someone had placed their hands over her eyes. She gave a little shriek.

'Who is it?' said a voice.

Her heart was pounding. She knew those hands and that

425

voice, but she controlled herself and said coolly, 'I have no idea. Pray, sir, remove your hands. I am not to be amused with such childish tricks.'

The hands were removed, and she was spun about to face Hawker, who was laughing down at her. 'So aloof, Miss Morland? Not amused? Oh, I am mortified!'

'You don't look mortified at all,' Fanny said crossly, annoyed with herself for being so disturbed by that white smile under the black moustache.

'Oh, but I am! To be snubbed by the beautiful Miss Morland — to be told one does not amuse — to be stigmatised as a bore — these are blows indeed! And I had hoped, in my impudence, that you had missed me!'

'Oh,' said Fanny, very loftily, 'have you been away? I had not noticed.'

Hawker laughed aloud. 'Brava! You are much improved, I may say, by your Season in Town! Yes, I had heard that the delicious Miss Morland was the most accomplished flirt in London, and now I see it was no more than the truth.'

Fanny felt her cheeks grow warm. 'Who says so? Who dares to say such a thing of me?'

'Why, the legion of those you torment, of course. Your victims, Miss Morland, are scattered to the four corners of the country. I meet them wherever I go. More particularly, I have been in the camp at Brighton lately, where you were the toast of the officers' mess. There was a certain Captain Daventry, whose heart is irretrievably broke —'

'Daventry? Nonsense! He had no heart to break,' Fanny said indignantly. 'Any more than you have, Lieutenant Hawker.'

'Wrong, Miss Morland! Wrong and wrong again. To begin with, I very definitely have a heart, and it's all too vulnerable where you are concerned. And second,' he went on quickly as Fanny gasped, 'I am no longer Lieutenant Hawker. The militia and I have parted company. It was an uneasy union from the beginning,' he went on, but musingly, as though he were speaking to himself, 'and condemned both partners to misery. Divorce was inevitable — and particularly since her dowry turned out to be not the tithe of what I expected. I thought I had taken a wealthy bride —'

'I have no idea what you are talking about,' Fanny said with dignity. 'And now, if you will excuse me, I must return to the dance. I am engaged to stand up with Lord Somercott for the next set.'

He snapped out of his reverie, and caught her hand, lifting it to his lips and kissing each finger separately. Fanny tried to release herself, but finding his grip too strong, let him have his way, feeling it would be too undignified to struggle. She glared at him in cold fury, hoping to disguise the mad fluttering of her senses at the warm touch of his lips and the brush of his moustache on her fingers.

'Lord Somercott? No, no,' he said between kisses. 'Too commonplace by far. You shall not dance with him, my dear Miss Morland. In fact, I have a distinct urge to make sure that you never dance with anyone but me, ever again!'

'You are impudent! Let me go!' she protested.

'But how shall I do that?' he went on as if she had not spoken. He separated the middle finger of her right hand and laid its tip against his lips. 'How to make sure of you? I could take you away, lock you up somewhere, and keep the key in my breast.' He smiled at her as if it were a joke, but the gleam of his eyes under the droop of his eyelids made her doubt that it was. 'But no, that would not do, would it? For though I kept your body, I would not have your heart, would I?'

'You would have nothing! How dare you speak to me like that!' she panted.

'No — and I would have everything, Miss Morland,' he said, looking into her eyes. Fanny felt ready to faint, hardly able to hold his gaze. Then there was a sound as of someone coming out from the ballroom, and in an instant Hawker had whirled her round, placing her hand perfectly correctly over his as if he were just about to lead her in to the dance. The gentleman who came out looked at them curiously, but if he noticed Fanny's high colour, he might have attributed it to the exertions of the afternoon.

'I think I hear the music beginning, ma'am,' Hawker said in a pleasant, normal voice. 'I believe this is our dance?'

She was as yet unable to speak, and went with him rather than attempt to argue further. Lord Somercott, searching for her a moment later, was more annoyed than surprised to see her standing in the set with another man.

'Who's that dancing with Fanny Morland?' he demanded of Sir Henry Hope, who was standing beside him.

'No idea,' said Sir Henry. 'There's an awful lot of people here who weren't invited. Heard Lady Aylesbury complainin' about it just now.' He examined the newcomer. 'Military fellow, by the look of him. Handsome, too. Often thought I might grow some whiskers — the ladies seem to like 'em.'

'He looks like an outsider to me,' Somercott said savagely. 'Like a damned butcher's dog.'

It was late when Major Wiske returned from headquarters, and the wedding celebrations were so plainly over at the house in Grosvenor Square that he hesitated for a moment about knocking. But when the doorkeeper opened to him, he said that her ladyship had left a message to say she was still up in her private sitting-room, and that if the Major called he was to go straight up.

The sitting-room was on the second floor, a small room adjoining Lucy's bedchamber, whose decorations of snuff and dark blue and rather heavy furniture suggested it had been a gentleman's dressing-room at some point in its life. Wiske scratched at the door and went in, to find Lucy sitting in a large leather chair by the fire, staring at the flames and brooding.

'I'm sorry I couldn't come sooner,' he apologised. 'Bathurst was there. Could hardly come away.'

'It doesn't matter,' she said absently, and waved her hand to a seat. 'There's wine on the table. You might pour some for me, too.'

'Did everything go off well?' he asked, handing her her glass. 'I'm sorry I missed the dancing. I was looking forward to standing up with you.'

'Hmm,' she said, her eyes still on the flames, and giving her a sympathetic look, he took his seat and remained silent, sipping the wine and waiting for her to come back to him.

At last she drew a profound sigh. 'I've been trying to make sense of it all,' she said.

'All what?'

'My life.'

'Oh,' he said. That seemed a daunting prospect.

'Seeing Minnie driving off in the carriage, with her bags strapped on behind, made me think of my own wedding. I was even younger than her, though of course I'd seen and done more. But the point is —' she paused.

'Hmm?' he prompted helpfully.

Lucy frowned. 'The point is, I married Chetwyn so that she could be born, that's all. And now she's married Sale so that — well, some other child can be born. And I don't understand any of it.' She looked up and met his eyes with a puzzled expression. 'What's happening to me, Danby? I never used to wonder about things. I never used to think about things at all. I just got on and did things and enjoyed them. Why am I like this now? I don't like it.'

'We're all changing,' he said. 'The world is changing.' He smiled. 'Mostly, I think, we're just getting older.'

'That's no help,' she said, and he saw the focus of her eyes change. 'Have you had your orders?' she asked abruptly.

'Yes,' he said. 'I've been recalled. I must leave the day after tomorrow.'

He saw her face set, and seem to age. He hadn't expected her to look so upset; and despite the flattering aspect of it for him, he felt he would have preferred her not to care, and be happy. He slipped from his chair and knelt in front of her, taking her cold hands and chafing them.

'Oh Lucy, my dear, don't look like that!'

'I was always having to say goodbye to Weston, too,' she said in a small voice. 'The last time he left, he said that when he came home again, it would be for good.' She moved her head, a tired gesture, like one seeking ease. 'Of course, as it turned out, he was right.'

'But I will come back, I promise you,' he said urgently.

'How can you promise that?' she said. 'It's not in your power to promise that.'

He felt helpless. 'The war won't last for ever. It can't last much longer.'

'We thought that after Trafalgar — seven long years ago. I was only thirteen years old when the war began, Danby. My children have never known a time of peace. Maybe it will go on for ever. Maybe it will go on until we're all dead.'

He looked at her urgently. 'Lucy, Lucy, don't . All I can say is that I love you, and I've always loved you. You're the light of life to me. I've got to go away, but I will come back. Please, please won't you marry me? Marry me tomorrow, before I go away.'

She gave him a tired smile. 'Tomorrow? Don't be silly.'

'I mean it,' he said. 'I can get a special licence. I love you, Lucy! What's the point of waiting any longer?'

She put her hands up and cupped his face, which was on a level with hers. 'How could I follow my own daughter up the aisle so closely? It would be ridiculous.'

'We'll keep it a secret,' he said, putting his hands on her shoulders. Touching her roused all his senses, and made it difficult for him to think. 'Oh God, I want to kiss you!'

'Kiss me then,' she said simply, and drew his face towards her. It made him feel strangely excited, to be held like that by her strong hands, to have her take the initiative. She kissed him as though she were the man, parting his lips with her tongue, probing for his. He pulled back while he still could.

'Marry me tomorrow,' he pleaded desperately.

She shook her head, but she was smiling, and her eyes were bright; then she glanced towards the door which led into her bedchamber. 'I'll marry you tonight instead,' she said.

Everything suddenly seemed very still, as though the world were holding its breath. 'Are you sure?' he whispered at last.

'Yes, I'm sure. Life is too uncertain. I realise that now. I don't want to miss anything.'

She stood up and held out her hand to him, and helped him up, and then led him to the door. His mind revolved with worries about the consequences of this rashness, what the servants would think, how he was going to shave in the morning; until his rejoicing body, singing with anticipation, finally managed to silence it.

The house seemed suddenly very quiet with Minnie and Polly gone, and Major Wiske overseas again. Most of the families were still in the country, and in the absence of sufficient callers or engagements to keep her mind occupied, Lucy decided to go down to Wolvercote to refresh herself with country air, quiet, and plenty of riding until the start of the Little Season. Fanny was fretful at having to leave London, but when challenged by Lucy to say what she feared she would be missing, she had nothing to say.

Once settled in at Wolvercote, however, Fanny found that it was very pleasant after all, and she and Lucy went for long rides together, and almost came to like each other. Each of them loved horses, and respected good horsemanship more than anything in the world, so there was sufficient ground for mutual admiration to spring up. With no gentlemen to impress, Fanny behaved in a natural, unstrained way, and they discussed horses, dogs and country matters quite pleasantly; and Parslow even suggested that Miss Morland might like to try Feather over a few jumps.

'She's going very nicely now, Miss,' he said. 'I think her ladyship will be wanting to take her out this season and shew her to hounds.'

Lucy's spirits revived so completely that in the second week of their stay, she arranged a cross-country race for fun, pitting herself against Fanny, Rosamund, Roland and Thomas, and putting up a prize of a guinea which she was quite determined to forfeit. Miss Trotton was particularly glad on Roland's behalf that he was to be allowed to join in the fun. She had been worried about him for some time, for she felt that his tutor, Mr Mansell, was too harsh and strict for the boy, and gave him too little liberty to run about and play. Roland was small for his age, and rather pale and quiet, and Miss Trotton feared that too harsh a regime might stunt the boy's growth as it had already cowed his spirit.

In a very oblique way, she had talked to Docwra about it, wondering if there were any way of persuading Lucy to intervene on Roland's behalf; but Docwra had shaken her head without much hope. It seemed strange to her that Lucy should care so little about Roland, considering he was Captain Weston's child, when she so doted on Thomas. But it seemed that she had relegated him in her mind to that limbo occupied by the children of her marriage, Chetwyn's children, whom she did not love, and could not care for. To Lucy, Roland was Chetwyn's heir, the new little Lord Aylesbury, and therefore Chetwyn's child. Docwra saw it, though she did not understand it.

But for the fortnight of their stay at Wolvercote, Miss Trotton begged a holiday for Roland, and Mansell granted it, glad of the time to himself, since he had a passion for fishing, and the lakes at Wolvercote were well-stocked. He went out early every morning with his tackle, a bound volume of Juvenal's poems, and a cloth-wrapped nuncheon of cold meat, cheese, and bread, and did not come back until after dark.

Miss Trotton had the pleasure of seeing pale, spindly Roland gradually straighten up, like a flattened plant, reaching towards the light and air. It was interesting to her to observe the growing friendship between him and Thomas, and particularly the way Thomas, four years the younger, shielded and protected Roland, while treating him with all the deference due to his rank. He was like a mediæval squire serving his knight — a servitude of dignity and affection.

When they returned to London, it was to the old house in Upper Grosvenor Street. The talk was of Bonaparte's invasion of Russia, and how his huge army had penetrated all the way to Borodino, about a hundred miles from Moscow, where an indecisive battle had been fought, resulting in huge slaughter on both sides.

The news from the Peninsula was not good: Wellington's force, marching on Burgos, had outstripped its supply train, including the guns and ammunition, by several days. By the time they had joined up again, the French in the fortress had had time to organise their defences, and resisted the siege. Meanwhile the other two French armies were marching up from Andalusia and Catalonia towards Madrid, obviously bent on retaking it.

Wellington, faced with the overwhelming numbers of the French, recalled Lord Hill from Madrid, met him on the road with his own force, and began to march back to Portugal to make winter camp. The disappointment in London was enormous, for everyone had thought victory in Spain was within reach, and now it seemed nothing had been gained, and that Wellington had been driven back exactly to where he had been two years ago.

Danby Wiske, in his letter to Lucy, painted the picture in more hopeful colours. 'We've shewn that despite their numbers, the French can do nothing against us. Soult and Joseph, to protect Madrid, have had to give up all the country south of the Tagus, and there the Spanish irregulars have taken control, and are even organising themselves into regular armies. We took twenty thousand prisoners at Madrid, three thousand guns, and all the French stores, and while we över-winter comfortably in Portugal, they will have a thin time of it in Spain.

'We must win in the end, dearest Lucy — it pains me that it

will take longer than I had hoped from earlier events, delaying the time that I can come back to you for good. I carry the memory of your sweetness close to my heart, and if the power of love can protect a man against shot and shell, you need have no fear for my safety.'

The long-dreaded letter from Captain Haworth had also arrived, in which he spoke of his hope that Africa was still making her way to him, and of his own enquiries, which he sent with every dispatch that left his ship; but his grief and pain were too plainly to be felt under the hopeful words for Lucy to be able to bear to reread it.

Town was still thin of company in the middle of October, when Lucy had an unexpected visitor.

'A Mr Morpurgo, my lady,' Hicks said with an anxious eye.

'Morpurgo? Oh, yes, I remember, the midshipman.'

'He asked after Miss Africa, my lady,' Hicks said dolefully.

'Oh, Lord!'

'Yes, my lady. I didn't like to take it upon myself to say anything, my lady.'

'You'd better send him up, Hicks. I wonder how it comes that he hasn't heard about her? He was serving aboard Haworth's ship.'

A few moments later, the young man came in, looking brown and salt-bleached, his front hair almost white, his eyes very blue. He was twenty-two now, very much a man and not a boy, his face firm with the experience of command.

'Lady Aylesbury, it's very good of you to receive me,' he said with a graceful bow.

'Not at all, Mr Morpurgo. It's kind of you to call. I suppose you bring a letter or message from Captain Haworth?'

'Well, ma'am, no doubt if he knew I was here, he would charge me with his compliments to you,' Morpurgo said, 'but in fact I parted company with the Commodore back in May. He was pleased to make me Acting-Lieutenant, and put me in command of one of the prizes — I suppose you heard about our action off Palermo, ma'am?'

'Yes, we read about it. It must have been very exciting,' Lucy said.

'It was, ma'am; and we took three prizes. Mine, the *Zephyr*, was badly holed, some of them below the waterline, and I had the d ... a hard time of it getting her back to Gibraltar.

Several times I thought we were for the bottom, but the men were wonderful! There's no-one works harder, ma'am, than a British Jack, especially when there's gold at the end of it!'

Lucy smiled. 'So you brought her in to Gibraltar safely? And what do you here?'

'Well, ma'am, we patched her up, and I was to bring her back to England, but there happened to be a squadron in port, with sufficient senior officers to hold the lieutenants' examinations, and Admiral Harvey kindly arranged for me to take mine before we set sail.'

'You passed, I take it?'

'Yes, ma'am, I'm glad to say I did! So now I've brought *Zephyr* in to Portsmouth to be docked, and posted up to London to hand in despatches, and now I have only to wait for a ship.'

'It won't be long, I'm sure,' Lucy said kindly. 'We need all our officers afloat, especially those who've distinguished themselves already.'

He beamed. 'You're too kind, ma'am! I hope you didn't think it impertinent of me to call on you like this?'

'Not at all. I'm glad to hear your news.'

'I hope you are all well? His lordship, and Lady Flaminia and Lady Rosamund?'

Lucy told him about Flaminia's marriage. 'Miss Haworth has gone with Lady Flaminia as her companion, so the house is very quiet.'

'And Miss Africa Haworth? She is well, I trust? I hoped she might be here, ma'am, so that I could pay my compliments to her. She and I are old shipmates, you know.'

Lucy drew breath. 'Yes, Mr Morpurgo, I know. I'm afraid I have some disagreeable news for you.'

Morpurgo listened in increasing astonishment and concern as Lucy told him about Africa's disappearance. 'But — but has nothing been done? Has no-one looked for her?'

Lucy kept her temper. 'To be sure, Mr Morpurgo, she has been sought diligently these five months. Did you think I would wash my hands of her?'

He flushed. 'I beg your pardon, ma'am. I didn't mean to suggest — of course, you will have done everything in your power.' He hesitated. 'Might I ask where you looked for her?'

Lucy told him briefly of her own and her agents' searches.

He listened attentively, his intelligence evidently at work behind his furrowed brow.

'Plainly,' he said, 'she didn't mean to disappear for ever. If she thought her father would approve of what she was doing, she must have expected him to learn of it at some time. So, if she hasn't written to him, and she hasn't gone to him —'

'We think she must still be on a ship somewhere, trying to do that very thing.'

Morpurgo shook his head. 'Forgive me, ma'am, but if she were aboard a King's ship, she, or news of her, would have reached her father by now. No, I believe she must have gone into hiding somewhere, intending to reveal herself when her father next comes to England. That means it must be somewhere where she can be sustained in the necessaries of life, and where she can hope to learn of her father's arrival.' He lapsed into thoughtful silence, and then an expression of illumination crept over his face which made Lucy's heart lift. 'I wonder —' he began.

'You have thought of the answer? You know where she is?'

'I don't know, ma'am. It's a possibility, that's all.'

'For God's sake, Mr Morpurgo, tell me!'

'Forgive me, ma'am, but I don't wish to raise your hopes uselessly. It is only a slender chance; but would you allow me to make certain enquiries on your behalf?'

'Of course,' Lucy said impatiently. 'Anything that may help — that may throw light on the matter. But tell me what it is you suspect. I may be able to help. I have money — agents — your task may be made easier.'

He shook his head. 'My enquiry is simply made. I need no help or money. I'll take leave of you now, if I may, Lady Aylesbury, and call again tomorrow, to let you know if I have met with any success.'

'Not until tomorrow?'

'Earlier perhaps, if I am in luck. Your servant, ma'am.'

He bowed himself out, leaving Lucy feeling as though she were suspended by a thread over a chasm.

CHAPTER TWENTY-TWO

A theatre during the daytime is a shabby place, smelling of dust and orange-peel; a place of unreality, a little sad, haunted by the ghosts of images. Not so a circus: here by day the hard work goes on, a real, down-to-earth matter of exertion and sweat and limber bodies. So Morpurgo discovered when he obtained entry to Astley's Amphitheatre by the simple method of sliding a half-crown into the hand of the burly doorman who was trying to keep him out.

'I've always wanted to watch a rehearsal,' Morpurgo said blandly as the coin disappeared.

'I never saw you, guv'nor. Musta slipped in be'ind me back,' said the doorman, gazing at the sky.

Inside there was a powerful odour of sawdust, manure, human sweat, and the prickling, foxy smell of caged animals. In the middle of the ring the slack-wire was up, and the wire-walkers were going through their balancing and stretching routines. Under the proscenium a troupe of dancers was practising, the regular thump of their feet unnaturally loud on the wooden stage in the absence of music; while down in the orchestra pit a lone musician was monotonously tuning a harp.

Morpurgo viewed it all with sharp interest, keeping as far as possible in the shadows and effacing himself, though no-one seemed disposed to pay any attention to him. He guessed that visitors of one sort or another were not uncommon, and that the doorman was more often looking at the sky than he would be likely to admit to his employers.

He didn't quite know what to do next. The idea of the circus had come to him like an inspiration, for in thinking of the visit he had paid here in Africa's company, he remembered suddenly how enthusiastic she had been, how she had spoken of nothing else for hours. If she had hidden herself, he reasoned, it must be somewhere that she could earn her living, amongst people who would not be likely to give her away, or to question her antecedents.

Africa was used all her life to dealing with the lower orders, in the shape of seamen, and knew how to get on with them and talk to them; she had also, since she could walk, run up and down ratlines, climbed and scrambled over spars and bowsprits, and balanced on footropes in a display of agility and control any circus tumbler might envy. There was also the consideration that if she had gone to Portsmouth, someone must have seen her. Morpurgo considered it impossible for her to have gone there and got aboard a ship without anyone's noticing; and if she didn't go to Portsmouth, the next most likely place was London. In London a person had more chance of concealing themselves; and there was also constant news about the comings and goings of His Majesty's ships.

So far so good; but if she were here, how was he to find her? She would not have given her real name, so to ask for her by it would be futile, and he suspected that enquiries on his part would only bring about a closing of the ranks amongst the circus people, and a look of blank ignorance on every face. His best plan was to wait and watch and see if she appeared, and if she did, to approach her quietly, if possible without her knowing. If she did not, he must think of some plausible excuse for searching further, in the hidden back quarters.

After some time, the slack-rope walkers finished their exercise, and there was an argument between a stout man whom, by his moustaches, Morpurgo took to be the ringmaster, and the mechanics, who, it seemed, didn't want the trouble of taking down the apparatus and later erecting it again. The ringmaster eventually raised his voice and his fist and stamped his foot a little, and the wire was taken down and the ring cleared. Shortly afterwards six black horses were led in by grooms and released, to canter around the ring under the direction of a muscular man with a long whip who stood in the centre and shouted orders at them.

Without the music, the routine had a curiously soporific effect. Morpurgo had sat down on a half-barrel in the shadows of a corner. It was hot and a little stuffy in the amphitheatre, and watching the black horses circle and reverse and do their simple manoeuvres, made complex only by the fact of their doing them in unison, he found his eyelids drooping. He

437

must have drifted off to sleep for a moment, for he jerked awake as his chin slipped down onto his chest, and looked guiltily towards the ring, to see that the black horses were being led out again, nodding their heads and snorting the dust from their flared nostrils. In the ring-entrance they were passed by another horse coming in, a big, heavily-built, broad-backed horse, being ridden astride by a slender and evidently feminine figure.

The Equestrienne! he thought. And then his heart lurched, and he rose involuntarily to his feet, as he realised why the figure looked so familiar — not because he had seen her perform before, or at least, not in this particular way. Even from this distance he could not mistake her, though her dark hair was bound up in a scarf like a gypsy, to keep it out of her eyes. So his guess had been right! He was filled with relief, and also with admiration for her resourcefulness. She had come to the one place where her particular, peculiar talents could be utilised.

The big horse began to canter slowly round, and Morpurgo watched, fascinated, as Africa stood upright, and balanced lightly on the balls of her feet on the gently-bouncing rump. It was nothing to her, he thought, after balancing on the yard-arm of an unpredictably-heaving ship. As she went through her practice, he began to edge nearer, making his way forward and sideways towards the archway through which the artists had been coming and going, which led, presumably, to the stables and beast-quarters. He was standing there when, having finished her routine, Africa jumped down lightly to the sawdust, rewarded the big horse with a piece of carrot, and led him out of the ring.

'Miss Haworth,' he said softly. She started so violently that it made the horse snort with alarm, and she turned to him, eyes wide. 'Hello, Africa,' he said.

'Morpurgo!' she exclaimed, staring as though she couldn't believe her eyes; and then she began laughing. 'Of all people! What are you doing here? How did you find me? Does anyone else know I'm here?'

Before he could answer any of the questions, somebody shouted at her to move the horse, and she said, 'I must put him back in his stall — it's the rule, they mustn't be kept standing about.'

'I'll come with you,' Morpurgo said firmly.

'All right,' she said, and laughed again. 'I won't run away from you. I'm glad to see you, in fact. How did you find me?'

'I've only just heard that you were missing,' he said, falling in beside her. 'As soon as I heard, I thought of the circus — it seemed obvious.'

'Not to anyone else, evidently,' she said, walking the horse through the archway and down a wooden tunnel. 'So, I suppose the game is up — you've come to fetch me home again?'

'No-one knows where I am yet,' he said. 'But you can't imagine how unhappy you've made everyone. Your father, Africa — he must be grieving for you, thinking you're dead.'

She looked surprised. 'But I wrote to him when I wrote to Aunt Lucy, to say I'd be quite all right, and that I'd see him when he came home.'

'I don't think he ever got that letter,' Morpurgo said. 'But even if he had, he must have feared the worst when you had disappeared so completely. No-one knew if you were alive or dead. Your poor aunt has obviously been worried almost to death.'

Africa looked stubborn. 'I'm sorry, I never meant to worry her. But I couldn't stay at the school any longer. You can't imagine, Peter! It was dreadful. Shut up like a cage-bird, I thought I should die. I *would* have died! I had to get out.'

'And so you came here?'

They passed from the tunnel into the stables, a long building lined with stalls on either side.

'I thought I could do something — tumbling or wire-walking or something,' she said, leading the big horse into a stall on the right, and attaching pillar-ropes to his headcollar. 'I didn't mind what it was, as long as I had somewhere to live and enough to eat. As it was, I was very lucky. The Equestrienne — you remember, we saw her perform the night we came here?' He nodded. 'Well, she'd got pregnant, and couldn't go on working much longer, and I said I could learn her tricks in a few days. They didn't believe me at first, but I did it, and they were so pleased, because she was their biggest attraction, and they thought they'd never replace her.'

Morpurgo shook his head in wonder. 'Africa, you're amazing!'

'Not at all — it's simple stuff. Anyone could do it, as long

439

as they could balance and understood horses. I used to do horseback tricks for Sophie when we were at Morland Place.' A wistful look came over her. 'How is Sophie? I do miss her.'

'You'll be able to find out for yourself soon,' he said pointedly.

She frowned. 'You mean to take me back? But Peter, I can't go back. Aunt Lucy will send me back to school. Besides, they need me here. It's not likely they'll find another Equestrienne, just like that.'

He loooked obdurate. 'You know you have to go back,' he said. 'If it helps, I don't think your aunt will send you back to school. I think you've made your protest sufficiently strongly. You can't stay here, Africa, you must see that.'

'Well, I must do tonight's performance, at least, and tell them that I'm going. It wouldn't be fair.'

'I can't let you,' he said.

'You said no-one else knows you're here?' she said. 'Well, then, one more night can't hurt, can it? You can come and watch my performance, if you like, and then take me away afterwards.' She sighed, and stroked the big horse's nose. 'It will be so dreadful to go back, but I suppose I always knew I'd be found sooner or later.'

'You wouldn't have been, if it weren't for me,' Morpurgo said guiltily. 'I'm sorry, Africa; but you really have made a lot of people very unhappy.'

'I'll forgive you, if you let me do my performance tonight,' she said cannily. 'You must, for no-one I know has seen it, and there must be someone to tell Papa how good I was.'

'That's another thing — how did you propose to find out when your father came back to England?'

'That's easy,' she said. 'I gave one of the children a penny to go down to the Admiralty every day and look at the lists put up on the gate of ships coming in.'

'How did you know he wouldn't betray you? He'd have got a lot more than a penny for telling your family where you were.'

'Circus people aren't like that,' Africa said.

The rediscovery of Africa, and her homecoming, was the sensation of the season, not only in the house but, since the news of what she had been doing inevitably leaked out, all through

440

London. That the famous Equestrienne had in fact been Lady Aylesbury's missing niece had everyone gossiping and exclaiming; and since news rarely travels very far without transmutation, and the fate of the original Equestrienne was soon muddled with that of her successor, Africa was variously supposed to have run away from school because she was pregnant, and given the child to the circus people to bring up; or to have been abducted by a circus-artist and made pregnant; or to have been a changeling all along, whom the circus people had at last claimed for their own.

The scandal Lucy had precipitated at the same age by running away to sea was nothing to this. Africa was notorious; people who had actually seen her perform were suddenly very popular as dinner-guests, until it gradually began to appear that there was hardly anyone in London who *hadn't* seen her perform. The glamour of the circus and a great deal of romantic nonsense about gypsies was mixed up with scandalous speculation about secret marriages and love-children; and Hicks was soon forced to take the knocker off the door to discourage callers, and to pull the downstairs blinds to prevent idlers from gawping from the street, and actually peering in through the windows in the hope of catching a glimpse of the Equestrienne herself.

Lucy's relief that she was found, and not lying dead in a ditch somewhere, was so profound that she had little emotion left for surprise or wonder. She felt she could hardly be censorious, considering her own escapade so long ago, and confined herself merely to rebuking Africa for having left them all to worry, when she might easily have sent a message at least to say she was alive and well. Morpurgo was the hero of the hour, though he effaced himself modestly. Lucy was mortified that Africa had been in London all the time, and less than two miles away, while Lucy and her agents had been scouring Portsmouth and the high seas for her; and that she had not thought of the answer for herself, though she possessed all the same information as Morpurgo.

The least she could do for him, she thought, was to use her influence with Their Lordships to get him commissioned into a ship at the earliest possible moment, which would also have the effect of removing him from London. As to Africa, she remained an unsolved problem. That she must leave London was plain, and as soon as possible, to allow the scandal to die down; but where could she be sent? No school or private house could hold her, short of tying her hand and foot and locking her up.

Morpurgo again came up with the answer. 'Could she not be sent to her father, ma'am?' he asked tentatively. 'I know it's what she wants, and it would remove her from all these staring eyes and wagging tongues.' From his fervent way of speaking, it was evident that he was under the misapprehension that the eyes and tongues were more of a threat to Africa than to her relatives.

Lucy considered the idea. At sea, Africa would be happy and good, protected and unobserved. She would not be at school and learning to be a lady, which was what her father wanted for her, and the correct procedure would be to consult Haworth before sending Africa out to him. But that would involve a great deal of time, and what was Lucy to do with the girl while she waited for a reply? At the very least, if he did not like it, he could send her straight back when she reached him, and make his own arrangements for his wayward daughter.

Lucy put the idea to Africa, and she was overjoyed. 'Oh Aunt, you are so good to me! It's what I want of all things! Even more than the circus!'

'I haven't made up my mind yet,' Lucy said. 'I don't even know if it can be done. I shall have to consult various people at the Admiralty.'

'Oh, it will be all right, I know it will,' Africa said rapturously. 'To be at sea again! The wind and the sky! To be with Papa!'

Lucy eyed her with a curious sympathy. 'I will see what can be done,' she said shortly. 'In the meantime, will you promise to behave yourself, and not draw any more attention to us?'

'Oh yes, dear Aunt, absolutely! I will do anything you tell me to. I'll hide in the attic if it will help.'

'I don't think that will be necessary. I think I had better send you down to Wolvercote for the time being. You can do lessons with Rosamund to pass the time, and there you'll be able to ride and walk without being stared at. But you must promise not to run away again.'

'Of course I won't,' Africa said. 'Oh thank you, Aunt Lucy!

442

You are the best aunt in the world. I knew you'd understand how I felt.'

All too well, Lucy thought drily, but she kept the thought to herself.

Fanny had been furious about the whole affair. She liked to be the centre of attention, and everyone had been too taken up with Africa to think of her. And then, when people did notice her, it was to ask questions about her cousin, and they gave her such peculiar smiles and looks! There were some kinds of fame, Fanny concluded, that one was better off without. Africa had made them a scandal and a laughing-stock, and brought shame on the family name.

She was very pleased when Africa departed for Wolvercote, and hoped that the notoriety would begin to fade away. Aunt Lucy was much preoccupied with trying to arrange for Africa to be sent back to her father, and their evening engagements had been disastrously curtailed; but at least it gave Fanny a welcome freedom for supervision. Her new maid, Beaver, was very good with clothes and hair, but not a little dim, and Fanny was able to manipulate her very easily. She had also made friends with the new groom, a callow and forward-looking youth called Gregory, who was pleased to do anything he was told for the sake of a shilling here and there.

Since Parslow was busy driving his lady in search of admirals and senior officials, it was Gregory who attended Fanny on her rides, and who drove her around the Park in the phaeton, or took her shopping in Bond Street with Beaver to carry the parcels. As long as one or both of the servants were with her, her reputation was safe, and she could meet Mr Hawker at prearranged times and places, and carry on the delicious oblique conversations with him that so fascinated her.

It occurred to Fanny more than once that she was falling in love with Hawker, and she resented it, and resisted the idea. Hawker was attractive and fascinating, but he was not titled or rich, and she did not want to marry him. Indeed, he wasn't eligible at all, and while she would have enjoyed a flirtation with him, as she had with so many other men she had no intention of marrying, she did not want him to disturb her peace, which he was all too prone to do.

She wondered sometimes if he were courting her for her

443

fortune, as others had already done; but then she had to admit to herself that he did not seem to be courting her at all. He treated her casually, almost with amusement, as if she were too young and unsophisticated to interest him seriously. Whenever they met, his eyes and voice caressed her in a way that distracted her senses; but he did not pursue her — it was always she who was the more eager for the next meeting. Every time they met she determined that this time it must be he who proposed it; and every time, when they parted and he was about to stroll away without having formed another assignation, she yielded, half ashamed, to her inner desires.

She did not clearly understand what he was doing in London, where he seemed on the fringes of society, not precisely included, nor denied. He was never at Almacks, nor at the balls or routs of the stuffier hostesses, but she met him here and there at lesser functions. One day, a week after Africa had gone down to Wolvercote, she met him by arrangement at the gate of the Park, and got down from the phaeton to walk with him, while Beaver walked a few paces behind, and Gregory drove at snail's pace behind them.

'How are things at Upper Grosvenor Street today?' he asked her.

'I hope you don't mean to ask me about my cousin,' she said quickly, 'for if anyone else mentions Africa to me, I shall scream. Every partner I had last night at Mrs Fauncett's wanted to know where she was. I was quite cutting to Mr Paston; and that odious Lavinia Fauncett asked me if I had seen any of Africa's costumes, and looked *so* at my head-dress that I could have scratched her eyes out.'

Hawker laughed aloud, and Fanny scowled. 'I don't know why you think it's amusing. And besides, why weren't you there? I thought we were engaged for the two last before supper?'

'I had a more pressing engagement with a pack of cards in St James's Square,' he said indifferently.

She raised her eyebrows, surprised and offended. 'You prefer playing cards to dancing with me?'

'Not prefer, Miss Morland,' he said. 'If things were otherwise, I should like nothing better than to dance with you all night, every night. But a man must live, and you do not pay me to dance with you.'

444

She stared at him. 'What can you mean?'

'I mean that I spent last night repairing my fortunes in a gaming-house,' he said, enjoying her innocence. 'I came out a hundred guineas up, which means I can pay enough of my bills to extend my credit.'

'Do you mean to tell me, Mr Hawker, that you live by gaming?' Fanny said, shocked.

He smiled. 'I do tell you so, Miss Morland. Why so surprised? It is not an uncommon thing. Your aunt's great friend Mr Brummell does the same, and no-one, surely, could be more respectable than he? Of course,' he added thoughtfully, 'he plays only in his clubs, where the bank passes from hand to hand, and a man with a cool nerve, like Mr Brummell, may win more often than he loses.' He eyed her questioningly. 'I told you that I had left the militia. How did you suppose I lived?'

'I never thought about it,' she said. She hardly ever thought about money — money was something that one gave to the lower orders in return for goods and services. All the adults she knew had plenty of it, without appearing to do anything for it. Of course, her grandfather went to his mills every day, and Uncle Ned went about the estate, but she did not associate these things directly with earning money. They were simply things they had to do, like going to church on Sunday, or visiting the sick, duties associated with their station in life. She knew Hawker was not rich, but she assumed he had an income from somewhere, like everyone else.

'No, I don't suppose you did,' he said. They walked on, and he did not speak, remaining deep in thought. Fanny grew restless, then peeved. She did not risk her aunt's wrath for the sake of being ignored.

'If you have nothing to say to me, Mr Hawker, I may as well leave you and drive on,' she said coolly.

'Very well,' he said absently. The hundred guineas he had won last night came nowhere near releasing him from worry, and his mind was deeply occupied in wondering how he was to manage, rather than in Fanny's sensitive vanity. It amused him to torment and flirt with her, but though he knew she was a great heiress, she was still too young to tempt him. Her fortune would not be released until she was twenty-one, and he had no illusions that her father would think him a good

445

enough match to release it earlier.

Fanny gave a little gasp at his reply, withdrew her hand sharply from his arm, and was about to flounce away when he caught her back, looking down into her flushed and angry face with amusement.

'No, no, Miss Morland, don't leave me in anger. That is not how friends part.'

'Friends? We are not friends, Mr Hawker, and I will leave you any way I wish,' she retorted a little breathlessly.

'Are we not, then? I hoped we were. Well, I see I cannot keep you — goodbye.' She hesitated, and he smiled his piratical smile. 'You do not take your leave. Does something remain to be said?' She bit her tongue to keep herself from asking, and seeing it, he chuckled and said, 'Where shall we meet again — that still remains to be asked. Who shall ask it? You or I?'

'Be assured I shall not,' she flung at him.

'No? Then I must. Or rather, I shall not ask you, I shall tell you. You have never been to Vauxhall Gardens, I believe? I think it's time you saw them, and the sooner the better. Tonight, Miss Morland, shall be the night.'

She gasped. 'I can't! They wouldn't let me.'

'Don't ask them, fool! All you need to do is to get out of the house. I shall meet you by the park railings opposite the end of your street, with a closed carriage, at half-past nine. I'll bring a domino and mask, and undertake to have you safe home by one o'clock.'

'How can I get out of the house?' she protested.

He shrugged. 'That's your affair. Your cousin managed it. Have you not the spirit for the adventure, Miss Morland? Perhaps I have invited the wrong girl. Perhaps Miss Haworth is more of a kindred spirit.'

Fanny glared. 'I am worth ten of her!'

'So I thought, or I would not have asked you. Will you be there?'

'Yes,' she snapped, and he laughed.

'I wonder. Time will tell. And now, goodbye, ma'am.'

Fanny had been fascinated by the idea of Vauxhall Gardens ever since she came to London, as Hawker well knew, but to slip out of the house unknown and to go there alone with a

446

man was something she knew to be so wicked that she quailed at the prospect. It was far worse than what Africa had done. If she were discovered, she would be ruined for ever. And yet she wanted to go: she wanted the adventure, and she wanted to be with him. She hated him to think her poor-spirited.

All day she turned the idea over in her mind, tugged this way and that, and her preoccupation was such that at dinner even Lucy noticed she was pale and quiet.

'Are you unwell, Fanny?' she asked.

Fanny took a deep breath. 'I'm afraid — I think I am, Aunt. I have the headache, a little.'

'Then you should not go to Mrs Underwood's this evening,' Lucy said, preparing for protest.

'No, Aunt. I think I would like to go early to bed. I do feel rather tired,' Fanny said.

That was enough to convince Lucy that she really was unwell. 'I hope you aren't sickening for something. If you're not better in the morning, I shall make up a dose for you.'

'Thank you, Aunt. If you will forgive me, I think I'll go to my room now,' Fanny said meekly, though her heart was pounding as she rose from the table and drifted away.

It took the contrivance of both her allies to get her out of the house. Firstly Beaver had to help her dress, and had to promise to convince anyone who asked that she was asleep in bed and mustn't be disturbed. When the time came to leave, Beaver smuggled her down the backstairs, where Gregory was keeping watch, to pick the right moment when all was quiet to slip her out into the service courtyard which gave onto the street. They were both to wait up, to reverse the process when she returned: he to smuggle her across the yard, and Beaver to open the door from within and escort her up the backstairs. Fanny was glad her father's allowance to her was so generous, for she knew from experience that servants' loyalty needed to be encouraged, especially when it involved staying awake after midnight.

The escape went so smoothly that her spirits rose, and she began to feel it was rather a good adventure after all. She had a moment's qualm that the carriage might not be waiting, that he might have forgotten or changed his mind, but there it was, standing by the railings with its lamps covered, a darker shape in the darkness under the trees. The driver made no sign of recognition as she approached, but the door opened silently and the step was let down, and a hand she knew reached out of the dark interior to help her in.

'Good girl,' Hawker said out of the shadows. 'You have spirit after all.'

She said nothing. She was half afraid that he might try to kiss her, but having put up the step, closed the door, and rapped on the ceiling, he settled back against the seat without touching her and said, 'Did you have any trouble getting out?'

'None at all,' she said proudly.

'What a shocking thing!' he said. 'It is scandalously easy for young women to escape supervision these days. No wonder so many of them are going to the bad.' She made no reply, puzzled as to whether he was serious or not. 'So, Fanny Morland, you have slipped the leash,' he said at last. 'Well, we shall have a merry evening together, and be damned to all cares and considerations!'

Then he lapsed into silence, and seemed so obviously disinclined for conversation that she would not expose herself any further, and was silent too. If he doesn't want to talk to me, he might as well not have brought me here, she thought, offended. The silence lasted all the way to Vauxhall, where, when the coach stopped, Hawker roused himself to give the driver instructions to be at the gate again at half-past twelve. Then he turned to Fanny.

'Now is the time to put on your mask, my dear Miss Morland. I think, as your cloak is plain and dark, we need not bother with the domino.'

She looked at him doubtfully, and he smiled more pleasantly than before. 'Come, we shall enjoy ourselves, I promise you. Or would you prefer to go home? We can turn round this minute if you do not like it.'

'That would be poor-spirited,' Fanny said with dignity. 'Give me the mask.'

'Brava! Spoken like a hero — or rather, heroine. Do you not think this is like an episode out of a novel?' She didn't answer. 'There will be fireworks later, you know,' he said cunningly. 'I should have hated you to miss them.'

Fanny loved the gardens from the first moment. The avenues of trees and shrubs, punctuated here and there by miniature summer-houses and temples, each containing a seat where lovers could sit and talk in seclusion, were lit by hundreds of coloured lanterns, and lamps contained in golden globes, like captive harvest moons floating in the dark foliage. At the centre in a large open space an orchestra was playing. Small private booths were arranged in a circle around it, where people could sit and take supper and watch the passers-by. There was dancing, too, in one rotunda, and a concert in the other, but it was evident that seeing and being seen, and pursuing assignations, were the principal occupations of the place.

Hawker had hired a booth to which he now conducted her, and soon a waiter brought them supper, featuring the wafer-thin slices of ham for which the gardens were famous. Hawker had evidently consulted her taste in ordering, for there was also cold chicken, oyster patties, little cakes, and an orange cream, and despite her earlier dinner, Fanny ate heartily of everything, enjoying the novelty of eating at such a time and in such a place. Hawker had ordered lemonade as well as champagne, and she was glad of the former, for the latter, though delightful, made her thirsty.

Afterwards they listened to the orchestra, and he talked amusingly about the passers-by, pointing out various people to her, criticising their *toilette*, telling her scandalous stories about them, and recognising masked people with an ease that made her anxious about her own disguise. The time flew past, and soon it was time for the fireworks to begin, after which they would have to leave. Hawker proposed strolling through the gardens to the water's edge where, he said, the view of the fireworks would be clearer.

They passed from one walk to another, increasingly secluded, until they came at the end of an alley to a white stone balustrade, beyond which the river glittered dimly in the light from the lanterns. It was very quiet, and Fanny felt all at once a little nervous. Now he will kiss me, she thought, and she didn't know whether she wanted him to or not. The champagne was singing in her veins, yet oddly her head felt quite clear. It was as if she were two people, one reckless and excited, the other cool and calculating.

She stood beside him at the balustrade, looking out over the dark water, waiting. She could hear him breathing, feel the warmth of his body radiating through the little space

449

between them. She had a distinct and piercing sense of him just at that moment, as though she had known him all her life, better than she knew anyone else; she knew him, skin and bones and muscles and blood; she knew he was hard and cold and untrustworthy, and that he would never hurt her, because in some way they belonged together. And at the very same moment, she knew that all this was nonsense.

'Well, Miss Morland,' he said, his voice coming familiar out of the darkness as if it were an extension of her own thoughts, 'have you had an agreeable evening?'

'Yes,' she said simply. 'I'm glad I came.'

'I'm glad too. I wanted to have one last, happy time with you.'

'Last?' she queried, feeling a little cold finger of breeze touch the back of her neck. She shivered. 'Are you going away?'

'I'm afraid so. I'm afraid I must.'

'For a long time?'

'I don't know. I hope not.' He paused. 'I have enjoyed seeing you happy this evening.' His words sounded so final that she shivered again, and he said, 'Are you cold, Fanny?'

He had never used her first name before, and it made her feel both protected and exposed at the same time. 'No,' she said, but he stepped closer all the same, turning her to face him and putting his arms round her.

'Little Fanny Morland,' he said softly, and his dark head stooped over her like some nemesis, cutting out what little light there was. She felt his lips on hers. It was a strange, strange sensation! She had never been kissed before, not by a man, not on the mouth. She didn't quite know what to make of it; but she knew she wanted something from him, and she put her hands up and took hold of him, to keep him there. His big, alien body was close to her, and she didn't know what to do with it, or with all the extraordinary feelings rushing through her; she only knew she felt hurt and disappointed when he pulled away from her.

'You're a fool, Fanny,' he said in a hard, bitter voice. 'And I'm a greater one. What the devil are we to do with each other?'

'Don't,' she said falteringly, not understanding him, only knowing she didn't want to feel separate from him; and then

450

there was an enormous explosion in the air above her, which made her jump and cry out, and a blinding flash of light drove her hands to her eyes.

Then Hawker was laughing loudly, like someone who has seen a danger pass by. 'It's only the fireworks, you goose! Look, Fanny, take your hands away, or you'll miss them! Look, look up into the sky!'

'Don't laugh at me!' she cried, but he pulled her hands away and turned her again towards the river. The sky was awash with coloured stars, comet-tails, cascades, and the river was a second sky mirroring the first, a black silken eternity filled with dazzling lights. 'It's beautiful!' she cried out in surprise.

'You're beautiful!' he shouted. He was still laughing, but she didn't mind it now, feeling that it was with her and not against her. He seized her wrists and tugged at her impatiently. 'We must go.'

'No! I want to see the rest!'

'We must go, I say! Come, Fanny, it's all over.'

He dragged her away from the water's edge into the dark alley, though the fires were still erupting overhead, and she went unwillingly because she must, his hand steely on her wrist.

'I don't want to go home,' she cried.

'You can't always do what you want,' he said.

'When will I see you again?' she asked, beginning to be breathless and a little frightened, dragged along behind him like a child. 'You're walking too fast! I shall stumble!'

'I won't let you fall,' he said tersely. It was an ungentle promise.

'When will I see you again?'

'I told you I was going away. I don't know when I will be back in London.'

'Before Christmas? I shall be going back to Yorkshire at Christmas. If you don't get back before Christmas, will you come up to York?'

They reached the gate, and he paused and looked down at her. By the light of the torches at the gate, she could see his face, but it was dark and unfathomable. 'Come to York? Why should I come to York?' he asked as if the question amazed him.

451

'To see me,' she faltered.

'Miss Morland, I repeat, you're a fool,' he said.

She felt tears burning in her eyes, and turned her face away and closed her teeth on her lip to stop it trembling. I won't let him see me cry, she thought, half in fury, half in grief. I will never let him see me cry! He's hateful! Cruel! I shall never think of him again.

She drew several deep breaths, and said in a voice which hardly trembled, 'Will you have the goodness to hand me into the carriage, Mr Hawker? If that is not asking too much of your manners.'

She saw a faint gleam of admiration in his eyes, before she lowered hers; and kept them rigidly on the ground as he opened the door, let down the step and handed her in; and then climbed in beside her. They rode in silence until they reached the place where he had met her, and the coach stopped.

'How will you get in?' he asked suddenly, and his voice sounded subdued. I have shamed him, she thought triumphantly.

'I have made my arrangements,' she said coolly. 'You have no need to concern yourself any further. I wish you goodnight, Mr Hawker, and thank you for an enjoyable evening.'

'Goodnight, Miss Morland,' he replied without emotion, opening the door and pushing the step down; but as she placed her hand on his to climb out, he gripped her fingers for the fraction of a second, and said, 'God bless you!'

She made no response, withdrawing her hand as soon as she was safely down, and walking away without another word or a backward glance.

BOOK THREE

The Heiress

'Do you remember me? or are you proud?'
Lightly advancing thro' her star-trimm'd crowd,
Ianthe said, and look'd into my eyes.
'A yes, and yes to both: for Memory
Where you but once have been must ever be,
And at your voice Pride from his throne must rise.'

Walter Savage Landor: *Ianthe's Question*

CHAPTER TWENTY-THREE

October 1813

Jasper Hobsbawn, emerging from a conference with a mechanic over a machine that was overheating, walked over to the window for a piece of rag on which to wipe his hands, and glancing out through the grimy pane, saw a familiar carriage in the yard below. With a silent curse, he threw down the rag and hurried downstairs.

In the outer office Cutler, the senior clerk, looked up apprehensively.

'Is Mr Hobsbawn here?' Jasper asked.

'No, Mr Jasper, sir, it's Miss Morland.'

'Deuce it is!' Jasper muttered. 'Where is she?'

'In th'office, Mr Jasper, lookin' at the books.'

'What?'

Cutler's eyes fawned. 'She axed me, Mr Jasper. What could I say?'

'No, quite right, it isn't your fault. Carry on, Cutler,' said Jasper briskly, and walked through into the inner office, which had always, until recently, been unassailably his own. Fanny was there, sitting at the desk, a voluminous black cotton wrapper over her pale muslin dress to protect it from ink and dust, her hair caught up behind under a very saucy hat decorated with three miniature arrows with rather dangerous-looking points. The books were spread open in front of her, and she was studying them with a frown of concentration between her brows.

'Well, Miss Morland, what a pleasant surprise to see you here,' Jasper said, controlling himself. 'And for the third time this month. Is there something I can do for you?'

Fanny looked at him briefly. 'No thank you, Mr Hobsbawn. Your servant gave me the books.'

'My *clerk* should not have done so,' Jasper said with faint asperity. 'Not without permission.'

Fanny raised an eyebrow. '*I* gave him permission,' she said shortly. She surveyed him dispassionately. 'I'm glad you are here, however. There are some questions I have to put to you. These items here, marked *Surg.* — what are they?'

'Surgeon's fees, Miss Morland.'

'So I imagined,' she said witheringly, 'but I say again, what are they? They are very high — much too high.'

'May I?' He came round the desk and looked over her shoulder, while she laid a dainty, nacreous finger against one figure and then another. 'The name beside the figure refers to the employee for whom the surgeon was called. This one, for instance — Rahilly — is one of the spinners who caught her arm in the machine. It had to be stitched.'

'By the surgeon? The apothecary could have done the job at half the cost. It is wasteful to call in the surgeon for small injuries,' Fanny said severely. 'And what is this one — O'Brien? I see there are three — no, four entries for O'Brien.'

'He slipped in the yard and put his foot down into a sump-hole containing a mechanical pump. Since the pump was operating at the time, the flying blades tore off his foot.' Jasper spoke unemotionally, but he hoped the words would cause her to quail or feel faint. 'I hope you don't think that was too trivial to warrant calling the surgeon?'

Fanny merely tapped the ledger page. 'Four visits?'

'The injuries were so severe that the boy eventually died of them,' he said harshly. O'Brien had been a favourite of his, a promising lad whom he had hoped to bring up to overseer one day.

'If they were so severe, you should not have called the surgeon at all,' Fanny said simply. 'You must have known it was a waste of time. Look at these figures! Two guineas, three guineas! Do you think this O'Brien was worth it? I doubt whether he did ten guineas' worth of work in his life.'

'It did not occur to me,' Jasper said in a trembling voice, 'to estimate the worth of the boy's life, before summoning help for him.'

'Well there you are, then,' Fanny said kindly. 'You should do so in future. And now, another thing — why are we still sending out work to this hand-weaver, when we have machines not running to full capacity? I have looked at his record in the putting-out book, and he is by far too slow.'

'Hargreaves' work is very good. He is slow at the moment because of an injury to his shoulder.'

'Then you should not send him any more work until he is fit again.'

Jasper breathed hard. 'Hargreaves is a good, loyal worker, who has been weaving pieces for us for twenty years, Miss Morland. He has a family to support. If I do not send him work, they will all starve.'

'That is nothing to the point,' Fanny said firmly. 'There is capital tied up in those machines — and in the spun cotton — which does not shew a return until we sell the cloth. If your Hargreaves cannot work, he must look to the parish, that's all.'

'I don't think there is anything you can tell me about the cotton business,' Jasper said angrily. 'Or about employing men —'

'Isn't there?' Fanny said. 'Do you think the men respect you more because you are soft with them?'

'I understand these people, Miss Morland. I grew up with them,' Jasper began, and stopped, reddening, as Fanny's eyes travelled over his plain, ill-fitting coat and paused involuntarily on his oil-blackened fingernails. Fanny, seeing the blush, was a little sorry to have embarrassed him. She had all her grandfather's determination and his love of progress and profit, but just a little more conciliation. Jasper was a useful man to have on her side, she knew, and she did not want to make an enemy of him.

'I understand, Cousin Jasper,' she said kindly, 'that some of the men seem like friends to you, but we cannot afford to waste money on people who can't or won't work. Perhaps you would not be so eager to do so, if the money involved was your own —'

He crashed his fists down onto the desk, making her jump, and leaned down so that his angry face was on a level with hers. 'The mills are mine,' he hissed. 'Mine by right of the labour and the love and the care, the hours and the sweat and, yes, the blood I have poured into them! And your grandfather knows it, Miss Morland! He may give you everything you ask for, and indulge you with your fancies, but he knows that the mills cannot be run by a woman.'

457

She raised a cool eyebrow. 'Cannot they, Mr Hobsbawn? Judging by what I see *here*, it seems to me they may be better run by some women than by some men. But we shall see.' She smiled. 'Let us not quarrel, however. I have brought an invitation from my grandfather to dine with us tonight at Hobsbawn House.'

He straightened up, perplexed. 'I don't understand you, ma'am. We have just been at outs, and now you ask me to *dine* with you?'

She stood up and began unbuttoning the wrapper. 'What is said between us in a business way need not interfere with our relationship in the social sphere, I hope? We are kin, Mr Hobsbawn; and my grandfather wishes us to be friends.'

Jasper stared at her, feeling frustrated. He remembered again the conversation he had had with Hobsbawn two years ago — oblique, embarrassing, humiliating — when Hobsbawn had hinted that he would like Jasper to marry his grand-daughter, Miss Fanny Morland.

Jasper had worked for Hobsbawn since he was a small child. He had been born in poverty and orphaned in it, and Hobsbawn had taken him into the mills, given him work and wages, trained him up, and finally made him mill-manager. He had everything to be grateful for, and he respected Hobsbawn, and loved the mills he had helped to raise from next to nothing.

He would never have set his sights higher, except that after Mrs Hobsbawn died, leaving only a daughter behind, Hobsbawn had let him know that he did not intend to marry again, and that, since he would not leave his mills to a female, they would one day come to him, Jasper, by right both of blood and desert. From then on, Jasper had worked every hour he was wakeful, had strained every nerve and muscle, had eaten and drunk and thought and dreamed Hobsbawn Mills, had lived for nothing but to expand and improve them.

Then there had come a series of reverses. Miss Hobsbawn had married — but the old man disapproved of her husband. She was with child — but the child was a girl. She bore a son — but the son died. Throughout all, Jasper had waited in the wings, uncomplaining, like a faithful wife with a philandering husband, while Hobsbawn's favour had waxed and waned. Then Fanny had come on that fateful visit, and Jasper had seen the old man's eyes light up, and a new spring come into his step.

But he could not leave the mills to an unprotected female. 'Woo her, Jasper,' had been the command. 'Marry her, and the mills will be yours through her.' No longer his by right, he thought bitterly, but as manager to that chit of a girl who looked at the dirt on his hands, and spoke to him kindly, as though he were a child or an idiot.

The terrible thing, the really terrible thing, was that it was possible. He had never been interested in women: in his life he had had too little leisure, and too little energy outside of his crippling working-hours to develop any taste for them. And women had never been interested in him, for few have the heart to be in love where there is no encouragement. But he could see that Fanny Morland was beautiful — not in a delicate, ethereal way, which he had always supposed women ought to be, but with a strong, healthy, vibrant beauty. He liked the hardness of her mind, too, though he deplored the hardness of her heart. His emotions on meeting her were complex. Mostly he wanted to put his hands round her white throat and squeeze and squeeze until he had throttled the life out of her; but sometimes he was forced painfully to acknowledge that while his hands were round her slender neck, he would find it hard not to kiss those full red lips, kiss them and kiss them —

'Woo my granddaughter,' had been the command. Aye, but what if she resists? Why should she want me? 'She'll have you, in the end, for the sake of the mills.' What does she care about the mills, lively, pretty thing with her gowns and hats and carriage-rides, and a dozen beaux in starched neckcloths hanging on her every word? 'Care about the mills? Why, man, she wasn't here five minutes before she started trying to wheedle 'em out of me. She wants the mills like a hanging man wants air.'

It had become increasingly clear that she did. No only that, but she had a most unfeminine grasp of business, a mathematical mind which could add a column of figures at a glance, a hardness and directness of thought and speech that Jasper deplored both as ugly, jarring, and horribly wasted on one of the soft sex. Miss Morland had been taught all manner of things at home she had no business learning, from mathematics to foreign languages, from latin to astronomy, from the running of an estate to the keeping of its books. And now, at the age of eighteen, and after a London Season to sharpen her wits, she had a cool, confident bearing which made it hard for Jasper to outmanoeuvre her; especially since he did not know, and could not find out, how much of her grand-father's designs concerning them she was a party to

'So Cousin, will you come?' she said now, smiling win-ningly. 'We have a turkey just fit to be eat, and I have asked the cook to make the little almond-cakes you like so much.' He hesitated still, angry and confused, and she smiled a little more. 'Or have you some other engagement? Sure, they cannot offer you such a good dinner as I will.'

'I have no other engagement,' he muttered gracelessly.

'Then you will come,' she said firmly; and held out her hand to him. It was that gesture which undid him, for it was done as openly and naturally as if she had never noticed that his hands were dirty, or his nails perpetually in mourning. 'So goodbye Mr Hobsbawn, until tonight. Grandfather will send the carriage for you.'

He felt the brief, firm grasp of her slender white hand, and then she was gone in a swirl of delicate muslin, ribbon and perfume. Her last words were a piece of kindness all her own, saving him the long, dark walk from the little stone house by Brindle Mill — the new acquisition — where he now lived. He knew that old Hobsbawn would never have thought of sending the carriage. 'He's a young man — let him walk,' would have been *his* attitude.

But *why* had she done it? He was no nearer to knowing that. All he knew was that she had exchanged for him an evening alone in a cheerless cottage, with cold bacon, bread and beer for his supper, for a warm, clean, brightly-lit house, comfortable chairs, good food, fine wine, pleasant conver-sation, and all the touches of softness and luxury his life had always been lacking. He stared around his dusty office, and smelled the elusive fragrance she had left behind, and he hated her.

Fanny had been feeling restless for a long time — indeed, on and off, since she left London at the end of her extended Season. She had cut Fitzherbert Hawker out of her heart, and

460

though the ruthless surgery had worked, and she no longer thought about him or cared about him, she felt curiously listless, at a loss, without her preference. Other men were so very dull in comparison with him — not that she ever did compare them, of course — and she couldn't take seriously any of the attempts to woo her that had taken place since then. She was gaining a reputation as a hardened flirt, she knew, but she could not help it. She laughed at the young men, or found them boring, and they didn't like it. To salve their wounded vanity, because she would not prefer them, they asserted that she would not have anyone.

The mamas did not like their darlings' being snubbed either. 'There's something disagreeably hard about Fanny Morland,' they would say. 'Something unfeminine — hoydenish — blue.' 'Fanny Morland is very blue — quite an eccentric, upon my life.' 'I do not like to see a young woman so immediately up to everything as Fanny Morland. London has quite spoiled her.'

She knew all these things were said of her, and she didn't care. She could not conceive that she would ever meet any man she could love enough to want to marry, since she was more strong and clever than they, and she could not endure to marry a weakling. So she had concentrated instead, since her return to Morland Place, on learning everything she could about the running of the estate. She found, as Miss Rosedale had told her again and again through her unheeding childhood, that there was something very satisfying in exercising the intellect. The harder she worked, and the more she learned, the more she liked it. One day she had found Uncle Ned asking her opinion about something — *Uncle Ned!* — and she had realised what it was that was happening to her. Business was more exciting than men and flirtations! Power was more thrilling than love! From that realisation, it was an obvious next step to turn her attention to her grandfather's mills.

There was no doubt that her grandfather loved her and favoured her, but how engrained was his prejudice against females? She could not be sure, even after another season of working on him, that he would indeed leave the mills to her. Well, if he did not leave them to her, he would leave them to Jasper, she reasoned; and so, she had better get to like Jasper, or at least get him to like her.

It was not easy. She could not like his person, and she despised his weakness, which had allowed him to remain subservient all his life, and which constantly erupted in foolish indulgence towards the mill-workers. He could not forget, she thought, that he was one of them by birth, and it told against him. Unless he could shake off his origins, he would never get anywhere — and it looked increasingly as though he were too old to shake them off. She did not want to trust him with her mills. He would not run them as ruthlessly as Grandpapa or she would; the hard task was to convince Grandpapa of that. He had grown used to relying on Jasper, and he was touchy about hearing him criticised. She had to tread warily.

When she returned to the carriage, she told the coachman to drive to Madame Renée's shop in King Street, to see whether her new gown was ready. It had been promised for Friday, but she thought if it were ready today, she might as well wear it at the assembly tomorrow night. There was a barouche drawn up at the kerbstone right opposite the shop, so the coachman had to pull up behind it, opposite the alley which ran down the side of the building. As the carriage stopped and Fanny looked out of the window, she was surprised to see a priest letting himself out of the little door which she knew led to Madame Renée's private quarters.

She knew who he was: a papist missionary priest who was said to do a great deal of good amongst the labouring poor of Manchester. She had never actually met him — though Grandfather was a papist himself, he disapproved of this Father Rathbone, as Fanny had learned the one time he had been mentioned in Grandfather's presence — but she had seen him around the town now and then. He had a rather raffish, piratical appearance which attracted her, reminding her just a little of a certain person.

She was even more surprised when she entered the shop a moment later to find it empty. She looked around impatiently, and then, in her usual direct way, walked briskly to the door at the back of the shop and went through into the back-room. It was filled with heaps of tacked and half-made gowns, bales of materials, busts and full-size mannequins, ledgers and papers and a spike overflowing with bills; and also a very shabby, rather soiled brocade-covered chaise-longue, before which stood Madame Renée, her skirt pulled up to her thigh as she fastened her garter around the one stocking she had on, the other being draped ready over her shoulder.

She turned with a gasp of dismay as Fanny came in, dropped her skirt, put her hands to her tousled head; and then, as Fanny raised a questioning brow, she reddened and said, 'Miss Morland! Why — what are you doing here? How did you get in? I was not expecting —'

'Evidently,' said Fanny coolly. 'The door was open. I came to see if my gown was ready.'

'But I locked the door! I made sure I had locked it! Did you not see the "closed" notice?'

Fanny suddenly remembered the priest in the alley, and began to feel this was no place for her. In any case, she would not bandy words with a mantuamaker. She turned away with a curl of the lip.

'If the gown is ready, you may send it to Hobsbawn House at once, if you please.'

'Wait! Miss Morland! I — I don't wish you to think — I had been feeling unwell, you see. I had the headache, and closed the shop so that I could lie down. I thought I had locked the door, but in my haste I suppose I must have forgot —'

Fanny made a gesture of dismissal with one hand and walked out, closing the door behind her. As she passed through the street door, she saw that there was, indeed, a notice propped in the corner of the frame saying 'Closed, owing to ill-health', which she had not seen as she entered. Madame Renée, of course, could not know that she had seen the priest leaving; she was flustered at having been caught tying her garter in a state of *déshabille*. Fanny reflected on it as she drove back to her grandfather's house. Information, however shocking, was always worth having. You never knew when it might become useful. She had learned that, she freely acknowledged, from her little cousin Rosamund.

Jasper Hobsbawn dressed in his best clothes and seated in the drawing-room at Hobsbawn House with a glass of sherry in his hand, still looked a little out of place. He was perfectly correctly dressed in a swallow-tail coat, white waistcoat and

463

small-clothes, and his hair had been drawn tidily into a queue at the back of his head with a bit of black ribbon; he had washed twice, and shaved himself so close his skin burned, and had scrubbed and gouged at his nails for fully twenty minutes; and he had made his housekeeper — his only servant — clean his shoes again.

But there still hung about him a kind of drab sourness of which he was as bitterly aware as his hostess could have been, though to be sure she was too well-mannered to show it to a guest in her own house. His skin, he knew, had the kind of dinginess which came from a restricted diet of bacon and dark bread: the dinginess of poverty. There was a meagreness about his body, which he felt most clearly when he looked at the bright eyes, clear skin, and firm rounded limbs of a young woman who had been cosseted and cared for all her life; who had eaten well and slept soundly between fine sheets and breathed clean air, unpolluted by the noise and dirt of the factories.

Fanny had been called away for a few minutes by the butler, and on her return, in answer to her grandfather's query, she said, 'It was only a messenger from the mantua-maker, Grandpapa, bringing my new gown for the assembly tomorrow.'

'Another new gown?' Hobsbawn said, pretending to frown. 'Why, Fan, you've more gowns than you can wear in a year! You'll ruin me with your mantuamaker's bills!'

Fanny, knowing that he liked nothing better than to spend money on her, and especially on her clothes, crossed the room to lean over the back of his chair and kiss his forehead.

'Oh, but Grandpapa,' she pouted prettily, 'it was such a lovely length of silk, I simply had to have it. It's French ivory, with little silver acorns embroidered all over it — you can't conceive how pretty! — and not at all expensive.'

'And what do you call *not expensive*?' Hobsbawn said, beetling his brows.

'Fifty guineas — but that includes making up,' Fanny said, playing along with him, pretending to think him angry. 'And I used the spider-lace off my old poplin for the trimming, instead of having new.'

'Why didn't you have new trimming? D'ye think I can't afford to buy my girl new clothes?' Hobsbawn said indignantly.

'I don't want you picking over old gowns, like some shop-keeper's daughter.'

Fanny laughed at his change of position. 'No, Grandpapa, but that lace is better than anything Madame Renée had. I got it in London when I came out, and it was Mechlin and cost eight shillings.'

'Eight shillings, eh?' Hobsbawn said happily.

'And Prudence Pendlebury came into the shop just after I'd bought the silk, and she was wild, because she had wanted it herself,' Fanny said, knowing how to please him. 'But there was only ten yards, and I took it all, for you know hems are wider this year.'

'Just as well — you'll do it more credit than ever Miss Pendlebury could,' Hobsbawn chuckled. 'And you are to wear this confection tomorrow, are you, Puss? I shall look forward to seeing it. You are going to the assembly, aren't you, Jasper?'

Jasper, who had been listening impatiently to this game, was startled at being addressed, and answered unwisely. 'The assembly? Not I!'

Hobsbawn frowned. 'And why not, may I ask? Our assem-blies are the finest in the North, let me tell you, young man, and there's many a person in York or even London who would not feel it beneath them to attend.'

Jasper looked down at his feet. His silk stockings had a tiny darn in them, which seemed to him horribly noticeable in the brightness of so many candles. 'It isn't that, sir. I'm not a great one for dancing, that's all.'

'Well, you don't have to dance — or at least, not all the time. It would look odd if you did not stand up for one or two, but the important thing is to be there, and let people see you. You shall go tomorrow, Jasper.'

'Really, sir, I would rather —'

'You'll go, I say,' Hobsbawn rolled over him. 'You shall go with us, in our carriage, and see Fanny in her new gown — that will be worth it alone, eh?'

Jasper looked up and met Fanny's eyes, but her expression was veiled. 'It would be a great honour, sir,' he said with an effort.

'And you shall dance with her,' Hobsbawn declared, as if he had just that moment thought of it. 'Fanny, you will stand

465

up for the two first with your cousin Jasper, do you hear?'

Fanny's long hazel eyes were as expressionless as a cat's. 'Yes, Grandpapa, certainly.'

She was so beautiful. He thought of her in white silk, with white roses in her thick, dark hair, and felt his palms sweating. He couldn't go to an assembly in darned stockings, and new ones were twelve shillings a pair; and the shirt and neckcloth he had on would have to be washed and dried, and his housekeeper had no idea of the proper starching of neckcloths and shirt-points. He would have to dance with Fanny Morland, knowing every eye was on him, judging him and finding him wanting.

In a desperate attempt to get away from such thoughts, he raised a subject he had intended to keep until he and Hobsbawn were alone together.

'Sir, I want to talk to you about the factory children. The hours they work are far too long — it makes them clumsy and prone to accidents, and the overseers can only keep them awake towards the end of the day by beating them.'

Hobsbawn looked at him in astonishment. 'What the deuce are you talking about, man?'

'They're working thirteen, fourteen hours a day — more, sometimes, when there's work to be made up. Half-grown children simply aren't strong enough for such labour. They fall asleep at the machines. Some of them are too tired even to eat when they stop for their meal.'

Fanny's eyes gleamed, and she drifted away to sit on a sopha at a little distance, the more comfortably to enjoy the spectacle of her cousin destroying himself.

'This is not the time nor the place to talk of such things.' Hobsbawn said, evidently controlling himself with an effort. 'This is a social visit, Jasper.'

Aware of Fanny out of the corner of his eyes, Jasper plunged on suicidally. 'Sir, I don't think there is a proper or an improper time to talk about matters so vitally important. There's a great deal of feeling in the town that factory hours are too long, and that the children should not work more than twelve hours a day, at least until they are sixteen years old.'

'A deal of feeling? Amongst whom? Jacobins and troublemakers? Luddites and revolutionaries?' Hobsbawn said, growing redder.

466

'Amongst masters, too,' Jasper said, quickly. 'There are a lot of mill-owners who are beginning to see that it's in their own interest to limit the children's hours.'

'How can it be in their interest?' Hobsbawn demanded contemptuously.

'Strong healthy children work better, sir.'

'Do they? Do they? Pamper them and make them idle, is that your idea? Children need discipline, and they're happier for it.'

'But these children aren't happy. You've only got to look at them — undersized, sickly, deformed. They're dying, Mr Hobsbawn! They come to work at eight years old, and they die at twelve.'

'Nonsense! The sickly ones would die anyway; and if they don't work, they'll die of hunger, so what do you want? We have to keep 'em going fourteen hours to get the work out of 'em, for they're an idle, thriftless lot. Aye, worse than the 'prentices I used to use, and that's saying a good deal.'

'Dead children do not work at all,' Jasper said.

'Well, well, there's plenty more where they came from,' Hobsbawn said indifferently. 'These Irish breed like dockside rats. Where d'you think they'd go for work if we didn't take 'em on, men like me? They should be damned grateful they've got jobs at all! And how d'you think they'd earn enough to live on, if they worked fewer hours?'

'We'd have to raise their wages,' Jasper said. Fanny made a sound like choked-off laughter, as Mr Hobsbawn's eyes seemed to bulge from his head.

'Work 'em fewer hours, and give 'em more money? And take on more of 'em, I suppose, to make up the work they're not getting through? By God, Jasper Hobsbawn, I used to think you had some sense, but now I think you must have lost a slate off your roof! Is that how you propose to run my mills? We'd be bankrupt within a year on your system!'

Jasper looked despairingly at him. 'No, sir, no, it wouldn't work like that. If they worked fewer hours, and ate better, they'd be stronger, and you'd get more work out of them — skilled work, too. There'd be fewer accidents, and accidents cost time and money. Less damage to the machines. Better products. It would pay handsomely, sir, in the end. It's — it's *wasteful* to work them to death. You wouldn't treat your

467

horses like that, would you? You'd think it madness to under-feed and overwork your carriage horses until they died, and then have to buy more, wouldn't you?'

Hobsbawn rose to his feet. 'I've heard enough of your raving. I think you must be light-headed. Perhaps it's hunger? Fanny, ring the bell, and let's have dinner. Now, not another word about it, Jasper! You're a guest in my house, and I'll thank you to remember it. Fanny, take Cousin Jasper's arm, will you, and talk to him about dancing or something. Ah, Bowles! We'll have our dinner now, if you please.'

Fanny could hardly believe her luck. All the next day she gloated over Jasper's folly in bringing up a subject which he must know was anathema to her grandfather. It was true there had been talk amongst reformers and clergymen about limiting the factory hours to twelve a day for children between nine and sixteen, and prohibiting children under nine from working in factories at all, but it always made grandfather very angry.

He had stopped using 'prentice children, partly because they were too expensive to keep, and partly because of the Act of Parliament which had been passed to protect them, which was an annoyance to masters. 'Free labour' children were the responsibility of their parents, so Hobsbawn and other masters like him reasoned. And the parents would not have welcomed a ban on work for their younger ones. Children in the home worked at one thing or another from the time they could walk — that was the natural order of things. To keep a great, grown thing of seven or eight idle, when it could be earning a living, all for the sake of some damned Jacobin or moist-eyed reformer, was the sheerest nonsense.

What Jasper had said about horses had given Fanny pause for an instant, for of course it would not make sense to work horses beyond their strength. Horses had to be cossetted; but then horses were a valuable commodity, which pauper children plainly were not. There had to be reason and moderation in all things. A two-hundred-guinea blood horse was a delicate creature, not easily replaced, and much capital was tied up in it. Pauper children belonged to their parents, and, as Grandpapa said, there were plenty more where they came from.

But it was obviously in Fanny's interests to encourage Jasper in his views, for nothing would better convince Grandpapa that he was not a fit person to inherit the mills. The next evening at the assembly, therefore, when they were standing at the head of the set, waiting for it to be completed. she set about making friends with him.

He was looking unusually smart, she thought, with new silk stockings, and a well-starched neckcloth for once, instead of the draggled, limp thing he usually sported; and his nails were almost clean, and his hair had been washed, and there was less of the sour smell that usually hung around him. She could not know, of course, the effort these improvements had cost him. All day he had avoided getting his hands dirty, to the surprise of his underlings; he had sent his shirt and cravat out to a laundress, at what he considered exorbitant expense, and bought new stockings; and had gone home from the mill early, having given his housekeeper instructions to have a copperful of hot water ready.

'T'ain't washing day, Mr Jasper,' she had protested.

'It's to wash myself in,' he had retorted, and she had shaken her head at him sadly. Working with them machines had turned his brain at last, she thought. She'd expected it for a long time.

'It's very kind of you to agree to stand up with me,' Fanny said with her best shy, modest look. 'I know that you don't care for dancing. It was very awkward of Grandpapa to insist upon it, for you could not well refuse.'

He eyed her cautiously, not sure what she was up to. 'I didn't mean I didn't care to dance — only that I am not a very accomplished dancer.'

'I'm sure that isn't so. I'm sure you dance very gracefully. Do you suppose there will be any waltzing? It's all the rage in London, though they don't allow it at Almacks. I'm not sure about it myself. Do you think it is improper, Mr Hobsbawn?'

'I've never seen it done,' he answered. Despite himself, he was being affected by the gentle, pleasant way she was talking. She seemed so very feminine, in her lovely white silk gown, trimmed with soft, creamy lace, with ribbons and flowers in her hair, it was impossible to think of her understanding account-books. 'I believe they tried to introduce it some years ago, didn't they?'

'Yes, so I understand, but it didn't take. The gentleman puts his arm around the lady's waist as part of the dance,' she explained, managing a modest blush, 'which is why some people think it shocking. But properly done, it looks very pretty.'

'I'm sure you would do it credit, Miss Morland,' he said.

It was quite a reasonable compliment, Fanny thought. She looked up under her eyelashes at him, and saw a gleam of something in his eyes which was not disapproval or indifference. 'I was very interested in what you were saying last night, Mr Hobsbawn,' she said in her softest tones. He looked wary, remembering her previously expressed indifference to the lot of mill-workers. 'When you spoke about the way we treat horses, I suddenly saw things in a very different light,' she hastened to explain. 'Of course, it is absurd and very shocking to work the children until they drop. Poor little things!'

Had she gone too far? No, it was all right. Some kind of intoxication was working on Jasper, and he was beginning to believe in her.

'I'm very glad you see it so, Miss Morland. You see, I grew up in the mills, and I have seen it all for myself, at first-hand. It is very hard, I know, for someone outside to understand the misery and suffering of these creatures. If I were to shew you a little child of eight years old, weeping at the end of the day with sheer exhaustion, too tired to eat what little food his parents can provide him with, his poor crooked bones aching so much he can hardly bear to lie down — why, I know it would touch you to the heart! You would want to cradle him in your arms for pity.'

Fanny shuddered involuntarily at the very idea of touching a deformed and odorous pauper-brat, but Jasper interpreted it his own way, and pressed her hand in grateful sympathy.

'But tell me, Mr Hobsbawn, what are you going to do next?' she went on. 'I'm sure it's of no use to try to persuade Grandpapa. He does not understand.'

'Not on his own, not when I am simply asking him to take my word for it,' Jasper agreed eagerly, 'but when there are enough people who think the same way — masters and employers and important people, whose opinion he respects — he will begin to see things in a different light. We are getting up a regular campaign, sending circular letters, and holding public meetings. There's to be one next week — I do hope you may be persuaded to come to it? It would be such a help to us.'

'I, sir — what use would I be to you?' Fanny said with a laugh.

He looked serious. 'Our ladies can be of the greatest possible use, in influencing their menfolk. Husbands listen to their wives a great deal more than is often reckoned, and Mr Hobsbawn values your opinion, too. If you were to come to the meeting — lend it your presence — it would be most encouraging. And if you insisted that you wanted to go, I don't believe your grandfather would refuse to accompany you.'

'Who is to speak at your meeting?' Fanny asked, without committing herself.

'We have some very distinguished speakers — Mr John Fielden, Dr Thomas Percival, Mr Gould, the merchant, and Sir John Hobhouse; and there are others who have agreed to sit on the platform in support, though they won't be speaking.'

'But you will speak, surely?' Fanny asked.

'I? No, I don't speak. It would be thought impertinence on my part — a mere mill-manager. We must have the great men up there, if we are to convince. No, my part is simply to organise.'

'That must be a great deal of work for you,' Fanny said, disappointed. The sight of Jasper on the platform addressing a meeting would have curdled Grandpapa's blood.

'I don't do it all alone,' he said with a smile. 'We have many willing helpers from amongst the middling sort — shopkeepers and clerks and so on. Father Rathbone and I are more the overseers of the effort —'

'Father Rathbone?' Fanny asked quickly.

'Yes — do you know him? He's a missionary, and does a great deal of good work amongst the poor. He has been involved in every campaign for the betterment of their lot for years. We couldn't do without his enthusiasm and experience.'

'No, I don't know him,' Fanny purred. 'Will he be at the meeting?'

'Of course — he will be the chairman, and introduce the speakers.'

Fanny smiled radiantly at him. 'I must certainly try to persuade Grandpapa to be there.'

Despite the eminence of the speakers, the mood of those attending the meeting was largely hostile to the proposal, and many had only gone hoping for the chance to shout them down. The financial crisis of 1811 was too recent to be forgotten. Indeed, the mills were only just settling into full-time working again, and there had been many mill-masters who fell by the wayside and went bankrupt. Not only that, but for two years the country had been convulsed with the activities of the Luddites, and though it was true that it had been mainly the Midlands, particularly Nottingham, which had suffered, no factory owner could think about frame-breakers without his blood rising. Only that January, seventeen Luddites had been hanged at York assizes, which was too close to home to be ignored.

The last thing the masters wanted was to be told to be kinder to their employees. Keep a firm grip on 'em, keep 'em down, make 'em work so they haven't time to get up to mischief — this was the kind of advice they would have welcomed. Times were hard; the war with America had curtailed markets, though the continent of Europe was now opening up again; profits were uncertain. Who was going to pay anyone more money for less work? It didn't make sense.

Jasper met Fanny and Mr Hobsbawn in the entrance. 'I'm so glad you came, sir,' he said. 'I've reserved seats for you and Miss Morland at the front. I know you don't agree with the motion to limit factory hours, but all I ask is that you listen to the speakers, and consider what they have to say. We have a physician here whose evidence I think will certainly give you food for thought.'

'Aye, well, I'll listen,' Hobsbawn said, 'but you won't persuade me. I only came because Fanny insisted.'

Jasper gave Fanny a smile of gratitude, and she lowered her eyes modestly. Hobsbawn had been outraged when she first suggested that they should go to the meeting, but she had pointed out that as Jasper was his manager, and people would inevitably associate his ideas with Hobsbawn's, it would be as well to find out what he was up to. 'Otherwise, Grandpapa, you won't know what it is you have to deny.'

'Aye, that makes sense, Puss,' Hobsbawn said. 'I don't

know what's got into Jasper lately. He seems to have lost his senses.'

'It's probably the people he's associating with, Grandpapa,' Fanny said sweetly.

'Eh? What? Who do you mean?' he said, startled.

'Oh, I don't know who they are; but I've often noticed,' she said wisely, 'that when a sensible man begins to behave foolishly, it's because he is keeping bad company, and coming under someone else's influence. Of course, it's usually female,' she added with a smile, 'but in Cousin Jasper's case —'

'Aye, there's sense in that,' Hobsbawn said thoughtfully. 'He's maybe been got hold of by some Jacobin. You're right, Fanny — we must go to this meeting, and see who he talks to.'

Even those who had gone to the meeting to heckle had no idea how much fun there was going to be right from the beginning. The grand speakers filed out and took their places on the platform, and then Father Rathbone, the tall, fiery-eyed missionary, entered and walked to the centre of the stage to open the meeting. Fanny felt her grandfather stiffen beside her, and glanced sideways to see his face suffusing with indignation. She had no idea why he disapproved of Rathbone, but it was good to have the soil ready prepared for what she was to plant next.

With a little cry to draw his attention to her, she put her hand over her face and turned to hide against her grandfather's shoulder.

'Why, Fanny, what's wrong?' he asked, instantly alarmed.

'Oh Grandpapa! It's that man! Oh, it's too dreadful!' she cried, muffled but perfectly audible. 'I must leave — Grandpapa, please take me home. I cannot remain in the same room with someone so —' She broke off with a little choke.

'Why, love, what is it?' Hobsbawn asked, bending over her. 'What man? D'you mean that priest-feller? What do you know about him?'

'Something too dreadful! I can't say it! Oh Grandpapa, to think of its being him that Cousin Jasper has been associating with!'

'But how do you know him, Fan? I made sure he should never come in your way.'

Fanny found that remark a little confusing, but shrugged it

473

off, intent on her own plan. Placing her lips as if reluctantly to her grandfather's ear, she whispered a sentence or two. His face mottled alarmingly.

'What!'

Fanny nodded, eyes lowered. 'It's perfectly true, I'm afraid,' she murmured, as one shocked and saddened. 'That's why I haven't ordered any more gowns from Madame Renée. I couldn't bear to be associated —'

'Right!' Hobsbawn said, rising to his feet like an angry mountain, drawing all eyes to him. 'Just you go along Fanny, and wait for me in the hallway. It isn't fit that you should hear what I'm going to say. I'll be with you in a few minutes to take you home after I've made sure,' he raised his voice, 'these good people know what kind of men are sponsoring this crackbrained notion! When I've done, there'll be no more talk of twelve-hour acts!' His voice rose to a bellow. 'Incitement to immorality, that's what it is, plain and simple!'

Fanny left the hall quickly, keeping her eyes down, and a limp hand to her brow as though she were near to fainting. It served very well to conceal the smile of satisfaction she could not keep from coming to her lips. Poor Cousin Jasper! She felt almost sorry for him.

CHAPTER TWENTY-FOUR

One October day, Lucy and Danby Wiske had ridden out to the ruins of the abbey at Godstow Bridge, taking a picnic meal with them of cold roast chicken, game pie, cheesecakes, and the new season's apples. They hitched the horses to a thorn tree and loosened their girths, and then found themselves a sheltered place on the turf amongst the ruined grey towers, and sat down with their backs to a broken wall to enjoy the warm autumn sunshine.

They ate slowly, with pleasure, and in silence, each occupied with private thoughts. They sat side by side, touching from shoulder to elbow, a cloth spread across their knees on which the food was laid. Just to the right of Lucy's head wild wallflowers were springing from a crack in the wall, attracting the attention of late bees; the little breeze which lives around the ruins was blowing the coarse crevice-grass, and singing just above their heads; the air smelled of warm turf and dry earth. Lucy was beginning to feel a little sleepy, when Danby drew a deep sigh, and she looked towards him, heavy-eyed but concerned.

'Is your leg hurting you? Shall I look at it again?'

'What, here? he said with a smile. He had taken a nasty sword wound in the thigh, which had not healed properly, and which had been draining his strength so much that his colonel had sent him home to recover. 'No, it doesn't hurt — itches abominably, though.'

'That's good. That means it's healing.'

'So you tell me,' he smiled. 'I was just thinking this is the wrong time to be out of the game, when so much is happening over there.'

'Poor Danby,' she said, amused. 'Who would have thought you'd turn out to be so bloodthirsty?'

'Not a matter of that,' he began to protest, and she squeezed his hand to shew it was a joke.

'Who would have thought also,' she went on, 'that things could change so much in such a short time? This time last year, we thought the war would go on for ever.'

'You did,' he corrected. 'It still may.'

'But so much has changed since then.'

'Boney's invading Russia was the turning point. Bit off more than he could swallow.'

'It was insanity,' Lucy said. 'After that, no-one could doubt that he's mad. Only a madman would have gone on so long just to reach Moscow: and for what?'

'The Russians did just as they ought. Refusing to face the French, luring them further and further from their supply bases. Weakening them with every mile into the heartland.'

'Captain Haworth said he didn't think Boney had any idea how large Russia was,' Lucy said. 'But I suppose if Moscow hadn't been burned down, it might have been different. He might have made that his base. I wonder who did set fire to it?'

'Don't suppose we'll ever know. But there would still have been the winter to get through.'

Bonaparte had reached Moscow in the middle of September, 1812. It had taken him three months to march to Moscow from the border, from which all his stores must be sent; with Moscow a smouldering ruin, there was nothing he could do but to march back, into the oncoming winter.

Stories were still filtering through about that nightmare retreat across Russia, but perhaps no imagination would ever be able to do justice to the sufferings of the men who made it. The severity of the Russian winter did what no troops in Europe could have managed. Bonaparte had crossed the Nieman in June with six hundred thousand men; the survivors straggling back over the frozen river in December numbered only fifty thousand. How many had been taken prisoner no-one knew; but by any reckoning half a million men had died, of cold, starvation, and the gangrene that follows frostbite — all for the Corsican's ambition.

'He shouldn't have abandoned his men like that, to save his own cowardly skin,' Lucy reflected. 'He should have stayed with them to the end, not gone posting off in a comfortable carriage, leaving them to die.'

'It isn't like that,' Danby was forced to say. 'A general must

476

save himself — no-one else to give orders. Wouldn't do any good for him to die with them.'

'It would have been best for everyone if he had,' Lucy said stubbornly.

'Astonishing that he managed to raise another army so soon,' Danby said with reluctant admiration. The Russians, pouring out from their country in Bonaparte's wake, had occupied Poland and Prussia. Prussia had declared war against France; cautious Austria had gone half way and declared itself neutral; and Sweden had agreed to join the alliance in exchange for Norway. Bonaparte's kingdom seemed to be falling apart.

Meanwhile, Wellington's new campaign of 1813 had achieved what last year's had failed to do, and driven the French out of Spain, back into France. Britain had joined the allies, offering gold to help the Russians keep a hundred and fifty thousand men in the field against the tyrant. Yet Bonaparte would not behave like a defeated man. Deserting the lost cause in Russia, he had posted to Paris, raised another army, and marched north into Prussia to retake Hamburg. Since then he had marched here and marched there, fought battles and won them; but he was losing men through casualties and desertions, and every loss strengthened the Allies. It was clear that he was no longer invincible in Europe.

'Well, I expect they'll manage to beat Boney without you,' Lucy said comfortingly. 'Lady Tonbridge told me last week that Lady Castlereagh told her that we're going to offer the French terms for peace. Something about natural frontiers — what are those?'

'It means that France would be confined to the land between the Alps, the Pyrénées and the Rhine,' Danby said. 'But I can't see Boney accepting. He'd have to give up Italy, which I believe he loves more than France; and Germany and Holland, and Belgium. And what about the colonies? I don't think he'll just tamely accept and lay down his arms. Why should he? We think we've got him cornered, but we've thought that before. A cornered fox is dangerous.'

'You're pessimistic,' Lucy said. 'What about the Allies? He can't fight everyone.'

'Alliances have been made before, and broken before,' Wiske said grimly. 'It isn't generally known, but back in

August, Austria was making secret negotiations with Boney for a separate peace between them, in return for certain territories dear to Austrian hearts.'

'The treacherous dogs!' Lucy said indignantly.

'Boney refused, of course, but it's a sign of what we have to contend with. Castlereagh's been writing to all the heads of government, begging them to stand united, saying that lasting peace can only come if everyone agrees on the terms, and doesn't go bargaining behind people's backs. So you see, we're not home and dry yet. I don't believe Boney will give in until he's cornered in his own capital without a single soldier to his name. And I want to be with Hookey when we march into Paris.'

Lucy stared into the middle distance. 'It's hard to imagine a Europe without Boney. We'll have to find someone else to blame for everything.' She looked at her companion. 'Well, I can understand your wanting to finish the game. You'll be fit enough to go back in a week or so, though that muscle will be weak for a while.'

He lifted her hand and kissed it, and she looked away, and changed the subject.

'Did you see much of Marcus when you were out there?'

'Yes, I saw quite a lot of him. He's a born soldier — taken to campaigning like a duck to water. Popular with the other officers, and his men adore him. Suits him down to the ground. I shouldn't be surprised if he didn't distinguish himself, if the war goes on long enough. You should have seen him at Vitoria — neck or nothing stuff! Took his men right through the French flank!'

'You'd better not say anything like that to the children,' Lucy said. 'Rosamund will have nightmares if she thinks Marcus is doing anything dangerous.'

Wiske looked amused. 'My dear Lucy, you underestimate Rosamund. She knows exactly how dangerous it is, and she's as proud as Lucifer of Marcus's exploits. She's not her mother's daughter for nothing.'

'What do you mean?'

'She wouldn't keep him from his duty any more than you would keep me from mine,' he said. 'There's one difference though — she'd marry Marcus tomorrow, if he asked her.'

'Don't be silly, she's just a child.'

478

'Why won't you marry me, Lucy? It makes no sense.'

'I can't explain it,' she said unhappily. 'Why must you ask? Don't you have enough of me as it is?'

'No,' he said steadily. 'You know I don't. You give me what you can too easily spare. You don't give me what I want.'

'What do you want, then?' she said, taking refuge in anger.

'You. Your self.'

She turned her head away. 'I don't know what you're talking about.'

'Yes you do. Lucy, please be honest with me. You said you would marry me when the war's over. If you want to marry me, then why wait? But if you said that just to keep me quiet, I beg you to tell me so. I wouldn't keep you to a promise you made unwillingly, or that you've thought better of. We can be friends again as we used to —'

'No we can't. You know we can't. Everything's changed now.'

'I don't want you to be unhappy,' he said desperately. 'You tell me what you want of me.'

'I don't know,' she said in a low voice. 'If I knew I would tell you. Maybe I don't want anything. How can I tell?'

They were both silent, staring at nothing. His own feelings for her were so unequivocal, that he did not understand how she could not understand her own.

'Would you prefer not to see me again?' he asked after a while, trying to keep his voice even.

'No!' she said sharply. She looked at him and sighed. 'Can't we just go on as we are for a while? And see what happens?'

'Yes, of course,' he said. 'If you like.' He did not add, what choice do I have? but they both heard the unspoken words all the same.

In March, 1814, Mathilde went on a long visit to her friend Lizzie Wickfield, who had just been delivered of her first child. Edward found the house very empty without her, and felt lost and restless. Nothing seemed comfortable without her, and no-one else's conversation made the evenings pass for him so quickly and delightfully.

It was the restlessness caused by Mathilde's absence that spurred him to sound Fanny out on the subject of his marrying. She had been so much more sensible lately, so much

479

more approachable, putting all her considerable energies into understanding the running of the estate rather than making mischief. He thought the time might be right at last to put his love on an official footing.

He sought Fanny out one day, finding her in the steward's room, where she was talking to Compton, the steward, and examining the stock books. Tiger ran to shove his cold nose into her hand, and she looked up as Edward appeared at the doorway. The black cotton wrapper she had had made for herself on her last visit to Manchester had become a familiar sight now, but when she didn't smile, it made her look rather formidable. Edward had to remind himself that she was only eighteen, and his niece to boot.

'Ah, Uncle Ned,' she said, 'I'm glad you're here — there's something I want to ask you. Those two geldings that were sold last year, a three-year-old and a four-year-old, to the Earl of Carlisle — they don't seem to be in the books. Why is that?'

'Of course they're in the books,' Ned said. 'All the bloodstock is registered at birth. I wrote 'em in myself.'

'No, I mean they don't appear as sales,' Fanny said. 'The price they fetched ought to have been written down in the ledger, but I can't find it.'

Ned smiled. 'Ah, that's because they were my own horses, not the estate's. I don't write my private sales in the estate ledgers, obviously — or your father's.'

'*Your* horses?' Fanny frowned.

Ned began to feel nervous. 'To be sure, Fanny: Ember and Gypsy Prince, the colts I bred out of my mare Firefly. You remember.'

Fanny's frown dissolved into a smile which made Compton excuse himself hurriedly. 'If you've finished with me, Miss Morland, I'll get back to my work.'

'Yes, Compton — and you may take these books with you. I've seen all I want for the moment.'

The steward gathered them up and beat his retreat. When they were alone, Edward began, 'Fanny, there's something I wanted to ask you — a sort of hypothetical question.'

'Just a moment please, Uncle Ned. We haven't dealt with the matter of the colts yet. As I remember, you sold them for three hundred guineas. Have I got that right? I heard you talking to Papa about it.'

'Yes, that's right,' Ned said. Fanny's memory for figures was formidable. 'What of it? It was a fair price for them. I thought Ember was going to be fast, but he got too heavy once he started putting on bone; and Gypsy —'

'But Uncle Ned, you've paid nothing into the estate accounts at all,' Fanny interrupted, still smiling. Ned stared, perplexed. 'I know they were bred out of your own mare; but she was covered in both cases, according to the stock book, by Icarus, a stallion owned by the estate. Did you pay any stud fees for either breeding?'

'No, of course not! But —'

'And then there's the question of their keep all these years — food, stabling, shoeing, farrier's bills. That amounts to quite a lot.'

'Now wait a minute, Fanny! I'm entitled to the keep of my horses,' Ned said angrily.

'Certainly you are — horses for your own use, that is. But when you are breeding and selling horses for a profit, I think it becomes a different matter, don't you?'

Ned glared at her. 'Is that what your grandfather's teaching you in Manchester? Is this how you mean to run the estate when it's yours?'

'It is mine,' Fanny retorted. 'You seem to forget that.'

'Oh no it isn't,' he snapped. 'Be very clear about that, Fanny — while the estate is held in trust for you, I am the sole arbiter of how it is run. All decisions are taken by me, and you have no right, no right at all, to question what I do.'

'Even if you attempt to defraud me?' she asked sweetly.

'Even if —? How dare you! Why, you impertinent minx —!' Edward was almost speechless with rage. 'If I were your father I'd box your ears, and teach you some manners, not to mention gratitude! When I think of all I've done for you over the years —'

'And you've been handsomely paid for it,' Fanny said, her eyes narrowing into green-gold slits as she lost her temper. 'You've taken a good living for yourself off my land, and I dare say you've laid up a tidy sum of money for yourself somewhere as well! Well you'll need every penny, for I promise you, you won't stay here a day to cheat me after I'm twenty-one!'

481

The moment the words were out, Fanny was sorry, for she knew how hard he worked, and had no real doubt about his honesty. But on the other hand, he had spoken to her disrespectfully, and seemed to behave as though Morland Place were his, not hers. She wondered how much of her inheritance was wasted, lost, frittered away, because of his unbusinesslike attitudes. It might come to thousands of pounds. No: she was sorry, and uneasy as a child must be who defies an adult for the first time, but she would not apologise.

Edward for his part felt murderous, and close to tears. To be accused of dishonesty, and by his own niece, for whom he had been working himself to a shadow for years, was too much to be borne. Little use now, he thought, to broach the question of marriage. It was all too plain what the answer would be! He would do better to leave straight away, and get himself a paid employment somewhere as steward, than to stay here and be despised and abused.

Yet even as he thought it, he knew that no paid employment would keep him in as much comfort as he enjoyed here. Not only that, but he was fifty years old, and he didn't want to leave his home now, and start again amongst strangers. And what about Mathilde?

'You may be sorry for those words one day,' was all he said, and he turned abruptly and left her.

Lizzie Wickfield was occupied in her favourite pursuits of eating sweetmeats and staring at her new baby, who was sleeping in a basket at her feet. She had grown very fat since her marriage, and seemed quite contented with her lot, and this contentment had finally tempted Mathilde into confiding in her over her increasingly worrying situation.

'I think you're very foolish,' Lizzie said frankly. 'He's much too old for you. I don't know how you can even think of it.'

'Mr Wickfield is a great deal older than you,' Mathilde pointed out stiffly.

'Yes, but he's well-to-do, and that makes all the difference. I have a nice house, and servants, and my own carriage, and plenty of pin-money. Your Mr Morland has nothing, has he? Suppose you did marry him, you'd have to go and live in a hovel, and do everything for yourself, and never had any new

482

clothes or anything nice to eat.'

'Don't be silly,' Mathilde said shortly. 'In any case, I should still love him.'

'No you wouldn't,' Lizzie said with a shrewd look. 'I've been thinking about it while you've been talking, and imagining my Mr Wickfield poor. And you know, without nice clothes, and a servant to shave and dress him, and a barber to cut his hair, well, I don't think I would care to be touched by him. After all, fifty is old, whichever way you look at it, and without comforts and luxuries, he would just be a poor old man, like those you see stone-picking in the fields.'

'Of course he wouldn't,' Mathilde said. 'His mind would still be the same wouldn't it? And his character.'

'Well, I don't know. I should think poverty would change those, too. You can't be nice and bookish and all those things when you haven't enough to eat. And old men don't smell very nice, dear. Think of that. Without lots of servants, you'd never be able to keep clean.'

'You are silly, Lizzie,' Mathilde laughed, but uncomfortably, unable to help feeling that there was some truth in what Lizzie was saying.

'If your Mr Morland were rich, or even if he had a reasonable income, I'd be happy for you, 'Tilda. But as it is, I think you ought to release yourself at once from this engagement, or whatever it is.'

'It isn't an engagement.'

'Then there's no difficulty, is there? You're young and pretty, and you could easily find yourself a nice young man to marry. That clergyman we met at the Phillipses the other night — what was his name?'

'Mr Rattray,' Mathilde said absently.

Lizzie looked approving. 'So you did notice him! Well, I thought he was very much struck with you. Why don't I ask Mr Wickfield to ask him to dinner? I'm sure a little trouble on your part would secure him. Wasn't he saying he's just come into a very nice living somewhere? And if he has his living, he'll be looking for a wife next.'

'Oh Lizzie,' Mathilde sighed, 'life isn't that easy, you know.'

'It's as difficult as you make it,' Lizzie said plainly. 'If you go making silly promises to old men with no money, it's bound to look difficult. I shall ask Mr Wickfield tonight about Mr Rattray. And you must put Mr Morland out of your head. I know you love him, and that he's a splendid person, but he's no right wasting your life with promises he can't keep, *and*,' she prevented Mathilde from interrupting, 'I'll go bail he's said the same thing himself, hasn't he?'

'Something like it,' Mathilde admitted. 'He's a gentleman, Lizzie. It's what you'd expect.'

'There are other gentlemen in the world,' Lizzie said implacably.

A ball at the Mansion House was considered a grand occasion in York, but Fanny decided her French ivory silk with the silver acorns quite good enough for it, especially as no-one in York society had seen it yet. She had two rows of plaited silk ribbon added around the hem, for ribbon trimming was all the rage that year, and it would be tiresome to have people think she didn't know. She also wheedled Madame's maid into doing her hair, for Marie had a better touch with it than Beaver, to whom she gave the hint that she had better learn a thing or two from the Frenchwoman, or find another position.

All in all, she thought as she looked critically at her reflection when Marie had finished, she looked as well as she ever had. Her figure had filled out beautifully, and though she was not particularly tall, she was so well proportioned that she made taller girls look too big. Her high colour and thick hair gave her a look of healthy vitality, which her cool and sophisticated air redeemed from any charge of rusticity; and her eyes, she knew, were fascinasting. They had an exciting, dangerous gleam to them which confident men found irresistible, and she preferred the company of confident men; though she danced a great deal with shy men, just to keep the confident ones in their place.

Fanny was going to the ball in the company of the Sales and Polly Haworth, who were staying at Shawes. Lady Barbara Morland's daughter, Barbarina, was seventeen, and to avoid being obliged to bear most of the expense of bringing her out by offering Chelmsford House for the ball, Roberta had hastily made up a party to go to Shawes for Easter, thereby making sure she was out of London for the Season.

As her party consisted of the Ballincreas and the Greyshotts, Roberta thought it a good excuse to invite the Sales, for she was curious to see how Flaminia was adapting to her new life. She hadn't seen her since the wedding.

After their honeymoon in Isleworth, Lord Harvey, apparently in need of company, had taken his bride and her companion up to Northumberland to stay with the Ballincreas for the shooting, and stayed on for Christmas and the hunting. After that they had gone on an extended tour of various relatives scattered around the country. When summer arrived, Flaminia, who was in an interesting condition, had been packed off to Stainton with her cousin, while Lord Harvey had gone down to Brighton to enjoy the company of old friends. Flaminia miscarried at three months, and remained in the country. Sale spent the Little Season in Town, Roberta knew, though she hadn't seen him herself, but had gone back to Stainton for the Christmas season, taking a party with him. The invitation to Shawes was readily accepted, and Roberta thought that Minnie and Polly must be in need of a change of scene.

When Roberta extended the invitation to Lucy, she seemed indifferent to the prospect of seeing her daughter again. Having married Flaminia creditably, she seemed to have cancelled her out of existence.

'But don't you want to see how she's doing?' Roberta asked, puzzled.

Lucy raised an eyebrow. 'Why should I? She's doing well enough, I'm sure. And if she isn't, there's nothing I can do about it, is there?'

'Oh, Lucy,' Roberta said reproachfully.

'Oh, Rob!' Lucy mocked. 'The reason I arranged a match for her, simpleton, was so that I could stop worrying about her. She's Lord Harvey's responsibility now, not mine.'

When the young people arrived, Roberta could see at once that there was no need to worry about Flaminia. She looked as healthy and untroubled as ever, plump and placid, dressed in fine style, and with a taste Roberta suspected owed something to Polly's direction. Even her disappointment of motherhood did not seem to have troubled her. When Roberta asked her, very carefully, if she had been very unhappy, she replied quite cheerfully, 'Oh, dear no. To be sure, Lord

Wyndham wanted us to have a son, but Harvey doesn't mind. I dare say we will have a child some time. For the moment I am just as happy as I am, for being in the family way is tiresome, and uncomfortable.'

Roberta was more surprised at the change in Polly: she seemed somehow to have faded. Though she had always been grave and reserved, it had never been possible not to notice her; but now her startling beauty was somehow less. After a closer study, Roberta realised that it was at least in part because of the way she was dressed, and had arranged her hair, which were dull and self-effacing. She seemed to have given up any idea of attracting a husband, to be content to dwindle into that most despised of creatures, a lady companion.

But she seemed pleased to be back in Yorkshire. Roberta had a word with Héloïse, and Héloïse drove over to tell Polly that she must feel free to come and go at Morland Place just as she liked, and that she had put a horse and groom specifically at her service. Minnie, similarly prompted by Roberta, assured Polly that she did not need her at all while she was staying at Shawes, and Polly needed no more persuasion to spend most of every day riding out alone, enjoying the freedom of solitude, and letting the fresh Yorkshire wind blow some colour into her cheeks.

Lord Harvey was more of an enigma. He treated his wife with courtesy, and with the sort of casual affection one might bestow on a rather foolish pet dog, but he spent as little time with her as possible, and seemed to forget all about her as soon as she was out of sight. Polly he ignored, never speaking to or even looking at her if he could help it. Roberta guessed that he had married because he had to, but rather resented the intrusion into his life of two females, and did his best to limit the intrusion as far as possible. His long sojourn first in Brighton and then in London, while his wife was at Stainton, seemed to confirm that.

He seemed to have lost weight since his wedding, and had a rather hectic, spent look about him. Roberta suspected he was drinking too much, and also probably philandering, perhaps seeing other married women, or consorting with the Muslin Company. It was a pity, she thought, that a married man could not satisfy himself at home; but of course all people were not as lucky as she and her two husbands had been.

When Roberta mentioned the Mansion House ball to her guests, she had not really thought they would want to attend, but to her surprise, Harvey Sale at once proclaimed himself eager to go. She had thought he would be too sophisticated to want to attend a ball in provincial York.

'Nonsense,' he said, 'why should York balls be less delightful than London ones? Minnie must have some dancing! She has been too much confined lately. She ought to have a little pleasure. Come, love, what do you say? You would like to go to the ball, would not you?'

Minnie smiled placidly. 'Oh, dear yes,' she said. 'I should like it of all things, if you wish to go.'

'Then it is settled,' Sale said firmly. 'Who else will join us?'

Lord Greyshott shuddered. 'Not I, I could never see the pleasure in dancing; and these country balls have nothing going on in the card-room but chicken whist and silver loo.'

'You are a monster of selfishness, Ceddie,' Maurice Ballincrea laughed. 'You know Mary cannot go, frail as she is, and I will not leave her; but you do not think of your own wife. Poor Helena must long for a little dancing.'

'She may go if she wants; *I* shan't stop her,' Greyshott said indifferently.

Helena shrugged. 'I had rather play billiards. I will play you, Maurice, for that ten guineas you won from me last night.'

'Paltry!' cried her brother. 'Make it fifty, Nell, or it's not worth standing up for.'

'Then it is just we three who are to go?' Sale said. 'You will all be sorry, when you hear what a splendid time we've had!'

Polly, her eyes averted, murmured that she did not want to go, but Sale turned at once to her, his eyes glittering a little unnaturally.

'Nonsense! You of all of us have the best right to go. Balls are especially for unmarried females; pleasure and dancing and falling in love are their property! I insist upon it, in your case. You *shall* go to the ball, Cousin Polly, and dance every dance. We shall chaperone you, and examine all the young men who offer for you, to make sure they're worthy.'

Polly looked distressed, but would not argue any further, and so it was decided; with the addition to the party of Fanny, to save Héloïse the task of chaperoning her. Fanny

487

was content with the arrangement, for she considered her cousins had both altered so much for the worse since their joint come-out, that they could only enhance her beauty by contrast. Well, to be fair, Minnie had not changed so very much, only she was plumper, and now that she dressed as a matron, she looked ten years older; but Polly had grown scrawny and plain, Fanny thought with some surprise, and seemed to have lost her taste in dress. She was dressed for this ball in the one shade of blue which did not become her, and had arranged her hair in such a strange way, as if she actually wanted to make herself look ugly!

As soon as they had shed their outer wraps and walked into the ballroom, Fanny was besieged by her usual group of admirers, the most faithful of whom were Horace Micklethwaite, Jack Appleby, handsome Henry Bayliss, whose father owned the newspaper, and Jack Dykes, the banker's son. They clamoured around her, complimented her appearance, begged for dances with her, and to be allowed to take her down for supper. Fanny charmed them all, a little absently, while looking around the room to see who else was there. The same old faces! she thought. No-one new to captivate; no-one she had the slightest chance of feeling a *tendre* for, to liven up her evening. She supposed she might dance with Lord Harvey Sale, just to annoy her suitors. Even the red coats scattered here and there did not raise a *frisson*, for she knew the wearers all too well.

She suddenly realised that she didn't see Tom Keating anyway. He was usually one of the first to approach her, and though he was growing more and more impossible, and drinking too much into the bargain, he was an amusing rattle while he was sober enough, and she didn't like to lose any of her following.

'Where is our friend Tom?' she asked abruptly, breaking into Henry Bayliss's rapturous admiration of her eyes. 'I do not see Tom Keating anywhere. Nor Edmund Somers,' she added with a frown. Another defection? It would not do!

They looked at each other a little awkwardly; then Horace Micklethwaite said, 'You haven't heard then? About Tom's sister?'

'Patience Skelwith? No, what of her?' Fanny said indifferently.

488

'She's dead,' said Micklethwaite. 'She died this morning. Tom's heartbroken — he was very close to poor Patience. And of course Edmund's her cousin — he wouldn't come to the ball with a black ribbon.'

'But what did she die of? She was perfectly healthy last time I saw her,' Fanny said in astonishment.

'Apparently she was taken ill a few days ago, with vomiting and cramps in the stomach,' Henry Bayliss said. 'My Uncle John, the physician, was called in, and treated her, but she just got worse and worse, and she died this morning.'

'Not a very good advertisement for your Uncle,' Fanny said. Her remark was greeted with a shocked silence, and then Jack Appleby giggled nervously.

'They say old Mrs Skelwith poisoned her. She always hated Patience,' he said.

'There's always a lot of loose talk about poison when some-one dies of this sort of thing,' Henry Bayliss said, looking at him sternly. 'If I were you, Jack, I wouldn't repeat it, or you'll find yourself in trouble.'

Jack looked subdued, and Fanny said impatiently, 'Well, it's very unfortunate for Tom and Edmund, but I don't think we should let it cast a shadow over the evening. After all, none of us was related to her.'

'We all knew her,' Horace said, a shade resentfully. 'We all liked her very much. You were at her wedding, Miss Morland.'

'Yes, I know. I was fond of Patience myself. But life must go on, you know. You all came here to dance, didn't you? Don't be such hypocrites.'

They looked at her uncomfortably, and then at their feet. Of course she was right, but it was not tactful of her to remind them of it quite so brutally. There was something — well, *unfeminine* about Fanny Morland sometimes.

Polly hadn't wanted to come to the ball, and hadn't expected to enjoy it when she got there. She had been approached by one or two gentlemen and asked to dance, but she had refused them, and remained at Minnie's side, silent, a little resentful, while Minnie was apparently quite happy just to watch the dancing. When the supper interval came, Minnie expressed herself surprised that the time had gone so quickly.

Everyone was in motion at once towards the supper-rooms. Lord Harvey had disappeared soon after they arrived — so much, Polly thought, for making sure Minnie had some dancing — so it was left to Polly to escort her cousin through the crowds, in the hope that they would be able to procure some supper, and somewhere to sit to consume it. In the press through the ballroom doors, Polly was separated from Minnie, and soon lost sight of her as she was thrust further ahead, and taller people interposed between them. It was then that she felt a hand on her arm, and turned her head to see Lord Harvey beside her.

'Let her go,' he said. 'I want to talk to you.'

'We're going in to supper. We didn't know where you were,' Polly said, not understanding him. His grip on her arm tightened. They came opposite another passage which led off at right-angles, and he tugged her out of the stream of people and into the passageway, which ran the width of the ballroom, behind the stage.

'What are you doing? Let me go,' she said angrily, trying to pull herself free.

'Don't struggle, Polly,' he said grimly. 'You'll draw attention to us and people will wonder what is happening.'

'They'll wonder anyway. We've no business being here,' she said. The corridor was completely featureless, a way between the two parallel passages on either side of the ballroom, along which the crowds were streaming towards the supper-rooms. 'Where are you taking me? Let me go, you're hurting my arm.'

No, not quite featureless. Half-way along, on the left, was a small, low door, whose knob Harvey grasped with his free hand.

'I've reconnoitred ahead, like a good campaigner,' he said. He glanced around. 'No-one's looking. Quick! In you go.'

He thrust open the door and, so that Polly should not resist, twisted his arm round her waist and whirled her through it. They were in an open space under the stage, evidently used for storage, for there were stacks of rout-chairs and folding card-tables, benches, heaps of dusty curtains, and boxes of all sizes. It was not dark, for all the way along there were small windows high up which let in the light from the passageway. It would be dangerous, probably to have lamps or candles in a place like this, Polly's mind reasoned in spite of herself and her predicament.

He released her, but stood between her and the door, as though he thought she might bolt. Polly stood, slowly rubbing her bruised wrist, looking at him thoughtfully, but saying nothing.

'Well, here we are,' he said nervously. 'I'm sorry to bring you to such a dusty place, but I had to be sure of being alone with you.'

'You didn't have to go to such lengths, surely? There must have been opportunities elsewhere to talk to me. Why make me come to this ball?'

'Because I had to trap you in a public place. At home — at Shawes — you can too easily avoid me; and there are always servants listening. And besides —'

'Yes?'

'I had a foolish desire to dance with you.'

Polly looked at him disbelievingly. 'Why didn't you ask me to dance, then? I should have refused you, but you didn't even ask.'

'Because you made me angry,' he said, suddenly stepping forward. 'This dress, for instance! Why did you put on this dress? It's hideous! And this,' he gestured at her head. 'Why have you dragged your hair back like that? Where are the little curls you used to wear round your face? You know it doesn't become you so.'

'What has it to do with you?' Her low voice vibrated with anger. 'I shall dress myself as I please, without consulting you, my lord!'

'You're deliberately trying to make yourself look ugly, and I won't have it!'

'*You* won't have it? What right do you have to object to anything I choose to do?'

'The right of loving you, Polly,' he said urgently. She flinched and looked away.

'You're a married man, my lord. Married to my cousin.'

'Don't call me that! Harvey, my name is Harvey!'

'I have no right to use it.'

'Right! You're always talking about rights! I didn't have any rights when it came to marrying. I was obliged to marry your cousin. There was nothing I could do about it. But it was

491

you I loved. I love you still.'

'Then I'm sorry for you,' she said harshly.

'Be sorry for yourself, too, for you love me! Oh my darling, this is torture!'

'Then you should have let me go,' she said angrily. 'After the first few weeks, when she could have got on without me. When you went to Northumberland, you should have let me go.'

'I couldn't. I have to have you near me, or my life is nothing. Polly, we've had all this out before. You promised you would stay —'

'If you behaved yourself.'

'And I have, haven't I? Minnie is happy, she has never suspected anything, not for an instant. But you haven't played fair.'

'What do you mean?' she said, alarmed.

He took the last step to her, and put his hands up to her head, and she felt his long fingers seeking out the pins that held her hair in place.

'This is what I mean,' he said.

'Stop it! Harvey, don't do that!'

'This, and that gown, and all the other hideous gowns you've made this last year.' He pulled out pins feverishly. 'You're the most beautiful creature I've ever seen, and you're trying to make yourself ugly. I can't bear it, Polly, do you hear?'

'Please, Harvey, don't —'

Her freed hair tumbled down her back. He thrust his fingers into it to either side of her head, and loosened it, pulling it forward to frame her face, and then his hands cupped her face and tilted it up to him.

'I've done my duty,' he said hoarsely, 'and I've done everything everyone asked of me, but I must have something, Polly. I know I can't have you, but I must be allowed to look at you, my beautiful, beautiful girl!'

'No, no you mustn't,' she moaned; but she was past struggling. His lips came down on hers, and after an instant she put her arms round him, and they were locked together in the embrace that had been denied them all this long time. He kissed her lips, her brow, her throat, her lips again.

'I love you, Polly. It was always you.'

492

'I love you too,' she said helplessly.

Their madness lasted only an instant. Voices sounded close at hand, startling them, and they thrust themselves apart as a group of people went past in the corridor, chatting and laughing. It came to Polly instantly what a wrong and sordid thing they were doing, secretively in this dusty place. It was dishonourable, it was weak, it was horrible. She drew away from him, and put her hands to her head.

'You must help me,' she said tersely. 'I cannot put it up on my own, without a mirror.'

'Yes, all right,' he said, subdued. 'Polly, I'm sorry; but you made me so angry.'

'You made me angry, too. Why did you go away all summer, and then all autumn too? Especially when Minnie needed you?'

'She didn't need me. She'll never need me. As long as she has you, she's happy. You will stay with her, won't you? Please, Polly, don't think of going away.'

'It's cruel to both of us to go on as we are. Cruel and dangerous.'

'No!' he said fiercely, and then, as she flinched, he said in a quieter, but still intense voice, 'No Polly. I promise you nothing like this will ever happen again. I will be absolutely correct towards you — to both of you. But you mustn't wear ugly clothes, or dress your hair like this: I can't bear it. Please, promise me you'll be beautiful. Let me have the pleasure of looking at you, and I promise everything will be all right.'

'Nothing can ever be all right,' she said. 'But I have nowhere else to go. I'll stay, because I have to.'

'No, because you want to,' he pressed her.

'That's the necessity,' she said unhappily.

Fanny had enjoyed the ball after all. A new group of officers from Fulford had arrived, and had rapidly singled her out as the prettiest girl in the room, so she had had the double pleasure of flirting and dancing with them, and of seeing her established courtiers looking jealous and angry. She had gone into supper with Henry Bayliss and Jack Dykes, and had managed to appear to look for Flaminia so as to sit with her, without any danger of actually finding her.

493

At the end of the supper interval she had retired to the ladies' room to dab a little powder on her shoulders, and adjust her hair; and when she came out and was walking back towards the ballroom, she suddenly felt an extraordinary sensation, as if an icy draught were touching the back of her neck. All the little hairs stood on end, and she shivered and turned round to see Hawker standing a little way off, watching her with those amused, knowing eyes.

She drew a breath of shock, dismay and delight. The first sight of him told her how much she had missed him, how much she had longed to see him again, though she denied it very firmly to herself, and she stood looking at him uncertainly, not knowing how she should greet him.

He thrust himself off from the wall against which he had been lounging, and came towards her with that lithe, easy grace which always made her think of a cat.

'Well, Miss Morland?' he said. 'I've been waiting here this half-hour for you to emerge. What do you ladies find to do in there?'

'Mr Hawker,' she said neutrally, with a slight curtsey.

His smile broadened. 'Is that all? Just "Mr Hawker" after all this time?'

'What else would you have me say?' she asked coolly.

'On your dignity, Fanny? Yes, and you were when we last parted, too.'

'Oh, you remember that, do you? And you will remember, then, how you behaved towards me — cold, indifferent, cruel! You have had the greeting you deserve, Mr Hawker,' she said, and turned away from him.

He caught her back, gently but firmly. 'Don't go yet. Let me look at you. By God, Fanny Morland, you're lovelier than ever! I like that gown, very much. Did you choose it yourself!'

'What interest have you in my gowns, pray?' she said sharply.

'I'm interested in everything about you. I've been watching you for a long time this evening, dancing with those callow boys, listening to their chatter, so horribly bored, and concealing it so well. Not from me of course — but I'm an old friend, and I know you better than they do.'

'You were here all the time?'

'Not all the time. I arrived half an hour before supper, and stood on the edge of the crowd, watching. But you didn't notice me.'

'Why didn't you approach me before now?' she asked a little stiffly.

'I wanted to see if you had missed me as much as I have missed you.'

'Nonsense! After the way we parted, the night you took me to Vauxhall —'

'Oh, Fanny, didn't you understand? I was trying to harden my heart against you! I knew I had to go away, and I didn't want to leave you. And I didn't want you to waste your life loving me, when I might never come back.'

'What are you talking about?' Fanny asked, intrigued despite herself. 'Why did you have to go away? You might please yourself, I suppose?'

'In time of war men cannot always do what they want,' he said obliquely.

'You can't mean you joined the army?'

He smiled. 'There are other ways of serving one's country, besides fighting.'

'You went on a diplomatic mission?' Her eyes were wide.

'I'm not at liberty to tell you anything,' he said. 'All I can say was that it was essential that I went, and that I had no knowledge of whether it would be in my power to return. But I'm here now, and we can forget all of that. I've come to see you, Fanny! Oh, you can't imagine how I have missed you, how I've thought of you, and our last night together at Vauxhall! Your sweetness then is one of my most treasured memories.'

'I've missed you too,' she admitted unwillingly. She glanced around. 'But we can't stand here — someone will come along and see us.'

'Then we'll go outside. I want to kiss you again, Fanny. I've dreamt of it so often.'

She trembled, but held firm. 'No, no, it's impossible! I must go back into the ballroom, or my name will be ruined. I am known here, you see. This is not London. What I do here matters.'

'Then I'll come and dance with you, if that's the best you can offer.'

'I'm engaged already,' she said. 'All my dances are taken.'

He took her hand and tucked it under his arm. 'Too bad,' he said. As they neared the ballroom he cocked an ear to the music which had just become audible. 'What's this? A Waltz? Can York be so very daring?'

Fanny was surprised too. 'I didn't think they would risk calling it. Probably not many people will take the floor.'

'All the better for us, then. We shall shew them how it should be done. Will you, Fanny?'

They stepped through the ballroom door. Only two couples had so far taken the floor, a little tentatively, and neither of them was performing the dance very well. It was, Fanny thought, a dance which demanded boldness, for to do it half-heartedly was to fail it in its essence. She suddenly wanted to shew them all, not simply how the dance should be done, but how life should be lived. They should all watch the beautiful Fanny Morland dancing with the most handsome man in the room.

'Yes, Mr Hawker,' she said, and turned to him, looping up her skirt as the people nearby fell away to give them passage. She trembled as Hawker took her hand, trembled even more as he placed his hand firmly round her waist; to be touched by a man so, in public, seemed almost indecent! And then the music got into her head, and poured down into her feet, and suddenly they were away, moving so rapidly over the floor it was like flying, whirling round and round, their steps perfectly matched. She saw the blur of faces watching as they passed, and didn't know if they watched in admiration or censure. What's more, she didn't care. To waltz with Hawker seemed the very pinnacle of bliss to her: she wished they might go on dancing like this for ever.

CHAPTER TWENTY-FIVE

In January 1814, Lord Castlereagh had gone in person to
Europe to co-ordinate the efforts of the Allies to decide a basis
for peace with France. He was charged with almost unlimited
discretion from the Cabinet and the Regent for this most
important role — a chance to make history. As John Anstey
said to Lucy, 'You could see he felt this was the moment he
had been preparing himself for.'

The talks were held at Chatillon, while in the south-west of
France, Wellington still pushed forward, and to the north,
Bonaparte still marched and fought against the allied armies.
The talks were limited to the four powers of England, Russia,
Prussia and Austria, Castlereagh himself sweeping aside the
suggestion that America and Spain ought to be included. The
discussions not only covered the question of the frontiers
France should be allowed, but who was to head the French
Government. Obviously, Bonaparte must be removed; the
Regent and the English Cabinet wanted a restoration of the
Bourbons, but the Csar favoured other aspirants, and there
was some thought of allowing the Empress Marie Louise to
rule as regent for Bonaparte's son, the King of Rome. It was
essential that whoever was chosen should command the loyalty
of the French people, or any treaty made would not be worth
the paper it was written on.

Meanwhile Wellington had pressed on to Bordeaux, where
the people rose to proclaim the restoration of the Bourbon
line; and the allied armies were closing on Paris. On 29
March, Marie Louise and her son fled the capital; Bonaparte
was still a hundred miles away, posting ahead of his army in
an attempt to reach Paris ahead of the Allies. On the thirtieth,
the Allies were fighting on the slopes of Montmartre, and
at four o'clock in the afternoon, General Marmont, whom
Bonaparte had left in charge in his absence, opened talks
with the Csar. An armistice was arranged, the capitulation

was signed, and the keys of the city were handed over, before Bonaparte had reached Fontainebleau.

On 1 April, the allied armies marched into Paris, led by Csar Alexander and the King of Prussia, and the Senate declared Bonaparte's abdication and the restoration of the Bourbon line, in the person of Louis XVIII. The former Emperor of half the world was to be given Elba for his new kingdom, a tiny island off the coast of Tuscany, between there and Corsica, where he had been born. His wife and son were not allowed to go with him, but were placed in the custody of her father, the Emperor of Austria. On 13 April, Bonaparte, in despair, attempted to kill himself by taking poison, but the attempt failed, and he recovered. On the twenty-first, he was travelling under heavy guard to his place of exile.

The news was greeted in London with almost as much astonishment as relief and joy. It was over! The war was over, and Bonaparte was deposed! It was incomprehensible that there should no longer be a Corsican Tyrant to struggle against, to threaten their security and take the lives of their men.

'I can't imagine what peace will mean,' Lucy said to George Brummell one day in May. 'How will we know it? Will it be any different?'

'Hardly different at all, I should think, except for those poor unfortunates who have earned their livelihood in the army or the navy. Don't you remember during the Peace of Amiens, how the clubs were full of half-pay officers with nothing to do?'

'Yes, I suppose the navy will be reduced again,' Lucy said. 'But surely the army won't be broken up immediately?'

'No, I should think there's bound to be an Army of Occupation to make sure the French behave themselves. Still, a large number will come home, you know, with back-pay to spend, and a terrible hunger for green baize.'

He smiled at the thought, and Lucy looked at him sharply. 'You mean, I suppose, to help lighten them of their load?'

He shrugged. 'They must lose to someone, so it had better be me. I will do it so much more gracefully.'

'Of course you will, George.' She hesitated before going on. 'I suppose things are all right with you? I know there have been difficulties —'

498

'Oh, since I found my lucky sixpence, I have done famously well,' he said airily. 'I told you at the time it would be a harbinger of good luck.'

'Its former owner evidently thought so,' Lucy said, 'since he drilled a hole in it. You had better take more care of it than he did. I wonder what happened to him?'

'I know what's happened to me, and it's quite delightful,' he said. 'And once the heroes are home, I may win enough to even pay my tailor. Though really, when I look at the size of his ridiculous bills, I feel he must be so rich it would make more sense for him to pay me.' Lucy laughed. 'The influx of heroes will be good for you, too, ma'am,' he went on. 'You will have a daughter to bring out next year, and a London teeming with officers is the best way I know to ensure of getting her off.'

'Oh, Rosamund won't care for any of them,' Lucy said wryly. 'She's too much her mother's daughter, cares for nothing but horses.'

'And her cousin,' Brummell suggested with a smile. 'Don't tell me her *tendre* for Captain Morland has worn away? It might not be a bad thing if they made a match of it at last.'

Lucy raised an eyebrow. 'Marcus thinks of her as a child. Besides, I don't suppose he has any idea of getting married.'

'When he comes back from the war he will; and Lady Rosamund is a child no longer.'

'Talking of matches, is it true, as I've heard, that you have been hanging out for a wife?'

Brummell shook his head. 'I am not yet reduced to *that*, I assure you. Charles Manners and I still have a scheme in hand which may make our fortunes at last. Marrying an heiress will be my last resort.'

Lucy said no more, but she was worried about her old friend, as she had been for some time. A year ago his style of life had finally outstripped his means, to the point where his unpaid bills were mounting daily. He was deep in debt, living on what he could win at play, and on the horses, a precarious sort of life at the best of times. It was true she had heard that he had been winning lately — Alvanley said he had won twenty-five thousand pounds in one evening at cards — but such luck could not be depended on.

He had also quarrelled fatefully with the Prince Regent,

and they were now not on speaking terms, which made it unpleasant for everyone who knew them both, as well as for Brummell. Indeed, there had been a very upsetting incident last year, when Brummell, Alvanley, Mildmay and Pierrepoint had given a fancy dress ball at the Argyle Rooms. No invitation had been sent to the Prince, but the Prince, hearing of the circumstances, had simply written to say he would be there. There was nothing to be done about it but to send him an invitation.

When the evening came, however, and the four hosts lined up at the entrance to receive the Prince, he had greeted the other three, but pointedly ignored Brummell. An awkward silence had fallen at this deliberate insult, in which Brummell was heard coolly and clearly to ask, 'Ah, Alvanley, who is your fat friend?' The story had gone rapidly round London, and though most of public opinion was on Brummell's side, it did not make his life any easier to be on bad terms with the Regent of England.

The Treaty of Paris occupied Castlereagh and the allied monarchs all through May, and was finally signed on the last day of the month. France was given her boundaries as they had been at the beginning of the war, in 1792, and her overseas possessions were to be restored to her, with the exception of Tobago, St Lucia and Mauritius.

'It seems much too generous,' Lucy said to John Anstey, who had walked in to take tea with her one evening when she was dining alone. 'When you think of all the trouble France has caused for the last twenty years —'

'Yes, but don't you see, the only settlement that could last would be one that the French themselves see as just and reasonable — otherwise they'd just break out again. It's for the same reason that France is to be allowed a five-year period before abolishing the slave-trade. That's annoyed the abolitionists, as you can imagine! They're calling Castlereagh all manner of unkind names; but the fact is that France has to restock her colonies, and if she's not allowed to, she'll simply break the treaty and we'll have it all to do again.'

Lucy looked unconvinced. 'I'd be happier if Bonaparte were dead, and the French completely subdued.'

'So would the Prussians,' Anstey said, 'but Castlereagh's after a settlement that leaves everybody at least content, and nobody too strong. A peaceful France, and good, solid barriers against anyone's future ambition. That's why the treaty also insists that Belgium should belong to Holland. A new state of the United Netherlands will keep France in check on her northern boundary.'

'It doesn't sound like much of a barrier,' Lucy commented. 'France has overrun Belgium and Holland before now.'

'Ah, but Prussia and Hanover will be behind them for support; and we're hoping to make stronger ties with the new state by a marriage treaty — our Princess Charlotte and the next Prince of Orange.'

'And what about a barrier in the south?'

'Piedmont,' John said promptly, 'with Austria at her back. It's all going to be a system of checks and balances, as neat as a clock. When Castlereagh's finished his job, we shall have a peace in Europe that will last for ever. Or as nearly for ever as anything can be in this uncertain world.'

'I hope you're right,' Lucy said. 'But I'd still feel happier if Boney were dead.'

One day in June, Fanny had herself driven into York to do some shopping, and met Hawker by prearrangement in Pavement. The market for corn, poultry, eggs and butter which thrived here made the street extremely crowded and noisy, and Fanny had protested a little at such a meeting-place. Shouldn't they rather meet somewhere quiet and secluded?

'Foolish!' he chided her. 'In a crowd, no-one can hear what you say, and you can see everyone, and everyone can see you. Who can lay a charge of clandestine behaviour against you? But in a quiet, secluded place, you never know who might be concealed, and listening.'

They strolled along, with Beaver behind them, chatting, or enjoying the silence of each other. Fanny could see his point now — they were both completely public, and completely concealed; and even sometimes, when the press of bodies forced them together, able to touch each other. She was happy. In the months since he had come back to York, she had seen him often, latterly almost every day, and she had ceased to struggle against the inevitable. She was in love with him. From the tiny acorn of that first meeting on the chapel stairs at Mathilde's ball, the most unlikely great oak had

501

flourished. What would happen next she had not contemplated; it was enough to enjoy the richness of colour and taste and texture that life now had, and to remember with a grateful shudder the grey monotone of the time when she had not been in love.

She had no doubts about him. When they had first met, she had been a child, and he an adult; but the passage of years had allowed her to catch up with him. She was his match, and his equal. He had seen and done more than she, of course, but she was sharp-witted and intelligent, and she could hold her own with him. They were right for each other, as he himself had said not long ago.

'We're both villains, Fanny, and we're both selfish. People will never like us much, because we say what we think, and we aren't sentimental, or hypocritical. We care most for our own skins and our own comfort, and so do they, but we aren't afraid to admit it. We aren't really very likeable, you know,' he added thoughtfully, 'except to each other.'

He had said many things, but he had never said he loved her, and it piqued her that she could not wring or trick the admission out of him. Sometimes, out of pride, she would be haughty with him. 'Dozens of young men are in love with me. I have more beaux than I can count on my fingers,' she would say. 'Why should I waste my time on you?'

'Because I understand you, my Fanny,' he would say with his piratical smile. 'They love you — if they love you at all — for qualities they think you have, or hope you have, or think you ought to have. But I value the qualities you really have — your ruthlessness, and shrewdness, and quick wit, and your bold temper, and your bold, bad eyes!'

Value — not *love*. It made her angry, and he would watch her with that knowing laughter in his eyes which always defeated her.

Today, however, she could tell he was preoccupied. He talked to her rather absently, and fell from time to time into silences that were not warm and companionable as usual, but distant and unhappy.

'What is it?' she asked after a while. 'Won't you tell me what's troubling you?'

He looked up. She knew he wouldn't insult her intelligence by telling her that nothing was wrong. 'Very well,' he said.

They were just passing the opening into the Shambles on their left, and with a little nod he turned her into it. There was a bench against the wall of the ruined church there, and he sat down and drew her down beside him. Beaver looked her astonishment, and took up an awkward position like a sentry at a little distance, looking this way and that and fiddling with her gloves.

'We're very conspicuous here,' Fanny said. 'We should not sit long.'

'If I had my way, we would sit where we liked and do what we liked,' he said savagely, 'and be damned to the old pussies.' She looked at him in surprise, and he gave her a rueful smile. 'Oh, you know my reaction to difficulty is always to take up cudgels. I haven't the patience to sit things out.'

'You've plenty of patience when it suits you,' Fanny said. 'Like a cat at a mouse-hole.'

'I'm afraid my days of watching for mice are in the past,' he said. He took her hand and held it between both of his. 'Listen Fanny, I know that you care for me, but I wonder how much?'

'You have no right to ask me for gauges of love, when you give me none,' she said coolly.

'No, no, my darling, you don't understand.' She jumped when he used the word 'darling', but he went on without seeming to notice. 'I'm not trying to test you — that would be the action of a coxcomb. Besides, I know my Fanny: she would tell me willingly that she loved me, but if I tried to coerce her, she would look at me haughtily and walk away.'

'It's as well you understand that,' Fanny said with an unwilling smile.

'Don't I tell you I know you? Very well, then, I will be honest with you. Pound dealing between us, nothing less. I love you, Fanny Morland. I think I've been half in love with you ever since you were a tangle-haired child, furious because you weren't allowed to go to the ball. But now it's much more than that. It's got to the stage where I can't manage without you. You are in my mind all the time, disturbing my thoughts, interfering with my former pleasures.'

'Probably just as well,' Fanny remarked. 'I can guess what they were.'

'Can you? Shame on you! But let me finish. I love you, and

503

I want to marry you. The only question is, do you love me enough to want to marry me? For I have to tell you that I am completely rolled up.'

'Rolled up?'

'Under the hatches. Penniless. I haven't a feather to fly with. In fact, if I don't come up with something soon, some reason to give my creditors hope, I shall either be forced to fly the country, or I shall end up in the Debtor's Prison over there.'

She looked at him in perplexity. 'How can you be rolled up? What were you living on before? You must have had money — where is it gone?'

He laughed. 'My dear little heiress, you can't conceive of someone's having no money, can you? I have been living on credit, simpleton! And now my credit has all but run out, and the duns are on my tail. A run of luck at macao or hazard would have done the trick, but the cards haven't been running my way lately.'

His use of the word *heiress* had made her think. 'Why have you told me this now?' she asked cautiously.

'Because I don't want to have to tip you the double, without your knowing why I've gone.' He eyed her shrewdly. 'Do you think I'm after your money, Fanny? Do you think I want to marry you because you're rich?'

'Of course not,' she said quickly. 'In any case, it wouldn't do you any good, because I don't inherit until I'm twenty-one.'

'I know that, goose. But that won't do for an answer, because you know, or you ought to know, that if I were to marry you, I should be able to raise almost unlimited credit on your expectations. So I ask again, do you think I want you for your money? Pound dealing, remember.'

She met his eyes steadily. 'I think you do really love me; and that you want my money too. And indeed, why shouldn't you? For if you had any money, I should want it. There's nothing wrong in that.'

He crowed with laughter. 'Fanny Morland, you're a woman in a million! In ten million! But I don't know that it mightn't have been better for both of us if you hadn't a fortune to your name, for then I could run away with you at once.'

'Don't be silly. It's much better to have money,' Fanny said sensibly.

'So it is. And do you love me enough to marry me, even though I'm penniless?'

'Are you proposing to me?'

'I am. I'd do it in better style, but the place and the time are not propitious.'

'I want to marry you,' she said evenly. 'But it may be difficult. I don't think my family will like the idea, if you really are penniless.'

'We won't tell them that,' Hawker said. 'In fact, we won't tell them anything just yet, if you don't mind, Fanny, not until we've accustomed them to my presence. I think I can raise the recruits for one last time, enough to stave off the duns for a month or two. We must work gently on your father — I fancy he's rather fond of you.'

Fanny stood up. 'We ought to walk on,' she said. She looked about her in a rather dissatisfied way. 'It isn't how I imagined being proposed to. And now I suppose I'm engaged, but with nothing to shew for it.'

'Poor Fanny, have I taken all the fun out of it? But don't fret. When the time comes, I'll propose to you again, with as much ceremony as you like. And when we're married, I think I can promise you'll find love a great deal more romantic than romance.'

In June the allied sovereigns came to London to celebrate the Treaty of Paris. Major Wiske was amongst the escort guard of honour who accompanied them, and as soon as his duties permitted, he set out to call on Lucy at Upper Grosvenor Street. On his way there, however, he suddenly lost his nerve, and decided to call in for a stiffener on the way at one of the clubs. Stephen's in Bond Street was the army officer's club, but he felt he had rather get away from his fellow-warriors for the moment, so he headed instead for White's.

He found it unexpectedly crowded, and there was evidently something untoward going on.

'What the deuce is the matter, Glenning?' he asked the porter as he gave him his hat. 'This place is very peculiar today.'

'Yessir, Major Wiske!' Glenning said promptly in his hoarse whisper — souvenir of some campaign in the Revolutionary War, when a shell exploded too close to him, and he inhaled the smoke. 'Hit's on account of this Maskewerade, sir, what the members is giving for the Hallied Soverings. Causing the club servants a lot of extra work, it is, sir, not but what the members aren't generous to a fault, sir, in the matter of — oh, thank you very much Major Wiske, sir!'

'You're an old reprobate, Glenning. Is anyone here that I know?'

'Mr Brummell and the rest of the Set is over at Burlington 'Ouse, sir, looking at the floor; but Lord Anstey went into the drawing-room a bit since.'

'Thank you, Glenning. I'll go and have a word.'

'Thank *you* sir. It's nice to 'ave you back Major Wiske, sir.'

John Anstey was reading the paper, but jumped up as Wiske came in and came towards him with his hands out.

'What a piece of luck! I've just ordered a bottle of claret, and it's poor sport drinking it alone. How are you, Wiske? Did you come over with the Sovereigns?'

'Yes, part of the guard of honour. Only just come off duty after eighteen hours at a run — thought I'd take a nip of something before going to Upper Grosvenor Street. I was beginning to wish I'd gone to Stephen's after all! What's all this about a masquerade?'

'Oh, the ball? We — the members of White's, that is — are giving a ball at Burlington House.'

'Yes, I gathered that, but why a masquerade?'

A waiter set a bottle of claret on the table beside them. Tipped off by Glenning, he had also brought two glasses.

'Prinny's idea. He thinks it will make it more informal, and allow some of the *demi-monde* to attend, which will make it more fun for him, and infinitely more naughty.'

'Good God! Julia Johnstone and Harriette Wilson and all that set?'

'That's right. But don't worry, old fellow — you can come in uniform if you like.'

'Thanks very much,' Wiske blinked. 'I hope Prinny isn't going to come as Henry VIII or anythin' embarrassing?'

'I doubt it, not with the Sovereigns there. What the Csar will think of it all I don't know — he was strictly brought up, so I hear. What's he like — have you had much to do with him?'

506

'Tall, good-looking, auburn hair and pink cheeks. Looks a good deal younger than his age. Acts it, too. Women all want to pet him. Perfectly affable, only rather earnest about things; have to watch what you're sayin'.'

'No trouble to me,' Anstey grinned, 'but there are others —! Prinny's been in a state, afraid someone's going to invite the Princess of Wales. He tried to get a rule set up about the tickets, that the members couldn't give them away to anyone but their own relatives. That way, the only person who could invite his wife would be him, and he'd be sure he wouldn't do it.'

Wiske smiled. 'Nothing's changed,' he said. 'How's Lucy?'

'Much the same — you know Lucy. She never was one to wear her heart on her sleeve.'

'I wonder,' Wiske said glumly.

'You do?'

'Wonder if I do know her.'

Anstey eyed him sympathetically, and poured him a glass of claret. 'It's none of my business, I know, old fellow, but if it will help to talk about it —'

Wiske drank appreciatively, and then said, 'I was thinking of asking your advice, actually. I mean, you must know Lucy better than anyone now.'

'Except that groom of hers, Parslow, but it might be difficult to confide in him,' John smiled. 'Well, yes, I've known Lucy all her life, since she was a little girl — all those years ago, when the world was young! It's hard to believe it now, when I remember those days. I was in love with her sister Mary — she was so beautiful! — and little Lucy was in love with a drunken old horse-doctor called Proom! She always was the oddest creature.' He returned from his brief reverie to catch Wiske's expression. 'Oh, I'm sorry, old fellow! Do go on. What was it you wanted to ask?'

'It's a bit delicate,' Wiske said, frowning. 'Quite in confidence?'

'Of course,' Anstey said, half puzzled, half amused. 'Lucy's welfare is very dear to my heart. I regard her rather as a sister.'

'Well, then,' Wiske said with difficulty, 'you know I'm very fond of her? More than that, really. Been in love with her for years, though I kept it to myself.' Anstey made a sympathetic noise in his throat. 'Well, a couple of years ago, I began to feel

507

that perhaps Lucy's feelings had changed. I took the chance and declared myself, and asked her to marry me.'

Anstey stifled his expression of surprise, and asked, 'And what did she say?'

'She accepted me, but said she wouldn't marry me until after the war.' Wiske frowned again. 'Thing is, every time I come back, I ask again, and I don't think she's unwilling, but she keeps to this business about the war. Don't know why. I've asked her, and she can't answer. But now the war is over, and I've got to go and — well, remind her of her promise, and I'm afraid —'

'Afraid she's changed her mind?'

'Not that, really. Afraid that if I don't ask her the right way, use the right words, she'll say no.' He looked at his friend. 'Is that nonsense? Touch of shell-shock, maybe? Too long in the firing-line, making my wits wander?'

'Not at all,' Anstey said seriously. 'I can perfectly understand your feelings.'

'You can?' Wiske seemed as surprised as pleased.

'Tell me — forgive me for asking — but does Lucy love you?'

'Hard to tell sometimes. You know what she is. But I think she does.'

'Then your path is clear. You must be firm with her. Don't stand any nonsense. Sweep her off her feet.'

'Really?'

'Really. If she argues, just kiss her, and keep kissing her until she stops.'

Wiske contemplated this pleasing notion. 'Think it will work?'

'Bound to. The trouble with Lucy is that she came to thinking very late in life, and now she does too much of it by way of compensation. And she's very loyal — I wouldn't be surprised if it weren't some nonsensical loyalty to Weston's memory that makes her hesitate. Your job will be to keep her occupied, so she hasn't time to think. That way she'll be happy. Here, have another glass of wine for courage, and then —'

'Sound the gallop?'

'Exactly. Forward the Tenth! Your health, Wiske, and Lucy's happiness! And be sure to invite me to the wedding.'

'Her ladyship is just on the point of going out, sir,' Hicks said when Danby enquired at the door. 'The horses will be brought round at any moment; but I'm sure her ladyship will be glad to see you.'

'Of course she will. Don't trouble yourself, Hicks, I'll find my own way up.'

'Very good, sir. Her ladyship is in the morning-room, I believe.'

He watched in well-concealed surprise as the Major positively ran up the stairs, taking the half-turn at a leap. A hint of wine on his breath, too, and a hectic look in the eye. Something was Up, Hicks thought, and if only he were ten years younger, he'd nip up the stairs after him and have a listen. But the horses would be here any instant, and that would be his excuse to go up and disturb them. By hovering outside a door, one could get to hear quite a lot, and be sure to intrude at the right moment to be told a little more.

Lucy was dressed in her riding habit, her hat, gloves and whip lying ready on the table. She was seated by the window, scrawling a letter in her round, childish hand, and when Wiske came in she didn't look up, but said, 'Yes, all right, Hicks, I shall be down directly.'

'It's not Hicks; it's me!'

She looked up. 'Danby! Why, I wasn't expecting you. When did you arrive? Why didn't Hicks announce you? I was just on the point of going out.'

'He told me. I said I'd come up anyway — not his fault. I got back last night, but I haven't had an instant to myself until now — not even long enough to scribble you a note.'

'You came with the Sovereigns, then? George and the rest are giving a ball for them at Burlington House —'

'Yes, I know about that. I didn't come here to talk about the ball.'

She eyed him cautiously. 'You sound rather odd. Are you all right?'

'Perfectly. Never better. The war's over, Lucy, and I've come to ask you to keep your promise.'

'My promise? Oh!' Lucy got up from the table and began to pace about, avoiding his eyes. 'Well, it's very sudden. I wasn't expecting you back just yet. There are lots of things to be thought about, arrangements — we have to talk things over —'

'Nothing to talk about that I can see,' he said simply. 'There's only one question to ask — will you marry me?'

'It's not that simple,' Lucy complained, pacing. 'There are dozens of things to be taken into consideration. I can't just be expected to make a decision on the instant like that —'

'You've had years to think about it,' he pointed out patiently.

'But I didn't know the war was going to end now, like this.'

'Lucy!' He caught her as she passed and made her face him, holding her lightly but firmly by the upper arms. 'There's only one question — do you love me? Will you marry me?'

'That's two questions,' she objected weakly.

'It's the same question,' he said firmly. 'The same answer will do for both; and I mean to be answered now.'

She looked at him, and for a moment he was distracted from his purpose by a new realisation of how much he loved her. This was no perfect, classical beauty's face. She was a mature woman now. There were lines — laughter-lines around the eyes, a frown-mark, he was sorry to say, between her brows, a crease in her upper lip from her habit of pulling it down between her teeth when she was vexed. The eyelids were softly creased, and there were a few silver hairs amongst the pale fawn of her perpetually disordered curls. She was unpredictable, difficult, brave, sometimes thoughtless, frequently careless, always loyal and truthful. She shook his senses; all the things she was were rooted so deep in him that every breath of hers tugged painfully at his heart.

'Do you love me?' he asked again, a little huskily.

'I won't be bullied,' she said, but the expression of her eyes had changed. She was not annoyed, or stubborn, or proud, only unsure; she watched him, shy, afraid, wanting to be convinced.

'I won't bully you,' he said, bending his face to hers, touching her lips with his, feeling her quiver. 'Only marry you, love you, care for you.' He kissed her, long and sweetly, and paused for breath. Her eyes half opened.

'But Danby —' she began to protest, though without conviction.

510

'Hmm?' he said, but folded her close against him and kissed her again. This time her eyes remained shut. 'Name the day, Lucy. How long do you need to get your wedding-gown made?'

She put an impatient hand round the back of his neck and pulled his mouth down to hers again. He wasn't quite sure what it was she murmured, but it sounded like 'Damn the wedding-gown!'

Hicks allowed a good five minutes of silence to elapse before he banged clumsily into the potted palm that stood in the passage beside the door, and turned the doorknob with a great deal of fumbling. When he stopped in, his lady was standing in the middle of the room, holding fast to the Major's hand, her cheeks so pink and her eyes so bright that she looked no more than twenty, and made Hicks's eyes go misty for a moment.

He cleared his throat. 'The horses are waiting, my lady,' he said.

'Thank you, Hicks. Have them sent back to the stables, if you please — I shan't be riding just yet,' Lucy said.

'Very good, my lady,' said Hicks, the imperturbable.

'And, Hicks, bring up a bottle of the Veuve Clicquot, will you, and two glasses. We have something to celebrate.'

'Yes, my lady,' Hicks said.

Lucy brought the hand that was holding her lover's forward so that it was clearly visible, and looked up at him with an expression of fondness and mischief and dependency and sheer high spirits, which made Hicks for an instant forget all about his varicose veins and want to dance.

'I'm going to marry the Major,' she said.

'Very good, my lady,' Hicks said, permitting himself a small smile of pleasure at his own *double entendre*. He backed out, closing the door, and out in the passage executed a very small four-step jig. 'And about time too,' he remarked to the potted palm with a satisfied nod.

Lucy's wedding to Major Wiske took place on 30 June at St George's, and though it couldn't hold a candle to Flaminia's for style or grandeur, it remained in the memory of most of the guests as the happiest wedding they were ever at.

George Brummell was groomsman, which alone would have bestowed on it the cachet of fashionableness; but add to that the fact that Danby Wiske was known and liked by everyone who mattered in the *ton*, and that everything Lucy did had always headed the society columns of the newspaper, and it became one occasion in the year that no-one wanted to confess they had missed.

Lucy looked very handsome, and affectingly nervous, in a gown of soft yellow silk with deep ruched silk trimming; and a delicious, high-crowned hat, trimmed with white marabou, knots and ribbons, which a dozen ladies tried to have copied in the week that followed, without success. Danby Wiske was in the full-dress uniform of the Tenth Hussars, which had been redesigned yet again that year. He looked very handsome in the blue pelisse with gold lace and buttons, the red-and-gold fringed sash, and gold-laced red shako, which complimented his fair good looks.

After the wedding they were driven back to Upper Grosvenor Street in an open barouche drawn by four white horses, to a breakfast few people ever forgot. The Prince Regent himself, as Colonel-in-Chief of the regiment, found time to drop in to propose the toast to the couple's health, and was heard to remark as he left, evidently reluctantly, to fulfil an official engagement, that it was 'the jolliest wedding he was ever at, by God, none of the usual stuffiness about it,' and that 'Lady Curricle had always been a favourite of his, and he'd be damned if he didn't do something for Wiske, who was as good a fellow as ever lived, and almost deserved his good fortune.'

The Prince had an unfortunate reputation for promising a great deal more than he ever performed, but in this case he proved as good as his word: Danby Wiske had been a personal friend of his for as long as Lucy had. In August there were widespread celebrations to mark the one hundred years of Hanoverian rule, and a number of honours were created to mark the happy occasion. Danby Wiske was made a viscount, promoted to Colonel, and given a staff appointment as Liaison Officer between Lord Castlereagh and Lord Wellington, who at the same time was raised to a Dukedom.

As a result, when the Peace Congress opened in Vienna in September, promising to be the most extended and glittering social gathering of all time, and Lord Castlereagh went out to head the negotiations which were to settle the future of Europe for all time, his enormous retinue included Colonel Lord Theakston and his lady, whose only care on the ship going across the channel seemed to be whether her horses would survive the crossing uninjured.

James had been increasingly anxious about Fanny's growing preference for the least suitable of her beaux. It was Louisa Anstey who first alerted him to the situation, which had been drawn to her attention by her sister-in-law, Meg Somers. Mrs Somers was bringing out her youngest daughter Jane, and was therefore present at every ball, rout and assembly in the area.

'Meg mentioned to me, and therefore I thought I ought to mention to you, Jamie,' Louisa said anxiously, 'that Fanny is beginning to be talked about, because of this Mr Hawker.'

'Mr Hawker? That fellow who was in the militia? What's he doing?'

'Well, Fanny stands up with him at every single ball,' Louisa said 'Oh, only for two dances — Fanny would never do anything improper, I'm sure — but sometimes they sit out and talk to each other, and it's always he who takes her to supper, and fetches her ices and so on.'

'Impudent dog,' James said, a little startled.

'Only, the thing is, Jamie,' she went on breathlessly, 'that everyone knows he's *not at all suitable*, for he must be ten years older than her, and he has what John calls a colourful reputation; and I'm *afraid*,' she screwed up her face in pain at having to speak ill of anyone, 'that he has debts with all the tradesmen, and *appears* to be entirely without means.'

James had thanked her, soothed her, and hurried home with the alarming intelligence to Héloïse, who appeared unmoved by it.

'Yes, he does hang around her,' she said serenly, not pausing in her hemming of a new dress for Benedict, whose vigorous career tended to make short work of his clothes. 'Have you not seen, after church on Sundays he waits for her at the door, and they talk while you are being civil to your friends.'

'I've never noticed particularly who she talks to after service,' he admitted. 'There are always half a dozen callow young men at her elbow, but I hardly know one from the other, and she treats them all alike, so I've never worried about it.' He frowned. 'How do you know about it?'

'Stephen tells me. He is my eyes and ears,' she said. She looked up, her head cocked enquiringly. 'For such a stern father, my James, you are sometimes very unnoticing.'

'I never thought she could get up to any mischief outside the Minster doors on a Sunday morning,' he said uncomfortably.

'I don't think she gets up to mischief. She is very careful to do nothing which is beyond the line of being acceptable.'

'Nevertheless, Louisa says she's being talked about, and Louisa is the least gossiping woman I know — apart from you, of course. It has to stop. I wish you'd told me before, Marmoset!'

'I didn't tell you, my love, for the very reason that if I did, you would probably go thundering in like a bull and forbid Fanny to see him again.'

'Damned right I would! It should have been stopped long ago!'

Héloïse put down her sewing. 'But no, you must not! Reflect a moment! Come, sit by me, and listen.'

He sat, looking at her with a perplexed frown. 'What then, Marmoset? You said I was an unnoticing father? Now I have noticed, why must I not do something about it?'

'If you go to Fanny and tell her she must not have anything to do with this man, do you think she will say "Very well, Papa", and obey you? Or will she rather scowl at you and stamp her foot and defy you? Picture to yourself, and tell me which is the more convincing portrait?'

James smiled unwillingly. 'Well, I suppose *forbidding* her might be a little extreme,' he admitted.

'It is why I have not spoken to her myself on the subject; for you know we go on very well, in general. But forbid her something, and she will want it all the more.'

'But, damn it, Héloïse, this man is unsuitable! He's deep in dun country, according to what Louisa said. Probably a gazetted fortune-hunter. I can't do nothing.'

'What I advise, *chéri*, is that you find out all you can about Mr Hawker. Ask some discreet questions at the club. You can do that so much better than I, or Stephen. And then, perhaps, we should have him to dinner.'

514

'What?'

'Why yes — with other people, of course, so that it shall not look too pointed.'

'But why the *deuce* —?'

'You cannot fight an enemy unless you can get near him,' she said quietly. 'Also, you must remember that you yourself began the acquaintance when you invited him to Mathilde's ball —'

'I didn't invite him. He came as a substitute, if you remember, brought by that other subaltern, the Irish one you didn't like.'

'Yes, I remember; but the invitation was issued in your name. Also he claims to be acquainted with Fanny's grandfather, and he did Fanny a great service in Manchester — though how much of truth there is in that story perhaps we shall never know. And he met her in London at a number of respectable houses, when she was under Lucy's chaperonage.'

'I didn't know that! How —'

'Stephen heard about it from Fanny's maid. So you see, the acquaintance is too long-standing to be broken off, unless there is some good reason, and I think this man will not give you reason, if he can help it.'

'Dangling after Fanny's fortune is reason enough, I should think.' James growled.

'To you — not to Fanny. She will probably tire of him soon, as long as she is not crossed, or forbidden to speak to him. Meanwhile, you must find out all you can about him, so that you can — discourage him, if it becomes necessary. There may be many things in his background that he would not care to have known.'

James reflected. 'Yes, you're right.' He lifted her hand and kissed it. 'As always, Marmoset.' He sighed and relapsed into thought again.

Héloïse watched him sympathetically, and after a while said comfortingly, 'After all, my James, Fanny is not so very susceptible. She is a very level-headed young woman, in fact, and has never yet lost her heart to any handsome face or charming manner. All the smartest beaux in York and London have tried, and failed, to make any mark on her.'

'Yes,' James said, but it didn't seem to comfort him. 'That's another worry. She's been out for three years, after all. She'll be nineteen soon, and she's never wanted to marry anyone. I'm beginning to fear she'll end up as an old maid. I wonder if we brought her out too young?'

Héloïse laughed, and rubbed his hand against her cheek. 'You are a dear fool, my James! The one minute to be afraid that she will want to marry, and the next to be afraid she won't.'

He smirked sheepishly. 'I just want her to be happy,' he said.

'Only that?' Héloïse said. '*Tiens*! Then we had better have recourse to prayer.'

James followed his wife's advice, and pursued discreet enquiries, and meanwhile gave a dinner-party to which he invited Hawker, amongst several other young people. He was disturbed to see Fanny in raptures over the news that her admirer was to come under her roof, although he had to admit that when the day came, she behaved in a perfectly calm and controlled way, and treated Hawker with a pleasant friendliness which suggested a long acquaintance, but was socially unexceptionable.

He was impressed by Hawker's behaviour: his manners were polished and unassuming; he was charming to Héloïse, respectful to the older gentlemen, spoke sensibly about whatever topic of conversation was raised, was grave or witty as the moment demanded, and paid no special attention to Fanny, or at least, none that was objectionable. The degree of their apparent intimacy dismayed James, even while he was puzzled by the quality of it, which suggested not so much a lover engaged in wooing, but something along the lines of an affectionate older brother, or perhaps a childhood playmate met again in maturity.

On the other hand, the more he learned about Hawker, the less he liked the situation. He was, as Louisa had said, deep in debt, with tradesman's bills of a long-standing nature, and apparently no means of paying them. He was a gamester, although from what he could gather, James guessed he played rather from necessity than out of gambler's fever.

Extending the delicate web of enquiry still further, James learned that when Hawker had been in the militia and stationed at Fulford, he had had a reputation for drinking too much, for keeping dubious company — like Black Tom, the notorious but uncatchable poacher and liquor-smuggler — and for consorting with the Muslin Company; though as to the latter charge, James could hardly blame him for that, considering his own past record. An unmarried man was entitled to take his pleasure that way, and he could not learn that Hawker had visited any Barques of Frailty since he had come to York in March of this year.

Meanwhile, the licence which had been granted to Hawker by his having been invited openly to dinner and acknowledged as an acquaintance meant that he was able to call at Morland Place, officially to pay his respects to Héloïse, but in reality to sit with Fanny for half an hour. There was nothing to object to in that — Héloïse made sure never to leave them alone together — but Hawker would sometimes invite Fanny to walk about the gardens, or go for a ride, or drive about the park. This was less satisfactory, though Héloïse, if she did not accompany them herself, which was not always possible, made sure that Fanny's maid went with them, and, if they were riding or driving, a reliable groom.

'Your scheme hasn't answered, Marmoset; it's only made things worse. She sees more of him than ever,' James complained.

Héloïse sighed. 'Yes, I know; but think, James, if she was forbidden to see him, she would probably do so in secret. At least there is nothing objectionable now. No-one can point the finger at her.'

'But people are saying that he means to marry her, and that I approve,' James cried, frustrated. 'And with his reputation, they *will* point the finger at her. There is nothing they might not think of her, if they think I believe she cannot do better than this — this — reprobate!'

'You must find out something about him, something enough to send him away,' Héloïse said. 'Why did he leave the militia, for instance? Perhaps he did something in Brighton. Why not ask Major Wiske if he can make an enquiry for you. He is very discreet.'

'Very well,' James said. 'But if he comes up with nothing, I shall just have to forbid her to see him any more. I can't stand by any longer and do nothing.'

He sent off an express the same day to Danby Wiske, who

agreed to find out what he could; and his reply came at last at the beginning of August, on the first day of race-week. James read, his brow darkening with anger at what he learnt of the man who dared to pursue his daughter; who would be hanging about their box at the Knavesmire, fetching Fanny ices, and expecting to be invited to the celebration balls and parties so that he could dance with her and strengthen his position still further.

'Now I have him!' he exclaimed in grim triumph, and rang the bell. In a moment Ottershaw came in. 'Where's Miss Fanny?' he asked.

'I believe she's in the rose garden with her ladyship, sir, cutting the flowers for the dinner tonight.'

'Send someone out, will you, and ask her to come to me immediately.'

'Very good, sir,' said Ottershaw.

CHAPTER TWENTY-SIX

James paced the room until Fanny came in.

'Yes, Papa? You wanted to speak to me?'

'Yes — come in. Close the door,' he said. The sight of her — so pretty in her gown of green cambric, with the long ruched sleeves and flounced hem, so womanly with her hair piled neatly at the back of her head, displaying her fragile jaw and slender neck — aroused all his most protective instincts, and made him long to kill the man who threatened her peace and well-being. 'Sit down, Fanny. I have something very particular to say to you about Mr Hawker.'

Fanny's eyes became wary, and she sat only on the edge of the armchair's seat, as if to be ready at any instant to get up again. 'Indeed, Papa? That's just as well — I wanted to talk to you about him myself.'

James ignored this, having worked himself up to his speech. 'I have been very worried, Fan, about how much that young man seems to be hanging about you. I've never liked it, but your stepmother persuaded me not to interfere —'

Fanny's brows rose. 'Madame persuaded you?'

'She thought it better to let things run their natural course. We both thought you would tire of him and send him about his business.'

'No, Papa, you don't understand,' Fanny began eagerly, but he held up his hand.

'Wait, let me finish. I have not been content to do nothing, however. I have made enquiries about Mr Hawker, and I have to tell you, Fanny, that his circumstances are straitened — in fact, his is deep in debt. He owes money everywhere, and the tradesmen —'

'I know.'

'You know?'

'He told me so himself, weeks ago,' Fanny said calmly.

'*He* told you?'

519

'Yes, Papa. Fitz and I are friends; there are no reserves between us. He told me that he was *rolled up*, and was living by what he could earn at play.'

'Good God, Fanny! If you knew that, why have you continued to encourage him?'

'I told you, Papa, we are *friends*.'

James looked grim. 'I think you will find, my love, that it is not friendship that is on his mind. He is in desperate straits, and unless I am much mistaken, it is marriage with you that he is hoping for, in order to rescue himself from what must otherwise follow —'

'Flight abroad, or debtor's prison,' Fanny supplied.

'Fanny, I wish you will take this seriously!' James said explosively.

'I do, Papa. I know he wishes to marry me; that is what I wanted to talk to you about — to ask your permission for Fitz and me to marry as soon as possible.'

'Fanny, for God's sake, you must be out of your senses! You cannot want to marry a fortune-hunter, a man unscrupulous enough to pursue an heiress — an under-age heiress — for the sake of her inheritance! You don't understand what —'

'No, it is you who does not understand!' Fanny retorted vehemently, rising to her feet. 'I wish to marry him because I love him, as he loves me.'

'Love doesn't come into it, Fan. He wants your money.'

'I told you, he has not kept his circumstances secret from me. We love each other, and that has nothing to do with money, though of course it is better that I have money, so that I can pay off his debts and set him up —'

'Fanny, you cannot be so naïve! He has pursued you in a way no honourable man would, lied to you —'

'He has not!'

'He told you he was in debt, but don't you see, that was simply part of his plan to make you trust him.'

'I do trust him. He would never hurt me. He has been honest with me. There is nothing you can tell me about him that I don't already know.'

'Did he tell you why he left the militia?' James asked quietly.

'No,' Fanny said, lifting her head a little, defiantly. 'I don't suppose it matters.'

'He changed from one regiment to another when his debts grew too great. While he was in Brighton, he ran up bills to such a degree that the tradesmen complained to his colonel, who was obliged to call in his commission. He owes money everywhere.' Fanny's cheeks were flushed, and her eyes glittered, but she did not speak. James felt sorry for what he knew must be her disillusionment, but he had to go on. 'There is more,' he said gently. 'I believe you met him in London during your come-out, just after he had left the militia. I think you probably did not know that during that time he was not only gaming, but had a hand in an illegal gaming-hell in a back-street of St James's. A shady place, Fanny, where innocent young men, fresh up to London, are robbed of their fortunes by sharpers with rigged packs of cards, and loaded dice. Do you understand what I'm saying?'

Fanny made no reply, only stared at him with hard, bright eyes.

'This gaming-hell was the property of a married woman, a Mrs Boyd-Carlson, of whom I'm sure you will not have heard, but she was notorious in the fringes of London society. Your Mr Hawker, I'm sorry to say, was her lover —'

'No!'

' — with the consent, or at least the complacency of her husband, but that hardly makes it any better. I'm sorry, Fan, but it was so. Everything began to get a little too hot for your *honest* Mr Hawker, and he concluded he would have to flee abroad for a time.'

'I know why he went abroad,' Fanny said eagerly. 'He was employed on a diplomatic mission, a secret one, but vital to the safety of the country!'

'No, darling, that wasn't it,' James said, almost unwillingly. 'The gaming club was drawing too much attention, prosecution was about to overtake him, and he fled to save himself. But that isn't the worst. He did not intend to flee alone. He attempted to take with him a wealthy heiress —' Fanny started visibly — 'a Miss Rickard, daughter of a city merchant. He tried to elope with her, Fanny, but fortunately the attempt failed, and he had to flee alone. You see what kind of man we are dealing with here.'

'It's lies, all lies!' Fanny cried passionately. 'I don't believe you! If you had known those things, you'd have spoken up

521

before. You've just made it up, to turn me against him.'

'Fanny, darling, use your wits! I've only just learned of these things myself. Look, here is the letter I received today — you may read it if you wish.' She jerked her head away angrily. 'I own I've never liked the look of him, but I didn't know how bad he was, and I'm persuaded you didn't either. Darling, I know it's a disappointment to you, but you are too sensible to ignore these facts.'

She turned her head back to him, and fixed him with a look which shook him, it was so hard and determined. There was nothing of the child, or even of the woman in that gaze. 'You're right, I didn't know all these things. But they don't make any difference to me. I mean to marry him, and it doesn't matter what you say to me, you won't change my mind.'

'But Fanny,' James said, shocked and dismayed, 'you must see now what he is about! You cannot still have any good opinion of him. You wouldn't defy me simply for the sake of defiance. You're nineteen, Fanny, not a child any longer. You know a little of the way the world works. This man is bad, unscrupulous, desperate —'

Her hands went down to her sides, and she spoke calmly. 'You don't understand even yet, do you? When I came back from London, I put him out of my mind. I didn't want to love him. I certainly didn't want to marry him. I know my own worth, Papa, as well as you do. Miss Morland of Morland Place — I wanted an earl at the very least! But it isn't like that now. When he came back, I saw it would not do. I love him. We are right for each other. Yes —' she forstalled James's interruption, 'yes, he wants my money. Probably he would pursue me for my fortune even if he didn't love me. But knowing that doesn't make any difference to what I feel for him; or he for me.'

James felt near to tears. 'Fanny, Fanny, if you could only hear yourself!'

'I will marry him, Papa.'

'No! I forbid it! I utterly forbid it! You will not see him again, and that's my last word on it. I will never give my consent to your marrying him, do you understand?'

He was shouting now, but she remained icy-calm, though her eyes were burning with intensity.

'I will marry him. You will give your consent, because if you do not, I will force your hand. I want no-one else, and I will make sure that no-one else will have me.'

'Fanny —!'

'Listen to me, Papa, I love him! There's nothing you can do about it. *I love him!*'

James stared at her, appalled, bewildered, afraid. There were tears on his cheeks now, tears of pity and of loss. His little girl, his lovely Fanny, whom he had adored since birth, had watched grow, had cherished and nurtured until she became a lovely and accomplished woman, was looking at him with the calm certainty of a martyr about to go to her death at the stake. His grief for her was like grief for her death. She would marry this utterly worthless man, and be destroyed, her heart broken, her loveliness wasted into dust. The strong, single-minded, devoted passion which had been his all her life was now turned in another direction, and poured out for another man, one so wholly unworthy of it, that nature itself protested at the idea, and he cried.

'It's madness,' he sobbed. 'Fanny, it's madness!'

She took a step forward and touched him, and he felt that she was trembling lightly, like a leaf vibrated by the wind. He flung his arms round her, and they hugged each other for an instant convulsively, and just for that moment she was his little girl again. But it was she who drew back.

'I will marry him, Papa,' she said softly. 'I think it would be best if you accepted that, and made the best of it. There will be settlements to arrange. His debts must be paid, and he must have an allowance until I am of age. I'll leave you now to think about it. But if you try to part us, I shall see him in secret, and that would be worse, wouldn't it? Think about that, Papa.'

She left him, closing the door quietly behind her, leaving James numb, as though he had just suffered a bereavement.

A public face had to be presented, The Morlands of Morland Place had to be visible in their box on every day of the races, or the world would conclude that something was seriously amiss. The first day was always a very social one, with friends and neighbours coming to pay their respects, to discuss the prospects for the week, and to try to wheedle some

523

information that might give rise to a profitable wager.

Edward, James and Héloïse, Mathilde, Fanny, Sophie, and the little boys with their nurses were all present, dressed in their best, smiling and nodding to their acquaintance, chatting to their friends. It was a fine day, though a little windy, with clouds running across the sun, throwing fast shadows which dimmed and then brightened the sunlight, as though someone were lowering and raising the wick of a lamp. The horses pranced, their manes and tails blowing sideways, the jockeys in their bright-coloured silks soothing them, patting their necks.

Of the party, only the children were wholly happy. James brooded silently. He had told no-one, not even Héloïse, the substance of the letter he had received, or of his interview with Fanny. He wanted time to think and devise a strategy before revealing even to his wife the extent to which Fanny had been corrupted by contact with this man. Héloïse glanced at him from time to time, concerned for him, knowing him unhappy. She looked at Fanny, and saw her bright and triumphant, glowing with some inner light that made her beautiful, and she could not draw any conclusions as to what had occurred between them.

Edward and Mathilde were also preoccupied, though that had become a normal state for them when in company with each other. Mathilde had returned from her visit to Lizzie Wickfield ill at ease and uncertain what to do for the best. She felt angry with herself for having doubts about her love for Edward, for her own inconstancy; and yet there seemed no prospect, now or in the future, of their love prospering. Edward was feeling equally despairing, knowing Fanny's sentiments towards him, and had determined that when Mathilde returned, he would speak to her, tell her that there was no hope, beg her to find someone else and not think of him again.

When they saw each other, however, neither found it in them to say what was necessary. Mathilde looked at Edward's grey head and lined face, and felt all the force of Lizzie's comments; yet he was so dear to her, and how could she hurt him by telling him she no longer wanted to marry him? Indeed, she didn't even know if that were true. It was hard to know precisely how she felt, when everything was hypothetical.

If it were in their power to be married, the answer might become clear to her. She felt a certain restraint with him, and she was aware that he knew it.

Edward looked at Mathilde, and loved her as he had always loved her. She was the only comfort he had in a grey world, the only pleasure, and he could not bring himself to cast her away. She had scolded him before for making decisions on her behalf, and he saw how wrong that was. But what right did he have to ask for her love when he could not offer her what she deserved, an establishment, security? He didn't know what to say to her; and he felt a certain restraint with her, and he was aware that she knew it.

Since then they had avoided being alone together, and when it was inevitable, they had behaved in a friendly, polite way, like old friends, rather than lovers. It had become a habit over the weeks, which, if not precisely what either wanted, at least made life in the same house tolerable. Yet they were both aware that it could not go on indefinitely. Sooner or later some decision was going to have to be made.

The Ansteys joined the Morlands in their box, with some of their vast brood of children. Little John was still at sea, of course, and Alfie and Ben, the next two sons, were strolling about somewhere with their contemporaries. The three little girls, Louisa, Mary and Charlotte, clustered round Sophie, their favourite, and admired every aspect of her appearance in an embarrassing chorus, which Sophie bore with good-naturedly, while young Henry, a hopeful sprig of six-and-a-half, headed straight for Nicholas, his exact contemporary, and bore him off to the back of the box to admire his new pet snail, which was concealed in his pocket.

Louisa sat down beside Héloïse, and dumped baby Aglaea on her lap — almost four and not quite such a baby, but a delight to Héloïse all the same — while John lounged against the front rail and chatted about the local news, and about Danby Wiske's preferment, which had just been announced. At that moment John Skelwith and his mother strolled past, and each gave a comprehensive bow of the head to ·the company. Half a dozen steps further on, Skelwith spoke a few words to his mother, and left her to walk on, while he returned to pay his respects more fully.

He was looking very drawn and weary, and was still in mourning, of course, for his wife, but he spoke cheerfully.

'I think we shall have a good day,' he said, addressing his remarks quite correctly to Héloïse, though his eyes strayed to Mathilde, sitting beyond her at the end of the row. 'I hope so, anyway, for I've persuaded Mother to come on the promise of it, and if the entertainment fails her, I shall never be able to get her out again.'

It was said in jest, but Héloïse could guess how much was behind the words. 'How is your mother, Mr Skelwith?' she said with sympathy. 'This sad business must have been a strain for her.'

His eyes met hers for a moment, and she read all the pain that he could not speak aloud. 'It has been very hard for her. She was fond of Patience, of course, but worse than that, I think, have been the unkind things that were said.'

'She must not — you must not, regard the wagging of spiteful tongues,' Héloïse said warmly. 'The only way to deal with loose talk is to ignore it.'

'Yes, ma'am, I know,' he said, wearily. 'But I'm afraid Mother cannot always be — rational — about such emotional subjects.'

Louisa spoke up. 'Is your mother in your usual seat, John dear? Then I shall go and speak to her. I'm sure she would like a little company.'

'Thank you, ma'am, I'm sure she would,' Skelwith said, though a trifle doubtfully. The truth was that he believed his mother's mind to have been unhinged by Patience's death and the talk which followed. Looking after her, coping with her unstable moods, was proving an increasing strain for him, more wearing than any grief he might have felt for the death of his wife. Indeed, looking after his mother in the immediate aftermath of Patience's death had prevented his feeling anything very much. He had not had the chance properly to mourn her.

Héloïse felt he would probably like the subject to be changed, and said, 'Tell me, Mr Skelwith, what do you fancy for the first race? You may speak frankly, for though I shall be obliged out of loyalty to place my shilling on James's colt, I would be glad to hear an unbiased opinion for once.'

He smiled. 'That makes it difficult for me, ma'am, for if I say I think he will win, you will think I am only being polite.'

'No, I promise I shall not,' Héloïse laughed. 'Ingot is a handsome fellow, isn't he? Such a lovely colour! I am never allowed to say that at home,' she confided, with a sideways glance at James, who was talking to Edward, 'for they call me a simpleton, and say that — how do you say it? — "handsome is as handsome does"?'

'I think he will perform handsomely enough to satisfy everyone,' Skelwith said, 'and I don't think you should be shamed out of admiring his looks. Between us, ma'am, I have always had a preference for that particular shade of chestnut myself.'

He did not look at Mathilde as he spoke, but she and Héloïse both knew where the remark tended. Her cheeks grew pink, and she lowered her eyes, and did not raise them when a moment later Skelwith addressed her in a gentle voice, saying, 'Is your shilling on Ingot too, Miss Nordubois, or have you some other preference? You, I am sure, might not be constrained in your choice by your relationship to Morland Place. You may choose freely, I'm persuaded, wherever your fancy directs you.'

Mathilde's heart was beating so rapidly that it was making her hands damp. She could hardly believe what she was hearing; but there was no mistaking his meaning. He wanted to know if there was any hope for him; telling her that his inclination was still towards her.

She had to say something, but hardly knew what. She did not know whether Edward had heard his words, or if he had heard, would understand their import. Héloïse, with the greatest of tact, had turned her head away from them, and was talking to the baby on her lap, playing pat-a-cake with it, to give them privacy.

'I — I hardly know, sir,' she managed at last. 'Certainly I am free to choose where I will, but I do not know which horse to prefer.'

'If you would permit me, I could guide your choice,' he said. 'Sometimes an outsider may see more clearly where your best advantage lies.'

She looked up and met his eyes, and read in them the old tenderness unabated. Thoughts followed each other in rapid succession through her mind. He was five months widowed, too short a time actively to pursue another woman; but in three or four months' time, there would be nothing to prevent a quiet courtship and betrothal. He had married Patience, but had always loved her. His mother would never countenance it. He was wealthy, kind, *young*. Oh Edward! Yet she liked him, she had always liked him. If she loved Edward so entirely, could she feel such a fluttering at Skelwith's words? She was lucky — more lucky than she deserved — to have a renewal of his interest, to be approached a second time. She was twenty-five, and portionless. But his mother hated her. And how could she break Edward's heart?

Skelwith continued to look at her tenderly, waiting for her answer. He had been thinking of her increasingly over the last few weeks. He had never ceased to love her, and the fact that she had remained single gave him encouragement to think that she might not be averse from a renewal of his suit. Even if she did not love him, even if her feelings were no more than friendly towards him, he could offer her the sort of establishment any women in her position must welcome; and he felt confident enough that, if they did marry, he could win her love, warm her feelings into something more than mere liking.

'Won't you tell me, Miss Nordubois, if you have chosen elsewhere?' he prompted her gently. 'A word will suffice — I will not plague you. But if your fancy is still free, may I not try to direct your choice?'

She wet her dry lips. 'I think — sir — I am not unwilling to listen to your advice — but I fear your mother may be wanting you. I should not like to be the cause of upsetting her.'

He understood her. 'You are not to be worrying about my mother, Miss Nordubois,' he said firmly. 'She is my responsibility, and mine alone.' He smiled at her. 'I must go to her now — but may I return later and mark your card for you?'

She hesitated, and then nodded. She saw him draw a deep breath, and thought for one dreadful moment he was going to kiss her; but he controlled his elation, and only murmured, 'God bless you!' before bowing a little wildly in the general direction of everyone, and taking his leave.

Héloïse turned back to Mathilde and said unemphatically, 'What a pleasant young man he is — so steady. Mathilde, *ma*

528

chère, don't you find this box a little airless? Why don't you take a little walk. I see the Miss Greys over there, and Miss Micklethwaite. I'm sure you would like to speak to them.'

'Thank you, Madame,' Mathilde said gratefully, and made her escape. Dear Madame, who knew that she simply could not sit still, but needed both movement and privacy to settle her disordered thoughts!

James barely controlled himself when Hawker strolled up to the box to pay his compliments. Only the awareness that any altercation would only draw public attention to what he wished above all to keep private, enabled him to bite his tongue and return Hawker's greeting with a nod. Hawker spoke to Fanny, using a form which was perfectly respectful and polite, but with a warmth of tone which Fanny returned, and which made James start up from his seat.

'Mr Hawker,' he said, 'would you oblige me by stepping aside for a few words?'

Hawker looked at Fanny with a raised brow, and she nodded briefly, which caused a lazy smile to curve his lips. 'Most certainly, sir,' he said to James. 'I am completely at your service. I will attend you at the box door.'

Damn his impudence, James thought, excusing himself to the company. Hawker met him in the passageway that ran behind the boxes, and gave him a curiously sympathetic look.

'Mr Morland,' he said, as soon as James appeared. 'I know your dearest wish at the moment must be to mill me down, but might I suggest, *not here?*'

'You damned scoundrel!' James exclaimed, but in a low voice.

'If we step across the road, sir, to the Hare and Heather, we might make use of a private parlour, and have our talk undisturbed,' Hawker went on. James could see the sense of it, though he hated Hawker the more for being undismayed at the prospect of what he was about to hear. Such self-confidence was positively insulting.

In the Hare and Heather, James made use of the landlord's privilege to take over one of the private rooms, curtly rejecting all offers of food and drink. As soon as they were alone, Hawker said genially, 'Now, sir, you may rant at me as you wish.'

'You unmitigated scoundrel! How dare you speak to me like that? Have you no shame?'

'Very little, I'm afraid,' Hawker said, seating himself on the edge of the table and folding his arms. 'I've never been able to afford it. You are aware, I am sure, of my financial circumstances.'

'I'm aware of all your circumstances. I may tell you that I have had a full report on your doings in Brighton and in London, and I cannot conceive how you ever had the effrontery to come anywhere near my daughter. But if you think you have the slightest chance of marrying her, and laying your hands on her fortune, you are very far astray, I can assure you!'

'Has Fanny spoken to you on the subject?' Hawker enquired evenly.

James felt his blood rising. 'What my daughter says to me is no concern of yours. And you will not use her name in that fashion, or I shall break your neck here and now.'

'I beg your pardon, sir! I meant no disrespect to Miss Morland. Indeed, I hold her in the greatest possible esteem.'

'You hold her in nothing! You are to have nothing further to do with her, do you hear? You will not speak to her, or see her, or — or write to her —'

'I beg your pardon, Mr Morland, but I cannot comply with your request.'

'It wasn't a request, damn you!'

'Miss Morland must have told you by now that she wishes to marry me, a prospect so wholly delightful to me that I could not by any means be brought to disappoint her.' James was speechless with rage, and Hawker took the opportunity to continue, eyeing the older man with that same odd sympathy. 'Let us be frank, sir! I can fully understand your feelings as a father. I am not the husband you would have wished for your daughter. In your place, I should be as loath as you must be to countenance the match: but the fact remains that I am Fanny's — Miss Morland's choice. She loves me, and I love her —'

'You damned unspeakable rascal! You want her fortune, that's all you love!'

Hawker frowned. 'You must think so, of course. And I confess that the money would be more than convenient to me —

530

it is a necessity, if I am not to go under. But I do wish you to understand that I love Fanny sincerely.'

'If you use her name again, I shall knock you down!' James cried out. Hawker was six inches taller than he, and almost twenty years younger, but there was nothing ridiculous in the threat at that moment. 'You love no-one and nothing but yourself, and if you think I will stand by and see my daughter ruined by an adventurer like you —'

Hawker sat in silence and let him rage, and when James had run out of words and breath, he said quietly, 'There is nothing you can do, sir. Miss Morland and I will be wed, for it is her choice. She must have told you so. If you try to prevent her, she will force your hand.'

James trembled all over, staring at Hawker with a sense of sick frustration. 'What is it you want, Hawker? Yes, I know very well! Well, I will pay you to go away and leave Fanny alone. I will settle your debts here, and give you a sum of money to set yourself up somewhere — anywhere — abroad.' Hawker shook his head silently. 'If you think you can get more by holding out, you are very mistaken. Fanny does not come into her estate until she is twenty-one, and by then you will be languishing in gaol. You had better take what's offered and get out while you can. I would not stoop to offer you money, but that I wish you to leave quickly, for Fanny's sake. Your debts settled, and a thousand pounds. That, I think you will agree, is handsome.'

'More than handsome,' Hawker said, and for a moment James's heart lifted. 'But I fear you have misunderstood me. It is not only the money — if it were, I would accept your generous offer with alacrity. But the fact is — and I deplore it myself — that I love Fanny, and I am as determined to marry her as she is to marry me. It is not a situation that I like. It makes me vulnerable, and I dislike to feel vulnerable. Come, sir, you must accept my word for it. Would I have stayed on here in York, risking arrest, in daily dread of the bailiffs, on the slender chance of marrying an heiress who is two years from inheriting?'

'I can prevent you,' James said in a low voice. 'You think you can coerce me into letting you marry her; perhaps you even contemplate elopement — I understand you have tried that before.' Hawker looked away. 'Well, I can lock Fanny up,

531

and keep her under lock and key until you are taken up, or forced to flee the country. What do you say to that, Mr Hawker?'

'I acknowledge that you could do that. But you will not.'

'Why not, pray?'

'Because you would not break her heart,' he said quietly.

James stared at him in silence for some time. Then he said, 'For God's sake, man, if you love her, why do you want to do this to her? Why do you want to ruin her?'

'I won't ruin her. I will make her happy. Ah, yes, I know that hurts! You don't want it to be true that I can make her happier than you can. I understand you, you see, Mr Morland. And you must try to understand me. I will be Fanny Morland's husband, and I will have the spending of her fortune; but I will never be the cause of her regretting, for a single moment, that she married me.'

James stared at him, appalled to be feeling the beginnings of sympathy for this man, and clenching his fists he cried, 'God damn you to hell, Hawker! You will not marry her! I will see you dead first!' And he stormed out.

Fanny came to see him the next morning. The formal dinner the night before had prevented any conversation between them, but she sought him out early, before the rest of the household was astir, and found him in the steward's room, sitting in the window-seat, staring out at nothing. His face was haggard, his eyes, as he looked up at her, were lost.

She came across to him and kissed his cold forehead, and pushed his hair back. 'You have ruffled it with your fingers,' she said gently. 'It looks like a bird's nest. Have you a comb about you?'

He produced one silently, and endured her touch as she combed his hair to her satisfaction. His heart felt as though it had been torn, and was bleeding.

'There,' she said at last. 'You are decent again.' She sat on the edge of the desk, facing him, her knees almost touching his, looking at him with love and pity. 'Come, Papa, you must not torture yourself. I hate to see you so unhappy. I love you, you know.'

'If you loved me —' he began in a low voice.

'No, don't say it,' she said quickly. 'You must not make

conditions: I do not. I say I love you, Papa; and because you love me, you will let me do as I want. I know that it is right for me, and the more countenance you lend it, the better. Don't you want me to be happy.?'

'You will not be happy with him!' he cried out in anguish.

She took his hand and stroked it. 'Yes, yes I will!' she said eagerly. 'You don't understand him, Papa, but I know him, better than I know myself. We will be happy together, you'll see. Speak to Uncle Ned for us, dearest Papa! Speak to him today. Let us announce our betrothal as soon as possible. I want to be married. Please, Papa, don't turn your face away from us.' He was silent, and she looked at him carefully. 'There was a time,' she said quietly, 'when you defied everyone — even respectability itself — for the person you loved. Don't make me do the same.'

'Oh God, Fanny!' he cried out, and held out his arms to her. She came to him, kneeling before him, allowing herself to be folded in his arms, feeling his tears on the crown of her head. He hugged her to him, rocking her in silent anguish; and when at last he released her and put her away from him, she saw the change in him. He looked exhausted beyond emotion.

'Very well,' he said. 'If it's what you truly want, I'll speak to Ned.'

'Thank you, Papa,' she said.

He shook his head. 'Go — go now. I can't bear any more. Oh Fanny!'

She went out quickly.

'Have you lost your senses? Fanny marry that fortune-hunter?' Edward said in astonishment. 'He owes money everywhere!'

'Yes, I know,' James said wearily, facing the long uphill struggle to persuade his brother of something he wanted even less himself. 'But it's Fanny's own choice. She's in love with him, and she's adamant that she wants to marry him.'

'Don't talk like a fool! You can't let her choose someone like that! Good God, Jamie, what kind of father are you? She's the biggest heiress in Yorkshire! You can't let her marry a penniless rogue like Hawker, just because she fancies she's in love with him!'

James tried a different tack. 'You think her love cannot be real because he's penniless? Can one only be in love with someone wealthy, then?'

Edward coloured slightly. 'Of course I don't mean that. But Fanny's just a girl — she doesn't know what she wants. She'll be in love with someone else in a week or two. And in any case,' he went on before James could interrupt, 'it's the duty of a father — and a trustee — to protect a young woman against making foolish marriages — and particularly against falling into the clutches of a fortune-hunter!'

'I think Hawker really does care for her,' James began.

'Fiddlesticks! He's after her money, and you know it! As soon as a betrothal was announced, he could raise credit against her expectations — that's what your precious Hawker's after. I've wondered at you before now, this year, letting her stand up with him at dances, letting him run tame about the house. I think you must have pigeons in your cock-loft, Jamie. Well I tell you this — I take my duties a little more seriously than you seem to. I certainly won't consent to this nonsensical idea of yours.'

It was a long and tiring day. When the racing was over, and everyone went back to Morland Place to dine and change for the Grand Ball at the Assembly Rooms, there was a feeling of tension and unhappiness, quite at odds with the holiday spirit which prevailed amongst the servants. Even the children felt it, and were subdued, and retired to their nursery-dinner and bedtime routine without any protest, glad to get away from the grown-ups.

The argument between Edward and James continued at intervals before and after dinner; while Fanny seemed unconcerned by all the undercurrents of which she could not be unaware, Héloïse looked anxious and tried to keep Sophie from being affected by the atmosphere, and Mathilde remained sunk in deep and complex reflection, and struggled to come to some understanding of herself.

At the ball, Hawker walked up to Fanny at once, and claimed her hand for the two first, and Edward, having waited in vain for James to send him about his business, stumped off to the card-room to cool his temper. An hour later, he sought out James with a particularly grim expression on his face, and asked him to step aside and speak to him. They found a quiet corner in one of the corridors, and Edward said in a low, urgent voice, 'Jamie, I've just been speaking to Colonel Brunton, and he's told me some things about our friend Hawker that I think you ought to know.'

James listened in silence to a recitation of the gaming-hell and elopement story. He had not told Edward — indeed, anyone — the whole of Hawker's infamy, thinking that if he was forced at last to accept him as a son-in-law, the fewer people who knew about it the better. But it seemed that it was already too late.

'Yes, I know,' he said when Edward had finished.

'You know?' Ned said in disbelief. 'You know all that, and you still want her to marry him?'

'I don't want it,' James said desperately. 'It's the last thing I want! But you must understand, Ned, that if we don't agree, she'll force our hands.'

'Poppycock! I won't be told what to do by a chit of a girl, even if you are so feeble-minded as to —'

'Listen!' James said desperately. 'If we refuse to allow her to marry, she will either elope with him, or — or she'll do something worse. *Do you understand me?* You know how determined Fanny is. She'll find a way to do it, even if we keep her locked in her room. And we can't keep her locked up for ever. The scandal will be far less if we put a brave face on it, and give our consent, make this man as respectable as we can, and just live the talk down.'

'It's insane,' Edward said plainly. '*You're* insane.'

'Then tell me what to do. You tell me what we *can* do.'

There was a silence as Edward ran through his thoughts; and then slapped his fist into his palm. 'Damnit, I won't have my hand forced.'

'There's no way out,' James said miserably. 'I've thought and thought. If Fanny were any other girl, we could just hold firm and refuse, but she means every word she says — you know she does. And if she elopes, or — or becomes pregnant, the scandal will be far worse.'

Edward breathed hard. 'I always said you spoiled her! You let her have her own way too much when she was a child!'

James stared at the ground. 'Don't you think I know that?' he said quietly.

Edward put a hand on his shoulder. 'I'm sorry, Jamie. I know this hurts you.' He thought for a while. 'Let me try talking to Hawker. He can't play on my heart-strings the way he can on yours. Maybe I can buy him off.'

'You can try,' James said without hope.

'Damn it, if he marries her, all this about the Rickard girl will come out. Everyone will think we condone that sort of thing. Our name will be ruined. We'll never live it down.'

'How is it going?' Hawker asked Fanny, as they stood up for their second dance together.

She shrugged. 'As well as can be expected. I hate to make them unhappy, you know. Oh Fitz, why can't things be easy?'

'A question I've asked myself all my life. But don't worry, darling, it will be all right once we're married. They'll see how happy you are, and they'll forgive me.'

'I don't think they'll ever forgive you,' Fanny said sadly.

'Well, then, we can ignore them. In two years you will be of age, and then you can do what you like. We can go abroad if you like —'

Her eyes widened. 'We can't do that,' she said. 'I have to be here, to take care of my estate.'

He raised an eyebrow. 'What do you think stewards and bailiffs are for, my sweet, simple darling? You don't have to do the work yourself.'

'You don't understand. Morland Place has never been run like that. The master or mistress *must* be there. It's like — like a kingdom; my kingdom.'

'Our kingdom, darling.'

'No, Fitz,' she said quietly. 'You may have the income to spend as you like, you may have all my money, and welcome to it, but Morland Place is mine, and mine alone.'

He looked down with admiration at her determined face, and raised her hand lightly to his lips. 'My love, I won't come between you and your subjects. Don't I tell you, I want you to be happy?'

Edward met Hawker at his club the next day. Edward had never liked the Maccabbees, and had always used Bookers, in Coney Street, which was less fashionable, but he found more solidly comfortable.

Ned determined from the beginning to be calm and business-like, feeling that this would have more effect on Hawker than an emotional outburst.

'You understand, Mr Hawker, that I am Miss Morland's trustee — her sole trustee? Any decisions about her estate, until she comes of age, are mine and mine alone.'

'I didn't know that, sir,' said Hawker, quite respectfully. 'I had assumed her father shared that agreeable duty.'

'You assumed wrongly. Now, as you can imagine, I am not at all in favour of the proposed match between you and Miss Morland.'

'I should be astonished, sir, if you were,' Hawker said pleasantly.

Edward frowned. 'By God, sir, you're a cool one! No wonder — but I digress. It may interest you to know that I have been this morning to see the family man of business, Mr Pobgee, of whom you may have heard.' Hawker nodded. 'And I have confirmed what I already knew, that there is no possible way for you to get your hands on Miss Morland's fortune, even if you marry her, until she comes of age. Two more years, Mr Hawker — have you thought of that?'

'I have, sir,' Hawker said calmly.

'Until then, I remain in complete control of all capital and income.'

'I understand that, sir.'

'Well, then,' Edward said, unnerved, 'you can't think I would give you anything?'

'I think, sir, that if — when I marry Miss Morland, you will be obliged to settle my immediate debts,' Hawker said, almost apologetically, 'or the name of Morland would become implicated in my unfortunate circumstances.'

'Very well, damn you, I concede that. But you'd be no better off, for I would not give you a penny more — and, what's more, I should make sure that the tradesmen understood the situation, and did not extend you any more credit.'

'That would be to admit to the world that you did not trust me. Surely you would not wish Miss Morland to become the subject of gossip and speculation?'

'You won't blackmail me that way, damn you,' Edward said, keeping his temper with an effort. 'I had sooner live with gossip, than part with a penny of Fanny's fortune for you to

537

fritter away.'

Hawker did not seem put out. He thought for a moment, and then said calmly, 'I think you would sooner not live with me at all. But if necessary, I can live comfortably enough at Morland Place for two years. It will soon pass. I shall have my shelter and food, horses to ride, Fanny's company. Perhaps you and I, sir, can play cards together of an evening. Are you fond of picquet?'

Edward glared at him. 'Damn your impudence, Hawker!'

'Damn anything you like, Mr Morland — for there I'll be.'

Now it was Edward's turn to think. 'Very well,' he said at last, 'now listen to me. I will consent to the marriage, pay your immediate debts, and pay you a pension for the two years of Fanny's minority if, and only if, you agree to live abroad for that period. I don't want to share my home with you. I don't want you under that roof at all, sullying my mother's memory, and the good name of my family. There have been Morlands at Morland Place for three hundred and fifty years, sir, and I have a responsibility to my ancestors, and to those who are to come after me.'

Hawker smiled softly. 'Of course, those who are to come will be Hawkers, won't they, not Morlands.'

Edward's face suffused. 'If you don't hold your tongue, sir, I shall knock you down!' he hissed.

'I beg your pardon, sir. It was very wrong of me,' Hawker said quickly.

'Well, what do you say? Do you agree to my proposition? For I may as well tell you, if you don't, you may go to hell as far as I am concerned.'

Hawker smiled. 'Well, sir, in view of the consideration that I should like to share your roof quite as little as you would like to share mine, and that I am rather fond of the Continent, and that it would suit me to travel abroad for a while, I accept your proposal — provided the pension, as you call it, is sufficient to maintain me in a suitable style.'

Edward grunted, and then settled down to the long negotiation over figures.

CHAPTER TWENTY-SEVEN

15 September was Fanny's wedding-day. She was to be married in the chapel at Morland Place, for though Edward didn't like it, the alternative, of St Edward's or the Minster, was far too public. Besides, as future mistress of Morland Place, she ought to be wed in the chapel: it was traditional. There would be no guests beyond the immediate family, and John and Louisa Anstey. There was already talk enough about the affair.

Speculation had been running high ever since the betrothal had been announced, and the family had been virtually under siege, unable to go beyond the estate boundaries without having to face impertinent curiosity. *Why* the wealthy heiress Fanny Morland should have been permitted to wed a penniless adventurer was a question to exercise every mind, high and low. The obvious conclusions were drawn, and sometimes even discarded. Those who had disliked Fanny now discovered they had always known she would come to a bad end. Those who had liked or admired her could only be puzzled, and assume there was more to Fitzherbert Hawker than met the public eye.

Edward had written in trepidation to apprise Mr Hobsbawn of the business, and prayed the old man had not heard the worst of the stories. A letter came in reply, full of outrage, demanding explanations, forbidding the nuptuals on pain of nameless consequences.

'I know the fellow, and he's paltry — a fortune-hunter, a nobody! I saw through him the moment I first clapped eyes on him, though it's true he did Fanny a great service at one time, and I was obliged to allow the acquaintance. But how comes it that you have so far forgotten your duty as to consent to this marriage? I demand that you put an end to the betrothal at once.'

Further correspondence resulted in Hobsbawn's threatening

539

to cut Fanny out of his will if the marriage went ahead; and then a long silence was succeeded by a letter from Mrs Murray, saying that her master had been taken ill of a seizure, but was a great deal better now. Fanny herself wrote, begging her grandpapa to forgive her if she had offended him, but that she had found a man entirely to her taste, and was determined to marry him. She asked permission to bring her husband to visit her dear grandpapa when they returned from their honeymoon. To that letter there was no reply, nor to her subsequent one. Fanny shrugged. For the moment, she must leave him to fret; but she felt sure that a visit later would enable her to bring him back round her thumb. Cousin Jasper was too far out of favour to get back into it so easily.

After the wedding-breakfast, Fanny and her husband were to leave straight away for London, Dover, Calais, Brussels, and Vienna, where they were to stay with Aunt Lucy for a few months and enjoy all the social events which surrounded the Peace Congress. Fanny, who had never been abroad, was thrilled at the idea, as well as quite seeing the point of removing herself and her husband from the environs of Morland Place until the scandal had died down.

The agreement between Hawker and Edward that he should live abroad for the next two years had been kept secret from Fanny, and it was for Hawker to break it to her when their honeymoon was over. How, when and where he did it, Edward was content to leave to Hawker. If Fanny refused to come home without her husband, as Ned very well thought she might, he did not mind in the least: the idea of Morland Place without Fanny suited him very well, though he kept these thoughts from James, who was miserable enough without them.

Héloïse found her sympathies very much divided in the weeks preceding the wedding. James must be her principal concern, and she did her best, day after day, to reconcile him to the business, reminding him that he would have resented any man who took his place in Fanny's heart, and representing Hawker in as favourable a light as possible. From her observations, she believed that Fanny really did love him, and she saw that there was a genuine intimacy between them. She did not entirely understand it, and it seemed sometimes almost a little sinister to her, but it was undeniably real, and she offered that, too, as comfort to James.

The wedding itself looked like being a grave, almost a sad affair, and in that her sympathies went out to Fanny. A woman's wedding-day was a very special thing, and if Fanny was marrying the man she loved, it ought to be an occasion she could remember without pain. Héloïse did everything she could to make it joyful and pleasant for Fanny; and Fanny therefore found her only ally in the house was the woman she had always held in hatred and suspicion, and was touched and grateful. A better understanding between them had been obtaining ever since Fanny came out; now at the last moment it warmed into the beginnings of affection.

Héloïse sought Fanny out one day, and asked her to come up to her bedchamber. There, on the bed, Fanny saw that Madame had laid out her own wedding-gown of fabulously expensive Chantilly lace.

'Of course, the style is old-fashioned, but the material is lovely, and as good as new. If you would like it, Fanny dear, it is yours, for your own wedding-gown. It can be made up however you like.'

Fanny touched the exquisite lace with appreciative fingers, and then looked up hesitantly, to see the sympathy in Madame's dark eyes.

'I really do love him, Madame,' she blurted out.

'Yes, Fanny, I know you do,' Héloïse said gently. 'And I believe he loves you, too.'

'Do you?' Fanny said gratefully.

'Yes. He is a strange man, but I can understand why you find him attractive. We cannot always choose whom we love. Seeing you together, I am reminded sometimes —' she hesitated.

'Yes, Madame?' Fanny prompted.

'Don't be offended, Fanny dear, but I am reminded of your father and me, as we were when we were your age. Each of us always knew what the other was thinking. All we wanted was to be together; but the fates were not with us,' she sighed.

'But that's how I feel — how we feel,' Fanny said eagerly. 'People don't understand. But he — he *knows* me, Madame. It's as if he can see into my head.'

'Yes, I know,' Héloïse nodded. 'I've seen it when you are together.'

Fanny looked at her stepmother warmly, wishing there were some way to reach out to her. 'I should like to have the lace, very much, Madame,' she said.

Héloïse smiled. 'Good. You will look lovely in it, *ma chère*.' She went towards the door, and then turned back. 'I hope you enjoy your wedding-day, Fanny. It should be a happy occasion. I shall talk to Monsieur Barnard about the wedding-breakfast. He will make his best effort for you.'

'Thank you, Madame,' Fanny said, a little wonderingly. How was it that she had never known how kind her stepmother was?

Barnard had listened to all the talk from the other servants, saying nothing, and reserving judgement, as was the prerogative of one who purported not to speak English. On the one hand, he had worked for the old mistress, and understood all the importance of responsibility and piety, and what qualities it was that made a Mistress of Morland Place. When Jemima died, he had gone to Héloïse, for he would not work for Fanny's mother. Since his return to Morland Place with Héloïse, he had regarded her as Mistress, and had inwardly shaken his head at Fanny's shortcomings. Of course, she had improved of late, but he still could not regard her as the true heiress. When she came of age, he would go with Héloïse, back to Plaisir.

But on the other hand, a wedding was a wedding, and he had no time for kitchen politics or gossip. So when Héloïse honoured him by coming to speak to him in person, he understood very well what she was saying, and had no hesitation in reassuring her.

'Everything shall be of the very best,' he said. 'No-one shall find fault, *chère madame*. The young miss shall not be disappointed.'

'I knew I could trust you,' Héloïse said. 'In the matter of the cake —'

'The cake — it shall be magnificent! A cathedral of a cake! Six strong men will be needed to lift it!' he promised.

Héloïse smiled. 'I am satisfied.'

'And the champagne — it will be of the very best, madame? Such a cake — one could not create a thing of such beauty, to be consumed with inferior wine,' Barnard said anxiously.

'Of the very best,' she said, and they exchanged a look of complete understanding.

The day dawned, and Héloïse woke and took her grieving husband into her arms and comforted him.

'You must not spoil the day for Fanny, my James,' she said gently. 'You must try to smile.'

'I can't feel it's right for her,' he said. 'I've tried, but I can't.'

'It's what she wants. She's happy, and she loves him. We must make it right, by supporting her, by making sure he is accepted. She needs us — she needs *you* — now as never before.'

'I should have killed him,' he whimpered into her shoulder. 'Called him out and shot him.'

'No, *mon âme*, don't say that.' She held him closer. 'Cry now, if you must, but afterwards, smile, my James. Smile at Fanny's wedding.'

'I'm losing her,' he said, and he did cry a little. But later, when he went to the door of the Blue Room, where Fanny had slept for the last eight years, to collect her; and she came out to him, looking tall and lovely in the Chantilly lace in which Héloïse had been married; and he saw the radiant joy in her eyes, the triumphant love which was not for him, and never would be again, he had no more desire to weep. His heart lay down and slept, and he took her on his arm, and led her down the chapel stairs to give her away with a calm smile.

Hawker was waiting, handsome and serious, and if he had not known the man, James might have thought him worthy of his girl, for he was a fine figure of a man, and his face was firm and intelligent. James felt as though he were in a dream, all through the service, and afterwards at the magnificent wedding-breakfast. He might have been eating ashes and drinking plain water, for all he noticed what he consumed. People were around him, but seemed separated from him by a transparent barrier, so that he could hear them only dimly. His eyes followed Fanny as she moved around, talking, laughing, going back always and again to the tall man who seemed to draw her — never straying far from his side, as a foal will not stray from its dam; but even Fanny seemed to exist in another world.

The post chaise arrived in the courtyard with the four horses — Fanny should not travel with a pair, not Fanny Morland of Morland Place! — and the bags were strapped on behind, and then they were saying goodbye. Fanny, now in a lovely blue-grey pelisse and a high-crowned bonnet trimmed with marabou, flung her arms round her father's neck, pressing a cheek to his which was warm and damp. He kissed her, and tasted salt.

'I love you, Papa,' she whispered, and was gone. The chaise circled the yard and drew out through the barbican, and they all waved, waved, and Fanny's hand waved back from one side of the carriage, and a man's hand from the other. The carriage passed from sight, and they all went back into the house and closed the door.

'It will be quiet without her,' Miss Rosedale said, pressing her large, white handkerchief to her eyes. 'Sophie, come and play something for us on the pianoforte. A little music to soothe us.'

'I don't know how it can be, but I feel hungry again,' John Anstey said.

'Come and have something more from the buffet, then. I could fancy a little of that salmon myself,' said Edward.

They all drifted away, and the hall emptied, leaving James standing where he was, just inside the door; and Héloïse a step away, watching him anxiously.

He looked up and met her eyes. 'I feel as if I've just buried her,' he said, and his own voice sounded very distant, all part of that same dream.

'Come,' she said, taking his arm and coaxing him along like an invalid. 'You're shivering. Come in to the fire.'

With all the turmoil over Fanny, and the subsequent arrangements for her wedding, Edward had seen little of Mathilde, and had had neither the time nor the inclination to think about their situation, far less to talk to her about it. But he knew things could not be allowed to go on as they were. Now that Fanny had married Hawker, there was no chance at all that Edward's fortunes would improve. As soon as Fanny came of age, she and her husband would turn them all out of doors, of that there was no doubt. Edward would have his three hundred a year, and the little he had managed to save.

On that he could set himself up comfortably in bachelor lodgings in the city, with a manservant, and a horse at livery, which was probably what his mother had envisaged for him.

But he could not establish himself in a house with a young wife; and there was one part of his mind which, albeit, reluctantly, began to wonder whether he even wanted to. He was fifty-two now, an old dog to be learning new tricks. Thrown out of his lifelong home in two years' time, he might settle pretty well in lodgings, with a quiet round of club, church, and friends' dining tables, hunt a little in the winter, take a gun out now and then, try not to think of Morland Place and that damned interloper.

But to struggle along in near-poverty with Mathilde would prevent him from sinking into a comfortable apathy. Every day would be a renewed battle for survival; he would be kept sharp, knowing, seeing, regretting. Suppose they should have a family? The thought of babies in poverty dismayed him. The thought of babies at all was uncomfortable. He had lived all his life without women, though there had been many he admired. He was too old — wasn't he? — to begin a new way of life now.

In fairness to Mathilde, he thought, he ought to tell her of his doubts; but before he had summoned up the courage to do so, something else had happened. Fanny's going away with her husband coincided with the end of John Skelwith's period of deep mourning. He might now with propriety enjoy a little more social intercourse, and to mark the occasion he paid a morning visit to his former mother-in-law, Augusta Keating. While he was sitting with her, Héloïse, Sophie and Mathilde were announced.

Though there was a little awkwardness at first, it soon passed, and while Héloïse kept Mrs Keating occupied, Skelwith chatted pleasantly to Sophie and Mathilde. The talk turned to the topic of books, on which all three had plenty to say, and it emerged that the ladies' next port of call was to be the circulating library on the corner of St Helen's Square. After half an hour they all rose to leave together, but when they reached the street, Héloïse announced that she wished to take Sophie to Peckett's, to be measured for a new pair of shoes.

'Then,' said Skelwith promptly, 'might I have the pleasure

of escorting you to the library, Miss Nordubois? If your lady-ship should find it acceptable?' he added politely to Héloïse. Héloïse, after briefly consulting Mathilde's face, and reading in its heightened colour and lowered eyes no great aversion to the scheme, consented, and proposed that they should all meet again at Enderby's, the draper's in Stonegate, in an hour's time.

John Skelwith offered Mathilde his arm, and they walked off down Coney Street, while Héloïse and Sophie turned in the other direction. They were silent at first, as Mathilde overcame her confusion at finding herself alone with her former admirer again, and Skelwith reflected on all the various complications of his life. Few of them had been his own fault, and he was determined that, if Mathilde would have him, there should at least be no misunderstanding to rob him of his happiness again.

They talked pleasantly of neutral topics all the way to the library, where he waited while she conducted her business, and then offered her his arm again, and turned in the direction of Stonegate. They had plenty of time before they were to meet the others, and it was a fine, warm September day. They strolled at an easy pace, and talked as they walked, finding again the similarities of mind which had given rise in former days to such a pleasant intimacy between them. John felt suddenly cheerful. The world was an agreeable place to live in after all; and Mathilde was, as she had always been, the dearest girl!

After a while, he said, 'I am very pleased to have this opportunity of talking to you, Miss Nordubois. There has been no occasion since the races, what with Miss Morland's wedding, and my continued state of deep mourning. But now I am into half-mourning, I hope you won't think it improper of me to raise a subject dear to my heart?'

Embarrassment made Mathilde's reply inaudible, but did not seem to convey unwillingness to be addressed.

'You know, I hope, how very much I have always admired you?' he began. 'When I spoke to you at the races, it seemed to me that you were not entirely indifferent to me. If I was mistaken, please forgive me; but if you would welcome, even if you would not wholly dislike, a return of my addresses, I should be happy and honoured to count myself again amongst your admirers.' She didn't answer, and he asked with a shade of anxiety, 'Are you — may I ask? — promised to another?'

Mathilde drew a long sigh. 'No, Mr Skelwith. I am not betrothed.'

He smiled. 'Then — dear Miss Nordubois, may I hope?'

She raised her eyes. 'Mr Skelwith, I know that your mother was very much against our friendship before. I don't know why, but I can guess.'

Skelwith coloured at the memory. How could it be? Had Mathilde heard a rumour from somewhere? For himself, he did not believe a word of it. His mother, he was sure, had been hysterical and had not known what she was saying. He had met James Morland many times since, and he had not betrayed any kind of consciousness towards him. 'I am sure my mother could have no reason to object to you,' he said awkwardly.

'But I am without birth or fortune, Mr Skelwith,' Mathilde said. His shoulders sank in relief.

'That, ma'am, can be no impediment. I have sufficient fortune to make it a matter of no importance whatever. I must tell you that my mother is old and frail, and she does not always mind what she says. But you must not let her upset you. I assure you she means nothing by it.'

Mathilde was silent, though not for the reasons he thought. After a while he said, 'My mother will get used to the idea eventually. I do not any longer allow her to interfere with my happiness. It may sound unfilial to you, but it is the only way. I'm sorry to say she is not always — entirely rational.'

Mathilde looked up and pressed his arm, moved by this difficult confession. 'You need not explain anything to me,' she said urgently.

He smiled. 'Dear Mathilde,' he said, cutting through the layers of time and social distance between them, 'we were such good friends. We enjoyed each other's company. All I ask is that you allow me to see you, to try to please you, try to win you. I don't expect you to fall into my arms the first minute I speak to you! But let me place myself at your service, and see if there is any possibility of making you love me.'

She felt grateful to him for his generosity, for loving her still, for not being too proud to admit it. She liked him — she had always liked him — and it seemed so long since she had enjoyed the simple pleasures of being wooed without complication. 'I should like you to try,' she said shyly.

His smile broadened. 'Excellent! You have made me very happy. Then, as a beginning, may I call for you tomorrow and take you out for a drive?'

'Yes,' she said. 'Thank you.'

They stood outside Enderby's, chatting, and the time seemed to fly past, so that they were both surprised when Héloïse and Sophie appeared, and apologised for being late. Skelwith took his leave, to walk the few steps to his house, further up Stonegate.

'Your servant, ma'am! Miss Morland! Until tomorrow then, Miss Nordubois.'

Héloïse led the way into the shop, and was soon deeply involved in the delicate business of matching ribbon. She was not too preoccupied, however, to say mildly to Mathilde, 'Are we to have the pleasure of seeing Mr Skelwith tomorrow, *ma chère*?'

Mathilde coloured a little. 'He is calling to take me driving, Madame. I hope you have no objection?'

'Not the least in the world,' Héloïse said, with some sinking of the heart. She had hoped that particular complication was a thing of the past. 'He is a very agreeable young man. Such pleasant manners. I can't decide between this colour, and this. What do you think, Mathilde? Which is the better match? Sophie, *mon ange*, hold them up by the window, in the light.'

But Mathilde was deep in contemplation of the interview she was honour-bound to have with Edward before tomorrow dawned, and was no help at all over the ribbon colours.

'Cousin Edward, may I speak to you?' Mathilde said, with considerable trepidation. She had hung about all day, trying to find an opportunity, but she never came across him alone. Now dinner was over, and tea had come and gone, and the evening was almost wasted. She had to take advantage of the chance of Héloïse's being out of the room for a moment, and James's being preoccupied at a little distance with the newspaper.

Edward looked up, and to Mathilde's surprise, seemed as confused as she felt. 'Yes, of course. In fact, I was wanting to speak to you.' They both looked doubtfully at James. Edward buckled his brow, and nodded towards the door. 'The steward's room,' he murmured.

No fire had been lit in the steward's room that evening, and the air struck a little chill. 'Are you cold?' Edward asked, looking at the grate in concern.

'No, no, I have a thick shawl,' Mathilde said quickly. She was in terror that, now they were alone, he would want to put his arms round her and kiss her, as they had used to do whenever life granted them a moment's privacy together. She no longer wanted his caresses. That fact alone must tell her that her feelings for him had changed; and the knowledge of her own inconstancy made her ashamed.

But Edward did not make any move towards her. He stood by the desk, his eyes down, tracing a pattern with one finger-tip as though he could not make up his mind to speak.

'Cousin Edward,' Mathilde began, drawing a deep breath to face the disagreeable task.

He looked up and interrupted her. 'My dear Mathilde, pray let me speak first. There is something that I must say, and I'm afraid I shall lose my courage if I delay. I should have spoken to you long before this, but somehow — well, at all events, I must speak now. While you were visiting your friend at Coxwold, I tried to speak to Fanny about our future, after she inherits the estate.' Mathilde drew a sharp breath. He went on, 'I'm sorry to say that she spoke in such hostile terms to me, that I've no doubt whatever she means to throw us both out as soon as she is of age. And you've seen what mark of man she has married. If you can doubt that that precious pair will want Morland Place to themselves —'

'No,' Mathilde said quietly. 'I have no doubt.' If he asks me now to marry him and live in poverty with him, how can I refuse? she thought miserably. It would be too cruel.

'You know my circumstances,' he went on. 'You know how small a provision I will have at that time — too little to support a wife in even the modicum of comfort. My dearest Mathilde,' he said with sudden vehemence, clenching his hands at his sides, 'I *cannot* ask you to marry me when I haven't the means to support you. Though I know it is a dreadful thing to do, a dishonourable thing, I must ask you to release me from our unofficial engagement.'

She stared at him in surprise, unable at once to speak, and he hurried on. 'You are angry with me, I can see. And I don't blame you. I have acted reprehensibly; but I trust you will believe that I never meant to hurt you. I know that Héloïse will always provide you with a home, more comfortable than I could make for you; and I am of the strongest hopes that, once you are free of me, you will still find a husband, a good, honest young man who can provide for you properly. Dear Mathilde, I do love you, and sincerely wish you well. Will you forgive me? Will you release me?'

Mathilde had to find words. She swallowed once or twice, and then said, 'Of course I forgive you. But there's nothing to forgive: it is I who am to blame, for insisting on our continuing with the engagement against your will. You said long ago that we should part, and I have been selfish in maintaining it. I hold you in the greatest esteem, and I hope we may continue good friends?'

She held out her hand, and he grasped it gratefully.

'We shall always be that. You have been everything that is generous,' he said. There was a pause. 'And now, what was it you wanted to speak to me about?'

'What? Oh, that — no, it's nothing. Nothing at all. If you'll excuse me, I think I would like to be alone for a little,' she said, and hurried out to find the solitude to settle her fluttering nerves.

Fanny adored Vienna; she loved being abroad, she loved the society — a mixture of dashing officers, diplomats, and the nobility of five nations — and she loved the heady, tingling feeling of power that filled the air: the intrigue, the negotiations, the unspoken alliances made and broken all in an evening upon the dance floor or across the green baize.

She loved gaming, and quickly became addicted to the new game of *roulette*, as well as to hazard, and the various card games, and billiards. She loved dancing, especially the waltz, which was not regarded here as anything untoward, and she never lacked for partners: pretty Mrs Hawker was the favourite of all the officers. She was filled with unappeasable energy, danced until four in the morning, and rose again at ten to be out riding in the park, driving in the Prater, to be rowed down the river Wien in a scrolled and gilded pleasure-boat, to picnic in the Wienerwald, or on the soft green curves of the hills that embraced the lovely grey and gold-domed city.

And in the evening there was the Opera, and the ballet, and the theatre; and dancing, dancing, dancing in a hundred handsome, baroque-fronted palaces whose great ballrooms glittered and shimmered with gilding and mirrors and crystal lustres and a thousand winking points of candlelight. Thanks to her Aunt Lucy, she moved in the inner circle which revolved about the Lord Castlereagh himself and the principal politicians of the five nations. Lady Theakston knew everyone, and carelessly presented generals and ambassadors and princes to her wondering niece. Mrs Hawker became known as a dashing rider, a cool gambler, a witty talker, and a tireless waltzer; and she knew how to flirt, too, daringly, but never beyond the line of what was agreeable.

Her husband watched her growing fame with amusement. 'You will be notorious, Fanny,' he said one morning as she sat up in bed devouring a large breakfast, despite her late night. 'Well for you that you have me here in the background to guarantee your respectability.'

She looked up from within the frame of her tumbled hair. Her yellow silk robe, embroidered with crimson birds of paradise, was slipping from her bare shoulders, and her fingers were sticky with cherry jam, and she disturbed his senses. 'I adore being a married woman!' she cried. 'I love being able to go where I please, and speak to anyone I like, and dance with anyone and drive with anyone, without all the old tabbies talking and shaking their heads! It is the best fun in the world!'

Hawker laughed. 'Is that all you like about being married?'

'Oh no,' she said promptly. 'I adore you, too.'

'Generous!' he said, sliding a hand inside her robe, and making her wriggle. Her eyelids drooped at once, but she said, 'Oh, let me finish my breakfast! Marcus is coming at ten with Colonel Brooke to take me to see the manoeuvres, and it takes Beaver for ever to curl my hair.'

Hawker removed his hand. 'Never turn away love, Fanny,' he said solemnly. 'There is no knowing if it will be offered again.'

Her eyes were instantly wide. 'Oh no! Don't say so! I didn't mean it, Fitz!' She flung herself against him across the tray,

551

upsetting her cup, and he felt her sticky fingers on the back of his neck and her lips on his. 'I love you so!' she cried, kissing him fervently. He returned her kisses with interest, and then detached her hands and licked the sweetness from them.

'It's all right, Fanny, I was only funning,' he said, giving her back her hands.

She pouted. 'Unscrupulous!' she remarked, setting her cup upright and mopping the mess carelessly with a damask napkin. 'One day, Fitzherbert Hawker, you'll go too far.'

'As you do every day, *cara mia.* Don't think I didn't see you flirting with Lord Hill last night!'

'Oh, but he's such a sweet old man,' she said quickly. 'He asked about you, too. I told him all about you.'

'Good God, Fanny, what have you said now?'

'The truth,' she said, watching him from under lowered lids. 'That you are a fine soldier and a brilliant diplomat. He was very interested.'

'You're learning to intrigue,' he said, shaking his head. 'So much for your innocence.' She laughed and spread cherry jam on another of the sweet rolls the hotel was famous for. 'You like it here, don't you, Fanny?'

'I love it! I wish we might stay for ever!'

He laughed. 'It may even be possible. You know what they are saying: "The Congress dances, but makes no progress"! It may be that Castlereagh and Metternich and the rest will go on talking for ever.'

'But aren't you happy?' she asked, detecting a touch of melancholy in his tone.

'Of course I am, love. It's just that I feel — restless, I suppose. It's so long since I've had nothing to worry about, that I feel a little lost. A life of unending pleasure was always my goal, but I'm not used to having it without struggle.'

Fanny shrugged. 'Then intrigue! Everybody else does.'

'I might have an affair, of course,' he pretended to muse. 'There are a great many handsome women in Vienna, and keeping it a secret from you would exercise my intellect.'

She eyed him warily. 'Whom had you in mind?'

'Oh, I don't know. There's Lady Castlereagh — she must want a lover as much as anyone, poor thing. And your aunt, Lady Theakston, is a very handsome woman.'

She laughed in relief. 'Oh, now I know you're only funning!

You would not care for Aunt Lucy — she is not at all your type, as prickly as a hedgehog, besides being as flat as a boy.' She glanced down complacently at the curves her yellow silk covered; they were even fuller now than before she was married. 'But talking of Aunt Lucy, she's asked us to her box at the Opera tonight. Should I accept, Fitz? I know we are dining with the Angleseys, but will they expect us to go to the Opera with them as well?'

'No, my darling, we can accept your aunt's invitation if you like. I dare say she will be inviting some high-ranking diplomat as well, to keep me amused while you're flirting with all the passing red-coats.'

Fanny finished her breakfast, and Hawker put the tray aside for her. 'I suppose I had better get up,' she said, stretching comfortably, like a cat. 'Aunt Lucy was talking the other day about going back to England. She has to bring out my cousin next Season, and says she might go home after Christmas. Will we have to go too?'

She had put the question idly, but Hawker eyed her carefully, and decided the moment had come.

'You may go home, Fanny, any time you like. I cannot.'

She looked surprised. 'What do you mean? Of course you can.'

'No, Fanny. There was an agreement — the condition on which I was allowed to marry you. I am not to set foot in England until you come of age.'

She paled. 'What are you talking about? This is nonsense, Fitz! Who made you promise such a thing?'

'Your honoured trustee, of course. He had no desire to be living under the same roof with me, and I can't say I entirely blame him.'

Her lips thinned with temper. 'He had no right! And why did you promise? There was no need — I told you they could not stop us marrying! Why didn't you trust me? But there is nothing he can do to enforce it, after all,' she reflected. 'You must ignore the promise. It was extracted unfairly, and does not count.'

'Fanny, darling, your uncle holds the purse-strings, don't you understand that? What do you think we are living on while we are here? How do you think we can afford to stay in this hotel? How do you think I pay for all your pretty clothes,' he said, caressing a silken curve, 'and the cases of wine and brandy, and the pleasant evenings of macao and hazard? Your uncle pays me a very handsome allowance, but on the condition that I live abroad for the next two years. If I return to England, he will stop the payments.'

'He can't! I won't let him!' she cried in fury.

'He can,' Hawker assured her calmly. 'He has complete discretion. You know that.'

'It's abominable!' she raged. 'He has no right to treat you so. You are my husband! Well, we'll defy him! You shall not be forced into exile because of that — that hateful old man!'

'I can't live on nothing, love. I am an expensive man,' he said gently.

'He can't stop my allowance. I shall give it to you. You shall have every penny.'

He kissed her hand. 'I honour your intentions,' he said, 'but it won't do. Your allowance is only just enough for you. You're a luxurious little thing, Fanny, and take a deal of keeping! But come, love, don't look so down! It's only two years — less than two years, now. The time will pass very quickly, and then we shall be able to do just as we please.'

'I don't want to be without you,' she said, close to tears. 'I can't bear it! Two years is a lifetime!'

He shrugged. 'Well, then, little one, stay here with me.'

She looked at him anxiously, her eyes dangerously bright, her lips trembling. 'How can I?' she said. 'I must go home. Morland Place is mine. I have to be there. There's no knowing what he will do if I'm away for long. He'll ruin it — he has no idea of business. And then there's Grandpapa's mills. He said he would cut me out of his will if I married you, and I must go and see him soon, to bring him round my thumb again. I know I can do it if I see him myself, but I dare not leave it too long. He's been ill, you know, and if he should die before I get to him —'

'Yes, I understand,' Hawker said. 'Business must come first. I quite see the necessity. You had better go home with your aunt after Christmas.'

'You will come too,' she said desperately.

'No, Fanny.'

'I'll make him increase my allowance, to make it enough!'

'Darling, listen to me,' he said, taking her hands. They

were cold, and he chafed them as he spoke. 'It isn't only the money, though that's a large part of it. But I don't want to live at Morland Place under your uncle's thumb, any more than he wants me to. It would be intolerable. Think of it, love! Your uncle and your father and stepmother, all hating me and disapproving of me; inspecting my actions, watching every penny I spend, looking at the clock when I come in or go out. And I'd have nothing to do all day. It would drive me mad. I couldn't do it, Fanny.'

She said nothing, staring at him miserably.

'You see that it's impossible, don't you?'

'You want to stay here,' she accused.

'Yes, I do,' he said frankly. 'There is so much happening — can't you feel it? The future of Europe is in the balance! And I am in the process — I didn't tell you this before — of finding myself something to do.'

'A diplomatic mission?'

'Of a kind.'

'Like the last time? The one that made you leave London after we went to Vauxhall Gardens?' she said bitterly.

'Oh Fanny, Fanny, you should have forgotten that! No, this time it's real. I was only half joking about Lady Castlereagh. I have been growing very friendly with her lately, and she is willing to drop a word in her husband's ear on my behalf. I have talents, Fanny, that haven't been used. I want to stretch myself, to take a hand in things! Can't you understand that?'

'I understand that you don't want to be with me,' she said, looking down at her fingers. Her eyelashes were wet.

'I do want to! Little simpleton, haven't I asked you to stay with me?' She was silent. 'Don't you want to be proud of your husband, Fan?' he said reproachfully. 'As I am of you? I don't try to keep you from your business. I'm proud of you, when you talk of your estate, and wanting to win back your place in your grandfather's will. If you say you must go home, I won't try to stop you. But you mustn't try to stop me either.'

'But Fitz,' she said at last, 'how can I bear to be without you?'

He took her in his arms. 'The time will soon pass, love. And then we'll be together for ever, until you're sick of me, and start to take lovers, and throw me out of the house to beg for my bread.' She made a little struggling movement. 'I was only joking, Fanny!' he protested.

But she thrust herself free from him, and he saw her face was cheese-white. 'I think I'm going to be sick,' she muttered. 'Oh Fitz —!'

He moved rapidly, grabbing the basin from the washstand, and then holding her hair back for her while she retched. When it was over, he brought the towel, the end damped from the ewer, and tenderly wiped her face.

'I'm sorry,' she murmured, raising swimming eyes to his. 'I don't know what's come over me.'

'Don't you?' he said with a suppressed smile. 'Fanny, love, when was your last flux?'

She looked uncomprehending, and then her eyes widened. 'You mean —?'

'It seems to me, love, that you haven't had one since we married,' he said. 'Had you really not noticed?'

'I didn't think about it,' she said, eyes downcast.

'Madam Innocent!' he said, amused. 'And don't you see how your pretty breasts are rounder than they were?' He bent his head to kiss her throat, and caress their fullness. 'My little, pretty wife, it seems to me you are quite obviously —'

'Pregnant!' she finished, her lips beginning to curve into a smile. 'Really? Do you really think so?'

'I know so.'

She laughed and flung her arms round his neck. 'Oh Fitz! But — are you happy about it?' she added anxiously.

'More happy than I can tell you,' he said, kissing her. 'What man could be other than happy in such a circumstance? You have a young Hawker in your belly, my love! And what a handsome child it will be, with my good looks and your intelligence —'

'No, the other way about!' Fanny said, her face rapturous. 'But when?' She began to calculate. 'Fitz, I think I must have held to my first mating!'

He laughed aloud. 'Your vocabulary, Mrs Hawker! You are not a horse, my love!'

'Well, but you are my stallion,' she said with a sly smile. 'How well we did, to make me pregnant so soon! Oh Fitz, I'm so happy! Shall we have a boy or a girl, do you think?'

'Certainly — one or the other, without a doubt,' he said genially. 'But, Fanny, this means you must certainly go home, and the sooner the better. It would not be fitting, or safe, for you to travel once you are far advanced in your pregnancy. Nothing must endanger your life, or that of our child.'

'Our first child!' Fanny breathed, still enraptured. Then she looked at him sharply. 'It is your first, isn't it?'

'The first I was ever aware of,' he said reassuringly. 'You had better speak to your aunt today, love. Tell her the good news, and ask her advice about travelling back to England. You must not go alone, that is certain. If Lady Theakston does not go, some other sensible, older lady must be found who is making the journey. It shouldn't be hard to find one — there is always someone going back and forth. I'll go with you as far as Calais, of course.'

Her lip trembled again. 'Oh Fitz, I don't want to be parted from you at such a time —!'

'Nor I from you, darling. But it can't be helped. It will be much better for you to have the baby at home. Think of it: our child will inherit Morland Place when we are gone.'

The trembling disappeared. 'Yes!' she said, her eyes bright, focused on the future. 'And he must be born in the Butts Bed. All the heirs are born in that bed, and our son must not be the exception.' Her focus shortened, and she looked into his eyes. 'Our son, Fitz!' she said softly. 'What wonderful words those are!'

'Yes,' he said, and drew her into his arms again. With Fanny at home, and delivered of a child, an heir, his position would be strengthened beyond dispute. A larger allowance for sure! And though he would miss her, two years would soon pass; and in the meantime, there was all the thrill of political intrigue, and Vienna, as he had said, was full of handsome women. He stroked her head tenderly, and thought of the glowing future before them. He had never thought of himself as a patriarch before, but now he saw very pretty pictures in his mind, of a handsome little boy, curly dark hair and his blue eyes; saw himself setting the boy on his first pony, teaching him to shoot and to box; saw the little creature running towards him, arms outstretched, face alight with love. It would be very agreeable indeed to be a father, he thought. And Fanny would be a very pretty, careless mother, and he would adore her even more than he did now.

He kissed Fanny's ear. 'Our son,' he murmured into it with satisfaction.

CHAPTER TWENTY-EIGHT

Fanny arrived at Morland Place at the end of January, having broken her journey by staying a few days in London with Lucy. London had seemed very flat after Vienna, especially as most of the families were still in the country; but there were compensations. It was pleasant to be admitted into the circle of the grown-ups, to flaunt her new status over the unmarried girls she met, to discuss babies with other young matrons, and to go where she liked without chaperonage.

She had brought back presents from Vienna for everyone, but she went out shopping for more, for the pleasure of visiting Bond Street and displaying the fur tippet Fitz had bought her as a going-home present. She bought herself another new hat, and found a very pretty shawl for Héloïse; she went into Rundell and Bridge's, and chose a stock-pin for her father, and then saw a gold snuff-box with lacquered paintings on five panels featuring erotic passages from the life of Zeus, which she thought very amusing, and which she had them wrap up and send to Fitz in Vienna; and finally she fell in love with a little enamelled gold music-box, the most charming thing, with a cunning little bird on the lid which opened its beak and wagged its tail when the music played.

'I'll have that, too,' she said, when the manager had demonstrated it. 'For the baby.'

'Madam?'

She smiled and nodded, and he blushed, and clicked his fingers for an assistant to wrap this second purchase.

'Shall I have it sent round to Lady Theakston's, madam?' he enquired, displaying the knowledge for which he scoured the society columns of the newspapers every morning.

'No, I'll take it with me. My carriage is outside,' said Fanny grandly. 'Thank you.'

'Thank *you*, madam. It's always a pleasure to serve you, madam,' he said effusively. Fanny felt she could never grow tired of hearing that sort of thing.

When she finally reached Morland Place, she was very tired, and glad to be home. Her father hugged and kissed her, dropped a few tears on her head, enquired tenderly after her health, and then repeated the process all over again. Miss Rosedale beamed with pleasure, the little boys were as excited as the dogs, and Sophie clasped her hands with glee and wanted to know what the boat journey had been like.

'I so long to go on a boat!' she cried. 'Was it very rough, Fanny? Were there huge waves?'

'No, of course not,' Fanny said, finding her half-sister's pleasure in seeing her again rather agreeable. 'We waited three days at Calais until the weather was calm enough to cross. The wind was strong, but that was all to the good — it made the crossing quicker. We did it in under three hours, which they tell me is very good; and the captain said I was a splendid sailor.'

'But you look tired, poor Fanny,' Héloïse said. 'We mustn't keep you standing here in the hall. Come in and sit by the fire, and let me take off your bonnet and gloves.'

It was good to sit down in the big chair by the fire in the drawing-room. She looked around her appreciatively at all the familiar objects: the dim old paintings of long-ago Morlands, the vast clock Grandpapa had given her parents on their wedding-day, the beautiful silver candlestick which had been found when the moat was drained and cleaned, the rosewood and ebony chess-table, the dainty little spindly-legged sewing table with the false drawers, the solemn bulk of the grand piano, on top of which reposed the Chinese bowl with a blue and scarlet dragon chasing its tail around the side.

Héloïse knelt before her and untied her bonnet-strings and lifted it off, and took off her gloves for her, and even unlaced her boots and removed them, and chafed her feet. It was very pleasant to be looked after like that: she had had so little mothering in her life.

'There, is that better?' Héloïse said when she had made her comfortable. 'Now a glass of wine will do you good. James, pour a glass for Fanny.'

'It will be very interesting to hear of your experiences, Fanny,' Miss Rosedale said. 'It was a marvellous opportunity

559

for you, to be present at such an historic time. I hope you were aware of it.'

'I was aware of everything,' Fanny said with a tired smile. 'I can't tell you how I loved Vienna! I felt so alive, with everything happening all around me. Sometimes it was almost as if there wasn't time to breathe! I didn't want to leave, ever. If it hadn't been for the baby —'

James pulled his chair nearer. 'I hope you talked about it to your Aunt Lucy, Fan,' he said earnestly. 'There's no-one whose advice you could better trust. What did she tell you? I wish we could make sure she would be on hand when the time comes. When is it due?'

'In June, I suppose,' Fanny said. She felt a little awkward discussing her pregnancy with her father, and was only glad Uncle Ned was not present — he was about the estate as usual. 'Where's Mathilde?'

'She has gone out riding with John Skelwith,' Héloïse answered her.

Fanny made a face. 'Oh, has she? Well I hope he may marry her this time, and take her off our hands.'

'Fanny!' Héloïse said reproachfully.

'It's embarrassing having a great girl of her age still unmarried and hanging about the house,' Fanny said. 'I should have been ashamed to stay single until I was twenty-five!'

'The house has been very quiet without you,' James said with a wry smile.

'Well, I can tell you, I haven't come home to be quiet,' Fanny said. 'I have come to stir you all up — and it looks as though you need it!'

'I suppose you won't be able to hunt this season, will you, Fanny?' Sophie said. 'That will be sad for you. We had the most wonderful hunt on Tuesday — we galloped four miles without a check, all the way from Hessay to the Roman Road past Tockwith! I wish you had been with us!'

'I was hunting in the Wienerwald just before Christmas,' Fanny said airily. 'The Csar complimented me on my seat, and said he wished he could shew me some Russian hunting. I thought I might go to St Petersburg one day, just to see.'

'You met the Csar of Russia?' Sophie said, as impressed as Fanny had intended her to be.

'How wonderful to be able to travel,' Miss Rosedale sighed. 'Of course, now the war is over, there's no reason why you shouldn't see lots of other countries.'

'I have to set my affairs in order first,' Fanny said. 'I shall have a look at the books tomorrow, Papa, and see what you have all been getting up to while I've been away. And then I must go and visit Grandpapa. Has anything more been heard from him?'

'Nothing,' Héloïse answered.

'Has anyone written to tell him I'm increasing?'

'No, ma chère. We thought you would want to write yourself.'

'Good.' Fanny nodded in satisfaction. 'That gives me an excuse to go and see him.'

'Another journey so soon — and in winter?' James said anxiously. 'I don't think it's wise, Fanny. Can't you just write to him?'

'No, Papa, it won't do. I have to make sure of the mills.'

'Oh, that!' James looked exasperated. 'Haven't you got enough, Fanny?'

'I could never have enough. And I've got a son to think about now,' she said firmly.

'How dynastic you sound!' James couldn't help laughing. 'But it may be a daughter, don't forget.'

'It's a boy,' Fanny said. 'I know.'

Fanny took a fortnight to 'set her affairs in order', before she departed on the visit to Manchester. Edward was more than glad to see her go. She had been openly hostile to him from the moment he arrived home on her first day back, and the following morning, disconcertingly early, she sought him out to take him to task for the promise he had extracted from Hawker to stay abroad.

'Everything we did, we did for your benefit,' Edward said hotly. 'God knows, the whole world revolves around Fanny Morland, and precious little thanks anyone has ever got for it! You've spent your life being contrary and causing trouble, and then you needs must decide to marry the most worthless man in Christendom —'

'That's the last time you ever speak of my husband like that, do you hear me?' she hissed, her eyes like slits of green-gold fire.

561

'You can't speak to me like that,' Edward said, half angry, half disdainful.

'Yes I can! Yes I will! You think you can do what you like, because you're my trustee, but one day I shall be powerful enough to crush you like a robin's egg! And if you ever say anything slighting about my husband again, I shall strike you!'

It had been a hard two weeks. Fanny found fault with everything, checked and checked again on Edward's work and figures in the most insulting way, letting the servants and estate-workers see that she didn't trust him. She appeared when she was least expected, silently, critically observing him; and in the evenings in the house she ignored him utterly, not according him even a civil nod as he came into the room. He would by far have preferred to retire to the steward's room of an evening, except that he would not be driven out of his own drawing-room by his own niece. It made things uncomfortable for everyone, and Héloïse begged James to intervene.

'It is intolerable to be forced to side with one or the other,' she said. 'If I talk to Edward, Fanny glares at me; and I cannot ignore him, and condone Fanny's rudeness.'

'Well, I'll talk to her,' James said, 'but I don't think it will do any good.'

'Tell her if she doesn't mind her temper, she will sour the baby's,' Héloïse suggested.

James tackled Fanny, and she listened to him with unexpected patience, but only said, 'He doesn't deserve my civility. He has deliberately separated me from my husband. He was always against Fitz, from the beginning.'

'Fanny, darling, we all were,' James said uncomfortably, 'and if you're reasonable, you can't blame us. It was our business to protect you, you must see that. We would have been failing in our duty if we hadn't tried to stop you making what we saw — everyone saw — as a bad marriage.'

'Well, I forgive you, because you love me. And Madame did her best to make my wedding-day happy. And Rosey minded her own business, and the others don't count. But I'll never forgive Uncle Ned. He'd better just watch his step from now on.'

James changed tack. 'Darling, there's another thing — I don't think you ought to be doing so much. You're working

562

far too hard. You must remember your delicate condition. You ought to be resting, and thinking about the baby.'

'Pho! The baby can take care of itself. Why, I hardly even shew yet,' Fanny said robustly.

'At least won't you forget about this trip to Manchester? And rest during the afternoons, if you're working during the mornings?'

She patted his hand. 'I can't, Papa. I know you're worried about me, but don't be. I'm very strong and healthy, you know that. I've never had a day's illness in my life.'

'That's true. But you've never been pregnant before,' he said.

'I must put everything in order, before I get too far along,' she said decidedly. 'You must understand that. By April I shall be too big to get about, and I'll have to spend my days lying on the sopha. Then you may brood over me as much as you like, and bring me caudles and cushions and rugs! But I must be sure everything is settled first, or I shall fret.'

James had to be content with that.

Fanny found the journey to Manchester more tiring than she expected. The winter had been mild, fortunately, and there was no snow to contend with, but the roads were heavily mired, and the slow jolting, with frequent stops while the horses hauled the carriage out of a particularly deep rut, was exhausting. Now in her fifth month, Fanny had been feeling very well, the bouts of sickness having disappeared, and a new access of energy filling her as her body adjusted itself to its new state. The journey, however, left her feeling nauseous, with an unpleasant headache, and at the end of seven hours in the chaise the first day, she was more than glad to reach Huddersfield, and to stop at The George, and bespeak a room and an early dinner.

After an hour's rest and a wash, she was refreshed enough to feel the pleasure of travelling alone, and of ordering her own dinner at a posting-house; though when the meal came, she was unable to do it proper justice. She slept heavily, and woke the next morning little refreshed, to face the second, but shorter leg of her journey. Once they were past Oldham, the roads were much improved, and the last eight miles were covered in only an hour, on a fine hard surface. At three o'clock they were clattering through the familiar crowded, grimy streets of Manchester. Fanny viewed the pall of smoke which drifted sideways in the damp air with indulgence: it was the symbol of prosperity; it was the smoke that was making wealth — her wealth.

When the carriage pulled up outside Hobsbawn House, Mrs Murray was waiting on the steps with the butler to greet her, her face wreathed in hypocritical smiles, which did not conceal from Fanny the sharpness of the eyes that scanned her as she stepped down from the chaise. Fanny might flatter herself that she 'hardly shewed', but one glance told Mrs Murray all. For a moment her face seemed to sharpen and age, and then her smile returned twice as wide, and she hurried forward.

'Oh Miss Morland — Mrs Hawker, I should say!' she enthused. 'What a wonderful thing! Pray allow me to offer you my heartiest congratulations, ma'am! I'm sure no-one guessed — but there, what a lovely surprise it will be for your grandpapa, ma'am! A little one on the way! Just the news to cheer him up!'

'Where is my grandfather?' Fanny demanded. 'Why isn't he here to greet me?'

'He's inside, ma'am, by the fire. He asked me to apologise to you, and bid you come straight in and warm yourself.'

'Is he ill?' Fanny asked sharply.

'No, ma'am, not ill — not precisely. But the weather is too sharp for him to wait about in the cold. The doctor advises against it, ma'am.'

'Doctor? Why is he consulting the doctor?'

'Oh, Mrs Hawker, your grandpapa is getting on in years, and after his unfortunate seizure last year — well, he hasn't ever been quite what he was. The shock which brought it on, ma'am — well, I'm sure there's no need to mention that again! But his nerves were much disordered, and the doctor says he mustn't be upset or over-stretched. Rest and quiet, that's what he needs. I'm sure you understand.'

'Oh yes,' Fanny said, fixing her with a gimlet eye. 'I understand everything, Mrs Murray, I assure you! Good afternoon, Bowles! Have my bags taken up to my room, will you. What time do you serve dinner?'

'Well, miss — ma'am, I should say,' the old man began to

564

mumble, but Mrs Murray broke in.

'Oh, your grandpapa don't take a regular dinner, Mrs Hawker, ma'am. Just a light something, on a tray, you know.'

'He'll take dinner today,' Fanny said firmly, and addressed the butler again. 'Send in some wine and biscuits at once, please, and have dinner ready for four o'clock — whatever cook can get ready. I find I'm very hungry after my journey.'

'Dinner, miss. Yes, miss,' Bowles said, blinking with pleasure. 'And wine. Straight away, miss.'

'Thank you Bowles. You need not come up with me, Mrs Murray. I can find my own way.'

Mrs Murray's lips thinned. 'I think I had better announce you, ma'am. The shock might be too much for Mr Hobsbawn, if you was to suddenly come upon him.'

'Fiddlesticks! He must have heard all the commotion by now, and he knows I'm coming. I'll find my own way, I said.'

Mrs Murray subsided unwillingly, saving Fanny the trouble of pushing her down the stairs. Fanny pulled off her bonnet and unbuttoned her pelisse as she went up to the first floor, and paused at the open door of the drawing-room. A bright fire was burning under the chimney, a fine, welcome sight, reflecting off the various shining surfaces in the room, glinting on china and glass, glowing on polished wood. The curtains were still open, shewing a glimpse of the waning day outside, and making, with their rich red velvet pile, a decided division between the cold gloom outside and the comfort inside. There was a smell of pot-pourri in the air, and there was a display of dried leaves and evergreens in a vase on the piano. Mrs Murray, Fanny reflected again, was a good house-keeper.

Her grandfather was seated in the wing-backed chair by the fire, as she had seen him on her first ever visit, just after her mother had died. He was hunched a little and staring into the fire, as he had been then, but the difference in him was enormous. He looked old now, shrunken and frail, and Fanny felt a breath of fear touch her. He had always been so vigorous, bestriding half her world immoveably like a colossus. Now she saw that he was mortal, that he might, indeed, die; and though he must do so to leave her his mills, she found that she didn't want him to. She discovered now, belatedly, that she loved the old man, and she didn't want him to die.

'Grandpapa,' she said softly. 'Grandpapa, I'm here. It's me, Fanny.'

He looked up, and for a moment his expression didn't change. She thought he did not know who she was. Has his mind gone, then? she wondered in panic. He looked at her expressionlessly.

'Grandpapa!' she said again, more urgently. 'It's Fanny!'

'I see you,' he said a shade irritably. 'And are you alone? Or have you brought that worthless husband of yours with you?'

'I'm alone,' she said. She crossed the room quickly and knelt down beside his chair, slid her hands under his, wound her fingers round his. His hands were smooth, chalk-dry, with hard, old-man's nails, like bird's claws. 'Grandpapa, aren't you pleased to see me? I've come all the way from York just to visit you.'

'You took your time about it,' he said.

For an instant she was puzzled — did he expect her to do the journey in one day? — and then she understood him. 'I've been abroad since my wedding,' she said. 'I only came home a fortnight ago. As soon as I could get away, I came straight to see you. You hurt me very much, you know, when you wouldn't answer my letter. It made me cry.'

His eyes focused on her at last, and she saw the pain in them. 'Hurt you?' he said, in a faint, sighing voice. 'Hurt you?'

'Grandpapa, please say you love me! I can't bear you to look at me like that!'

'Oh Fanny, why did you marry him?' he cried suddenly in anguish. 'My little Fanny! You could have had anyone! Anyone!'

'But you see, Grandpapa, I didn't want anyone,' she said. 'I love him as you loved my grandmother. And when you love someone, no-one else will do, don't you see?'

He stared a moment longer, and then with an inarticulate sound, he put his arms round her. She put hers round his neck, and they hugged each other.

'Fanny! My little Fanny!' he cried into her neck.

After a moment, Fanny released herself, and pushed him back into the chair, laughing now, though her eyes were wet. 'Oh Grandpapa, I knew you'd understand! We're alike, you and I — you've always said so. I love him so much,

Grandpapa, and he loves me too. If you could see how much, you'd forgive him for marrying me.'

'Aye, well, he'd better love you, that's all,' Hobsbawn growled. 'And what have you been doing abroad, you minx? Dancing the waltz in Vienna, I'll be bound!'

'Yes, and talking to all the great men, and playing *roulette*! But now I'm home to take care of my business. Fitz stayed on in Vienna. I didn't want to leave him, but business must come first, of course.' She knew he would like this, and he did. He smiled approvingly, and patted her cheek.

'Right! You're right there. But we must have a glass of wine, Fanny — a glass of claret. Ring the bell for Bowles. And you must want your dinner. I shall have to order something for you. I don't know what there may be. I haven't been taking dinner myself recently —'

'I know. I heard that from Mrs Murray, and it won't do, Grandpapa,' Fanny said sternly. 'Slops on a tray! You must take care of yourself, and not let Mrs Murray coddle you like an invalid. She thinks you're an old man, you know.'

He gave a papery chuckle. 'Aye, you're right, Puss! Well, we'll have a fine dinner today, and share a bottle of claret, like the old days. Your poor dear mother had a fine taste in claret —'

'Yes, I know,' she smiled. 'It's all arranged already, Grandpapa. I spoke to Bowles on the way in.' She kissed his sunken cheek, and the touch of it under her lips made her feel as though a giant hand had clenched round her heart. He was old! Death and mortality were like great rifts that drained the happiness from the world. She wanted to press life into his hands like a bounty, pour it into his lap out of her own abundance. She had so much of it: she could spare him enough to keep him from the dark. She did not want to lose him now that she had come at last to know and appreciate him.

'Grandpapa, I have something to tell you — something you'll like,' she said eagerly, looking into his eyes, smiling into him. 'Perhaps you've guessed already?'

'Guessed? No, Fan, what is it?' he said, looking bewildered.

'Grandpapa, there's another Hobsbawn on his way,' she said. Still he stared. 'I'm with child, Grandpapa! I'm going to have a baby!'

Slowly it sank in, slowly the realisation dawned. He stared

567

at her wonderingly, looked down at her belly, and then back to her face, and a joy so luminous filled his eyes that she wanted to cry and laugh at the same time.

'A baby? Fan, a baby?'

She nodded. 'Are you pleased?'

'Pleased? A baby? By God,' he suddenly roared like the Joseph Hobsbawn of old, 'a baby! Pleased? I should by God think I am pleased!'

The door opened at that instant, and Bowles began shuffling in, balancing a tray precariously in his knotted old grasp.

'Bowles!' Hobsbawn roared. Bowles uttered a little cry of alarm, and the tray wavered perilously, making the glasses rock. 'Bowles, take that stuff away and bring us champagne! Champagne, I say! Miss Fanny's going to have A BABY!'

Bowles's toothless mouth curved into a gap from which a dry, whistling laugh came sighing, and Hobsbawn began laughing too, banging his hands down on the arms of the chair in childlike delight. Bowles was shaking all over, his shoulders twitching, his eyes wet; Hobsbawn stamped his feet and roared.

'A baby, a new Hobsbawn! Bless my soul! A baby!'

Fanny, kneeling on the floor between them, turned her head this way and that, from one wheezing old man to the other, smiling at their pleasure, at their absurd delight. And then suddenly she felt the most extraordinary sensation, which sent her eyebrows climbing, made her mouth drop open with astonishment. Careless of modesty, she pressed her hands to her belly, and felt again the little fluttering, trapped-bird movement that had rippled across it. Something was alive, where before there had been nothing.

'The baby's moving,' she whispered. And suddenly she was crying too, pressing her hands to her belly, her mouth bowed like a child's, while a pandemonium of delight raged all around her.

Two horses, one bay, one chestnut, came cantering along the track from Long Marston, up the side of Cromwell's Plump, and were pulled up on the top, and stood tossing their heads and champing their bits as the cold wind lifted their manes. The February sky was grey, white-grey behind, with gull-coloured clouds, ragged at the edges, rolling fast beneath; but the moor was still green after the mild winter, gashed with the brown of the tracks and roads, and fringed with the pinkish fuzz of distant woods.

Mathilde gazed out over it, feeling the stillness and the breadth.

'It's so peaceful,' she said at last. 'It's lovely to hear nothing but the wind, and the silence underneath. And it's a good silence — not full of undertones and hostility.'

'Are things bad at Morland Place, then?' John Skelwith asked.

'It's just Fanny and Cousin Edward,' Mathilde said unhappily. 'They hate each other so — I'm sure it can't be good for Fanny's baby. And when they don't quarrel, it's worse than when they do.' She couldn't tell John the rest — how guilty she felt, seeing Edward's isolation, his loneliness, his friendlessness. He worked so hard, and Fanny was so unjust. 'It can't go on like that,' she sighed. 'Month after month — it will drive everyone to distraction. Madame's taken to sitting in the nursery to get away from it.'

He looked at her thoughtfully. 'There's no need for you to endure it any longer,' he said. 'You know my feelings for you. Let me take you away, and give you a home of your own.' She looked at him uncertainly. 'Mathilde, what is it? I'm asking you to marry me.'

'Oh John, it's just — well, I still wonder about your mother. She doesn't like me, you know.'

'Nonsense!'

'It's true! I know she doesn't say anything, but I've seen the way she looks at me. And if ever I mention Morland Place, or the family, she glares at me as if she'd like to kill me.'

'It's your imagination. Mother never smiles at anything or anyone — not even me,' he teased gently.

'I can't help it, John. I would like to marry you, but I can't exchange one hostile home for another.'

Trooper sighed and spread his weight comfortably, but Vanity moved restlessly, and Mathilde let her turn round and face the other way, and pushed her up closer to Trooper, so that she and John were facing each other.

'Is that the only reason you hesitate?' he asked at last. 'Do you really want to marry me?'

She thought of being away from Morland Place, of having

a husband of her own, an establishment, security, freedom. 'Yes,' she said. 'Yes, I do.'

'Well then, I'll tell you how we'll arrange matters: you and I won't live with my mother. She can stay in the house in Stonegate, and I'll find her a lady-companion to live with her, and you and I will have a new house all our own.'

'Do you mean it?' she asked wonderingly.

'Of course I do. And what's more, we'll design it and build it ourselves — a completely new, modern house, with everything just as we want it. No more nasty, cramped old mediæval rooms, and crooked stairs, and sloping ceilings. Everything straight, square, bright, full of light and air. And a proper garden, so that you can have a shrubbery to walk in, and a flower-garden, and everything just as it should be. It's a nonsense for the leading master-builder in the North to live in that old ruin in Stonegate. Our house shall be our advertisement to the world! What do you think?'

'It sounds wonderful,' Mathilde said. 'But you won't want to leave your mother. I don't want to force you to choose between us.'

He reached for her hand. 'There's no question of choice. Dearest, I want to marry you. I don't want to lose you a second time. Mother will be all right, I'll see to that. You mustn't feel that you're forcing me to anything.'

'Well, if you're sure —'

'Quite sure. And you?' She nodded, smiling, and he squeezed her hand. 'Next month, then — what do you say? As soon as I'm out of mourning. I don't want to wait any longer. Name a date.'

She laughed. 'March the twelfth,' she said at random.

He lifted her hand and kissed it. 'That's a promise, mind! You've said it, and you can't go back on it now.'

Mathilde announced her engagement late that evening, just before bedtime, with a blush, a conscious look, and a faint hesitation which Héloïse found so touching that she suppressed her instant reaction of dismay and hurried forward to embrace and congratulate her.

'It is wonderful news, *chérie*,' she said warmly. 'He is an excellent young man, and I am sure you will be very happy together.'

'Thank you, Madame,' Mathilde said, the more gratefully because the only other two occupants of the room, Edward and James, were evincing no pleasure in the news at all. James was staring at nothing, his expression devoid of any emotion, and Edward had turned his face away and was looking into the fire. Mathilde saw out of the corner of her eye the hunch of Edward's shoulders, and wondered uneasily what he was feeling. His appearance was the epitome of unease, but was it regret, envy, relief, or simply embarrassment which made him unable to meet her eye?

Héloïse was now turning to her husband, urging him, with a hint of reproach, to add his congratulations to hers.

'It will be a fine establishment for her, won't it, James?' she said.

'Oh — certainly. First rate,' James said with an effort.

'And it is not such a surprise to us really,' Héloïse went on, catching his eye pointedly, 'for Mr Skelwith has been visiting so regularly, we should have guessed it was in the air.'

James met her look. Yes, they should have guessed it; but torn between wanting the best for Mathilde and wanting no more complications in their lives, they had preferred to ignore the situation and hope it would go away. But something more must be said, something warmer. James made the effort.

'I'm very happy for you, my dear,' he said, and managed a smile. 'Does he — does he really care for you?'

'Yes — I believe so,' Mathilde said, looking a little wonderingly from him to Madame and back. 'He is everything that is kind — and I care for him, too,' she added in a little burst.

James rose and went forward to embrace her in his turn, and said with real warmth, 'However good a young man he is — and I hear nothing but good of him — he will have a better wife in you than he deserves! And I shall make sure to tell him so when next I meet him. I wish you every happiness, Mathilde. God bless you, my dear.' And he kissed her heartily, winning an approving nod from his wife.

'Thank you,' Mathilde said, a little bright-eyed from so much emotion. 'Thank you both for everything — so many kindnesses —' And with an incoherent and hasty goodnight, she left the room.

A moment later Edward got up and went out too, and James and Héloïse were left alone together. They exchanged a

571

long and eloquent look, at the end of which James said merely, 'Damn!'

Héloïse returned to her seat by the fire and studied her hands, her brow puckered. We shall never be rid of him, she thought. We shall see him every day, and have to hide our knowledge and our feelings. We shall be haunted by him for the rest of our lives — and what when he and Mathilde have children? They will be James's grandchildren. How will we bear it?

She wondered if James had thought about that aspect of it, and looked up to find him regarding her with a mixture of pain and resignation which told her he had realised everything there was to realise about the situation.

'The sins of the father seem about to be visited on the father,' he said at last. 'If I could have known what the outcome would be —'

'You would still have done the same,' Héloïse said. 'You were young and foolhardy. It is not possible to be as wise at eighteen as —'

'There's no excuse, Marmoset! Don't try to find one for me. I have embroiled myself damnably, but what is worse, I have embroiled others, too. If they should ever find out —! And then there's you, love — you shouldn't be put into such a position, you who are all goodness, who never in your life —'

'Oh, no James, don't say it!' She was on her feet interrupting with a bright, angry look. 'Am I not a sinner? Yes, you know I am — and more, more than you know!' She pressed her hands together and made the painful confession. 'I have been so jealous, so jealous! You cannot imagine. I have thought such things —!'

He was astonished. 'Jealous? Of whom? Not of Mary?'

'Yes!' she cried fiercely. 'Of both your Marys! Of anyone who had you before me! Of anyone who had any part of you that I have not had!'

'Darling —!'

'Yes, you see me now in my true colours! I am not your saint, your angel! I am weak and foolish and sinful, and I love you so, my James, that I burn with rage for every instant of your life that I have missed! And for the children of you that I should have borne!' He stared at her in almost comic dismay, and she took a deep, quivering breath and lowered her hands,

572

and resumed in a nearly normal voice. 'So it is right that I should be punished too.'

He shook his head, though whether it was a denial or merely a gesture of suffering she did not know; and then he held out a hand to her, and she came to him to be folded in and comforted. Cradled against his broad chest, she grew calm again. His cheek was resting on the top of her head; after a while she felt the movement as he suddenly smiled, and she made an interrogative noise.

'I was just thinking,' he explained, and she heard the amusement in his voice, 'that poor Mathilde couldn't have known what a bomb she was dropping on us! The poor creature probably thought she'd be giving us pleasure — expected us to be delighted with her news.'

Héloïse tilted her head back to look up into his face, and was glad to see the mischief alight again in his eyes.

'Do you think we tried hard enough to be pleased?' she asked.

'We must make sure that she never knows we were otherwise,' James said ruefully. 'Poor Mathilde!'

Héloïse rested her head on his chest again. 'Sophie will be delighted. She will say all the things Mathilde longs to hear. And I suppose Fanny will be glad,' she added, but with hesitation.

'Of course she will,' James said defensively. 'Why shouldn't she be?'

Edward caught up with Mathilde in the hall, where she was lighting her candle to go up to bed. He had followed her from the room with no clear idea of what he meant to say, knowing only that something must be said, and that he had behaved churlishly in not offering her his congratulations.

She looked up as he reached her, and regarded him enquiringly, but with a faint apprehension which touched him, and filled him with a sudden rush of natural, warm affection.

'Mathilde, my dear,' he began, and then stopped. He had been about to apologise, but it suddenly seemed presumptuous to suppose an apology necessary. He had asked her to release him; she had done so. He had urged her to find another; she had done so. What more was there to say? Except that he loved her very much, and he needed suddenly to tell her so in some way which would not burden her with embarrassment or guilt. 'I am so very happy for you,' he said at last.

'Are you, Cousin Edward?' she said — not with hostility, but simply wanting to be sure.

'Can you doubt it? I want you to be happy — that's what I have always wanted.'

'But do you like him? Do you think I am right to accept him?' It occurred to her that to Edward alone had she revealed, long ago, her reasons for not wishing to marry John Skelwith the first time he had courted her. He would think she was now accepting her suitor for purely mercenary reasons. Perhaps he might even think that she loved him, Edward, still, and was quite callously seeking a material advantage in accepting John Skelwith. 'I do — *care* for him, you know,' she added anxiously.

Edward smiled. 'I'm sure you do. He is a very likeable, worthy young man, and evidently much attracted to you. To resume his addresses to you after so long shews him to be constant. I think you have every chance of being happy with him, and I sincerely wish you so.'

But all this was only words, he thought impatiently. The complexity of loving her and wishing her well and being glad for her and wanting her for himself was such that any attempted explanation was bound to sound insincere. Touch was better, more truthful. He reached for her hand, at the same instant as she put down the candle she was holding and reached out for his.

He took both her hands in his and now the smile they exchanged was without restraint, the smile of two dear and loving friends. He took her in his arms for the last time, and she accepted his embrace and remembered all the times she had found comfort there, and felt tears in her eyes, of regret for the past and gladness for the future, of compassion and affection.

'We shall always be friends, shan't we?' she said against his shoulder.

Edward felt one last pang, that had things been different, she would have been wholly his. He pressed her close just once, and then released her.

'Of course. Always,' he said.

She picked up her candle and with a shy smile went away, climbing the stairs to bed. He watched her go with a sense of loss which had nothing to do with her actions or feelings. He had lost something of himself. He was an old man, and love had come too late for him, and he had not had the courage to seize it and commit himself to it, to take the chance when it was offered. It would not be offered again. Now she would marry Skelwith (of all people! And who knew what complications might arise in the future?) But it was not that Skelwith had won her, it was that he had let her go, and with her had let go some vital part of himself — not quite hope, but something like it.

She climbed the stairs, holding the candle before her, and he watched in silence as the golden flame receded upwards, bending and wavering with her movement, throwing her shadow longer and longer, until at last it turned the corner and left him and the hall below in darkness.

The month flew past. Three days before Mathilde's wedding-day, the family was gathered in the evening in the drawing-room. The weather had turned very cold the last couple of days, and the hills were powdered with snow, putting Héloïse in an apprehension for her flower-garden, where a number of species had been lured by the mild winter into budding early.

There was a silence in the room, broken only by the ticking of the clock, the cracking and spitting of the fire, and the soft sound of the piano, where Sophie was touching odd notes almost at random, while she dreamed of ball gowns and handsome young men. She was to come out this Season: as soon as Mathilde's wedding was over, Héloïse was to take her to London, and she was to be launched with Cousin Rosamund from Aunt Lucy's house. She had heard again and again, and never tired of, Fanny's stories about her come-out, and she was looking forward to her own beyond measure. Of course, she was no Miss Morland of Morland Place. She was not even pretty. But she had not lacked admirers. People liked her, and wanted to talk to her, and at the parties she had been to this last year, where members of the opposite sex were present, it had been around her that they had clustered, rather than around the pretty Miss Laxton or the witty Miss Greaves.

Mathilde, Héloïse and Miss Rosedale were sitting around the large circular table. Héloïse and Miss Rosedale were sewing flounces on the hem of Mathilde's wedding-gown, while Mathilde embroidered flowers on the yoke of a silk night-gown. Once or twice her mind had strayed to a contemplation of the first occasion on which she would wear the nightgown, and she had surprised herself into blushes. She couldn't imagine what was going to happen. She knew about horses and sheep and chickens, of course, but her imagination baulked at applying that knowledge to human beings. She was only glad that it was going to be John Skelwith who was with her that night, for she thought it was likely to be deeply embarrassing. He was so kind, and such a friend, she caught herself sometimes thinking absurdly that she could not have endured facing it with anyone but him.

James was reading the paper in the chair at one side of the fire, and dozing a little. The fire was very warm, and he had eaten a large dinner, and had read the paper once already that day. He had taken recently to wearing spectacles for reading, and when he dozed, they slipped down to the end of his nose. Héloïse looked across at him from time to time, and smiled affectionately, thinking how much more she loved him when he looked absurd and vulnerable.

Fanny, sitting in the chair to the other side of the fire, also looked across at him, and felt irritated. If he wants to sleep, why doesn't he go to bed? she thought. And if he wants to read, why doesn't he move away from the fire? She hated him to look silly, as he did when his spectacles slipped. She felt it reflected on her when her father looked silly. She had a great deal to vex her at the moment. She had quarrelled fiercely again that day with Edward — who was sitting with his back pointedly to her, playing chess with Father Aislaby — and felt all the frustration of not being able to have her own way on her own estate.

Then also she was now beginning her seventh month of pregnancy, and she was getting large and uncomfortable. She missed her husband dreadfully, and was fretting because he had not written for a fortnight. His last letter was in her pocket, and she had re-read it so often she knew it almost by heart. He was enjoying himself — well, she wouldn't want him not to, but he ought to be as miserable without her as she was without him. He *said* he missed her, of course — but then in the next paragraph he was talking about a certain Lady Ballantyre, who was amusing and witty, and lodging, too conveniently, in the same street.

And then, to cap it all, she had eaten too much, or too fast, at dinner, and she had indigestion. Perhaps it was the lobster cutlets, she thought. Or perhaps that bitter sauce on the duck had been too rich. But she was uncomfortable, unhappy, and bored, and she wanted to snap at everyone. Thank heaven all the fuss over Mathilde's wedding would soon be over, and there would be one person fewer to eat her out of house and home. Edys Cowey — who had become quite friendly now that she was Mrs Percival Bolter, and who was a stinging gossip — had told her something rather intriguing about John Skelwith after church last Sunday, and though she was not sure if she believed it, it was interesting to speculate. She knew her father had been wild in his youth, though to look at him now, she thought disgustedly, as his head fell forward and his spectacles slithered down like something scuttling for freedom, you would never think it. Mind you, to look at John Skelwith's mother, you wouldn't think anyone could ever have fancied her. She was a little touched in the upper works now, so Edys said. She had certainly glared at the whole Morland party like a madwoman, and refused to answer anything anyone said to her.

Mathilde was being married at St Edward's, not in the chapel. Fanny had put her foot down about that — though Madame had said soothingly that she had never meant Mathilde's wedding to be held in the chapel anyway. Madame had also insisted on paying for everything out of her own pocket, which was as it should be, and Fanny, on that understanding, had agreed that the wedding-party could come to Morland Place afterwards for the wedding-breakfast.

There had been some fun when that was announced, for Mrs Percy Bolter said that old Mary Skelwith had utterly refused to set foot in Morland Place, and frightened her son nearly into fits about it. He was such a *stick*, Fanny thought. Just right for Mathilde — she was lucky to get him, with that hair and those freckles. Still, Fanny had to admit that he did the right thing on that occasion — told his mother she could either go to the breakfast and behave herself, or go straight home from the church. Mrs Skelwith had said she would go straight home, so John was apparently going to give out at the last minute that she'd been taken ill — not very ill, just too ill to go to the breakfast. And they'd do very well without her, Fanny thought.

At that moment there was the sound of someone knocking violently on the house door. Everyone looked up and exchanged startled glances. James woke from his latest doze and said 'Eh? What? Who's that?'

'Who on earth can that be, at this time of night?' Edward said.

Mathilde looked apprehensively at Héloïse. Sudden alarms usually meant bad news, and bad news in her case meant something that would affect her wedding plans. Héloïse reached across the table and patted her hand reassuringly, but she looked uneasy. No matter how far in the past it was, her experience of living through the Terror always made her fear the worst from sudden interruptions at night.

There were voices out in the hall, Ottershaw's measured tones, someone answering, agitated. Mathilde's eyes widened. She was sure it was John's voice. Old Mrs Skelwith has died, she thought, and the wedding will have to be cancelled. I knew something like this would happen!

Fanny thrust herself abruptly out of her chair. 'For God's sake,' she growled, 'what's going on?' She walked to the door and opened it, and vented some of her irritation by shouting for Ottershaw. A moment later he appeared with John Skelwith behind him, tousled and wind-blown, his face red from the sharpness of the night air, his person liberally splashed with mud. What a clown! Fanny thought. I'm glad he was never a beau of mine.

'What's all the noise about, Ottershaw?' she said sharply. 'And what are you doing here at this time of night, Mr Skelwith? Can't your passion contain itself until morning?'

'Oh, I beg your pardon, ma'am —' Ottershaw began flutteringly, but Skelwith thrust past him and stood before Fanny, looking hard into her eyes.

'I'm sorry to disturb you, Mrs Hawker, but some news has come to my hand — very grave news. I felt I must take the first opportunity of letting you all know.'

She smelled the ale on his breath. 'This news came to you

in the Hare and Heather, I take it?' she said, poisonously sweet.

'Fanny, dear, ask Mr Skelwith to come in,' Héloïse suggested gently from within the drawing-room. Fanny returned to the fire with a bad grace, and Skelwith stepped in, while Ottershaw hung about outside the door, which no-one had remembered to shut, hoping for enlightenment.

In the full light of the drawing-room, Skelwith looked white and shocked. Everyone's attention was on him — even James was wide awake now.

'I was in the Hare and Heather,' he said. He licked his lips, which seemed dry. 'That's how I got the news so soon. I made sure you wouldn't have heard it yet, off the main road as you are. I rode straight here across the fields —'

'In the dark? Oh John, that was dangerous!' Mathilde couldn't help exclaiming. 'You might have gone into the beck.'

He glanced at her distractedly, then turned his attention to James, to Edward, and then to Héloïse. 'The news is from London. It's — I don't know how to tell you. Boney's out! He's escaped from Elba, and landed in France.'

Héloïse gave a little cry, and stood up, and her chair fell over with a thud. 'Dear God, no!' she cried. 'The monster is loose again?'

'Is it true? Good God, man, is it sure?' Edward cried.

Skelwith nodded. 'Sure enough. It was known by our agent in Florence a week ago, but apparently everyone thought he would make for Italy, and the news got held up somewhere. He headed instead for France — that's why our ships didn't intercept him. The whole thing was obviously planned to the last detail. He landed near Antibes on the first of March with an army — I don't know how many. God knows where he is now.' He passed a hand over his face wearily. 'Wellington's in Vienna. There's no army anywhere near him — I don't know what's to stop him reaching Paris. London's in turmoil — they say 'Change has gone quite mad, and Lloyds is in a panic, and wanting to double their rates. It's clear what *they* think is going to happen.'

Héloïse was staring at nothing, her eyes wide and shocked. 'Now it will begin all over again,' she whispered. 'Another twenty years of bloodshed! God help us all!'

And then Fanny gave a strange cry, and they all turned to look at her, and watched in disbelief as the colour drained quite visibly from her face. Even her lips were white, and her eyes seemed to be starting from her head.

'Fanny, what is it?' Miss Rosedale said quickly, rising to her feet.

'A pain,' Fanny whispered, hardly moving her lips. Her whole body was rigid, as if she feared any movement would shatter her.

'Where? What sort of pain?' Héloïse asked. Fanny said nothing, only stood there, her eyes bulging with terror. 'Fanny, answer me!'

'It's the baby!' she cried out in a terrible voice. 'It's too soon! Not now! Oh not now! It can't be!' She turned to her father, thrusting out her hands at him pleadingly; instinctively at this moment, it was to him she turned, like a child. Her voice rose to a scream. 'It's too soon — it'll die! It's too soon! Papa, make it stop! *Make it stop!*'

It was all over. Dawn came at last: no sunrise, little more than a slight alleviation of darkness, a grey wet sky hanging low over the mute earth. The house was silent and cold. In the drawing-room, the fire had sunk to a handful of embers, and no-one had remembered to make it up. The candles had burnt out in the sockets. They had been sitting for the last two hours in the creeping light of morning: Mathilde had drawn the curtains back, the only movement anyone had made for some time.

James sat as though he would never move again. It was impossible to believe. She was so strong, so healthy. He relived, wearily, the moment when Héloïse had come out from the bedchamber to where he waited in the passage, and looked at him, and he had known that where his child was before, now there was nothing. How could someone exist one moment and not the next? It was impossible to believe. His thoughts trudged wearily round the same circle. Last night, only last night, she had sat there opposite him, full of life and energy and vigour. It was she who had stood up and gone to the door when Skelwith came. She had shouted, with that edge of irritation to her voice, to find out what was going on. She of all of them was filled with vital force. She couldn't, she couldn't be dead.

Héloïse came in, and they all lifted their heads dully to look at her. She pushed her hair from her face in a tired gesture and walked across to sit heavily in the chair opposite James.

'It's all finished,' she said. 'You can go up, if you want.' She and Marie had been laying out the body. Sarah and Jenny had helped clean up the room. There had been a great deal of blood: she had not given up her life easily. Matty had washed the baby, weeping her easy, healing tears over it. Héloïse could not bear the force of the pity that pulled at her at the sight of it. A boy after all — Fanny had said all along it was a boy, and she was proved right. Perfect, but so tiny, too tiny ever to have lived. It had never breathed air, dead already when it came, three months too soon, into this harsh world.

James looked up. 'She's not alone? You didn't leave her alone?'

Héloïse shook her head. 'Miss Rosedale is with her. You can go and see her, if you want.'

But he shook his head. He didn't want to see her dead, while she was still warm and alive in his mind. He wanted to keep her as he still remembered her from last night, alive enough to be bad-tempered. All too soon, he knew, she would fade and be gone; but not yet, not yet.

The long, long silence went on.

'What do we do now?' James asked at last, speaking to Héloïse, as if there were no-one else present. For him, there was no-one. Everything else he had loved was lying cold and still in the blue bedchamber, all life spent in one last, fierce, heroic struggle.

Héloïse met his eyes. 'I don't know,' she said. She sounded exhausted beyond thought. 'I don't know what there is to do.'

And James knew there was no escape, that she really was dead, and that there was nothing to do any more, only sit here, in silence, and endure this pain. He folded his hands in his lap, and let it have its way.

While the world shook with terror at the escape of Bonaparte from his prison of Elba — too fragile a cage, surely, ever to have held such a powerful eagle — Morland Place brooded, barely aware of the cataclysmic events that were convulsing

581

Europe, turning its face from the world and looking inward on its own grief. Comprehension was hard to achieve. If it had not been so sudden! If it had been anyone but Fanny! The house had rung with the sound of her healthy young voice and the tale of her misdeeds since she was first able to walk. She had caused everyone so much trouble and anxiety; the words 'Where's Fanny?' had so often been uttered in trepidation; she had been so very much *there*, sometimes hard to love, but always impossible to ignore; that a world in which she did not exist seemed simply implausible.

Edward remembered every harsh word he had ever said to her, particularly the last ones; and though he had never loved her, he felt the emptiness she had left behind. Father Aislaby remembered the times he had only just managed to restrain himself from slapping her, and the times he had failed. Sophie grieved for her sister with the simplicity of her open nature, and the little boys clung to their mother's skirt, bewildered by the atmosphere in the house. Miss Rosedale went over every treasured memory of her stormy pupil, every little triumph, every small token of Fanny's growing love and esteem. Héloïse remembered how much closer they had grown lately, and remembered that affectionate, grateful look Fanny had given her when she had offered her the lace for her wedding-gown.

And James remembered the day Fanny was born, when his mother had placed her in his arms, only minutes old, her transparent skin still pulsing with the force of new life flowing through her. From that moment onward, she had held his heart in the palm of her small hand, and he had watched her grow and change, bud and flower, with astonishment that he could have had any part in making something so strong and separate, so utterly unlike him, so full of vigour. She had never ailed a thing in her whole life. She had never known illness. She had raged and stormed through their lives, brought James grey hairs of anxiety over what she might do next, and he had loved her absolutely. For twenty years, there had been Fanny, first and foremost and unforgettable. Now her strong life had been cut off, and there was no Fanny. She was dead, gone, finished. All that was left was the shroud and the coffin, the painful words of the mass, and the dark vault, and the forgetting.

'We will never be the same. Nothing will ever be the same again,' Sophie had said, sobbing with her head in his lap. 'Why did Fanny have to die? It isn't *fair*!'

James touched her dark head, tried to feel the love for her he knew existed, but it wouldn't come, like the tears that were trapped somewhere deep inside him and wouldn't flow. Sophie cried, and he patted her vaguely, answered her somehow. Héloïse watched him, but didn't come near him, knowing with some instinct deeper than words that he could not bear to be touched. Some time he would come to her, and take comfort of her, but not now. After a while, she came and took Sophie away, and held her on her lap and hugged her, watching James from out of another world, a world where things happened. He was trapped like a fly in amber, held in the boredom of grief, the monotony of bereavement, caught in a world where nothing would ever happen any more, but the repeated remembering that Fanny was dead.

On the day of the funeral, Mr Pobgee came to the house, and asked the butler if he could see her ladyship.

Ottershaw, who cared deeply about etiquette, and more than ever at a time like this, allowed himself to raise an eyebrow. 'Mr Morland and Mr James are in the drawing-room, sir,' he suggested.

'No doubt, my good man,' said Pobgee patiently, 'but I would still like the favour of an interview with her ladyship.'

'Her ladyship is much engaged,' Ottershaw said disapprovingly. 'I will enquire if she is at liberty. If you would care to wait, sir —'

'Is there anyone in the steward's room? I will wait there, then. I should like to see her ladyship privately, if you please.'

It was some time before Héloïse joined him, looking older than her years, and very plain in crow-black crape. The news, conveyed to her at length by Ottershaw, that the family lawyer wished to see her, had started a train of thoughts which had not troubled her before. The shock of Fanny's death had been so great that it had not been possible yet to wonder how it would affect any of them materially: of all the aspects of Fanny's self that had occupied their minds, the fact of her being the heiress had not been one.

Material considerations had been confined to the immediate

problems of the funeral, and mourning-clothes. Mathilde's wedding had had to be postponed, of course, and Sophie's come-out would have to be put off. Poor Mr Hawker would have to be informed, and Mr Hobsbawn — what would the news do to him? But what would happen to them all in the long run, it had not yet crossed her mind to wonder.

'Mr Pobgee,' she said, holding out her hand civilly. All the burden of the funeral arrangements had naturally fallen on her shoulders, but she did not allow it to appear that it was very inconvenient to have him take up her time just now. 'I hope you haven't been waiting long?'

He waved that aside. 'It's good of you to see me, ma'am. May I offer my deepest condolences? Such a shocking thing! It must be very hard for you all to bear. It seems so much worse when a young person is taken from us. In the nature of things, we don't expect to outlive our children.'

Héloïse nodded painfully, and sat down, offering him a seat by a gesture of her hand. 'You have come, I suppose, about the inheritance,' she said.

'Yes, ma'am, I have. Of course, I will arrange a formal reading of her late ladyship's will in due course, but I thought —'

'Her late ladyship's?' Héloïse queried.

'Just so,' Pobgee said gently.

'I don't understand,' Héloïse said.

'Lady Morland left the estate in trust for Miss Morland — Mrs Hawker, I should say. It did not become hers absolutely until she reached the age of twenty-one. As her demise has occurred before that age, the clauses in the will concerning the trust become invalid, and a further clause takes its place.' He looked at her sympathetically, knowing she was not really taking in his words. He began again. 'Do you remember ma'am, just after Lady Morland's death, that I came to see you?'

'Yes, to give me the cedar-wood box,' Héloïse said, grateful for something concrete to attach her mind to.

'Just so. And I also told you that there was another provision in her will that concerned you, but that I was not at liberty to divulge it until and unless certain circumstances existed.' Héloïse nodded. 'I have to tell you that those circumstances now exist.'

584

'Sir?'

'In plain language, ma'am, Lady Morland's will provided that in the event of Miss Morland's death without issue before attaining her majority, the whole estate was to come to you.'

Héloïse stared at him. 'You are not serious?'

'I never jest about matters of business,' he said gravely.

Héloïse tried to assemble her thoughts; and suddenly remembered that day long ago when she had walked with Jemima in the gardens at Shawes. It came back to her so vividly that she might almost have been there. She remembered the heat of the gravel under her thin sandals, the aromatic, evocative smell of box, the sound of the bees in the lavender bushes: all as fantastic as another world on this grey March day. She remembered the sound of Jemima's voice, though she couldn't see her face. 'I wanted to leave Morland Place to you —' she had said. 'I wanted you to have my kingdom —'

'She recognised me as her heiress, as the countess had recognised her,' she murmured to herself.

'My lady?' Pobgee enquired.

She looked up. 'You are sure, Mr Pobgee? That everything comes to me?'

'Everything, ma'am. The whole estate, as it would have gone to Miss Morland — Mrs Hawker. Of course, there are various provisions in the matter of pensions and small bequests —'

He talked on, but Héloïse no longer heard his voice. Morland Place was hers, she thought, pleasure not yet winning over astonishment. The house and the moat and the stableyard and the gardens; the little chapel, with its marble memorials, its exquisite fan-tracery, and the generations of ancestors sleeping peacefully in the vault, trusting the honour and the name of Morland to those who still strived in the living world above their quiet heads.

She thought of the orchards, the fields, the woods and streams, the farms, the town property, all hers; the horses and the sheep, the chickens in the fowl-yard and the pigeons in the dovecote; the wine in the cellar and the treasure in the strong-room; the peacocks on the kennel-roof and the swans on the moat —

'No, not the swans; the swans belong to the King,' she said

aloud, cutting Pobgee off in mid-sentence. He looked at her enquiringly, and she realised he hadn't understood her, because she had spoken in French. But somehow for the moment she couldn't seem to find any English; her poor bemused brain wouldn't work properly. 'Her kingdom,' she tried to explain. 'She left me her kingdom, because she knew I would take care of it.'

'My lady? Are you all right? Shall I call someone?' poor Pobgee asked anxiously.

Héloïse put her hands to her face, and felt that her cheeks were wet, and a sound escaped her which was something like a sob. Her long regency was over, and she was Mistress of Morland Place in truth. It was not just, she wanted to explain; but it was right.

'Poor Fanny,' she said. 'Oh poor Fanny!'

586

DYNASTY 1:
THE FOUNDING

Cynthia Harrod-Eagles

Triumphantly heralding the mighty Morland Dynasty – an epic saga of one family's fortune and fate through five hundred years of history. A story as absorbing and richly diverse as the history of the English-speaking people themselves.

The Founding

Power and prestige are the burning ambitions of Edward Morland, rich sheep farmer and landowner.

He arranges a marriage. A marriage that will be the first giant step in the founding of the Morland Dynasty.

A dynasty that will be forged by his son Robert, more poet than soldier. And Eleanor, ward of the powerful Beaufort family. Proud and aloof, and consumed by her secret love for Richard, Duke of York.

And so with *The Founding*, The Morland Dynasty begins – with a story of fierce hatred and war, love and desire, running through the turbulent years of the Wars of the Roses.

DYNASTY 2: THE DARK ROSE

Cynthia Harrod-Eagles

The marriage of Eleanor Courtenay and Robert Morland heralded the founding of the great Morland Dynasty. Now, Paul, their great grandson, is caught up in the conflict of Kings and sees, within his family, a bitter struggle bearing seeds of death and destruction.

And Nanette, his beloved niece, maid-in-waiting to the tragic Anne Boleyn, is swept into the flamboyant intrigues of life at court until, leaving heartbreak behind, she is claimed by a passionate love.

A magnificent saga of revenge, glory and intrigue in the turbulent years of the early Tudors as the Morlands crest the waves of power.

DYNASTY 3: THE PRINCELING

Cynthia Harrod-Eagles

The third volume in the magnificent Dynasty series.

Elizabeth I is now England's Queen and the Catholic
Morlands are threatened by the upsurge of Protestantism.
They must seek new spheres of influence if they are to
restore the family fortunes.

John, heir to Morland Place, rides north to wed the daughter
of Black Will Percy, a Borderland cattle lord. He learns
through blood and battle how to win proud Mary's heart.

Lettice, his gentle sister, is married to the ruthless,
ambitious Scottish baron, Lord Robert Hamilton, who
teaches her the bitter lesson of survival in the bleak and
treacherous court of Mary Queen of Scots.

Continuing the powerful story begun in *The Founding* and *The
Dark Rose*, *The Princeling* sees the Morlands fighting for their
religion, their inheritance and their love.

DYNASTY 4: THE OAK APPLE

Cynthia Harrod-Eagles

England has prospered during the long years of Charles I's reign. But peace is suddenly and violently shattered by the outbreak of brutal civil war between King and parliament.

Edmund Morland sees his family divided when his eldest son, Richard, brings home a young Puritan bride while Kit is drawn to the dashing Royalist cavalry of Prince Rupert.

Amid bitterless and disillusion the war grinds on, severing husband from wife, brother and brother, and Edmund struggles grimly to preserve the Morland fortune intact, estranged from his sons, and alienated at last even from his beloved wife, Mary.

DYNASTY 5:
THE BLACK PEARL

Cynthia Harrod-Eagles

THE BLACK PEARL continues to unfold the memorable
saga of the Morland Dynasty.

The years of Cromwell's Commonwealth had been long and
cruel for the Morlands, but with the restoration of
Charles II, hope is reborn.

For Ralph Morland, Master of Morland Place, the return of
the King is a chance to rebuild the family estates and fortune.
For the beautiful and ambitious Annunciata, the Restoration
brings a journey to London – a journey that leads to the
amours and intrigues of Charles's Court and to the
unlocking of her mysterious past.

A new age is dawning – a time of healing wounds – but
uncertainty, conflict and sorrow await them both before they
can win the most coveted prize of all.

sphere

To buy any of our books and to find out
more about Sphere and Little, Brown Book Group,
our authors and titles, as well as events and
book clubs, visit our website

www.littlebrown.co.uk

and follow us on Twitter

@LittleBrownUK
@LittleBookCafe
@TheCrimeVault

To order any Sphere titles p & p free in the UK,
please contact our mail order supplier on:

+ 44 (0)1832 737525

Customers not based in the UK should contact
the same number for appropriate postage
and packing costs.